OXFORD WORLD'S CLASSICS

THE RED AND THE BLACK

STENDHAL (Henri Beyle) was born on 23 January 1783 in Grenoble, where his father was a lawyer and his maternal grandfather a doctor. He lost his mother at the age of 7. After distinguishing himself in mathematics at the Ecole Centrale in Grenoble, he moved to Paris in 1799 intending to study for admission to the Ecole Polytechnique, but preferred to make his début in the world of art and literature. He was employed at the Ministry of War, and took part in the Napoleonic campaigns in Italy, Germany, Austria, and Russia from 1800 to 1814. At the fall of the Empire he settled in Milan, where he began to write on painting and music. Returning to Paris in 1821, he lived as a dandy in high society, publishing a treatise on love in 1822, his first novel *Armance* in 1827, followed by *Le Rouge et le Noir* in 1830.

The last phase of his career was spent as a diplomat in Italy, with postings as Consul in Trieste and then Civitavecchia. He was awarded the Légion d'honneur in 1835. The *Chartreuse de Parme*, a novel of military and romantic adventure set in Italy, appeared in 1839. Stendhal died of a stroke in 1842 during a period of leave in Paris. His remaining fictional and autobiographical works were published posthumously. His literary achievement went largely unrecognized during his lifetime, and it was left to later generations to appreciate his penetrating psychological and social insights and his ironical humour.

CATHERINE SLATER was Fellow and Tutor in French Language and Linguistics at Lady Margaret Hall, Oxford from 1971 to 1987, and is now an Honorary Research Fellow. She works in Bristol at Hewlett-Packard's European research laboratories.

ROGER PEARSON is a Fellow and Praelector in French at The Queen's College, Oxford, and the author of *Stendhal's Violin: a Novelist and his Reader* (Clarendon Press, 1988). He has also edited Stendhal's *The Charterhouse of Parma* for Oxford World's Classics.

OXFORD WORLD'S CLASSICS

For over 100 years Oxford World's Classics have brought
readers closer to the world's great literature. Now with over 700
titles—from the 4,000-year-old myths of Mesopotamia to the
twentieth century's greatest novels—the series makes available
lesser-known as well as celebrated writing.

The pocket-sized hardbacks of the early years contained
introductions by Virginia Woolf, T. S. Eliot, Graham Greene,
and other literary figures which enriched the experience of reading.
Today the series is recognized for its fine scholarship and
reliability in texts that span world literature, drama and poetry,
religion, philosophy and politics. Each edition includes perceptive
commentary and essential background information to meet the
changing needs of readers.

OXFORD WORLD'S CLASSICS

STENDHAL

The Red and the Black
A Chronicle of the Nineteenth Century

Edited and Translated with Notes by
CATHERINE SLATER

With an Introduction by
ROGER PEARSON

OXFORD
UNIVERSITY PRESS

OXFORD
UNIVERSITY PRESS

Great Clarendon Street, Oxford OX2 6DP

Oxford University Press is a department of the University of Oxford.
It furthers the University's objective of excellence in research, scholarship,
and education by publishing worldwide in

Oxford New York

Athens Auckland Bangkok Bogotá Buenos Aires Calcutta
Cape Town Chennai Dar es Salaam Delhi Florence Hong Kong Istanbul
Karachi Kuala Lumpur Madrid Melbourne Mexico City Mumbai
Nairobi Paris São Paulo Shanghai Singapore Taipei Tokyo Toronto Warsaw

with associated companies in Berlin Ibadan

Oxford is a registered trade mark of Oxford University Press
in the UK and in certain other countries

Published in the United States
by Oxford University Press Inc., New York

Translation and Notes © Catherine Slater 1991
Introduction, Further reading, and Chronology © Roger Pearson 1991

The moral rights of the author have been asserted

Database right Oxford University Press (maker)

First published as a World's Classics paperback 1991
Reissued as an Oxford World's Classics paperback 1998
Reissued 2009

British Library Cataloguing in Publication Data

Data available

Library of Congress Cataloging in Publication Data

Stendhal, 1783–1842.
[Rouge et le noir. English]
The red and the black: a chronicle of the nineteenth century / Stendhal;
translated by Catherine Slater; with an introduction by Roger Pearson.
p. cm.—(Oxford world's classics)
Translation of: Le rouge et le noir
Includes bibliographical references.
I. Slater, Catherine. II. Pearson, Roger. III. Title. IV. Series.
[PQ2435.R7E5 1991] 843'.7—dc20 90–47949

ISBN 978–0–19–953925–3

15

Printed in Great Britain by
Clays Ltd, Elcograf S.p.A.

CONTENTS

The Red and the Black

BOOK ONE

INTRODUCTION

THE RED AND THE BLACK is a shocking novel. One of the
principal shocks which it administers comes in Book II,
Chapter 35, and the reader who is not already privy to the
nature of this shock would be well advised to treat this
introduction as a postface. For, as Stendhal himself wrote: 'the
essential thing about a novel must be that the reader who
begins it one evening should stay up all night to finish it: to
reveal a novel's plot in advance would therefore be tantamount
to robbing him of the greater part of his interest in it.'

To reveal it in the case of *The Red and the Black* would be
robbery indeed. One of the principal themes of the novel
concerns the value of unpredictability in an age of the only too
predictable, and one of its intended delights for the Happy
Few[1] to whom it is dedicated is precisely the liberating effect
of surprise upon the imagination. 'The novel is like a bow,'
wrote Stendhal, 'the body of the violin *which gives back the
sounds* is the reader's soul.' *The Red and the Black*'s status as a
World's Classic depends substantially on the moral and aesthetic worth of its shockingness, and a reader coming to this
novel for the first time will need to have undergone some state
of shock before he or she can consult the sounds given back by
their soul, the better then to decide whether its classic status is
justified.

When *The Red and the Black* was first published on 13
November 1830, it was a novel ahead of its time. In a curious
way this was literally so since its title-page bore the date 1831
and a reconstruction of the historical time-scale within the
novel suggests that the events of the last few chapters take
place also in 1831. But it was ahead of its time principally
because it was uncomfortably topical, and topicality is the
aspect of the novel which Stendhal stressed when he tried to
have his own review of it published anonymously in a Floren-
tine literary review two years later. 'The author', he writes,

---

[1] On 'the Happy Few', see note to p. 1 on p. 530.

'dared recount an adventure which took place in 1830.' Even more daringly the author pulled no punches in his depiction of contemporary society, and this 'Chronicle of 1830' presents a comprehensive and damning account of France at the time. Stendhal spent much of his life in Italy, but between 21 November 1821 and 6 November 1830 he had lived in Paris. His chronicle is based on first-hand experience and the information of well-placed friends.

The reader meets a wide variety of social representatives ranging from the inmates of Valenod's workhouse to the king himself, and while each level of society appears superficially different, hypocrisy, deviousness and callous self-interest are omnipresent. This is part of 'the truth, the truth in all its harshness' proclaimed by the first epigraph in the novel. Julien Sorel's mercenary father with his peasant cunning, the seminarists who wish for a quiet life and a full stomach, the counter-revolutionary aristocrats plotting the invasion of their own country, Rênal and Valenod swapping political parties for their opportunistic convenience, these are the paltry players in the sordid drama of post-Napoleonic France. Chélan, Pirard and Chas-Bernard provide honourable exceptions for the Church and, among the vapid youth of Restoration Paris, Croisenois at least is man enough to die defending Mathilde's reputation, but generally the picture is bleak. Add to this the industrialization of Verrières and the environmental nonchalance of its mayor, the increasing power of the new money and its tasteless attempts to imitate the old, the propagandistic purpose and architectural inadequacy of the restoration of the abbey at Bray-le-Haut, the feud between the Jansenists and the Jesuits, and the all-pervasive influence of the Jesuits' secret society, the Congregation, and the sheer scope of Stendhal's indictment becomes readily apparent.

One important element seems, however, to be missing: the July Revolution of 1830. Where are those three 'Glorious Days' which saw the overthrow of the reactionary Bourbon king Charles X, his replacement by the supposedly more liberal Orleanist Louis-Philippe and the advent of the so-called Bourgeois Monarchy? Nowhere, except for an ironically understated and dismissive reference in the fictional Publisher's Note with which the novel begins. And why are there two sub-titles: 'A Chronicle of the Nineteenth Century' and 'A Chronicle of 1830'? Are they perhaps satirically synonymous? Even this momentous year has changed nothing: regimes may come and go, but cant and conventionality still rule.

The marked topicality of *The Red and the Black* may not always strike a modern reader, of course, but if one substitutes the politics and personalities of one's own day and thinks what one's reaction might be then, it becomes evident that Stendhal was playing with fire. He was also breaking new ground. As Erich Auerbach has stated in his celebrated study *Mimesis*: 'in so far as the serious realism of modern times cannot represent man otherwise than as embedded in a total reality, political, social and economic, which is concrete and constantly evolving—as is the case today [1946] in any novel or film—Stendhal is its founder.' No wonder the author of *The Red and the Black* thought that his literary merits would not be recognized for another fifty years. The contemporary reader might, like Balzac, have seen the pertinence of Stendhal's 'chronicle', but he may well have been too caught up personally in the issues presented to be able to view them within the larger and less timebound context to which the novel also offers imaginative access.

Be that as it may, the contemporary reader would almost certainly have been disconcerted, not to say scandalized, by the main story which the novel has to tell—namely, how a carpenter's son attempts to murder his ex-mistress, the mayor's wife, during Mass. That was simply not what novelists should be writing about, and anyway, of course, the whole thing was quite implausible. Here, however, the laugh would have been on the reader since the story is based on, and the novel originally inspired by, two court cases which Stendhal read about in the *Gazette des Tribunaux*. This publication, which appeared every weekday and contained full and largely reliable accounts of court proceedings, provided Stendhal with some of his favourite reading matter. He found it 'very entertaining' and to be both incontrovertible testimony to the power of human passion, which the decorum of polite society but thinly concealed and contained, and an invaluable source of information about the everyday lives of ordinary French men and women.

The two cases which caught the novelist's attention concerned Antoine Berthet and Adrien Lafargue, two murderers who met with remarkably different fates. Berthet was a short, thin man with a pale complexion, the son of a blacksmith in Brangues. He had spent four years in a seminary in Grenoble training to be a priest when, at the age of 21, ill health forced him to leave; and his protector, the village priest, secured him a post as tutor to one of the children of M. and Mme Michoud, a well-to-do couple who lived in Brangues. Whether Mme Michoud became his mistress remains uncertain, but some aspect of their relationship led to Berthet's dismissal after a year. After two years in another seminary, Berthet returned to Brangues in 1825 and began to write to Mme Michoud accusing her of having got him the sack and of being the mistress of his successor as tutor. There followed a series of reverses: expulsion from another seminary in Grenoble after one month, dismissal—again after one year—from a post as tutor to the de Cordon family, possibly because he seduced Mlle de Cordon and possibly after M. de Cordon had received a letter from Mme Michoud. Although M. Michoud was trying behind the scenes to help Berthet and actually got him a job working for a notary, Berthet became increasingly bitter and blamed his repeated failure to be accepted by a seminary (and the consequent frustration of his ambition to become a priest) on Mme Michoud, whom he now repeatedly threatened to murder. On Sunday 22 July 1827, during Mass in the church at Brangues, Antoine Berthet shot Mme Michoud twice and then himself. Both survived. Berthet was subsequently found guilty of attempted murder 'with all aggravating circumstances' and sentenced to death. He was executed on 23 February 1828.

Adrien Lafargue was treated rather more leniently than Berthet. A cabinet-maker by trade, he was a good-looking, well-spoken young man of 25 whose work had brought him temporarily to the town of Bagnères-de-Bigorre in the Pyrenees. At his lodgings the daughter of the house, called Thérèse, was a married woman who claimed to have been left by her husband. She took to Lafargue, and they became lovers.

Though he had a fiancée in Bayonne, Lafargue became sincerely attached to Thérèse and was therefore all the more put out one morning to find her in bed with a painter. Accepting her story that this was a former lover whose sentimental appeal to their shared past had vanquished her scruples, Lafargue forgave her. On his uncle's advice he then moved out of the lodgings, but continued to see Thérèse. She, however, tired of him, particularly when he refused to lend her some money, and soon she had the police forbid him to see her or to enter her house. Embittered by what he saw as an abuse of his sincerity and tolerance and bent on ridding the world of 'a nasty piece of work', Lafargue resolved to shoot her. On 21 January 1829 he went to her in her room. He fired once and missed, fired a second time and killed her. Fearing she was not dead, he then slit her throat. After this, as he had intended, he shot himself, but there was only powder in the pistol and he survived. He was found guilty of voluntary but unpremeditated manslaughter under grave duress, and sentenced to a mere five years' imprisonment.

The Berthet case provided Stendhal with the main shape of his plot together with many incidental details, while the Lafargue case led him to speculate that energy and strength of purpose of the kind once evinced by Napoleon were now to be found only amongst the working classes, and that the great men of the future would come not from the etiolated ranks of the aristocracy or the bourgeoisie but from those whose characters were still forged on the anvil of an unsheltered existence. Such is part of the message of *The Red and the Black*, and indeed of Julien Sorel's speech at his trial. Energy, sincerity, imagination and a certain nobility of soul: these are the qualities so lacking in the world of Verrières and Paris, yet these are the qualities which are absolutely necessary to the pursuit of happiness.

Plainly Julien Sorel has these qualities himself, and Stendhal's unflinching exposé of what, in his proposed review, he called 'a land of affectation and pretension' is illuminated by the central presence of this young and energetic hero. Julien sets out to conquer the society of his time by playing it at its own game of hypocrisy while yet remaining free from moral taint by virtue of his own lucidity. Just when it seems that he may have lost this lucidity, he rejects the false image of himself contained within Mme de Rênal's letter to the Marquis de la Mole and in an act of murderous passion recovers his real self. The violence of the deed stands as testimony to its integrity, and the aftermath—the willing acceptance of responsibility, the discovery of happiness, the poetic remembrance of things past—points to a form of authenticity that is the quarry of every Stendhalian hero.

More than one hundred and fifty years after *The Red and the Black* first appeared this has now become the orthodox way to read the novel, but in 1830 it would not have been an easy lesson for the reader to assimilate. Consequently he might well have been left cold by the numerous comic aspects which enliven the narrative (such as Julien's trouserless departure at the end of Book I or the various shenanigans with ladders), and which combine with its more tragic moments to provoke that blend of laughter and tears which Stendhal so treasured as an effect of the *opera buffa* of Mozart and Cimarosa. Equally the narrator's delicious sense of irony may have struck the reader as simply irritating. For *The Red and the Black* to work, he or she has got to have some sympathy for its central character, and if a sense of moral outrage takes over, then the scandalized reader is suffering from that emotion which Stendhal repeatedly stated that he least wanted to stir: 'impotent hatred'.

Such a reader may also have been put off by another shocking aspect of the novel: its style. *The Red and the Black* may not describe the July Revolution, but it was itself a revolution. The bastions of supposed good taste and novelistic propriety are stormed with resolve. Not for Stendhal the sonorous periods of Chateaubriand and the rhetorical grand gestures of Victor Hugo. Not for him either the navel-regarding intricacies of confessional novels like Chateaubriand's *René* and their anguished portraits of pathological passivity. He had already poked fun at these in his first novel *Armance* (1827). Instead he aimed now at a narrative which would have something of the energy and directness of its low-born protagonist. While he later felt that he might have gone too far and that his prose in *The Red and the Black* had been too angular and staccato in effect, he need not have feared, because he succeeded in producing a narrative whose lean and vigorous tone and constant forward impetus not only suggest the no-nonsense approach of the young man in a hurry but have also prevented the novel from dating. We may no longer have an immediate sense of the boldness of the novel's topicality, but we cannot fail to be aware of its principal stylistic hallmark: its presentness.

This presentness is apparent from the very first page of the novel. You are there walking up the main street of Verrières, you can see M. de Rênal, you can hear the dreadful din of his nail factory. The first chapter and a half of the novel are in the present tense, but even after the narrative has moved through a series of subtly modulated changes of temporal gear into the conventional mode of a story-in-the-past, the sense of presentness remains and is constantly reinforced throughout the novel. The present tense dominates *The Red and the Black*. It is the tense of the narrator and his ubiquitous interpolations, be they geographical (about Verrières, Paris, or even the Rhine), sociological (about the behaviour patterns of provincials or Parisians or about how seminarists eat a boiled egg), sententious (life is like this, or that) or simply chatty (by the way, I forgot to tell you, I must confess that...). It is the tense also of the putative reader to whom reference is periodically made in the course of the novel (you think Julien is being silly, you don't like these reception rooms), and it is the tense of the characters themselves—in their dialogue, their interior monologues, and their letters.

The sense of urgent actuality which is so characteristic of *The Red and the Black*—and which makes it such a good read—is created in further ways. There is almost no anticipation of subsequent events in the novel, so that the narrator comes over not as someone already in the know but as one who is as eager as we are to get on with things. The future, it seems, is as unpredictable for him as for us. By the same token he takes care not to delay us with flashbacks. There are a number at the beginning, inevitably, when he has to fill us in on some of the background, but mostly the narrative obeys the rules of the chronicle, which by definition is 'a detailed and continuous register of events in order of time' (*OED*). On five occasions, however, it is almost as if the narrator has been overtaken by events, and we find him being obliged to interrupt the onward surge of the narrative to go back and supply supplementary detail. These five occasions are five key moments in the plot: Julien's first visit to Mme de Rênal's bedroom, Mathilde's declaration of love to Julien by letter, the shooting of Mme de Rênal, the day of the trial, and the execution of Julien. In each case the shock value of a major turning-point is preserved by postponing narration of the preliminary events which immediately lead up to it.

Throughout the novel we are continually being surprised and kept on our toes in this way. The pace of the narrative is extraordinarily rapid, in places quite implausibly—and entertainingly—so, and the viewpoint from which the events are recounted varies constantly. One minute we are immersed in Julien's thoughts, the next he has already written the letter he was thinking of and we are learning of the recipient's reaction. Sometimes such a switch will occur within a single sentence, and there may be several within the shortest of paragraphs. By the sheer speed and unpredictability of its unfolding *The Red and the Black* creates that very excitement and imaginative zestfulness which it finds so deplorably absent from the world it describes.

The reader may meet with other surprises. One of the main lessons of the novel would seem to be that it is dangerous to preconceive the future. As Julien reflects in prison upon his past life, he realizes that he was distracted from the happiness and fulfilment he could have found with Mme de Rênal by his overriding ambition to seek fame and fortune. Because his head was filled with all sorts of fantasies, many of them derived from what he had heard and read about Napoleon, he was less able to appreciate the value of what reality was offering him. As if to reinforce this lesson Stendhal plays on his reader's expectations within the novel in such a way as to lead him or her into similar error. Repeatedly we are inveigled into speculating about Julien's future, both by what some of the characters predict for him and by the parallels which immediately

suggest themselves between his life and that of various historical and literary figures.

Thus the various references to Julien's desire to seek fame
and fortune, together with the recurring possibility that he is a
foundling, put one in mind—and would most certainly have
put a reader of 1830 in mind—of the typical eighteenth-
century novel plot which is so playfully exemplified in one of
Stendhal's favourite novels, Fielding's *Tom Jones*. Is *The Red
and the Black* to be another novel about the parvenu, we may
wonder. Or are we reading the biography of another Napoleon,
the man whom Julien so much admires? Or of another
Richelieu? Or perhaps of a revolutionary hero in the mould of
Danton, or Robespierre, or Mirabeau? Just before Julien
shoots Mme de Rênal, it seems that many of these predictions
may have been correct. The parvenu has arrived: money and
title, an officer's rank and the most brilliant match in Paris, all
are his. 'When you come to think about it,' he reflects, 'my
story's ended, and all the credit goes to me alone' (11.34).

But then comes the letter from Mme de Rênal, written at the
dictation of her confessor and describing him as another
Tartuffe. This portrait is so at variance with the person he
believes himself to be that he goes off to destroy the supposed
purveyor of this distorted image by doing the last thing one
would expect a mercenary and falsely pious hypocrite to do.
While he then spends the remainder of the novel trying to sort
out who he really is ('to see clearly into the depths of his soul':
11. 44), we also have to answer the same questions: who is
Julien? what does he stand for? We see that there is no
substance in the idea that he is a foundling, we remember that
he has been thoroughly uninterested in money all along, we
note that, unlike Napoleon, he owes his commission to patronage not prowess and that he resembles him only in so far as he
resembles Mathilde's father imitating him at parties, and we
recognize that, while Julien may have a chip on his shoulder,
he is no political radical and has none of the idealism of a
Danton. Even his speech at the trial, we are carefully informed,
is an act of bravado brought on by the insolent look in the eyes
of the gloating Valenod. Nor is he indeed Tartuffe. His
ambition to 'make his fortune' is a nebulous boyish dream of

somehow bettering himself, in all senses, not the project of a would-be property tycoon.

The shooting of Mme de Rênal explodes our preconceptions of the end of the novel just as surely as it does Julien's, and it is for this reason that foreknowledge of it may falsify a first reading of *The Red and the Black*. Subsequent readings, on the other hand, may bring one no nearer to understanding it! Critical opinion about this crucial turn of events has varied widely in respect both of its significance and of its aesthetic merits. The notorious view expressed by Emile Faguet at the end of the last century was that the shooting was implausible and provided irrefutable evidence of novelistic amateurishness. Quite definitely not one of the Happy Few, Faguet argued that a clever schemer like Julien would be mad to throw it all away because of a bad reference from Mme de Rênal. What's more, the Marquis de la Mole still had a pregnant daughter to marry off and the daughter in question had pretty firm views as to whom she wanted for a husband. Since Faguet, a number of people have tried to defend Stendhal by saying that Julien is indeed mad, that is, that he acts in a kind of somnambulistic trance and is therefore not entirely responsible for his actions. While there is some evidence in the text for Julien being in something of a state, it is insufficient to sustain such a thesis. More persuasive are those who have argued in terms of an act of vengeance and who have noted that, because Mme de Rênal is a woman, Julien is denied the opportunity of clearing his name by challenging the offender to a duel. Most persuasive of all, perhaps, is the view that the very inexplicability of the act makes it true to life. It is a crime of passion and, as such, not reducible to the tidy comprehensibility of the rational. By the same token, on the level of novelistic technique, it constitutes an act of defiance, a refusal to tell the story as if it were like many other similar stories, an assertion that the central event of this novel is unique: just as its main character is not like other heroes of history and literature but is, as he is so often described in the book, someone quite out of the ordinary.

But what lessons can we draw from the experiences of this man who shoots the woman he loves? That we should not preconceive our lives, that we should live for the moment and be ready to pounce on those fleeting moments of happiness which life occasionally offers? That love, and love alone, holds the key? Yes, partly, but the rich and subtle ironies, indeed the comedy and the pathos, of *The Red and the Black* derive substantially from the ambiguity surrounding these questions. True, at the end of the novel it does seem as if imagination, that error which 'bears the mark of a superior man' (II. 19) as the narrator calls it, is to be mistrusted. Imagined futures have led both Julien and the reader astray, and Mathilde's desperate determination to relive the violent romance of her sixteenth-century ancestors begins to look increasingly suspect and sterile. She alone is not surprised by the shooting, for it corresponds to so many of her fantasies, yet these bear little relation now to the increasingly authentic nature of Julien's experience. Like him we too may be 'tired of heroism' (II. 39). But earlier in the novel Mathilde's energy and imagination seemed commendable, as did her disdainful rejection of easy mediocrity. Were we wrong to commend her? No, just as we may not be right to see Julien discovering any universally applicable recipe for happiness at the end of the novel.

For why in fact did Julien pass up the happiness on offer at Vergy? Because he might have been bored. He himself reflects on this question:

Could happiness be so near at hand?... A life like this doesn't involve much by way of expenditure; I can choose whether to marry Mlle Elisa [Mme de Rênal's maid] or become Fouqué's partner... But a traveller who has just climbed a steep mountain sits down at the summit and finds perfect pleasure in resting. Would he be happy if forced to rest for ever?' (I. 23)

For all that Vergy epitomizes some cherished Stendhalian values and for all that Julien's pursuit of happiness could well have ended there, imagination says no. Energy, curiosity and exploration are as important as the trusting repose of reciprocated love. It may even be better to travel than to arrive. The pursuit may matter more than the happiness.

However perfect the view from the mountain-top, there are other peaks to climb, and Julien's wise analogy points to the tragic disjunction between happiness and imagination which

lies at the very heart of *The Red and the Black* and is its
principal concern. From the start Julien has been faced with
an ancient dilemma: 'like Hercules, he found himself with a
choice—not between vice and virtue, but between the unrelieved mediocrity of guaranteed well-being, and all the heroic
dreams of his youth' (I. 12). Heroically he defends himself
against the lure of 'dreary caution' (I. 14), heroically he
abandons the bliss of Vergy, and heroically he rejects the
worldly achievements of M. Julien Sorel de la Vernaye: 'in
short, what made Julien a superior being was precisely what
prevented him from savouring the happiness which came his
way. Every inch the young girl of sixteen who has delightful
colouring, and is foolish enough to put on rouge to go to a ball'
(I. 15). This rouge is the added highlight that imagination
lends to life; not the knowing artifice of black ambition but the
gratuitous and unthinking enhancement of blood-red vitality,
the wanton assertion that there is more to be had from life
even than all the bounty life may already have bestowed. It is
make-up as make-believe. And it is this very quality of
uncalculating passion which brings Julien the red ribbon of the
cross of the Legion of Honour to wear against the unyielding
blackness of his clerical habit, a sign of life to cheer the
'uniform of [his] century' (II. 13) which he wears 'like someone
in mourning' (II. I). For the Marquis de la Mole, when Julien
appears before him in red and black, he is an equal, an
aristocrat by nature, a 'superior man', and for us too. He
belongs to that other Legion of Honour, the one founded by
Stendhal after the manner of Napoleon, whose members,
though not legion, make it a point of honour to 'judge life with
[their] imagination' (II. 19) and whose names—Octave (in
Armance), Julien, Lucien (in *Lucien Leuwen*), and Fabrice (in
The Charterhouse of Parma)—have a Roman ring to recall the
energy and *virtù* upon which an earlier empire was founded.

Alas, Julien also resembles that other young Roman, St
Clement. The real St Clement was the third pope and in no
way military, but the statue of Stendhal's saint is depicted as
representing a 'young Roman soldier' who has met a violent
end: 'he had a gaping wound in his neck which seemed to be
oozing blood' (I. 18). This last detail, the thousand candles

which illuminate the mortuary chapel containing the statue and relic of the saint, the swooning girls, all come to mind at the end of the novel when the decapitated Julien is buried in 'that little grotto magnificently lit by an infinite array of candles', and Mathilde bears off her capital relic amidst the throng of mountain villagers who have come like pilgrims to witness this strange rite. Julien the latter-day apostate is revealed to be more akin to an early Christian martyr. Imagination not only leads Julien away from happiness, it leads him to premature death: 'the red' brings 'the black'.

The wounded neck represented on the statue of St Clement is but one of the several details in the novel which foreshadow Julien's crime and execution and thereby create a sense of fateful inevitability in the mind of the retrospective reader. What may have appeared random now takes on a providential quality. The parallels established by the prospective reader— parvenu, foundling, Napoleon, revolutionary hero—may now be replaced by the figure of the man of destiny, the man of exceptional passion and energy whose life is punctuated by intimations of premature mortality and whose superiority is the cause of his downfall. We may remember the piece of paper in the pew in Verrières church and its reference to the execution of one Louis Jenrel. We may smile that Julien notes only that 'his name ends like mine' (1. 5), whereas it is an exact anagram of his own, and we may even be led by this to realize that Julien Sorel and Louise de Rênal are anagramatically almost united. We note the crimson drapery and the red light that turns the holy water to blood, and later how the red damask with which, after a funeral service, the abbé Chas-Bernard transforms Besançon Cathedral to celebrate Corpus Christi provides a prophetic backdrop to Mme de Rênal's collapse. And the crimson curtains are duly drawn when Julien shoots Mme de Rênal at the moment of the elevation of the Host, the Body of Christ. Verrières is even the French for 'church windows'.

And might we not also note that, when Julien takes his 'first step' in Verrières church, this is said to be a 'station'; that he is tried on a Friday; that there are three days during which he can appeal; that he shares his champagne with two petty criminals; that Fouqué must, like Joseph of Arimathaea, plead for his mortal remains; that he is consistently referred to as the son of a carpenter. At the beginning of the novel we learn that Julien could recite the New Testament by heart: was he unwittingly foretelling his future? Has Julien been crucified for the values he proclaims by a society that fears the radical threat they pose? Has the man who won the cross of the Legion of Honour for his energy and imagination been nailed to the cross of bourgeois reaction? After all, we know who made the nails: M. de Rênal.

The road which Julien travels in *The Red and the Black* is a *via dolorosa*. But wherein lies redemption? Do we look askance at Julien's imagination and exclaim, as Mirabeau does in the epigraph which precedes the shooting of Mme de Rênal: 'O God, give me mediocrity!' (II. 35)? Do we content ourselves with the view that what led Julien away from the paradise of Vergy was mere foolish ambition and that the ultimate truth of the novel lies in his prison-idyll with Mme de Rênal and the discovery of his unique self? Julien, then, is a man saved at the last minute from the error of his ways? Perhaps, even, the lovers are reunited in death? Redemption, according to this line of thinking, would lie in sincerity and true love.

Or do we prefer to revert to the heroic outlook of our prospective view of Julien and see him once more in terms of other people, as indeed a man of destiny, not—as it turns out—of military or political destiny so much as a quasi-religious one? Is it perhaps only through imagination that the world can be redeemed? Through the actions of great men with vision enough to transcend the predictable and the orthodox? Through literature too? Did *The Red and the Black* condemn itself to critical death in order to redeem the world of 1830?

On 16 August 1819 at St Peter's Fields in Manchester workers demonstrated in favour of better working conditions and, as C. W. Thompson has recently brought to light, they carried red and black flags. Troops intervened and many of the demonstrators met their deaths, the working class its Peterloo. On 29 July 1830 in Paris during the July Revolution a red and black flag was seen flying from the Vendôme column signifying a fight to the death. On 25 February 1830 at the first night of *Hernani* red and black tickets were issued to the claque chosen to champion Victor Hugo's new romantic drama within the last bastion of Classical taste, the Comédie Française. What better title could Stendhal have chosen for his hard-hitting critique of contemporary society which abolishes the conventional happy ending of marriage combined with the acquisition of wealth and enhanced social standing and substitutes that of unmercenary, classless adultery, and which turns the life of a peasant who attemps murder during Mass into a modern version of the Life of Christ?

The Red and the Black is a shocking novel, but it offers no design for living. It presents the incompatibility of happiness and imagination as a problem without solution, a problem illustrated by events in 1830 but for which a solution has been, and will be, sought in every age. Unlike Julien and Mathilde after their reading, the reader of *The Red and the Black* is left not with heroic preconceptions but with the resonance of an unanswered question, the resonance of a violin which has been played on with tact and expertise. The reader is thus in a better position to obey the golden rule which Stendhal laid down for himself in a diary entry of May 1804: 'regard everything I've read to date about man as a prediction; believe only what I have seen for myself. *Joy, happiness, fame, all is upon it.*'

ROGER PEARSON

NOTE ON THE TEXT

Le Rouge et le Noir was first published on 13 November 1830. The present translation is based on P.-G. Castex's edition of the text published in the Classiques Garnier series in 1973.

FURTHER READING

READERS wishing to consult the French text of *The Red and the Black* (*Le Rouge et le Noir*) may rely on either of the following annotated editions:

(i) ed. Michel Crouzet (Paris, Garnier-Flammarion, 1964)
(ii) ed. P.-G. Castex (Paris, Garnier frères, 1973)

Almost all Stendhal's works have been translated into English at one time or another, some repeatedly. Those wishing to read further novels by Stendhal in translation might next try his other undisputed masterpiece, *The Charterhouse of Parma*, which is available in C. K. Scott Moncrieff's version (reissued by the Zodiac Press, 1980) or in Penguin Classics (translated by Margaret Shaw, 1958). *Armance*, the first as well as the shortest of his three completed novels, is available in C. K. Scott Moncrieff's translation (republished by the Soho Book Company in 1986) or in that of Gilbert and Suzanne Sale (Merlin Press, 1960). *Lucien Leuwen*, his longest but unfinished novel, may be read in H. L. R. Edward's translation (London, 1951).

The Penguin Classics series includes *Love* (translated by Gilbert and Suzanne Sale, 1957) and the autobiographical work *The Life of Henry Brulard* (translated by J. Stewart and B. C. J. G. Knight, 1973). Of further interest is Richard Howard's translation of two shorter narratives *The Pink and the Green. Mina de Vanghel* (Hamish Hamilton, 1988); the *Lives of Haydn, Mozart and Metastasio by Stendhal (1814)*, translated and edited by Richard N. Coe (London, 1972); and the same translator's *Life of Rossini* (London, 1970). Extracts from Stendhal's correspondence may be read in *To The Happy Few. Selected Letters*, translated by Norman Cameron in 1952 and reissued with an introduction by Cyril Connolly by the Soho Book Company in 1986.

The most useful biography of Stendhal in English is by Robert Alter (in collaboration with Carol Cosman): *Stendhal. A Biography* (Allen and Unwin, 1980).

Critical studies in English devoted solely to *The Red and the Black* include:

John Mitchell, *Stendhal: 'Le Rouge et le Noir'* (Edward Arnold, 1973)

Stirling Haig, *Stendhal: 'The Red and the Black'* (Landmarks of World Literature, Cambridge University Press, 1989)

Recent critical studies in English which contain chapters on *Le Rouge et le Noir* include:

Ann Jefferson, *Reading Realism in Stendhal* (Cambridge University Press, 1988)

Roger Pearson, *Stendhal's Violin: A Novelist and his Reader* (Clarendon Press, Oxford, 1988)

Other general critical works on Stendhal in English include:

Robert M. Adams, *Stendhal: Notes on a Novelist* (the Merlin Press, 1959)

Victor Brombert, *Stendhal. Fiction and the Themes of Freedom* (University of Chicago Press, 1968)

F. W. J. Hemmings, *Stendhal. A Study of his Novels* (Clarendon Press, Oxford, 1964)

Geoffrey Strickland, *Stendhal. The Education of a Novelist* (Cambridge University Press, 1974)

Margaret Tillett, *Stendhal. The Background to the Novels* (Oxford University Press, 1971)

Michael Wood, *Stendhal* (Elek, 1971)

A CHRONOLOGY OF
STENDHAL (MARIE-HENRI BEYLE)

1783:   23 January: born in Grenoble into well-to-do family.

1790:   23 November: death of his mother Henriette (*née* Gagnon).

1799:   After three successful years at the Ecole Centrale, is recommended to apply to the Ecole Polytechnique in Paris. Arrives on 10 November but prefers not to take the entrance examination.

1800:   Family connections bring him a job at the Ministry of War. His visit to Milan at the end of May marks the beginning of a lifelong love affair with Italy. 23 September: appointed to a commission as sub-lieutenant in the cavalry (of Napoleon's army in Italy).

1801–2: Granted sick leave and resigns his commission on returning to Paris, where he devotes more time to study and to his many attempts to write a comedy.

1804–5: Falls in love with an actress, Mélanie Guilbert. Follows her to Marseille, where he briefly finds employment with a colonial import and brokerage firm.

1806:   Returns to Paris without Mélanie. Departs to join Napoleon's army in an administrative position. Posted to Brunswick.

1809:   Working in Vienna. Illness keeps him from the battle of Wagram.

1810–11: Returns to Paris and promotion. Presented to the empress. Spends three months in Italy. Affair with Angela Pietragrua. Works on a history of Italian painting.

1812:   Leaves Paris for Russia with dispatches. After a month in Moscow departs just before the main retreat.

1814:   Paris occupied by the Allies. Signs declaration recognizing the Bourbon restoration. 20 July: leaves Paris to live in Milan.

1815:   Publishes his *Vies de Haydn, de Mozart et de Métastase*. End of the affair with Angela Pietragrua.

1816–17: Meets Lord Byron at La Scala. Publishes his *Histoire de la peinture en Italie* and *Rome, Naples et Florence en 1817* (in which he uses the pseudonym 'Stendhal' for the first time). Begins work on a life of Napoleon.

1818: 4 March: beginning of his great and unrequited passion for Matilde Dembowski (*née* Viscontini).

1819: 20 June: death of his father Chérubin, who leaves him some minor debts rather than the fortune he had expected. Passing friendship with Rossini.

1820–1: Working on *De l'amour*. Suspected by his left-wing friends of being a French agent, and by the authorities of involvement in left-wing plots. Departure from Milan and Matilde. Return to Paris.

1822: Publishes *De l'amour*. Begins regular contributions (until 1828) on the Parisian cultural scene to English periodicals, such as the *New Monthly Magazine*.

1825: 1 May: death of Matilde Dembowski.

1827: Publishes his first novel, *Armance*.

1829: 25–6 October: his 'first idea' of *Le Rouge et le Noir*.

1830: 8 April: signs contract with Levavasseur for publication of *Le Rouge et le Noir*. 25 September: after considerable persistence finally offered the post of consul in Trieste. 6 November: departure from Paris, after making a written proposal of marriage to Giulia Rinieri (which is refused). 13 November: publication of *Le Rouge et le Noir*. Arrival in Trieste. Accreditation refused.

1831: 11 February: appointed consul in Civitavecchia. 5 March: publication of second edition of *Le Rouge et le Noir* (in pocket-book format). 25 April: accredited as consul by the Holy See.

1833: Begins elaboration of short stories on the basis of late Renaissance manuscripts discovered in Rome. These stories, posthumously dubbed his *Chroniques italiennes*, are published at periodic intervals in the *Revue des Deux Mondes* during the late 1830s.

1834: Starts work on *Lucien Leuwen* but abandons the novel some 700 pages later when, on 23 September 1835, he hears of the abolition of the freedom of the press—by his employers.

1835: Awarded the cross of the Legion of Honour for services to literature (would have preferred it for services to diplomacy). 23 November: begins work on his autobiography, the *Vie de Henry Brulard*, which he abandons on 17 March 1836: 'The subject exceeds the saying of it.'

1836: 24 May: arrives in Paris on leave, which he manages to protract until 1839.

1838: Dictates *La Chartreuse de Parme* in its entirety between 4 November and 26 December.

1839: 6 April: publication of *La Chartreuse de Parme*. 13 April: begins work on *Lamiel*, his last, unfinished novel. 24 June: leaves Paris to resume office as consul and is back at his desk on 10 August.

1840: 1 January: suffers first stroke. 25 September: Honoré de Balzac publishes elogious review of *La Chartreuse de Parme* (in which he also tells its author how he could have written it better).

1841: Further illness. 15 September: granted sick leave. 22 October: leaves for Paris.

1842: 22 March: collapses in the street after dinner with the Minister of Foreign Affairs and dies in his lodgings at 2 a.m. the following morning. 24 March: buried in the cemetery of Montmartre. Desired epitaph: 'Arrigo Beyle Milanese. Scrisse. Amò. Visse.'

THE RED AND THE BLACK

A Chronicle of 1830

TO THE HAPPY FEW*

PUBLISHER'S NOTE*

THIS work was ready for publication when the great events of July* supervened and left French minds rather unreceptive to creations of the imagination. We have reason to believe that the pages which follow were written in 1827.*

BOOK ONE

The truth, the truth
in all its harshness.

DANTON*

CHAPTER 1

A small town

Put thousands together
Less bad.
But the cage less gay.

HOBBES

THE small town of Verrières may be regarded as one of the prettiest in the Franche-Comté.* Its white houses with their steeply pitched roofs of red tile are spread over a hillside where clumps of sturdy Spanish chestnuts mark out the slightest dips in the terrain. The river Doubs flows several hundred feet beneath the old town walls, built in former times by the Spaniards and now fallen to ruin.

Verrières is sheltered on its northern side by a high mountain ridge, part of the Jura range. Right from the earliest cold spells in October the jagged peaks of the Verra are covered with snow. A mountain stream which comes tumbling down from the heights passes through Verrières on its way to join the Doubs, and supplies power to numerous sawmills. This simple form of industry provides a reasonably comfortable living for the majority of the inhabitants, who are peasants rather than townsfolk. The wealth acquired by this little town does not, however, come from the sawmills, but rather from the factory where painted fabrics are produced in the Mulhouse tradition.* This is the source of the general prosperity which, since the fall of Napoleon, has enabled all the house-fronts in Verrières to be refurbished.

You have scarcely set foot in the town before you are deafened by the din from a noisy and fearful-looking machine. Twenty massive hammers come thundering down with a noise to set the cobbles shaking, and are lifted up again by a wheel driven by the waters of the stream. Each one of these hammers makes countless thousands of nails every day. It is the task of pretty, fresh-cheeked girls to hold out the little pieces of iron which the enormous hammers beat speedily into nails. This rough-looking work is one of the activities which the traveller who ventures for the first time into the mountains separating France from Switzerland finds most surprising. If on his arrival in Verrières the traveller asks who owns this fine nail factory which deafens people as they go up the main street, he will be told in the drawling local accent: 'Ah! that belongs to his worship the mayor.'

If the traveller stops but a moment in the main street of Verrières, which climbs up from the bank of the Doubs almost to the top of the hill, you can bet a hundred to one he will see a tall man appearing on the scene with the look of someone going about important business. As he passes, all hats are raised with alacrity. His hair is turning grey, and grey is what he wears. He is a member of several orders of knighthood,* he has a high forehead and a Roman nose, and his face is not without a certain overall regularity: people even think at first sight that it combines the dignity befitting a village mayor with that special charm which can still be found in someone rising fifty. But soon the traveller from Paris is shocked by a certain look of self-satisfaction and complacency mingled with an indefinable hint of narrow-mindedness and lack of imagination. You feel in the end that the wit of this man does not go beyond making sure he is paid on the dot whatever is owed to him, and leaving it to the last possible moment to pay back what he himself owes.

Such is the mayor of Verrières, M. de Rênal. He walks solemnly across the road and disappears from sight into the town hall. But if the traveller continues his stroll he will notice, a hundred yards or so further up, a rather fine-looking house and, through the iron gate next to it, some very splendid gardens. The skyline beyond is formed by the hills of

Burgundy, and seems expressly created to please the eye. This view allows the traveller to forget the poisonous atmosphere of petty financial intrigue which is beginning to stifle him.

He is told that this house belongs to M. de Rênal. The profits from his sizeable nail factory have enabled the mayor of Verrières to put up this fine dwelling in solid stone which he is in the process of completing. His family, it is said, is of Spanish origin from way back, and has been settled in the region, so they maintain, since well before it was conquered by Louis XIV.*

Since 1815 his involvement with industry has been a source of embarrassment to him: the events of 1815* made him mayor of Verrières. The walls supporting the terraces of his magnificent garden which runs down step by step to the Doubs are also a reward for M. de Rênal's expertise in the iron industry.

When in France you must not expect to come across the kind of picturesque gardens that are found on the outskirts of manufacturing towns in Germany like Leipzig, Frankfurt or Nuremberg. In the Franche-Comté, the more walls a man builds, the more his land bristles with rows of stones laid one on top of another, the greater his claim to his neighbours' respect. M. de Rênal's gardens with their walls everywhere are further admired because he spent a fortune purchasing some of the small plots of land on which they are sited. Take, for instance, that sawmill which caught your eye by its striking location on the bank of the Doubs as you entered Verrières, and where you noticed the name SOREL written in gigantic letters on a board set above the roof: six years ago it used to occupy the site on which the wall of the fourth terrace of M. de Rênal's gardens is now being built.

For all his pride, the mayor had to enter into lengthy negotiations with old Sorel, a tough and stubborn peasant if ever there was one. He had to hand over a handsome sum in gold coin to get him to move his mill elsewhere. As for the *public* stream which powered the saw, M. de Rênal managed to have it diverted, using the influence he commands in Paris. This favour was granted him after the 182– elections.* For each acre he took from Sorel, he gave him four on a site five hundred yards downstream on the banks of the Doubs. And although this position was much more advantageous for his trade in deal planks, old Mr Sorel, as he is called now that he has grown rich, found a way to screw out of his neighbour's impatience and *obsessive greed for land* the sum of 6,000 francs as well.

It is true that this arrangement has come in for some criticism from the right-thinking individuals in the neighbourhood. Once on a Sunday four years ago when M. de Rênal was on his way back from church in his mayor's robes, he noticed from a distance how old Mr Sorel, with his three sons gathered round him, smiled as he looked in the mayor's direction. That smile was a fatal flash of illumination for the mayor: now he can't help thinking he might have been able to drive a better bargain over the exchange.

To win public esteem in Verrières, the main thing, while of course building walls in great number, is to avoid any design brought over from Italy by the stonemasons who come through the gorges in the Jura in the springtime on their way up to Paris. An innovation of this kind would earn the foolhardy landowner a lasting reputation for *unsound views*, and discredit him for ever in the eyes of the wise and sensible folk who mete out esteem in the Franch-Comté.

In actual fact, these wise folk keep everyone there in the grip of the most irksome *despotism*. This dirty word sums up why it is that life in a small town is unbearable to anyone who has dwelt in the great republic called Paris. Public opinion— and you can just imagine what it's like!—exercises a tyranny that is every bit as *mindless** in small towns in France as it is in the United States of America.

CHAPTER 2

A mayor

> Does dignity then count for nothing,
> sir? It is respected by fools, held in awe
> by children, envied by the rich, and
> despised by any wise man.
>
> BARNAVE*

FORTUNATELY for M. de Rênal's reputation as an administrator, a massive *retaining-wall* was needed to shore up the public promenade which runs along the hillside a hundred feet or so above the course of the Doubs. From this excellent vantage-point you get one of the most picturesque views in the whole of France. But every spring, rainwater used to erode the path away, leaving deep gullies and making it quite impassable. This drawback affected everyone, and put M. de Rênal in the fortunate position of having to immortalize his term of office by building a wall twenty foot high and some eighty yards long.

The parapet of this wall cost M. de Rênal three journeys to Paris, because the last Minister of the Interior but one had declared himself utterly opposed to the promenade at Verrières. The parapet now rises four feet above ground level, and, as if in defiance of all ministers past and present, it is now being dressed with slabs of solid stone.

How many times, as I stood there leaning my chest against those great blocks of fine blue-grey stone, musing on the Paris balls I had left behind the day before, have I gazed down into the valley of the Doubs! Beyond it on the left bank there are five or six winding valleys with tiny streams at the bottom clearly visible to the naked eye. You can see them cascading down into the Doubs. The heat of the sun is fierce in the mountains here, and when it shines overhead the musing traveller is sheltered by the magnificent plane trees on this terrace. They owe their rapid growth and their fine blue-green foliage to the new soil which the mayor had the builders bring

up to put behind his huge retaining-wall. For in spite of
opposition from the town council, he widened the promenade
by more than six feet (which I welcome, although he is an
Ultra* and I am a liberal), and in his opinion and that of M.
Valenod, who has the good fortune to be master of the
workhouse in Verrières, this terrace is now fit to be compared
to the one at Saint-Germain-en-Laye.*

For my part, I have only one criticism of the AVENUE DE
LA FIDÉLITÉ (you can read its official name in fifteen or
twenty places on marble plaques which have earned M. de
Rênal yet one more decoration); what I dislike about it is the
barbarous way the municipality pollards these leafy planes to
the quick, giving them low, round, smooth heads which make
them look like the commonest of vegetables from the allot-
ment, when they are crying out to be left in the magnificent
shapes they display in England. But the mayor's will is
tyrannical, and twice a year all the trees belonging to the
commune have their branches mercilessly amputated. Local
liberals claim, not without some exaggeration, that the hand of
the official gardener has become far heavier since M. Maslon
the curate adopted the habit of appropriating the cuttings for
himself.

This young clergyman was sent from Besançon some years
ago to keep an eye on Father Chélan and a number of other
incumbents of neighbouring parishes. An old army surgeon
who had fought in the Italian campaigns and had retired to
Verrières—a man who in his lifetime managed to be both a
Jacobin* and a Bonapartist at once, according to the mayor—
was bold enough one day to complain to his worship about the
way these fine trees were being periodically mutilated.

'I like shade,' replied M. de Rênal with the right degree of
aloofness for addressing a surgeon who is a Member of the
Legion of Honour.* 'I like shade, and I have *my* trees pruned
to give shade; I can see no other use for a tree when, unlike
the serviceable walnut, it *doesn't bring in any money*.'

BRINGING IN MONEY: this is the key phrase which settles
everything in Verrières. It sums up the habitual thinking of
more than three-quarters of its inhabitants.

Bringing in money is the consideration which settles everything in this little town you found so pretty. The newcomer who decides to visit it, won over by the beauty of the cool, deep valleys round about, imagines to begin with that its inhabitants appreciate what is beautiful. They are always talking about the beauty of the locality, and it is undeniable that they value it highly; but this is because it attracts a number of travellers from elsewhere with the means to line the innkeepers' pockets, and thereby, through local taxes, to *bring money to the town.*

On a fine morning in autumn, M. de Rênal was strolling along the Avenue de la Fidélité with his wife on his arm. While listening to her husband solemnly talking away, Mme de Rênal was keeping an anxious eye on the activities of three small boys. The eldest, who might have been eleven, kept on going over to the wall, far too often for her liking, and making as if to climb on to it. A gentle voice was then heard calling 'Adolphe', and the boy had to abandon his daring venture. Mme de Rênal looked about thirty, but was still a rather pretty woman.

'He might well come to regret it, this fine gentleman from Paris,' M. de Rênal was saying. He looked indignant, and his face was paler than usual. 'It isn't as though I had no friends at Court...'

But although I do wish to spend two hundred pages telling you about the provinces, I shall not be uncivilized enough to subject you to the long-windedness and *deliberately roundabout ways* of a provincial dialogue.

This fine gentleman from Paris, so loathsome to the mayor of Verrières, was none other than a M. Appert* who had succeeded two days previously not merely in getting inside the prison and the workhouse in Verrières, but also the hospital which was run as a charity by the mayor and the chief landowners of the neighbourhood.

'But what harm can this gentleman from Paris do you,' Mme de Rênal asked timidly, 'since you're most scrupulously honest in administering what is given to the poor?'

'His only reason for coming is to *apportion* blame, and then he'll get articles written in newspapers with liberal leanings.'

'You never read them, my dear.'

'But people gossip about these radical articles; it's all very distracting for us, and it *prevents us from going about our good works*.[1] For my part I shall never forgive the priest.'

[1] This is a historical fact. [Stendhal's note.]

CHAPTER 3

Care of the poor

A virtuous priest who is a stranger to intrigue
is a godsend to any village.

FLEURY*

YOU should know that the priest of Verrières, an old man of
eighty who none the less had a constitution and character of
iron, thanks to the invigorating mountain air, was entitled to
visit the prison, the hospital and even the workhouse at any
hour of the day or night. It was precisely at six o'clock in the
morning that M. Appert, bearing an introduction from Paris
to the priest, had had the wisdom to turn up in an inquisitive
little town. He had gone straight to the presbytery.

Reading the letter addressed to him by the Marquis de la
Mole, a peer of France and the richest landowner in the
provinces, Father Chélan remained plunged in thought.

'I'm old and well loved here,' he said to himself under his
breath, 'they wouldn't dare!' Turning at once to the gentleman from Paris, with a look in which despite his great age
there shone that sacred fire which betokens pleasure in carrying out a fine action with some degree of risk attached, he
said:

'Come with me, sir, and while we're in the presence of the
gaoler and more particularly of the warders in the workhouse,
be so good as to refrain from commenting on what we shall see
there.' M. Appert realized he was dealing with a stalwart
character: he followed the venerable priest round the prison,
the hospice and the workhouse, asking a good many questions
but despite some odd replies never allowing himself to express
the slightest sign of disapproval.

The visit lasted several hours. Father Chélan invited M.
Appert to dinner with him, but the latter said he had letters to
write: he did not want to compromise his generous escort any
further. Around three o'clock the two gentlemen went off to
finish inspecting the workhouse and then returned to the

prison. On the doorstep they found the gaoler, a bow-legged giant of a man six foot tall; his unprepossessing face had become hideous with terror.

'Ah! sir,' he said to Father Chélan on catching sight of him, 'isn't this gentleman I see with you M. Appert?'

'And what if he is?' replied the priest.

'You see, since yesterday I've been under the strictest instructions delivered from the prefect by a gendarme who must have galloped hard through the night, not to let M. Appert into the prison.'

'I concede, M. Noiroud, that this traveller I have with me is M. Appert. Do you recognize my right to enter the prison at any hour of the day or night, and to take with me anyone I please?'

'Yes, Father Chélan,' said the gaoler in a low voice, hanging his head like a bulldog reluctantly cowed into submission by fear of the stick. 'But remember, Father Chélan, I've a wife and children, and if anyone tells on me, I'll get the sack. My job's all I've got to live off.'

'I should be just as put out to lose mine,' replied the good priest, sounding more and more agitated.

'But there's all the difference!' retorted the gaoler. '*You* have an income of eight hundred pounds,* Father Chélan, everyone knows you do—a nice bit of property...'

These are the events which, in numerous versions rich with commentary and exaggeration, had for the past two days been stirring up all the spiteful passions in the little town of Verrières. At this particular moment they formed the subject matter of the little discussion which M. de Rênal was having with his wife. That morning he had gone to the priest's house taking with him M. Valenod, the master of the workhouse, to express their dissatisfaction in the strongest possible terms. Father Chélan had no one to protect him and he realized the full implications of their words.

'Well, gentlemen! I shall be the third priest in the neighbourhood to be stripped of his office at the age of eighty.* I've been here for fifty-six years; I've baptized almost all the inhabitants of the town, which was scarcely more than a village when I arrived. Every day I marry young folk whose grandparents I married in times gone by. Verrières is my family, but I said to myself on seeing the stranger: "This man from Paris may indeed be a liberal, there are only too many of them around; but what harm can he do our paupers and our prisons?"'

When criticism of his conduct from M. de Rênal and especially M. Valenod had reached a pitch of severity, the old priest had exclaimed in a quavering voice:

'All right then, gentlemen, have me removed from office! It won't stop me living in these parts. Everyone knows that forty-eight years ago I inherited a field which brings in eight hundred pounds. I shall live off this income. I don't put any money by in a position like mine, gentlemen, and maybe that's why I'm not so afraid when there's talk of dismissing me from it.'

M. de Rênal was on very good terms with his wife, but, not knowing what to reply to her hesitantly repeated question: 'What harm can this gentleman from Paris do to the prisoners?', he was about to lose his temper, when she let out a cry of alarm. Her second son had just climbed on to the top of the terrace wall and was running along it, although there was a drop of more than twenty feet from the wall to the vineyard on the other side. Fear of startling her son and making him fall stopped Mme de Rênal from calling out to him. Eventually the child, laughing at his feat of daring, glanced at his mother and saw how pale she was; he jumped down on to the path and ran over to her. He got a good scolding.

This little incident gave a new turn to the conversation.

'I'm determined to take on young Sorel, the sawyer's son, as part of the household,' said M. de Rênal. 'He can keep an eye on the children, who are becoming rather a handful for us. He's a young priest, or as good as, knows his Latin, and the children will learn a great deal from him; he's made of stern stuff, according to Father Chélan. I shall give him three hundred francs and his keep. I did have some doubts about his morality, as he was the blue-eyed boy of that old surgeon who was a member of the Legion of Honour and came to board at the Sorels' on the strength of being a cousin of theirs. The fellow may well really have been a secret agent of the liberals. He used to say that our mountain air did his asthma good, but there's no proof of that. He had taken part in all *Buonaparté's* campaigns in Italy, and even, so they say, voted 'no' to the Empire* in the past. This liberal taught young Sorel Latin, and left him the stock of books he had brought with him. So I should never have thought of putting the carpenter's son* in charge of our children, had the priest not told me, on the very day before the incident which has just made us enemies for good, that young Sorel has been studying theology for three years with the intention of going to the seminary. So he isn't a liberal, and he does know Latin.

'This arrangement works out in more ways than one,' went on M. de Rênal, glancing at his wife with a diplomatic look on his face. 'Valenod is as proud as anything of the two fine Normandy cobs he has just bought for his barouche; but he hasn't got a tutor for his children.'

'He might well get in before us with this one.'

'So you approve of my plan?' said M. de Rênal with a smile to thank his wife for the excellent idea she had just had. 'Right, that's settled then.'

'Heavens above! my dearest, you are quick to make up your mind!'

'That's because I'm a person of character, I am, and this much was obvious to the priest. Let's make no bones about it, we're surrounded by liberals here. All the cloth merchants are envious of me, I know for certain they are; and two or three of them are getting filthy rich. Well, you see, I like the idea of their seeing M. de Rênal's children going past on their walk, in the charge of *their tutor*. Everyone will be impressed. My grandfather would often tell us how in his youth he'd had a tutor. It may cost me as much as a hundred crowns, but it must be reckoned a necessary expenditure to maintain our station.'

This sudden resolve left Mme de Rênal deep in thought. She was a tall, well-built woman who had been the local beauty, as they say in the mountains round here. She had an artless air about her, and a youthful way of walking. To the eyes of a Parisian, this natural charm, full of lively innocence, would even have been enough to conjure up thoughts of sweet pleasure. Had she known she had this kind of success, Mme de Rênal would have felt deeply ashamed of it. Her heart was quite untouched by coquetry or affectation. M. Valenod, the wealthy master of the workhouse, was believed to have tried to win her favours, but with no success. This had cast a dazzling light on her virtue since this M. Valenod, a tall, powerfully built young man with a ruddy complexion and big black sidewhiskers, was one of those vulgar, brazen, loud individuals who are called handsome fellows in the provinces.

Mme de Rênal, who was extremely shy and seemed highly impressionable,* was especially disturbed by M. Valenod's constant movements and his loud voice. What the people of Verrières call the pleasures of the flesh were something totally alien to her, and this had given her the reputation of being very proud of her origins. Nothing could have been further from her thoughts, but she had been delighted to find the townsfolk visiting her less often. I shall not conceal the fact that she was considered silly by *their* ladies, because she never tried to manipulate her husband, and let slip the most marvellous opportunities of getting him to buy hats for her in Paris or Besançon. As long as she was left to wander alone in her beautiful garden she never uttered a word of complaint.

She was a naïve creature who had never ventured so much as to judge her husband and admit to herself that she found him boring. She imagined without putting it into words that no husband and wife enjoyed a more tender relationship. She was particularly fond of M. de Rênal when he talked to her about his plans for their children, one of whom he destined for the army, the next for the magistracy and the third for the Church. In short, she found M. de Rênal far less boring than all the other men of her acquaintance.

This conjugal opinion was well founded. The mayor of Verrières had a reputation for wit and above all for good taste, which he owed to the half-dozen jokes he had inherited from an uncle. Old Captain de Rênal had served in the Duke of Orleans'* infantry regiment before the Revolution, and when he went to Paris he was admitted to the duke's salons. There he had set eyes on Mme de Montesson,* the famous Mme de Genlis, and M. Ducrest, the creator of the Palais-Royal. These characters made all too frequent appearances in M. de Rênal's anecdotes. But gradually it had become an effort for

him to remember things which had to be recounted with such
subtlety, and for some time now he had not repeated his
anecdotes about the House of Orleans except on grand occasions. Since, moreover, he was extremely polite except when
the conversation was about money, he was rightly considered
to be the most aristocratic person in Verrières.

CHAPTER 4

Father and son

E sarà mia colpa
Se cosi è?
MACHIAVELLI*

'MY good lady* really is pretty shrewd!' said the mayor of
Verrières to himself at six o'clock the following morning as he
was walking down to old Mr Sorel's mill. 'Whatever I may
have said to her to maintain a fitting show of superiority, it
hadn't occurred to me that if I don't take on the young abbé*
Sorel, who is said to know Latin like an angel, the master of
the workhouse, that eternal agitator, could well have the very
same idea, and snap him up first. How smugly he'd talk about
his children's tutor!... Now will this tutor wear a cassock once
he's in my employment?'

M. de Rênal was pondering this question when he caught
sight of a peasant in the distance, a man nearly six foot tall,
who seemed very busy at this early hour of the morning
measuring pieces of wood stacked up along the towpath by the
Doubs. He did not look at all pleased to see his worship
approaching, for his pieces of wood were blocking the path,
and had been stacked there contrary to regulations.

Old Mr Sorel—for it was the man himself—was most
surprised and still more pleased at the unusual proposition
which M. de Rênal was making to him in respect of his son
Julien. This did not prevent him from listening with that air
of surly gloom and indifference which the inhabitants of these
mountains are so good at putting on to cover up their cunning.
Having been slaves at the time of Spanish rule, they still keep
this characteristic of the Egyptian fellah's countenance.

Sorel's reply at first consisted entirely of a lengthy recital of
all the formulas of respect he knew by heart. While he was
reeling off these empty words with an awkward smile which
increased the shifty, almost deceitful look he habitually wore
on his face, the old peasant's fertile mind was trying to work

out what could possibly induce such an important person to take his good-for-nothing son into his own household. He was thoroughly dissatisfied with Julien, and Julien was the one for whom M. de Rênal was offering him the undreamed of wage of three hundred francs a year, with his keep and even his clothes thrown in. This last demand, which old Mr Sorel had had the brilliant idea of putting forward out of the blue, had been accepted forthwith by M. de Rênal.

The mayor was struck by this request. Since Sorel isn't delighted and overcome by my proposition, as of course he should be, it's clear, he said to himself, that he's received offers from another quarter. And where can they come from if not from friend Valenod? M. de Rênal tried in vain to get Sorel to make a deal on the spot, but the old peasant's scheming mind was dead against it. He wanted, so he said, to consult his son, as if in the provinces a rich father consults a penniless son except for form's sake.

A water-driven sawmill consists of a shed on the banks of a stream. The roof is held up by a frame supported on four stout wooden posts. Eight to ten feet off the ground, in the middle of the shed, there is a saw which goes up and down while a very simple mechanism pushes a piece of wood against it. A wheel powered by the stream drives this dual mechanism: to raise and lower the saw and to push the piece of wood gently towards it so that it gets cut into planks.

As he approached his mill, old Mr Sorel called out to Julien in his stentorian voice. No one answered. The only people visible were his elder sons, giant-like figures armed with heavy axes, who were squaring off the fir logs they were going to take to the saw. They were intent on cutting accurately along the black lines drawn on the pieces of wood, and each blow of their axes sent huge chips flying. They did not hear their father's voice. He made his way over to the shed, and on entering looked in vain for Julien in the place where he should have been—by the saw. He sighted him five or six feet higher up, astride one of the roof timbers. Instead of giving his attention to supervising the operation of the whole machine, Julien was reading. Nothing was more repugnant to old Sorel. He might perhaps have forgiven Julien his slender build, ill-suited to heavy manual labour and so unlike that of his elder brothers; but he could not abide this obsession with reading—he could not read himself.

He called Julien two or three times to no avail. It was not so much the noise of the saw as his absorption in his book that prevented the young man from hearing his father's thundering voice. At length, in spite of his age, the latter jumped nimbly onto the tree-trunk which was being sawn up, and from there to the cross-beam supporting the roof. A violent blow sent the book flying out of Julien's hands into the stream; a second blow delivered just as violently sideways across the top of his head made Julien lose his balance. He was just about to fall down twelve feet or more right into the moving levers of the machine and be broken to bits, but his father caught him with his left hand as he fell.

'You lazybones, you! won't you ever stop reading your blasted books while you're on duty by the saw, eh? You can read 'em in the evening when you go off wasting your time at the priest's, if I may make a suggestion.' Julien was stunned by the force of the blow and covered in blood, but he started down towards his official post next to the saw. There were tears in his eyes, not so much on account of the physical pain as for the loss of his beloved book.

'Down with you, you brute, I want to talk to you.' The noise of the machine again prevented Julien from hearing this command. His father, who had got down and did not want to go to the trouble of climbing back onto the machine, fetched a long pole used for knocking down walnuts and banged him on the shoulder with it. Julien was scarcely on the ground before old Sorel pushed him roughly along in front of him in the direction of the house. God knows what he's going to do to me, the young man said to himself. As he passed, he looked sadly into the stream where his book had fallen: it was the one he treasured more than all the rest, the *St Helena Chronicle*.*

His cheeks were flushed and he kept his eyes on the ground. He was a small, frail-looking young man of eighteen or nineteen, with irregular but delicate features, and a roman nose. His large dark eyes which in moments of calm suggested a reflective streak and a fiery temperament, shone at that instant with an expression of the most ferocious hatred. He had a low forehead framed by dark chestnut hair, and when he was angry, this gave him a fierce expression. Among the countless varieties of human face, it would be difficult to imagine a more strikingly individual one. His slim and shapely figure suggested nimbleness rather than strength. Right from early childhood his deeply pensive air and his pallor had convinced his father that he would not survive, or that if he did he would be a burden on his family. The butt of everyone's scorn at home, he hated his brothers and his father. He was always beaten in the games played on Sundays in the town square.

It was less than a year since his pretty face had begun to win him allies among the girls. Despised by everyone for his frailty, Julien had adored the old army surgeon who one day dared to speak to the mayor about the plane trees.

The surgeon would sometimes pay old Mr Sorel a day's wages for his son, and would teach him Latin and history, that is, all the history he knew: the Italian campaigns of 1796. On his death he had bequeathed him his Legion of Honour cross, the arrears on his half pay, and thirty or forty books, the most precious of which had just landed in the *public stream* that had been diverted at his worship's expense.

As soon as he stepped inside the house, Julien was pulled to a halt by the heavy hand of his father on his shoulder. He trembled in the expectation of a beating.

'Answer me without lying,' bellowed the harsh voice of the old peasant in his ear, while his hand turned him round like a child's hand turning a tin soldier. Julien's big black eyes, welling with tears, were met by the malicious little grey eyes of the old carpenter who looked as if he wanted to read into the depths of his soul.

CHAPTER 5
Striking a bargain

Cunctando restituit rem
ENNIUS*

'ANSWER me without lying if you're capable of it, you revolting bookworm! How do you know Mme de Rênal? When have you spoken to her?'

'I've never spoken to her,' replied Julien, 'I've only ever seen the lady at church.'

'Then you must have looked at her, eh? you cheeky devil!'

'Never! You know I only have eyes for God in church,' Julien added with a hypocritical look on his face, specially designed, as he thought, to ward off further blows.

'There's something going on here, all the same,' retorted the wily peasant, and he fell silent for a moment. 'But I won't get anything out of you, you blasted hypocrite. As a matter of fact, I'm going to be rid of you, and my saw will do all the better for it. You've won over Father Chélan or his likes, and they've found you a fine situation. Go and pack your bundle, and I'll take you off to M. de Rênal's, where you're going to be tutor to the children.'

'What'll I get for it?'

'Your board and lodging, your clothing and three hundred francs in wages.'

'I don't want to be a servant.'

'No one's talking about being a servant, you dolt! Would I want my son to be a servant?'

'But then who am I going to have my meals with?'

This question threw old Sorel. He realized that if he said any more he might put his foot in it. He lost his temper with Julien, swearing profusely at him and accusing him of being greedy, and went off to consult his other sons.

Julien saw them soon afterwards, leaning on their axes, deep in council. He watched them for a long time, but was unable to guess what they were saying, so he went and stationed himself on the far side of the saw to avoid being caught spying. He wanted to think about this unexpected news which was changing his destiny, but he felt incapable of acting prudently. His imagination was completely taken up with picturing what he would see in M. de Rênal's fine house.

I must give up the whole idea, he said to himself, rather than sink to eating with the servants. My father will try to make me, but I'd rather die. I've got fifteen francs and eight sous in my savings; I'll run away tonight and get to Besançon in two days by cutting across country on paths where I'm in no danger of meeting an officer of the law. There, I'll enlist in the army and, if need be, cross into Switzerland. But that means goodbye to any chance of bettering myself, goodbye to all my ambition, and goodbye to the priesthood—that fine profession which opens all doors.

This horror of eating with the servants was not natural to Julien; he would have done far more distasteful things as a means to fortune. He got this repugnance from Rousseau's* *Confessions*, the one book his imagination drew on to help him picture the world. The collected bulletins of Napoleon's great army and the *St Helena Chronicle* completed his Koran. He would have given his life for these three works. He never put his faith in any other. In accordance with one of the old army surgeon's sayings, he regarded all the other books in the world as a pack of lies, written by rogues to better themselves.

Along with his fiery temperament, Julien had one of those amazing memories which so often go with silliness. To win over old Father Chélan, on whom it was plain to him that his own future lot depended, he had learnt off by heart the whole of the New Testament in Latin. He also knew J. de Maistre's book *On the Pope*,* and believed as little in the one as in the other.

As if by mutual agreement, Sorel and his son avoided speaking to each other for the rest of the day. At dusk Julien went off to have his theology lesson from the priest, but did not consider it wise to say anything to him about the strange proposal his father had received. It may be a trap, he said to himself, I must pretend to have forgotten all about it.

Early next morning M. de Rênal summoned old Sorel, who

kept him waiting well over an hour before he finally turned
up, making innumerable excuses the moment he was inside
the door, with a little bow between each one. By dint of
enumerating all kinds of objections, Sorel gathered that his son
would eat with the master and mistress of the house, and on
days when they had company, alone in a separate room with
the children. Becoming ever more inclined to raise difficulties
the more genuinely keen he detected his worship to be, and
being in any case full of mistrust and amazement, Sorel asked
to see the bedroom where his son would sleep. It was a large,
very decently furnished room, but the three children's beds
were already in the process of being moved into it.

This circumstance was a revelation to the old peasant. He at
once asked confidently to see the suit of clothes his son was to
be given. M. de Rênal opened his desk and took out a hundred
francs.

'With this money your son will go to M. Durand the draper
and have a full black suit made to order.'

'And even if I took him out of your service,' said the
peasant, suddenly forgetting to speak with respect, 'he'd keep
this black suit?'

'I dare say.'

'Well then!' said Sorel in drawling tones, 'there only remains
one thing for us to agree on—the money you'll give him.'

'What!' exclaimed M. de Rênal indignantly. 'We agreed on
that yesterday: I'm giving him three hundred francs. I think
that's a lot, maybe too much.'

'That was your offer, I don't deny it,' said old Sorel,
speaking even more slowly; and, with a stroke of genius which
will only surprise those unfamiliar with peasants from the
Franche-Comté, he added, looking straight at M. de Rênal,
'We've had a better offer.'

A look of consternation came over the mayor when he heard
this. But he pulled himself together, and after a masterly
dialogue lasting over two hours, in which no word was said at
random, the peasant's shrewdness got the better of the rich
man's, the latter not having to rely on shrewdness for his
livelihood. All the detailed arrangements which were to govern
Julien's new existence were hammered out: not only were his

wages fixed at four hundred francs a year, but they had to be paid in advance, on the first of each month.

'Right then! I'll give him thirty-five francs,' said the mayor.

'To make a round number,' said the peasant *ingratiatingly*, 'a man as rich and generous as your worship will surely go up to thirty-six francs.'*

'All right,' said the mayor, 'but that's the end of the matter.'

This time, anger made him sound resolute. The peasant saw that he must stop there. It was then M. de Rênal's turn to score some points. He was adamant that he would not hand over the first month's pay of thirty-six francs to old Sorel, who was most anxious to receive it on his son's behalf. It occurred to M. de Rênal that he would be obliged to describe to his wife the role he had played in all this bargaining.

'Hand back the hundred francs I gave you,' he said in annoyance. 'M. Durand owes me something. I shall go with your son to have the black cloth cut.'

After this display of strength, Sorel wisely reverted to his expressions of respect: a good quarter of an hour was taken up in flowery phrases. Eventually, seeing that there really was nothing more to be gained, he took his leave. He ended his last bow with these words:

'I shall send my son up to the château.'

This was what the mayor's subordinates called his house when they wanted to please him.

Once back at his sawmill, Sorel looked in vain for his son. Wary of what might happen, Julien had gone out in the middle of the night. He wanted to take his books and his Legion of Honour cross to a place of safety. He had carted everything off to the house of a friend of his, a young timber merchant called Fouqué who lived up in the mountains behind Verrières.

When he reappeared, his father greeted him with: 'God only knows, you damned idler, if you'll ever have enough decency to repay me the cost of your food which I've been advancing you all these years! Get your rags together and be off with you to his worship's house.'

Julien was astonished not to be beaten, and left in haste. But as soon as he was out of sight of his dreaded father, he slackened his pace. He thought it would be in the interests of his hypocrisy to make a Station* in the church.

Does the word *hypocrisy* surprise you? Before being able to apply this terrible term to himself, the young peasant had already advanced some way along the path of his spiritual development.

In early childhood Julien had seen some dragoons from the sixth regiment on their way back from Italy, tying their horses to the barred windows of his father's house; they wore long white coats and had helmets with long black plumes, and the sight of them made him crazy about the army. Later, he would listen enthralled while the old army surgeon recounted the battles of Lodi bridge, Arcola and Rivoli.* He noticed how the old man's eyes lit up as he glanced at his Legion of Honour cross.

But when Julien was fourteen, they began to build a church in Verrières that may well be called magnificent for such a small town. Julien was particularly struck by the sight of four marble pillars; they became famous in the region for the deadly hatred they aroused between the justice of the peace and the young curate sent from Besançon, who was reputed to be a spy from the Congregation.* The justice of the peace was on the point of losing his job, at least that is what was generally believed. Hadn't he dared to fall out with a priest who nearly every fortnight went to Besançon where, rumour had it, he saw Monsignor the bishop?

At this point the justice of the peace, who had a large number of children, passed several sentences which appeared unjust; they were all directed against those inhabitants who read *Le Constitutionnel*.* It was a victory for the orthodox party. The sums involved were admittedly only of the order of four or five francs; but one of these small fines had to be paid by a nailmaker who was Julien's godfather. In his fury this man exclaimed: 'What a change! To think that for over twenty years the justice of the peace was considered such an upright citizen!' Julien's friend the army surgeon was dead by then.

Quite suddenly Julien stopped talking about Napoleon. He announced that he was intending to become a priest, and he was constantly to be seen at his father's sawmill engaged in

learning off by heart a Latin Bible which the priest had lent
him. The kindly old man was astonished at his progress and
spent long evenings teaching him theology. Julien never
uttered anything but pious sentiments in his presence. Who
could have guessed that this face, as pale and gentle as a girl's,
hid the unshakable determination to risk a thousand deaths
rather than fail to make his fortune!

For Julien, making his fortune meant first and foremost
getting out of Verrières; he loathed his native town. Everything
he saw there froze his imagination.

From early childhood, there had been occasions when he
was carried away by his own fantasies. At such times he
imagined with rapture that one day he would be introduced to
the pretty women of Paris, and would succeed in drawing
himself to their attention by some glorious deed. Why shouldn't
he be adored by one of them, just as Bonaparte, still penniless,
had been adored by the dazzling Mme de Beauharnais?* For
years now, Julien had never let an hour of his life pass without
telling himself that Bonaparte, an obscure lieutenant without
fortune, had made himself master of the globe with his sword.
This thought consoled him for his sufferings, which he
believed to be great, and increased any pleasure which came
his way.

The building of the church and the sentences passed by the
justice of the peace were a sudden flash of illumination for
him. He was struck by an idea which drove him almost crazy
for several weeks, and finally took hold of him with the
overwhelming force characteristic of the very first idea a
passionate individual believes he has thought of himself.

When Bonaparte first made a name for himself, France was
afraid of being invaded; military prowess was necessary and in
fashion. Nowadays you find priests of forty earning a hundred
thousand francs, in other words three times as much as the
famous generals in Napoleon's army. They need people to
back them up. Look at that justice of the peace, such a level-
headed and honest man up till now, dishonouring himself at
his age for fear of displeasing a young curate of thirty! The
answer is to be a priest.

Once, in the midst of his new-found piety, when Julien had

been studying theology for two years, he was betrayed by a sudden eruption of the inner fire which was consuming him. It happened at a dinner given by Father Chélan for a gathering of priests, at which the kindly host had presented Julien as a prodigy of learning: he went and praised Napoleon with great vehemence. Afterwards, he strapped his right arm to his chest, pretending he had dislocated it while moving a fir trunk, and kept it in this uncomfortable position for two months. After this corporal punishment he forgave himself. This was the young man of nineteen, looking puny for his age, indeed unlikely to be taken for more than seventeen at the very most, who with a small bundle clasped under his arm was preparing to enter the magnificent church in Verrières.

He found it dark and deserted. All the windows of the building had been draped with crimson material for a feast-day, and as a result the sun's rays streaming in produced a dazzling light-effect of the most awe-inspiring and religious kind. Julien shuddered. Alone in the church, he took a seat in the finest-looking pew. It bore the arms of M. de Rênal.

On the hassock Julien noticed a piece of paper with printing on it, spread out there as if meant to be read. He looked at it closely and saw:

Details of the execution and last moments of Louis Jenrel, executed at Besançon on the…

The paper was torn. On the back, the first few words of a line could be read. They ran: *The first step*.

Who can have put that paper there? Julien wondered. Poor wretch, he added with a sigh, his named ends like mine… and he crumpled up the piece of paper.

On his way out, Julien thought he saw blood beside the stoup of holy water; some of it had been spilled, and the light coming through the red drapings over the windows made it look like blood.

After a while Julien felt ashamed of his secret terror.

Could I be a coward! he said to himself. '*To arms!*'

This expression, which recurred so often in the old surgeon's accounts of battles, had heroic symbolism for Julien. He stood up and walked quickly in the direction of M. de Rênal's house.

In spite of this fine resolve, as soon as he caught sight of it twenty yards in front of him he was seized with overwhelming shyness. The iron gate was open; it looked magnificent to him, and he had to go inside.

Julien was not the only person to feel deep agitation at his arrival in the house. Mme de Rênal with her excessive shyness was put out at the thought of this stranger who, by the very nature of his duties, was constantly going to come between herself and her children. She was accustomed to having her sons sleeping in her bedroom. That morning a good many tears had been shed when she had seen their little beds moved into the quarters set aside for the tutor. She asked her husband in vain to have her youngest child Stanislas-Xavier's bed brought back into her room.

Feminine delicacy was carried to excess in Mme de Rênal. She conjured up the most disagreeable image of a boorish, ill-kempt individual, empowered to scold her children solely because he knew Latin, a barbarous language on account of which her sons would be beaten.

CHAPTER 6

Boredom

Non so più cosa son,
Cosa facio.
MOZART (*Figaro*)*

WITH the lively and graceful demeanour which came naturally
to her when she was not in company, Mme de Rênal was coming
out into the garden through the French window of the
drawing-room when she noticed the figure of a young peasant
standing by the front door. He was scarcely more than a boy,
and his pale face showed signs of recent tears. He was wearing
a spotless white shirt and carrying a very clean jacket of thick
mauve wool under his arm.

The peasant boy had so fair a complexion and such gentle
eyes that Mme de Rênal's romantically inclined nature led her
to imagine at first that he might be a girl in disguise, coming
to ask some favour of the mayor. She felt a surge of pity for
the poor soul standing there at the front door and obviously
not daring to raise a hand to the bell. She went over to him,
distracted for a moment from the deep distress which the
prospect of a tutor in the house was causing her. Julien was
facing the door and did not see her coming. He started when a
gentle voice said right in his ear: 'What have you come for,
dear?'

Julien turned round in a flash, and, struck by the gracious
look in Mme de Rênal's eyes, forgot some of his shyness. Soon,
astonished at her beauty, he forgot everything, even what he
was there for. Mme de Rênal had repeated her question.

'I've come to be tutor here, madam,' he told her at last,
thoroughly ashamed of the tears he was doing his best to wipe
away.

Mme de Rênal was struck speechless. They were standing
very close together, looking at each other. Julien had never
been spoken to gently by a person so well dressed—particularly
a woman with such a dazzling complexion. Mme de Rênal gazed

at the big teardrops poised on the young peasant's cheeks, which had now turned from pale to deep crimson. She soon began to laugh with the uncontrollable mirth of a girl; she was laughing at herself, unable to take in the full extent of her good fortune. Was it possible? was this the tutor she had imagined as an unkempt, shabby priest who would come to scold and cane her children?

'Can it be, sir,' she said to him at last, 'that you know Latin?'

The term *sir* so astonished Julien that he took a moment to reflect.

'Yes, madam,' he said shyly.

Mme de Rênal was so happy that she plucked up the courage to say to Julien: 'You won't scold the poor children too much, will you?'

'Me, scold them?' said Julien in surprise. 'Why should I?'

'You will be sure, sir, won't you,' she added after a short pause, in a voice which grew more and more emotional by the moment, 'to be kind to them. Do you promise me you will?'

To hear himself addressed again as *sir* in all seriousness, and by so well dressed a lady, was far beyond anything Julien had anticipated. Whenever he had built castles in the air in his youth, he had always told himself that no real lady would ever deign to speak to him until he had a fine uniform. Mme de Rênal, for her part, was completely beguiled by Julien's exquisite complexion, his large dark eyes and his lovely hair, which was curlier than usual because he had just cooled himself off by dipping his head in the trough under the public drinking fountain. To her great delight, she detected the shy look of a young girl in this fateful tutor whose sternness and rebarbative appearance she had so dreaded on her children's account. For a temperament as quiet as Mme de Rênal's, the mismatch between her fears and what she now saw was a major upheaval. She eventually recovered from her surprise, and was astonished to find herself on her own doorstep with this young man almost in his shirtsleeves, and standing so close to him too.

'Shall we go in, sir?' she said to him in some embarrassment.

In all her life Mme de Rênal had not been so deeply moved

by a wholly pleasurable sensation; never had so charming an apparition come as a sequel to such alarming fears. So these lovely children of hers, the objects of her tender care, wouldn't fall into the hands of a dirty, ill-tempered priest. As soon as she was inside the hall she turned to face Julien who was timidly following her. His look of astonishment at the sight of such a fine house was a further source of charm to Mme de Rênal. She couldn't believe her eyes; it seemed to her that the tutor would surely be wearing a black suit.

'But is it true, sir,' she asked him with the same hesitation and in mortal dread of being wrong, so great was the happiness her supposition gave her, 'that you really know Latin?'

These words wounded Julien's pride and broke the spell he had been living under for the past quarter of an hour.

'Yes, madam,' he replied, endeavouring to muster a chilly look, 'I know Latin as well as Father Chélan does, and he's sometimes even good enough to say better.'

Mme de Rênal thought Julien had a very fierce look on his face; he had stopped some feet away from her. She went up to him and said quietly: 'You won't give my children the cane, will you, not the first few days, even if they don't know their lessons?'

A voice so gentle and almost pleading from a lady of such beauty caused Julien to forget at once what he owed to his reputation as a Latin scholar. Mme de Rênal's face was close to his, and he caught the fragrance of a woman's summer clothes—something quite breathtaking to a simple peasant. Julien blushed deeply and said with a sigh in scarcely audible tones: 'Never fear, madam, I shall obey your every word.'

It was only at that moment, when her anxiety about her children was completely dispelled, that Mme de Rênal was struck by how extremely good-looking Julien was. The almost feminine cast of his features and his air of embarrassment did not appear at all ridiculous to a woman who was excessively shy herself. She would have been frightened by the overt masculinity which is commonly thought an essential ingredient of good looks in a man.

'How old are you, sir?' she asked Julien.

'Nearly nineteen.'

'My eldest son is eleven,' Mme de Rênal went on, completely reassured, 'he'll almost be a companion for you; you'll be able to reason with him. His father once decided to thrash him, and the child was ill for a whole week, even though he wasn't beaten at all hard.'

How different things are for me, thought Julien. Only yesterday my father beat me. How lucky these rich people are!

Mme de Rênal had already reached the stage of reading what was going on in the tutor's mind, down to the finest subtleties. She took his wistful expression for shyness and tried to encourage him.

'What's your name, sir?' she asked with a delicacy of tone which thoroughly charmed Julien's feelings, although he was quite unaware of what was going on.

'I'm called Julien Sorel, madam. I'm very nervous at coming into a strange household for the first time in my life; I shall need you to protect me and to forgive me a good many things in the early days. I never went to secondary school, I was too poor. I've never talked seriously to anyone apart from my cousin the army surgeon who's a member of the Legion of Honour, and Father Chélan our priest. He'll put in a good word for me. My brothers have always beaten me: don't believe them if they say nasty things about me to you. Forgive my mistakes, madam; I shall never intend any wrong.'

Julien was gaining confidence during this long speech. He looked closely at Mme de Rênal. Such is the effect of perfect grace when it is a natural part of someone's character—especially when the person it adorns does not take pains to cultivate it—that Julien, who was a great connoisseur of feminine beauty, would have sworn at that moment that she was no more than twenty. He was at once struck with the bold idea of kissing her hand. He soon took fright at his idea, but a moment later said to himself: It would be cowardice on my part not to carry out an action which may prove useful to me, and lessen the disdain which this beautiful lady probably feels for a poor workman only just wrested from his saw. Possibly Julien felt somewhat encouraged at remembering the term *handsome lad* which he had heard some of the girls use a number of times on Sundays over the last six months. While this inner debate was going on, Mme de Rênal had been giving him one or two words of instruction on how to make a start with the children. Julien's struggle to take hold of himself made him turn very pale again, and he said awkwardly:

'I'll never beat your children, madam; I swear before God I won't.'

As he uttered these words, he plucked up the courage to take Mme de Rênal's hand and raise it to his lips. She was astonished at his gesture, and when she thought about it, shocked. As the weather was very hot, her arm was quite bare under her shawl, and it had been completely uncovered when Julien raised her hand to his lips. After a moment or so she was cross with herself, feeling that she had not been quick enough to take offence.

Hearing the sound of voices M. de Rênal came out of his study and said to Julien with the solemnity and smooth condescension he assumed when officiating at weddings in the town hall: 'It is essential that I have a word with you before the children see you.'

He ushered Julien into a room and asked his wife to remain with them, despite her desire to leave them alone. Once the door was shut, M. de Rênal sat down gravely.

'Father Chélan tells me you are diligent and well-behaved. Everyone here will treat you with respect, and if I am pleased with you I shall arrange a modest settlement for you at a later date. My wish is that you should have no further dealings with your family or friends, as their manners are not fitting for my children. Here are thirty-six francs for the first month; but I must have your word that you will not give a single penny of this money to your father.'

M. de Rênal was furious with the old man for having been more cunning than himself over this deal.

'Now, *sir*—for everyone here is under orders to call you "sir", and you will appreciate the advantage of entering a respectable household—now, sir, it is not appropriate for the children to see you dressed in a jacket. Have the servants seen him?' M. de Rênal asked his wife.

'No, my dear,' she replied, looking deeply pensive.

'So much the better. Put this on,' he said to the astonished young man, handing him one of his own frock-coats. 'And now we shall call on M. Durand, the draper.'

When, over an hour later, M. de Rênal returned home with the new tutor dressed entirely in black, he found his wife sitting in the same spot. She felt her peace of mind return in Julien's presence: studying him closely made her forget to be afraid of him. Julien had no thoughts for her; despite all his mistrust of fate and of mankind, he was at that moment still only a child at heart. It seemed to him that aeons had passed since that moment three hours ago when he had stood trembling in the church. He noticed how aloof Mme de Rênal was looking, and took it she was angry because he had dared to kiss her hand. But the sense of pride he derived from the feel of clothes so unlike the ones he was accustomed to wearing put him in such an abnormal state of excitement, and he was so anxious to hide his delight, that every movement he made seemed jerky and uncontrolled. Mme de Rênal gazed at him with astonishment in her eyes.

'A little gravity, sir,' said M. de Rênal to Julien, 'if you wish to be respected by my children and my servants.'

'Sir,' replied Julien, 'I feel uncomfortable in these new clothes. I'm only a poor peasant, and I've never worn anything but jackets. With your permission, I'll go and retire to my room.'

'What is your opinion of our new acquisition?' M. de Rênal asked his wife.

In an almost instinctive reaction—one which certainly escaped her conscious awareness—Mme de Rênal concealed the truth from her husband.

'I'm by no means as delighted as you are with this peasant lad. Your attentions will give him ideas above his station, and you'll be obliged to dismiss him before the month is up.'

'Well then! we'll dismiss him; it will have cost me a hundred francs or so at most, and Verrières will have grown used to seeing a tutor in charge of M. de Rênal's children. This end could not have been achieved if I had left Julien in workman's attire. When I dismiss him, I shall of course retain the full black suit I've just ordered from the draper. He will only keep

what I found ready-made at the the the tailor's, and had him put
on.'

The hour that Julien spent in his room seemed a brief
moment to Mme de Rênal. The children, who had been told of
the new tutor's arrival, were besieging their mother with
questions. At last Julien made his appearance. He was a
changed man. It would have been incorrect to say that he was
grave: he was gravity incarnate. He was introduced to the
children, and spoke to them in a manner which astonished
even M. de Rênal.

'I am here, young gentlemen,' he said to them as he wound
up his address, 'to teach you Latin. You know what it means
to say your lessons. Here is the Holy Bible,' he went on,
showing them a pocket-sized volume bound in black. 'More
specifically it is the story of Our Lord Jesus Christ, the part
we call the New Testament. I shall often have you say your
lessons, so now you take me through mine.'

Adolphe, the eldest of the three children, had taken the
book.

'Open it up—at random,' Julien continued, 'and give me
the first word of any verse. I shall recite the Holy Book, which
we all must live by, word for word until you stop me.'

Adolphe opened the book and read out a word, and Julien
recited the whole page as fluently as if he had been speaking
his native tongue. M. de Rênal gazed at his wife in triumph.
The children, seeing their parents' astonishment, were looking
on wide-eyed. A servant came to the drawing-room door, and
still Julien went on speaking Latin. The servant stood stock-
still at first, and then vanished. Soon the mistress's chambermaid and the cook appeared at the door; by then Adolphe had
already opened the book in eight different places, and Julien
was still reciting with the same fluency.

'Bless my soul! there's a fine young priest for you!' exclaimed
the cook, who was a good-hearted and very pious girl.

M. de Rênal's self-esteem was bothering him. Far from
thinking of putting the tutor to the test, he was wholly
engrossed in racking his brains for a few words of Latin. He
eventually managed to bring out a line of Horace. Julien's only
Latin was the Bible. He replied with a frown: 'The sacred

ministry which is my calling forbids me to read so profane a poet.'

M. de Rênal quoted a fair number of lines purportedly from Horace. He told his children all about Horace, but the children were so struck with admiration that they scarcely paid any attention to what he was saying. They were gazing at Julien.

As the servants were still at the door, Julien thought it right to prolong the ordeal.

'Now,' he said to the youngest of the children, 'Master Stanislas-Xavier must also give me a passage from the Holy Book.'

Little Stanislas, bursting with pride, read out the first word of a verse as best he could, and Julien recited the whole page. To complete M. de Rênal's triumph, while Julien was in the midst of reciting, in came M. Valenod, the owner of the fine Normandy cobs, and M. Charcot de Maugiron, the sub-prefect* of the district. This scene earned Julien his title of *sir*: even the servants did not dare withhold it from him.

That evening the whole of Verrières flocked to M. de Rênal's house to see the wonder. Julien replied to everyone in gloomy tones which discouraged familiarity. His fame spread so fast through the town that a few days later M. de Rênal, fearful of losing him to someone else, invited him to sign an undertaking for two years.

'No, sir,' replied Julien coldly, 'if you wanted to dismiss me, I should be obliged to leave. An undertaking which is binding on me without putting you under any obligation is not equitable, and I cannot accept it.'

Julien handled matters so skilfully that less than a month after his arrival in the house, he was even respected by M. de Rênal himself. As the priest was on bad terms with both M. de Rênal and M. Valenod, there was no one to betray Julien's former passion for Napoleon, and he never spoke of him but with horror.

CHAPTER 7
Elective affinities*

Their only way of touching a heart is to wound it.
MODERN AUTHOR

THE children adored him, but he did not like them at all: his mind was on other things. Whatever the little rascals did, he never lost his patience. He was a good tutor to them—cold, fair, imperturbable and yet much loved, because his arrival had somehow dispelled the boredom in the house. For his part he felt nothing but hatred and loathing towards the high society he had been admitted to, right down at the bottom end of the table, it's true, which perhaps explains the hatred and the loathing. There were some ceremonial dinners where he had great difficulty in containing his hatred for everything surrounding him. On one occasion—it was the feast of St Louis*—when M. Valenod was holding forth at M. de Rênal's house, Julien was on the point of giving himself away; he escaped into the garden, saying he wanted to see what the children were up to. All this praise of honesty! he exclaimed, you'd think it was the only virtue there was. And yet what esteem, what servile respect for a man whose fortune has obviously doubled and even tripled since he's been in charge of the workhouse! I'm ready to bet he even makes a profit on the funds set aside for the foundlings, those paupers whose wretchedness gives them a more sacred claim than anyone else! Ah! what monsters! what monsters! I too am a sort of foundling, hated by my father, my brothers and my whole family.

A few days before the feast of St Louis, when Julien had been out walking alone reciting his prayer book in a little wood called the Belvedere which overlooks the Avenue de la Fidélité, he had tried in vain to avoid meeting his two brothers whom he could see from a distance coming towards him down a lonely path. Such jealousy had been stirred up in these two coarse labourers by their brother's fine black suit, by his exceedingly clean appearance, and his genuine disdain of them, that they had thrashed him and left him senseless and covered in blood. Mme de Rênal, who was out walking with M. Valenod and the sub-prefect, chanced to come through the wood; she saw Julien lying on the ground and took him for dead. She was so stricken that M. Valenod became quite jealous.

His alarm was premature. Julien thought Mme de Rênal exceedingly beautiful, but he hated her on account of her beauty: it was the first reef which had almost wrecked his fortune. He spoke to her as little as possible, so as to erase the memory of that passionate impulse on the first day which had made him kiss her hand.

Elisa, Mme de Rênal's chambermaid, had lost no time in falling in love with the young tutor, and she often confided in her mistress. Mlle Elisa's love had earned Julien the hatred of one of the valets. One day he overheard the man saying to Elisa: 'You won't speak to me any more, now that this filthy tutor is in the house.' Julien did not deserve this insult, but as a good-looking fellow he instinctively took twice as much care as before over his personal appearance. M. Valenod's hatred of him increased twofold as well. He declared publicly that such vanity ill suited a young abbé. Barring the cassock, Julien indeed wore ecclesiastical dress.

Mme de Rênal noticed that he spoke to Mlle Elisa more often than usual, and she discovered that the cause of these exchanges was the plight Julien found himself in on account of his very scant wardrobe. He had so little linen that he was obliged to have it laundered very frequently elsewhere, and Elisa proved useful to him over these small services. Mme de Rênal was touched by such extreme poverty, which she had not suspected: she felt an urge to give him presents, but didn't dare. This inner resistance was the first painful feeling Julien caused her. Until then the name Julien had been synonymous for her with a feeling of joy that was pure and entirely of the mind. Tormented by the thought of Julien's poverty, Mme de Rênal spoke to her husband about making him a present of some linen:

'How gullible you are!' he replied. 'The very idea of it! Why on earth give presents to a man we are entirely satisfied with, and who gives us good service? If he neglected his appearance, now that would be the moment to reawaken his zeal!'

Mme de Rênal was humiliated by this way of looking at things; it would never have struck her before Julien's arrival. She could not help thinking to herself, every time she noticed how extremely clean the young abbé's admittedly simple attire was: 'Poor boy, how does he manage?'

Gradually she came to pity Julien for everything he lacked, rather than feeling shocked by it.

Mme de Rênal was one of those provincial women who may well strike you as foolish during the first fortnight of your acquaintance. She had no experience of life, and did not cultivate conversation. She was sensitive and aloof by nature, and the instinct for happiness present in all human beings made her disregard—most of the time—the actions of the vulgar characters in whose midst chance had cast her.

She would have been noted for her spontaneity and liveliness of mind if she had been given any kind of education. But as an heiress, she had been brought up by nuns who were fervent worshippers of the Sacred Heart of Jesus, and were filled with violent hatred for all Frenchmen who were enemies of the Jesuits. Mme de Rênal had had enough sense to reject as absurd everything she had learnt at the convent, and to forget it pretty rapidly; but she did not replace it with anything, and ended up totally ignorant. The flattery which had come her way very early on as the heiress to a large fortune, together with a marked bent for fervent religious zeal, had set her upon a completely inward-looking way of life. Beneath an appearance of the most civil concern for others and total denial of her own will, which the husbands in Verrières held up as an example to their wives, and M. de Rênal drew great pride from, her inner frame of mind stemmed in fact from the most haughty of temperaments. A princess renowned for her pride takes infinitely more notice of what her noblemen are doing round about her than this seemingly gentle and modest woman took of all her husband's words and actions. Until Julien arrived, she had not really taken any notice of anything except her children. Their minor ailments, their sorrows, their little joys absorbed all the tenderness of this soul whose only passion in life had been God, when she was at the Sacred Heart in Besançon.

Without her deigning to say so to anyone, if one of her sons had a bout of fever she was reduced to virtually the same state as if the child had been dead. A burst of coarse laughter, a shrug of the shoulders accompanied by some trite maxim on the folly of women, had always been the response when her need to confide in someone had led her to share anxieties of this kind with her husband in the early years of their marriage. Jocular reactions like these, especially where her children's illnesses were concerned, simply turned the knife in Mme de Rênal's wounded heart. This was what she found in place of the obsequious and cloying flattery of the Jesuit convent where she had spent her youth. She learnt about life through suffering. Too proud to talk about this sort of misery even to her friend Mme Derville, she imagined that all men were like her husband, or M. Valenod or the sub-prefect Charcot de Maugiron. Vulgarity and the most brutish insensitivity to anything that did not involve money, rank or orders of knighthood; a blind hatred of any argument that stood in their way—these seemed to her to be the natural attributes of the other sex, like wearing boots and a felt hat.

After all these years Mme de Rênal was still not accustomed to the ways of these money-driven folk in whose midst she had to live.

Hence her attraction to the young peasant Julien. She discovered sweet pleasures, all gleaming with the charm of novelty, in the communion of spirit with someone so noble and proud. Mme de Rênal had soon forgiven him his extreme ignorance which was yet one more source of charm to her, and the roughness of his manners which she succeeded in tempering. She found him worth listening to, even when the conversation was on the most trivial of subjects, even when it was about some poor dog that had got run over crossing the road by a peasant's cart going at a trot. The sight of such suffering caused her husband to let out one of his loud laughs, whereas she saw Julien's beautiful, exquisitely arched black eyebrows draw together in pain. Little by little she formed the view that generosity, nobility of soul and humanity only existed in this young abbé. She felt for him all the sympathy and even the admiration which these virtues inspire in someone of good breeding.

In Paris, Julien's situation with regard to Mme de Rênal would very soon have become more straightforward; but in Paris, love is born of fiction. The young tutor and his shy mistress would have found three or four novels, and even couplets from the Théâtre de Madame,* clarifying their situation. The novels would have outlined for them the roles they had to play, and given them a model to imitate; and sooner or later Julien would have been forced by his vanity to follow this model, albeit without pleasure and perhaps with overt reluctance.

In a small town in the Aveyron* or the Pyrenees, the slightest incident would have been rendered decisive by the torrid climate. Beneath our more sullen skies, a young man without means, who is only ambitious because his delicate sensibility makes him crave some of the pleasures afforded by money, has daily dealings with a woman of thirty, genuinely virtuous, absorbed by her children, and never looking to novels for examples on which to model her conduct. Everything proceeds slowly, everything develops gradually in the provinces; it is all more spontaneous.

Often, when she thought of how poor the young tutor was, Mme de Rênal would be moved to tears. One day Julien caught her actually weeping.

'Oh madam, can some misfortune have struck you?'

'No, my dear,' she replied; 'call the children, and we'll go for a walk.'

She took his arm and leant on it in a way which struck him as odd. It was the first time she had addressed him as *my dear*.

Towards the end of the walk Julien noticed that she kept blushing. She slackened her pace.

'You'll have heard', she said without looking at him, 'that I'm sole heir to a rich aunt who lives in Besançon. She showers me with presents... My sons are getting on so well... so remarkably well... that I'd like to press you to accept a small gift as a token of my gratitude. Just a few sovereigns to get you

some linen. But...' she added, blushing still more deeply, and
at this point she broke off.

'What, madam?' exclaimed Julien.

'It would serve no purpose', she went on, lowering her head,
'to mention this to my husband.'

'I am humble, madam, but I am not base,' retorted Julien,
stopping in his tracks and drawing himself up to his full
height, his eyes blazing with fury. 'That's something you
should have thought about. I'd be no better than a servant if I
put myself in the position of hiding from M. de Rênal anything
whatsoever concerning *my money*.'

Mme de Rênal was dumbfounded.

'His worship the mayor', Julien continued, 'has paid me five
times thirty-six francs since I took up residence in his house.
I'm ready to show my accounts book to him or to anyone
else—even to M. Valenod who hates me.'

This outburst left Mme de Rênal pale and trembling, and the
walk finished without either of them finding a pretext for
starting up the conversation again. Any thought of loving Mme
de Rênal became more and more impossible for a proud spirit
like Julien's. As for her, she felt fresh respect and admiration
for him; she had been reprimanded by him. Under the guise
of making up for the humiliation she had involuntarily caused
him, she allowed herself to indulge him with the most tender
attentions. The novelty of these ways was a source of happiness
to Mme de Rênal for a week. Their effect was to soothe Julien's
anger in part; he was very far from seeing in them anything
which might resemble a personal liking.

That's what these rich people are like, he reflected, they
humiliate you, and then think they can make up for it all by a
few ridiculous gestures!

Mme de Rênal took all this too much to heart and was as yet
too much of an innocent to be able to refrain from telling her
husband, despite her resolutions to the contrary, what she had
offered Julien and how she had been rebuffed.

'How on earth', replied M. de Rênal in extreme vexation,
'could you tolerate a refusal from a mere *servant*?'

And as Mme de Rênal protested at this term:

'I am speaking, madam, as the late Prince de Condé* did

when he presented his chamberlains to his new wife: "*All these people*", he said to her, "*are our servants.*" I have read you that passage from Besenval's Memoirs* which is quite essential for an understanding of precedence. Anyone who isn't a gentleman, and lives in your house and receives a wage, is your servant. I shall have a word or two with this M. Julien, and give him a hundred francs.'

'Oh, my dear!' said Mme de Rênal, trembling, 'Then at least don't do it in front of the servants!'

'Quite so, they might be envious and with good reason,' said her husband as he went off, thinking about the relative size of the sum.

Mme de Rênal collapsed on to a chair, almost fainting with misery. He's going to humiliate Julien, and it's all my fault! She was revolted by her husband, and hid her face in her hands. She vowed never to go confiding again.

When she next saw Julien, she was trembling all over, and her chest felt so constricted she was unable to utter a single word. In her embarrassment she took hold of his hands and squeezed them.

'Well now, my dear,' she said at last, 'are you pleased with my husband?'

'How could I fail to be?' Julien answered with a bitter smile. 'He gave me a hundred francs.'

Mme de Rênal looked at him as if she did not know what to make of this.

'Give me your arm,' she said with a note of bravery in her voice that Julien had never heard before.

She was bold enough to venture as far as the bookseller's in Verrières, in spite of his terrible reputation for liberal views. There she chose books to the value of ten louis which she gave to her sons. But these were books she knew Julien wanted. She insisted there and then, in the bookseller's shop, that each of her sons write his name in the books which fell to his share. While Mme de Rênal was feeling glad that she was somehow able to make amends to Julien in this audacious manner, he was astonished at the number of books he saw displayed at the bookseller's. Never had he dared set foot in so profane a spot. His heart was thumping. Far from having any mind to guess

what was going on in Mme de Rênal's heart, he was deep in
thought about ways and means for a theology student to
procure himself some of these books. He eventually came up
with the idea that it would be possible with a little skill to
persuade M. de Rênal that his sons ought to be set exercises
on the history of the famous gentlefolk born in the region.
After working at it for a month, Julien saw his idea catch on;
so much so that when speaking to the mayor some time later,
he was bold enough to risk suggesting a course of action which
would be altogether more onerous for the noble mayor: it
involved contributing to the wealth of a liberal by taking out a
subscription with the bookseller. M. de Rênal was willing to
agree that it was wise to acquaint his eldest son *de visu** with a
number of works he would hear mentioned in conversation
when he was at the Military Academy; but Julien found that
the mayor drew the line at going any further. He suspected
there must be some hidden reason, but was unable to fathom
what it might be.

'I was thinking, sir,' he said to him one day, 'that it would
be highly unsuitable for the name of a worthy gentleman such
as a member of the Rênal family to appear in the sordid files of
the bookseller.'

M. de Rênal brightened visibly.

'It would also be a very bad mark for a poor theology
student', Julien went on in humbler tones, 'if it could one day
be discovered that his name had been on the files of a
bookseller who hired out books. The liberals would be able to
accuse me of having requested the most infamous books. Who
knows if they mightn't even go as far as writing in after my
name the titles of these wicked books.'

But Julien was losing the scent. He could see the mayor's
face taking on a look of embarrassment and ill-temper. Julien
stopped talking. I've got my man, he said to himself.

A few days later, when the eldest boy asked Julien in the
presence of M. de Rênal about a book announced in *La
Quotidienne*,* the young tutor replied:

'To avoid giving the Jacobin party* any cause for scoring a
victory, and yet to enable me to answer Master Adolphe, it

would be possible to have a subscription taken out with the bookseller in the name of the lowest of your servants.'

'Now that's not a bad idea at all,' said M. de Rênal, obviously quite delighted.

'All the same, it would have to be laid down,' said Julien with that solemn and almost sad expression which so becomes certain people when they see the fulfilment of aspirations they have cherished the longest, 'it would have to be laid down that the servant may not take out any novels. Once inside the house, these dangerous books could corrupt Mme de Rênal's women, and the servant himself.'

'You're forgetting political pamphlets,' added the mayor in a superior voice. He wanted to hide his admiration for the clever *mezzo-termine** devised by his children's tutor.

Julien's life was thus made up of a series of little negotiations; and making a success of them preoccupied him much more than the feeling of special liking which he could easily have read in Mme de Rênal's heart if only he had wished to.

The psychological situation in which he had found himself all his life continued to apply in the mayor of Verrières's house. There, just as at his father's sawmill, he deeply despised the people he lived with, and was hated by them. Every day he could see from the way the sub-prefect or M. Valenod or other friends of the household related recent happenings they had witnessed, how out of touch they were with reality. If an action struck him as admirable, it was bound to be the one to attract the censure of the people around him. His private response was always: What monsters or what fools! The amusing thing is that with all his pride, it often happened that he didn't understand a word of what was being discussed.

In all his life he had never talked sincerely to anyone except the old army surgeon, and the few ideas he had were about Bonaparte's campaigns in Italy, or about surgery. His youthful courage took pleasure in detailed descriptions of the most painful operations; he said to himself: I wouldn't have batted an eyelid.

The first time Mme de Rênal tried to have a conversation with him that did not concern her children's upbringing, he began to talk about surgical operations. She turned pale and begged him to stop.

Julien's knowledge went no further. And so, as he spent his days with Mme de Rênal, the strangest of silences fell between them as soon as they were alone together. In the drawing-room, however humble his air, she detected in his eyes a look of intellectual superiority towards any and every visitor to her house. But she had only to find herself alone with him for an instant to see him visibly embarrassed. This worried her, for her feminine instinct told her that this embarrassment did not spring from tenderness.

Basing himself on some vague idea picked up from an account of high society as seen by the old army surgeon, Julien felt humiliated as soon as silence fell at any time when he was in the company of a woman, as if he were to blame personally for this silence. His feeling was infinitely more distressing when he and the woman were alone together. His imagination, filled with the most exaggerated, the most Spanish of notions about what a man should say when he is alone with a woman, offered him nothing in his plight but suggestions which could not be entertained. His soul was up in the clouds, and yet he was unable to break the most humiliating of silences. His look of severity during his long walks with Mme de Rênal and the children was thus increased by the most cruel suffering. He despised himself horribly. If he was unfortunate enough to force himself to speak, he found himself saying totally ridiculous things. To crown his wretchedness, he could see his own absurdity and magnified it to himself; but what he could not see was the expression in his eyes: they were so beautiful, and revealed such an ardent spirit, that like good actors they sometimes put a charming gloss on words that scarcely deserved one. Mme de Rênal noticed that when he was alone with her he never succeeded in saying anything memorable unless he was distracted by some unforeseen event, and was not thinking about turning a nice compliment. As the friends of the family never treated her to any new and brilliant ideas, she revelled in Julien's bursts of wit.

Since the fall of Napoleon, any appearance of gallantry has been strictly banned from provincial mores. People are afraid of being deprived of office. Rogues look to the Congregation for support, and hypocrisy has made great strides even among the liberal classes. Boredom has become acute. The only pleasures left are reading and agriculture.

Mᵐᵉ de Rênal, the rich heiress of a devout aunt, and married at sixteen to a respectable gentleman, had never in her life experienced or witnessed anything remotely resembling love. It was really only her confessor, the worthy Father Chélan, who had talked to her about love, in connection with M. Valenod's advances; and he had given her such a disgusting picture of it that all the word conjured up in her mind was the idea of the most abject debauchery. She treated as an exception—or even as something quite outside the realm of nature—the kind of love she had encountered in the very small number of novels which chance had put in her path. Protected by this ignorance, Mᵐᵉ de Rênal went her way perfectly happy, with Julien constantly in her thoughts, and it never occurred to her that she might have the slightest cause for self-reproach.

CHAPTER 8

Minor events

Then there were sighs, the deeper for suppression,
And stolen glances, sweeter for the theft,
And burning blushes, though for no transgression.
Don Juan, C. I, st. 74*

THE angelic sweetness which Mme de Rênal's character and
her present happiness bestowed upon her only became clouded
when her thoughts turned to her chambermaid Elisa. The girl
inherited some money, and went to confess to Father Chélan
that she had it in mind to marry Julien. The priest was
genuinely delighted at his friend's happiness; and he was
greatly surprised when Julien announced to him in resolute
tones that Mlle Elisa's proposal was not acceptable to him.

'Beware, dear boy, of what your heart is up to,' said the
priest with a frown. 'I congratulate you on the strength of your
vocation, if that's the only reason why you spurn a more than
adequate fortune. I've been the priest here in Verrières these
fifty-six years, and yet all the signs are that I'm about to be
dismissed from office. It distresses me greatly, although I do
have an income of eight hundred pounds. I'm telling you this
detail so that you don't have any illusions about what awaits
you if you go into the priesthood. If you're thinking of courting
men in high office, it's a sure road to eternal damnation. You'll
be able to make your fortune, but you'll have to trample on
the poor and wretched, flatter the sub-prefect, the mayor—
anyone held in esteem—and serve their passions. Such conduct, which is known in society as worldly wisdom, need not
for a layman be totally incompatible with salvation; but with
our calling, we have to choose; you either make your fortune
in this world or the next, there's no half-way house. So think
about it, my dear fellow, and come back to me in three days'
time with your final answer. I dimly perceive in the depths of
your character a smouldering ardour which doesn't signal the
sort of moderation and complete renunciation of worldly
advantages that are essential in a priest. I predict great things

of your intellect; but if you'll allow me to say so,' the kindly priest added with tears in his eyes, 'I shall fear for your salvation if you go into the priesthood.'

Julien was ashamed of the emotion he felt; for the first time in his life, he could see that someone cared for him; he savoured his tears, and went off to hide them in the deep woods above Verrières.

Why am I in this state? he wondered to himself at last; I feel I would willingly give my life a hundred times over for kind old Father Chélan, and yet he's just proved to me that I'm a mere idiot. He's the crucial one I have to deceive, and he sees straight through me. This secret ardour he was talking about is my ambition to make my fortune. He thinks I'm unworthy to be a priest, at the very moment when I imagined that by sacrificing an income of fifty louis I would give him the highest opinion of my piety and my vocation.

In future, Julien went on, I shall only count on the parts of my character that I've put to the test. Whoever would have predicted that I'd get any pleasure from shedding tears! Or that I should feel affection for someone who proves to me that I'm a mere idiot!

Three days later Julien had found the pretext he should have been armed with right from the start: it was a piece of slander, but does that matter? He admitted to the priest with much hesitation that he had been put off the proposed marriage from the outset by a consideration which he could not go into because it would be damaging to a third party. This was tantamount to impugning Elisa's conduct. Father Chélan detected in Julien's attitude a sort of vehemence that was entirely worldly, and altogether different from the kind which should have inspired a young Levite.

'Dear fellow,' he said to him, pursuing the matter, 'you'd do better to become an honest country squire, learned and worthy of respect, than be a priest without a calling.'

Julien replied very ably to these fresh admonishments as far as language went: he was able to produce the words that a fervent young seminarist would have used. But his tone of voice in uttering them, and the ill-disguised vehemence which shone in his eyes, caused great alarm to Father Chélan.

You mustn't take too dim a view of Julien's future prospects. He could come up with just the phrases required by a cautious and wily hypocrisy. That's not bad at his age. As far as tone and gesture were concerned, he lived among country folk, and had been deprived of great models to imitate. Later on, he had only to be given the opportunity to associate with such gentlemen and he at once became admirable in gesture as well as in word.

Mme de Rênal was astonished that her chambermaid's new fortune did not make her any happier; she noticed how the girl was constantly visiting the priest, and coming back with tears in her eyes. At last Elisa spoke to her of her marriage.

Mme de Rênal felt as though she had fallen ill; a kind of fever prevented her from sleeping; she only revived when she had her maid or Julien with her. She could think of nothing but the two of them, and the happiness they would experience in their married life. The little house where they would have to live in poverty on an income of fifty louis imprinted itself on her imagination in the most charming colours. Julien could very easily become a barrister in Bray, the sub-prefecture two leagues* away from Verrières; in which case she would see him from time to time.

Mme de Rênal genuinely believed that she was going to go mad; she told her husband, and eventually fell ill. That very evening, while her maid was attending to her, she noticed that the girl was crying. She loathed Elisa at the time, and had just been short with her; she apologized for it. Elisa's tears only increased; she said that if her mistress would allow it, she would tell her all her troubles.

'Go on,' replied Mme de Rênal.

'Well you see, madam, he's turned me down; people must have said nasty things to him about me out of spite, and he believes them.'

'Who's turned you down?' Mme de Rênal asked, hardly able to breathe.

'Who do you think, madam?' replied the maid, sobbing. 'Mr Julien, of course. Father Chélan couldn't overcome his reluctance; because, you see, Father Chélan thinks he shouldn't refuse an honest girl on the grounds she's been a chambermaid. After all, Mr Julien's father's only a carpenter; and how did he earn his living before he came to Madam's?'

Mme de Rênal had ceased to listen; the surfeit of happiness had almost deprived her of her senses. She asked her maid to confirm several times over that Julien had given a definite refusal which ruled out the possibility of going back to a more sensible decision.

'I want to make a last attempt,' she told her maid. 'I shall speak to Mr Julien.'

After lunch the next day, Mme de Rênal gave herself the sweet pleasure of pleading her rival's cause, and seeing Elisa's hand and fortune steadfastly spurned for an hour on end.

Gradually Julien dropped his stilted replies, and ended up answering Mme de Rênal's sensible arguments with some degree of wit. She could not withstand the flood of happiness which overwhelmed her after so many days of despair. She suddenly felt quite unwell. When she had recovered and was comfortably settled in her room, she sent everyone away. She was deeply astonished.

Could I be in love with Julien? she asked herself at last.

This discovery, which at any other moment would have plunged her into remorse and deep agitation, remained a matter of intellectual contemplation for her: she was very struck by it, but somehow indifferent. She was so exhausted by everything she had just been through that she had no emotional energy left to experience any feelings.

Mme de Rênal tried to settle to her needlework, and fell into a deep sleep. When she awoke, she did not experience as strong a sense of alarm as she should have done. She was too happy to be able to put a bad interpretation on anything. This good provincial woman was so naïve and innocent that she had never tortured her soul to try and force it to experience some new nuance of feeling or unhappiness. Before Julien's arrival she had been completely absorbed by the volume of work which, in regions remote from Paris, is the lot of a good mother and housewife; and she thought of passions as we think of the lottery: inevitably a confidence trick, and a source of happiness pursued only by madmen.

The bell rang for dinner; Mme de Rênal blushed deeply when

she heard Julien's voice as he brought the children in. She had become quite cunning since falling in love, and to explain away her flushed appearance she complained of a terrible headache.

'That's the way with all women,' M. de Rênal replied with a loud laugh. 'There's always something needing mending with those machines!'

Though accustomed to this kind of wit, Mme de Rênal was shocked by his tone of voice. To distract herself, she looked at Julien's face; had he been the ugliest of men, he would still have been attractive to her at that moment.

Careful to copy the habits of people at Court, M. de Rênal took up residence at Vergy as soon as the first fine days of spring arrived. This is the village made famous by the tragic adventure of Gabrielle.* A few hundred yards from the picturesque ruins of the old gothic church, M. de Rênal owns an old château with four turrets and a garden laid out like the one at the Tuileries,* full of boxwood borders and walks lined with chestnut trees pruned twice a year. A neighbouring field planted with apple trees provided a place for walks. There were about ten magnificent walnut trees at the bottom of the orchard; their great canopy of leaves rose to a height of some eighty feet.

'Each one of these cursed walnuts costs me half an acre's worth of harvest,' M. de Rênal would say whenever his wife admired them. 'Wheat won't grow in their shade.'

The sight of the countryside struck Mme de Rênal as quite new, and she marvelled at it to the point of ecstasy. The feeling within her made her witty and decisive. Two days after their arrival in Vergy, when M. de Rênal had gone back to town on civic business, Mme de Rênal hired some workmen at her own expense. Julien had given her the idea of a little sandy path which would wind through the orchard and under the great walnut trees, allowing the children to go for walks in the early morning without getting their shoes drenched with dew. This idea was carried out less than twenty-four hours after being thought up. Mme de Rênal spent the whole day happily in Julien's company, giving instructions to the workmen.

When the mayor of Verrières returned from town, he was most surprised to find the path finished. Mme de Rênal was equally surprised to see him back; she had forgotten about his existence. For two months he talked peevishly about the audacity of carrying out so important an *improvement* without consulting him; but Mme de Rênal had done it at her own expense, which consoled him a little.

She spent her days running about the orchard with her children, and chasing after butterflies. They had made big hood-shaped nets out of pale-coloured gauze to catch the *lepidoptera* with. This was the barbarous name that Julien taught Mme de Rênal to use. For she had had M. Godart's excellent study* sent over from Besançon, and Julien told her all about the peculiar habits of these poor creatures.

They were mercilessly stuck with pins on to a large cardboard frame which was also set up by Julien.

This at last provided Mme de Rênal and Julien with a topic of conversation, and he was no longer condemned to suffer the terrible torture inflicted on him by moments of silence.

They talked endlessly to each other, and with considerable interest, although always on wholly innocent subjects. This busy and cheerful life of activity suited everyone except Mlle Elisa, who found herself overwhelmed with work. 'Not even at carnival time,' she would say, 'when there's a ball at Verrières, has Madam ever taken so much trouble over her appearance; she changes dresses two or three times a day.'

As our intention is to flatter no one, we shall not deny that Mme de Rênal, who had lovely skin, had some dresses cut to leave her arms and bosom very exposed. She had a very good figure, and this way of dressing suited her wonderfully.

'You've never *been so young*, Mme de Rênal,' she was told by her friends from Verrières who came to dine at Vergy. (This is a local expression.)

The strange thing is—and it will scarcely be believed by people like ourselves—that Mme de Rênal had no conscious intention in taking so much trouble. It afforded her pleasure; and without giving any other thought to it, she did in fact devote all the time she was not catching butterflies with the children and Julien to dressmaking with Elisa. The only time she went into Verrières to shop was when she fancied some new summer dresses that had just been brought from Mulhouse.

She arrived back in Vergy bringing with her a young woman who was one of her relatives. Since her marriage Mme de Rênal had been drawn imperceptibly closer to Mme Derville, who had once been her companion at the Sacred Heart.

Mme Derville was much amused by what she called her cousin's wild ideas. 'I'd never think of that on my own,' she would say. These sudden notions, which would have been called impulses in Paris, were something Mme de Rênal felt ashamed of when she was with her husband, as though they looked foolish; but Mme Derville's presence encouraged her. At first she imparted her thoughts to her in a timid voice; but when the two ladies were alone together for some while, Mme de Rênal's mind became far more adventurous, and a long morning on their own passed in a flash, leaving the two friends in ebullient spirits. On this visit, the sensible Mme Derville found her cousin much less ebullient and far happier.

Julien for his part had lived like a real child since the beginning of his stay in the country, as happy chasing after butterflies as his young charges were. After so much constraint and careful scheming, now that he was alone, away from the public gaze, and instinctively quite unafraid of Mme de Rênal, he gave himself up to the sheer pleasure of living, which is so intense at that age, and when you're in the most beautiful mountains in the world.

From the very moment she arrived, it seemed to Julien that Mme Derville was a friend. He lost no time in showing her the view from the far end of the new path under the great walnuts; it is indeed equal if not superior to the very finest that Switzerland or the Italian lakes can offer. If you go up the steep slope which starts a few feet from that spot, you soon find yourself overlooking deep ravines with oak woods growing along their edges, which extend almost to the river itself. It was to the summit of these sheer crags that Julien, feeling happy, free and even something more—lord of the household—would take the two ladies, and delight in their admiration for these sublime views.

'I find it just like the music of Mozart,' said Mme Derville.

His brothers' jealousy and the presence of a despotic and ill-tempered father had spoilt Julien's enjoyment of the country-side round Verrières. At Vergy he had no such bitter memories, and for the first time in his life he found himself with no enemies. When M. de Rênal was in town, which was a frequent occurrence, he plucked up the courage to read. Soon, instead of reading at night, taking care at that to conceal his lamp inside an overturned vase, he felt able to indulge in sleep. During the day, between the children's lessons, he would come to these rocks with the book which alone ruled his conduct and was the object of his delight. It was at once a source of happiness, ecstasy and consolation to him in moments of discouragement.

Certain things which Napoleon says about women, and a number of passages discussing the merits of novels fashionable during his reign, now gave Julien for the very first time the kind of thoughts that any other young man of his age would have long since been entertaining.

The summer heatwave arrived. They took to spending their evenings beneath an enormous lime tree just outside the house. It was totally dark there. One evening, Julien was talking excitedly, deriving intense enjoyment from the pleasure of expressing himself eloquently, and to young women too. As he gesticulated, he touched Mme de Rênal's hand which was resting on the back of one of those painted wooden chairs which are often put in gardens.

The hand was withdrawn very soon; but Julien decided it was his *duty* to ensure that this hand would not be withdrawn when he touched it. The idea of a duty to carry out, and a risk of suffering ridicule or rather a feeling of inferiority if he failed in it, immediately removed all pleasure from his heart.

CHAPTER 9

An evening in the country

Guérin's painting of Dido: a charming sketch.

STROMBECK*

HE had a strange look in his eyes the next day when he met Mme de Rênal; he observed her as if she were an enemy he was going to have to fight. This look, so different from his expression the day before, caused Mme de Rênal to lose her head: she had been indulgent towards him, and he seemed angry. She could not tear her gaze away from his.

The presence of Mme Derville allowed Julien to say less and spend more time on what was preoccupying him. His sole concern throughout the whole of that day was to fortify himself by reading the work of inspiration which always retempered his soul.

He cut short the children's lessons considerably, and later, when Mme de Rênal's presence served to recall him to the single-minded pursuit of his personal glory, he decided it was absolutely essential that she should allow her hand to remain in his that very evening.

As the sun went down and brought the decisive moment nearer, it caused Julien's heart to beat strangely. Night fell. He observed, with a sense of joy which took an enormous weight off his chest, that it was going to be a very dark one. The sky was laden with big clouds driven by a sultry wind, and it seemed to portend a storm. The two ladies remained out walking very late. Everything they did that evening seemed strange to Julien. They were enjoying this weather, which for some delicate souls seems to increase the pleasure of affection.

Eventually they all sat down, with Mme de Rênal next to Julien, and Mme Derville by her friend. Julien's mind was quite taken up with what he was going to attempt, and he could find nothing to say. The conversation flagged.

Will I be as fearful and as wretched when my first duel

comes along? Julien wondered, for he was too wary both of himself and of others to fail to perceive his own state of mind.

In his mortal anguish, any form of danger would have seemed preferable to him. How many times he longed for some sudden business to crop up which would oblige Mme de Rênal to return to the house and leave the garden! The effort which Julien had to make to control himself was too violent for his voice not to be profoundly affected by it. Soon Mme de Rênal's voice became unsteady too, but Julien did not notice. The fearful battle being waged by his sense of duty against his nervousness was too painful to leave him in a state to observe anything besides himself. The château clock had just struck a quarter to ten, and he had still not ventured anything. Outraged at his own cowardice, Julien declared to himself: At the precise moment when ten o'clock strikes, I shall carry out what I have been promising myself all day I shall do this evening, or else I shall go up to my room and blow my brains out.

After a final period of anxious waiting, during which Julien was almost beside himself from excess of emotion, ten strokes rang out from the clock above his head. Each chime of the fateful bell reverberated in his chest, causing a kind of physical reaction there.

At last, as the final stroke of ten was still ringing, he reached out his hand and took Mme de Rênal's, which she immediately withdrew. Not quite knowing what he was about, Julien grasped it again. Although thoroughly moved himself, he was struck by the icy coldness of the hand he was taking. He squeezed it with convulsive strength; there was one last attempt to remove it from his grasp, but in the end the hand remained in his.

Happiness flooded over him; not that he was in love with Mme de Rênal—it was just that a fearful torture had ceased. To prevent Mme Derville from noticing anything, he felt it incumbent upon him to speak; his voice was now ringing and loud. Mme de Rênal's, on the other hand, betrayed so much emotion that her friend thought she was ill and suggested going indoors. Julien sensed the danger at once: If Mme de Rênal goes in to the drawing-room, I shall be back in the terrible situation I've been in all day. I've held this hand for too short a time for this to count as a victory won.

Just as Mme Derville was repeating her suggestion that they go indoors to the drawing-room, Julien gave a firm squeeze to the hand that had been abandoned to him.

Mme de Rênal, who was already rising from her seat, sat down again and said in expiring tones:

'I do indeed feel a little ill, but the fresh air is doing me good.'

These words confirmed Julien's happiness, which at that moment was intense. He talked, forgetting all pretence, and seemed the most agreeable of men to the two friends listening to him. Yet there was still a lack of courage in this sudden fit of eloquence. He was in mortal dread that Mme Derville, wearied by the wind which was beginning to get up before the storm, should decide to go indoors to the drawing-room alone. This would have left him on his own with Mme de Rênal. It was almost by chance that he had had the blind courage which suffices for action; but he sensed that it was beyond his powers to say the simplest of words to Mme de Rênal. However gentle her reproaches, he was going to be defeated, and the advantage he had gained would be wiped out.

Fortunately for him that evening, his moving and grandiloquent speeches found favour with Mme Derville, who often found Julien uncouth like a child, and scarcely amusing. As for Mme de Rênal, with her hand in Julien's she was not thinking about anything; she was letting life take its course. The hours they spent beneath that great lime tree, which according to local tradition had been planted by Charles the Bold* were a long stretch of happiness for her. She listened in rapture to the moaning of the wind in the dense foliage of the lime, and the patter of isolated raindrops which were beginning to fall on its lower leaves. Julien failed to notice an incident which would have greatly reassured him: Mme de Rênal, who had been obliged to take her hand out of his because she rose to help her cousin pick up a pot of flowers which the wind had just blown over at their feet, had no sooner sat down again than she gave him back her hand with scarcely any reluctance, as if this were already an agreement between them.

Midnight had struck long ago; the time came at last to leave the garden. They went their separate ways. Mme de Rênal, carried away by the happiness of love, was so innocent that she hardly reproached herself at all. Happiness drove away sleep. A leaden sleep took hold of Julien, who was wearied to death by the battles which had been raging in his heart all day between nervousness and pride.

The next day he was woken up at five; and—a cruel blow for Mme de Rênal had she but known it—he hardly had a thought for her. He had *done his duty, his heroic duty*. Filled with happiness at this thought, he locked himself into his room and gave himself up with new-found pleasure to reading about the deeds of his hero.

When the bell rang for lunch, the bulletins of the Great Army had made him forget all the advantages he had won the day before. He said casually to himself as he went downstairs to the drawing-room: I must tell this woman I love her.

Instead of the deeply amorous glances he was expecting to encounter, he was greeted by the stern face of M. de Rênal, who had arrived back from Verrières two hours previously, and did not hide his displeasure at finding that Julien had spent the whole morning without attending to the children. Nothing could be more ugly than this self-important man when he was out of temper and believed he was entitled to show it.

Each sharp word from her husband pierced Mme de Rênal's heart. As for Julien, he was so deep in ecstasy, so preoccupied still with the great happenings which had unfurled before his eyes for hours on end, that at first he could scarcely bring his attention down to the level required to take in the harsh words with M. de Rênal was uttering. In the end he said rather abruptly:

'I was ill.'

The tone of this reply would have stung a man far less touchy than the mayor of Verrières. It crossed his mind to answer Julien by dismissing him forthwith. He was only prevented from doing so by the maxim he had adopted of never showing undue haste in business.

This young fool, he soon said to himself, has acquired something of a reputation in my house; Valenod may offer him employment, or else he will marry Elisa, and in either case he will be able to mock me deep down in his heart.

For all his wise thoughts, M. de Rênal none the less gave vent to a stream of coarse language which began to exasperate Julien. Mme de Rênal was on the point of bursting into tears. No sooner was lunch over than she asked Julien to give her his arm for a walk, and leaned on him in a gesture of friendliness. But to everything that Mme de Rênal said to him Julien could only mutter in reply:

'*That's the rich for you!*'

M. de Rênal was walking close beside them; his presence increased Julien's anger. He noticed suddenly that Mme de Rênal was leaning on his arm in a marked manner; this gesture appalled him, he pushed her violently away and freed his arm.

Luckily M. de Rênal did not see this fresh piece of impertinence. It was only observed by Mme Derville: her friend was overcome with tears. At that moment M. de Rênal began to throw stones to drive off a peasant girl who had taken a wrong path and was crossing the corner of the orchard.

'Monsieur Julien, I beg you, control yourself; consider that we all have our moments of ill-temper,' said Mme Derville quickly.

Julien looked coldly at her with eyes which reflected the most supreme disdain.

His look astonished Mme Derville, and would have done so even more if she had fathomed what it really expressed. She would have read in it a glimpse of hope of the most atrocious revenge. It is doubtless such moments of humiliation that create the Robespierres* of this world.

'This Julien of yours is very aggressive, he frightens me,' Mme Derville said to her friend in a low voice.

'He has every reason to be angry,' the latter replied. 'After the astonishing progress which the children have made at his hands, what does it matter if he spends one morning without speaking to them. You must agree that men are very hard.'

For the first time in her life, Mme de Rênal felt a kind of desire to get her revenge on her husband. The dire hatred which Julien was nursing against the rich was about to explode. Fortunately M. de Rênal summoned his gardener and was kept busy getting him to block off the illicit path across the orchard with bundles of thorny twigs. Julien did not utter a single word in response to the solicitous attentions paid to him during the remainder of the walk. M. de Rênal had hardly left them before the two friends, claiming to be tired, had each of them asked him for an arm.

Flanked by these two women whose cheeks were flushed with deep embarrassment and discomfiture, Julien's haughty pallor and his glum and resolute air formed an odd contrast. He despised these women and every kind of tender feeling.

So! he said to himself. I don't even get an income of five hundred francs to finish my studies! Wouldn't I just like to tell him where he gets off! Absorbed by these harsh thoughts, he was irritated by what little he deigned to take in of the two friends' soothing words: they struck him as empty, silly, ineffectual—in a word, *feminine*.

In the course of talking for the sake of talking, and trying to keep the conversation alive, Mme de Rênal chanced to mention that her husband had returned from Verrières because he had done a deal for some maize straw with one of his farmers. (In this part of the country, maize straw is used to fill under-mattresses.)

'My husband won't be joining us again,' added Mme de Rênal. 'With the help of the gardener and his valet, he'll be busy finishing off the job of renewing the mattresses in the house. This morning he put maize straw in all the beds on the first floor, and now he's on to the second.'

Julien changed colour; he gave Mme de Rênal a strange look and soon drew her aside, as it were, by quickening his pace. Mme Derville let them go on ahead.

'Please save my life,' he said to Mme de Rênal, 'only you can do it; for you know the valet loathes me mercilessly. I must confess to you, madam, that I have a portrait; I've hidden it inside the under-mattress on my bed.'

At these words Mme de Rênal grew pale in her turn.

'You alone, madam, can go into my room right now; please search, without letting anyone see what you are doing, in the corner of the under-mattress nearest to the window, and you'll find a little box of smooth black cardboard.'

'And there's a portrait inside it!' said Mme de Rênal, scarcely able to remain on her feet.

Her demoralized look did not pass unnoticed by Julien, who hastened to take advantage of it.

'I've a second favour to ask of you, madam: I beg you not to look at this portrait, it's my secret.'

'It's a secret!' repeated Mme de Rênal in a faint voice.

But although she had been brought up among people proud of their fortunes, and only moved by financial interest, love had already planted generosity in Mme de Rênal's heart. Cruelly wounded as she was, she had an air of the most straightforward devotion when she asked Julien the necessary questions to enable her to carry out her errand properly.

'So,' she said to him as she went off, 'it's a little round box of black cardboard, nice and smooth.'

'Yes, madam,' Julien replied with the hard look which danger gives to men.

She went up to the second floor of the house, as pale as if she were going to her death. To complete her wretchedness, she felt herself on the point of being taken ill; but the necessity of doing Julien a service restored strength to her.

'I must have that box,' she said to herself as she quickened her step.

She heard her husband talking to his valet in Julien's very room. Luckily they went through into the children's bedroom. She lifted the mattress and plunged her hand into the straw underneath it with such violence that she took some of the skin off her fingers. But although she was very sensitive to minor pain of this kind, she was unaware of anything on this occasion, for almost simultaneously she felt the smooth surface of the cardboard box. She seized it and slipped away.

No sooner was she relieved of the fear of being surprised by her husband than the horror instilled in her by the box almost caused her to be well and truly taken ill.

So Julien's in love, and I've got the portrait of the woman he loves in there!

Sitting on a chair in the entrance to this set of rooms, Mme de Rênal was racked by all the torments of jealousy. Her extreme ignorance was again of service to her at the moment, since her pain was tempered by astonishment, Julien appeared, seized the box without a word of thanks or any other kind, and ran into his room where he lit a fire and burned it on the spot. He was pale and shattered, greatly exaggerating the extent of the risk he had just run.

Napoleon's portrait, he said to himself, shaking his head, found hidden in the room of a man who openly professes such hatred for the usurper! found by M. de Rênal, such an extreme *Ultra* and in such a state of anger! and to crown my rashness, on the white card at the back of the portrait there are lines written in my own hand, which leave no doubt about the excess of my admiration! And each of these passionate outbursts is dated—there's one from the day before yesterday!

All my reputation gone, destroyed in a moment! said Julien to himself as he saw the box go up in flames, and my reputation is my only asset; it's all I have to live by... and what a life at that, by God!

An hour later, fatigue and self-pity inclined him towards a tender mood. On meeting Mme de Rênal he took her hand and kissed it with more sincerity than he had ever shown. She blushed with happiness and almost at the same instant pushed Julien away with jealous anger. His pride, which had been so recently wounded, made him act foolishly at that point. All he saw in Mme de Rênal was a rich woman; he let go of her hand with disdain and strode off. He went and walked round the garden, deep in thought. Soon a bitter smile appeared on his lips.

Here I am walking about undisturbed like a man who is master of his own time! I'm not looking after the children! I'm laying myself open to being humiliated by M. de Rênal, and he'll be quite right. Julien ran to the children's room.

The caresses of the youngest boy, for whom he had much affection, soothed his burning pain a little.

He at least doesn't despise me yet, Julien thought. But soon he reproached himself with this diminution of his pain as a fresh sign of weakness. These children fondle me just as they would the hunting pup that was bought yesterday.

CHAPTER 10

A generous heart and a meagre fortune

> But passion most dissembles, yet betrays,
> Even by its darkness; as the blackest sky
> Foretells the heaviest tempest.
>
> *Don Juan,* C. I, st. 73.

M. DE RÊNAL, who was going round all the rooms in the house, returned to the childrens' room with the servants who were bringing back the mattresses. The sudden appearance of this man was the last straw for Julien.

Looking paler and more sombre than usual, Julien rushed towards him. M. de Rênal stopped and glanced at his servants.

'Sir,' Julien said to him, 'do you think that with any other tutor your children would have made the same progress as with me? If your answer is no,' he went on without giving M. de Rênal a chance to reply, 'then how can you dare reproach me with neglecting them?'

M. de Rênal had no sooner got over his fright than he inferred from the strange manner he observed the little peasant adopt that he was in possession of some advantageous offer from elsewhere, and that he was about to leave his service. Julien's anger increased as he spoke:

'I can make a living without you, sir,' he added.

'I am genuinely disturbed to see you so upset,' replied M. de Rênal with something of a stammer. The servants were some way off, busy putting back the beds.

'That doesn't satisfy me, sir,' Julien went on, quite beside himself with anger. 'Consider the disgraceful language you used to me—and in the presence of ladies, too!'

M. de Rênal understood only too well what Julien was asking for, and he was torn by a painful conflict. Julien did indeed exclaim in a real fit of rage:

'I know where to go, sir, when I leave your house.'

At this M. de Rênal pictured Julien installed in M. Valenod's establishment.

'Well then, sir!' he said to him at last with the sigh and the look he would have produced for summoning a surgeon to perform the most painful of operations, 'I grant your request. Starting from the day after tomorrow, which is the first of the month, I shall give you fifty francs a month.'

Julien felt like laughing and was completely taken aback; all his anger had vanished.

I didn't despise this animal enough, he said to himself. This is no doubt the greatest apology such a petty mind is capable of.

The children, who were listening to this scene with mouths agape, ran off into the the garden to tell their mother that Mr Julien was terribly angry, but he was going to get fifty francs a month.

Julien followed them out of habit, without even looking at M. de Rênal, whom he left in a state of profound vexation.

That makes a hundred and sixty-eight francs that M. Valenod is costing me, said the mayor to himself. It's essential I have stern words with him about his contract to provide supplies for the foundlings.

A moment later Julien was back again face to face with M. de Rênal:

'I must speak to Father Chélan about my conscience; may I most respectfully inform you that I shall be absent for a few hours.'

'Ah! my dear Julien,' said the mayor with a laugh that rang utterly false, 'all day if you wish, and all tomorrow, my dear fellow. Take the gardener's horse to get to Verrières.'

There he goes, M. de Rênal said to himself, to give an answer to Valenod; he hasn't promised me anything, but I'll have to let the young hothead simmer down.

Julien made a quick escape and climbed up through the thick woods which lead from Vergy to Verrières. He did not want to get to Father Chélan's immediately. Far from wishing to inflict on himself a further scene of hypocrisy, he needed to sort out what was going on inside himself, and to attend to the welter of feelings which were agitating him.

I've won a battle, he said to himself as soon as he was safely in the woods, out of anyone's sight. So I've won a battle!

This word depicted his situation to him in a favourable light, and restored some of his peace of mind.

Here I am with a salary of fifty francs a month: M. de Rênal must have been well and truly frightened. But what of?

This meditation on what could possibly have frightened the happy and powerful man who had made him fume with rage only an hour beforehand completed the process of calming Julien down. He almost responded for a moment to the bewitching beauty of the woods he was walking through. Enormous blocks of bare rock had at one time fallen from the mountainside into the middle of the forest. Tall beeches grew almost as high as these rocks, which afforded delightfully cool shade only a few feet away from spots where the heat of the sun's rays would have made it impossible to stop.

Julien paused an instant for breath in the shade of these great rocks, and then resumed his climb. Soon a narrow, barely visible track used only by goatherds took him to the top of a huge rock, where he stood in the certainty of being away from all humankind. His physical location made him smile, depicting for him the position he yearned to attain in the spiritual sphere. The pure air in these high mountains imparted serenity to him, and even joy. The mayor of Verrières was indeed in Julien's eyes still the representative of all the rich and the impudent on earth; but he sensed that for all the violence of his reactions, there was nothing personal about the hatred which had moved him. If he were to stop seeing M. de Rênal, he would have forgotten him in a week—him, his fine house, his dogs, his children and all his family. I've forced him, I don't understand how, to make an enormous sacrifice. Imagine! More than fifty crowns* a year! Only an instant before, I had extracted myself from dire danger. That makes two victories in one day; the second brings me no credit, I shall have to get to the bottom of it. But tomorrow is time enough for painstaking investigation.

Standing on the top of his great rock Julien gazed at the sky which glowed in the August sunshine. Cicadas were chirruping in the field beneath the rock, and when they fell silent all was stillness around him. At his feet he could see the countryside for twenty leagues round about. A sparrowhawk which had taken wing from the great rocks above his head came into view from time to time as it wheeled its great circles in silence. Mechanically, Julien's eyes followed the bird of prey. He was struck by its serene, powerful movements; he envied such strength, he envied such isolation.

Such was Napoleon's destiny; would it one day be his?

CHAPTER 11
In the evening

Yet Julia's very coldness still was kind,
And tremulously gentle her small hand
Withdrew itself from his, but left behind
A little pressure, thrilling, and so bland
And slight, so very slight that to the mind
'Twas but a doubt.

Don Juan, C. I, st. 71

IT was necessary nevertheless to put in an appearance in Verrières. By a stroke of good luck, Julien ran into M. Valenod on leaving the presbytery, and hastened to tell him of the increase in his salary.

Once back in Vergy, Julien did not go down to the garden until night had fallen. He was worn out by the many powerful emotions which had shaken him during the course of the day. What shall I say to them? he worried to himself as he thought of the ladies. He was a long way from realizing that his mind was precisely on the level of the petty circumstances which normally absorb the whole of women's attention. Julien was often unintelligible to Mme Derville, and even to her friend, and in his turn he only half understood all the things they said to him. Such was the effect of the strength, and if I may be permitted the expression, the grandeur of the passionate impulses which rocked this ambitious young man's inner being. Within this strange individual, almost every day was stormy.

As he went into the garden that evening, Julien was all prepared to take an interest in the pretty cousins' ideas. They were waiting impatiently for him. He took his customary seat next to Mme de Rênal. It soon became pitch dark. He wanted to take hold of a white hand which he had seen beside him for some time resting on the back of a chair. There was some hesitation, but at length the hand was withdrawn in a way which indicated pique. Julien was inclined to take that for an answer and to continue brightly with the conversation, when he heard M. de Rênal approaching.

Julien's ears were still ringing with the rude words from that morning. Wouldn't it be a way of mocking this so-and-so who has everything fortune can offer, he said to himself, if I took possession of his wife's hand, and in his presence too? Yes I'll do it, *I* will—the person he treated with so much scorn.

After this the calm that came so unnaturally to Julien was very soon banished; he desired frenetically, and without being able to think of anything else, that Mme de Rênal consent to yield him her hand.

M. de Rênal was angrily talking politics: two or three industrialists in Verrières were definitely getting richer than he was, and were trying to go against him in the elections. Mme Derville was listening to him. Annoyed at his haranguing, Julien drew his chair close to Mme de Rênal's. Darkness hid all his movements. He was bold enough to lay his hand very close to the pretty arm left bare by the dress. He was aroused and took leave of his senses; he put his cheek to this pretty arm and dared to touch it with his lips.

Mme de Rênal quivered. Her husband was only a few feet away; she hastily gave Julien her hand, and at the same time pushed him away a little. As M. de Rênal continued his diatribe against people with nothing to their name and Jacobins who grew rich, Julien smothered the hand which had been abandoned to him with passionate kisses, or at least so they seemed to Mme de Rênal. Yet the poor woman had had proof on that fateful day that the heart of the man she adored without admitting it to herself belonged to another! For the whole of Julien's absence she had been in the throes of a deep distress which had caused her to reflect.

Goodness! Could I be in love! she said to herself. Could this be love I feel! I'm a married woman, and I've fallen in love! But, she said to herself, I've never felt for my husband this sinister madness which makes me unable to take my mind off Julien. He's really only a child full of respect for me. It'll only be a passing madness. What does it matter to my husband what feelings I may have for this young man! M. de Rênal would be bored by my conversations with Julien on matters of the imagination. He only thinks about his business. I'm not taking anything away from him to give it to Julien.

There was no hypocrisy there to taint the purity of this innocent soul, led astray by a passion she had never experienced. She was deceived, but unwittingly, and yet some virtuous instinct within her had taken fright. These were the struggles disturbing her when Julien appeared in the garden. She heard him speak, and almost at the same instant saw him sit down beside her. She was quite carried away by this delightful happiness which for the past fortnight had astonished her even more than it had seduced her. She never knew what to expect. After a few moments, however, she said to herself: Is Julien's presence enough to wipe out all his wrongs? She took fright, and that was when she withdrew her hand from his.

The passionate kisses, the like of which she had never experienced, caused her to forget at once that perhaps he loved another woman. Soon he was no longer guilty in her eyes. The abrupt end to a poignant grief, born of suspicion, and her present of happiness, beyond anything she had even dreamed of, filled her with ecstatic feelings of love and mad gaiety. It was a delightful evening for everyone except the mayor of Verrières, who was unable to forget those industrialists on the make. Julien stopped thinking about his black ambition and his plans that were so difficult to execute. For the first time in his life he was carried away by the power of beauty. Lost in a sweet and aimless dream quite alien to his character, gently clasping a hand he could admire for its flawless prettiness, he listened distractedly to the rustle of the lime leaves in the gentle night breeze, and the dogs down at the mill by the Doubs barking in the distance.

But the emotion he felt was a pleasure not a passion. On returning to his room there was only one thing he desired to make him happy: to take up his favourite book. At twenty, the thought of the wide world and the impact you can have on it overrides everything else.

Soon, however, he put the book down. Thinking about Napoleon's victories had given him a new insight into his own. Yes, I've won a battle, he said to himself, but I must take advantage of it, I must crush the pride of this proud gentleman while he is in retreat. That would be Napoleon all over. I must ask for three days' leave to go and see my friend Fouqué. If he refuses to grant it, I'll spell out my terms to him again; but he'll give in.

Mme de Rênal was unable to sleep. It seemed to her that she had not lived until that moment. She could not take her mind off the pleasure of feeling Julien smothering her hand with ardent kisses.

Suddenly the dreadful word *adultery* came to her. All the revolting images that the vilest debauchery can imprint on the idea of sensual love came crowding into her imagination. These ideas did their best to tarnish the tender and divine images she had of Julien and of her happiness in loving him. The future appeared to her in terrible colours. She saw herself as despicable.

It was a dreadful moment; she was entering uncharted territory. The previous day she had tasted a happiness never experienced before; now she suddenly found herself plunged in atrocious misery. She had no conception of such suffering, and it clouded her reason. She thought for an instant of confessing to her husband that she feared she was in love with Julien. It would have allowed her to talk about him. Fortunately her memory supplied her with a precept given her long ago by her aunt, on the eve of her wedding. It was about the dangers of confiding in a husband, who is after all a master. The excess of her misery made her wring her hands.

She was carried this way and that by contradictory and painful images. At one moment she was afraid of not being loved; at the next, the dreadful thought of her crime tortured her as if she were to face the pillory the next day in the public square of Verrières, with a placard explaining her adultery to the populace.

Mme de Rênal had no experience of life; even when fully awake and in complete command of her reasoning powers, she would not have perceived any gap between being guilty in the eyes of God, and being subjected in public to the rowdiest display of public scorn.

When she was able to rest her mind from the dreadful idea

of adultery and all the ignominy which, in her opinion, this crime carries in its wake, and when she came to think of the sweet pleasures of living innocently with Julien, just as in the past, she found herself engulfed in the horrible thought that Julien loved another woman. She could still see him grow pale when he feared he had lost his portrait of her, or would compromise her by letting it be seen. For the first time, she had caught an expression of fear on a face so calm and noble. He had never shown any sign of being moved like this on her account or her children's. Her excess of grief reached the full pitch of distress which the human mind is given to endure. Without realizing it, Mme de Rênal cried out and woke her chambermaid. Suddenly she saw the brightness of a lamp by her bed and recognized Elisa.

'Are you the one he loves?' she exclaimed in her madness.

The chambermaid was astonished at the dreadful state of confusion she found her mistress in, and luckily paid no attention to these strange words. Mme de Rênal noticed how unguarded she had been: 'I'm feverish,' she said to her, 'and a bit delirious, I think. Stay with me.' Fully wakened by the need to pretend, she felt less unhappy; her reason regained the hold it had lost while she was half asleep. To free herself from the chambermaid's fixed stare, she ordered her to read from the newspaper; and it was to the drone of the girl's voice reading a long article from the *Quotidienne* that Mme de Rênal made the virtuous resolve to treat Julien with exemplary coldness when she next saw him.

CHAPTER 12

A journey

In Paris you find elegant people; there
may be people of character in the
provinces.

SIEYÈS*

By five o'clock the next morning, before Mme de Rênal
appeared, Julien had obtained three days' leave from her
husband. Contrary to his expectations, Julien found himself
wishing to see her again; he kept thinking of her pretty hand.
He went down into the garden; she took her time to make an
appearance. If Julien had loved her, he would have glimpsed
her behind the half-closed shutters on the first floor, pressing
her forehead against the glass. She was watching him. At last,
in spite of her resolve, she made up her mind to go out into
the garden. Her usual pallor had given way to a heightened
flush. This highly innocent woman was clearly agitated: a
feeling of constraint and even of anger destroyed the expression
of deep serenity, seemingly above all the vulgar concerns of
life, which gave her angelic face so much charm.

Julien hurried over to her, admiring the fine arms that could
be glimpsed through a shawl she had put on in haste. The cool
of the morning air seemed to heighten still more the colours of
a complexion which the night's turmoil had rendered all the
more receptive to every impression. Her beauty was unpretentious and touching, yet enhanced by qualities of mind that are
not found among the lower classes; and it seemed to reveal to
Julien a faculty of his own being that he had never experienced
before. Completely absorbed in admiring the charms discovered by his avid gaze, Julien had no thoughts for the
friendly welcome he was expecting to receive. He was all the
more astonished at the show of icy coldness with which the
lady tried to greet him, and in which he even thought he
detected the intention of putting him in his place.

The smile of pleasure died on his lips: he remembered the
rank he occupied in society, and especially in the eyes of a

noble and rich heiress. In a moment, his face showed nothing but aloofness and anger at himself. He felt violently resentful at having delayed his departure for over an hour, only to be given such a humiliating reception.

Only a fool, he said to himself, gets angry with other people: a stone falls because it's heavy. Won't I ever grow up? When on earth will I acquire the good habit of letting these people have only so much of my soul as their money has paid for? If I want their esteem and my own, I must show them that it's only my poverty that enters into dealings with their riches, but that my heart is a hundred miles away from their insolence, in a sphere so high up that it's out of reach of their petty marks of disdain or favour.

While these sentiments were crowding into the young tutor's mind, his mobile features took on a fierce expression of suffering pride. Mme de Rênal was completely flustered by it. The cold look of virtue she had wanted to greet him with gave way to an expression of interest—one lit by surprise at the sudden change she had just observed. The idle words which people exchange in the morning about their health, or the beauty of the day, dried up for both of them at once. Julien, whose judgement was not clouded by any passion, soon found a way to show Mme de Rênal how little he considered himself to be on terms of friendship with her; he said nothing to her of the short journey he was about to embark on, took his leave and left.

As she watched him go, aghast at the sullen disdain she could read in his expression which had been so amiable the previous evening, her eldest son ran up from the bottom of the garden and said as he kissed her:

'We've got a holiday: Mr Julien is off on a journey.'

At these words Mme de Rênal felt a deathly chill come over her: she was unhappy through her virtue, and more unhappy still through her weakness.

This new turn of events absorbed all her imagination; she was carried far beyond the wise resolves which had come to her during the terrible night she had just gone through. It was no longer a matter of resisting so charming a lover, but of losing him for ever.

She had to appear at lunch. To crown her misery, M. de Rênal and Mme Derville talked of nothing but Julien's departure. The mayor of Verrières had noticed something out of the ordinary in the firmness with which he had requested his leave.

'This little peasant has no doubt got an offer from someone else in his pocket. But this someone, even if it were M. Valenod, must be a bit downcast at the sum of six hundred francs which the annual outlay now amounts to. Yesterday, in Verrières, the person will have asked for three days' grace to think it over; and this morning, so as not to have to give me an answer, the little gentleman ups and leaves for the mountains. To be obliged to reckon with a wretched workman who plays at being impertinent, what a pass we've come to!'

Since my husband, who's unaware how deeply he has wounded Julien, thinks he's going to leave us, what am I to believe myself? wondered Mme de Rênal. Ah! it's all settled!

So that she could at least shed tears in peace, and not have to answer Mme Derville's questions, she said she had a terrible headache and went to bed.

'That's women for you,' said M. de Rênal again, 'there's always something wrong with these complicated machines.' And he went off with a sneer.

While Mme de Rênal was suffering the cruellest effects of the terrible passion which chance had brought upon her, Julien was journeying cheerfully through the loveliest vistas which mountain landscapes can afford. He had to cross the high ridge north of Vergy. The path he was following climbed gradually through great beechwoods, cutting countless zigzags on the face of the high mountain which marks out the valley of the Doubs to the north. The traveller's gaze soon passed over the lower slopes which flank the course of the Doubs on the south side, and penetrated as far as the fertile plains of Burgundy and the Beaujolais. Insensitive as this ambitious young man was to such beauty, he could not help stopping from time to time to contemplate so vast and impressive a view.

At length he reached the summit of the high mountain which you have to pass by on this cross-country trail in order to reach the lonely valley where his friend Fouqué the young timber merchant lived. Julien was in no hurry to see him, or for that matter any other fellow human. Hidden like a bird of prey among the bare rocks which crown the high mountain, he could spy from afar any man who might happen to draw near him. He discovered a small grotto in the almost vertical face of one of the crags. He made for it and was soon installed in this retreat. Here, he said to himself with delight shining in his eyes, no man can do me any harm. He had the idea of indulging in the pleasure of writing down his thoughts, a most dangerous undertaking for him anywhere else. A square stone slab did duty as a desk. His pen flew back and forth: he was oblivious of his surroundings. At last he noticed that the sun was setting behind the distant hills of the Beaujolais.

Why don't I spend the night here? he said to himself; I've got some bread and *I'm free!* The sound of these grand words filled him with jubilation; his hypocrisy prevented him from being free even in Fouqué's house. With his head resting on his hands, Julien sat in the grotto feeling happier than ever in his life before, stirred by his fancies and the happiness which freedom brought. Without paying particular attention to it, he saw all the rays of the sunset fade away one by one. In the midst of this great darkness his imagination was lost in the contemplation of what he fancied he would one day find in Paris. There was first of all a woman of far greater beauty and more refined wit than he had ever encountered in the provinces. He was passionately in love, and was loved in his turn. If he left her side for a brief moment, it was to go and win glory, and earn even greater love from her.

Even if one were to credit him with Julien's imagination, a young man brought up amid the sorry truths of Parisian society would have been awakened at this point in his romance by a chilling sense of irony; the great deeds would have vanished along with the hope of accomplishing them, giving way to the well-known maxim: If you leave your mistress, you run the risk, alas! of being deceived two or three times a day. The young peasant saw nothing coming between him and the most heroic deeds, apart from lack of opportunity.

But an impenetrable night had driven away the daylight, and Julien still had two leagues to go to get down to the hamlet where Fouqué lived. Before leaving the little grotto, Julien lit a fire and carefully burned everything he had written.

He caused his friend great astonishment by knocking at his door at one in the morning. He found Fouqué busy doing his accounts. He was a tall, rather awkwardly built young man, with coarse, hard features, an endlessly long nose, and plenty of good-nature hidden beneath this repellent exterior.

'Have you had a quarrel with your M. de Rênal, then, to bring you to my doorstep unexpectedly like this?'

Julien reported to him—in a suitable version—the events of the previous day.

'You stay here with me,' Fouqué said to him. 'I see that you've got to know M. de Rênal, M. Valenod, the sub-prefect Maugiron and Father Chélan; you've grasped the subtleties of these people's characters; you're now fit to take part in auctions. You're better at sums than I am, so you can keep my accounts. My trade brings me in a lot of money. Every day I miss excellent business because it's impossible to do everything myself, and I'm afraid that anyone I take on as a partner will prove to be a rogue. It's less than a month since I let Michaud from Saint-Armand make six thousand francs; I hadn't seen him for six years, and I met him by chance at the auction in Pontarlier.* Why shouldn't it have been you who made those six thousand francs, or at any rate three thousand? For you see, if I'd had you with me that day, I'd have started bidding for that plot of timber, and the rest of them would soon have let me have it. Come and be my partner.'

This offer put Julien in a bad mood, as it interfered with his train of fantasy. Throughout supper, which the two friends prepared for themselves like Homeric heroes, since Fouqué lived alone, he showed Julien his accounts and proved to him how advantageous his trade in timber was. Fouqué had the highest opinion of Julien's intelligence and character.

When at last Julien was alone in his little pine-board room, he said to himself: It's true that I can earn several thousand francs here, and then be in a better position to take up a career as a soldier or a priest, according to what's in fashion in France at that time. The little nest egg I'll have accumulated will smooth out all the minor difficulties in my way. With time to myself in these mountains, I'll be able to dispel some of my terrible ignorance about the things that concern all these salon people. But Fouqué has given up thought of getting married, and he keeps telling me that solitude makes him unhappy. It's obvious that if he takes a partner who hasn't any capital to put into his business, he must be hoping to get himself a companion who'll never leave him.

Am I going to deceive my friend? Julien exclaimed in annoyance. This individual whose usual means of salvation were hypocrisy and a total lack of sympathy, was unable on this occasion to bear the thought of the slightest insensitivity towards a man bound to him by ties of friendship.

But suddenly Julien cheered up: he had a reason for refusing. Just think, I'd feebly go and lose seven or eight years of my life! I'd end up being twenty-eight; but at that age Bonaparte had his greatest achievements behind him. By the time I've earned a bit of money as a nobody by going from one timber auction to the next and winning favours from a handful of subordinate rogues, who can guarantee that I'll still have the sacred fire you need to make a name for yourself?

The next morning, with an air of perfect composure, Julien told the honest Fouqué, who considered the matter of their partnership as settled, that his calling to the sacred ministry did not allow him to accept. Fouqué was completely taken aback.

'But do you realize', he repeated, 'that I'm making you a partner, or if you prefer, I'll give you four thousand francs a year? And you want to go back to your M. de Rênal who despises you like the dirt on his boots! Once you've got a pile of two hundred gold louis in front of you, what's to stop you from going to the seminary? I'll tell you something else: I'll make it my business to get you the best living in the neighbourhood. For you see,' added Fouqué, lowering his voice, 'I supply firewood to important people like M. ——, M. —— and M. ——. I give them the finest varieties of oak, and they only pay me the price of deal for it, but never was money better spent.'

Nothing could shift Julien from his vocation. Fouqué ended up thinking him slightly mad. On the third day Julien said

goodbye to his friend early in the morning in order to spend
the day amid the crags on the high mountain peak. He found
his little grotto again, but his peace of mind was gone; his
friend's proposition had robbed him of it. Like Hercules he
found himself with a choice—not between vice and virtue, but
between the unrelieved mediocrity of guaranteed well-being,
and all the heroic dreams of his youth. It shows I haven't got
real determination, he said to himself; and it was this doubt
which caused him the greatest anguish. I'm not made of the
stuff of great men, since I'm afraid that eight years spent
earning my living may drain me of the sublime energy which
gets extraordinary feats accomplished.

CHAPTER 13

Openwork stockings

A novel is a mirror you turn this way
and that as you go down a path.

SAINT-RÉAL*

WHEN Julien caught sight of the picturesque ruins of the old church in Vergy, he realized that for the past three days he hadn't thought once about Mme de Rênal. When I left the other day, that woman reminded me of the immeasurable distance between us; she treated me like a workman's son. No doubt she wanted to show me she regretted having abandoned her hand to me the evening before... What a pretty hand it is, though! and what a charming, noble look in that woman's eyes!

The option of making his fortune with Fouqué gave a degree of flexibility to Julien's reasoning, which was now less often flawed by annoyance and an acute sense of his own poverty and low standing in the eyes of the world. From the heights of his metaphorical promontory he was able to pass judgement—and he so to speak looked down—on both extreme poverty and the comfortable circumstances which he still called wealth. He was a long way from taking a philosophical view of his position, but he was lucid enough to feel *different* after his little journey into the mountains.

He was struck by how extremely agitated Mme de Rênal looked while listening to the short account of his journey which she had begged him to give her.

Fouqué had had plans to get married, but had been unlucky in love. He had confided at length in his friend during the course of their conversations together. Having found happiness too soon, Fouqué had discovered that he was not the only one to be loved. Julien had been astonished by everything he was told; he had learned so much that was new to him. His solitary life, fed entirely by his imagination and his wariness, had distanced him from any possible source of enlightenment.

Life for Mme de Rênal during his absence had been one long

series of different ordeals, all of them unbearable; she was genuinely ill.

'Now above all,' Mme Derville said to her when she saw Julien return, 'in your state of health, you're not to go into the garden this evening; the damp air would only make you much worse.'

Mme Derville was astonished to observe that her friend, who was always being taken to task by M. de Rênal for her excessively plain way of dressing, had just acquired some openwork stockings and some charming little shoes newly arrived from Paris. Mme de Rênal's sole distraction for the past three days had been to cut out and get Elisa to run up a summer dress in a lovely fine fabric at the height of fashion. The dress only just got finished a few minutes after Julien's return; Mme de Rênal donned it there and then. Her friend was no longer in any doubt. She's in love, poor wretch! Mme Derville said to herself, and she understood all the strange manifestations of her illness.

She observed her talking to Julien. Pallor replaced her crimson flush. Anxiety was depicted in her eyes which gazed into the young tutor's. Mme de Rênal was expecting him to explain himself at any moment, and announce that he was either leaving the household or staying. After a terrible struggle, Mme de Rênal at last plucked up courage to ask him, in a trembling voice which betrayed all her passion:

'Will you be leaving your pupils to take a position elsewhere?'

Julien was struck by Mme de Rênal's quavering voice and the look on her face. That woman's in love with me, he said to himself. But it's only a passing moment of weakness which her pride is ashamed of, and once she's no longer afraid that I'll leave, her haughtiness will be back. This vision of their respective positions came to Julien like a flash, and he answered hesitantly:

'I should find it very hard to leave such nice children—and *so well born* too—but it may perhaps be necessary. One does have oneself to think about too.'

As he uttered the words *so well born* (this was an aristocratic expression which Julien had recently picked up), Julien was fired with a deep feeling of animosity.

In the eyes of this woman, he said to himself, *I* don't count as well born.

Mme de Rênal listened to him in admiration at his brilliance and his good looks, and her heart was wrung at the prospect he held out to her that he might indeed leave. All her friends from Verrières who had come to dine at Vergy during Julien's absence had seemed to be deliberately outdoing one another in complimenting her on the amazing young man whom her husband had had the good fortune to unearth. Not that they understood a thing about the children's educational progress. It was the ability to recite the Bible by heart, and in Latin what's more, that had filled the inhabitants of Verrières with an admiration that may well last a century.

Julien, who did not talk to anyone, knew none of this. If Mme de Rênal had kept any of her composure, she would have complimented him on the reputation he had earned himself, and once Julien's pride had been soothed, he would have been gentle and amiable with her—all the more so as he found her new dress delightful. Mme de Rênal, who was also pleased with her pretty dress, and Julien's comments to her on it, had wanted to take a stroll round the garden; but she soon confessed that she was quite incapable of walking. She had taken the traveller's arm, and far from renewing her strength, the feel of his arm against hers robbed her of all the strength she had.

It was dark. No sooner had the party sat down than Julien asserted his established privilege and dared to put his lips to his pretty neighbour's arm and take her hand. He was thinking of how forward Fouqué had been with his mistresses, not of Mme de Rênal; the term *well born* still rankled in his heart. He felt his hand being squeezed, but it gave him no pleasure. Far from deriving any pride, or at least some gratitude from the feelings which Mme de Rênal betrayed that evening by quite unmistakable signs, he remained virtually unmoved by her beauty, her elegance and her unspoilt charm. Purity of mind and the absence of any hostile emotion are no doubt responsible for prolonging youth. The face is where the first signs of ageing appear with the majority of pretty women.

Julien was sulky all evening. Until then, he had only felt anger at fate and at society, but since Fouqué had offered him an unworthy means of becoming comfortably off, he felt resentment against himself. Lost in his own thoughts, although he did from time to time say a few words to the ladies, Julien eventually let go of Mme de Rênal's hand without even noticing. The poor woman was utterly shattered by this gesture: she read it as a symbol of her fate.

Had she been sure of Julien's affection, her virtue might perhaps have found the strength to resist him. Fearful of losing him for ever, she was led astray by her passion to the point of taking hold of Julien's hand which he had distractedly left resting on the back of a chair. Her gesture brought the ambitious young man to himself: he would have liked it to be witnessed by all those snobbish noblemen who gave him such patronizing smiles at table when he was down at the far end with the children. This woman can't despise me any more: in which case I must respond to her beauty; I owe it to myself to become her lover. Such an idea would never have occurred to him before his friend so innocently confided in him.

The sudden resolve he had just made provided him with a welcome distraction. He said to himself: I must have one of these two women. He realized he would have much preferred to make advances to Mme Derville; not because she had more charm, but because she had only ever seen him as a tutor respected for his learning, and not as a carpenter's lad with a woollen jacket folded under his arm, as he had first appeared to Mme de Rênal.

It was precisely as a young workman blushing to the roots of his hair as he stood at the front door of her house not daring to knock, that Mme de Rênal pictured him at his most charming.

Continuing to review his situation, Julien realized that it was out of the question to think of conquering Mme Derville, who was probably aware of Mme de Rênal's fondness for him. Forced to return to her, he asked himself: What do I know of this woman's character? Merely this: before I went away, when I took hold of her hand she withdrew it; today, I withdraw my hand and she grasps it and squeezes it. It's a fine opportunity to pay her back for all the times she's disdained me. Heaven knows how many lovers she's had! Maybe she's only settled for me because it's so easy for us to see each other.

This, alas, is the unfortunate consequence of too much civilization! At twenty, the heart of a young man who has had some education is utterly remote from the carefree abandon without which love is often only the most tedious of duties.

I owe it to myself all the more to succeed with this woman, continued Julien's petty vanity, since if ever I make my fortune, and the humble job of tutor is held against me, I shall be able to insinuate that love cast me in that role.

Once more Julien moved his hand away from Mme de Rênal's, and then he took hold of it again in a tight grasp. As they were going back into the drawing-room towards midnight, Mme de Rênal said to him under her breath:

'Will you be leaving us? Will you be going?'

Julien replied with a sigh:

'I must indeed leave, because I love you passionately, and it's a sin... such a sin for a young priest!'

Mme de Rênal leaned on his arm, with such abandon that she felt the warmth of Julien's cheek against hers.

These two individuals each spent a very different kind of night. Mme de Rênal's mind was uplifted by feelings of the purest ecstasy. A flirtatious young girl who falls in love early grows used to the turmoil of love; when she reaches the age of true passion, the charm of novelty has worn off. As Mme de Rênal had never read any novels, all the facets of her happiness were new to her. No sorry truths were there to chill her, not even the spectre of the future. She saw herself as happy in ten years' time as she was at that moment. Even the thought of her virtue, and the fidelity she had sworn to M. de Rênal, which had caused her such agitation a few days previously, came to her now in vain and was banished like an unwelcome guest. I shall never yield anything to Julien, said Mme de Rênal to herself. We'll go on living just as we've lived for the past month. He'll be a good friend.

CHAPTER 14

A pair of English scissors

*A girl of sixteen had a complexion
like a rose, and she put on rouge.*

POLIDORI*

As for Julien, Fouqué's offer really had taken all his pleasure away: he was incapable of settling on any course of action. Alas! Perhaps I lack character; I'd have been no good as one of Napoleon's soldiers. At any rate, he added, my little intrigue with the lady of the house will keep my mind occupied for a while.

Fortunately for him, even in this minor incident, his offhand words were a poor reflection of what was going on inside him. He was afraid of Mme de Rênal because she had such a pretty dress. In his eyes this dress was the vanguard of Paris. His self-esteem was reluctant to leave anything to chance or to the inspiration of the moment. On the basis of what Fouqué had confided in him, and the little he had read about love in his Bible, he drew up a highly detailed plan of campaign for himself. And since without admitting it he was extremely agitated, he wrote this plan down.

The next morning, Mme de Rênal found herself alone with him for a moment in the drawing-room.

'Is *Julien* your only name?' she asked him.

This flattering enquiry left our hero at a loss for an answer. It was a detail that had not been anticipated in his plan. Had it not been for this silly idea of making a plan, Julien's sharp wits would have served him well, and the effect of surprise would only have increased the sharpness of his perceptions.

He reacted ineptly, and his ineptness took on exaggerated proportions in his mind. Mme de Rênal was quick to forgive him for it. She read it as evidence of charming candour. And the very thing she found lacking in this man held to be so brilliant was precisely a look of candour.

'Your young tutor fills me with deep mistrust,' Mme Derville would say to her from time to time. 'He looks to me as if he's always thinking, and never acts uncalculatingly. He's devious.'

Julien remained profoundly humiliated by the misfortune of having failed to find a reply to Mme de Rênal.

A man of my sort owes it to himself to recover from this setback; and taking advantage of the moment when they were moving from one room to the next, he decided it was his duty to give Mme de Rênal a kiss.

Nothing could have been less well prepared, or given less pleasure to either of them; nothing could have been more unwise. They only just escaped being seen. Mme de Rênal thought he had gone mad. She was terrified and above all shocked. This piece of foolishness reminded her of M. Valenod.

What would happen to me, she asked herself, if I were alone with him? All her virtue returned to her when love was thus eclipsed. She made sure that one of her children was always by her side.

It was a boring day for Julien: he spent the whole of it ineptly putting his plan of seduction into effect. He did not once look at Mme de Rênal without his glance having some reason behind it; yet he was not so silly that he failed to see he was not succeeding in being agreeable, let alone seductive.

Mme de Rênal could not get over her astonishment at finding him so inept and at the same time so bold. It's the timidity of love in a man of intellect! she said to herself at last with unutterable joy. Could it possibly be that he has never been loved by my rival!

After lunch Mme de Rênal returned to the drawing-room to receive a visit from M. Charcot de Maugiron, the sub-prefect of Bray. She was working at a little tapestry frame that stood high off the floor. Mme Derville was at her side. In this position, in full daylight, our hero saw fit to move his boot forward and press it against Mme de Rênal's pretty foot with its openwork stocking and pretty little shoe from Paris which clearly attracted the eye of the gallant sub-prefect.

Mme de Rênal took extreme fright. She dropped her scissors, her ball of wool, and her needles, and Julien's gesture could pass off as an inept attempt to prevent the scissors he had seen starting to slide from actually falling to the ground. Fortunately, this little pair of English steel scissors broke, and Mme de Rênal gave full vent to her regrets that Julien had not been closer to her side.

'You noticed them falling before I did, you could have stopped them; but instead, all you achieved in your eagerness was to give me a hefty kick.'

All this deceived the sub-prefect, but not Mme Derville. This handsome fellow has some pretty foolish manners! she thought. The etiquette of a provincial capital does not forgive transgressions of this sort. Mme de Rênal found an opportunity to say to Julien:

'Be careful, I order you to.'

Julien realized how inept he had been, and it put him in a bad temper. He debated at length with himself whether he ought to take offence at the expression *I order you to*. He was silly enough to think: she could say to me *I order you to* if it were something to do with the children's upbringing, but in responding to my love, she puts us on an equal footing. You can't love without *equality*...; and his mind wandered off completely into platitudes about equality. He angrily repeated to himself a line of Corneille* that Mme Derville had taught him a few days previously:

... ...   Love
Creates equalities, it does not seek them out.

Since Julien obstinately persisted in playing Don Juan despite never having had a single mistress in his life, he was unutterably foolish all day. He only had one sound idea. Fed up with himself and with Mme de Rênal, he was contemplating with dread the approach of evening, when he would be seated in the garden by her side in the dark. He told M. de Rênal he was going to Verrières to see the priest; he left after dinner and did not return until well into the night.

In Verrières Julien found Father Chélan in the midst of moving house: he had finally been stripped of his office, and was being replaced by M. Maslon the curate. Julien lent a hand to the kindly old priest, and was inspired to write to Fouqué to say that the irresistible calling which he felt for the sacred ministry had prevented him at first from accepting his kind offer, but that he had just seen such a flagrant example of injustice that it might perhaps be more advantageous to his salvation not to enter holy orders.

Julien congratulated himself on his cunning in turning the sacking of the priest of Verrières to his own advantage to leave the door ajar for himself to return to the world of trade if, in the battle raging in his mind, dreary caution got the better of heroism.

CHAPTER 15

The crowing of the cock

Amour en latin faict amor;
Or donc provient d'amour la mort,
Et, par avant, soulcy qui mord,
Deuil, plours, pièges, forfaits, remords.
LOVE'S BLAZON*

HAD Julien had any of the shrewdness he so gratuitously imagined himself to possess, he would have been able to congratulate himself the next day on the effect produced by his trip to Verrières. His absence had wiped out the memory of his inept antics. That day too he was rather sullen. Towards evening, a ludicrous idea occurred to him, and he imparted it to Mme de Rênal with singular intrepidity.

They were hardly seated in the garden when, without waiting for it to be sufficiently dark, Julien put his lips to Mme de Rênal's ear and, at the risk of compromising her most horribly, said:

'Madam, this very night I shall come to your room at two o'clock, I've got something to say to you.'

Julien trembled lest his request be granted; his seducer's role was such a horrible burden on him that if he had been able to follow his inclination, he would have withdrawn to his room for several days, and avoided seeing the ladies. He was aware that his expert behaviour the previous day had ruined all the promising signs of the day before that, and he was genuinely at a loss which way to turn.

Mme de Rênal responded with real, unforced indignation to the impertinent announcement that Julien had been bold enough to make to her. He thought he detected scorn in her short reply. There is no doubt that this reply, uttered in a low tone, had contained the phrase *how dare you*. Under the guise of saying something to the children, Julien went off to their room, and on his return he took a seat beside Mme Derville, a long way away from Mme de Rênal. He thus made it impossible for himself to take her hand. The conversation was serious, and Julien made a very good showing, apart from one or two moments of silence while he was racking his brains. Oh why can't I think up a really good move, he said to himself, to force Mme de Rênal back into giving me those unequivocal demonstrations of fondness which led me to believe three days ago that she was mine!

Julien was extremely put out by the almost hopeless state into which he had got his affairs. Yet nothing would have embarrassed him more than success.

When they all went their own ways at midnight, his pessimism convinced him that he had earned Mme Derville's scorn, and that he had probably fared no better in the eyes of Mme de Rênal.

In this state of ill-temper and great humiliation, Julien was unable to fall asleep. He couldn't have been further from the thought of giving up all pretence, all strategy, and of living from one day to the next with Mme de Rênal, perfectly content like a child with the happiness that each day brought him.

He exhausted his mind thinking up clever moves, and then the next moment he decided they were absurd; in short, he was in an exceedingly miserable mood when the château clock struck two.

The noise roused him as the crowing of the cock roused St Peter. He realized the time had come to embark on the most arduous of undertakings. He hadn't given any further thought to his impertinent proposal since making it; it had been so badly received!

I told her I'd go to her room at two o'clock, he said to himself as he got up. I may indeed be inexperienced and coarse as befits a peasant's son—Mme Derville has made that only too clear to me—but at least I won't be feeble.

Julien was right to congratulate himself on his courage; he had never imposed a more arduous obligation on himself. He was shaking so much as he opened his door that his knees gave way under him, and he was forced to lean against the wall for support.

He had no shoes on. He went and listened at M. de Rênal's door, and heard the sound of his snoring. He was bitterly disappointed. So there was no excuse now for not going to her.

But what on earth would he do there? He had no plan, and even if he had had one, he felt in such turmoil that he would have been in no state to follow it.

At last, suffering infinitely more than if he had been walking to his death, he turned down the little corridor leading to Mme de Rênal's bedroom. He opened the door with a shaking hand, making a terrible noise as he did so.

The room was lit: a nightlight was burning in the chimney-place. He wasn't expecting this new misfortune. On seeing him come in, Mme de Rênal sprang out of bed. 'You wretch!' she cried. There was a bit of confusion. Julien forgot his idle plans and reverted to his natural role: not to find favour with such a charming woman struck him as the height of misfortune. His only response to her words of reproach was to fling himself at her feet and clasp her knees. As she spoke extremely harshly to him, he burst into tears.

Some hours later, when Julien left Mme de Rênal's room, one could say, in novelettish style, that he had nothing left to desire. For the love he had inspired and the unexpected impression made on him by her seductive charms had given him a victory which would never have been achieved by all his clumsy skill.

But, in the sweetest moments, he was still the victim of a bizarre pride, and aspired to play the role of a man accustomed to subjugate women: he tried unbelievably hard to spoil his endearing characteristics. Instead of being attentive to the ecstasy which he aroused, and the expressions of remorse which heightened its intensity, he was constantly beset by the idea of *duty*. He was afraid of terrible remorse and eternal ridicule if he deviated from the ideal model he had set himself to follow. In short, what made Julien a superior being was precisely what prevented him from savouring the happiness which came his way. Every inch the young girl of sixteen who has delightful colouring, and is foolish enough to put on rouge to go to a ball.

Terrified out of her wits by the sudden appearance of Julien, Mme de Rênal was soon in the throes of the most cruel fears. She was intensely stirred by Julien's tears and his despair.

Even when she had nothing left to refuse him, she pushed

Julien away from her with genuine indignation, only to fling herself back into his arms. There was no forethought apparent in this sequence of behaviour. She believed herself damned beyond reprieve, and sought to conceal the sight of hell from herself by smothering Julien with the most passionate of caresses. In short, nothing would have been lacking to our hero's happiness, not even a passionate sensuousness in the woman he had just conquered, if he had but known how to enjoy it. Julien's departure did not put an end to the storms of passion which buffeted her in spite of herself, or to her struggles with the remorse that devoured her.

Good Lord! Being happy, being loved—is that all there is to it? This was Julien's first thought on returning to his room. He was in that state of astonishment and uneasy agitation which overwhelms a person who has just obtained something long desired. You're in the habit of desiring, you can't find anything to desire any more, but you don't yet have any memories. Like a soldier returning from parade, Julien was intently engaged in reviewing all the details of his conduct.

'I didn't fail, did I, in any of the things I owe to myself? Did I play my part properly?'

And what part was it? That of a man accustomed to dazzling success with women.

CHAPTER 16

The day after

He turn'd his lips to hers, and with his hand
Call'd back the tangles of her wandering hair.
Don Juan, C. I, st. 170

FORTUNATELY—for Julien's image—Mme de Rênal had been too agitated, too astonished to notice the foolishness of the man who in an instant had become everything in the world to her.

As she entreated him to leave, seeing the dawn about to break, she said:

'Oh! my goodness! if my husband has heard any noise, it's the end of me.'

Julien, who had time to turn a fine phrase, remembered this one:

'Would you leave this world with regret?'

'Ah! very much at this moment! but I wouldn't regret having known you.'

Julien thought it befitted his dignity to make a point of going back to his room in broad daylight, defying prudence.

The constant attention with which he studied his every action in the mad hope of appearing a man of experience did have one fortunate consequence: when he saw Mme de Rênal again at lunch, his behaviour was a masterpiece of prudence.

For her part she could not look at him without blushing deeply, and she could not exist for a moment without looking at him; she was aware of her discomfiture, but her efforts to conceal it only made matters worse. Julien only glanced up at her once. At first, Mme de Rênal admired his prudence. Soon, seeing that this single glance was not repeated, she became alarmed: Can it be that he doesn't love me? she wondered. Alas! I'm rather old for him; there's ten years difference between us.

As they moved from the dining-room into the garden, she squeezed Julien's hand. Taken aback by such an extraordinary sign of love, he gave her a passionate look, for she had seemed very pretty to him at lunch, and while keeping his eyes lowered, he had spent the time going over her charms in his mind. This look consoled Mme de Rênal; it did not banish all her anxieties, but her anxieties almost entirely banished her remorse towards her husband.

At lunch this husband of hers had not noticed anything. The same could not be said of Mme Derville: she thought that Mme de Rênal was on the verge of succumbing. Throughout the whole day her bold and forthright friendship did not spare Mme de Rênal any innuendo designed to portray in hideous colours the danger she was in.

Mme de Rênal ached to be alone with Julien; she wanted to ask him if he still loved her. In spite of the unvarying sweetness of her temper, there were several occasions when she almost gave her friend to understand how unwelcome her interference was.

That evening in the garden Mme Derville arranged things so well that she found herself sitting between Mme de Rênal and Julien. Mme de Rênal, who had conjured up an exquisite image of the pleasure of squeezing Julien's hand and putting it to her lips, was unable to address a single word to him.

This setback increased her agitation. She was consumed with remorse over something: she had scolded Julien so much for his imprudent act in coming to her room the previous night, that she was now in fear and trembling that he would not come that evening. She left the garden early and went and settled herself in her room. But unable to contain her impatience she came and pressed her ear to Julien's door. In spite of the uncertainty and the passion consuming her, she did not dare go in. To do so seemed to her the most infamous step, for it features in a provincial saying.*

The servants had not all gone to bed. Prudence at length dictated that she return to her room. Two hours of waiting were two centuries of torment.

But Julien was too faithful to what he called duty to fail to carry out in every detail what he had laid down for himself.

As one o'clock was striking he slipped quietly from his room, made sure that the master of the house was deeply asleep, and made his appearance in Mme de Rênal's room. That day he found greater happiness in the arms of his love, for his thoughts dwelled less constantly on the role he had to play. He had eyes to see with and ears to hear. What Mme de Rênal said about her age contributed to his feeling of increased assurance.

'Alas! I'm ten years older than you! How can you love me!' she repeated to him aimlessly, because the idea of it oppressed her.

Julien could not grasp this misfortune, but he saw that it was real enough, and he forgot almost all his fear of being ridiculous.

The silly idea of being regarded as an inferior lover because of his humble birth vanished as well. As Julien's rapture gradually reassured his timid mistress, so she recovered a little happiness and the ability to judge her lover. Luckily he showed virtually no signs on that occasion of the stilted manner which had made the previous day's encounter a victory but not a pleasure. If she had noticed the attention he devoted to acting a part, this sad discovery would have robbed her of all happiness for ever. She could only have taken it as a sad result of the age-gap between them.

Although Mme de Rênal had never thought about theories of love, difference in age follows close on difference in fortune as being one of the great commonplaces of provincial humour whenever it comes to joking about love.

It was only a matter of days before Julien, regaining the full ardour of his youth, was head over heels in love.

I must admit, he said to himself, that she's as sweet-natured as an angel, and it would be difficult to be prettier.

He had almost completely lost the idea of the role he had to play. In an unguarded moment he even confided all his worries to her. This confession fanned into a blaze the passion he inspired. So I never had a happy rival! said Mme de Rênal to herself in ecstasy. She plucked up courage to question him on the portrait he had been so concerned about; Julien swore to her that it was the picture of a man.

At times when Mme de Rênal still had enough composure to reflect, she couldn't get over her astonishment that such happiness should exist, and that she had never suspected it.

Ah! she mused, if only I'd known Julien ten years ago when I was still considered pretty!

Julien was very far removed from such thoughts. His love still stemmed from ambition, from the joy of knowing that he, a poor wretch so deeply despised, could possess such a noble and beautiful woman. His acts of adoration, his excitement at the sight of his loved one's charms, eventually reassured her about the difference in their ages. If she had had any of the worldly wisdom which women of thirty have possessed for quite some time in more civilized parts of the country, she would have feared for the duration of a love which only seemed to feed on novelty and flattered self-esteem.

At moments when Julien forgot his ambition, his rapturous admiration extended to the very hats, the very dresses that Mme de Rênal wore. He could not have enough of the pleasure of smelling their perfume. He opened her mirrored wardrobe and spent hours on end admiring the beauty and the style of everything he found there. Leaning against him, his mistress looked at him, while he looked at the jewels and garments which might have composed a trousseau on the eve of a wedding.

I might have married a man like that! Mme de Rênal thought from time to time. What a passionate creature! What an enchanting life together!

Julien for his part had never come so close to these terrible instruments of feminine artillery. It just isn't possible, he said to himself, that there's anything more beautiful to be had in Paris! At this point he could find no further obstacle to his happiness. Often his mistress's sincere admiration and her rapture caused him to forget the futile theory which had made him so unnatural and almost ridiculous at the beginning of their liaison. There were moments when, in spite of his habitually assumed hypocrisy, he found it extremely comforting to confess to this grand lady who so admired him how ignorant he was of a host of little customs. His mistress's rank seemed to raise him up above himself. Mme de Rênal on her side derived the sweetest of mental enjoyment from providing instruction in this way, in a host of little matters, to a young man so full of genius, who was universally regarded as someone who would one day go far. Even the sub-prefect and M. Valenod could not help admiring him; and they seemed to him the less foolish for it. As for Mme Derville, she was far from having such sentiments to express. In despair at what she guessed to be going on, and realizing that her wise counsel was becoming distasteful to a woman who had literally lost her head, she left Vergy without offering any explanation, and none was asked of her. Mme de Rênal shed one or two tears over it, but it soon seemed to her that her bliss had only increased. This departure gave her virtually the whole of the daytime alone with her lover.

Julien was all the more ready to give himself up to the delightful company of his beloved since, whenever he was alone with himself for too long, Fouqué's fateful proposition returned to the forefront of his mind to unsettle him. In the early days of his new life, there were moments when Julien, who had never loved or been loved by anyone, found such delightful pleasure in being sincere that he was on the point of telling Mme de Rênal of the ambition that had up till then been the be-all and end-all of his existence. He would have liked to seek her opinion on the strange temptation which Fouqué's proposition held out for him, but a little happening put any frankness out of the question.

CHAPTER 17

First deputy

> O, how this spring of love resembleth
> The uncertain glory of an April day,
> Which now shows all the beauty of the sun
> And by and by a cloud takes all away!
>
> TWO GENTLEMEN OF VERONA

ONE evening at sunset he sat deeply musing beside his mistress at the bottom of the orchard, far from any intruder's gaze. Will such sweet moments last for ever? he wondered. His mind was preoccupied with the difficulty of adopting a profession, and he resented this great new burden which brings an end to childhood and spoils the early years of poverty-stricken youth.

'Ah!' he exclaimed, 'Napoleon really was a man sent from God for the young men of France! Who will replace him? Without him, what will become of the unfortunate people—even those richer than I am—who can just scrape together what it takes to pay for a good education, but haven't got enough money at twenty to buy their way into a career! Whatever we do', he added with a deep sigh, 'this fateful memory will always prevent us from being happy!'

All of a sudden he saw Mme de Rênal frown and take on a cold and disdainful look: this way of thinking struck her as something to be expected of a servant. Brought up in the knowledge that she was extremely wealthy, it seemed to her to go without saying that Julien was too. She loved him infinitely more dearly than her life, and was quite indifferent to money.

Julien was nowhere near guessing these thoughts. Her frown brought him down to earth again. He had enough presence of mind to modify what he said and give the noble lady sitting on the grassy bank beside him to understand that the words he had just repeated had been heard by him on his visit to his friend the timber merchant. They represented the way of thinking of the ungodly.

'Very well then! Don't mix with people like that any more,'

said Mme de Rênal, still with a trace of the frosty air that had suddenly replaced an expression of the utmost tenderness.

Her frown, or rather the regret he felt at his rash words, was the first setback to the illusion beguiling Julien. He said to himself: She's kind and sweet, and has a strong attachment to me, but she was brought up in the enemy camp. They must be particularly afraid of the class of spirited young men who receive a good education but haven't enough money to embark on a career. What would become of these same nobles if it fell to our lot to fight them with equal arms! Imagine me as mayor of Verrières for instance. I'm well-intentioned and honest just like M. de Rênal is underneath! I'd soon get the better of the curate, M. Valenod and all their skullduggery! Justice would soon triumph in Verrières! It wouldn't be their talents that put obstacles in my way. They're forever groping in the dark.

Julien's happiness reached the verge, that day, of becoming lasting. In the event our hero lacked the courage to be sincere. He needed to be bold enough to engage battle—and that *forthwith*. Mme de Rênal had been astonished by Julien's words, because the men in her circle said repeatedly that what made the return of Robespierre* possible was first and foremost the young men from the lower orders who had been too well educated. Mme de Rênal's chilly air lasted some while, and struck Julien as very marked. You see, the fear of having indirectly said something disagreeable to him had replaced her distaste for his unsuitable remarks. This unhappiness was vividly reflected in her countenance, which was usually so pure and innocent when she was happy and away from tedious company.

Julien no longer dared let his fancies run free. Calmer and less madly in love, he decided it was unwise to visit Mme de Rênal in her bedroom. It was better for her to come to his; if one of the servants noticed her moving about the house, any number of reasons could be found to explain her conduct.

But this arrangement had its disadvantages too. Julien had received from Fouqué some books which as a theology student he could never have requested from a bookseller. He did not dare open them except at night. Often he would have been very glad not to be interrupted by a visit which, as recently as the evening before the little scene in the orchard, would have put him in a state of anticipation quite unconducive to reading.

He owed to Mme de Rênal a totally new understanding of the books he read. He had been bold enough to question her about a host of little things that are unfamiliar to a young man born outside society, and stop his comprehension in its tracks, however much natural ability one is prepared to credit him with.

This education of love given by an extremely ignorant woman was a great joy. Julien was able to gain a direct perspective on society as it is today. His intelligence was not offended by the account of what it had been at other times, two thousand years ago or only sixty years back, in the time of Voltaire* and of Louis XV.* To his unutterable delight the scales fell from his eyes and he at last understood the goings-on in Verrières.

In the foreground there emerged some very complicated intrigues which had been plotted over the past two years in the prefect of Besançon's entourage. They received support in the form of letters emanating from Paris, written in the most illustrious quarters. The aim was to make M. de Moirod—he was the most pious man in the region—the first and not the second deputy to the mayor of Verrières.

He had a rival in the person of an extremely rich manufacturer whom it was vital to keep down in the position of second deputy.

Julien at last understood the veiled remarks he had overheard when the high society of the locality came to dine with M. de Rênal. This privileged society was deeply preoccupied by the business of selecting a first deputy, which the rest of the town and in particular the liberals never even suspected was an issue. What made this a matter of importance was that, as everyone knows, the east side of the main street in Verrières needs to be moved back more than nine feet, for this street has become a royal highway.

Now if M. de Moirod, who owned three houses requiring to be moved back, succeeded in becoming first deputy, and later on mayor of Verrières in the eventuality of M. de Rênal's being chosen for the Chamber of Deputies,* M. de Moirod would turn a blind eye and it would be possible at the same time to make unnoticeable minor repairs to the houses which project onto the public highway in such a way that they would last a hundred years. In spite of the great piety and honesty universally recognized in M. de Moirod, everyone was sure he would be *accommodating*, for he had a large number of children. Among the houses which had to be moved back, nine belonged to the élite of Verrières.

In Julien's eyes this intrigue was far more important than the history of the battle of Fontenoy,* which he first saw mentioned in one of the books Fouqué had sent him. There were things which had astonished Julien over the past five years, ever since he had begun to pay evening visits to the priest. But as discretion and humility of mind are the first qualities required of a theology student, it had always been impossible for him to ask any questions.

One day Mme de Rênal was giving an order to her husband's valet, Julien's enemy.

'But madam, today's the last Friday in the month,' the man replied with a strange look.

'All right then,' said Mme de Rênal.

'Now look,' said Julien, 'he's off to that hay barn which used to be a church and has recently been taken over again for divine office; but what's he going to do there? This is one of the mysteries I've never been able to solve.'

'It's a very salutary but rather peculiar institution,'* replied Mme de Rênal. 'Women aren't admitted; the only thing I know about it is that they all address one another as equals.* Our servant, for instance, will meet M. Valenod there, and this proud and silly man won't take any offence at hearing himself addressed familiarly by Saint-Jean, and he'll answer him in the same vein. If you really want to know what goes on there, I'll ask M. de Maugiron and M. Valenod for details. We pay twenty francs per servant so as to stop them cutting our throats one day.'

Time flew by. The memory of his mistress's charms kept Julien's mind off his black ambition. The need to avoid talking to her about dreary, rational matters, since they belonged to opposing parties, added without his realizing it to the happiness he owed to her, and to the hold she was gaining over him.

At times when the presence of children with too much understanding reduced them to speaking exclusively the language of cold reason, Julien sat perfectly docile, gazing at her with love shining in his eyes, listening to her explaining the way of the world. Often, in the midst of an account of some piece of cunning roguery connected with a road or the supply of goods, Mme de Rênal's mind would suddenly wander to the point of incoherence; Julien would have to scold her, and she would indulge in the same affectionate gestures with him as with her children. For there were days when she had the illusion of loving him like her own child. Wasn't she always having to answer his naïve questions about countless simple things that a well-born child is familar with by the age of fifteen? A moment later, she admired him as her master. His genius was such as to frighten her; every day she thought she discerned more clearly in this young abbé a man destined for greatness. She saw him as pope, she saw him as prime minister like Richelieu.*

'Will I live long enough to see you in your glory?' she asked Julien. 'There's a place waiting for a great man: religion and the monarchy need one.'

CHAPTER 18

A king in Verrières

Are you only fit to be flung aside like the
corpse of a people, without a soul, and with
no blood left in its veins?

BISHOP'S ORATION
at the Chapel of St Clement

ON the third of September at ten in the evening an officer of
the law woke the whole of Verrières as he galloped up the main
street with the news that his majesty the King of —— was
arriving the following Sunday; it was then Tuesday. The
prefect gave permission, or rather orders, for a guard of honour
to be formed; as much pomp and ceremony as possible had to
be laid on. A messenger was dispatched to Vergy. M. de Rênal
arrived during the night to find the whole town in turmoil.
Everyone claimed a right to this, that or the other. Those with
least to do hired balconies to see the king's arrival.

Who shall command the guard of honour? M. de Rênal saw
immediately how important it was, in the interest of the houses
that had to be moved back, that M. de Moirod should have
this charge. It might serve as a credential for the post of first
deputy. There was no impugning M. de Moirod's zeal—it was
beyond compare—but he had never ridden a horse in his life.
He was a man of thirty-six, timorous in all respects, and he
was equally afraid of falling off and of appearing ridiculous.

The mayor summoned him at five o'clock in the morning.

'You observe, sir, that I seek your advice as if you already
held the post that all good citizens wish to see you occupy. In
this unfortunate town, factories are flourishing, the liberal
party is acquiring millions, it is set on getting into power, and
will turn anything to advantage. Let us think of the interests
of the king, of the monarchy and above all of our sacred
religion. Who, sir, in your opinion, can be entrusted with the
command of the guard of honour?'

In spite of his terrible fear of horses, M. de Moirod ended
up accepting this honour as he might have done martyrdom. 'I

shall manage to adopt a suitable manner,' he told the mayor. There was barely enough time left to adapt the uniforms which had served seven years before when a prince of the blood had passed through.

At seven o'clock Mme de Rênal arrived from Vergy with Julien and the children. She found her drawing-room filled with liberal ladies who were preaching the need for unity among the parties, and had come to beg her to exhort her husband to include some of their number in the guard of honour. One of them claimed that if her husband were not selected, he would go bankrupt from grief. Mme de Rênal lost no time in getting rid of all these people. She seemed very preoccupied.

Julien was amazed and even more annoyed that she made a mystery to him of what was agitating her. I saw it coming, he said to himself bitterly; her love is eclipsed by the delightful prospect of having a king as guest in her house. She's dazzled by all the fuss. She'll love me again once the ideas of her caste have stopped bothering her.

The amazing thing was that he loved her all the more for it.

The decorators and upholsterers were beginning to fill the house; he hovered for a long time in vain waiting for a chance to say something to her. At last he caught her coming out of his own room carrying one of his suits. They were alone. He attempted to speak to her. She ran off refusing to listen to him. What a fool I am to love a woman like this; ambition is driving her as mad as her husband.

She was even madder: one of her great desires, which she had never confessed to Julien for fear of shocking him, was to see him dressed, if only for a day, in something other than his dreary black suit. With truly admirable skill for a woman so straightforward, she secured the agreement first of M. de Moirod and then of the sub-prefect M. de Maugiron that Julien be appointed guard of honour in preference to five or six young men who were the sons of very well-to-do manufacturers, and at least two of whom were models of piety. M. Valenod, who was intending to lend his barouche to the prettiest woman in town and show off his fine Normandy cobs, agreed to give one of his horses to Julien, the individual he hated most of all. But all the guards of honour owned or had borrowed one of those beautiful sky-blue outfits with two colonel's epaulettes in silver, which had been so dazzling seven years before. Mme de Rênal wanted a new outfit, and she only had four days left to send off to Besançon and have despatched from there the dress uniform, the arms, the hat etc.—everything required by a guard of honour. The amusing thing about it all is that she thought it unwise to have Julien's outfit made in Verrières. She wanted it to be a surprise for him, and the town too.

Once he had dealt with the guards of honour and the matter of public support, the mayor had to organize a grand religious ceremony, as the King of —— did not wish to pass through Verrières without visiting the famous relic of St Clement which is preserved at Bray-le-Haut,* a short league away from the town. A large number of clergy had to be present, and this proved the most difficult matter to arrange; Father Maslon, the new priest, wanted at all costs to ensure that Father Chélan would not be there. M. de Rênal achieved nothing by representing to him that this would be a rash step. The Marquis de La Mole, whose ancestors had been governors of the province for so long, had been chosen to accompany the King of ——. He had known Father Chélan for thirty years. He would be certain to ask after him on arrival in Verrières, and if he found him in disgrace, he was the kind of man to go and fetch him out from the little house he had retired to, accompanied by as much of the procession as he could muster. What a slap in the face!

'I shall be dishonoured here and in Besançon', replied Father Maslon, 'if he appears among my clergy. A Jansenist,* by God!'

'Whatever you may say about it, my dear Father,' retorted M. de Rênal, 'I shall not expose the administration in Verrières to the risk of a snub from M. de La Mole. You don't know him: he's an orthodox figure at Court, but here in the provinces he's a satirical, sardonic fellow given to jokes in poor taste, and always out to embarrass people. He's quite capable, simply to amuse himself, of making a laughing-stock of us in front of the liberals.'

It was not until well into the Saturday night, after three days of negotiations, that Father Maslon's pride gave way to the mayor's fear, which was gradually turning into courage. He was obliged to write an unctuous letter to Father Chélan, begging him to attend the ceremony in honour of the Bray-le-Haut relic—if, that is, his advanced years and his infirmities allowed him to do so. Father Chélan requested and obtained a letter of invitation for Julien, who was to accompany him as an under-deacon.

From Sunday morning onwards thousands of peasants came in from the mountains round about and flooded the streets of Verrières. It was a glorious sunny day. At last, at about three o'clock, a great stir ran through the whole crowd: a huge fire could be seen on a peak two leagues away from Verrières. This signal announced that the king had just set foot inside the département.* Immediately, the pealing of all the bells, and repeated volleys from an old Spanish cannon belonging to the town, betokened its joy at this great event. Half the population climbed onto the roofs. All the women were at their balconies. The guard of honour set off. The dazzling uniforms were admired; everyone recognized a relative or a friend. They laughed at M. de Moirod's fear as he kept a cautious hand always at the ready to grab the pommel of the saddle. But one comment put all others into oblivion: the first rider in the ninth column was an exceedingly handsome fellow, very slender, whom no one recognized at first. Soon a shout of indignation from some quarters and an astonished silence from others signalled a universal reaction. People recognized this young man riding one of M. Valenod's Normandy cobs as young Sorel the carpenter's son. A unanimous shout went up against the mayor, particularly from the liberals. What! Just because this little workman dressed up as an abbé was tutor to his brats, he had the nerve to appoint him guard of honour, over the heads of M. —— and M. ——, who were rich manufacturers! 'These gentlemen', said a banker's good lady, 'should certainly deliver a public snub to this little upstart born in squalor.' 'He's sly as they come, and wearing a sabre,' replied her neighbour. 'He'd be treacherous enough to slash them in the face.'

Comments from noble circles were more dangerous. The ladies wondered whether the mayor alone was responsible for this monstrous impropriety. The general consensus gave him credit for scorning the accident of low birth.

While all these things were being said about him, Julien was the happiest of men. Bold by nature, he was better on horseback than the majority of young men in this hill town. He could see in the women's eyes that their attention was on him.

His epaulettes shone more brightly because they were new. His horse reared up every few minutes and he felt on top of the world.

His happiness knew no bounds when, as they passed near the old ramparts, the noise of the small cannon caused his horse to break ranks. By sheer good luck he did not fall off, and from then on he felt like a hero. He was one of Napoleon's aides de camp and was leading the charge against a battery.

There was one person happier than he. First she had seen him go past from one of the windows of the town hall; then, getting into her barouche and quickly making a big detour, she arrived in time to tremble when his horse broke ranks and carried him off. Finally, by having her barouche gallop out of the town by another gate, she managed to join the road which the king was due to pass along, and was able to follow the guard of honour only twenty paces behind, in a cloud of noble dust. Ten thousand peasants shouted 'Long live the king!' when the mayor had the honour of addressing his majesty. An hour later, when all the speeches were over and the king was about to enter the town, the small cannon began to fire again in rapid bursts. There followed an accident, not for the cannoneers who had proved their mettle at Leipzig* and Montmirail, but for the first-deputy-to-be, M. de Moirod. His horse deposited him gently in the only dung-heap along the main road, causing a mighty stir because he had to be dragged out of it so that the king's carriage could pass.

His majesty alighted at the fine new church, which was adorned that day with all its crimson draperies. The king was due to dine and then get back into his carriage immediately afterwards to go and venerate the famous relic of St Clement.

The king had no sooner reached the church than Julien galloped off in the direction of M. de Rênal's house. There, with much regret, he exchanged his lovely sky-blue outfit, his sabre and his epaulettes for the familiar shabby black suit. He climbed on to his horse again and a short while later he was at Bray-le-Haut, which crowns the top of a very fine hill. Enthusiasm makes these peasants proliferate, thought Julien. You can't move for them in Verrières, and there are more than ten thousand of them here around this ancient abbey. Half-ruined by vandalism under the Revolution,* it had been magnificently restored since the Restoration,* and there was beginning to be talk of miracles. Julien joined Father Chélan, who scolded him roundly and handed him a cassock and a surplice. He dressed in haste, and followed Father Chélan who was off to find the young Bishop of Agde*—a nephew of M. de La Mole who had been recently appointed, and had been entrusted with showing the relic to the king. But the bishop was nowhere to be found.

The clergy were getting impatient. They were waiting for their spiritual head in the gloomy gothic cloisters of the ancient abbey. Twenty-four priests had been gathered together to represent the original chapter of Bray-le-Haut, composed before 1789 of twenty-four canons. After spending three-quarters of an hour deploring the bishop's youth, the priests thought it fitting that the Reverend Dean should withdraw to warn Monsignor that the king was about to arrive, and that it was exceedingly urgent to take their places in the chancel. Father Chélan had been made dean in virtue of his great age; despite his annoyance at him, he beckoned Julien to follow him. Julien looked very good in his surplice. By some myster-ious trick of ecclesiastical toilette he had smoothed his lovely curly hair down flat; but by an oversight which increased Father Chélan's rage, beneath the long folds of his cassock could be seen his guard of honour's spurs.

When they arrived at the bishop's lodgings, tall, richly dressed footmen scarcely deigned to reply to the old priest that Monsignor was not at home to visitors. They scoffed at him when he tried to explain that in his capacity as dean of the noble chapter of Bray-le-Haut he was privileged to be received at any time by the officiating bishop.

Julien's haughty temperament was shocked by the footmen's insolence. He set off at a run through the dormitories of the ancient abbey, rattling all the doors he passed. A very small one yielded to his efforts, and he found himself in a cell in the midst of Monsignor's valets, dressed in black with chains round their necks. His hurried look made these gentlemen believe that he had been summoned by the bishop, and they let him pass. He went on a few steps and found himself in an immense and extremely dark gothic hall, panelled throughout in dark oak; all but one of the ogive windows had been bricked up. The crudeness of this masonry was not disguised in any way, and contrasted sadly with the ancient magnificence of the woodwork. Richly carved wooden stalls adorned the two long sides of this hall so renowned among Burgundian antiquaries, which Charles the Bold had built in about 1470 in expiation for some sin or other. On these stalls you could see all the mysteries of the Apocalypse worked in wood of different colours.

Julien was touched by this melancholy magnificence spoilt by the sight of the bare bricks and fresh white plaster. He stood still in silence. At the far end of the hall, near the only window which let in the light, he saw a hinged mirror on a mahogany stand. A young man in a purple robe and a lace surplice, but with nothing on his head, was standing three paces from the mirror. It seemed a strange piece of furniture to have in such a place, and it had probably been brought from the town. Julien thought the young man looked exasperated; his right hand was solemnly giving blessings in the direction of the mirror.

What can this mean? he wondered. Is this young priest carrying out some preparatory ceremony? Perhaps he's the bishop's secretary... he'll be insolent just like the footmen... oh well, never mind, let's have a try.

He moved forward and walked fairly slowly down the length of the hall, his gaze firmly directed towards the solitary window and fixed on the young man, who continued to give blessings which were slowly executed but indefinitely repeated, without a moment's respite.

As he approached, Julien was better able to make out his look of annoyance. The richness of the surplice adorned with lace caused him to stop involuntarily a few paces from the magnificent mirror.

It's my duty to speak, he told himself at length; but the beauty of the hall had stirred his emotions, and he was ruffled in advance by the harsh words that were going to be spoken to him.

The young man saw him in the glass, turned round, and suddenly dropping his angry look said to him in the gentlest of tones:

'Well, sir! Has it been fixed at last?'

Julien was flabbergasted. As the young man turned towards him Julien saw the pectoral cross on his chest: he was the Bishop of Agde. So young, thought Julien; seven or eight years older than me at the very most!...

And he felt ashamed of his spurs.

'Monsignor,' he replied timidly, 'I've been sent by the dean of the chapter, Father Chélan.'

'Ah! He's been most warmly recommended to me,' said the bishop in polite tones which added to Julien's delight. 'But I do beg your pardon, sir, I mistook you for the person who is supposed to be bringing me back my mitre. It was carelessly packed in Paris; the silver brocade is horribly damaged at the top. It'll look really most dreadful,' added the young bishop with a sorrowful expression, 'and to crown it all they're making me wait.'

'Monsignor, I'll go and fetch the mitre, if your lordship allows.'

Julien's lovely eyes did the trick.

'Please do, sir,' the bishop replied with engaging politeness. 'I need it right away. I'm terribly sorry to keep the Reverend Fathers of the chapter waiting.'

When Julien reached the middle of the hall he turned back to look at the bishop and saw that he had started giving blessings again. What on earth is all this? Julien wondered. It's no doubt some necessary ecclesiastical preparation for the

ceremony about to take place. On reaching the cell where the
valets were, he saw the mitre in their hands. These gentlemen
yielded in spite of themselves to Julien's imperious look, and
handed him Monsignor's mitre.

He felt proud to be carrying it: his pace as he walked across
the hall was slow, and he held it with respect. He found the
bishop seated in front of the mirror; but from time to time his
right hand would still give another blessing in spite of its
fatigue. Julien helped him put on his mitre. The bishop shook
his head from side to side.

'Ah! It'll stay put,' he said to Julien with an air of satisfaction. 'Would you mind stepping back a bit?'

The bishop then went quickly to the middle of the hall and,
as he walked back with slow steps towards the mirror, he
resumed his expression of annoyance, and solemnly gave out
blessings.

Julien was rooted to the spot with astonishment; he was
tempted to draw conclusions, but didn't dare. The bishop
stopped and, looking at him with an air which rapidly lost
some of its solemnity, said:

'What do you think of my mitre, sir? Does it look good?'

'Very good, Monsignor.'

'It isn't too far back? That would look a bit silly; but nor
must it be worn pulled down over the eyes like an officer's
shako.'

'It looks very good to me.'

'The King of —— is accustomed to clergy who are venerable and no doubt extremely solemn. I shouldn't wish, particularly in view of my age, to look insufficiently serious.'

And the bishop began to pace up and down again giving out
blessings.

It's clear, said Julien, at last daring to draw the right
conclusion; he's practising giving the blessing.

A few moments later:

'I'm ready,' said the bishop. 'Kindly go, sir, and inform the
Reverend Dean and Fathers of the chapter.'

Soon Father Chélan, followed by the two most senior priests,
entered by a very large, magnificently carved door that Julien
had not noticed. But this time he remained in his place, right

at the back, and could only see the bishop over the shoulders of the clergy who were crowding round the door.

The bishop made his way slowly across the hall; when he reached the threshold the priests lined up in procession. After a brief moment of confusion the procession set off, striking up a psalm. The bishop walked last, between Father Chélan and another very old priest. Julien slipped in right next to Monsignor as Father Chélan's attendant. They went down the long corridors of Bray-le-Haut abbey, gloomy and damp in spite of the brilliant sunshine. At length they reached the portico of the cloisters. Julien was struck dumb with admiration at such a beautiful ceremony. The ambition reawakened in him by the bishop's extreme youth and the sensitivity and exquisite politeness of this prelate were all warring to win his heart. This politeness was quite another matter from M. de Rênal's, even on his good days. The higher you rise towards the first rank in society, Julien thought, the more examples you find of these delightful manners.

As the procession entered the church by a side door, a fearful din suddenly shook the ancient vaulting: Julien thought it was collapsing. It was the little cannon again; it had just arrived, pulled by eight galloping horses, and it had hardly arrived and been lined up by the cannoneers who had fought at Leipzig before it was firing five shots a minute as if it were pointing at the Prussians.

But this splendid noise had no more effect on Julien; he had no thoughts for Napoleon and military glory. So young, he thought, and bishop of Agde! Where is Agde anyway? And how much is the income? Maybe two or three hundred thousand francs.

Monsignor's footmen appeared with a magnificent canopy; Father Chélan took one of the poles, but in fact it was Julien who carried it. The bishop took up his station beneath it. He really had managed to make himself look old; our hero's admiration knew no bounds. Anything can be done with a bit of skill! he thought.

The king entered. Julien had the good fortune to see him from very close up. The bishop addressed him with unction,

adding just a shade of emotion that was very flattering to his
majesty.

We shall not repeat the description of the ceremonies at
Bray-le-Haut; they filled the columns of all the newspapers in
the département for a fortnight afterwards. Julien heard from
the bishop's address that the king was descended from Charles
the Bold.

Later it was one of Julien's duties to check all the accounts
relating to expenditure on the ceremony. M. de La Mole, who
had obtained a bishopric for his nephew, had determined to
pay him the compliment of taking care of all the expenses. The
ceremony at Bray-le-Haut alone cost three thousand eight
hundred francs.

After the bishop's address and the king's reply, his majesty
stationed himself under the canopy and then knelt very piously
on a hassock near the altar. The chancel was lined with stalls,
and these stalls were raised two steps above the stone floor.
The last of these steps provided a seat for Julien at Father
Chélan's feet, rather like a trainbearer next to his cardinal in
the Sistine Chapel in Rome. There was a *Te Deum*, clouds of
incense, and endless volleys of musket and artillery fire; the
peasants were intoxicated with happiness and piety. A day like
that undoes the work of a hundred issues of the Jacobin press.

Julien was six paces away from the king, who was praying
with real fervour. He noticed for the first time a short man
with a lively expression wearing a suit that was virtually
unadorned. But he had a sky-blue sash* over this very plain
garb. He was closer to the king than many other nobles whose
costumes were so heavily embroidered with gold that, as Julien
put it, you couldn't see the cloth. He learned a few moments
later that this was M. de La Mole. He thought he looked
haughty and even insolent.

This marquis wouldn't be polite like my handsome bishop,
he thought. Ah! the priesthood makes a man gentle and wise.
But the king has come to venerate the relic, and I see no relic.
Where has St Clement got to?

A little cleric next to him informed him that the venerable
relic was in the upper part of the building in an *ardent chapel**
permanently lit by candles.

What's an *ardent chapel?* wondered Julien.

But he was unwilling to ask for an explanation of the expression. His attention increased.

On the occasion of a visit by a sovereign prince, etiquette has it that the canons do not accompany the bishop. But as he set off for the chapel of rest the Bishop of Agde summoned Father Chélan; Julien was bold enough to follow him.

After climbing a long flight of stairs, they reached a door which although very small had magnificent gilding all round its gothic frame. The work looked as if it had been carried out the previous day.

In front of the door knelt a group of twenty-four girls belonging to the most distinguished families in Verrières. Before opening the door, the bishop knelt down in the midst of these very pretty young girls. While he prayed out loud, they seemed overwhelmed with admiration for his fine lace, his gracious manner and his young and gentle countenance. This spectacle caused our hero to lose the last vestiges of his reason. At that moment he would have fought for the Inquisition, and in all sincerity too. Suddenly the door opened. The little chapel was revealed, ablaze with light. On the altar you could see more than a thousand candles, divided into eight rows separated from one another by sprays of flowers. The sweet smell of the purest incense billowed out of the sanctuary door. The freshly gilded chapel was very small but extremely high. Julien noticed that on the altar there were candles more than fifteen foot tall. The girls could not restrain their cries of admiration. The only people to be let into the little vestibule of the chapel were the twenty-four girls, the two priests and Julien.

Soon the king arrived, followed only by M. de La Mole and his grand chamberlain. The guards themselves remained outside on their knees, presenting arms.

His majesty positively hurled rather than flung himself on to the prie-dieu. Only then did Julien, who was wedged against the gilded door, catch a glimpse—from under the bare arm of one of the girls—of the charming statue of St Clement.* He was hidden beneath the altar, in the garb of a young Roman soldier. He had a gaping wound in his neck which seemed to be oozing blood; the artist had surpassed himself. His dying eyes, still full of grace, were half closed. The beginnings of a moustache adorned his charming mouth which, half closed too, still seemed to be in prayer. At this sight the girl next to Julien shed copious tears; one of her tears fell onto Julien's hand.

After a moment of prayer in the most profound silence, broken only by the distant sound of bells from all the villages in a radius of ten leagues, the Bishop of Agde asked the king's permission to speak. He ended a brief, very moving speech with some simple words which were all the more effective.

'Never forget, young Christians,' he said, addressing the girls, 'that you have seen one of the greatest kings on earth kneeling before the servants of this dread and almighty God. These servants are weak, persecuted and put to death on earth, as you can see from St Clement's ever-bleeding wound, but theirs is the triumph in heaven. You will, young Christians, won't you, always remember this day? You will abhor the ungodly. You will be ever faithful to this God who is so mighty, so dread, and yet so loving.'

At these words the bishop rose authoritatively.

'Do you promise me you will?' he said, holding out his arm as one inspired.

'We promise we will,' said the girls, breaking down in tears.

'I receive your promise in the name of the dread and mighty God!' added the bishop in a thundering voice. And the ceremony was ended.

The king himself was weeping. Not until much later did Julien feel composed enough to ask where the saint's bones were that had been sent from Rome to Philip the Good,* Duke of Burgundy. He learned that they were concealed in the charming wax statue.

His Majesty deigned to allow the maidens who had waited on him in the chapel to wear a red ribbon embroidered with the words: HATRED TO THE UNGODLY, ETERNAL ADORATION.

M. de La Mole had ten thousand bottles of wine given out to the peasants. That evening in Verrières the liberals found a pretext for laying on infinitely better illumination than the royalists. Before leaving, the king paid a visit to M. de Moirod.

CHAPTER 19

Thinking brings suffering

The grotesque side of day-to-day events
stops you seeing the real misery of
passions.

BARNAVE

As he was putting back the everyday furniture in the room
that M. de La Mole had used, Julien found a sheet of very stiff
paper folded in four. He read at the bottom of the first page:

'To the Most Hon. the Marquis de La Mole, Peer of France,
Knight of the King's orders' etc., etc.

It was a petition in large handwriting, like a cook's.

My Lord Marquis,
    All my life I have had religious principles. I faced the bombs at
Lyon when it was under siege in '93 of cursed memory.* I take
communion; I go to Mass every Sunday at the parish church. I have
never failed in my paschal duty, even in '93 of cursed memory. My
cook, before the Revolution I had servants, my cook uses no meat or
fat on Fridays. In Verrières I enjoy widespread and, if I may say so,
deserved respect. I walk under the canopy at processions, next to our
Reverend Father and his worship the mayor. I carry a big candle on
grand occasions bought with my own money, for all of which there
are certificates in Paris at the Ministry of Finance. I ask your lordship
to grant me the lottery office* in Verrières, which cannot fail to fall
vacant soon one way or another, as the present holder is very ill, and
anyway votes the wrong way at elections, etc.

DE CHOLIN

In the margin of this petition was a note of support signed
De Moirod, which began with this line:

'I had the honour of speaking to you *yesserdy** about the
worthy citizen making this request', etc.

So, even this idiot Cholin shows me the path I must follow,
said Julien to himself.

A week after the King of ——'s visit to Verrières, what
surfaced from the innumerable lies, silly interpretations, ridiculous discussions etc., etc. which had focused successively on

the king, the Bishop of Agde, the Marquis de La Mole, the ten thousand bottles of wine, poor old fall-in-the-mud Moirod who, in the hope of getting a cross, did not venture outside his house until a month after his fall—what surfaced was the sheer indecency of having *catapulted* Julien Sorel, a carpenter's son, into the guard of honour. You should have heard the rich manufacturers of painted cloth on the subject, men who grew hoarse in the café morning and evening preaching equality. That haughty woman, Mme de Rênal, was the author of this abomination. And the reason for it? The lovely eyes and glowing cheeks of the little abbé Sorel made it abundantly plain.

Shortly after the return to Vergy, Stanislas-Xavier the youngest child threw a fever; Mme de Rênal was suddenly overcome by terrible remorse. It was the first time she had reproached herself for her love with any consistency; she seemed to understand, as if by a miracle, how gross was the immorality she had allowed herself to get caught up in. In spite of her deeply religious nature, up until then she had not considered the enormity of her crime in the eyes of God.

In the past, at the convent of the Sacred Heart, she had loved God with passion; she started to fear him likewise in her new situation. The battles which ravaged her soul were all the more terrible because there was nothing rational in her fear. Julien discovered that any attempt at rationalization aggravated rather than soothed her: she took it as the language of hell. However, since Julien himself was very fond of little Stanislas, he was more welcome when he talked to her of the boy's illness. This soon took a very serious turn. Then unremitting remorse deprived Mme de Rênal even of the ability to sleep; she retreated into a desperate silence: had she opened her mouth, it would have been to confess her crime to God and to mankind.

'I entreat you,' Julien would say to her as soon as they found themselves alone, 'don't say anything to anyone; let me be the only recipient of your troubles. If you still love me, don't say anything: your words can't take the fever away from our little Stanislas.'

But his endeavours to console her had no effect; he did not

know that Mme de Rênal had taken it into her head that to appease the wrath of the jealous Almighty, she had to hate Julien or else see her son die. It was because she felt she could not hate her lover that she was so wretched.

'Keep away from me!' she said one day. 'In the name of God, leave this house: it's your presence here that's killing my son.'

'God is punishing me,' she added in a low voice, 'he is just. I worship his justice; my crime is horrendous, and there I was living without remorse! It was the first sign of abandoning God: I must be doubly punished.'

Julien was deeply touched. He could not detect any hypocrisy or exaggeration in this. She thinks she's killing her son by loving me, and yet, poor thing, she loves me more than her son. This is the source, I'm convinced, of the remorse that's killing her; these are truly noble sentiments. But how did I manage to inspire a love like this: I'm so poor, so badly brought up, so ignorant, even sometimes so crude in my ways?

One night, the child's fever was at its height. Around two in the morning M. de Rênal came to see him. The child, racked with fever, was exceedingly flushed and failed to recognize his father. Suddenly Mme de Rênal flung herself at her husband's feet: Julien saw that she was going to confess everything and ruin herself for ever.

By good luck M. de Rênal was very put out by this strange gesture.

'Goodnight! goodnight!' he said as he turned to leave.

'No, listen to me!' exclaimed his wife kneeling before him and trying to hold him back. 'You must learn the whole truth. It's my fault that my son is dying. I gave life to him, and I am taking it from him. Heaven is punishing me, in the eyes of God I'm guilty of murder. I must bring about my own downfall and my own humiliation; perhaps this sacrifice will appease the Lord.'

If M. de Rênal had been a man of any imagination, he would have understood everything.

'Romantic nonsense,' he exclaimed pushing away his wife who was trying to clasp his knees. 'This is all a whole lot of romantic nonsense! Julien, summon the doctor at daybreak.'

And off he went to bed. Mme de Rênal fell on her knees, half unconscious, thrusting Julien away with a convulsive gesture when he tried to come to her aid.

Julien stood amazed.

So this is adultery! he said... Could it possibly be that those two-faced priests... are right? That men who commit so many sins are privileged to know the real workings of sin? What a peculiar state of affairs!

For twenty minutes now since M. de Rênal had withdrawn, Julien had watched the woman he loved kneeling with her head resting on the child's little bed, motionless and almost unconscious. Here's a woman of superior genius plunged in the very depths of misery because of knowing me, he said.

Time is racing by. What can I do for her? I must make up my mind. In this situation it isn't a question of what I want any more. What do I care about other people and their insipid little comedies? What can I do for her... leave her? But I'd be leaving her alone in the grip of the most appalling grief. Her automaton of a husband is more of a hindrance than a help to her. He'll say some harsh word to her through being so crude; she may go mad and fling herself out of the window.

If I leave her, if I stop watching over her, she'll confess everything to him. And who knows, perhaps in spite of the inheritance she's due to bring him he'll cause a scandal. She may tell all, great heavens! to that b... idiot of a Father Maslon, who uses a six-year-old's illness an as excuse for not budging from this house, and with an ulterior motive too. In her grief and her fear of God she forgets everything she knows about the man; she only sees the priest.

'Go away!' said Mme de Rênal to him all of a sudden, opening her eyes.

'I'd lay down my life over and over again to know what would be of greatest help to you,' Julien replied. 'I've never loved you so much, my darling angel, or rather it's only now that I begin to adore you as you deserve. What will become of me far away from you, with the knowledge that you're unhappy through my fault! But let's not think about my suffering. All right, I'll go, my love. But if I leave you, if I cease to watch over you, to be constantly there between you

and your husband, you'll tell him all, you'll ruin yourself. Just
think how ignominiously he'll drive you from his house; the
whole of Verrières, the whole of Besançon will talk of this
scandal. You'll be made into the guilty party; you'll never get
over the shame of it...'

'That's what I want,' she exclaimed, rising to her feet. 'I
shall suffer: so much the better.'

'But you'll also bring about his own ruin with this abominable scandal!'

'But I'll be humiliating myself, I'll be flinging myself into
the mire; and perhaps in so doing I shall save my son. Perhaps
this humiliation in front of everyone is a form of public
penitence? As far as I can judge in my weakness, isn't this the
greatest sacrifice I can make to God?... Perhaps he will deign
to accept my humiliation and leave me my son! Show me
another more painful sacrifice and I'm ready for it.'

'Let me punish myself. I'm guilty too. Do you want me to
retreat to the Trappist monastery? The austerity of life there
may appease your God... Oh heavens! Why can't I take
Stanislas's illness upon myself...?'

'Oh, you really love him, you do!' said Mme de Rênal, getting
up and flinging herself into his arms.

At the same moment she pushed him away in horror.

'I believe you! I believe you!' she went on, sinking to her
knees again. 'Oh my only friend! Oh why aren't you Stanislas's
father? Then it wouldn't be a horrible crime to love you more
than your son.'

'Will you allow me to stay, and to love you from now on just
like a brother? It's the only only expiation that makes sense; it
may appease the wrath of the Almighty.'

'And what about me?' she cried, getting up and clasping
Julien's head in both hands, and gazing at it at arm's length,
'what about me, am I to love you like a brother? Is it in my
power to love you like a brother?'

Tears were starting to run down Julien's face.

'I shall obey you,' he said falling at her feet. 'I shall obey
you whatever you order me to do; it's all that's left for me. My
mind is struck blind; I can't see what to do. If I leave you,
you'll tell your husband everything; you'll ruin yourself and

him too. There's no way, after this ridicule, that he'll ever be chosen for the National Assembly. If I stay, you'll think me the cause of your son's death, and you'll die of grief. Do you want to try out the effect of my departure? If you like, I'll punish myself for our wrongdoing by leaving you for a week. I'll go and spend it in a retreat of your choosing. In the abbey at Bray-le-Haut, for instance: but swear to me that during my absence you won't confess anything to your husband. Just think that I won't ever be able to come back if you say anything.'

She promised, he left, but was recalled after two days.

'It's impossible for me to keep my oath without you. I shall tell my husband if you aren't there constantly to order me with your eyes to keep silent. Each hour of this abominable life seems to me to last a whole day.'

At last heaven took pity on this wretched mother. Gradually Stanislas emerged from danger. But the illusion was shattered, her reason had grasped the extent of her sin; she was unable to regain her stability. Her remorse remained, and it was as you would expect in a heart of such sincerity. Her life was heaven and hell: hell when she did not have Julien with her, heaven when she was at his feet. 'I don't have any illusions left,' she said to him even at times when she dared to indulge her love to the full. 'I'm damned, damned beyond remission. You are young, you yielded to my seduction, heaven may forgive you; but I am damned. I know from a sure sign: I'm afraid. Who wouldn't be afraid at the sight of hell? But deep down I don't repent. I'd commit my sin again if it had to be committed. If heaven would just refrain from punishing me in this world and through my children, then I shall have more than I deserve. But what about you at least, my own Julien,' she exclaimed at other moments, 'are you happy? Do I love you enough for your liking?'

Julien's mistrustfulness and his touchy pride, which were particularly in need of a love full of sacrifices, did not hold out in the face of a sacrifice so total, so indubitable and so constantly renewed. He adored Mme de Rênal. For all that she's a noblewoman, and I'm a workman's son, she still loves me... I'm not a valet she uses to fulfil the functions of a lover. With this fear removed Julien fell victim to all the follies of love, and all its deadly uncertainties.

'At any rate', she exclaimed on seeing his doubts about her love, 'let me make you truly happy for the short time we have to spend together! Let's be quick about it; maybe tomorrow I won't be yours any more. If heaven strikes me through my children, it'll be no use my trying to live solely in order to love you, trying not to see that my crime is what's killing them. I shouldn't be able to survive such a blow. Even if I wanted to I wouldn't be able to; I'd go mad.

Ah! if only I could take your sin upon myself, just as you made me such a generous offer of taking on Stanislas's burning fever!'

This great spiritual crisis changed the nature of the feeling which bound Julien to his mistress. His love was no longer merely admiration for her beauty and pride at possessing her.

Their happiness was henceforth of a far superior nature, the fire which consumed them was more intense. They had moments of excitement filled with madness. Their happiness would have seemed greater in the eyes of society. But they never recovered the sweet serenity, the cloudless bliss, the straightforward happiness of the early days of their romance, when Mme de Rênal's only fear was of not being loved enough by Julien. Their happiness sometimes took on the appearance of crime.

In the happiest and seemingly most tranquil moments, Mme de Rênal would suddenly cry out: 'Ah! God Almighty! I can see hell,' as she gripped Julien's hand convulsively. 'What horrible tortures! I've richly deserved them.' She clasped him to her, clinging to him like ivy to a wall.

Julien would try in vain to calm this soul in turmoil. She took his hand and smothered it with kisses. Then, relapsing into gloomy brooding: 'Hell,' she said, 'hell would be a mercy for me. I'd still have a few days to spend with him on earth; but hell beginning on earth, the death of my children... Yet perhaps for that price my crime would be forgiven me... Ah! God Almighty! Do not grant me mercy at that price. These poor children haven't trespassed against you; I'm the guilty one, I alone: I love a man who isn't my husband.'

Then Julien would see Mme de Rênal reach moments of apparent tranquillity. She tried to take hold of herself, she wanted not to poison the very existence of the one she loved.

In the midst of these alternating bouts of love, remorse and pleasure, the days sped by for them like a flash of lightning. Julien lost the habit of reflection.

Mlle Elisa went off to Verrières to attend to a little lawsuit she had there. She found M. Valenod in high dudgeon against Julien. She hated the tutor, and often spoke of him to M. Valenod.

'You'd ruin me, sir, if I revealed the truth!...' she said to him one day. 'Masters are all in cahoots when it comes to important things... There are some revelations that don't get forgiven to poor servants...'

After these ritual preambles, which M. Valenod's impatient curiosity found a way of curtailing, he learned the most mortifying things for his self-esteem.

This woman, the most distinguished in the neighbourhood, on whom he had lavished such attentions for six years, and unfortunately in full view and knowledge of everyone; this proud woman, whose rebuttals had caused him to blush on so many occasions, had just taken for a lover a little workman dressed up as tutor. And as if that weren't enough to spite the master of the workhouse, Mme de Rênal adored this lover.

'And', added the chambermaid with a sigh, 'Mr Julien didn't put himself to any trouble to make this conquest, he didn't abandon his usual coldness one bit for Madam.'

Elisa had not had any firm proof until they were in the country, but she thought the affair had started much earlier.

'That's no doubt the reason', she went on in pique, 'why some while back he refused to marry me. And like a silly idiot, I went and asked Mme de Rênal's advice, and begged her to speak to the tutor.'

That very evening M. de Rênal received a long anonymous letter sent from town with his newspaper, informing him in the minutest detail of what was going on in his house. As he read this letter written on blue-tinted paper, Julien saw him grow pale and cast hostile glances in his direction. The mayor

did not get over his discomfiture for the remainder of the
evening, and Julien achieved nothing when he tried to butter
him up by asking him to explain the genealogy of the best
families in Burgundy.

CHAPTER 20

Anonymous letters

Do not give dalliance
Too much rein: the strongest oaths are straw
To the fire i' the blood.

TEMPEST

As they were leaving the drawing-room at about midnight, Julien had time to say to his mistress:

'We must avoid seeing each other this evening: your husband has his suspicions; I'd swear that long letter he was reading with so many sighs is an anonymous one.'

Fortunately, Julien was in the habit of locking himself into his room. Mme de Rênal had the mad idea that this warning was just an excuse for not seeing her. She lost her head completely and came to his door at the usual time. Hearing a noise in the corridor, Julien instantly blew out his lamp. Someone was trying to open his door: was it Mme de Rênal? Was it a jealous husband?

Very early the next morning the cook, who was Julien's ally, brought him a book: on the cover he read these words in Italian: *Guardate alla pagine 130.**

Julien trembled at her rashness, looked for page 130 and found pinned to it the following letter, written in haste, tear-stained and full of spelling mistakes.*

Normally Mme de Rênal was very careful over spelling: he was touched by this detail and temporarily forgot the terrible rashness.

So you didn't want me to come to you last night? There are moments when I think I've never read into the depths of your soul. The look in your eyes terrifies me. I'm afraid of you. God Almighty! Can it be that you've never loved me? If so, let my husband find out about our romance, let him shut me up in an eternal prison, in the country, away from my children. Perhaps God wills it this way. I'll soon die. But you'll be a monster.

Don't you love me? Are you tired of my follies and my remorse, you ungodly creature? Do you wish to ruin me? I'll give you an easy way to do it. Go on, show this letter to the whole of Verrières, or rather, just to M. Valenod. Tell him I love you, no, don't utter such blasphemy, tell him I adore you, that life only began for me the day I set eyes on you; that in the wildest moments of my youth, I'd never even dreamed of happiness like you've brought me; that you've had the sacrifice of my life, and you're getting the sacrifice of my soul. You know that the sacrifice is even greater than that.

But what does a man like that know about sacrifices, anyway? Tell him, tell him to annoy him that I defy all ill-wishers, and that there's only one misfortune left in the world for me—to see a change of heart in the only man who makes my life worth clinging to. How glad I shall be to lose it, to offer it up as a sacrifice and be rid of my fears for my children!

Don't be in any doubt about it, my dear, if there's an anonymous letter, it comes from that hateful creature who pursued me for six years with his loud voice, his accounts of his jumping feats on horseback, his brazen smugness, and the endless enumeration of all his good points.

Is there an anonymous letter? You beast, that's what I wanted to discuss with you; actually no, you did the right thing. Hugging you in my arms, perhaps for the last time, I'd never have been able to discuss things coolly, as I'm doing now on my own. From now on our happiness won't be so straightforward any more. Will you be in the least bit put out by it, Julien? Yes, on days when you haven't received some entertaining book from M. Fouqué. The sacrifice is made: tomorrow, whether or not there's an anonymous letter, I'm going to tell my husband that I've received an anonymous letter too, and that he's got to pay you to go elsewhere, he's got to find a decent excuse and send you back to your family right away.

Alas! my dear, we shall be separated for a fortnight, maybe a month! There now, I'll do you justice, you'll suffer as much as I shall. But in the end this is the only way to counteract the effect of that anonymous letter; it's not the first one that my husband has received, and about me, what's more. Alas! how I used to laugh at them!

The whole aim of my conduct is to make my husband think that the letter comes from M. Valenod; I have no doubt that he's the author of it. If you leave the house, be sure to go and live in Verrières. I'll see to it that my husband has the idea of spending a fortnight there, to show fools that there's no coolness between him and me. Once you're in Verrières, be friendly with everyone, even the liberals. I know that all the good ladies will seek you out.

Don't go and quarrel with M. Valenod or cut his ears off, as you were saying one day; on the contrary, show him all your charm. The main thing is that people in Verrières should believe that you are going to enter Valenod's household, or anyone else's, to instruct their children.

That's what my husband will never be able to stand. Were he to resign himself to it, well, at least you'll be living in Verrières, and I shall see you from time to time. My children who love you so much will go and visit you. Oh God! I feel as if I love my children the more because they love you. What remorse! How will all this end... My mind is wandering... Anyway, you understand how to behave; be gentle, polite, not supercilious with these coarse individuals, I entreat you on my knees: they will decide our fate. Don't doubt for a moment that in dealing with you my husband will follow the dictates of *public opinion*.

It's up to you to provide me with the anonymous letter; arm yourself with patience and a pair of scissors. Cut out from a book the words you'll find below; then stick them with gum on to the sheet of blue-tinted paper I enclose; it came from M. Valenod. Be prepared for your room to be searched; burn the pages of the book you have mutilated. If you can't find the words ready made, have the patience to compose them letter by letter. To spare you trouble, I've done the anonymous letter a bit too short. Alas! If you no longer love me, as I fear, how long you must be finding mine!

ANONYMOUS LETTER

Dear Madam,

All your little goings on are well-known; but the individuals who have an interest in putting a stop to them are informed. As a last vestige of friendship for you, I urge you to detach yourself completely from the little peasant. If you have the sense to do it, your husband will believe that the communication he has received is false, and he will be allowed to remain in error. Consider that I know your secret; tremble, unfortunate woman; as from now, I want to see you *keep to the straight and narrow*.

As soon as you have finished sticking together the words which make up this letter (did you recognize the Master's way of talking?), come out into the house, I'll meet you.

I'll go into the village and come back looking upset, and indeed I really will be. God Almighty! what am I risking, and all because you *thought you detected* an anonymous letter. Anyway, with my face distraught I shall give my husband this letter which a stranger has handed to me. What *you* must do is go for a walk along the forest track with the children, and don't come back till dinner time.

From the top of the rocks you can see the dovecot tower. If our affairs are going well, I'll put a white handkerchief there; if not, there'll be nothing.

You unfeeling creature! won't your heart show you a way to tell me that you love me before you set off for this walk? Whatever may happen, you can be sure of one thing: I shan't go on living for a single day after our final separation. Ah! unworthy mother! These last two words I've just written are completely empty, dear Julien. They don't affect me at all; I can only think of you at this moment, I only wrote them so as not to be blamed by you. Now that I see myself on the brink of losing you, what's the point of hiding anything? Yes, let my soul appear black as hell to you, but let me not lie to the man I adore! I've been only too guilty of deception already in my life. There now, I forgive you if you don't love me any more. I haven't any time to reread my letter. It seems to me a small price to pay with my life for the days of happiness I've just spent in your arms. You know they will cost me more than that.

CHAPTER 21

Dialogue with a master

Alas, our frailty is the cause, not we:
For such as we are made of, such we be.
TWELFTH NIGHT

JULIEN derived a childish pleasure from piecing words together for an hour on end. As he was leaving his room he ran into his pupils and their mother; she took the letter so straightforwardly and courageously that he was terrified by her calm.

'Has the gum dried enough?' she asked him.

Is this the woman who was driven so wild by remorse? he thought. What are her plans at this moment? He was too proud to ask her; but she struck him as more attractive than perhaps ever before.

'If this goes wrong,' she added with the same composure, 'everything will be taken away from me. Bury this cache somewhere in the mountains; it may be my only resource one day.'

She handed him a small red morocco case,* filled with gold and a few diamonds.

'Off you go now,' she said to him.

She kissed the children, the youngest one twice. Julien stood there motionless. She walked away from him swiftly and without looking at him.

From the moment he had opened the anonymous letter, M. de Rênal's life had been quite ghastly. He had not been so agitated since a duel he had almost fought in 1816, and, to do him justice, at that time the prospect of being shot had made him less wretched. He examined the letter from all angles: Isn't this a woman's handwriting? he said to himself. In that case, what woman wrote it? He ran through all the women he knew in Verrières without being able to fix his suspicions on any one of them. Might a man have dictated the letter? What man? The same uncertainty again; he was envied and no doubt hated by the majority of men he knew. I must consult my wife, he said to himself through force of habit, getting up from the chair in which he was slumped.

He was hardly up before he exclaimed: 'God Almighty!' and banged his head with his fists. She's the one I've got to be specially wary of: she's my enemy at this moment. And from sheer anger, tears welled up in his eyes.

As a just reward for the emotional barrenness which is a matter of practical wisdom in the provinces, the two men M.de Rênal feared most at that moment were his two most intimate friends.

After these two, I've got maybe ten friends, and he ran through them, reckoning as he did so how much solace he might hope to derive from each of them. 'All of them! All of them!' he exclaimed in rage, 'will get the greatest of enjoyment from my frightful misadventure.' He was lucky enough to be, he believed, much envied, and with good cause too. In addition to his splendid house in town, which the King of —— had just honoured in perpetuity by sleeping there, he had done up his château in Vergy very nicely indeed. The façade was painted white and the windows were fitted with beautiful green shutters. He took a moment's comfort from the thought of this magnificence. The fact is that this château could be seen from three or four leagues away, to the great detriment of all the neighbouring country houses or so-called châteaux, which had been left the humble grey colour that weathering had produced.

M. de Rênal could count on the tears and pity of one of his friends, the churchwarden of the parish; but he was an idiot who shed tears over anything. This man, however, was his only recourse.

'What wretchedness can be compared with mine!' he exclaimed in rage. 'What isolation!'

Can it be, wondered this man who was genuinely to be pitied, can it be possible that I haven't a friend to turn to for advice in my misfortune? For I'm losing my reason, I can feel it! Ah! Falcoz! Ah! Ducros! he exclaimed bitterly. These were the names of two childhood friends whom he had estranged by his haughty behaviour in 1814. They were not noble, and he had wished to alter the equal footing which had marked their relations since childhood.

One of them, Falcoz, an intelligent, warm-hearted man who was a paper merchant in Verrières, had bought a printing press in the main town of the département, and had started up a newspaper. The Congregation had determined to ruin him: his newspaper had been condemned and his printer's licence withdrawn. In these sad circumstances he had tried writing to M. de Rênal for the first time in ten years. The mayor of Verrières thought it his duty to reply like an ancient Roman: 'If the king's minister did me the honour of consulting me, I should say to him: "Do not scruple to ruin all provincial printers, and turn printing into a monopoly like tobacco."' This letter to a close friend was admired by the whole of Verrières at the time, and M. de Rênal was now appalled to recall its terms. Who could have told me that with my rank, my fortune, and my decorations, I should need him one day? Tossed by fits of anger such as these, now directed against himself, now against everything round about him, he spent a terrible night; but fortunately he did not think to spy on his wife.

I'm used to Louise, he said to himself, she's familiar with all my business; even supposing I were free to marry tomorrow, I shouldn't find anyone to replace her. At that point he went along with the idea that his wife was innocent; this view of matters did not impose on him the need to show any force of character, and suited him much better; what a common occurrence it is, anyway, to see women slandered!

'What the devil!' he exclaimed suddenly, striding fitfully up and down. Am I to put up with her mocking me with her lover as if I were a nobody, or a vagabond? Must the whole of Verrières laugh me to scorn for turning a blind eye? Just think what they said about Charmier! (He was one of the neighbourhood's notorious cuckolds.) When his name is mentioned, doesn't a smile pass over everyone's lips? He's a good barrister, but who on earth ever talks of his oratorical skills? 'Ah! Charmier!' they say, 'Bernard's Charmier': that's what they call him—by the name of the man who's the cause of his shame.

Thank heavens, thought M. de Rênal at other moments, I haven't got a daughter, and the way I'm going to punish their mother won't prejudice the establishment of my children; I can surprise that little peasant with my wife, and kill them both; in that case, the tragic side of the adventure will perhaps remove the ridicule from it. This idea appealed to him; he pursued it in every detail. The penal system is on my side, and whatever happens, our Congregation and my friends on the jury will save me. He examined his hunting knife which was exceedingly sharp; but the thought of blood frightened him.

I can thrash this impertinent tutor and drive him from the house; but what a furore in Verrières and even throughout the département! After Falcoz's newspaper had been banned, when its editor-in-chief came out of prison, I helped to ensure that he lost his job worth six hundred francs. They say this scribbler is daring to show his face again in Besançon, he can offer me up cleverly to public ridicule, and in such a way that it will be impossible to take him to court. Take him to court!... The impertinent fellow will find innumerable ways of insinuating that he has told the truth. A gentleman who maintains his station as I do is hated by all plebeians. I shall get into those frightful Paris newspapers; oh heavens! what a calamity! to see the ancient name of Rênal plunged into the mire of ridicule... If ever I travel I shall have to change my name. What! give up this name which is my glory and my strength. What depths of misfortune!

If I don't kill my wife, but instead drive her from the house in ignominy, she has her aunt in Besançon who will hand over her fortune to her directly. My wife will go and live in Paris with Julien; Verrières will come to hear of it, and once again I'll be taken for a dupe. At this point the unhappy man noticed from the dimness of his lamp that day was beginning to break. He went out into the garden for a breath of fresh air. At that moment he was almost resolved not to create a scandal, chiefly on the grounds that a scandal would thoroughly delight his friends in Verrières.

The walk in the garden calmed him down a little. 'No,' he exclaimed, 'I shan't deprive myself of my wife, she's too useful to me.' He pictured with horror what his house would be like without his wife; the only female relative he had was the Marquise de R——, who was old, weak in the head and spiteful.

A very sensible idea occurred to him, but to carry it out would have required strength of character far in excess of what little the poor man possessed. If I keep my wife, he said, I know myself, one day when I get impatient with her I'll reproach her with her infidelity. She's proud, we'll quarrel, and all this will happen before she has inherited her aunt's money. How I shall be mocked then! My wife loves her children, everything will revert to them in the end. But *I* shall be the laughing-stock of Verrières. What! they'll say, he didn't even manage to get his revenge on his wife! Wouldn't it be better to stick to suspicions and not try to prove anything? In that case I tie my hands, and can't reproach her with anything subsequently.

A moment later M. de Rênal was seized again by wounded vanity and laboriously recalled all the ploys quoted in the billiard room of the *Casino** or *Noble Circle* of Verrières when someone with the gift of the gab interrupts the pool to have a joke at the expense of a cuckolded husband. How cruel these jibes seemed to him now!

God! Why is my wife not dead! then I'd be impervious to ridicule. Why am I not a widower! I'd go and spend six months in Paris in the best circles. After this moment of happiness conjured up by the idea of widowerhood, his imagination returned to the means of ascertaining the truth. Should he emerge at midnight, after everyone had gone to bed, to spread a thin layer of bran in front of the door to Julien's room? Next morning at dawn he would see the footprints.

'But that method's no good,' he cried out in a sudden fit of rage, 'that sly minx Elisa would notice, and the household would soon know that I'm jealous.'

In another story told at the *Casino*, a husband had ascertained his misfortune by sealing up the doors to his wife's and the gallant's bedrooms by means of a little wax and two strands of hair.

After so many hours of uncertainty, this method of shedding light on his fate seemed to him to be decidedly the best, and he was thinking of using it when, at a bend in one of the paths, he met this wife whom he would have liked to see dead.

She was coming back from the village. She had gone to hear Mass in the church at Vergy. A tradition of most dubious reliability in the eyes of the cold man of reason, but one she believed in, has it that the little church used today was the chapel of the château belonging to the squire of Vergy. This idea obsessed Mme de Rênal for the whole of the time she was intending to spend praying in this church. She had a constant image of her husband killing Julien while out hunting, as if by accident, and then making her eat his heart* in the evening.

My fate, she told herself, depends on what he's going to think when he listens to what I have to say. After this fateful quarter of an hour, I may not find another opportunity to speak to him. He isn't a man of sense, controlled by reason. Otherwise I could use my feeble reasoning powers to foresee what he's going to do or say. *He* will decide our common fate, he has the power to do it. But that fate depends on my cunning, my skill in guiding the thoughts of this unpredictable mind turned blind by anger and prevented from seeing half of what's going on. God Almighty! I need talent, I need a cool head, where do I get them from?

She regained her calm as if by magic on entering the garden and seeing her husband from a distance. His rumpled hair and clothes signalled that he had not slept.

She handed him a letter with the seal broken but refolded. He did not open it but stared at his wife with wild eyes.

'This is an abomination', she said to him, 'that was handed to me as I was passing round the back of the solicitor's garden, by a disreputable-looking man claiming to be acquainted with you and to owe you a debt of gratitude. I demand one thing of you: that you send this Mr Julien off packing back to his family, right away.' Mme de Rênal uttered his name hastily, perhaps a little too soon, in order to be rid of the fearful prospect of having to utter it.

On seeing the joy which her words produced in her husband, she was overcome with the same feeling herself. She realized from the way he was staring at her that Julien had guessed right. Instead of lamenting this genuine misfortune, she thought to herself: what a genius, what perfect intuition! And in a young man still lacking any experience! Will any doors remain closed to him later on! Alas! then his successes will make him forget me.

This little act of admiration for the man she adored rid her completely of her nerves.

She congratulated herself on what she had done. I haven't been unworthy of Julien, she said to herself with a sweet inner glow of pleasure.

Without saying a word for fear of committing himself, M. de Rênal examined the second anonymous letter composed, the reader will remember, of printed words stuck on to a sheet of blue-tinged paper. I am being mocked in any event, M. de Rênal said to himself, overwhelmed with fatigue.

Yet more slander to examine, and my wife's the cause of it again! He was on the point of subjecting her to the coarsest of insults, when the prospect of the Besançon inheritance stopped him just in time. Devoured by the need to vent his destructive urge on something, he crumpled up the paper on which this second anonymous letter had been written, and began striding off; he needed to get away from his wife. A few moments later he returned to her, in a calmer frame of mind.

'You must take a decision and dismiss Julien,' she said to him at once; 'after all, he's only a workman's son. You can make him a small payment in compensation, and anyway he's very learned and will easily find himself another post, for instance with M. Valenod or the sub-prefect de Maugiron who both have children. In this way you won't be doing him any harm...'

'You're talking just like the silly idiot you are,' thundered M. de Rênal. 'What sense can anyone expect from a woman? You never pay any attention to what is reasonable; how can you possibly know a thing? your happy-go-lucky outlook and your laziness only give you energy for chasing after butterflies, you feeble creatures that we are unfortunate enough to have in the midst of our families!...'

Mme de Rênal let him have his say, and it went on for a good while; he was *getting shot of his anger*, as the local expression goes.

'Sir,' she answered him at last, 'I speak as a woman impugned in her honour, that is to say in the most precious thing she has.'

Mme de Rênal remained completely unruffled throughout the whole of this painful conversation on which hung her chance of going on living under the same roof with Julien. She tried to produce ideas she thought most likely to guide the blind anger of her husband. She had been unmoved by all the insulting remarks he had addressed to her, she wasn't even listening, she was thinking about Julien at the time. Will he be pleased with me?

'This little peasant on whom we have showered kindness and even presents may be innocent,' she said at last, 'but he is none the less the pretext for the first affront I've received... Sir! when I read this abominable missive, I vowed to myself that either he or I would leave your house.'

'Do you want to cause a scandal to dishonour me and yourself too? You give rise to a lot of bad feeling in Verrières.'

'It's true: most people envy the prosperous state which your wise administration has secured for yourself, your family and the town... All right! I shall entreat Julien to ask you for a period of leave to go and spend a month with that timber merchant in the mountains—a worthy friend for this little workman.'

'Don't you take any kind of action,' replied M. de Rênal quite calmly. 'What I insist on above all is that you should not speak to him. You would do it in anger and set him and me at loggerheads; you know how touchy the little gentleman is.'

'The young man has no sense of propriety,' went on Mme de Rênal, 'he may be learned—you're the judge of that—but underneath he's nothing but a real peasant. As far as I'm concerned, I've never thought well of him since he refused to marry Elisa; it was a guaranteed fortune; and all because she sometimes pays secret visits to M. Valenod.'

'Ah!' said M. de Rênal, raising his eyebrows quite excessively, 'what was that? Did Julien tell you that?'

'Not exactly; he has always talked to me about his calling for the sacred ministry; but believe you me, the first calling for common people like him is to earn their bread. He led me to understand clearly enough that he was aware of these secret visits.'

'And *I* was quite unaware of them, *I* was!' exclaimed M. de Rênal, full of fury once more and stressing his words. 'Things happen in my house that I'm unaware of... What, was there ever anything between Elisa and Valenod?'

'Ha! That's ancient history, my dearest,' laughed Mme de Rênal, 'and perhaps nothing wicked happened. It was at the time when your good friend Valenod wouldn't have been displeased if people in Verrières had thought that a little affair was developing between him and me—perfectly platonic, of course.'

'I thought as much at one time,' exclaimed M. de Rênal, hitting his head furiously as he made one discovery after another, 'and you never said anything to me about it?'

'Was there any need to cause two friends to quarrel for the sake of a little flight of vanity from our dear Master? You name me a society woman to whom he hasn't sent some extremely witty and even flirtatious letters!'

'Did he write to you by any chance?'

'He writes a lot.'

'Show me those letters at once, I order you to!' and M. de Rênal drew himself up to a full six foot.

'I shall certainly not,' came the reply, gentle almost to the point of nonchalance, 'I'll show them to you one day, when you're behaving better.'

'This very instant, by God!' shouted M. de Rênal, intoxicated with anger, and yet happier than he had been for the past twelve hours.

'Do you swear to me', said Mme de Rênal very gravely, 'that you will never quarrel with the master of the workhouse on the subject of these letters?'

'Quarrel or no quarrel, I can take the foundlings from him; but', he went on furiously, 'I want those letters at once; where are they?'

'In a drawer of my desk; but I certainly won't give you the key.'

'I'll find a way of breaking into it,' he shouted as he ran off to his wife's room.

He did indeed use an iron bar to smash a valuable writing-desk in veined mahogany obtained in Paris that he often used to buff up with his coat-tail when he thought he saw some mark on it.

Mme de Rênal had run up the hundred and twenty steps to the top of the dovecot; she was fastening the corner of a white handkerchief to one of the iron bars of the little window. She was the happiest of women. She gazed with tears in her eyes towards the great woods on the mountain. No doubt, she said to herself, Julien is underneath one of those leafy beeches, watching out for this good-luck signal. She strained her ears for a long time, then cursed the birdsong and the monotonous chirruping of the cicadas. If it weren't for this unwelcome noise, a shout of joy from the great rocks might have reached as far as here. Her avid gaze devoured the vast slope of dark greenery, smooth as a meadow, formed by the tops of the trees. How can he not have the wit, she said to herself quite overcome, to invent some signal to tell me that his happiness equals mine? She did not come down from the dovecot until she grew afraid that her husband might come and fetch her.

She found him in a state of fury. He was running through M. Valenod's anodyne prose, which was quite unaccustomed to being read with so much emotion.

Taking advantage of a pause in her husband's outbursts which allowed her to make herself heard:

'I keep coming back to this idea of mine,' said Mme de Rênal, 'It would be a good thing for Julien to go on a journey. Whatever his talent for Latin, he's only a peasant after all, who is often coarse and lacking in tact; every day, thinking he's being civil, he pays me exaggerated compliments in poor taste which he learns by heart from some novel...'

'He never reads novels,' snapped M. de Rênal; 'I've made sure of that. Do you think I'm the kind of master to be blind and unaware of what goes on in his household?'

'All right! If he doesn't read these ridiculous compliments anywhere, he invents them, in which case, more fool him. He must have spoken about me in this vein in Verrières...; and without supposing as much as that', said Mme de Rênal with the look of someone making a discovery, 'he must have spoken like that in front of Elisa, and that's to all intents and purposes as good as speaking in front of M. Valenod.'

'Ah!' shouted M. de Rênal shaking the table and the whole set of rooms by slamming down his fist as hard as is humanly possible, 'The printed anonymous letter and Valenod's letters are written on the same paper.'

'About time too!' thought Mme de Rênal; she put on a dumbfounded look at this discovery, and feeling too weak to add anything further, she went off and sat down on the sofa at the far end of the drawing-room.

From then on the battle was won; she had a hard time preventing M. de Rênal from going off to have words with the supposed author of the anonymous letter.

'How can you fail to understand that making a scene to M. Valenod without adequate proof is the most signal piece of ineptitude? You are envied, sir, and who is to blame? Your talents. Your wise administration, your buildings in such good taste, the dowry I brought you, and especially the substantial inheritance we may expect from my good aunt—people grossly exaggerate its size, but still—all this has made you the most important figure in Verrières'.

'You're forgetting my birth,' said M. de Rênal, with a hint of a smile.

'You are one of the most distinguished noblemen in the provinces,' Mme de Rênal went on eagerly; 'if the king were free and could do justice to high birth, you would no doubt be a member of the house of peers, etc. And with such a splendid position in society, do you really wish to give envious tongues food for comment?

To speak to M. Valenod about his anonymous letter amounts to proclaiming throughout the whole of Verrières—no, throughout Besançon, indeed throughout the whole of the provinces—that this little commoner, perhaps rather unwisely admitted to the family circle of *a Rênal*, has found a way of insulting him. Supposing these letters you've just turned up were to prove that I had responded to M. Valenod's love, you ought to kill me, I should richly deserve it; but you shouldn't show him any anger. Think how all your neighbours are just waiting for an excuse to get their revenge for your superiority;

think how in 1816 you did your bit to get certain people arrested. That man taking refuge on his roof...'*

'What I'm thinking is that you are showing no consideration or friendship towards me,' exclaimed M. de Rênal with all the bitterness evoked by a memory of this kind, 'and I wasn't made a peer!...'

'I'm reflecting, my dear,' went on Mme de Rênal with a smile, 'that I shall be richer than you, I've been your companion for twelve years, and all these considerations ought to give me the right to a say in what goes on, especially in the matter concerning us today. If you prefer a Mr Julien to me', she added with ill-disguised pique, 'I'm ready to go and spend a winter with my aunt.'

This remark was uttered *most appositely*. There was a firm ring to it beneath a veneer of politeness; it settled matters for M. de Rênal. But, as is the custom in the provinces, he went on speaking for a long time, he went back over all the arguments; his wife let him have his say, there was still anger in his voice. At length, two hours of pointless chatter wore down the strength of a man who had been in a fit of rage all night. He settled the line he would take with M. Valenod, Julien and even Elisa.

Once or twice during this great scene Mme de Rênal was on the verge of feeling some sympathy for the very real misfortune of this man who had been her friend for twelve years. But true passions are selfish. Besides, she was expecting at every moment that he would confess to having received an anonymous letter the previous evening, and this confession was not forthcoming. Mme de Rênal's peace of mind was incomplete without knowledge of what might have been suggested to the man in whose hands lay her fate. For in the provinces husbands control public opinion. A husband who complains brings ridicule upon himself, something which is becoming daily less dangerous in France; but his wife, if deprived by him of money, sinks to the level of a woman forced to work for a living on a pitiful wage, and what's more, right-minded folk will scruple to employ her.

An odalisque in a harem may love the sultan through thick and thin; but he is all-powerful, and she has no hope of stealing his authority from him by a series of little acts of cunning. The master's vengeance is terrible and bloody, but military in its generosity: a dagger blow ends it all. The blows are dealt by public scorn when a husband kills his wife in the nineteenth century; he does it by closing all salon doors to her.

Mme de Rênal's feeling of danger was rudely awakened when she returned to her room; she was shocked at the state of chaos she found it in. The locks on all her pretty little caskets had been forced; several blocks of the parquet floor had been prised up. He would have had no pity on me! she said to herself. Fancy ruining this parquet floor in contrasting wood that he's so fond of; when one of his children comes in with wet shoes, he turns red with anger. And now it's ruined for good! The sight of this violence rapidly banished her last reproaches to herself for her over-hasty victory.

Shortly before the dinner bell, Julien returned with the children. During the sweet course, when the servants had withdrawn, Mme de Rênal said very curtly to him:

'You expressed the wish to me to go and spend a fortnight in Verrières; M. de Rênal is agreeable to granting you leave. You may go when you see fit. However, so that the children don't waste their time, their Latin proses will be sent to you every day for you to correct.'

'My mind is made up', M. de Rênal added in very sour tones, 'not to grant you more than a week.'

Julien read in his features the anxiety of a deeply tormented man.

'He hasn't yet settled on a course of action,' he said to his mistress when they were alone together for a moment in the drawing-room.

Mme de Rênal gave him a rapid account of everything she had done since the morning.

'The details can wait until tonight,' she added laughing.

Aren't women perverse! thought Julien. What pleasure, what instinct drives them to deceive us!

'I find you both enlightened and blinded by your love,' he said to her somewhat coldly; 'your conduct today is admirable; but is it prudent for us to try to see each other tonight? This house is lined with enemies; just think of the passionate hatred Elisa feels for me.'

'That hatred is very like the passionate indifference I must suppose you feel for me.'

'Even if I were indifferent, I must rescue you from the danger I've put you in. If chance has it that M. de Rênal speaks to Elisa, one word from her may reveal all to him. What's to stop him from hiding near my room, well armed...'

'What! not even any courage!' said Mme de Rênal with all the hauteur of a daughter of the nobility.

'I shall never stoop to speak of my courage,' said Julien coldly, 'It's beneath me. Let the world judge according to deeds. But', he added taking her hand, 'you cannot conceive how attached I am to you, and what a joy it is for me to be able to take leave of you before this cruel absence.'

CHAPTER 22

Modes of behaviour in 1830

Speech was given to men to conceal their
thoughts.

R. P. MALAGRIDA*

JULIEN had no sooner arrived in Verrières than he began to
reproach himself for his conduct towards Mme de Rênal. I'd
have despised her like a feeble little woman if, out of weakness,
she'd messed up her scene with M. de Rênal. She pulls it off
like a diplomat, and I go and sympathize with the victim who
is my enemy. My action smacks of petty-mindedness; my
vanity is shocked because M. de Rênal is a man! What a vast
and illustrious company I have the honour of belonging to: I'm
just an idiot.

Father Chélan had refused the lodgings that the most
influential liberals in the locality had vied with one another in
offering him when his removal from office drove him from the
presbytery. The two rooms he had rented were cluttered up
with his books. Wishing to show Verrières what a priest was
worth, Julien went and fetched a dozen deal planks from his
father and carried them on his own back all the way along the
main street. He borrowed some tools from an old friend and
had soon constructed a sort of bookcase in which he put away
Father Chélan's books.

'I thought you'd been corrupted by worldly vanity,' said the
old man to him with tears of delight. 'This certainly redeems
the childish indulgence of wearing a dazzling guard of honour's
uniform, which made you so many enemies.'

M. de Rênal had instructed Julien to lodge in his house. No
one suspected what had happened. Three days after his arrival,
Julien received a visit in his own room at the top of the stairs
from no less important a personage than the sub-prefect M. de
Maugiron. It was only after two lengthy hours of insipid gossip
and long laments over the wickedness of men, the lack of
honesty of the people in charge of administering public funds,

the dangers besetting this poor France of ours, etc., etc., that
Julien at long last saw the subject of this visit come up. They
were already on the upstairs landing, and the poor tutor in
semi-disgrace was ushering out with all due respect the future
prefect of some fortunate département, when the latter was
pleased to turn his mind to Julien's prospects, to praise his
moderation in matters of material interest, etc., etc. At last, as
M. de Maugiron was embracing him in the most genial fashion,
he came out with the proposition that Julien leave M. de Rênal
and take up employment in the household of an official who
had children to *edicate*,* and who, like King Philip,* would
offer up thanks to heaven not so much for having given them
to him as for having ensured they were born in the vicinity of
Mr Julien. Their tutor would enjoy a salary of eight hundred
francs payable not by the month—'which is not the practice
among the nobility,' said M. de Maugiron—but quarterly and
always in advance.

It was Julien's turn, after an hour and a half of waiting in
boredom for his cue to speak. His reply was perfect, and above
all it was as long as an episcopalian homily; it implied
everything, and yet said nothing directly. You would have
found in it at one and the same time respect for M. de Rênal,
veneration for the public in Verrières and gratitude towards
the illustrious sub-prefect. The sub-prefect, astonished to find
a more jesuitical mind than his own, tried in vain to get a
straight answer. Julien was delighted to seize this opportunity
of practising his skills, and he began his reply all over again in
different terms. Never has an eloquent minister, wishing to
get through the end of a session when the Chamber appears to
be trying to wake up, used more words to say less. M. de
Maugiron had hardly left before Julian burst into uncontrollable laughter. To take advantage of his jesuitical verve, he
wrote a nine-page letter to M. de Rênal, reporting to him
everything that had been said to him, and humbly asking for
his advice. The rascal didn't actually tell me the name of the
person making the offer! It'll be M. Valenod, who takes my
exile in Verrières to be the effect of his anonymous letters.

Once he had sent off his despatch, Julien, feeling as contented as a sportsman who at six o'clock on a fine autumn

morning steps out on to a plain abounding in game, went off
to seek Father Chélan's advice. But before he reached the good
priest's house, heaven, who had treats in store for him, set M.
Valenod in his path, and Julien did not conceal from him that
his heart was torn:

A poor lad like himself must devote himself wholeheartedly
to the calling which heaven had planted in his heart, but one's
calling was not everything here below on earth. To till the
Lord's vineyard fittingly, and not to be altogether unworthy of
so many learned co-workers, it was necessary to study; it was
necessary to spend two very costly years in the seminary at
Besançon; it was therefore becoming indispensable to put by
some savings, which was far easier on a salary of eight hundred
francs paid quarterly than with six hundred francs that got
eaten up month by month. On the other hand, did it not seem
that by putting him in close contact with the de Rênal children,
and particularly by inspiring him with a special fondness for
them, heaven was making it plain to him that this was not the
right moment to give up this education in favour of another?...

Julien reached such heights of perfection in this kind of
eloquence, which has replaced the swiftness of action found
under the Empire, that he ended up boring himself with the
sound of his own words.

On returning to the house he found one of M. Valenod's
valets in full livery, who was scouring the town for him with a
note inviting him to dinner that very day.

Julien had never set foot in the man's house; only a few days
before, he could think of nothing else but ways of giving him
a sound beating without being hauled up before a police court.
Although dinner was only announced for one o'clock, Julien
thought it more respectful to present himself at twelve-thirty
in the master of the workhouse's study. He found him oozing
self-importance in the midst of a host of files. His broad black
sidewhiskers, his enormous mass of hair, his smoking-cap
sitting askew on the top of his head, his huge pipe, his
embroidered slippers, the fat gold chains criss-crossing his
chest—the entire set-up befitting a provincial financier who
fancies himself a ladies' man—did not impress Julien; he only
dwelt the more on the beating he owed him.

He asked to have the honour of being introduced to Mme Valenod; she was at her toilette and could not receive anyone. In compensation, he had the benefit of being present while the master of the workhouse attended to his own. Afterwards they went to Mme Valenod's suite, and she introduced the children to him with tears in her eyes. This lady, one of the most eminent in Verrières, had the coarse features of a man, which she had daubed with rouge for this grand ceremony. Throughout it, she laid on a full display of maternal pathos.

Julien's thoughts were on Mme de Rênal. His mistrustful nature only allowed him to be susceptible to the kind of memories that are evoked by opposites, but he was then deeply stirred by them. This mood was increased by the appearance of the master's house. He was shown round it. Everything was magnificent and brand new, and he was told the price of each piece of furniture. But Julien felt there was something base about it which smacked of stolen money. Even down to the servants, everyone there seemed to be composing their faces to keep scorn at bay.

The inspector of taxes, the man in charge of indirect levies, the officer of the law and two or three other public officials arrived with their wives. They were followed by a few wealthy liberals. Dinner was announced. It occurred to Julien, who was already in a hostile frame of mind, that on the other side of the dining-room wall were wretched prisoners whose portion of meat had perhaps been fraudulently skimped to pay for all this luxury in poor taste that was intended to bowl him over.

They may be hungry at this very moment, he said to himself. He felt a lump in his throat, and found it impossible to eat and almost even to speak. Things became far worse a quarter of an hour later; in the distance they heard some snatches of a popular song, rather vulgar, it must be admitted, sung by one of the workhouse inmates. M. Valenod caught the eye of one of his men in full livery; he disappeared, and soon the singing was heard no more. At this moment, a valet was offering Julien some Rhine wine in a green glass, and Mme Valenod was careful to point out to him that this wine cost nine francs a bottle, purchased from the producer. Holding out his green glass Julien said to M. Valenod:

'That indelicate song isn't being sung any more.'

'I should damn well hope not!' replied the master triumphantly. 'I had the beggars reduced to silence.'

These words were too much for Julien; he had the manners, but not yet the heart befitting his station. In spite of all the hypocrisy which he had practised so often, he felt a large tear rolling down his cheek.

He tried to hide it behind the green glass, but it was absolutely impossible for him to do justice to the Rhine wine. *Stopping him singing*! he said to himself. Oh my God! and you suffer this to happen!

Fortunately no one noticed his misplaced compassion. The inspector of taxes had struck up a royalist song. During the din of the refrain, sung by everyone in chorus, Julien's conscience was murmuring: So there you see the stinking riches you will acquire, and you will only enjoy them under these conditions and in like company! You may well get a post worth twenty thousand francs, but you will be obliged, while gorging yourself on meat, to prevent the poor prisoner from singing; you will host dinners on money stolen from his wretched pittance, and throughout your dinner he will be even more unhappy! Oh Napoleon! how sweet it was in your day to rise to fortune through the dangers of battle; but to be a coward and increase a poor wretch's suffering...!

I confess that the weakness shown by Julien in this monologue gives me a very poor opinion of him. He would be a worthy colleague for those yellow-gloved conspirators who set out to change the entire way of life of a great country, and do not wish to have to reproach themselves with the slightest scratch.

Julien was brought back to his role with a violent jolt. It wasn't to indulge in daydreaming and sit in silence that he had been invited to dine in such good company.

A retired manufacturer of painted cloth, who was a corresponding member of the Academies of Besançon and Uzès, turned to him from right down the far end of the table to ask him whether what people said about his astonishing achievements in the study of the New Testament was true.

There was a sudden deathly hush; a New Testament in

Latin appeared as if by magic in the hands of the learned member of two academies. On Julien's reply, half a Latin sentence was read out at random. He recited on: his memory served him faithfully and the prodigious feat was admired with all the rowdy energy to be expected at the end of a dinner. Julien looked at the glowing faces of the ladies; several of them were quite pretty. He had singled out the wife of the tax inspector with the fine voice.

'I am ashamed in all honesty to go on speaking Latin for so long in front of the ladies,' he said, looking at her. 'If M. Rubigneau (he was the member of the two academies) will be good enough to read out a Latin sentence at random, then instead of continuing with the Latin text, I shall try to translate it impromptu.'

This second ordeal put the crown on his reputation.

Among the company were a number of wealthy liberals who, as the happy fathers of children in the running for scholarships, had undergone sudden conversions since the last mission.* In spite of this subtle political move, M. de Rênal had never consented to entertain them in his house. These worthy characters, who only knew Julien by reputation and through having seen him on horseback on the day of the King of ——'s triumphal entry, were now his rowdiest admirers. When will these fools grow tired of listening to this biblical idiom which they can't make head or tail of? he thought. But on the contrary the idiom amused them by its unfamiliarity; it made them laugh. It was Julien who grew tired.

He rose gravely as six o'clock was striking and mentioned a chapter of Ligorio's new theology* which he had to learn in order to be able to recite it to Father Chélan on the following day. 'For my profession', he added engagingly, 'is to make others say their lessons and also to say my own.'

There was much laughter and admiration; this is what passes for wit in Verrières. Julien was already on his feet, and everyone rose in spite of decorum; such is the power of genius. Mme Valenod kept him for a further quarter of an hour; he simply had to hear the children saying their catechism; they got into the most comic of muddles which he was the only one to perceive. He was careful not to point them out. What ignorance of the first principles of religion! he thought. At last he made his farewells and thought he could escape; but he had to endure a fable by La Fontaine.*

'This author is highly immoral,' Julien told Mme Valenod, 'there's one particular fable, about Messire Jean Chouart,* that dares to pour ridicule on what is most worthy of veneration. It is roundly condemned by the best commentators.'

Before he left, Julien received four or five invitations to dinner. 'This young man is a credit to the département,' exclaimed a chorus of exceedingly merry guests. They even went so far as to speak of an allowance drawn from municipal funds to give him the wherewithal to continue his studies in Paris.

While this rash idea was echoing round the dining-room, Julien had made his way nimbly to the carriage entrance. 'Ah! you swine! you swine!' he expostulated under his breath three or four times in a row, enjoying the pleasure of breathing the fresh air.

He felt every inch the aristocrat at that moment—the very same Julien who had been so shocked for ages at the disdainful smile and the haughty superiority which he detected beneath all the marks of courtesy shown to him in M. de Rênal's house. He couldn't help feeling the immense difference. Even forgetting, he said to himself as he left, the matter of stealing money from the poor prisoners, and stopping them singing, what's more! Did M. de Rênal ever take it into his head to tell his guests the price of each bottle of wine being served to them? And when this M. Valenod starts enumerating all his properties, which he keeps on doing, he can't speak of his house, his estate, etc. if his wife is present without saying *your* house, *your* estate.

This lady, apparently so sensitive to the pleasure of owning property, had just created an abominable scene at dinner when a servant had smashed a stem glass and thus *ruined one of her sets of twelve*; and the servant had replied with the utmost insolence.

What a household! Julien said to himself. They could give me the half of all they steal, and I still wouldn't want to live with them. One fine day I'd betray myself; I'd be unable to refrain from expressing the disdain I feel for them.

He was obliged, however, on Mme de Rênal's instructions, to attend several dinners of the same sort; Julien became all the rage: his guard of honour's outfit was forgiven him, or rather, this piece of rashness was the true cause of his success. Soon the only topic of concern in Verrières was who would win the battle to obtain this learned young man—M. de Rênal or the master of the workhouse. Together with Father Maslon these gentlemen formed a triumvirate which for a good many years had tyrannized the town. The mayor was an object of envy, the liberals had grievances against him, but he was, after all, noble and destined for a position of superiority, whereas M. Valenod's father hadn't even left him so much as an income of six hundred pounds. In his case, people had had to switch from feelings of pity for the shabby apple-green suit universally associated with him in his youth to envy for his Normandy cobs, his gold chains, his clothes sent from Paris—all his present prosperity.

Amid the sea of faces in this unfamiliar milieu, Julien thought he discerned an honourable man; he was a geometer by the name of Gros,* and had the reputation of being a Jacobin. Julien, who had committed himself to the line of only ever saying things that seemed false to him, was unable to get beyond mere suspicions in regard to M. Gros's opinions. He received thick packages of Latin proses from Vergy. He was advised to visit his father often, and he fell in with this dreary necessity. In short, he was patching up his reputation rather well, when one morning he was very surprised to be woken up and feel two hands covering his eyes.

It was Mme de Rênal who had made a trip to town and, running up the stairs four at a time, leaving the children playing with a favourite rabbit that was of the party, had reached Julien's room just before they did. It was a blissful moment, all too brief: Mme de Rênal had disappeared when the children arrived with the rabbit, which they wanted to show their friend. Julien welcomed them all warmly, even the rabbit. It seemed to him that he was back with his family again; he felt that he loved these children, that he enjoyed chattering with them. He was astonished at the sweetness of their voices, at how simple and noble their little ways were; he needed to cleanse his imagination of all the vulgar modes of behaviour, all the disagreeable thoughts tainting the air he breathed in Verrières. You couldn't get away from fear of doing without, you couldn't get away from luxury and dire poverty tearing each other's hair out. The people he dined with would indulge, on the subject of the joint of meat, in revelations that were humiliating for them and nauseating for anyone listening.

'You nobles, you have reason to be proud,' he said to Mme de Rênal. And he described to her all the dinners he had put up with.

'So you've become all the rage!' And she laughed heartily at the thought of the rouge that Mme Valenod felt obliged to put on whenever she was expecting Julien. 'I think she has designs on your heart,' she added.

Lunch was delectable. The presence of the children, though inhibiting at first sight, in fact increased the general happiness. These poor children were beside themselves with joy at seeing Julien again. The servants had not failed to relate to them that he was being offered two hundred francs extra for *edicating* the little Valenods.

In the middle of lunch Stanislas-Xavier, still pale after his serious illness, suddenly asked his mother how much his silver cutlery and the tankard he drank from were worth.

'Why do you ask?'

'I want to sell them to give the money to Mr Julien, so he isn't a *sucker* for staying with us.'

Julien hugged him with tears in his eyes. His mother wept openly while Julien, who had taken Stanislas on his lap, explained to him that he shouldn't use the word *sucker*, which in that sense was a lackey's way of talking. Seeing the pleasure he was giving Mme de Rênal, he tried to explain, using picturesque examples that amused the children, what being a sucker meant.

'I understand,' said Stanislas, 'it's like the crow who's silly enough to drop his piece of cheese, and the fox gets it, and he was a flatterer.'

Mme de Rênal was overcome with joy, and smothered her children in kisses, which she could hardly do without leaning a little on Julien.

Suddenly the door opened: it was M. de Rênal. The stern look of displeasure on his face contrasted strangely with the tender delight that his presence dispelled. Mme de Rênal turned pale; she felt in no state to deny anything. Julien decided to speak, and in a loud voice began to tell his worship how Stanislas had wanted to sell his silver tankard. He was sure that this story would not go down well. To begin with, M. de Rênal frowned from sound habit at the very word *silver*. 'When this metal is mentioned,' he would say, 'it's always the preface to some call on my purse.'

But in this instance there was more to it than a question of what could be obtained with silver; there was an increase in the level of suspicion. The look of happiness on the faces of his family in his absence was unlikely to improve matters with a man ruled by such prickly vanity. As his wife was praising the gracious and witty manner in which Julien suggested new ideas to his pupils:

'Yes! Yes! I know, he makes me odious to my children; it's easy enough for him to be infinitely more agreeable to them than I am, being, when it comes down to it, the master in this house. Everything nowadays conspires to cast odium on *legitimate* authority. Poor France!'

Mme de Rênal did not pause to examine the niceties of the reception she was getting from her husband. She had just glimpsed a chance of spending twelve hours with Julien. She had a host of purchases to make in town, and declared that she insisted on going to dine in a cabaret; in spite of everything her husband could say or do, she stuck to her idea. The children were delighted at the very mention of the word *cabaret*,* uttered with such pleasure by the prudishness of our times.

M. de Rênal left his wife in the first fashion shop she entered; he had to go off and pay some calls. He was more sullen on his return than in the morning; he was convinced that the whole town was engrossed with him and Julien. In actual fact no one had yet given him cause to suspect the offensive aspect of public gossip. What had been relayed to the mayor was exclusively concerned with whether Julien would remain in his household at six hundred francs, or would accept the eight hundred francs offered by the master of the workhouse.

The master himself, on meeting M. de Rênal in company, *gave him the cold shoulder*. This behaviour was not unpremeditated; few things are done heedlessly in the provinces: feelings are so rare there that they are exploited to the full.

M. Valenod was what is known, a hundred leagues from Paris, as a *swaggerer*—that is: a vulgar fellow of brazen and coarse disposition. His triumphant existence since 1815 had reinforced his promising tendencies. He reigned, so to speak, in Verrières under the orders of M. de Rênal; but he was much more active, did not blush at anything, meddled in everything, was constantly on the go, writing, speaking, forgetting humiliations, having nothing personal at stake; so much so that in the end his influence had come to outweigh his master's in the eyes of the ecclesiastical authorities. M. Valenod had more or less said to the local grocers: give me the two most foolish from among you; to the legal profession: show me the two most ignorant; to the medical practitioners:* name me the two greatest charlatans. When he had done gathering together the most brazen representatives of every trade, he had said to them: let's reign together.

These people's ways wounded M. de Rênal's susceptibilities. Valenod's vulgarity was not offended by anything, not even by the flat contradictions that little Father Maslon did not spare him in public.

However, in the midst of all this prosperity, M. Valenod needed to indulge in minor acts of effrontery to protect his self-image from the blatant truths which, as he was well aware, everyone was entitled to bring to his attention. His activity had been stepped up since the state of alarm he was left in by the visit of M. Appert; he had made three journeys to Besançon; he wrote several letters for each post; he despatched others using the services of strangers who called at his house at nightfall. He had perhaps been wrong to have old Father Chélan removed from office, since this vindictive act had caused him to be regarded by a number of pious ladies of good birth as a profoundly wicked man. Besides, doing this favour had put him completely under the thumb of the vicar-general, M. de Frilair, and he received strange instructions from him. This was the state of his politicking when he succumbed to the pleasure of writing an anonymous letter. To cap his embarrassment, his wife announced to him that she wanted to have Julien in her household; her vanity had taken a fancy to the idea.

In this situation M. Valenod foresaw a decisive confrontation with his former associate M. de Rênal. The latter would address harsh words to him, which he didn't mind that much; but he might write to Besançon and even to Paris. A cousin of some minister or other might suddenly descend on Verrières and take over the workhouse. M. Valenod considered aligning himself with the liberals: that was why a number of them were invited to the dinner at which Julien had performed. He would have got powerful support against the mayor, but elections might come along, and it was patently obvious that the workhouse and a vote the wrong way were incompatible. An account of this politicking, astutely surmised by Mme de Rênal, had been given to Julien while he offered her his arm to walk from one shop to another, and had gradually taken them as far as the Avenue de la Fidélité, where they spent several hours almost as undisturbed as at Vergy.

During this time M. Valenod was attempting to avert a decisive confrontation with his former protector by adopting an audacious stance towards him himself. That day the strategy worked, but it increased the mayor's ill-temper.

Never had vanity in conflict with petty love of money in all its harshest and meanest aspects put a man in a more wretched state than that afflicting M. de Rênal when he went into the *cabaret*. Never, on the other hand, had his children been more full of joy and good cheer. This contrast put the finishing touches to his pique.

'I'm not welcome in my family, so I see!' he said as he came in, trying to make his tone of voice sound forceful.

By way of reply, his wife took him on one side and urged on him the need to get Julien out of the way. The hours of happiness she had just enjoyed had given her the necessary poise and firmness to carry out the plan of action she had been meditating for the past fortnight. What really succeeded in upsetting the poor mayor of Verrières through and through was that he knew jokes were being made openly in town about his attachment to his *cash*. M. Valenod was as generous as a thief, while he himself had behaved more prudently than outstandingly in the last five or six collections in aid of the Brotherhood of St Joseph,* the Congregation of the Virgin, the Congregation of the Holy Sacrament etc., etc., etc.

Among the gentry of Verrières and its neighbourhood, cunningly listed on the collecting brothers' register in order of the magnitude of their donations, M. de Rênal's name had been observed more than once down on the bottom line. It was to no avail that he said he *earned nothing* himself. This is no joking matter for the clergy.

CHAPTER 23

The woes of a civil servant*

Il piacere di alzar la testa tutto l'anno è
ben pagato da certi quarti d'ora che bisogna
passar.

CASTI*

BUT let us leave this petty man to his petty fears; why did he
take a man with a generous heart into his house when what he
needed was the soul of a valet? Why isn't he any good at
choosing his servants? The normal course of events in the
nineteenth century is that when a powerful member of the
nobility encounters a man of generosity, he kills him, exiles
him, imprisons him, or humiliates him so much that the other
man is foolish enough to die of grief. By chance in this
instance, the man of generosity is not yet the one to suffer.
The great misfortune afflicting small towns in France and
elected governments like the one in New York, is that they
cannot forget that there exist individuals like M. de Rênal. In
the midst of a town of twenty thousand inhabitants these men
shape public opinion, and public opinion is dreadful in a
country that has its Charter.* A man endowed with a noble
and generous spirit, someone who might even have been your
friend, but lives a hundred leagues away, will judge you by
public opinion in your town, and this is shaped by the fools
who by sheer chance were born noble, rich and moderate. Woe
betide you if you stand out from the herd!

Immediately after dinner the family left for Vergy; but two
days later Julien found them all back again in Verrières.

An hour had not gone by before he discovered to his great
surprise that Mme de Rênal was keeping a secret from him. She
broke off her conversations with her husband as soon as he
appeared, and seemed almost to wish him to go away. Julien
did not wait to be asked twice. He became cold and reserved;
Mme de Rênal noticed and did not seek any explanation for it.
Is she going to find a successor to me? Julien wondered. And
so intimate with me only the day before yesterday! But they

say that's how these great ladies go about things. Just like kings: never more attentive than to the minister who will find his fall from favour announced in a letter awaiting him back at his house.

Julien noticed that in these conversations which ceased abruptly when he approached, there was often talk of a large house belonging to the commune* of Verrières; it was old, but spacious and convenient, and it was sited opposite the church in the busiest part of town. What can there be in common between this house and a new lover! Julien said to himself. In his distress he repeated to himself the pretty couplet by François I which felt new to him because it was not a month since Mme de Rênal had taught it to him. How many vows, how many caresses had given the lie at the time to each of these lines!

> Woman is a fickle thing,
> Mad the man who trusts her.*

M. de Rênal left by post horses for Besançon. He decided on this journey in the space of two hours, and appeared to be in considerable torment. On his return, he flung down on the table a fat package wrapped in grey paper.

'Here's this silly business,' he said to his wife.

An hour later, Julien saw the billsticker making off with the fat package; he hastened off after him. I'll find out the secret at the first street corner.

He waited impatiently behind the billsticker as he daubed the back of the notice with his big brush. It was hardly in position before the curious Julien read a detailed announcement concerning the letting by auction of the large old house which had so often been mentioned by name in M. de Rênal's conversations with his wife. The assignment of the lease was announced for two o'clock on the following day, in the municipal hall, when the third candle burned out. Julien was very disappointed; he found the deadline really rather close: how would there be time for all rival bidders to be informed? But in any case this notice, which was dated two weeks previously, and which he read from start to finish in three different spots, told him nothing at all.

He went to look round the house that was to be let. The porter, not seeing him approach, was saying mysteriously to a neighbour:

'Hmm! Waste of time! Father Maslon promised him he can have it for three hundred francs; and as the mayor dug his heels in, he was summoned to the bishop's palace by the vicar-general M. de Frilair.'

Julien's arrival appeared to disturb the two friends greatly, for they did not add another word.

Julien did not miss the assigning of the lease. There was a great crowd in a poorly lit hall; but they were all eyeing one another up and down in an odd way. All eyes were turned towards a table where Julien saw three short candle-ends burning on a tin plate. The auctioneer was shouting: *Three hundred francs, gentlemen!*

'Three hundred francs! That's a bit steep!' said a man under his breath to his neighbour. Julien was standing between them. 'It's worth more than eight hundred; I intend to up that bid.'

'Might as well save your breath! What good'll it do you making enemies of Father Maslon, M. Valenod, the bishop, his dreadful vicar-general de Frilair, and the rest of the clique.'

'Three hundred and twenty francs!' called out the other.

'Stupid dolt!' retorted his neighbour. 'And look, if that isn't one of the mayor's spies!' he added, pointing to Julien.

Julien wheeled round to punish this remark; but the two Franche-Comté locals were no longer paying any attention to him. Their composure restored his own. At that moment the last candle went out, and the auctioneer's drawling voice assigned the house for nine years to M. de Saint-Giraud, head clerk at the prefecture in ——, for the sum of three hundred and thirty francs.

As soon as they mayor had left the hall, the comments began.

'That's thirty francs Grogeot's rashness has earned the commune,' said someone.

'But M. de Saint-Giraud', said someone else, 'will get his revenge on Grogeot; he'll not enjoy that.'

'What a disgrace!' said a fat man on Julien's left, '—a house

I'd have given eight hundred francs for, I would—for my factory, and I'd have done a good deal.'

'Come off it!' replied a young manufacturer of liberal persuasion, 'doesn't M. de Saint-Giraud belong to the Congregation?* Haven't his four children got scholarships? Poor man! The commune of Verrières has to pay him a supplementary income of five hundred francs, that's all.'

'And to think that the mayor wasn't able to prevent it!' remarked a third man. 'Because he's an Ultra, he is, bully for him! But he doesn't steal.'

'Doesn't steal?' rejoined someone else. 'No, but that gullible stooge does, whenever Simon Says. It all goes into a great big common kitty, and everything gets shared out at the end of the year. But there's little Sorel over there; let's be off.'

Julien went home in a very bad temper; he found Mme de Rênal extremely depressed.

'Have you come from the auction?' she asked him.

'Yes, madam, and I had the honour of being taken for his worship's spy.'

'If he had listened to me, he would have gone off on a journey somewhere.'

At that moment M. de Rênal appeared; he was exceedingly glum. No one spoke a word over dinner. M. de Rênal instructed Julien to follow the children to Vergy; the journey was depressing. Mme de Rênal tried to console her husband:

'You should be used to it, my dear.'

That evening, they were sitting in silence round the family hearth; the sound of the beech-logs burning was the only distraction. It was one of those moments of gloom that occur in the most united families. One of the children shouted excitedly:

'A ring at the door! A ring at the door!'

'Confound it! If that's M. de Saint-Giraud coming to set me off again under the pretence of thanking me,' exclaimed the mayor, 'I'll give him a piece of my mind; it's more than I can take. I suppose Valenod's the one he has to thank for it, and I'm the one to be compromised. What can I say if those cursed Jacobin papers go and get hold of the story, and turn me into a Mr Five-and-Ninety?'*

A very handsome man with big black sidewhiskers was following the servant into the room at that very moment.

'Your worship, I am il Signor Geronimo.* Here is a letter for you which the Chevalier de Beauvaisis, the attaché at the embassy in Naples, handed me when I left; that was only nine days ago,' added Signor Geronimo cheerfully, looking at Mme de Rênal. 'Signor de Beauvaisis, your cousin and my good friend, madam, tells me you know Italian.'

The Neapolitan's good humour transformed this gloomy evening into a very cheerful one. Mme de Rênal insisted on giving him supper. She had the whole house in a bustle; she wanted at all costs to take Julien's mind off the label *spy* that had rung in his ears twice on that day. Signor Geronimo was a famous singer, a man of good breeding and yet full of gaiety— qualities rarely found together any more in France. After supper he sang a little *duettino* with Mme de Rênal. He told some delightful stories. At one in the morning the children protested loudly when Julien suggested it was their bedtime.

'Just this one story,' said the eldest.

'It's my own story, Signorino,' replied Signor Geronimo. 'Eight years ago, I was a young pupil like you at the Naples Conservatoire—I mean I was your age; but I didn't have the honour of being the son of the illustrious mayor of the pretty town of Verrières.'

These words made M. de Rênal sigh; he looked at his wife.

'Signor Zingarelli,'* went on the young singer, overdoing his accent a little as it made the children splutter with laughter, 'Signor Zingarelli was an exceedingly strict master. People do not like him at the Conservatoire; but he expects them to behave all the time as if they did like him. I used to go out as often as I could; I went to the little San-Carlino theatre, where I heard music fit for the gods: but, great heavens, how was I to scrape together the eight sous it cost to get into the stalls? A huge sum,' he said looking at the children, and they burst out laughing. 'Signor Giovannone,* the director of the San-Car-lino, heard me sing. I was sixteen: "This child's a real treasure," he said.

"Would you like me to sign you on, dear boy?" he came over to ask me.

"And how much will you give me?"

"Forty ducats a month." Gentlemen, that's a hundred and sixty francs. I thought I saw the heavens opening up before me.

"But what can be done," I asked Giovannone, "to ensure that the strict Signor Zingarelli lets me out?"

"*Lascia fare a me.*"'

'Leave it to me!' exclaimed the eldest child.

'Exactly, my little lord. Signor Giovannone says to me: "*Caro*, first of all let's make a little undertaking." I sign, and he gives me three ducats. I'd never seen so much money. Then he tells me what I have to do.

'The next day I ask to see the terrible Signor Zingarelli. His old valet shows me in.

"What do you want from me, wretched boy?" asks Zingarelli.

"Maestro," I said, "I repent for all my misdeeds; I'll never escape from the Conservatoire again by climbing over the iron gate. I'll work twice as hard."

"If I wasn't afraid of spoiling the loveliest bass voice I've ever heard, I'd put you in prison on bread and water for a fortnight, you rascal!"

"Maestro," I went on, "I'll be a model for the whole school, *credete a me.** But I ask one favour of you, if anyone comes asking for me to sing elsewhere, refuse to let me go. I beg you, say you can't."

"And who the devil do you think will come asking for a rotten number like you? Will I ever give permission for you to leave the Conservatoire? Are you trying to poke fun at me? Be off with you! Be off with you!" he shouted, trying to kick me up the b... "Or watch out for dry bread in prison."

'An hour later, Signor Giovannone calls on the director:

"I've come to ask you to make my fortune," he says, "let me have Geronimo. If he sings in my theatre, I'll be able to marry off my daughter this winter."

"What do you want with this unruly fellow?" asks Zingarelli. "I'm against it; you shan't have him; and anyway, even if I were to agree to it, he'll never be willing to leave the Conservatoire; he's just sworn to me he won't."

"If it's only a matter of his wishes," says Giovannone gravely, pulling my undertaking from his pocket, "*carta canta*!* Here's his signature."

'At once Zingarelli tugs at the bell-pull in fury:

"Expel Geronimo from the Conservatoire," he shouted, seething with rage. I was duly expelled, laughing my head off. That same evening I sang the aria *del Moltiplico*. Punchinello wants to get married and is counting out on his fingers the things he will need in his household, and he keeps getting muddled over his sums."'

'Oh! I beg you, sir, do sing us this aria,' said Mme de Rênal.

Geronimo sang and everyone laughed themselves to tears. Signor Geronimo did not go to bed until two in the morning, leaving the family enchanted by his good manners, his obliging nature and his jollity.

The next day M. and Mme de Rênal handed him the letters he needed at the French Court.

So, it's deceit everywhere, thought Julien. There's il Signor Geronimo going to London with a salary of sixty thousand francs. If it hadn't been for the know-how of the director of the San-Carlino, his divine voice might not have been discovered and admired until ten years later... Goodness me, I'd rather be a Geronimo than a Rênal. He isn't so highly honoured in society, but he doesn't have the distress of making assignments like the one today, and his life is full of gaiety.

One thing astonished Julien: the solitary weeks he had spent in Verrières in M. de Rênal's house had been a happy time for him. He had only experienced revulsion and gloomy thoughts during the dinners that had been put on for him; in this solitary house, was he not able to read, write and think without being disturbed? He wasn't dragged from his brilliant flights of fancy at every moment, first by the harsh necessity of studying the workings of a base mind, and then by the need to outwit it through hypocritical actions or words.

Could happiness be so near at hand?... A life like this doesn't involve much by way of expenditure; I can choose whether to marry Mlle Elisa or become Fouqué's partner... But a traveller who has just climbed a steep mountain sits down at the summit and finds perfect pleasure in resting. Would he be happy if forced to rest for ever?

Mme de Rênal's mind had come to entertain dire thoughts. In spite of her resolve, she had told Julien about the whole business of the assignment. He'll make me forget all my oaths, so it seems! she thought.

She would have sacrificed her own life without hesitating to save her husband's if she had seen him in danger. She was one of those noble, romantic creatures for whom seeing the possibility of a generous action and not carrying it out gives rise to almost as much remorse as does a crime actually committed. Nevertheless, there were black days when she could not banish the image of the surfeit of happiness that would overwhelm her if she were suddenly widowed and able to marry Julien.

He loved her sons much more than their father did; despite his stern even-handedness, he was adored by them. She was well aware that in marrying Julien she would have to leave Vergy with its beloved shade. She pictured herself living in Paris, continuing to give her children the education that everyone admired. Her children, herself, Julien—all perfectly happy.

Strange is the effect of marriage as it has been fashioned by the nineteenth century! The boredom of married life is sure to kill off love when love precedes marriage. And at the same time, as a philosopher would say, it soon induces in people rich enough not to work a profound sense of being bored with all quiet pleasures. And, among women, only the most unresponsive of natures are not predisposed by it towards love.

Philosophic reflection makes me forgive Mme de Rênal, but she was not forgiven in Verrières, and without her suspecting it, the entire town thought of nothing else but the scandal of her passion. Because of this great affair, the inhabitants were far less bored that autumn than usual.

Autumn and part of winter passed all too quickly. It was time to leave the woods of Vergy. High society in Verrières began to grow indignant that its anathemas were having so little effect on M. de Rênal. Within the space of a week, a number of solemn individuals, who make up for their habitual seriousness by the pleasure they derive from carrying out this kind of mission, planted in him the most cruel of suspicions, couched, however, in the most moderate of terms.

M. Valenod, who was playing things very cautiously, had secured Elisa a position with a highly regarded noble family in which there were five women. Fearing, as she said, that she wouldn't find a position during the winter, Elisa had only asked this family for about two-thirds of what she received at the mayor's. On her own initiative this girl had had the excellent idea of going to make her confession to the former priest Father Chélan and at the same time to the new one, with the aim of telling both of them all about Julien's amorous exploits.

The day after his arrival, at six o'clock in the morning, Father Chélan summoned Julien.

'I'm not asking you any questions,' he said to him; 'I beg you, and if need be I order you not to tell me anything; I demand that within three days you leave for the seminary in Besançon, or for your friend Fouqué's house, since he's still minded to offer you a magnificent future. I have fixed everything in advance, made all the arrangements, but you must go, and not return to Verrières before a year is up.'

Julien did not reply; he was considering whether his honour should feel slighted at the concern shown on his behalf by Father Chélan, who was not after all his father.

'Tomorrow at this same hour I shall have the honour of seeing you again,' he said at last to the priest.

Father Chélan, who was counting on the full force of his authority to get the better of so young a man, spoke at great length. Adopting the most humble stance and countenance to cushion himself, Julien did not open his mouth.

Eventually he left and ran off to warn Mme de Rênal, whom he found in despair. Her husband had just spoken to her with a certain degree of openness. The natural weakness of his character, backed by the prospect of the Besançon legacy, had swayed him to consider her perfectly innocent. He had just told her about the strange state in which he had found public opinion in Verrières. The public were wrong, they were led astray by envious tongues, but still, what was to be done?

For a moment Mme de Rênal entertained the illusion that

Julien might accept M. Valenod's offer and remain in Verrières. But she was no longer the straightforward, shy woman she had been a year ago; her fateful passion and her remorse had enlightened her. She soon suffered the pain of convincing herself, as she listened to her husband, that a separation, at least for the time being, had become essential. *Once he's away from me, Julien will revert to his ambitious schemes that come so naturally to someone who's penniless. And look at me, God Almighty! I'm so rich! and so pointlessly as far as my happiness is concerned! He'll forget me. Engaging as he is, he will be loved, and will love in return. Ah! how wretched I am... What have I got to complain of? Heaven is just; I didn't have the virtue to put a stop to the crime, and now heaven is depriving me of my judgement. All I had to do was to win Elisa over with a little money—nothing would have been easier for me. I didn't take the trouble to reflect for a moment, the wild fantasies of love took up all my time. I'm done for.*

Julien was struck by one thing as he gave Mme de Rênal the terrible news of his departure: he did not meet with any selfish objections. She was obviously making efforts not to cry.

'We must be steadfast, my dearest.'

She cut off a lock of her hair.

'I don't know what I shall do,' she said, 'but if I die, promise me you'll never forget my children. Whether you're far away or close by, strive to make gentlemen of them. If there's another revolution, all the gentry will be slaughtered, their father may emigrate on account of that peasant who was killed on a rooftop. Watch over the family... Give me your hand. Farewell, my dear one! These are our last moments. Once this great sacrifice is made, I hope that in public I shall have the courage to think about my reputation.'

Julien was expecting signs of despair. The simplicity of this farewell touched him.

'No, this isn't the way I shall accept your farewells. I shall leave; they wish me to; you do yourself. But three days after my departure I shall come back to visit you during the night.'

Mme de Rênal's existence was transformed. So Julien did care for her, since he had thought up the idea of seeing her again himself! Her terrible sorrow was transformed into one of the most intense pangs of joy she had experienced in her whole life. Everything became easy for her. The certainty of seeing her lover again rid these last moments of all their heartrending qualities. From that instant on, Mme de Rênal's conduct, like her countenance, was noble, firm and perfectly appropriate.

M. de Rênal soon returned home; he was beside himself. He finally told his wife about the anonymous letter he had received two months previously.

'I intend to take it to the Casino, show everyone that it comes from that despicable Valenod whom I raised from nothing and made into one of the richest members of the bourgeoisie in Verrières. I'll shame him with it in public, and then I'll fight a duel with him. This is more than I can take.'

I might be a widow, God Almighty! thought Mme de Rênal. But at virtually the same instant she said to herself: If I don't prevent this duel, as I undoubtedly can, I shall be my husband's murderer.

Never had she handled his vanity with such skill. In less than two hours she brought him round to the view, using arguments that he himself produced, that it was essential to show more friendliness than ever to M. Valenod, and even to take Elisa back into the house. Mme de Rênal needed courage to make up her mind to see this girl again, as she had been the cause of all her misfortunes. But the idea came from Julien.

At last, having been put on the right track three or four times, M. de Rênal managed, unaided, to hit upon the idea— a very onerous one financially—that what would be most disagreeable for him would be if Julien, in the midst of all the hubbub and tittle-tattle in Verrières, were to remain there as tutor to M. Valenod's children. It was obviously in Julien's interest to accept the master of the workhouse's offer. What was vital for M. de Rênal's reputation, on the contrary, was that Julien should leave Verrières and enter the seminary in Besançon or Dijon. But how could he be persuaded, and then, what would he live on?

Seeing that a financial sacrifice was imminent, M. de Rênal was in greater despair than his wife. For her part, after this conversation she was in the position of a generous-hearted man who, weary of life, has just taken a dose of *stramonium*: all his actions are now pure clockwork, as it were, and he has no further interest in anything. Thus it was that Louis XIV found himself saying as he lay dying: *When I was king*. An admirable phrase!

The next day, as soon as it was broad daylight, M. de Rênal received an anonymous letter. This one was in the most insulting style. The most vulgar terms applicable to his situation stood out on every line. It was the work of some envious person of subordinate station. This letter brought him back to the idea of fighting a duel with M. Valenod. Soon his courage extended to ideas of executing it immediately. He went out alone and called at the armourer's for some pistols which he ordered to be loaded.

In fact, he said to himself, even supposing the strict administration of the Emperor Napoleon were to make a comeback, I personally don't have a jot of shady business to reproach myself with. At the very most I turned a blind eye, but I have solid letters in my desk authorizing me to do so.

Mme de Rênal was terrified by her husband's cold anger; it revived the dire thought of widowhood which she found so hard to banish. She closeted herself with him. For several hours on end she talked to him in vain: the new anonymous letter made him adamant. She finally managed to transform a courageous determination to deliver a slap in the face to M. Valenod into the courage to offer six hundred francs to Julien for a year's board and lodging in a seminary. With a thousand curses on the day he had had the ill-fated idea of taking on a tutor, M. de Rênal forgot the anonymous letter.

He consoled himself a little with an idea which he did not impart to his wife: with a bit of skill, and exploiting the romantic ideas in the young man's head, he hoped to get him to agree, for a lesser sum, to refuse M. Valenod's offer.

Mme de Rênal had far greater difficulty in proving to Julien that since, to suit her husband, he was sacrificing a position worth eight hundred francs that was being publicly offered him by the master of the workhouse, he need have no scruples in accepting a sum in compensation.

'But', Julien kept on saying, 'I've never, not even for a moment, had any intention of accepting that offer. You've got me too accustomed to an elegant life-style; the vulgarity of those people would finish me off.'

The iron hand of cruel necessity broke Julien's will. His pride offered him the illusion that he could accept the sum offered by the mayor of Verrières as a mere loan, and make out a note to him specifying repayment in five years with interest.

Mme de Rênal still had several thousand francs hidden in the little grotto in the mountains.

She offered them to him in fear and trembling, sensing only too clearly that she would meet with an angry refusal.

'Do you wish', Julien said to her, 'to turn the memory of our love into something abominable?'

Finally Julien left Verrières. M. de Rênal was extremely happy, for when the fateful moment came to accept money from him, the sacrifice proved too great for Julien. He refused point-blank. M. de Rênal flung his arms round his neck with tears in his eyes. Julien had asked him for a character reference, and in his enthusiasm he could not find terms sufficiently glowing to extol his conduct. Our hero had five louis in savings, and was counting on asking Fouqué for a similar sum.

He was deeply moved. But a league away from Verrières, where he was leaving behind so much love, his only thoughts now were for the pleasure of seeing a capital, a big martial city like Besançon.

During this brief three-day absence, Mme de Rênal was deceived by one of love's most cruel tricks. Her life was bearable, for between her and ultimate unhappiness there was this last meeting she was to have with Julien. She counted the hours and the minutes separating her from it. At last, during the night after the third day, she heard the agreed signal from afar. After braving countless dangers, Julien appeared before her.

From that moment on she had but a single thought: I'm seeing him for the very last time. Far from responding to her lover's excitement, she was like a corpse virtually devoid of life. If she forced herself to tell him she loved him, it came out so unnaturally as almost to prove the contrary. Nothing could take her mind off the cruel idea of eternal separation. Suspicious Julien believed for a moment that he was already forgotten. His hurt words to this effect were only greeted with large tears running down her cheeks in silence, and almost convulsive squeezes of the hand.

'But great heavens! how do you expect me to believe you?' Julien replied to the cold protestations of his mistress; 'You'd show infinitely more signs of genuine friendship to Mme Derville, to a mere acquaintance.'

Mme de Rênal was petrified and did not know what to answer:

'It isn't possible to be more unhappy... I hope I'm going to die... I feel my heart growing chill...'

These were the longest answers he could get out of her.

When dawn made departure necessary, Mme de Rênal's tears stopped completely. She saw him fix a knotted rope to the window without uttering a word, without returning his kisses. It was in vain that Julien said to her:

'We've now reached the situation you so ardently wished for. From now on you'll live without remorse. Whenever your children are the least bit ailing you won't any longer imagine them in their graves.'

'I'm vexed that you can't kiss Stanislas,' she said to him coldly.

Julien ended up being profoundly struck by the absence of any warmth in the embraces of this living corpse; he was unable to think of anything else for several leagues. His heart was wrung, and before he crossed over the mountain, as long as he could still see the church steeple in Verrières, many were the times he looked back.

CHAPTER 24

A capital city

So much noise, so many busy people!
So many ideas for the future in the head of
a twenty-year-old! What distractions for
love!

BARNAVE

AT last, on a distant mountainside, he caught sight of the
black walls of the citadel of Besançon. How different it would
be for me, he said with a sigh, if I was coming to this noble
martial city to be a sub-lieutenant in one of the regiments in
charge of defending it!

Besançon is not only one of the prettiest towns in France, it
abounds in generous-hearted and intelligent people. But Julien
was only a little peasant, and had no means of approaching any
men of distinction.

He had obtained a plain suit from Fouqué, and he was
wearing this outfit when he crossed the drawbridge. With his
head full of the history of the siege of 1674,* he was keen to
see the ramparts and the citadel before shutting himself away
in the seminary. On two or three occasions he was on the point
of being arrested by the sentries; he was going into places to
which the military authorities refuse the public access, in order
to be able to sell twelve or fifteen francs' worth of hay every
year.

The height of the walls, the depth of the moats, the fearsome
look of the cannon had kept him occupied for several hours,
when he passed in front of the big café on the boulevard.
He stood stock still in admiration; in spite of reading the word
café written in large letters above the two huge doors, he still
couldn't believe his eyes. He struggled to overcome his nervousness; he plucked up the courage to go in, and found
himself in a room thirty or forty paces long, with a ceiling at
least twenty foot high. That day everything was magical for
him.

Two games of billiards were under way. The waiters were

calling out the scores; the players were running round the
tables cluttered with spectators. Great whiffs of tobacco smoke
streaming from every mouth enveloped all heads in a blue
cloud. The tall stature of these men, their rounded shoulders,
their heavy tread, their huge sidewhiskers, the long frock-coats
draped round them—everything caught Julien's eye. These
noble children of ancient Bisontium only spoke to shout; they
assumed the poses of fearsome warriors. Julien was rooted to
the spot in admiration; his thoughts were on the sheer size and
the magnificence of a great capital like Besançon. He felt
nothing like bold enough to request a cup of coffee from one
of those haughty-looking gentlemen who were calling out the
billiards score. But the girl behind the bar had noticed the
attractive figure of this young bourgeois from the country who,
standing three paces away from the stove with his little bundle
under his arm, was contemplating the fine white plaster bust
of the king. This barmaid, a tall Franche-Comté lass with a
lovely figure, dressed just right to do honour to a café, had
already said twice, in a quiet voice aiming not to be heard by
anyone but Julien: 'Sir! Sir!' Julien looked into two big blue
eyes filled with kindness, and saw that he was the person being
addressed.

He walked briskly over to the bar and the pretty girl, as he
would have marched to face the enemy. In this great action,
his bundle fell to the floor.

Imagine the pity our little provincial is going to arouse in
those young Parisian schoolboys who at the age of fifteen are
already adept at sauntering into a café with the most distinguished of airs! But these boys who have so much style at
fifteen become *common* at eighteen. The intense reserve found
in the provinces is sometimes overcome, and it then brings out
will-power. As he went over to this beautiful girl who deigned
to speak to him: I must tell her the truth, thought Julien, who
was growing brave through triumphing over his reserve.
'Madam, this is the first time in my life I've come to Besançon:
I'd like to have a roll and a cup of coffee—I can pay.'

The barmaid smiled a little and then blushed; she was afraid
of hearing the billiard players direct quips and ironic comments

at this attractive young man. He'd be frightened off and wouldn't come back.

'Take a seat here near me,' she said, showing him a marble table almost completely hidden by the enormous mahogany bar projecting into the room.

The girl leaned out over the bar, which gave her the opportunity to display her superb figure. Julien noticed it; his ideas underwent a rapid shift. The beautiful girl had just put down a cup, some sugar and a roll in front of him. She was hesitating to call a waiter for the coffee, realizing that his arrival would put an end to her tête-à-tête with Julien.

Julien was pensive, comparing this fair, sparkling beauty with certain memories which often disturbed him. The thought of the passion he had inspired banished almost all his nervousness. The beautiful girl only had a moment; she read Julien's gaze.

'This pipe smoke is making you cough, come for breakfast before eight o'clock tomorrow: at that time, I'm almost alone.'

'What's your name?' asked Julien with the caressing smile of nervousness reassured.

'Amanda Binet.'

'Will you allow me to send you, in an hour's time, a little bundle the size of this one?'

The beautiful Amanda thought for a moment.

'They've got their eye on me: what you're asking may compromise me; all the same, I'll go off and write down my address on a card for you to put on your bundle. You can send it to me without any worries.'

'I'm called Julien Sorel,' said the young man; I have neither relatives nor acquaintances in Besançon.'

'Ah! I understand,' she said delightedly, 'you're here to study law.'

'Alas! no,' Julien replied, 'I'm being sent to the seminary.'

The light in Amanda's face was instantly extinguished by a look of the most total discouragement; she called a waiter: she felt able to now. The waiter poured Julien some coffee without looking at him.

Amanda was taking money at the bar; Julien felt proud of having dared to speak; a quarrel broke out at one of the billiard tables. The shouts and denials of the players echoing round the enormous room created a din that amazed Julien. Amanda was looking dreamy and had her eyes lowered.

'If you like, mademoiselle,' he said to her suddenly in confident tones, 'I'll say I'm your cousin.'

This little air of authority appealed to Amanda. This young man isn't a nobody, she thought. She said to him very quickly, without looking at him, since she was keeping a watchful eye to see if anyone was coming up to the bar:

'I'm from Genlis, near Dijon; say you're from Genlis too, and a cousin of my mother's.'

'I'll be sure to.'

'Every Thursday at five o'clock in summertime the young gentlemen from the seminary pass by in front of the café.'

'When I go past, if you're thinking of me, have a bunch of violets in your hand.'

Amanda looked at him in astonishment; this look turned Julien's courage into temerity; yet he blushed deeply as he said to her:

'I feel I love you with the most passionate love.'

'Do lower your voice,' she said to him with a terrified look.

Julien was thinking of calling up some passages he had read in an incomplete volume of *La Nouvelle Héloïse** that he had found at Vergy. His memory served him well. He had been reciting *La Nouvelle Héloïse* for a good ten minutes to a delighted Mlle Amanda, and was feeling pleased with his bravery, when suddenly the belle of the Franche-Comté assumed an icy glare. One of her lovers was on the doorstep of the café.

He walked over to the bar, whistling and swinging his shoulders in step; he looked at Julien. Instantly, the latter's imagination, always veering to extremes, was filled exclusively with thoughts of a duel. He turned extremely pale, pushed his cup away, assumed a self-confident air and stared closely at his rival. While this rival had his head lowered, intent on pouring himself a glass of brandy at the bar like an old customer, Amanda ordered Julien with a glance to lower his gaze. He obeyed, and for two minutes remained motionless in his seat, pale, resolute and wholly absorbed in what was to come; he

looked really impressive at that moment. The rival had been
astonished at Julien's eyes; downing his brandy in one go, he
said a word to Amanda, stuck his two hands in the side pockets
of his heavy frock-coat and went over to one of the billiard
tables, blowing the air out of his mouth as he looked at Julien.
The latter stood up in a fit of rage; but he did not know how
to go about being insulting. He put down his little bundle and
walked towards the billiard table, swinging his hips as best he
could manage.

It was to no avail that prudence said to him: Look, with a
duel the moment you arrive in Besançon, your ecclesiastical
career is ruined.

So what, let no one say I let a cheeky devil get away with
it.

Amanda observed his courage; it made a nice contrast with
the naïvety of his manners; it was the work of an instant for
her to prefer him to the tall young man in the frock-coat. She
got up, and while appearing to be gazing after someone who
was passing in the street, she quickly came and stationed
herself between him and the billiard table.

'Be careful not to give that gentleman dirty looks, he's my
brother-in-law.'

'What do I care? He stared at me.'

'Do you want to make me unhappy? Maybe he did stare at
you, perhaps he's even going to come over and talk to you. I
told him you're a relative of my mother's and you've just
arrived from Genlis. He's from the Franche-Comté, and he's
never been further than Dôle,* on the way to Burgundy; so
you can say what you like, there's nothing to fear.'

Julien was still hesitating; she added very quickly, her
barmaid's imagination supplying her with lies in plenty:

'Maybe he did stare at you, but that was when he was asking
me who you are. He's a man who's *boorish* to everybody; he
didn't mean to insult you.'

Julien was keeping an eye fixed on the so-called brother-in-
law; he saw him purchase a number for the pool being played
at the further of the two billiard tables. Julien heard his loud
voice shouting in menacing tones: *I'm stepping in now.* He

slipped quickly behind Mlle Amanda and began to walk towards the billiard table. Amanda grabbed him by the arm:

'Come and pay me first,' she said to him.

That's right, thought Julien, she's afraid I'll leave without paying. Amanda was as agitated as he was and very flushed; she handed him his change as slowly as she could, while repeating to him in a low voice:

'Leave the café this instant, or I won't love you any more; but I love you a lot, actually.'

Julien did indeed leave, but taking his time. Isn't it my duty, he kept repeating to himself, to go and stare and puff at that rude individual? This uncertainty kept him for an hour on the boulevard outside the café; he was watching for his man to come out. He did not appear and Julien went away.

He hadn't been in Besançon for more than a few hours and already he had notched up a sense of failure. The old army surgeon had once given him a few fencing lessons in spite of his gout; this was all the knowledge Julien could muster in the service of his anger. But this embarrassment would not have mattered a whit, had he but known how to show his annoyance otherwise than by delivering a slap in the face; and if it came to a punch-up, his rival, an enormous man, would have beaten him and left him there.

For a poor devil like me, said Julien to himself, with nobody to protect me and no money, there won't be much difference between a seminary and a prison; I must leave my plain clothes in some inn or other, and resume my black suit. If ever I manage to get out of the seminary for a few hours, I can perfectly well go and see Mlle Amanda wearing my plain clothes. It was a fine piece of reasoning, but Julien went past all the inns without daring to enter a single one.

At last, as he was going past the Ambassadors Hotel for a second time, his anxious gaze met that of a fat woman, still fairly young, with a ruddy complexion and a happy, cheerful air. He went up to her and told her his story.

'Of course, my fine little Father,' said the mistress of the Ambassadors, 'I'll keep your plain clothes for you, and I'll even get them dusted off regularly. In this weather it isn't a good idea to leave a cloth suit undisturbed.' She took a key and led him off to one of the rooms herself, advising him to make a note of what he was depositing.

'Lord a mercy! Don't you look dandy like that, Father Sorel, sir!' said the fat woman to him when he came down to the kitchen. 'I'll be seeing to it you get a good dinner put in front of you; and', she added in a low voice, 'it'll not cost you more than twenty sous, instead of the fifty that everyone else pays; for we've surely got to go easy on your little *nest egg*.'

'I've got ten louis,' Julien retorted with some pride.

'Oh Lord!' replied the good hostess in alarm, 'don't talk so loud; there's a lot of good-for-nothings in Besançon. You'll have it nicked in next to no time. Above all, don't ever set foot in those cafés, they're full of good-for-nothings.'

'Really!' said Julien; the term set him thinking.

'Don't come anywhere except my place; I'll see to it there's coffee made for you. Remember that here you'll always find a friend and a good dinner for twenty sous; that means something, I trust. Go and sit yourself down, I'll be serving you myself.'

'I don't feel like eating,' Julien said to her, 'I'm too upset, I'm going into the seminary when I leave here.'

The good woman did not let him leave until she had filled his pockets with supplies. At last Julien set off on his way to the terrible place; the hostess gave him directions leaning out through the top section of her door.

CHAPTER 25

The seminary

Three hundred and thirty-six dinners at
83 centimes, three hundred and thirty-six
suppers at 38 centimes, chocolate for those
entitled to it; how much profit is there to
be made from my submission—
and from theirs?

THE BESANÇON VALENOD*

HE caught sight of the gilded iron cross on the door from a
long way off; he approached slowly; his legs seemed to be
giving way beneath him. So this is the hell on earth that I
shan't be able to escape from! Eventually he made up his mind
to ring the doorbell. The noise resounded as in a desolate
spot. Ten minutes later a pale man dressed in black came to
let him in. Julien looked at him and at once lowered his gaze.
The porter had a strange face. The bulging green irises of his
eyes were rounded like a cat's; the motionless lines of his
eyelids proclaimed the absence of any possible sympathy; his
thin lips spread in a semicircle over a set of protruding teeth.
However, this face did not proclaim criminality so much as the
kind of total impassivity that arouses far greater terror in the
young. The only feeling that Julien's rapid glance could detect
in this long, pious face was a profound disdain for everything
that anyone might wish to say to him unless it concerned the
interests of heaven.

Julien made an effort to look up and, in a voice trembling
from the pounding of his heart, explained that he wished to
speak to M. Pirard, the master of the seminary. Without
uttering a word, the man in black beckoned to him to follow.
They went up two flights of a wide staircase with wooden
banisters and sagging steps which sloped right down on the
side away from the wall, and looked about to collapse. A small
door with a large graveyard cross above it made of deal painted
black was opened with difficulty, and the porter showed him
in to a gloomy, low room with whitewashed walls, decorated

with two large pictures blackened with age. There Julien was left on his own; he was shattered, his heart was thumping; he would have been glad to have dared to cry. A deathly silence reigned throughout the house.

When a quarter of an hour had gone by, seeming like a whole day to Julien, the sinister-faced porter reappeared on the threshold of a door at the far end of the room, and without deigning to speak, beckoned to him to come forward. He went into a room even bigger than the first and very poorly lit. The walls were likewise whitewashed, but it was unfurnished. Only in a corner by the door did Julien see as he passed a deal bed, two wicker chairs and a little slatted pine armchair without cushions. At the other end of the room, next to a little window with yellowing panes, adorned with tatty vases of flowers, he caught sight of a man sitting at a table, wearing a shabby cassock; he appeared to be angry, and was picking up little squares of paper one by one from a heap, and tidying them away on this table after writing one or two words on each. He did not notice Julien's presence. The latter was standing motionless in the middle of the room, exactly where he had been left by the porter, who had gone out again shutting the door behind him.

Ten minutes went by thus; the ill-dressed man was still writing. Julien's emotion and terror were such that he felt as if he were about to collapse. A philosopher would have remarked, perhaps wrongly: 'It's the violent impression made by ugliness on a sensibility meant to love what is beautiful.'

The man writing looked up; Julien only noticed after a moment or two, and even when he did, he went on standing stock still as if the terrible look which was fastened on him had struck him a mortal blow. Julien's eyes were swimming: he had difficulty in making out a long face covered with red blotches everywhere except on the forehead, which displayed a deathly pallor. Between the red cheeks and the white forehead shone two small black eyes such as would frighten the bravest of men. The broad expanse of forehead was outlined by thick, smooth, jet-black hair.

'Are you going to come closer then? yes or no?' the man said at last, impatiently.

Julien went forward unsteadily, and at length, on the point of collapse and paler than he had ever been in his life before, he stopped three paces away from the little deal table covered with squares of paper.

'Closer,' said the man.

Julien went forward a little more, stretching out his hand as if trying to lean on something.

'Your name?'

'Julien Sorel.'

'You're very late,' came the response, and again the terrible eyes transfixed him.

Julien was unable to bear this gaze; stretching out his hand as if to support himself, he fell prostrate on the floor.

The man rang a bell. Julien had only lost the use of his eyes and the strength to move; he heard footsteps approaching.

Someone picked him up and put him in the little deal chair. He heard the terrible man saying to the porter:

'He fell down in a fit, so it would appear; this really is the limit.'

When Julien was able to open his eyes, the red-faced man was writing away again; the porter had disappeared. I must be brave, our hero said to himself, and above all hide my feelings: he felt violently sick; if I have an accident, God knows what they'll think of me. At last the man stopped writing, and looking sideways at Julien:

'Are you in a fit state to answer me?'

'Yes, sir,' said Julien in a feeble voice.

'Ah! that's fortunate.'

The man in black had half-risen from his seat and was impatiently looking for a letter in the drawer of his pine table, which creaked as it opened. He found it, sat down slowly, and turned to Julien again with a look fit to wrest from him the little life that remained:

'You are recommended to me by Father Chélan: he was the best priest in the diocese, a man of virtue if ever there was one, and my friend for the last thirty years.'

'Ah! It's M. Pirard I have the honour of speaking to,' said Julien in expiring tones.

'So it would appear,' retorted the master of the seminary, looking at him in annoyance.

His little eyes flashed with twice the intensity, and there was a twitching of the muscles at the corners of his mouth. It was the face of a tiger savouring in advance the pleasure of devouring its prey.

'Chélan's letter is brief,' he said, as if speaking to himself. '*Intelligenti pauca*;* in this day and age, one can scarcely write too little.' He read aloud:

I am sending you Julien Sorel, of this parish, whom I baptized coming up for twenty years ago; son of a wealthy carpenter, who gives him nothing, however. Julien will be an outstanding worker in the Lord's vineyard. Memory and intelligence are not lacking, and there is a capacity for thought. Will his calling be a lasting one? Is it sincere?

'*Sincere*!' repeated Father Pirard in astonishment, looking at Julien; but the priest's gaze was already less lacking in humanity. '*Sincere*!' he repeated, lowering his voice, and he went on reading:

I am asking you to give Julien Sorel a scholarship; he will earn it by sitting the necessary examinations. I have introduced him to a little theology, the good, old-fashioned theology of men like Bossuet,* Arnault and Fleury. If you do not find this individual to your liking, send him back to me; the master of the workhouse, whom you know well, is offering him eight hundred francs to be tutor to his children. I am at peace within, thank the Lord. I am growing accustomed to the terrible blow. *Vale et me ama.**

Father Pirard, slowing down his voice as he read the signature, uttered the word *Chélan* with a sigh.

'He's at peace,' he said; 'and indeed, his virtue deserved this reward; may God grant it to me, if the need arises!'

He raised his eyes to heaven and made the sign of the cross. At the sight of this sacred sign, Julien felt some lessening of the profound horror that had chilled his blood ever since he had set foot in this house.

'I have here three hundred and twenty-one candidates aspiring to the holiest of states,' Father Pirard said at last in a tone of voice that was severe but not unkind. 'Only seven or eight of them come to me with recommendations from men like Father Chélan; thus among the three hundred and twenty-one, you are going to be the ninth. But my protection means neither favour nor indulgence; it means increased watchfulness and severity in dealing with vices. Go and lock this door.'

Julien made an effort to walk, and managed not to collapse. He noticed that a little window near the door into the room looked out over the countryside. He looked at the trees; the sight of them made him feel better, as if he had caught sight of some old friends.

'*Loquerisne linguam latinam* (Do you speak Latin)?'* Father Pirard asked him as he returned.

'*Ita, pater optime* (yes, most excellent Father),' replied Julien, gradually coming to himself again. One thing was certain: never had any man in the world seemed less excellent to him than Father Pirard in the half hour that had just gone by.

The conversation continued in Latin. The expression in the priest's eyes softened; Julien regained a certain degree of composure. How feeble I am, he thought, to be overawed by these appearances of virtue! I bet this man is quite simply a rogue like Father Maslon; and Julien congratulated himself on having hidden almost all his money in his boots.

Father Pirard examined Julien on theology, and was surprised at the extent of his knowledge. His astonishment increased when he grilled him specifically on the Holy Scriptures. But when he came to questions on the doctrine of the Church Fathers, he observed that Julien had scarcely even heard of St Jerome, St Augustine, St Bonaventure, St Basil, etc., etc.

Come to think of it, Father Pirard pondered, this is indeed that fatal tendency towards Protestantism that I've always blamed in Chélan. A thorough, too thorough knowledge of the Holy Scriptures.

(Julien had just been talking to him, without being questioned on the subject, about the *actual* time when Genesis, The Pentateuch etc. were written.)

Where does all this endless reasoning over the Holy Scriptures lead to, thought Father Pirard, apart from *independent scrutiny*, in other words the most appalling Protestantism? And alongside this rash learning, nothing about the Church Fathers to counterbalance this tendency.

But the master of the seminary's amazement knew no bounds when he questioned Julien about the authority of the pope, and expecting to meet with the maxims of the old Gallican Church, found that the young man recited to him the whole of Joseph de Maistre's book.

Strange man, this Chélan, thought Father Pirard. Did he show him this book to teach him to mock it?

It was to no avail that he questioned Julien to try and find out whether he seriously believed in the doctrine of Joseph de Maistre. The young man merely answered from memory. From then on, Julien really excelled, he felt in full control of himself. After a very lengthy examination, it seemed to him that Father Pirard's severity towards him was now a mere matter of form. Indeed, were it not for the principles of austere gravity that for the past fifteen years he had forced himself to adopt towards his theological students, the master of the seminary would have embraced Julien in the name of logic, such were the clarity, precision and sharpness he observed in his replies.

There's a bold and sound mind, he said to himself, but *corpus debile* (the body is weak).

'Do you often collapse like that?' he asked Julien in French, pointing at the floor with his finger.

'It was the first time in my life; the porter's face had chilled me with terror,' Julien added, blushing like a child.

Father Pirard almost smiled.

'There you have the effect of the vain pomp of this world; you are accustomed, so it seems, to laughing faces—true theatres of falsehood. Truth is austere, sir. But our task here below is austere too, is it not? You'll have to watch out that your conscience guards against this weakness: *Too much sensitivity to vain external graces*.

'If you were not recommended to me,' Father Pirard resumed in Latin, with obvious pleasure, 'if you were not recommended to me by a man like Father Chélan, I should speak to you in the vain language of this world to which you seem only too accustomed. The full scholarship you are requesting, let me tell you, is the most difficult thing in the world to obtain. But Father Chélan has deserved very little indeed by his fifty-six years of apostolic toil if he cannot have a scholarship at the seminary in his gift.'

After these words Father Pirard advised Julien not to join any secret society or Congregation without his consent.

'I give you my word of honour I won't,' said Julien with the heartfelt warmth of a gentleman.

The master of the seminary smiled for the first time.

'That expression is out of place here,' he said. 'It is too reminiscent of the vain honour of worldly men which leads them to commit so many lapses, and crimes as often as not. You owe me holy obedience in virtue of paragraph seventeen of Pope Pius V's Bull *Unam Ecclesiam*.* I am your ecclesiastical superior. In this house, to hear, my dearest son, is to obey. How much money have you got?'

Now we're getting there, said Julien to himself, that's what the 'dearest son' was all about.

'Thirty-five francs, Father.'

'Make a careful note of how you spend this money; I shall expect you to give me an account of it.'

This painful session had lasted three hours; Julien summoned the porter.

'Put Julien Sorel in cell nº 103,' Father Pirard instructed this man.

As a great honour, he was giving Julien a separate room.

'Take his trunk there,' he added.

Julien looked down and recognized his own trunk standing opposite him; he had been staring at it for the past three hours and had not recognized it.

When he reached nº 103, which was a little closet of a room eight foot square on the top floor of the house, Julien observed that it looked out on to the ramparts; beyond them you could see the lovely plain separated off from the town by the river Doubs.

What a delightful view! exclaimed Julien; as he spoke to himself thus, he had no feeling for the meaning of these words. The feelings of such intensity that he had experienced in the short time he had been in Besançon had completely drained his strength. He sat down by the window on the only wooden chair in the cell and fell at once into a deep sleep. He did not hear the supper bell, nor the one for vespers; he had been forgotten.

When the first rays of the sun woke him the following morning, he found himself lying on the floor.

CHAPTER 26

The world or what the rich man lacks

> I am alone on earth, no one deigns to think of me.
> All those I see making their fortunes have an
> effrontery and a hardness of heart that I do not detect
> in myself. They hate me for my easy good-nature. Ah!
> I shall soon die, either of hunger or from unhappiness
> at finding men so hard-hearted.
>
> YOUNG*

HE hastily brushed off his suit and went downstairs; he was late. An assistant master scolded him severely; instead of attempting to justify himself, Julien folded his arms over his chest:

'*Peccavi, pater optime*' (I have sinned, I confess the error of my ways, O Father), he said with a contrite air.

This beginning was a great success. The more acute of the seminarists saw that they were dealing with a man who was well beyond the rudiments of the profession. Recreation time came round. Julien became an object of general curiosity. But his only response was reserve and silence. In accordance with the maxims he had drawn up for himself, he considered his three hundred and twenty-one fellow students as enemies; the most dangerous of all in his eyes was Father Pirard.

A few days later, Julien had to choose a confessor; he was presented with a list.

Heavens above! who do they take me for? he said to himself. Do they think I can't *read between the lines*? And he chose Father Pirard.

Without his suspecting it, this step was decisive. A very young little seminarist, a native of Verrières, who had declared himself Julien's friend from the very first day, informed him that if he had chosen Father Castanède the vice-master of the seminary he would perhaps have acted with greater prudence.

'Father Castanède is the enemy of Father Pirard, who is suspected of Jansenism,' the young seminarist added in Julien's ear.

All the first moves made by our hero who thought himself so cautious were, like the choice of a confessor, acts of sheer thoughtlessness. Led astray by all the presumptuousness of an imaginative young man, he took his intentions for facts and believed himself to be a consummate hypocrite. His folly led him so far as to reproach himself with his successes in this art born of weakness.

Alas! It's my only weapon! In another age, he said to himself, eloquent actions in the face of the enemy would have been my way of *earning my living*.

Satisfied with his conduct, Julien looked around him; everywhere he saw outward signs of the purest virtue.

Nine or ten seminarists lived in the odour of sanctity and had visions like St Theresa and St Francis when he received the stigmata on Mount Verna* in the Apennines. But it was a great secret, their friends concealed it. These poor youths with visions were nearly always in the infirmary. Some hundred others combined a robust faith with tireless application. They made themselves ill from overwork, but failed to learn much. Two or three stood out from the rest through genuine talent, among their number a certain Chazel; but Julien felt remote from them, and they from him.

The remainder of the three hundred and twenty-one seminarists were nothing but boorish individuals who could not be relied on to understand the Latin words they repeated day in day out. Almost all of them were peasants' sons who preferred to earn their living by reciting a handful of Latin words than by tilling the soil. It was this observation that allowed Julien right from the start to forecast rapid success for himself. In any form of service there is a need for people of intelligence, he reflected, for after all there's a job to be done. Under Napoleon I'd have been a sergeant; among these future parish priests, I shall be a vicar-general.

All these poor devils, he went on, have been manual labourers since childhood, and lived on junket and black bread until arriving here. In their cottages they only ate meat five or six times a year. Like Roman soldiers who considered war to be a time for rest, these boorish peasants are thrilled with the delights of the seminary.

The only thing Julien ever read in their dour gaze was the satisfaction of physical need after dinner and the anticipation of physical pleasure before the meal. It was among people like these that he had to distinguish himself; but what Julien did not know, and everyone was careful not to tell him, was that to be first in the various classes in dogma, ecclesiastical history etc., etc. that are attended in a seminary, constituted in their eyes nothing less than a *sin of pride*. Since Voltaire, since the institution of government by two Chambers,* which is basically nothing more than *mistrust and independent scrutiny*, and gives the mind of nations the bad habit of being mistrustful, the Church of France seems to have grasped that books are her real enemies.* Submission of the heart is everything in her eyes. Success in studies, even sacred ones, is suspect in her eyes, and rightly so. Who is to prevent the superior man from going over to the other side like Sieyès* or Grégoire!* The Church clings in trembling to the pope as if he were the only chance of salvation. The pope alone can try to paralyse individual scrutiny by the pious pomp of his Court ceremonies, and to make an impression on the sick and weary minds of worldly folk.

Julien half-perceived these various truths, which all the words uttered in a seminary none the less go to belie, and he fell into a bout of profound melancholy. He worked very hard, and soon succeeded in learning things of great use to a priest, but totally false in his eyes, and of no interest to him whatsoever. He believed there was nothing else for him to do.

So have I been forgotten by everyone on earth? he wondered. He was unaware that Father Pirard had received and cast into the fire one or two letters with a Dijon postmark, in which despite the conventions of the most proper style, signs of the most ardent passion showed through. Great remorse seemed to be wrestling with this love. So much the better, thought Father Pirard; at least the woman this young man once loved isn't an impious one.

One day Father Pirard opened a letter which seemed half obliterated by tears; it was an eternal farewell. 'At last', said the writer to Julien,

Heaven has granted me the grace to hate not the agent of my sin, for he will always be what I hold most dear in the world, but my sin in itself. The sacrifice is made, my dear. And not without tears, as you can see. The salvation of those I am committed to—ones you loved so dearly—overrides everything else. A just but terrible God will not any longer be able to avenge on them their mother's crimes. Farewell, Julien, be just towards your fellow men.

This last part of this letter was almost totally illegible. The writer gave an address in Dijon, and yet hoped that Julien would never answer, or at least would do so in words that a woman who had returned to the path of virtue could hear without blushing.

Julien's melancholy, compounded by the indifferent food supplied to the seminary by the purveyor of dinners at eighty-three centimes, was beginning to affect his health, when one morning Fouqué suddenly appeared in his room.

'At last I've managed to get inside. I've come to Besançon five times—no fault of yours—just in order to see you. Stony faces every time. I posted someone at the seminary door; why the devil don't you ever go out?'

'It's an ordeal I've imposed on myself.'

'You seem to me to have changed a lot. At last I'm setting eyes on you again. Two five-franc coins in fine silver have just taught me that I was a mere idiot not to have produced them on the very first visit.'

The conversation between the two friends was endless. Julien changed colour when Fouqué said to him:

'By the way, have you heard? Your pupils' mother has fallen into excesses of devotional piety.'

And he spoke in that casual tone which makes such a strange impression on passionate beings whose dearest concerns are being thrown into turmoil unbeknown to the speaker.

'Yes, my good friend, the most fanatical piety. They say she goes on pilgrimages. But to the eternal shame of Father Maslon who spied on poor Father Chélan for so long, Mme de Rênal would have none of him. She goes to confession in Dijon or Besançon.'

'She comes to Besançon?' asked Julien, flushing all over his brow.

'Pretty often,' replied Fouqué with a questioning look.

'Have you got any copies of *Le Constitutionnel* on you?'

'What did you say?'

'I'm asking if you've got any copies of the *Le Constitutionnel*, Julien went on in the calmest of voices. 'They sell for thirty sous each here.'

'What! liberals, even in the seminary!' exclaimed Fouqué. 'Poor France!' he added, adopting the hypocritical voice and the dulcet tones of Father Maslon.

This visit would have made a deep impression on our hero if, on the very next day, something said to him by the little seminarist from Verrières who struck him as immature had not led him to make an important discovery. Since his arrival in the seminary, Julien's conduct had been nothing but a succession of false moves. He laughed bitterly at himself.

If the truth be told, the important actions in his life were skilfully conducted; but he did not pay attention to details, and the clever operators in a seminary only look at details. So he already had the reputation among his contemporaries of being a *free thinker*. He had been betrayed by a host of petty actions.

In their eyes he was guilty of this monstrous vice: *he thought and formed opinions independently*, instead of blindly following *authority* and example. Father Pirard had been of no help to him; he had not addressed a single word to him outside the confessional, where in any case he listened more than he spoke. Matters would have been very different if he had chosen Father Castanède.

As soon as Julien perceived his folly, he ceased to be bored. He determined to discover the full extent of the damage and, to this effect, he emerged to some degree from the haughty and obstinate silence with which he rebuffed his fellows. This was the moment for them to get their revenge on him. His advances were met with a scorn which verged on derision. He recognized that since his arrival in the seminary there had not been a single hour, especially during recreations, which had not told either for or against him, which had not increased the number of his enemies, or won him the goodwill of some seminarist of sincere virtue or slightly less boorish than the others. The damage to be made good was immense, the task exceedingly difficult. From then on Julien's attention was constantly on the watch; he had to map out a completely new character for himself.

The movements of his eyes, for instance, gave him a great deal of trouble. Not without reason do the inhabitants of such places keep theirs lowered to the ground. What presumption I had in Verrières! Julien said to himself; I thought I was living, when all I was doing was preparing myself for life; here I am at last in the world as I shall find it for as long as I play this part, surrounded with real enemies. What a tremendous strain, he went on—maintaining this hypocrisy every minute of the day; it makes the labours of Hercules pale in comparison. The Hercules of modern times is Sixtus V,* who for fifteen whole years succeeded by his modesty in deceiving forty cardinals who had known him as fiery and haughty throughout the whole of his youth.

Learning counts for nothing here! he reflected in disgust; progress in dogma, in sacred history, etc., only receives lip-service. Everything that is said on this matter is designed to ensnare crazy idiots like me. Alas! my only merit lay in my rapid progress, in the way I grasped this rubbish. Can it be that in the end their assessment of my achievement is the right one? Do they judge it as I do? And I was foolish enough to be proud of it. The top marks I always get have only served to make dogged enemies for me. Chazel, who is more learned than I am, always throws some blunder or other into his essays which puts him down to fiftieth place; if he comes first, it's because he isn't thinking. Ah! how useful one word, just a single word from Father Pirard would have been to me!

From the moment Julien was disabused, the long exercises in ascetic piety such as rosary five times a week, canticles to the Sacred Heart, etc., etc., which he used to find so deadly boring, became his most interesting moments of action. By reflecting severely about himself, and trying above all not to exaggerate his own capabilities, Julien did not aspire from the outset, like the seminarists who served as models to the others, to use every moment to perform *significant* actions, that is, ones proving a kind of Christian perfection. In a seminary, there is a way of eating a boiled egg which declares the progress made in devotional life.

Would the reader, who is perhaps smiling, kindly deign to remember all the *faux pas* made by the Abbé Delille* in eating an egg when invited to breakfast with a great lady at the Court of Louis XIV.

Julien attempted first of all to achieve the *non culpa*, that is the state of a young seminarist whose way of walking, moving his arms, eyes, etc. do not, it is true, indicate anything worldly, but do not yet reveal a being absorbed by the idea of the other world and the *pure nothingness* of this one.

Julien was constantly coming across sentences written in charcoal on the walls of the corridors, such as: 'What are sixty years of trials, set against an eternity of bliss or an eternity of boiling oil in hell?' He did not despise them any more; he realized that they had to be kept constantly before his eyes. What shall I be doing all my life? he would ask himself; selling the faithful their place in heaven. How is this place to be made manifest to them? By the difference between my outward appearance and that of a layman.

After several months of unfaltering application, Julien still looked as if he were *thinking*. His way of moving his eyes and holding his mouth did not betoken implicit faith ready to believe and to uphold anything, even at the cost of martyrdom. Julien was annoyed to see himself outshone in this art by the most boorish peasants. There were good reasons why they did not look as if they were thinking.

What endless trouble he took to attain that facial expression of fervent and blind faith, ready to believe and suffer anything, that is so often encountered in monasteries in Italy, and of which Guercino* has left us laymen such perfect models in his church paintings.[1]

On high feast days the seminarists were served sausages with sauerkraut. Julien's neighbours at table noticed that he was indifferent to this delight; that was one of his first crimes. His companions took this as an odious characteristic of the most

[1] See, in the Louvre, François, Duke of Aquitaine laying down his breastplate and putting on a monk's habit, n. 1130. [Stendhal's note.]

stupid hypocrisy; nothing made him more enemies. 'Look at this bourgeois, look at this stuck-up prig,' they said, who pretends to scorn the finest sustenance, sausages with sauer-kraut! Shame on the swine! the snob! the creature of damnation.

Alas! the ignorance of these young peasants, my fellows, is an immense advantage to them, exclaimed Julien in moments of discouragement. On their arrival in the seminary the teacher doesn't have to rid them of the fearful number of worldly ideas that I bring with me and they read on my face, try as I may.

The most boorish of the little peasants who arrived at the seminary were studied by Julien with a degree of attention bordering on envy. At the point where they were stripped of their coarse woollen jackets and put into black habits, all they had in the way of education was an immense and limitless respect for *dry and liquid* assets, as the expression goes in the Franche-Comté.

This is the sacramental and heroic way of expressing the sublime idea of *cash*.

Happiness for these seminarists, as for the heroes of Voltaire's novels, consists chiefly in dining well. Julien found in nearly all of them an innate respect for any man wearing a suit of *fine cloth*. This sentiment appreciates at its true value, and even below, the *distributive justice* that is meted out by our courts. 'What can you win', they would often repeat among themselves, 'from fighting a *big 'un* in court?'

This is the term used in the Jura valleys to designate a wealthy man. You can just imagine their respect for the wealthiest entity of all: the Government!

Not to smile with respect at the very name of the prefect is viewed by the peasants in the Franche-Comté as rashness: and rashness, where the poor man is concerned, is swiftly punished by a shortage of bread.

Having been choked, as it were, at the outset by a feeling of scorn, Julien ended up experiencing pity: it was a frequent occurrence for the fathers of the majority of his companions to return home to their cottages on winter evenings to find neither bread, nor chestnuts nor potatoes. It's hardly surprising, then, Julien reflected, if their idea of a happy man is first and foremost someone who has just had a good dinner, and next someone who owns a good set of clothes! My fellow students have a firm vocation, that is to say they regard the priesthood as a long continuation of this happiness: to dine well and have warm clothes in winter.

Once, Julien happened to hear a young seminarist with the gift of imagination say to his companion:

'Why shouldn't I become pope like Sixtus V who kept swine?'

'They only make Italians pope,' replied the friend; 'but they'll draw lots among us, that's for sure, for posts as vicar-general, canon and maybe bishop. Father P——, the Bishop of Châlons, is a cooper's son: that's my father's trade.'

One day, in the middle of a dogma class, Father Pirard summoned Julien to his presence. The poor young man was delighted to leave the physical and moral atmosphere he was plunged in.

Julien was greeted with the same reception in the master's study as had so terrified him on the day he entered the seminary.

'Explain to me what is written on this playing card,' he said to him with a look such as to make him sink into the ground.

Julien read:

Amanda Binet, at the Café de la Girafe, before eight o'clock. Claim to be from Genlis, and my mother's cousin.

Julien saw what immense danger he was in; Father Castanède's police had stolen this address from him.

'The day I set foot here', he replied staring at Father Pirard's forehead, for he could not bear his terrible gaze, 'I was in fear and trembling: Father Chélan had told me it was a place full of sneaking and beastliness of all kinds; spying and denunciation among friends are encouraged here. This is the wish of heaven, to show young priests what life is really like, and to fill them with aversion for the world and its pomp.'

'Are you lecturing me!' exclaimed Father Pirard in fury. 'You young scoundrel!'

'In Verrières', Julien went on unmoved, 'my brothers beat me when they had reason to be jealous of me...'

'Come to the point! Come to the point!' shouted Father Pirard, almost beside himself.

Not in the least intimidated, Julien resumed his narrative.

'The day I arrived in Besançon, at about midday, I was hungry and went into a café. My heart was filled with repugnance for such a profane place; but I thought my breakfast would cost me less there than in an inn. A lady who appeared to be the mistress of the establishment took pity on my novice's look. "Besançon is full of good-for-nothings," she said to me, "I'm afraid for you, sir. If you were to land in any trouble, appeal to me, get a message to me before eight o'clock. If the porters at the seminary refuse to run your errand, say you are my cousin and a native of Genlis..."'

'I'll have the truth of all this blarney checked,' exclaimed Father Pirard, who was unable to stand still and was pacing about the room.

'To his cell at once!'

The priest followed Julien and locked him in. The latter at once began going through his trunk, where he kept the fatal card hidden like a treasure at the bottom. Nothing was missing from the trunk, but a number of things had been disturbed; yet the key never left his person. How fortunate, said Julien to himself, that during the time I was blind to the set-up, I never accepted leave to go out, which Father Castanède was always offering me with a kindness I now understand. I might perhaps have been weak enough to change my clothes and go and call on the lovely Amanda; I'd have brought about my own ruin. When they despaired of exploiting the information in this way, then in order not to waste it, they used it as it stands as a means of denouncing me.

Two hours later the master summoned him.

'You were not telling lies,' he said to him with a look that was less severe; 'but keeping an address like that is an act of imprudence of a gravity you cannot conceive. Wretched child! In ten years' time, perhaps, you will suffer for it.'

CHAPTER 27

First experience of life

The present moment, by God! is the ark
of the Lord. Woe betide him who touches it.

DIDEROT*

THE reader will obligingly allow us to give very few clear and
precise facts about this period in Julien's life. Not that they
are lacking, far from it; but what he lives through in the
seminary is perhaps too black for the moderate tones we have
sought to preserve in these pages. One's contemporaries who
undergo certain ordeals cannot recall them without experiencing a horror which paralyses any other pleasure, even that of
reading a story.

Julien had little success with his attempts at hypocrisy in the
matter of gesture; he fell into bouts of repugnance and even of
total demoralization. He wasn't succeeding, and in a lousy
career, what's more. The least little bit of outside help would
have sufficed to restore his morale—the difficulty to be overcome was not that great—but he was alone like a frail craft
abandoned in the middle of the ocean. And even if I did
succeed, he told himself, think of having to spend a lifetime in
such bad company! Gluttons who only think about the bacon
omelette they'll wolf down at dinner, or men like Father
Castanède for whom no crime is too black! They'll rise to
power; but God Almighty, at what price!

The will of man is powerful, I read this everywhere; but is
it sufficient to overcome repugnance like this? The task of
great men has been easy up till now; however terrible the
danger, they saw beauty in it; and who can understand, apart
from me, the ugliness of everything surrounding me?

This was the most taxing moment of his life. It would be so
easy for him to enlist in one of the fine regiments garrisoned in
Besançon! He could become a Latin teacher; he needed so
little to live on! But that would mean goodbye to his career, to

any future for his imagination: it was death. Here is a detailed account of a typical dreary day.

In my presumption I congratulated myself so often on being different from the other young peasants! Well, I've lived long enough to see that *difference breeds hatred*, he said to himself one morning. This great truth had just been brought home to him by one of his most stinging failures. He had worked away for a week at currying favour with a pupil who lived in the odour of sanctity. He had walked round the recreation ground with him, listening submissively to a load of rubbish fit to send anyone to sleep. Suddenly a storm blew up, there was a crash of thunder and the saintly pupil shouted out, pushing Julien rudely away:

'Listen, it's everyone for himself in this world; I don't want to be blasted by thunder: God may strike you down for impiety, like a Voltaire.'

Gritting his teeth in rage and looking wide-eyed at the lightning-rent sky: I'd deserve to go under if I fall asleep during the storm! exclaimed Julien. Let's try and win over another prig.

The bell rang for Father Castanède's Church History class. These young peasants who lived in such fear of the harsh toil and the poverty of their fathers learned that day from Father Castanède that the Government, that most fearsome of creatures in their eyes, only exercised real and legitimate power because this had been delegated to it by God's vicar on earth.

'Make yourselves worthy of the pope's kindnesses by the sanctity of your lives, and by your obedience; be *like a rod in his hands*,' he went on, 'and you will obtain a superb post where you will command like a leader, remote from all interference; a permanent post with a third of the salary paid by the Government and two-thirds by the faithful, who are educated by your preaching.'

At the end of the class Father Castanède stopped in the recreation ground.

'It is indeed appropriate to say of a parsh priest: the worth of the office is no more nor less than that of the holder,' he said to the pupils who were standing in a circle round him. 'I have known, as sure as you see me here, certain mountain parishes where the perks were worth more than those of many a town priest. There was as much money, not to mention fat capons, eggs, fresh butter and countless little luxuries; and in places like that, the priest is incontrovertibly cock of the roost: no one gives a good meal without inviting him, honouring him, etc.'

No sooner had Father Castanède gone up to his room than the pupils split off into groups. Julien was not included in any; he was left out like a black sheep. In every group he saw a pupil toss a coin in the air, and if he guessed right in the game of heads or tails, his fellows concluded that he would soon have one of these parishes rich in perks.

Then came the anecdotes. Such and such a young priest who, after scarcely a year's ordination, had offered a domesticated rabbit to an old priest's housekeeper, had got himself chosen as curate, and only a few months later—for the old priest very soon died—he had taken over his excellent parish for him. Another had succeeded in getting himself appointed successor to the parish in an exceedingly prosperous country town by attending the palsied old priest's every meal, and carving up his chickens for him with style.

The seminarists, like young men in any career, exaggerate the effect of these little ways and means that seem to be magic and catch the imagination.

I must, thought Julien, get the hang of these conversations. When they were not discussing sausages and good parishes, they talked about the worldly side of ecclesiastical doctrines; about rifts between bishops and prefects, mayors and parish priests. Julien saw the idea of a second God appearing, but this was a far more fearsome and more powerful God than the other: this second God was the pope. They said amongst themselves, but in lowered voices, and when they were quite sure of not being overheard by Father Pirard, that if the pope does not go to the trouble of appointing all the prefects and all the mayors in France, this is because he has entrusted this task to the King of France by naming him the Firstborn Son of the Church.

It was about this time that Julien decided there was some advantage to his reputation to be derived from Joseph de

Maistre's book *On the Pope*. He most certainly astonished his fellows; but it was yet another disaster. He aroused their enmity by expounding their own opinions better than they could themselves. Father Chélan had been unwise on Julien's account, just as he was on his own. Having given him the habit of arguing straight and not being taken in by idle words, he had neglected to tell him that in someone who is not highly regarded, this habit is a crime; for all sound arguments cause offence.

Julien's eloquence thus became a fresh crime on his record. By concentrating their thoughts on him, his fellow students came up with a single expression to sum up all the horror he aroused in them: they nicknamed him MARTIN LUTHER; chiefly, they said, on account of that infernal logic of his which makes him so proud.

A number of young seminarists had fresher complexions and could well be considered more handsome than Julien, but he had white hands and could not conceal certain habits of personal cleanliness. This asset did not count as one in the dreary house into which Fate had cast him. The dirty peasants he lived among declared that he had very decadent morals. We are afraid of wearying the reader with an account of our hero's countless misfortunes. For instance, some of the toughest of his fellows tried to adopt the habit of thrashing him; he was obliged to arm himself with an iron compass and announce— by means of signs, though—that he would make use of it. Signs cannot serve to such advantage in a spy's report as words can.

CHAPTER 28

A procession

> Every heart was moved. The presence of
> God seemed to have come down into these
> narrow Gothic streets, bedecked on every
> side and liberally strewn with sand by the
> good offices of the faithful.
>
> YOUNG

IT was no use Julien making himself small and foolish, he could not get anyone to like him, he was too different. And yet, he said to himself, all these teachers are discriminating people chosen from among thousands; how come they don't appreciate my humility? Only one of them seemed to take advantage of his readiness to believe anything and to appear to be completely gullible. This was Father Chas-Bernard, precentor at the cathedral where for the past fifteen years he had been led to expect the office of canon; while waiting, he taught sacred rhetoric at the seminary. During the period before his enlightenment, this was one of the classes where Julien most regularly came top. Father Chas had followed this up with marks of friendship towards him, and at the end of his class he would readily link arms with him to take one or two turns round the garden together.

What's he working round to? Julien wondered. He was amazed to see that Father Chas would spend hours on end talking to him about the cathedral vestments. It possessed seventeen braided chasubles in addition to the mourning vestments. Great hopes were placed on the aged wife of the Président de Rubempré; for over seventy years this ninety-year-old lady had preserved her wedding dresses made of sumptuous fabrics from Lyon interwoven with gold. 'Just imagine, dear fellow,' said Father Chas stopping in his tracks and opening his eyes wide, 'these fabrics stand up by themselves, there's so much gold in them. It's widely believed in Besançon that in her will the président's wife increases the cathedral *treasure* by more than ten chasubles, not to mention four or five capes for high feasts. I'll go further,' added Father Chas lowering his voice, 'I have reason to suppose that the président's wife will leave us eight magnificent torches in silver-gilt that are presumed to have been bought in Italy by the Duke of Burgundy, Charles the Bold, to whom one of her ancestors was favourite minister.'

But what's this man working round to with all this stuff about old clothes? Julien wondered. This skilful preparation has been going on for ages, and nothing is coming of it. He must mistrust me a lot! He's more skilful than all the rest of them—you can guess their secret aims as easily as anything in a couple of weeks. I get it, this fellow's ambition has been suffering for fifteen years!

One evening, in the middle of their instruction on the use of arms,* Julien was summoned to see Father Pirard, who said to him:

'Tomorrow is the feast of Corpus Christi. Father Chas-Bernard needs you to help him adorn the cathedral; go and obey.'

Father Pirard called him back and added with an air of commiseration:

'It's up to you to see if you want to exploit the opportunity to wander off into the town.'

'*Incedo per ignes*,'* Julien replied (I have hidden enemies).

On the following morning, as soon as it was full daylight, Julien made his way to the cathedral with lowered gaze. The sight of the streets and the bustle beginning to take over the town did him some good. On all sides people were adorning the house-fronts for the procession. All the time he had spent at the seminary seemed now like a mere moment to him. His thoughts were on Vergy and on pretty Amanda Binet whom he might well meet, as her café was not far off. He caught sight of Father Chas-Bernard from a distance, standing in the door of his beloved cathedral; he was a portly man with a radiant face and an open expression. That day he was in jubilation: 'I was waiting for you, my dear son,' he exclaimed as soon as he caught sight of Julien, 'I bid you welcome. Today's task will be long and arduous; let us fortify ourselves with a first

breakfast; the second will come at ten o'clock during High
Mass.'

'It is my wish, Father,' Julien said to him gravely, 'not to be
alone for a single instant; may I beg you to note', he went on,
pointing to the clock above their heads, 'that my time of arrival
is one minute to five.'

'Ah! those nasty little wretches in the seminary are making
you afraid! You're a bit silly to think about them,' said Father
Chas. 'Is a path any the less beautiful for having thorns in the
hedges bordering it? Travellers go on their way and leave the
nasty thorns to fester where they are. But anyway, to work,
dear boy, to work.'

Father Chas was right to say the task would be arduous. On
the previous evening there had been a grand funeral ceremony
at the cathedral; no one had been able to prepare anything, so
it was necessary in the space of a single morning to deck all the
gothic pillars which form the three naves with a sort of draping
of red damask rising to a height of thirty feet. The bishop had
had four decorators brought from Paris by mail-coach, but
these gentlemen could not cope with everything, and far from
encouraging their clumsy Besançon workmates, they made
matters worse by laughing at them.

Julien saw he would have to go up the ladder himself, and
his agility served him well. He took upon himself to direct the
efforts of the local decorators. Father Chas watched in delight
as he leaped from ladder to ladder. When all the pillars were
decked in damask, it was a matter of going to position five
enormous bunches of feathers on top of the great canopy above
the high altar. An elaborate centrepiece of gilded wood is
supported by eight spiralling columns in Italian marble. However, to reach the centre of the canopy above the tabernacle,
the only access was along an old wooden ledge possibly riddled
with woodworm and forty feet from the ground.

The sight of this difficult climb had extinguished the Parisian decorators' gaiety which had sparkled so conspicuously till
then; they looked up from below, argued a lot, and did not go
up. Julien seized hold of the bunches of feathers and ran up
the ladder. He positioned them perfectly on top of the crown-
shaped decoration in the centre of the canopy. As he came

down the ladder, Father Chas-Bernard clasped him in his arms:

'*Optime*,' exclaimed the kindly priest, 'I shall tell Monsignor.'

Breakfast at ten was very jolly. Father Chas had never seen his church looking so beautiful.

'Dear disciple,' he said to Julien, 'my mother hired out chairs in this venerable basilica, so I was nurtured in this great edifice. Robespierre's Terror ruined us; but although only eight at the time, I was already serving Masses in private houses, and I was fed on days when Mass was celebrated. No one could fold a chasuble better than I, the braid never got creased. Since Napoleon's reinstatement of religious worship, I have had the good fortune to be in charge of everything in this venerable basilica. Five times a year my eyes behold it bedecked with these lovely adornments. But it has never been so resplendent, never have the widths of damask been so beautifully hung as today, so closely moulded to the pillars.'

At last he's going to tell me his secret, thought Julien, here he is talking to me about himself; he's feeling expansive. But nothing rash was said by this man for all his signs of exaltation. And yet he has worked hard, he's happy, Julien said to himself, there's been no stinting on the good wine. What a man! What an example to me! He gets the gong. (This was a vulgar expression he had picked up from the old surgeon.)

As the *Sanctus* from the High Mass rang out, Julien made as if to put on a surplice to follow the bishop in the magnificent procession.

'What about thieves, dear fellow, what about thieves!' exclaimed Father Chas. 'You're not thinking. The procession is about to go out; the church will be left deserted; we'll watch over it, just the two of us. We'll be very lucky if all that goes missing is a couple of lengths of that fine braid encircling the base of the pillars. That's yet another gift from Mme de Rubempré; it comes from the famous count her great-grandfather; it's pure gold, dear boy,' added the priest into his ear, with an air of obvious excitement, 'nothing is fake! I'm putting you in charge of inspecting the north aisle, don't leave it. I'll do the south aisle and the main nave. Watch out for the confessionals; that's where the thieves plant their ladies to keep an eye open for the moment our backs are turned.'

As he finished speaking, the third quarter after eleven struck, and the great bell at once pealed out. It rang full swing; these solemn, resonant peals moved Julien. His imagination was no longer on earth.

The smell of incense and of the rose leaves scattered in front of the holy sacrament by little children dressed up as St John brought his exaltation to full pitch.

The deep tones of this bell ought not to have aroused in Julien anything other than the thought of twenty men labouring for fifty centimes each, maybe assisted by fifteen or twenty of the faithful. He ought to have been thinking of the wear on the ropes, on the beam, and of the danger from the bell itself, which falls every other century; thinking of ways of reducing the wages of the bellringers, or of paying them with some indulgence or other grace drawn from the Church's treasure trove without shrinking her purse.

Instead of such wise reflections, Julien's soul, uplifted by the great masculine resonance of the pealing bell, had wandered off in flights of fantasy. He will never make a good priest, or a great administrator. Souls which are moved like that are fit at the very most to produce an artist. Here, Julien's presumption breaks forth in its full glory. As many as fifty, maybe, of his fellow seminarists, made attentive to the nitty gritty of life by public hatred and Jacobinism, depicted to them as lying in wait behind every hedge, would only have thought, on hearing the great cathedral bell, of the wages of the ringers. They would have considered with Barême's* genius whether the degree of emotion aroused in the public was worth the money paid to the bellringers. If Julien had wished to think of the material interests of the cathedral, his imagination would have overshot the target, and fixed upon economizing forty francs in manufacturing, thereby missing the opportunity of saving an expenditure of twenty-five centimes.

While the procession moved slowly through Besançon on one of the loveliest days you can imagine, stopping at the resplendent altars of repose* put up by each official body in a

bid to outshine the others, the church remained plunged in
deep silence. It was pleasantly cool in the half-light; the smell
of flowers and incense still lingered there.

The silence, the deep solitude, the cool of the long naves
made Julien's dreaming all the sweeter. He did not fear
disturbance from Father Chas, who was busy in another part
of the church. His soul had almost cut free from its mortal
body, which was walking slowly up and down the north aisle
that had been entrusted to Julien's guard. He was all the more
at ease since he had made sure that the confessionals only
contained a few pious women; his eyes looked without seeing.

However, he was half recalled from his absent state by the
sight of two strikingly well dressed women kneeling down, one
in a confessional, and the other, right next to the first, against
a chair. He looked without seeing; but whether from a vague
sense of duty, or whether out of admiration for the noble and
simple dress of these ladies, he noticed that there was no priest
in the confessional. How odd, he thought, that these beautiful
ladies are not kneeling in front of one of the altars of repose, if
they are pious; or stationed to their advantage in the front row
of a balcony, if they belong to high society. How shapely that
dress is! How graceful! He slackened his pace to get a better
view of them.

The one who was kneeling in the confessional turned her
head a little to one side on hearing the noise of Julien's
footsteps in the depths of this great silence. All of a sudden she
gave a little cry and began to feel faint.

As her strength left her, this lady fell backwards from her
kneeling position; her friend, who was close by, rushed foward
to come to her aid. At the same moment, Julien saw the
shoulders of the lady who was falling backwards. A twisted
necklace of large natural pearls that was very familiar to him
caught his gaze. Imagine his feelings on recognizing the hair:
it was Mme de Rênal! The lady who was trying to support her
friend's head and prevent her from falling right over backwards
was Mme Derville. Julien rushed forward, quite beside himself;
Mme de Rênal's fall might well have brought her friend down
too if Julien had not supported them both. He saw Mme de
Rênal's head, pale and totally inert, lolling on her shoulder.

He helped Mme Derville to rest this charming head against a wicker chair; he was on his knees.

Mme Derville turned round and recognized him.

'Be off with you, sir, be off!' she said to him in tones of the utmost fury. 'It's vital she doesn't see you again. The sight of you must indeed be appalling to her, she was so happy before you came along! Your behaviour is atrocious. Be off with you; go away if you have any shame left.'

These words were spoken with such authority, and Julien felt so weak at that moment, that he did go away. She's always hated me, he said to himself, thinking about Mme Derville.

At the same moment, the nasal chanting of the first priests in the procession echoed round the church; it was coming back in. Father Chas-Bernard called Julien several times without his hearing to begin with: he finally came over, and finding Julien behind a pillar where he had taken refuge more dead than alive, took him by the arm. He wanted to present him to the bishop.

'You're not feeling too good, my boy,' said the priest to him on seeing him so pale and scarcely in a fit state to walk. 'You've been working too hard.' The priest gave him his arm. 'Come along, sit you down on the holy water clerk's little bench behind me; I'll hide you.' They found themselves next to the main door. 'Take it easy, we've a good twenty minutes yet before Monsignor appears. Try to gather your strength together; when he passes, I'll lift you up: I'm strong and sturdy in spite of my age.'

But when the bishop passed by, Julien was trembling so much that Father Chas gave up the idea of presenting him.

'Don't be too upset,' he said to him, 'I'll find another opportunity.'

That evening he arranged for ten pounds of candles to be sent over to the seminary chapel, 'candles that had been thrifted by Julien's care, and the speed with which he had had them extinguished.' Nothing could have been further from the truth. The poor man was totally extinguished himself; he had not had a single idea in his head since seeing Mme de Rênal.

CHAPTER 29

First promotion

He knew his times, he knew his
département, and he is now rich.
THE PRECURSOR*

JULIEN had not yet emerged from the trance-like state into
which he had been plunged by the incident in the cathedral,
when he was summoned one morning by the stern Father
Pirard.

'I have just had a letter from Father Chas-Bernard speaking
well of you. I am reasonably pleased with your behaviour in
general. You are extremely rash and even scatterbrained—
despite appearances; however so far, your heart has been in
the right place, and it's even a generous one; you have a
superior mind. All in all, I detect a spark in you that mustn't
be neglected.

'After fifteen years' toil, I am on the point of leaving this
establishment: my crime is to have let the seminarists go their
own way, and to have neither protected nor worked against
the secret society you spoke to me about in the confessional.
Before leaving, I want to do something for you; I should have
acted two months ago, for you deserve it, had you not been
denounced on account of Amanda Binet's address that was
found in your room. I am making you an instructor for the
New and the Old Testament.'

Overwhelmed with gratitude, Julien did think of flinging
himself to his knees and thanking God; but he yielded to a
more spontaneous impulse. He went up to Father Pirard, took
his hand and raised it to his lips.

'What's all this?' exclaimed the master, looking displeased;
but Julien's eyes spoke even more revealingly than his gesture.

Father Pirard looked at him in astonishment, like a man
who for many a long year has been out of the habit of
encountering delicate emotions. This attention betrayed the
master; his voice altered.

'Well yes, there it is, my boy, I've grown attached to you. Heaven knows that it really is in spite of myself. I should be just, and have neither hatred nor love for anyone. Your career will be difficult. I detect in you something offensive to the vulgar. You will be dogged by jealousy and slander. Wherever Providence may put you, your companions will never see you without hating you; and if they pretend to like you, it will be to betray you all the more surely. There's only one remedy for this: have no recourse to anyone but God, who has made it necessary for you to be hated as a punishment for your presumption; let your conduct be pure; it's the only resource I can see for you. If you hold fast to the truth with an invincible embrace, sooner or later your enemies will be confounded.'

It was so long since Julien had heard a friendly voice that he must be forgiven for an act of weakness: he broke down in tears. Father Pirard held out his arms to him; it was a truly comforting moment for both of them.

Julien was wild with delight; this promotion was the first to come his way; the benefits were immense. To have any conception of them, you have to have been condemned to spend months on end without a moment to yourself, in direct contact with contemporaries who are importunate at the very least and for the most part intolerable. Their shouts alone would have been enough to unsettle a delicate constitution. The rowdy glee of these well-fed, well-dressed peasants was incapable of expressing itself unassisted, and did not consider itself complete unless they were shouting with all the lung-power they could muster.

Now Julien dined alone, or virtually so, an hour later than the other seminarists. He had a key to the garden and could go for walks there at times when it was deserted.

To his great astonishment, Julien observed that the others hated him less; he was expecting, quite on the contrary, that the hatred would increase. His secret desire not to be spoken to, which was only too apparent and won him so many enemies, was no longer a mark of ridiculous disdain. In the eyes of the boorish creatures who surrounded him, it was a rightful sense of his own dignity. The hatred grew noticeably less, especially among his younger fellow seminarists who had become his pupils and were treated by him with considerable courtesy. Gradually he even acquired some supporters; it became bad form to call him Martin Luther.

But what's the point of naming his friends and his enemies! All *that* is sordid, and it's all the more sordid, the more genuine the vocation. Yet men like this are the only moral teachers available to the common people, and how would the latter fare without them? Will newspapers ever succeed in replacing priests?

Since Julien's new promotion, the master of the seminary made a point of never speaking to him without witnesses. This conduct was a measure of prudence for master as well as disciple; but it was above all an *ordeal*. The unvarying principle of the strict Jansenist Pirard was: Is a man worthy in your eyes? Put obstacles in the way of everything he desires, everything he undertakes. If his worth is genuine, he will find the means to overturn or get round the obstacles.

It was the hunting season. Fouqué had the idea of sending a stag and a wild boar on behalf of Julien's family. The dead animals were left in the passage between the kitchen and the refectory. That was where all the seminarists saw them on their way in to dinner. They were an object of great curiosity. For all that it was dead, the boar frightened the younger ones; they fingered its tusks. No one talked of anything else for a week.

This gift, which put Julien's family into the segment of society deserving respect, dealt envy a deadly blow. He was a superior being to whom fortune had given her accolade. Chazel and the most distinguished among the seminarists made overtures to him, and might almost have complained to him that he had not informed them of his family's wealth, and had thus put them at risk of failing to show due respect for money.

The army came round for conscripts; Julien, as a seminarist, was exempt. He was deeply stirred by this incident. So there's an end for ever to the moment when, twenty years ago, a heroic life would have begun for me!

He was walking alone in the seminary garden, and he overhead a conversation between some stonemasons who were working on the boundary wall.

'That's it then, better be off, they're doin' another conscription.'

'*Last* time round, what a doddle! there was masons becomin' officers, becomin' generals, I'm tellin' yer.'

'An' just look at it now! Only beggars goin' off. Anyone with the *means* stays back 'ome.'

'If you're born poor as a church mouse, you stay that way— that's all there is to it.'

'Talkin' of that, is it true what they're sayin', that *he's* dead?' asked a third mason, joining in.

'It's the big 'uns are sayin' that, see! They were right scared of *him*.'

'What a difference; work was work in his day! And to think he was betrayed by his marshals! Talk of traitors!'

This conversation consoled Julien somewhat. As he moved away he repeated to himself with a sigh:

The only king remembered by the crowd!*

The season for examinations came round. Julien answered brilliantly; he observed that Chazel himself was trying to display all his learning.

On the first day, the examiners appointed by the notorious vicar-general de Frilair were exceedingly put out to find themselves constantly having to give first place on their lists, or at the very least second, to this Julien Sorel who had been pointed out to them as the blue-eyed boy of Father Pirard. Bets were laid in the seminary that Julien would be put first on the final ranking list, which carried with it the honour of dining with Monsignor the bishop. But at the end of a session bearing on the Church Fathers, a clever examiner who had questioned Julien on St Jerome and his passion for Cicero moved on to Horace, Virgil and the other profane writers. Unknown to his fellows, Julien had learned off by heart a large number of passages from these authors. Carried away by his success he forgot where he was, and at the examiner's repeated insistence, he recited and paraphrased several of Horace's odes with great ardour. After letting him plait a rope for his own neck for some twenty minutes, the examiner suddenly changed countenance and sourly reproached him for the time he had wasted on these profane studies, and the useless or criminal ideas with which he had filled his head.

'I am a fool, sir, you are quite right,' said Julien with a humble air, recognizing the clever strategy that had trapped him.

The examiner's ploy was considered a dirty trick, even at the seminary, but this did not prevent Father de Frilair—that clever operator who had so skilfully organized the network of the Congregation in Besançon, and whose despatches to Paris struck fear into the hearts of judges, prefect and even the general staff of the garrison—from putting the number 198 in his powerful hand against Julien's name. He was delighted at this chance to mortify his enemy the Jansenist Pirard.

For ten years his overriding concern had been to take the mastership of the seminary from him. Father Pirard, who followed for himself the plan of conduct he had outlined to Julien, was sincere, pious, devoid of intrigue, attached to his duties. But heaven in its wrath had endowed him with a bilious temperament, of the kind that is deeply affected by insults and hatred. None of the slights intended for him were lost on this fiery soul. He would have handed in his resignation time and time again, but he believed himself to be of some use in the post in which Providence had placed him. I am preventing the spread of Jesuitism and idolatry, he told himself.

At the time of the examinations he had not spoken to Julien for as long as two months, and yet he was ill for a week when, on receiving the official letter announcing the ranking in the examination, he saw the number 198 opposite the name of the pupil he regarded as the star of the establishment. The only consolation for this stern character came in concentrating all his means of surveillance on Julien. He was overjoyed to discover in him neither anger, nor plans for revenge, nor loss of morale.

A few weeks later Julien was startled at the sight of a letter he received: it bore a Paris postmark. At last, he thought Mme de Rênal has remembered her promises. A gentleman signing himself Paul Sorel and claiming to be a relative of his was sending him a note of hand worth five hundred francs. The writer added that if Julien continued to study the good Latin authors with the same success, a similar sum would be sent to him every year.

She's done it, it's *her* kindness! thought Julien, overcome with tenderness, she wants to console me; but why isn't there a single word of friendship?

He was wrong about the letter: Mme de Rênal, guided by her friend Mme Derville, was wholly engrossed in her deep remorse. In spite of herself she did often think of the strange being who had come into her life and thrown it into turmoil, but the last thing she would have done was write to him.

If we spoke in the language of the seminary we might recognize a miracle in this sending of five hundred francs to Julien, and say that it was Father de Frilair himself that heaven was using to make this gift to Julien.

Twelve years previously, the Abbé de Frilair had arrived in Besançon with the slimmest of portmanteaux which, according to rumour, contained all this worldly wealth. He was now one of the richest landowners in the département. In the course of this rise to prosperity, he had bought one half of a piece of land, the other portion of which fell by inheritance to M. de La Mole. Hence a great lawsuit between these characters.

In spite of his dazzling existence in Paris and the offices he held at Court, the Marquis de La Mole sensed that it was dangerous to fight a vicar-general in Besançon who had the reputation of making and unmaking prefects. Instead of soliciting a bribe to the tune of fifty thousand francs, disguised under some heading or other allowed by the budget, and conceding to the Abbé de Frilair this paltry lawsuit worth fifty thousand francs, the marquis took umbrage. He believed himself to be in the right—indubitably in the right!

Now if it is permitted to say so: what judge does not have a son or at least a cousin who needs help to get on in the world?

To enlighten those who are really blind, the Abbé de Frilair took Monsignor the bishop's carriage and went in person to give the cross of the Legion of Honour to his barrister. M. de La Mole, somewhat thrown by the posture of his opponent, and sensing that his lawyers were weakening, sought advice from Father Chélan, who put him in touch with Father Pirard.

These contacts had been going on for several years at the

time of our story. Father Pirard threw his passionate character
into this affair. In constant touch with the marquis's lawyers
he studied his case and, finding justice on his side, went about
openly canvassing support for the Marquis de La Mole against
the all-powerful vicar-general. The latter was outraged at the
impertinence of it, and coming from a little Jansenist, what's
more!

'Just take a look at this Court nobility which thinks itself so
powerful!' Father de Frilair would say to his intimate acquaintance. 'M. de La Mole didn't even send a wretched cross to his
agent in Besançon, and he'll let him fall from office just like
that. And yet, so I gather from letters, this noble peer doesn't
let a week pass without going to show off his Blue Sash* in the
Lord Chancellor's salon, whoever he happens to be.'

Despite all Father Pirard's activity, and the fact that M. de
La Mole was always on the best of terms with the Minister of
Justice and more particularly his departments, all that he had
managed to achieve after six years' effort was not losing his
case outright.

In constant correspondence with Father Pirard over a matter
they both pursued with passionate interest, the marquis
eventually came to appreciate the priest's cast of mind. Gradually, despite the great gulf between their social positions,
their correspondence took on a tone of friendship. Father
Pirard told the marquis of the attempts to force him by a
succession of public affronts to resign his position. In his anger
at the infamous strategy, as he saw it, that had been deployed
against Julien, he recounted his story to the marquis.

Although exceedingly rich, this great lord was no miser. Not
once had he been able to get Father Pirard to accept anything,
not even reimbursement of the postal charges incurred for the
lawsuit. He seized upon the idea of sending five hundred francs
to his favourite pupil.

M. de La Mole took the trouble to write the accompanying
letter himself. This made him think of the priest.

One day, the latter received a short note which entreated
him, on a pressing matter, to make his way forthwith to an inn
in the suburbs of Besançon. There he found M. de La Mole's
steward.

'His lordship the marquis has instructed me to bring you his barouche,' the man told him. 'He hopes that having read this letter you will see fit to leave for Paris, in four or five days' time. I shall use such time as you are good enough to specify in visiting his lordship's lands in the Franche-Comté. After which, on the day that suits you, we shall leave for Paris.'

The letter was short:

Rid yourself, my dear sir, of all the tiresome cares of the provinces; come and breathe some calm air, in Paris. I am sending you my carriage, which has orders to await your resolve for four days. I shall await you myself in Paris until Tuesday. All that I need, sir, is for you to say 'yes', and I shall accept in your name one of the best livings in the neighbourhood of Paris. The richest of your future parishioners has never set eyes on you, but is more devoted to you than you can possibly imagine; he is the Marquis de La Mole.

Without realizing it, the stern Father Pirard loved this seminary rife with his enemies, which had been the focus of all his thoughts for the past fifteen years. M. de La Mole's letter was like the appearance of the surgeon called in to perform a cruel and necessary operation. It was certain that he would be dismissed from his office. He arranged to meet the steward three days hence.

For forty-eight hours he was in a fever of uncertainty. Eventually he wrote to M. de La Mole and drafted a letter to Monsignor the bishop, a masterpiece of ecclesiastical prose, if rather lengthy. It would have been difficult to couch it in a more irreproachable style, or one exuding more sincere respect. And yet this letter, intended to give Father de Frilair an uncomfortable hour in the presence of his superior, voiced all the subjects of serious complaint, and went into the instances of sordid petty harassment which, though endured with resignation for six years, were now forcing Father Pirard to leave the diocese.

His firewood was stolen from his woodpile, his dog was poisoned, etc., etc.

Once the letter was finished, he sent someone to wake Julien who, at eight in the evening, was already asleep like all the seminarists.

'You know where the bishop's palace is?' he said to him in stylish Latin. 'Take this letter to Monsignor. I shall not conceal from you that I am sending you in among the wolves. Be all eyes and ears. No lying in your answers; but bear in mind that anyone questioning you might well take genuine delight in being able to do you harm. I am indeed glad, my boy, to give you this experience before leaving you, for I make no secret of it to you: the letter you bear is my resignation.'

Julien stood there motionless, he was fond of Father Pirard. It was to no avail that the voice of prudence said to him: once this upright man has left, the Sacred Heart faction will demote me and maybe even expel me.

He was unable to think of himself. What was bothering him was a sentence he was trying to phrase politely, and he felt genuinely at a loss how to do it.

'What's up, dear fellow, aren't you going?'

'You see, Father,' said Julien timidly, 'I gather that in all your long period of administration, you haven't put any savings by. I've got six hundred francs.'

Tears prevented him from going on.

'*This too will be noted*,' said the ex-master of the seminary coldly. 'Off you go to the bishop's palace, it's getting late.'

Chance had it that Father de Frilair was on duty in the bishop's parlour that evening; Monsignor was dining at the prefecture. So Julien handed the letter to Father de Frilair himself, but without knowing who it was.

Julien was astonished to see this priest boldly opening the letter addressed to the bishop. The handsome face of the vicar-general soon expressed a mixture of surprise and keen pleasure, and became even more grave. While he was reading, Julien, who was struck by his prepossessing countenance, had time to study it. It was a face which would have had more gravity about it, had it not been for the extreme cunning which showed in certain features, and might even have reached the point of signifying untrustworthiness if the owner of this fine face had ceased for an instant to keep it under control. The long projecting nose formed a single, perfectly straight line, and unfortunately gave to what was in other respects a highly distinguished profile the unmistakable likeness of a fox. Be that as it may, this priest who seemed so taken up by Father Pirard's resignation was attired with an elegance that Julien found much to his liking, and had never encountered in a priest before.

Julien only discovered later what Father de Frilair's special talent was. He knew how to amuse his bishop, an amiable old man who was cut out for life in Paris, and viewed Besançon as a place of exile. The bishop had very poor eyesight and passionately loved fish. Father de Frilair took the bones out of the fish served up to Monsignor.

Julien was silently watching the priest rereading the letter of resignation when the door suddenly burst open. A richly dressed footman hurried through; Julien only had time to turn round towards the door; he caught sight of a little old man wearing a pectoral cross. He prostrated himself: the bishop gave him a kindly smile and passed on. The handsome priest followed him, and Julien remained alone in the parlour to admire its pious splendour at his leisure.

The Bishop of Besançon, a man of intelligence who had been sorely tried but not broken by the long hardships of the Emigration,* was over seventy-five and supremely indifferent to what would happen in ten years' time.

'Who is that seminarist with a discerning look in his eye that I think I glimpsed as I passed?' asked the bishop. 'Aren't they all supposed, according to my rule, to be in bed at this hour?'

'This particular one is wide awake, I can promise you, Monsignor, and he brings great news: the resignation of the sole remaining Jansenist in your diocese. The terrible Father Pirard has at last got the message.'

'Has he indeed!' said the bishop with a laugh, 'I defy you to replace him with anyone his equal. And to demonstrate the extent of his worth, I shall invite him to dine with me tomorrow.'

The vicar-general attempted to put in a few words on the choice of a successor. The prelate, disinclined to talk business, said to him:

'Before ushering in the next one, let's find out a bit about how this one comes to be leaving. Send for that seminarist: the truth is found in the mouths of babes.'

Julien was summoned: I'm going to find myself between two inquisitors, he thought. He had never felt braver.

When he entered, two tall valets attired more elegantly than M. Valenod himself were in the process of disrobing Monsignor. The prelate saw fit to question Julien on his studies before getting on to the subject of Father Pirard. He talked a bit about dogma and was astonished. He soon moved on to the humanities, to Virgil, Horace and Cicero. Those names, thought Julien, earned me my 198th place. I've nothing to lose, let's try a brilliant performance. He succeeded; the prelate, himself an excellent humanist, was delighted.

At dinner at the prefecture a young girl of well-deserved reputation had recited her poem about Mary Magdalene.* The bishop was well launched on the subject of literature, and soon forgot Father Pirard and all matters of business in the interests of debating with the seminarist whether Horace was rich or poor. The prelate quoted several odes, but at times his memory was sluggish and Julien immediately recited the whole ode with a demure air; what struck the bishop was that Julien maintained a conversational tone throughout; he uttered his twenty or thirty lines of Latin as if he were talking about what went on in his seminary. They talked at length about Virgil and Cicero. At the end the prelate could not resist complimenting the young seminarist.

'It would be impossible to improve on the education you have received.'

'Monsignor,' said Julien, 'your seminary can offer you a hundred and ninety-seven candidates far less unworthy than myself of your esteemed approbation.'

'How can this be?' asked the prelate, astonished at this figure.

'I can supply official proof to back what I am most humbly claiming in front of Monsignor. In the annual examination at the seminary, when I replied on the very subjects which now earn me Monsignor's approbation, I was put in 198th place.'

'Ah! he's Father Pirard's little blue-eyed boy!' exclaimed the bishop, laughing and turning to Father de Frilair. 'We should have expected as much; but that's fair play. I'm right in thinking, am I not, my boy,' he added turning to Julien, 'that they woke you up to send you here?'

'Yes, Monsignor. I've only ever been out of the seminary once on my own, and that was to go and help Father Chas-Bernard adorn the cathedral on Corpus Christi day.'

'*Optime*,' said the bishop; 'so you were the one who showed such courage in putting the bunches of feathers up on the canopy, were you? They make me tremble every year; I'm always afraid they'll cost me a man's life. My boy, you will go far; but I don't wish to halt your career, which will be a brilliant one, by starving you to death.'

And on the bishop's orders, biscuits were brought in with some Malaga wine; Julien did honour to them, and Father de Frilair even more so, knowing how his bishop loved to see people tucking in with good cheer.

The prelate, feeling more and more pleased with the way his evening was ending, spoke for a moment on ecclesiastical history. He noted a complete lack of understanding in Julien. The prelate moved on to the moral state of the Roman Empire under the emperors in Constantine's century. The end of paganism was accompanied by the same state of anxiety and doubt which afflicts gloomy and bored minds in the nineteenth century. Monsignor observed that Julien had scarcely even heard of Tacitus.

Julien replied candidly, much to the prelate's astonishment, that this author was not to be found in the library at the seminary.

'I am highly delighted,' said the bishop gaily. 'This gets me out of a spot: for the past ten minutes I've been trying to think of a way to thank you for the agreeable evening you have procured me, and most unexpectedly, I'm sure. I was not expecting to find a learned doctor in one of the pupils at my seminary. Even though the gift may not be all that canonical, I wish to give you a set of Tacitus.'

The prelate had eight superbly bound volumes brought to him, and insisted on inscribing the title-page of the first one in his own hand with a compliment in Latin for Julien Sorel. The bishop prided himself on his fine Latin; his last words to him were spoken in a serious tone which marked a complete contrast with the rest of the conversation:

'Young man, *if you behave well*, one day you will have the best living in my diocese, and not a hundred leagues from my bishop's palace either; but you must *behave well*.'

Weighed down with his books, Julien left the bishop's palace in great astonishment as midnight was striking.

Monsignor had not said a word to him about Father Pirard. Julien was particularly astonished at the extreme civility of the bishop. He could not conceive of such urbanity of manner allied with so natural an air of dignity. Julien was particularly struck by the contrast when he saw the sombre Father Pirard again, waiting impatiently for him.

'*Quid tibi dixerunt?*' (What did they say to you?) he bellowed out at him, as soon as he caught sight of him.

When Julien stumbled a little over translating into Latin what the bishop had said:

'Speak in your own tongue, and repeat Monsignor's exact words, without adding or suppressing anything,' said the ex-master of the seminary with his harsh voice and his profoundly inelegant manners.

'What a strange present from a bishop to a young seminarist!' he said as he leafed through the splendid Tacitus, seemingly appalled by the gold leaf.

Two o'clock was striking when, after a fully detailed account, he allowed his favourite pupil to go back to his room.

'Leave me the first volume of your Tacitus with Monsignor the bishop's flattering dedication,' he said to him. 'That line of Latin will act as your lightning-conductor in this house after I am gone. *Erit tibi, fili mi, successor meus tamquam leo quærens quem devoret.* (For to you, my son, my successor will be as a roaring lion, seeking whom he may devour.)

The following morning Julien found something odd about the way his companions spoke to him. It made him all the more reserved. So this is the effect of Father Pirard's resignation. The whole establishment knows about it, and I'm thought of as his favourite. There must be an element of insult in this way of behaving; but he was unable to detect it. On the contrary, there was an absence of hatred in the eyes of everyone he encountered going through the dormitories: What does this mean? It must be a trap, let's play things carefully. Eventually the little seminarist from Verrières said to him with a laugh: *Cornelii Taciti opera omnia* (the complete works of Tacitus).

At these words, which were overheard, it seemed as if they were all trying to outdo one another in their compliments to Julien—not only on the magnificent present he had received from Monsignor, but also on the two-hour long conversation with which he had been honoured. They knew everything, right down to the smallest details. From that moment on, there was no more envy; they curried servile favour with him: Father Castanède, who only the previous day had been the ultimate in rudeness to him, came up to him and took him by the arm to invite him to lunch.

Through a fatal flaw in Julien's character, the insolence of these boorish creatures had hurt him deeply; their servility revolted him and gave him no pleasure.

About midday, Father Pirard said farewell to his pupils, making a point of delivering a stern speech to them. 'Do you want worldly honours', he said to them, 'and every kind of social advantage, the pleasure of commanding others, of holding the law in contempt, and of getting away with being insolent to everyone? Or do you want your eternal salvation? The least alert among you have only to open your eyes to tell these two paths apart.'

No sooner had he left than the devout followers of the Sacred Heart of Jesus* went off to the chapel to strike up a *Te Deum*. No one in the seminary took the ex-master's speech seriously. 'He's very miffed at being dismissed,' was the comment in all quarters; not a single seminarist was simpleminded enough to believe that anyone could voluntarily renounce a post which offered so many contacts with big suppliers.

Father Pirard went and installed himself in the finest inn in Besançon; and purporting to have some (non-existent) business to attend to, he determined to spend two days there.

The bishop had invited him to dine; and to tease his vicargeneral de Frilair, he was trying to show him off to his best advantage. They were in the middle of the sweet course when the strange news arrived from Paris that Father Pirard had been appointed to the magnificent living at N——, four leagues from the capital. The good prelate offered him his sincere congratulations. He detected in this whole affair a *well-played trick* which put him in excellent humour and gave him the highest opinion of the priest's talents. He gave him a magnificent certificate in Latin, and reduced the Abbé de Frilair to silence when he took the liberty of remonstrating with him.

In the evening, Monsignor went to impart his admiration to the Marquise de Rubempré's salon. It was tremendous news for Besançon high society; everyone was lost in conjecture about this extraordinary favour. They pictured Father Pirard as a bishop already. Those with most discernment thought M.de La Mole had become a minister, and they took the liberty that day of smiling at the imperious airs which the Abbé de Frilair gave himself in society.

On the following morning Father Pirard was almost followed about the streets, and shopkeepers came to their doorsteps when he went to canvass the magistrates instructed with the marquis's case. For the first time ever he was given a civil reception. Outraged by everything he saw, the stern Jansenist worked a long stint with the barristers he had chosen for the Marquis de La Mole, and he then left for Paris. He was self-indulgent enough to tell two or three college friends who accompanied him to the barouche and much admired its coat-of-arms that, having administered the seminary for fifteen years, he was leaving Besançon with five hundred and twenty francs in savings. These friends embraced him with tears, and said amongst themselves: 'Dear Father Pirard might have spared himself this lie, it makes him look just too ridiculous.'

Blinded by the love of money, the common herd was not capable of understanding that Father Pirard's sincerity was the source of the energy he had needed to battle on alone for six years against Marie Alacoque,* the Sacred Heart of Jesus, the Jesuits and his bishop.

CHAPTER 30

A man of ambition

There is only one form of nobility: the title
of *duke; marquis* is ridiculous, the word
duke makes people look round.

EDINBURGH REVIEW

THE Marquis de La Mole welcomed Father Pirard without any of the mannerisms of a great lord—so polite and yet so insulting to anyone who sees them for what they are. It would have been a waste of time, and the marquis was sufficiently engrossed in important affairs to have no time to lose.

For the past six months he had been involved in an intrigue to get the king and the nation to accept the choice of a particular Cabinet,* which would, as a sign of gratitude, make him a duke.

The marquis had been asking his lawyer in Besançon in vain over the years for a clear and succinct statement about his lawsuits in the Franche-Comté. How could the famous barrister have explained them to him when he didn't understand them himself?

The little square of paper handed to him by the priest explained everything.

'My dear Father Pirard,' said the marquis when he had despatched in less than five minutes all the customary expressions of politeness and concern about personal matters, 'my dear Father Pirard, in the midst of all my supposed wealth, I have no time to pay serious attention to two small concerns that are actually pretty important; my family and my affairs. I take care of the fortune of my noble house on a broad front, and I am in a position to advance it considerably; I take care of my pleasures, and that's what comes before all else, at least in my eyes,' he added, on surprising a look of astonishment in those of Father Pirard. Although himself familiar with the ways of the world, the priest was filled with wonder at hearing an old man speak so frankly of his pleasures.

'You can of course get people to work for you in Paris,'

continued the great lord, 'but you find them tucked away up on the fifth floor, and as soon as I approach a man, he sets himself up with a flat on the second floor and his wife sets herself up with a day to be "at home"; as a result, no more work, no more effort except what goes into being or seeming to be a man of high society. That's all they think about as soon as they get enough to eat.

'When it comes to my lawsuits specifically, and what's more—to each case taken separately—I have lawyers killing themselves; why, one of them died on me from a bad chest only the day before yesterday. But when it comes to my affairs in general, would you believe it, sir? for three years now I've given up all hope of finding a man who, while writing on my behalf, will deign to give any serious thought to what he's doing. But anyway, all this is merely by way of a preface.

'I respect you, and I would even make so bold as to add, although this is the first time I've set eyes on you, that I like you. Are you willing to be my secretary, with a salary of eight thousand francs a year, or even twice that much? I should still be the gainer out of it, take my word for it; and I'll make it my business to reserve your fine living for you, for the day when we no longer suit each other.'

The priest refused; but towards the end of the conversation, the genuine plight in which he saw the marquis suggested an idea to him.

'I've left behind in the depths of my seminary a poor young man who, if I'm not mistaken, is going to come in for some nasty persecution there. If he were just a simple monk, he would already be *in pace**.

'Up until now, all that this young man has been acquainted with is Latin and the Holy Scriptures; but it's not impossible that one day he may manifest great talents either for preaching or for the care of souls. I do not know what he will do, but he has the sacred fire within him, and he's capable of going far. I was counting on handing him over to our bishop, if ever one had come our way who had something of your attitude towards men and their affairs.'

'What are your young man's origins?' asked the marquis.

'He is said to be the son of carpenter from the mountains

round our way, but I'm more inclined to believe that he's the illegitimate son of some wealthy man. I observed that he received an anonymous or pseudonymous letter with a note of hand worth five hundred francs.'

'Ah! you mean Julien Sorel,' said the marquis.

'How do you come to know his name?' asked the priest in astonishment; and as he blushed at his question,

'That I shan't tell you,' replied the marquis.

'Well now!' went on the priest, 'you could try making him your secretary, he has energy and understanding; in short, it's worth a try.'

'Why not?' said the marquis; 'But would he be the sort to let the chief of police or anyone else slip him a bribe to spy on my household? That's my only reservation.'

Favourably reassured by Father Pirard, the marquis took a thousand-franc note:

'Send this to Julien Sorel for his journey; arrange for him to be brought to me.'

'It's obvious', said Father Pirard, 'that you live in Paris. You are unfamiliar with the tyranny which oppresses us poor provincials, especially priests who are no friends of the Jesuits. They won't let Julien Sorel leave, they'll manage to cover themselves with the cleverest of excuses, they'll say in their reply to me that he's ill, that the post must have lost the letters, etc., etc.'

'I shall convey a letter from the minister to the bishop one day soon,' said the marquis.

'There's a precaution I was forgetting,' said the priest: 'although of very lowly birth, this young man has a noble heart; he'll be of no use if his pride is ruffled; you would turn him into an idiot.'

'I like the sound of that,' said the marquis. 'I'll make him my son's companion, will that do?'

Some time after this, Julien received a letter in an unknown hand bearing a Châlons postmark; in it he found a warrant payable through a merchant in Besançon, and instructions to go to Paris without delay. The letter was signed with an invented name, but on opening it Julien had started: a leaf had fallen to the ground at his feet; this was the sign he had agreed on with Father Pirard.

Less than an hour later, Julien was summoned to the bishop's palace, where he was received with thoroughly paternal kindness. While quoting Horace, Monsignor complimented him very skilfully on the lofty destiny awaiting him in Paris, in such a way as to invite an explanation from him by way of thanks. Julien was unable to say anything, primarily because he knew nothing, and Monsignor conceived a great esteem for him. One of the minor palace priests wrote to the mayor who hastened to come in person with a signed passport which had the bearer's name left blank.

That evening before midnight Julien was at his friend Fouqué's house; the latter's prudence was more surprised than enchanted by the future that seemed to await his friend.

'What you'll end up with', said this liberal voter, 'is a governmental post that'll force you into some action which will be decried in the newspapers. Your shame will be the way I get news of you. Remember that even financially speaking, it's better to earn a hundred louis in a good timber-yard belonging to you than to receive four thousand francs from any government, even King Solomon's.'

Julien did not see anything in all this beyond the petty-mindedness characteristic of the rural middle class. He was at last about to appear on the stage of great events. Delight at going to Paris, which he imagined stocked with clever people—adroit schemers and hypocrites, but as civil as the Bishop of Besançon and the Bishop of Agde—eclipsed everything else for him. He made out to his friend that Father Pirard's letter deprived him of his free will.

At about noon on the next day he arrived in Verrières, the happiest of men; he was counting on seeing Mme de Rênal again. He went first of all to call on his first patron, the kindly Father Chélan. He met with a stern reception.

'Do you feel under any obligation to me?' asked Father Chélan without replying to his greeting. 'You're going to have lunch with me, meanwhile someone will go and hire another horse for you, and you will leave Verrières *without seeing anybody here*.'

'To hear is to obey,' replied Julien with his best seminary face; and the remainder of the time was spent on theology and fine Latin scholarship.

He mounted his horse, rode a league, after which, on spying a wood and no one to see him enter, he plunged into it. At sundown he sent the horse away. Later, he went into a peasant's dwelling, and the man agreed to sell him a ladder and to follow him with it as far as the Avenue de la Fidélité in Verrières.

'It's a poor draft evader I've been following... or a smuggler,' said the peasant as he took leave of him, 'but what of it! my ladder's fetched a good price, and it's not as though I hadn't had a few ups and downs in my life too.'

The night was exceedingly dark. As one o'clock approached, Julien walked into Verrières weighed down by his ladder. He climbed down as soon as he could into the bed of the stream which runs through M. de Rênal's magnificent gardens at a depth of ten feet, in a passage between two walls. Julien easily climbed over with the ladder. How will the guard dogs greet me? he wondered. That's the big question. The dogs barked and raced towards him; but he whistled softly and they came and fawned all over him.

Then he went up through the terraces one after the other although all the gates were locked, and it was easy for him to get himself right under the window of Mme de Rênal's bedroom which, on the garden side, is only nine or ten feet above the ground.

There was a little heart-shaped opening in the shutters which Julien knew well. To his great sorrow, this little opening was not lit from inside by a nightlight.

'Oh my God!' he said to himself, 'Mme de Rênal isn't in this room tonight! Where on earth will she be sleeping? The family is in Verrières, because I met the dogs; but I may encounter M. de Rênal himself or some stranger in this room with no light, and then what a scandal!'

The wisest thing was to retreat; but this course of action filled Julien with horror. If it's a stranger, I'll run hell for leather, leaving my ladder behind; but if it's her, what reception will I get? She has fallen into repentance and the most extreme piety, without any conceivable doubt; but then, she still has some memory of me since she has just written to me. This consideration decided him.

Trembling at heart, yet resolved to see her or perish in the attempt, he flung some pebbles against the shutter; no answer. He leaned his ladder up next to the window and knocked on the shutter himself, gently at first, then more loudly. However dark it is, someone could still fire a shot at me, thought Julien. This idea reduced the mad enterprise to a question of bravery.

This room is unoccupied tonight, he thought, or else whoever's sleeping there must be awake by now. So there's no need to take any more precautions on that account; the only thing I must try to avoid is being heard by the people sleeping in the other rooms.

He climbed down, positioned his ladder against one of the shutters, climbed back up again and, passing his hand through the heart-shaped opening, was very soon fortunate enough to find the wire that was fixed to the fastening which held the shutter to. He pulled on this wire; he felt with a surge of unutterable joy that the shutter was no longer fast and was yielding to his pull. I must open it little by little, and let my voice be recognized. He opened the shutter enough to pass his head inside, repeating softly as he did so: '*It's a friend.*'

He reassured himself by careful listening that nothing was disturbing the deep silence in the room. But there most certainly wasn't a nightlight in the fireplace, even half burnt-out; it was a very bad sign.

Watch out for a shot! He paused to reflect; then he braved himself to knock at the window-pane with one knuckle: no answer; he knocked more loudly. Even if I have to smash the pane, I must carry this through. In the midst of his loud knocking, he thought he glimpsed in the depths of the pitch darkness something like a white shadow crossing the room. At last there was no doubting it, he saw a shadow which seemed to be advancing extremely slowly. Suddenly he saw a cheek pressed against the glass where his eye was.

He jumped and withdrew a little. But the night was so black that even at that distance he was unable to tell whether it was Mme de Rênal. He feared a first cry of alarm; he could hear the dogs prowling and half-snarling round the foot of his ladder. 'It's me,' he repeated quite loudly, 'a friend.' No answer; the white phantom had disappeared. 'I beg you to open the window for me; I must speak to you, I'm so unhappy!' And he knocked away as if he would smash the glass.

There was a faint grating sound; the fastening on the casement window was yielding; he pushed one half in and jumped lightly into the room.

The white phantom was receding; he took it by the arms; it was a woman. All his thoughts of courage vanished. If it's her, what's she going to say? Imagine his reaction when he realized from her little cry that it was Mme de Rênal!

He clasped her in his arms; she was trembling, and scarcely had the strength to push him away.

'You wretch! What are you doing?'

Only with great difficulty could her strangled voice get these words out. Julien detected genuine indignation in it.

'I've come to see you after fourteen months of the most cruel separation.'

'Get out! Leave me this instant. Ah! Father Chélan, why did you prevent me from writing to him? I should have forestalled this outrage.' She pushed him away with quite extraordinary force. 'I repent my crime; heaven has deigned to enlighten me,' she repeated in a broken voice. 'Get out! Be off with you!'

'After fourteen months of unhappiness, I shall certainly not leave you without talking to you. I want to know everything you've done. Ah! I've loved you enough to deserve a frank account... I want to know everything.'

In spite of herself, Mme de Rênal found her heart swayed by this tone of authority.

Julien, who was holding her in a passionate embrace and resisting her attempts to break free, stopped clasping her in his arms. This movement reassured Mme de Rênal somewhat.

'I'm going to pull in the ladder', he said, 'so it doesn't compromise us if some servant or other is roused by the noise and goes on a tour of inspection.'

'No! Get out! On the contrary, you get out of here!' came the genuinely furious reply. 'What do I care about other people? It's God who sees the frightful scene you're making, and he'll punish me for it. You're taking cowardly advantage of the feelings I once had for you, but don't have any more. Do you understand, Mr Julien?'

He was bringing in the ladder very slowly so as not to make any noise.

'Is your husband in town, my love?' he said to her tenderly, not in order to defy her, but carried away by old habits.

'Don't speak to me like that, I implore you, or I'll call my husband. I'm guilty enough as it is for not having sent you away, whatever the consequences. I pity you,' she said to him, trying to wound his pride, which she knew to be so touchy.

This refusal to use terms of affection, this brusque way of breaking so tender a bond, which he was still taking for granted, brought Julien's love to a pitch of fervour.

'What! is it possible that you don't love me any more!' he said to her with one of those cries from the heart that are so difficult to listen to unmoved.

She did not answer; as for him, he wept bitterly.

In all honesty he did not have any strength left to speak.

'So I'm completely abandoned by the only being who has ever loved me! What's the point of going on living now?' All his courage had ebbed away as soon as he did not have to fear the danger of confronting a man; everything had vanished from his heart except love.

He wept for a long time in silence. He took her hand, she tried to withdraw it; yet after one or two almost convulsive attempts, she abandoned it to him. It was pitch dark; they both found themselves sitting on Mme de Rênal's bed.

What a change from how things were fourteen months ago! thought Julien; and his tears welled up all the more. So absence is quite sure to destroy all human feelings!

At last, embarrassed at his silence, Julien said in a voice choked with tears: 'Be so good as to tell me what has been happening to you.'

'No doubt', replied Mme de Rênal in a hard voice which sounded somehow curt and reproachful towards Julien, 'my misdemeanours were known throughout the town at the point when you left. There had been so much recklessness in your actions! Some while later—I was in despair at the time—our esteemed Father Chélan came to see me. He tried for ages in vain to get me to confess. One day, he had the idea of taking me to the church in Dijon where I made my first communion. There, he was bold enough to broach the subject himself...' Mme de Rênal broke off in tears. 'What a moment of shame! I confessed everything. That kindly man was good enough not to crush me under the weight of his indignation: he shared my affliction. At that time I was writing letters to you every day which I didn't dare send; I used to hide them away carefully, and when I was too unhappy I shut myself up in my room and reread my letters.

'Finally Father Chélan got me to agree to give them to him... Some of the more guardedly written ones had been sent off to you; you didn't answer.'

'I swear to you, my love, that I never received a single letter from you at the seminary.'

'Good God! who can have intercepted them?'

'Just think what my sorrow was like: up until the day I saw you in the cathedral I didn't know if you were still alive.'

'God granted me the grace to understand how deeply I was sinning against him, against my children, against my husband,' Mme de Rênal went on. 'He has never loved me the way I used to believe that you loved me...'

Julien flung himself into her arms, quite genuinely with nothing in mind, just beside himself with love. But Mme de Rênal pushed him away and went on with some determination:

'My esteemed friend Father Chélan gave me to understand that in marrying M. de Rênal, I had pledged him all my affections, even feelings I was ignorant of and had never experienced before our ill-omened affair... Since the great sacrifice of handing over those letters which were so dear to me, my life has flowed on if not happily, then at least reasonably peacefully. Don't throw it into turmoil; be a friend to me... my best friend.' Julien smothered her hands in kisses; she could feel that he was still in tears. 'Don't cry, I feel so sorry for you... It's your turn to tell me what you've been doing.' Julien was unable to speak. 'I want to know what sort of life you lead at the seminary,' she repeated, 'and then you'll have to go.'

Without thinking about what he was saying, Julien spoke about all the intrigues and countless manifestations of jealousy he had encountered at first, and then of the more peaceful life he had led since being appointed an instructor.

'It was at that point', he added, 'that after a long period of silence doubtless intended to impart to me what I can see only too clearly now, that you no longer loved me or cared in the least about me...'. Mme de Rênal squeezed his hands. '—it was at that point that you sent me the sum of five hundred francs.'

'I never did any such thing,' said Mme de Rênal.

'It was a letter postmarked Paris and signed Paul Sorel, to allay any suspicions.'

A short discussion arose on the possible source of this letter. Their psychological stance changed. Without realizing it, Mme de Rênal and Julien had abandoned their tone of formality; they had reverted to one of tender friendship. It was so dark they could not see each other, but there was something in their voices which gave everything away. Julien slipped his arm round her waist; it was a very risky gesture to make. She tried to shift his arm, but he rather cleverly caught her attention at that very moment with an interesting element in his story. The arm was somehow forgotten and remained where it was.

After a good many conjectures about the source of the letter with five hundred francs in it, Julien had taken up his story again; he was more in control of himself now that he was talking about his past life, which interested him very little in comparison with what was happening to him at that moment. His attention focused entirely on the way in which his visit was going to end. 'You'll have to leave,' a brisk voice still kept on telling him at intervals.

What a disgrace for me if I'm shown out! I'll feel so mortified it'll poison my whole life, he said to himself, she'll never write to me. God knows when I'll ever come back to this part of the world! From that moment on, everything blissful in Julien's situation rapidly faded from his heart. Sitting beside a woman he adored, virtually clasping her in his arms, in the very room where he had been so happy, in the midst of total darkness, perceiving very clearly that for some time now she had been crying, feeling from the heaving of her breast that she was indeed sobbing, he had the misfortune to become a cold schemer, almost as calculating and cold as when, in the recreation ground of the seminary, he found himself the victim of some nasty joke from a fellow seminarist who was tougher than he was. Julien spun out his story, and told of the unhappy life he had led since leaving Verrières. So, said Mme de Rênal to herself—after a year's absence, when he was almost entirely deprived of anything tangible to foster memories, while here I was forgetting him, he only had thoughts for the happy days he had spent at Vergy. Her sobs grew more violent. Julien saw how well his story had worked. He realized he had to try his last resort: he moved abruptly to the letter he had just received from Paris.

'I've taken my leave of Monsignor the bishop.'

'What! you're not going back to Besançon! Are you leaving us for ever?'

'Yes,' said Julien resolutely; 'Yes, I'm leaving a place where I'm forgotten even by the one I've loved most dearly in my life, and I'm leaving it never to set eyes on it again. I'm going to Paris...'

'You're going to Paris, my love!' came Mme de Rênal's more than audible cry.

Her voice was almost choked with tears and revealed her overwhelming emotion. Julien needed this encouragement: he was about to try a move which might settle everything against him; and before this outburst, since he couldn't see a thing, he was totally unaware of the effect he was succeeding in producing. He hesitated no longer; fear of regretting his conduct later gave him perfect self-control; he added coldly as he got up:

'Yes, madam, I am leaving you for ever, I wish you happiness; farewell.'

He walked a few steps towards the window; he was already in the process of opening it. Mme de Rênal sprang after him and flung herself into his arms.

And so it was that after three hours of dialogue Julien obtained what he had so passionately desired for the first two. Had it come a little sooner, this return to tender feelings, this total eclipse of Mme de Rênal's remorse, would have given truly divine happiness; being thus obtained by skill, they afforded no more than mere pleasure. In spite of his mistress's entreaties, Julien insisted on lighting the nightlight.

'Do you want me to be without any memory of having seen you?' he said to her. 'Shall the love that I don't doubt is shining in those enchanting eyes of yours then be lost on me? Shall the whiteness of this pretty hand then be invisible to me? Just think, I'm leaving you for a very long time maybe!'

Mme de Rênal was unable to refuse anything when faced with this thought which reduced her to tears. But dawn was beginning to sketch in the sharp outlines of the fir trees on the mountain slope to the east of Verrières. Instead of leaving, Julien, intoxicated with the sweetness of love, asked Mme de Rênal if he might spend the whole day hidden in her room and only set off the following night.

'Why not?' she replied. 'This fatal relapse takes away all my self-respect and brings about my eternal misfortune.' And she clasped him to her heart. 'My husband is a changed man, he has his suspicions; he thinks I've been taking him in over this whole business, and he's behaving with great resentment towards me. If he hears the slightest noise, that's the end of me, he'll turn me out of the house like the wretch I am.'

'Ah! that's one of Father Chélan's expressions,' said Julien. 'You wouldn't have spoken to me like that before my cruel departure for the seminary; you loved me then!'

Julien was rewarded for the detachment with which he had uttered these words: he saw his beloved quick to forget the danger she was in from the presence of her husband and become mindful of the far greater danger of seeing Julien doubt her love. The daylight was fast growing brighter and the room was clearly lit; Julien rediscovered all the sweet satisfactions of pride when he was able to see so charming a woman in his arms again, and almost at his feet—the only one he had ever loved, and one who, only a few hours previously, had been totally overwhelmed by the fear of a terrible God and by devotion to her duties. Resolutions fortified by a year of constancy had not been able to withstand his courage.

Soon they heard stirrings in the house; something she had not thought of brought a sudden worry to Mme de Rênal.

'That beastly Elisa is going to come into the room, what's to

be done with this enormous ladder?' she asked her lover;
'where are we to hide it? I'm going to take it up to the attic,'
she exclaimed all of a sudden somewhat playfully.

'But you have to go through the manservant's room,' said
Julien in astonishment.

'I'll leave the ladder in the corridor, I'll call the servant and
send him off on an errand.'

'Make sure you think up something to say in case the servant
notices the ladder in the corridor as he goes past.'

'Yes, my angel,' said Mme de Rênal, giving him a kiss. 'And
you make sure you hide under the bed pretty quick if Elisa
comes in here while I'm gone.'

Julien was astonished at this sudden gaiety. So, he thought,
when some material danger is at hand, far from worrying her,
it restores her gaiety because she forgets her remorse! What a
truly superior woman! Ah! there's a heart where it's glorious
to reign! Julien was delighted.

Mme de Rênal took hold of the ladder; it was clearly too
heavy for her. Julien was making his way over to help her,
admiring her elegant figure which proclaimed the very opposite
of strength, when suddenly, without any assistance, she seized
the ladder and removed it as she might have done a chair. She
carried it rapidly to the corridor on the third floor, where she
laid it on its side along the wall. She called the servant, and to
give him time to get dressed, she went up to the dovecot. Five
minutes later when she returned to the corridor she found no
ladder there. What had happened to it? If Julien had been
outside the house, this danger would scarcely have bothered
her. But as things stood, what if her husband were to see the
ladder! It could be dreadful. Mme de Rênal ran all over the
place. At length she discovered the ladder under the eaves
where the servant had taken and even hidden it. This circumstance was most odd; it would have alarmed her before.

What do I care, she thought, what happens in a twenty-four
hours' time when Julien has gone? Won't everything then be
sheer horror and remorse for me?

She had a sort of vague feeling that she would have to end
her life, but what of it? After what she had taken to be an
eternal separation, he had been restored to her, she was with

him again, and what he had done in order to reach her showed such love!

As she recounted the incident of the ladder to Julien:

'What shall I reply to my husband', she said to him, 'if the servant tells him he's found this ladder?' She mused for a moment. 'It'll take them twenty-four hours to track down the peasant who sold it to you.' And flinging herself into Julien's arms and clasping him in a convulsive embrace: 'Ah! to die, to die like this!' she cried, smothering him with kisses; 'but you mustn't die of hunger,' she said laughing.

'Come on; the first thing is for me to hide you in Mme Derville's room, which is always kept locked.' She went and stood guard at the far end of the corridor, and Julien ran across.

'Be careful not to open if anyone knocks,' she said to him as she locked him in; 'in any case, it would only be the children in jest while they are playing together.'

'Bring them out into the garden, beneath this window,' said Julien, 'so I can have the pleasure of seeing them; make them talk.'

'Yes, yes,' Mme de Rênal called out to him as she went away.

She soon returned with some oranges, some biscuits and a bottle of Malaga wine; it hadn't been possible for her to steal any bread.

'What's your husband doing?' asked Julien.

'He's drawing up deals with peasants.'

But eight o'clock had struck, and there was noise coming from all over the house. If no one had seen Mme de Rênal, they would have looked for her everywhere; she was obliged to leave him. She was soon back, flying in the face of caution, to bring him a cup of coffee; she was in fear and trembling lest he die of hunger. After lunch she managed to bring the children underneath the window of Mme Derville's bedroom. He found them much grown, but they had taken on a common air, or else his ideas had changed.

Mme de Rênal talked to them about Julien. The eldest responded warmly and regretted his old tutor; but it appeared that the younger ones had almost forgotten him.

M. de Rênal did not go out that morning; he was constantly going up and down stairs all over the house, busily transacting deals with peasants to whom he was selling his potato crop. Right up until dinner time Mme de Rênal did not have a moment to spare for her prisoner. Once dinner was announced and served, she took it into her head to make off with a plate of hot soup for him. As she was silently approaching the door of the room he was in, carrying this plate with great care, she found herself face to face with the servant who had hidden the ladder that morning. At this moment, he too was moving silently along the corridor as if listening. Julien had probably been walking about unguardedly. The servant went off in some embarrassment. Mme de Rênal went boldly into Julien's room; seeing her made him tremble.

'You're afraid,' she said to him; 'I'm ready to brave all the dangers in the world without turning a hair. There's only one thing I fear, it's the moment when I'm alone after you've gone.' And she ran off again.

'Ah!' said Julien to himself in a state of exaltation, 'remorse is the only danger dreaded by this sublime being!'

At last evening came round. M. de Rênal went to the Casino. His wife had declared she had a frightful migraine; she withdrew to her room, hastened to dismiss Elisa, and rapidly got up again to go and let Julien in.

It appeared that he was genuinely starving. Mme de Rênal went to the larder to fetch some bread. Julien heard a loud cry. Mme de Rênal returned and told him how when she had gone into the unlit larder, made her way over to a dresser where the bread was stored, and stretched out her hand, she had touched a woman's arm. It was Elisa who had let out the cry that Julien had heard.

'What was she doing there?'

'Stealing a few sweetmeats, or else spying on us,' said Mme de Rênal with total indifference. 'But luckily I found a dish of pâté and a large loaf.'

'What's that in there, then?' asked Julien, pointing to the pockets of her apron.

Mme de Rênal had forgotten that since dinner they had been full of bread.

Julien clasped her in his arms with the most intense passion; she had never seemed so beautiful to him. Even in Paris, the thought ran obscurely through his mind, I'll never manage to meet such a noble character. She had all the awkwardness of a woman unaccustomed to ministrations of this sort, and at the same time the real courage of someone who only fears dangers of another order, ones that strike an altogether different kind of terror.

While Julien was eating supper with a hearty appetite, and his beloved was teasing him about the frugality of the meal, for she could not bear to talk seriously, the door of the room was suddenly rattled with great force. It was M. de Rênal.

'Why have you locked yourself in?' he shouted to her.

Julien only just had time to slip under the sofa.

'What! you're fully dressed, dear!' said M. de Rênal as he came in; 'you're having some supper, and you've locked your door!'

On any ordinary day this question, uttered in the most formal of conjugal tones, would have alarmed Mᵐᵉ de Rênal, but she sensed that her husband only had to bend down a little to catch sight of Julien; for M. de Rênal had flung himself onto the chair where Julien had been sitting only a moment ago opposite the sofa.

The migraine served as an excuse for everything. While her husband in his turn was giving her a lengthy blow-by-blow account of the pool he had won at billiards in the Casino—'a pool of nineteen francs 'pon my word', he added—she caught sight of Julien's hat, there on a chair right in front of them. Her nerve strengthened, she began to undress and, at a certain moment, moving swiftly behind her husband, she flung a dress over the chair with the hat on it.

At last M. de Rênal left. She begged Julien to begin his account of his life in the seminary all over again. 'Yesterday I wasn't listening, all I was thinking about while you were speaking was forcing myself to send you away.'

She was recklessness itself. They were talking very loud; it might have been two in the morning when they were interrupted by a violent thump on the door. It was M. de Rênal again.

'Let me in right away, there are thieves in the house!' he was saying. 'Saint-Jean found their ladder this morning.'

'This is the end of everything!' cried Mᵐᵉ de Rênal, flinging herself into Julien's arms. 'He'll kill us both, he doesn't believe this business about thieves; I'm going to die in your arms, happier in death than ever I was in life.' She made no move to answer her husband who was losing his temper; she was passionately kissing Julien.

'You must save Stanislas's mother,' he said to her with a look to be obeyed. 'I'm going to jump into the courtyard from the window of your closet and escape into the garden, the dogs know me. Fasten my clothes into a bundle and throw it into the garden as soon as you can. Meanwhile, let your door be broken open. Above all, don't admit to anything, I veto it; far better for him to live with suspicions than certainties.'

'You'll be killed when you jump!' was her only reply and her only anxiety.

She went with him to the window of the closet; then she took the time to hide his clothes. At last she opened the door to her husband who was seething with rage. Without uttering a word he looked round the room, looked round the closet and left abruptly. Julien's clothes were flung down to him, he grabbed them and raced down to the bottom of the garden in the direction of the river Doubs. As he ran, he heard a bullet whistle past, and at the same time the sound of a shot.

That's not M. de Rênal, he thought, he's not a good enough shot. The dogs were running along silently at his side, a second shot must have shattered the leg of one of them for it began to howl piteously. Julien leaped over a terrace wall, did fifty yards or so under cover, and then set off in flight again in a different direction. He heard voices calling to one another, and was quite certain he saw the servant his enemy firing a shot; a farmer came out too and fired some random shots from the other side of the garden, but by then Julien had reached the bank of the Doubs and was putting on his clothes.

An hour later he was a league away from Verrières on the road to Geneva; if they have any suspicions, thought Julien, the Paris road is where they'll look for me.

End of Book One

BOOK TWO

She isn't pretty, she has no rouge on.

SAINTE-BEUVE*

CHAPTER 1

Pleasures of the countryside

O rus quando ego te adspiciam

VIRGIL*

'THE gentleman must be here to catch the mail-coach to Paris?' asked the keeper of an inn where he stopped to eat.

'Either today's or tomorrow's, it hardly matters to me,' Julien replied.

The mail-coach arrived while he was feigning indifference. There were two empty seats.

'Well I never! if it isn't my old friend Falcoz!' said a passenger travelling from the Geneva direction to the traveller who was boarding the coach at the same time as Julien.

'I thought you were settled in the neighbourhood of Lyon,' said Falcoz, 'in a delightful valley near the Rhône.'

'Settled my foot! I'm running away.'

'What! running away? You of all people, Saint-Giraud, with your air of respectability, have you committed some crime or other?' asked Falcoz with a laugh.

'Might as well have done, I'm telling you! I'm running away from the abominable life of the provinces. I love the freshness of the woods and rustic peace and quiet, as you know; you've often accused me of being a romantic. I could never stand any talk of politics, and now politics is driving me out.'

'Which party do you support?'

'None, and that's my undoing. This is the sum total of my politics: I like music and painting; a good book is an event in my life; I'm about to be forty-four. How much longer have I got to live? Fifteen, twenty, thirty years at the very most? Well now! I maintain that in thirty years' time, ministers will be a bit more skilled, but just as honest as they are today. The history of England offers me a mirror for our future. There'll always be a king trying to increase his prerogative; the wealthy inhabitants of the provinces will always be kept awake at night by ambition to be elected to the Chamber of Deputies and by the fame and hundreds of thousands of francs earned by Mirabeau:* they'll call this being liberal and caring about the people. The wish to become a peer or a gentleman of the Chamber will always spur on the Ultras. On the ship of State, everyone will want to turn a hand to the sails, for the work is well paid. So will there never be even the tiniest bit of room for a mere passenger?'

'Quite so, quite so, that must be great fun with your calm temperament. Is it the last election* that's driving you out of your province?'

'My misfortune dates from further back. Four years ago, I was forty years old and in possession of five hundred thousand francs; I'm four years older today, and probably fifty thousand francs the poorer, which I'm going to lose on the sale of my château at Monfleury near the Rhône—a superb site. In Paris I was weary of this perpetual role-playing one is forced into by what you call nineteenth-century civilization. I yearned for good-natured simplicity. So I went and bought a piece of land in the mountains near the Rhône. Nothing could be as beautiful in the whole wide world.

'For six months the village curate and the local landowners sought me out; I invited them to dinner; "I've left Paris", I told them, "so as never again in all my life to talk politics or hear it talked of. As you see, I don't subscribe to any newspaper. The fewer the letters the postman brings me, the happier I am."

'The curate didn't see things this way; I soon became the target for innumerable forms of harassment, indiscreet requests, etc. I wanted to donate two or three hundred francs a year to the poor, and I'm asked to give the money to pious associations:* the Brotherhood of St Joseph, the Association of the Blessed Virgin, etc. I refuse, and I'm then insulted over and over again. I'm stupid enough to take offence. I can no longer leave home in the morning to go and enjoy the beauty of our local mountains without coming across some trouble which drags me away from my contemplations and is an unpleasant reminder of human beings and their wickedness. During Rogation Day processions, for instance, with their chanting that I enjoy (it's probably a Greek melody), my fields are no longer blessed "because", says the curate, "they belong to one of the ungodly." Some cow belonging to a pious old peasant woman dies, and she says it's because there's a pond nearby owned by me the infidel, a philosopher from Paris; and a week later I find all my fish floating belly up, poisoned with lime. I'm harassed on all sides, in all sorts of ways. The magistrate, who's a decent fellow, but fears for his post, always passes judgement against me. The peace of the countryside is hell to me. Once everyone saw that I had been dropped by the curate, who leads the Congregation in the village, and that I wasn't backed by the retired captain, who leads the liberals, they all got their knives into me, right down to the stonemason I'd kept in business for the past year, and the cartwright who tried to get away with diddling me when he repaired my ploughs.

'In order to have some support and to win at any rate some of my lawsuits, I became a liberal; but as you say, along came those wretched elections, my vote was solicited...'

'For a stranger?'

'Not at all, for a man I know only too well. I refused—how dreadfully rash! From then on, I had all the liberals to cope with as well, and my position became intolerable. I think if it had occurred to the curate to accuse me of murdering my housekeeper, there would have been twenty witnesses from both parties who would have sworn they saw the crime committed.'

'You want to live in the country without furthering the passions of your neighbours, without even listening to their gossip: what a blunder!...'

'Well anyway, I've put things right. Monfleury is up for sale, I stand to lose fifty thousand francs if need be, but I'm full of joy, I'm leaving this hellhole of hypocrisy and hassle. I'm going to seek solitude and rustic peace in the only place they are to be found in France, in a fourth-floor flat in Paris overlooking the Champs-Elysées. And what's more, I've even reached the point of considering whether I shan't begin my political career, in the neighbourhood of Saint-Philippe du Roule,* by handing back the consecrated bread to the parish.'

'None of this would have happened to you under Bonaparte,' said Falcoz, his eyes glinting with anger and regret.

'That's all very well, but why didn't he manage to stay put, this Bonaparte of yours? Everything I suffer from today is his work.'

At this point Julien became doubly attentive. He had realized from his first words that the Bonapartist Falcoz was the former friend of M. de Rênal whom the latter had repudiated in 1816; and that the philosopher Saint-Giraud must be a brother of the chief clerk at the prefecture of —— who was adept at getting himself allocated houses belonging to local communes for very reasonable sums.

'And all that is the work of your friend Bonaparte,' went on Saint-Giraud. 'A gentleman, as harmless as they come, with forty years and five hundred thousand francs to his credit, can't settle in the provinces and find peace there; Bonaparte's priests and nobles drive him out.'

'Ah! don't speak ill of him,' exclaimed Falcoz. 'Never has France risen so high in the esteem of nations as during the thirteen years of his reign. That was a time when there was greatness in everything ever done.'

'Your emperor—the devil take him—', went on the man of forty-four, 'was only great on his battlefields, and when he restored the finances around 1802. What's to be made of all his later actions? With his chamberlains, his pomp and his official functions at the Tuileries, he gave us a new edition of all the silly trappings of the monarchy. It had been revised, and would have done for another century or two. The nobles and the priests preferred to go back to the old edition, but they haven't got the iron hand you need to sell it to the public.'

'There speaks a former printer!'

'Who's driving me off my land?' continued the printer in

anger. 'The clergy, whom Napoleon recalled with his Concordat* instead of treating them as the State treats doctors, barristers or astronomers, simply seeing them as citizens, without worrying about what business they engage in to try to earn their living. Would there be impertinent gentlemen around today, if your Bonaparte hadn't created barons and counts? No, the fashion for them had gone out. Next in line after the clergy, it was the minor country noblemen who vexed me most, and forced me to become a liberal.'

The conversation was endless; the text of it was something France will ponder for the next half-century. As Saint-Giraud repeated over and over again that it was impossible to live in the provinces, Julien timidly volunteered the example of M. de Rênal.

'Goodness me, young man, that's a good one!' exclaimed Falcoz; 'he's turned himself into a hammer in order not to be an anvil, and a terrible hammer at that. But I see old Valenod is more than a match for him. Do you know that scoundrel? He's the real one. What'll your M. de Rênal say when he finds himself stripped of his office one of these fine mornings, and old Valenod put in his place?'

'He'll be left staring his crimes in the face,' said Saint-Giraud. 'So you know Verrières, do you, young man? Well, Bonaparte—heaven confound him and all his monarchist trappings—Bonaparte made possible the reign of men like M. de Rênal and Father Chélan, which brought in its wake the reign of Valenods and Maslons.'

This gloomy political conversation astonished Julien and kept his mind from wandering down sensuous paths.

He was not particularly struck by the first sight of Paris glimpsed in the distance. The castles he was building in the air about the fate awaiting him had to vie with the ever vivid memory of the twenty-four hours he had just spent in Verrières. He swore to himself that he would never abandon his loved one's children, and would give up everything in order to protect them if the folly of the clergy were to land us with a republic and persecution of the nobility.

What would have happened on the night of his arrival in Verrières if, just as he was leaning his ladder against the window of Mme de Rênal's bedroom, he had found the room occupied by a stranger or by M. de Rênal?

But then what bliss, for the first two hours, when his loved one genuinely wanted to send him away, and he pleaded his cause sitting beside her in the dark! A person of Julien's sensibility is pursued by such memories throughout a lifetime. The remainder of this encounter was already merging with the earlier phases of their affair fourteen months previously.

Julien was roused from his deep dreaming by the coach coming to a halt. They had just driven into the courtyard of the post-house in the Rue Jean-Jacques Rousseau. 'I want to go to La Malmaison,'* he said to a cab which drew up.

'At this hour, sir, what for then?'

'None of your business! Get a move on.'

All true passion is concerned only with itself. This is why, it seems to me, passions are so ridiculous in Paris, where your neighbour is always claiming you should spend time thinking of him. I shall refrain from describing Julien's emotions at La Malmaison. He wept. 'What! in spite of the ugly white walls built this year, which break up the park?'* 'Yes, sir: for Julien, as for posterity, nothing separated Arcola, St Helena and La Malmaison.'

In the evening Julien hesitated a long time before setting foot in the theatre: he had strange ideas about this place of perdition.

A deep-seated mistrust prevented him from admiring the living city of Paris; he was only moved by the monuments left behind by his hero.

So here I am in the centre of intrigue and hypocrisy! This is where the protectors of Father de Frilair hold sway.

In the evening of the third day, curiosity got the better of his plan to see everything before presenting himself to Father Pirard. The priest explained coldly to him what sort of life was awaiting him in M. de La Mole's household.

'If in a few months' time you aren't being of use, you will return to the seminary, but by the front door. You are going to reside with the marquis, who is one of the greatest noblemen in France. You will wear a black suit, but like someone in mourning, not like a man in holy orders. I insist on your continuing your theological studies three times a week in a seminary to which I shall give you an introduction. Every day at noon you will take up your post in the marquis's library; he intends to employ you to write letters in connection with lawsuits and other business. The marquis jots down briefly in the margin of each letter he receives the kind of reply that is called for. I have made the claim that in three months' time you would be in a position to draft these replies, so that out of a dozen you hand to the marquis for his signature, he'll be able to sign eight or nine. In the evening, at eight o'clock, you will tidy up his study, and at ten you will be free.

'It may be', Father Pirard went on, 'that some old lady or some soft-spoken man will let you glimpse enormous advantages elsewhere or will quite crudely offer you gold in exchange for showing them the letters received by the marquis...'

'Oh, sir!' exclaimed Julien, flushing.

'It is odd', said the priest with a bitter smile, 'that for all your poverty, and after a year in a seminary, you should still go in for displays of righteous indignation. You must have been pretty blind!'

'Could this be his blood that speaks?' the priest muttered under his breath, as if talking to himself. 'The strange thing is', he added, looking at Julien, 'that the marquis knows you... I don't know how. He's giving you a salary of one hundred louis to begin with. He's a man who only acts on impulse, that's the flaw in his character; he will vie with you in acts of childishness. If he is satisfied, your salary may rise later on to as much as eight thousand francs.

'But you must be well aware', Father Pirard continued sourly, 'that he's not giving you all this money for nothing. You have to make yourself useful. If I were in your position, I should say very little, and above all never a word on matters about which I knew nothing.

'Ah!' he said, 'I've made some enquiries for you; I was forgetting M. de La Mole's family. He has two children, a daughter, and a son of nineteen, the height of elegance, a sort of madman who never knows what he's going to be doing from one moment to the next. He has wits and courage; he fought in the Spanish War.* The marquis hopes, I don't know why,

that you will become a friend to the young Count Norbert. I
said you were a great Latin scholar, perhaps he's counting on
your teaching his son a few stock phrases on Cicero and Virgil.

'In your position I should never let myself be teased by this
handsome young man; and before yielding to his advances,
which are exquisitely polite, yet a bit spoilt by irony, I should
get him to repeat them more than once.

'I shall not conceal from you that the young Count de La
Mole is bound to despise you to begin with, because you are
merely one of the lower middle classes. His own ancestor
belonged at Court, and had the honour of having his head cut
off in the Place de Grève* on the 26th of April 1574 for
involvement in a political plot. You, on the other hand, are the
son of a carpenter from Verrières, and what's more, in the pay
of his father. Weigh up these differences carefully, and study
the history of this family in Moreri;* all the flatterers who dine
in their house make what they call delicate allusions to it from
time to time.

'Watch out how you reply to the jokes made by his lordship
Count Norbert de La Mole, squadron commander in the
Hussars and future peer of France, and don't come to me with
your complaints later on.'

'It seems to me', said Julien, going very red, 'that I shouldn't
reply at all to a man who scorns me.'

'You have no idea what that kind of scorn is like; it will only
manifest itself through exaggerated compliments. If you were a
fool, you might be taken in by them; if you wished to make your
way in the world, you would have to be taken in by them.'

'If the day comes when none of this appeals to me any more,
will I be thought an ungrateful creature if I return to my little
cell n° 103?'

'It's more than likely,' replied Father Pirard, 'that all the
hangers-on in the marquis's entourage will slander you, but I
shall appear in person as a witness. *Adsum qui feci.** I shall say
that this resolution was prompted by me.'

Julien was distressed by the bitter and almost hostile tone he
detected in Father Pirard's voice; it utterly spoilt his reply.

The fact is that Father Pirard had prickings of conscience
over his affection for Julien, and suffered a kind of religious

terror from becoming so directly involved in the fate of another person.

'You will also encounter', he added with the same bad grace, as if fulfilling a painful duty, 'you will also encounter her ladyship the Marquise de La Mole. She's a tall, fair-haired woman, pious, haughty, exquisitely polite and even more of a nonentity. She's the daughter of the old Duc de Chaulnes, so renowned for his aristocratic prejudices. This great lady is a kind of compendium in high relief of what constitutes the essential character of women of her rank. *She* doesn't conceal the fact that having ancestors who fought in the Crusades is the only asset she values. Money comes a long way behind: does that surprise you? We're not in the provinces any more, dear fellow.

'In her salon you will hear a number of great lords speaking of our princes in tones of striking flippancy. Whereas Mme de La Mole lowers her voice in respect every time she names a prince and especially a princess. I shouldn't advise you to say in her presence that Philip II* or Henry VIII were monsters. They were KINGS, which gives them inalienable rights to claim respect from everyone, especially from individuals of no birth such as you and me. Nevertheless', Father Pirard added, 'we are priests, for she will take you to be one; in this capacity, she considers us as menservants necessary to her salvation.'

'Father,' said Julien, 'it seems to me that I shall not spend long in Paris.'

'That's fine! But you must be aware that the only way to fortune, for a man of our cloth, is through great lords. With that indefinable trait in your character which remains a mystery, at least to me, if you don't make your fortune, you'll be persecuted; there's no middle way for you. Don't be deceived. Men see that they cause you no pleasure in conversing with you; in a country like ours where social values are what count, you are heading for misfortune if you don't win people's respect.

'What would have become of you at Besançon if it hadn't been for this whim of the Marquis de La Mole? One day you will understand just how extraordinary what he is doing on your behalf is, and, if you aren't a monster, you will be eternally grateful to him and his family. How many poor priests, more learned than you, have lived for years in Paris on the fifteen sous from their regular mass and the ten sous from their disputations at the Sorbonne!... Remember what I told you last winter about the early years of the unruly Cardinal Dubois.* Could your pride make you imagine, by any chance, that you are more talented than he was?

'Take me, for instance, a quiet and undistinguished man: I was expecting to die in my seminary; I was childish enough to become attached to it. Well! I was about to be removed from office when I handed in my resignation. Do you know how much my fortune amounted to? I had five hundred and twenty francs of capital, no more no less; not a single friend, and scarcely two or three acquaintances. M. de La Mole, whom I'd never set eyes on, got me out of this tight spot; he only had to breathe the word, and I was offered a living where all the parishioners are well-to-do-folk, above vulgar vices, and the income makes me feel ashamed, it's so disproportionate to the amount of work I do. I've only been speaking to you at such length in order to knock a bit of sense into that head of yours.

'There's something else: I have the misfortune to be short-tempered; it's possible that you and I may cease to be on speaking terms.

'If the haughty ways of the marquise or her son's bad jokes make their household totally unbearable for you, I advise you to finish your studies in some seminary thirty leagues from Paris, preferably to the north rather than the south. In the north there is more civilization, and fewer injustices; and', he added, lowering his voice, 'I have to confess that the proximity of Parisian newspapers frightens petty tyrants.

'If we continue to take pleasure in each other's company, and the marquis's household doesn't suit you, I offer you a post as my curate, and I'll give you a half-share of what the parish brings in. I owe you this and more besides', he added, interrupting Julien's expressions of thanks, 'for the most unusual offer you made me in Besançon. If instead of five hundred and twenty francs I had had nothing, you would have saved me.'

Father Pirard had abandoned his cruel tone of voice. To his

great shame, Julien felt tears coming into his eyes; he was dying to fling himself into his friend's arms; he couldn't refrain from saying to him, with as manly an air as he could muster:

'I've been loathed by my father ever since the cradle; it was one of my great afflictions; but I shan't complain about my luck any more; I've found a new father in you, sir.'

'Come now, come now,' said the priest in some embarrassment; then added, hitting very aptly upon the sort of remark that the master of a seminary would make: 'You must never say *luck*, my boy, always say *Providence*.'

The hackney cab stopped; the coachman lifted the bronze knocker on an enormous door: it was the HOTEL DE LA MOLE; and so that passers-by should be in no doubt about it, these words could be read on a black marble plaque above the door.

This piece of affectation did not go down well with Julien. They're so afraid of Jacobins! They see Robespierre and his cart* behind every hedge—to the point where it's quite ridiculous, yet there they go labelling their houses so that when there's an uprising the rabble can recognize and plunder them. He imparted this thought to Father Pirard.

'Ah! poor boy, you will soon be my curate. What an appalling idea you've just had!'

'It seems as simple as anything to me,' said Julien.

The gravity of the porter and especially the cleanliness of the courtyard had filled him with admiration. It was a beautiful sunny day.

'What magnificent architecture!' he said to his friend.

It was one of those houses with very flat fronts in the Faubourg Saint-Germain,* built around the time of Voltaire's death.* Never have fashion and beauty been so far apart.

CHAPTER 2

Entry into society

Ridiculous and touching memory: the salon where
one made one's first appearance at eighteen, alone
and without patronage! A woman's glance was
enough to intimidate me. The harder I tried to please,
the more awkward I became. I got quite the wrong
ideas about everything; either I was confiding with
no justification; or I saw a man as an enemy because
he had looked at me gravely. But at that time, in the
midst of the terrible misfortunes caused by my
shyness, how really fine a fine day was!

KANT*

JULIEN stood dumbfounded in the middle of the courtyard.

'Do try to look as if you had your wits about you,' said
Father Pirard; 'you have these horrible ideas, and then you act
just like a child! What's happened to Horace's *nil mirari*?*
(Never show any enthusiasm.) Just think that this tribe of
lackeys, on seeing you established here, will try to make fun of
you; they will see in you an equal who has been unjustly put
above them. Beneath outward appearances of good nature,
kind advice, and a desire to guide you, they will try to get you
to put your foot in it in a big way.'

'I defy them to,' said Julien, biting his lip, and he resumed
all his wariness.

The rooms which these gentlemen went through on the first
floor before reaching the marquis's study would have seemed
to you, my good reader, as dismal as they were magnificent.
Were you to be offered them just as they are, you would refuse
to inhabit them; they are a land of yawns and of dreary
argument. They increased Julien's delight. How can anyone
be unhappy, he thought, who inhabits so splendid a realm!

At length the gentlemen reached the ugliest of the rooms in
this superb suite: it had scarcely any daylight. There they
found a small thin man, with bright eyes and a fair wig. Father
Pirard turned to Julien and introduced him. It was the

marquis. Julien had great difficulty in recognizing him, he had such an air of civility about him. He no longer looked like the great lord of lofty mien whom he remembered from Bray-le-Haut Abbey. It seemed to Julien that his wig had far too much hair in it. Thanks to this impression he was not in the least intimidated. This descendant of Henry III's friend* struck him at first as having a rather unimpressive appearance. He was exceedingly thin and never kept still. But Julien soon observed that the marquis's civility was far more agreeable to his interlocutor than even the Bishop of Besançon's. The interview was over in three minutes. As they went out, Father Pirard said to Julien:

'You stared at the marquis as if he were a picture. I'm no great expert in what these people call politeness—you'll soon know more about it than I do—but all the same, the boldness of your gaze struck me as far from polite.'

They had got back into a hackney cab again; the driver stopped near the boulevard. Father Pirard showed Julien into a suite of large rooms. Julien noticed that there was no furniture. He was looking at a magnificent gilded clock depicting a subject he thought highly indecent, when a most elegant gentleman came up to him wreathed in smiles. Julien made a half-bow.

The gentleman smiled and put his hand on his shoulder. Julien started and leapt backwards. He flushed with anger. Father Pirard, despite his gravity, laughed till the tears ran down his cheeks. The gentleman was a tailor.

'I'm giving you your freedom again for two days,' the priest told Julien as they went out; 'only then can you be introduced to Mme de La Mole. Anyone else would watch over you as if you were a girl during these first moments of your sojourn in this new Babylon. Go and sin right away, if sin is to be your fate, and I shall be delivered from the weakness that makes me concerned about you. The day after tomorrow, in the morning, this tailor will have two suits brought to you; you will give five francs to the boy who fits them. And by the way, don't let these Parisians come to know the sound of your voice. If you say a word, they'll discover the secret of making fun of you. They have a way of it. Be at my lodgings at noon the day after tomorrow... Go on, go and sin... I was forgetting, go and order some boots, some shirts and a hat from the addresses noted here.'

Julien was looking at the handwriting.

'It's the marquis's hand,' said Father Pirard; 'he's an active man who foresees everything, and who prefers to do things himself than to give orders. He's taking you on in order for you to spare him this kind of bother. Will you have sufficient wits to carry out properly all the things that this quick thinker will indicate to you by the merest hints? Only the future will tell: watch out for yourself!'

Julien presented himself without a single word to the tradesmen indicated by the addresses; he noticed that this caused him to be received with respect, and the bootmaker wrote his name down in his book as M. Julien de Sorel.

At the Père-Lachaise cemetery,* a most obliging gentleman, who turned out to be even more liberal in his remarks, volunteered to point out to Julien the tomb of Marshal Ney,* deprived of the honour of an epitaph by a clever piece of politics. But when he parted from this liberal who, with tears in his eyes, almost clasped him in his arms, Julien no longer had his watch on him. This was the experience that had enriched Julien when at noon two days later he presented himself to Father Pirard; the latter looked hard at him.

'Perhaps you are going to become a fop,' said the priest severely. Julien looked like a very young man in high mourning; as a matter of fact, it suited him very well, but the good priest was too much of a provincial himself to see that Julien still had that way of moving his shoulders which in the provinces denotes both elegance and self-importance. On seeing Julien, the marquis judged his graces so differently from Father Pirard that he asked him:

'Would you have any objection to M. Sorel's taking dancing lessons?'

The priest was rooted to the spot.

'No,' he replied at last, 'Julien isn't a priest.'

Running up a little hidden staircase two steps at a time, the marquis went himself to settle our hero into a pretty-looking attic looking out over the huge garden of the house. He asked him how many shirts he had obtained from the linener.

'Two,' replied Julien, intimidated to see such a great lord stoop to details of this kind.

'Fine,' went on the marquis with a serious air and a curt and imperious note in his voice which set Julien thinking. 'Fine! Get another twenty-two shirts. Here's the first quarterly instalment of your salary.'

As he went down from the attic, the marquis called out to an old man: 'Arsène, you will attend to M. Sorel's wants.' A few minutes later, Julien found himself alone in a magnificent library; it was a delectable moment. So as not to be caught unawares in this state of emotion, he went and hid in a little dark corner; from there he cast his rapturous gaze over the shining spines of the books: I shall be able to read all this, he said to himself. And how could I dislike it here? M. de Rênal would have believed himself dishonoured for ever if he had done one hundredth of the things the Marquis de La Mole has just done for me.

But let's see what fair copies I've got to do. Once the work was finished, Julien dared to approach the books; he almost danced for joy on finding an edition of Voltaire. He ran and opened the library door in order not to be taken by surprise. Then he gave himself the pleasure of opening each one of the eighty volumes. They were magnificently bound, it was the work of the best craftsman in London. This was more than enough to bring Julien to a pitch of admiration.

An hour later, the marquis came in, looked at Julien's work and noticed with astonishment that Julien wrote *possible* with a single *s*: *possible*.* Could everything Father Pirard told me about his learning be pure fabrication! Deeply disappointed, the marquis said to him gently:

'You're a bit unsure of your spelling, aren't you?'

'That's right,' said Julien without thinking in the very least about the damage he was doing himself; he was touched by the marquis's displays of kindness, which reminded him of the arrogant tone of M. de Rênal.

I'm wasting my time over this whole experiment with a

young abbé from the Franche-Comté, thought the marquis; but I did so need someone I could rely on!

'*Possible* is spelled with a double *s*,' the marquis told him; when your work is finished, look up in the dictionary any words you are unsure how to spell.'

At six o'clock the marquis sent for him. He looked with obvious pain at Julien's boots: 'I have myself to blame for it, I didn't tell you that every day at five thirty you must go and dress.'

Julien looked at him uncomprehendingly.

'I mean put on stockings. Arsène will remind you; today I shall make your excuses.'

As he finished speaking, M. de La Mole ushered Julien into a drawing-room resplendent with gilding. On comparable occasions, M. de Rênal never failed to quicken his pace in order to gain the advantage of going through the doorway first. This petty vanity of his former employer caused Julien to tread on the marquis's heels, which was exceedingly painful for him on account of his gout. 'Oh! he's clumsy into the bargain,' said the latter to himself. He introduced him to a tall, imposing-looking woman. It was the marquise. Julien thought she had an insolent air, rather like Mme de Maugiron, the wife of the sub-prefect of the Verrières district, at the St Charles's day* dinner. Somewhat thrown by the extreme magnificence of the drawing-room, Julien did not hear what M. de La Mole was saying. The marquise scarcely deigned to look at him. There were a number of men there, among whom Julien was unutterably delighted to recognize the young Bishop of Agde, who had deigned to speak to him a few months back at the Bray-le-Haut ceremony. The young prelate must have been alarmed by the tender gaze which Julien in his timidity cast in his direction, and he did not trouble to recognize this provincial.

The men gathered in this drawing-room seemed to Julien to have an air of gloom and constraint about them; people speak softly in Paris, and do not exaggerate trifling matters.

A good-looking young man with a moustache, a very pale complexion and a very slim figure came in at about half-past six; he had an exceedingly small head.

'You *will* always keep people waiting,' said the marquise, as he kissed her hand.

Julien realized that this was the Count de La Mole. He found him charming right from the start.

Can it be possible, he wondered, that this is the man whose offensive jokes are to drive me from this house!

After he had scrutinized Count Norbert for a while, Julien noticed that he was wearing boots and spurs; and I'm supposed to wear shoes, apparently like an inferior. They sat down to table. Julien heard the marquise saying something stern in slightly raised tones. Almost at the same time he caught sight of a young lady with exceedingly fair hair and a most elegant figure, who came and sat down opposite him. He did not find her in the least attractive; however, on looking attentively at her, he thought to himself that he had never seen such beautiful eyes; but they signalled great emotional coldness. Later on, Julien decided that they had an expression of watchful boredom that none the less remains mindful of the duty to appear imposing. And yet Mme de Rênal had really beautiful eyes, he said to himself, she was always being complimented on them; but they had nothing in common with this pair. Julien did not have enough experience to discern that it was the fire of repartee that shone from time to time in the eyes of Mlle Mathilde, as he heard her called. When Mme de Rênal's eyes lit up, it was with the fire of passions, or from warm-hearted indignation at the tale of some unkind action. Towards the end of the meal, Julien hit upon a word to express the sort of beauty in Mlle de La Mole's eyes: they glitter, he said to himself. Apart from this, she had a cruel likeness to her mother, whom he disliked more and more, and he stopped looking at her. In contrast, Count Norbert seemed admirable to him from every point of view. Julien was so captivated that it did not occur to him to be jealous and to hate him for being richer and nobler than he was.

Julien thought the marquis looked bored.

At about the time the second course was being served, he said to his son:

'Norbert, I should like you to be kind to M. Julien Sorel

whom I've just taken on to my staff, and intend to turn into somebody if at all *posible*.

'He's my secretary,' the marquis said to his neighbour, 'and he spells *possible* with only one *s*.'

Everyone looked at Julien, who bowed his head rather too markedly in Norbert's direction; but on the whole, the expression on his face went down well.

The marquis must have mentioned the kind of education Julien had received, for one of the guests challenged him on Horace: talking about Horace was precisely how I succeeded with the Bishop of Besançon, Julien said to himself, it seems they only know this author. From then on, he had himself well under control. The effort was made easy for him because he had just decided that Mlle de La Mole would never be a woman in his eyes. Since being in the seminary, he defied men to do their worst, and was not easily intimidated by them. He would have been perfectly calm and collected if the dining-room had been less magnificently furnished. What actually overawed him still further was two mirrors, both eight foot high, in which from time to time he would glance at his interlocutor while speaking of Horace. His sentences were not too long for a provincial. He had beautiful eyes, and nervousness made them shine, now hesitantly, now radiantly when he had given a good answer. He was deemed to be agreeable. This kind of examination added a spark of interest to a solemn dinner. The marquis signalled to Julien's interlocutor to push him hard. Could it possibly be that he knows something! he thought.

In his replies Julien improvised ideas, and he lost enough of his nervousness to display not wit—something impossible for anyone who doesn't know the idiom used in Paris—but fresh ideas, even if they were lacking in polish and inappositely presented. And everyone saw that he knew Latin perfectly.

Julien's opponent was a member of the Académie des Inscriptions* who happened to know Latin; he found Julien to be a very fine humanist, lost his fear of making him blush, and tried in earnest to put him on the spot. In the heat of battle Julien at last forgot the magnificent furnishings in the dining-room, and reached the point of putting forward ideas about the Latin poets that his interlocutor had not seen anywhere in print. As a gentleman he gave the young secretary credit for them. By a stroke of good fortune, they embarked on a discussion about whether Horace was poor or rich: an amiable, sensuous and carefree man who wrote poetry for his own enjoyment like Chapelle,* the friend of Molière and La Fontaine; or a poor devil of a poet laureate imitating the Court and writing odes for the king's birthday like Southey, Lord Byron's accuser. They talked about the state of society under Augustus and under George IV; in both periods the aristocracy was all-powerful, but in Rome it had had power wrested from it by Maecenas, who was only a mere knight, while in England it had more or less reduced George IV to the state of a Venetian doge. This discussion appeared to rouse the marquis from the state of torpor in which boredom had kept him submerged at the beginning of the dinner.

Julien was at a complete loss over all the modern names like Southey, Lord Byron, George IV, which he was hearing for the first time. But it escaped no one's notice that whenever the conversation turned to events that had happened in Rome, knowledge of which could have been gleaned from the works of Horace, Martial, Tacitus etc., he displayed an unquestionable superiority. Julien did not hesitate to take over several of the ideas he had got from the Bishop of Besançon in the famous discussion he had had with that prelate; they went down more than well.

When everyone was tired of talking about poets, the marquise, who made it her rule to admire whatever entertained her husband, deigned to look at Julien. 'The uncouth manners of this young abbé may perhaps conceal a man of learning,' the academician sitting near her said to the marquise; and Julien caught snatches of this. Ready-made comments suited the mistress of the house's intelligence well enough; she adopted this one on Julien, and felt pleased with herself for inviting the academician to dinner. He entertains M. de La Mole, she thought.

CHAPTER 3

The first steps

This huge valley filled with brilliant
lights and so many thousands of men
dazzled my eyes. Not a single one knows
me, they are all my betters. My head is
swimming.

Poemi dell'avvocato REINA*

VERY early the next morning, Julien was writing out fair copies of letters in the library when Mlle Mathilde came in by a little communicating door very cleverly hidden with book spines. While Julien was admiring this invention, Mlle Mathilde seemed most astonished and somewhat put out to encounter him there. With her hair in curl-papers Julien thought she looked hard, haughty and almost masculine. Mlle de Là Mole had found her own way of stealing books from her father's library without letting it show. Julien's presence made that morning's errand fruitless, which vexed her all the more as she was coming to fetch the second volume of Voltaire's *Princess of Babylon*,* a worthy complement to an eminently royalist and religious upbringing that was a masterpiece of the Sacred Heart! At nineteen this poor girl was already in need of the zest of wit in order to find a novel interesting.

Count Norbert appeared in the library around three o'clock; he was coming to study a newspaper in order to be able to talk politics that evening, and was delighted to encounter Julien, whose existence he had forgotten about. He behaved exemplarily towards him; he offered to take him riding.

'My father is giving us time off until dinner.'

Julien understood the force of this *us* and was utterly charmed by it.

'My goodness, your lordship,' said Julien, 'if it were a matter of felling a tree eighty foot high, squaring it off and sawing it into planks, I'd make a good showing, if I may make so bold as to say so; but riding a horse—I've not done that more than six times in my whole life.'

'Well, this'll be the seventh, then,' said Norbert.

Actually, Julien remembered the King of ——'s triumphal entry into Verrières and thought himself most expert on horseback. But coming back from the Bois de Boulogne,* right in the middle of the Rue du Bac,* he fell off as he swerved suddenly to avoid a cab, and he plastered himself in mud. It was lucky for him that he had two suits. At dinner, wishing to say something to Julien, the marquis asked him about his outing; Norbert hastened to reply in general terms.

'His lordship is full of kindness towards me,' Julien added, 'I thank him for it, and I appreciate it fully. He deigned to have me ride the more docile and handsome of the horses; but of course he couldn't tie me on, and for want of this precaution I fell off right in the middle of that very long street, near the bridge.'

Mlle Mathilde tried in vain to conceal a fit of laughter; her indiscretion then requested details. Julien acquitted himself in a perfectly straightforward manner; he had style without realizing it.

'I think this young priest will go far,' said the marquis to the academician; 'a provincial being straightforward in a situation like that! It's never been seen before and won't be again; and what's more, he's recounting his misfortune in the presence of *ladies!*'

Julien put his hearers so much at their ease over his mishap that at the end of dinner, when the general conversation had taken another turn, Mlle Mathilde questioned her brother about the details of the unfortunate incident. As she persisted in her questioning, and Julien caught her eye several times, he plucked up courage to reply directly, although he had not been addressed, and all three of them ended up laughing just like three young inhabitants of a village in the depths of a wood.

The next day Julien went to two theology classes, and then returned to transcribe some twenty letters. Settled down next to him in the library he found a young man dressed with considerable care, but his appearance was unimpressive and his face spelled envy.

The marquis came in.

'What are you doing here, Monsieur Tanbeau?' he asked the newcomer sternly.

'I thought... ,' replied the young man with an ingratiating smile.

'No, sir, you didn't *think*. You are trying this on, and it's a failure.'

Young Tanbeau got up in fury and marched out. He was a nephew of Mme de La Mole's friend the academician, and he hoped to become a man of letters. The academician had secured the marquis's agreement to engage him as a secretary. When Tanbeau, who worked in a remote room, had found out about the favour bestowed on Julien, he wanted to share it, and had come along in the morning to set up his writing things in the library.

At four o'clock, after some hesitation, Julien was bold enough to call on Count Norbert. The latter was about to go riding and was embarrassed, for he was exquisitely polite.

'I think', he said to Julien, 'that you will soon be going to riding school; and in a few weeks' time I'll be delighted to go out on horseback with you.'

'I wanted to have the honour of thanking you for all your kindness towards me. Be assured, sir,' Julien added with a very serious air, 'that I am most conscious of everything I owe you. If your horse isn't wounded as a result of my clumsiness yesterday, and if he's free, I should like to ride him before dinner.'

'Goodness me, my dear Sorel, on your own head be it! Just assume that I've put to you all the objections that prudence requires; the fact is that it's four o'clock, we've no time to lose.'

Once he was mounted:

'What do you have to do to avoid falling off?' Julien asked the young count.

'Lots of things,' replied Norbert, laughing his head off. 'For instance, lean back.'

Julien set off at a fast trot. They were on the Place Louis XVI.*

'Hey! you young hothead,' said Norbert, 'there are too many carriages, and what's more, driven by rash fools! Once you're on the ground, their tilburies will run right over you; they're not going to risk spoiling their horses' mouths by pulling them up short.'

Twenty times over, Norbert saw Julien on the verge of falling off; but eventually the ride ended without an accident. On their return the young count said to his sister:

'Let me introduce a bold daredevil to you.'

At dinner, speaking to his father from the far end of the table, he did justice to Julien's boldness; it was all that could be said in praise of his way of riding a horse. Earlier in the day the young count had heard the men who were grooming the horses in the courtyard retailing Julien's fall in order to poke outrageous fun at him.

In spite of so much kindness Julien soon felt himself totally isolated in the midst of this family. All their customs struck him as peculiar, and he was always getting things wrong. His blunders were the delight of the valets.

Father Pirard had gone off to his parish. If Julien is a frail reed, let him perish, he thought; if he's a man of character, let him manage on his own.

CHAPTER 4

The Hôtel de la Mole

What is he doing here! could he be
enjoying himself? might he be aiming to
be liked?

RONSARD*

IF everything seemed strange to Julien in the noble drawing-room of the Hôtel de La Mole, the pale young man dressed in black seemed in his turn most peculiar to the individuals who deigned to notice him. Mme de La Mole suggested to her husband that he send him out on business on days when they had important people to dine.

'I'd like to persevere to the end with this experiment,' the marquis replied. 'Father Pirard claims that we are wrong to shatter the self-respect of the people we take into our household. *You can only lean on something that offers resistance,** etc. This fellow is only out of place because he cuts such an unfamiliar figure, and anyway, he's a deaf-mute.'

To get things straight for myself, Julien reflected, I must write down the names of the people I observe coming to this salon, and make a note of their characters.

At the top he put five or six hangers-on who made a point of being nice to him on the off-chance, believing him to be in favour through a whim of the marquis's. They were pathetic creatures, more or less spineless; but it must be said in praise of this class of men to be found nowadays in the salons of the aristocracy: they were not equally spineless to everyone. You might well see one of them letting himself be put down by the marquis, but taking exception to a harsh word addressed to him by Mme de La Mole.

The masters of the house had too much pride and too much boredom ingrained in their characters; they were too accustomed to behaving outrageously in order to dispel boredom for there to be any hope of their making real friends. But except on rainy days and in moments of ferocious boredom, which were rare, they were always deemed to be exquisitely polite.

If the five or six hangers-on who showed such paternal friendship to Julien had deserted the Hôtel de La Mole, the marquise would have been exposed to long bouts of solitude; and in the eyes of women of this rank, solitude is frightful: it is the emblem of *disgrace*.

The marquis behaved perfectly towards his wife; he made sure that her salon was adequately adorned; not with peers—he felt his new colleagues* were not noble enough to come to the house as friends, and not amusing enough to be admitted as inferiors.

It was only much later that Julien got to the bottom of these secrets. High politics, which is a talking point in middle-class establishments, is only touched upon in those of the marquis's class in times of distress.

Even in this weary century, the need to be entertained still holds such sway that even on days of grand dinners, no sooner had the marquis left the drawing-room than everyone else fled. Provided there was no joking at the expense of God, the clergy, the king, the powers that be, artistic and literary figures currently enjoying favour at Court, or indeed any part of the establishment; provided that no good word was spoken for Béranger,* the opposition press, Voltaire, Rousseau, or anything venturing to be in any way outspoken; provided above all that there was never any mention of politics, it was permissible to discourse freely on any subject.*

Not even an income of a hundred thousand crowns or a Blue Sash gives licence to contest a salon charter of this kind. An idea with the slightest spark in it seemed like a piece of rudeness there. In spite of the refined taste, the exquisite politeness, the desire to be agreeable, boredom was stamped on every brow. Young men who came out of duty, fearful of talking about anything which might arouse the suspicion that they were thinking, or again of betraying some forbidden reading-matter, fell silent after one or two elegant remarks about Rossini and the weather.

Julien observed that the conversation was usually kept alive by two viscounts and five barons whom M. de La Mole had known during the Emigration. These gentlemen enjoyed incomes of between six and eight thousand pounds; four of them supported *La Quotidienne** and three *La Gazette de France*. One of them had a daily anecdote to relate from the Court in which the word *admirable* was not spared. Julien noticed that he wore five decorations, while the others on the whole only had three.

On the other hand there were ten footmen in livery to be seen in the antechamber; and throughout the evening ices or tea were served every quarter of an hour, and at midnight there was a kind of supper with champagne.

This was the reason why Julien sometimes stayed on until the end; in point of fact, he could scarcely understand how anyone could listen seriously to the usual conversation in this magnificently gilded drawing-room. Sometimes he looked at the participants to see whether they mightn't actually be talking tongue in cheek. Good old Joseph de Maistre, whom I know off by heart, said it all infinitely better, he thought, and yet he's boring enough.

Julien was not the only one to notice the mental asphyxia. Some found consolation in consuming quantities of ice-cream; others in the pleasure of being able to say for the rest of the evening: 'I've just come from the Hôtel de La Mole, where I heard that Russia... etc.'

Julien learned from one of the faithful that less than six months ago Mme de La Mole had rewarded assiduous attendance for over twenty years by making poor Baron Le Bourguignon into a prefect, after he had been a sub-prefect since the Restoration.

This great event had retempered the zeal of all these gentlemen; they would have taken offence at trifles before, from now on they never took offence at anything. Only rarely was the lack of courtesy blatant, but Julien had already overheard two or three brief little exchanges at table between the marquis and his wife that were extremely hurtful to those seated near them. These noble personages did not conceal their sincere contempt for anyone unconnected with people who *rode in the king's carriages*.* Julien observed that the word *Crusade* was the only one which brought to their faces an expression of deep seriousness mingled with respect. Ordinary respect was always tinged with condescension.

In the midst of this magnificence and this boredom Julien was interested in nothing but M. de La Mole; he was pleased to hear him protest one day that he had had nothing to do with the promotion of poor Le Bourguignon. This was a way of paying respect to the marquise: Julien knew the truth from Father Pirard.

One morning when the priest was working with Julien in the marquis's library on the never-ending Frilair lawsuit:

'Father,' said Julien suddenly, 'is it one of my duties to dine with her ladyship, or is it a kindness they are showing me?'

'It's a signal honour!' answered the priest, scandalized. 'Not once has M. N—— the academician, who has been assiduous in his attentions for the past fifteen years, been able to obtain it on behalf of his nephew M. Tanbeau.'

'For me, Father, it's the most irksome part of my job. I was less bored at the seminary. I sometimes even see Mlle de La Mole herself yawning, and she at any rate ought to be accustomed to the civility of the family's friends. I'm afraid of falling asleep. I beg you, get permission for me to go and dine for forty sous in some obscure inn.'

Father Pirard, a genuinely self-made man, was highly appreciative of the honour of dining with a great lord. While he was attempting to make Julien understand this sentiment, a slight noise made them look round. Julien saw Mlle de La Mole listening. He blushed. She had come to fetch a book and had heard everything; Julien went up in her esteem. There's a man who wasn't born on his knees, she thought, like that old priest. God, he's ugly!

At dinner Julien did not dare look at Mlle de La Mole, but she was good enough to speak to him. That day they were expecting a large party, and she entreated him to stay. Young ladies in Paris are not very fond of middle-aged company, particularly if badly dressed. Julien had not needed much sagacity to discern that M. Le Bourguignon's colleagues who stayed on in the drawing-room had the distinction of being the usual butt of Mlle de La Mole's quips. That day, whether or not she was putting it on, she was merciless to the bores.

Mlle de La Mole was the centre of a little group which gathered almost every evening behind the marquise's enormous wing chair. Among them was the Marquis de Croisenois, the Comte de Caylus, the Vicomte de Luz and two or three other young officer friends of Norbert's or his sister's. These gentlemen sat on a large blue sofa. At the other end of the sofa from where the brilliant Mathilde sat, Julien would be stationed in silence on a small, rather low wicker chair. This modest post was envied by all the hangers-on; Norbert made it acceptable to seat his father's young secretary there by speaking to him or mentioning his name once or twice in an evening. That day Mlle de La Mole asked him how high the hill was on which the citadel at Besançon is built. Julien was utterly incapable of saying whether this hill was higher or lower than Montmartre. He often laughed with all his heart at the things that were said in this little group; but he felt incapable of thinking up anything comparable. It was like a foreign language that he understood but could not speak.

Mathilde's friends were doing running battle that day against the people arriving in the vast drawing-room. Friends of the family were given preference, being better known. You can just imagine how attentive Julien was: everything interested him, both the substance of the matter and the way it was joked about.

'Ah! here's M. Descoulis,' said Mathilde, 'he isn't wearing his wig any more; is he wishing to get the post of prefect through sheer genius? He's putting that bald forehead of his on show, which he says is full of lofty thoughts.'

'He's a man who knows the whole world,' said the Marquis de Croisenois; 'he also frequents my uncle the cardinal. He's capable of keeping up a lie with each one of his friends for years on end, and he's got two or three hundred friends. He knows how to nurture friendship, it's his special talent. As sure as you see him there, by seven in the morning in winter he's already covered in filth from standing on the doorstep of some friend or other.

'He has a quarrel from time to time, and writes seven or eight letters for this tiff. Then he makes it up, and does seven or eight letters for his effusions of friendship. But where he really excels is in the frank and sincere outpourings of the gentleman who bears no grudges. This ploy surfaces when he has some service to request. One of my uncle's vicars-general is wonderful when he describes M. Descoulis's life since the Restoration. I'll bring him along for you.'

'Bah! I wouldn't believe that sort of thing; it's professional jealousy among the lower orders,' said the Comte de Caylus.

'M. Descoulis will go down in history,' went on the marquis; 'he took part in the Restoration with the Abbé de Pradt,* M. de Talleyrand and M. Pozzo di Borgo.'

'The man has had millions passing through his hands,' said Norbert, 'and I can't imagine he comes here to rake in my father's witticisms, which are often abominable. "How many times have you betrayed your friends, my dear Descoulis?" he shouted to him the other day from the far end of the table.'

'But is it true that he's betrayed people?' said Mlle de La Mole. 'Who hasn't?'

'What's this?' said the Comte de Caylus to Norbert, 'you're entertaining M. Sainclair in your house, the notorious liberal; and what the devil does he come here for? I must go over and speak to him, and get him talking; they say he's so witty.'

'But how will he go down with your mother?' said M. de Croisenois. 'His ideas are so extravagant, so generous, so independent...'

'Just look,' said Mlle de La Mole, 'there's the independent fellow bowing and scraping to M. Descoulis, and grasping his hand. I almost thought he was going to raise it to his lips.'

'Descoulis must be more in with the Government than we thought,' M. de Croisenois replied.

'Sainclair comes here to get into the Academy,' said Norbert; 'look at him, Croisenois, look at him greeting the Baron L——.'

'He'd be less base going down on his knees,' added M. de Luz.

'My dear Sorel,' said Norbert, 'you who have wits, but have only just come up to Paris from your mountains: try never to greet anyone the way that great poet* does, were he God the Father himself.'

'Ah! here's the man of wit to end all wit, his lordship the Baron Bâton,' said Mlle de La Mole, lightly mimicking the footman who had just announced him.

'I think even your servants make fun of him. What a name, the Baron Bâton!*' said M. de Caylus.

'"What's in a name?" he said to us the other day,' went on Mathilde. '"Imagine the Duc de Bouillon* announced for the first time; all the public needs, where I'm concerned, is a little familiarity..."'

Julien left the vicinity of the sofa. With little appreciation as yet of the delightful subtleties of lighthearted banter, if he was to laugh at a joke he expected it to have some rational basis. All he saw in the exchanges of these young people was the tone of universal denigration, and he was shocked by it. With the straitlaced outlook of a provincial or an Englishman, he went so far as to detect envy in it, and he was certainly quite wrong there.

Count Norbert, he thought, whom I've seen writing three rough copies of a twenty-line letter to his colonel, would be happy indeed if he had written a page like one of M. Sainclair's in his whole life.

Moving unnoticed because of his insignificance, Julien went over to several groups in succession; he was following the Baron Bâton at a distance, and wanted to hear him speak. This man with such great wit wore a worried look, and Julien only saw him recover a little composure once he had thought up three or four clever remarks. It struck Julien that this kind of wit needed breathing space.

The baron was unable to say anything punchy; he needed at least four sentences of six lines in order to sparkle.

'This man holds forth, he doesn't converse,' someone was saying behind Julien. He turned round and flushed with pleasure when he heard the Comte Chalvet's name mentioned. He's the most subtle man of this century.* Julien had often seen his name in the *St Helena Chronicle* and the fragments of history dictated by Napoleon. The Comte Chalvet expressed himself tersely; his sallies were lightning flashes, well-aimed, brilliant and profound. If he spoke on some matter, the discussion was instantly seen to be advanced. He adduced facts, it was a pleasure to listen to him. What is more, in politics he was a shameless cynic.

'I'm an independent,' he was saying to a gentleman wearing

three medals, whom he appeared to be making fun of. 'Why
do people expect me to be of the same opinion today as I was
six weeks ago? In that case, my opinion would rule me like a
tyrant.'

Four solemn young men standing round him pulled faces;
these gentlemen don't appreciate flippancy. The count saw
that he had gone too far. Luckily he caught sight of honest M.
Balland, like Tartuffe* in his honesty. The count began talking
to him: the group closed in, realizing that poor Balland was
going to be slaughtered. By dint of moralizing and morality, in
spite of being horribly ugly, and after a début in society that it
is delicate to relate, M. Balland married an exceedingly rich
woman who died; then another exceedingly rich woman, who
is never seen in society. He enjoys an income of sixty thousand
pounds in all humility, and has his own flatterers. The Comte
Chalvet spoke to him of all this and showed no mercy. There
was soon a circle of some thirty people gathered round them.
Everyone was smiling, even the solemn young men, the bright
hopes of the century.

Why does he come to M. de La Mole's salon, where he is
clearly a sitting target, Julien wondered. He went over to
Father Pirard to ask him.

M. Balland made his escape.

'Good!' said Norbert, 'that's one of my father's spies gone;
there's only the little cripple Napier left.'

Could that be the answer to the riddle? thought Julien. But
in that case why does the marquis entertain M. Balland?

The stern Father Pirard was scowling in a corner of the
drawing-room as he listened to the footmen announcing guests.

'This must be a thieves' den,' he said like Bazilio,* 'I only
see suspect individuals arriving.'

For the stern priest was unfamiliar with the workings of
high society. But through his friends the Jansenists, he had
very precise notions about the kind of men who only make
their way into salons by putting their great finesse at the service
of all parties, or thanks to their scandalous fortunes. For a few
minutes that evening he replied out of the abundance of his
heart to Julien's pressing questions; then he stopped short,
disturbed at always having to speak ill of everyone, and

reproaching himself with it like a sin. A bilious Jansenist who believed in the duty of Christian charity, his life in society was a struggle.

'What a face that Abbé Pirard has!' Mlle de La Mole was saying as Julien approached the sofa.

Julien felt irritated, and yet she was right. Father Pirard was undeniably the most upright man in the salon, but his blotchy red face twitching from the torments of his conscience made him look hideous at that moment. And now go and believe in physiognomy, thought Julien; it's at the very moment when Father Pirard's delicacy reproaches him with some peccadillo that he looks atrocious; whereas the face of that Napier, who is a spy known to everyone, is stamped with pure, serene happiness. Father Pirard had nevertheless made great concessions to the party of his allegiance; he had taken on a servant, he was very well dressed.

Julien noticed something strange in the salon: all eyes turned to the door, and there was a sudden hush. The footman was announcing the notorious Baron de Tolly, on whom the elections had recently fixed everyone's gaze. Julien moved forward and saw him very clearly. The baron was president of one of the electoral colleges:* he had the bright idea of doing a vanishing trick with the little squares of paper bearing votes for one of the parties. But to compensate for this, he replaced them as he went along by other little pieces of paper bearing a name that was to his liking. This decisive manœuvre* was noticed by some of the voters who hastened to compliment the Baron de Tolly on it. The fellow was still pale from this great affair. Uncharitable souls had uttered the term 'hard labour'. M. de La Mole gave him a cold reception. The poor baron made his escape.

'If he's leaving us so soon, it's to go and see M. Comte,'* said the Comte Chalvet, and everyone laughed.

Surrounded by several great lords who said nothing, and the schemers—most of them corrupt, but all of them sharp-witted—who were arriving in succession that evening at M. de La Mole's salon (there was talk of him for a ministry), little Tanbeau was making his début. If his perceptions as yet lacked subtlety, he made up for it, as we shall see, by the energy of his words.

'Why not condemn this man to ten years' imprisonment?' he was saying as Julien drew near his group. 'The depths of a dungeon is the place to lock up reptiles; they must be left to die in the dark, otherwise their poison is stimulated and becomes more dangerous. What's the point of fining him a thousand crowns? He's poor, I grant you—so much the better; but his party will pay on his behalf. What was called for was a fine of five hundred francs and ten years in the dungeons.'

Good grief! whoever is this monster they are talking about, then? thought Julien, admiring the vehement tones and staccato gestures of his colleague. The thin, drawn little face of the academician's favourite nephew was hideous at that moment. Julien soon discovered that the man in question was the greatest poet of the age.*

'You monster!' exclaimed Julien half out loud, and warm-hearted tears welled up in his eyes. Ah, you little beggar! he thought, I'll get even with you for those words.

Yet these, thought Julien, are the lost children of the party which has the marquis as one of its leaders! And as for the illustrious man he's slandering—just imagine how many medals, how many sinecures he might have collected if he had sold himself, I'm not saying to the servile ministry of M. de Nerval,* but to one or other of that succession of reasonably honest ministers we've seen in office!

Father Pirard signalled to Julien from a distance; M. de La Mole had just said something to him. But when Julien, who at that moment was listening with lowered gaze to the moanings of a bishop, was free at last and could make his way over to his friend, he found him monopolized by the abominable little Tanbeau. This little monster loathed Father Pirard for being the source of the favour shown to Julien, and was there to win him over.

When will death deliver us from this man of corruption? It was in these terms, biblical in their force, that the little man of letters was referring at that moment to the respectable Lord Holland.* It was to his credit that he was thoroughly versed in the biographies of living men, and he had just done a rapid review of all the men who could aspire to some influence under the reign of the new king of England.*

Father Pirard moved off into an adjoining room; Julien followed him.

'The marquis doesn't like scribblers, I warn you; it's his only aversion. Make sure you know Latin and Greek—if you can, the history of the Egyptians, the Persians, etc., and he will honour you and give you patronage as a scholar. But don't go writing a single page in French, and above all not on serious matters above your station in society, or he might call you a scribbler and take against you. How come you live in a great lord's house and don't know the Duc de Castries's* saying about d'Alembert and Rousseau: "Express an opinion on everything, they would, and they haven't so much as a thousand crowns in income".'

Everything gets found out, thought Julien, here just as in the seminary! He had written nine or ten fairly bombastic pages: it was a sort of historical eulogy of the old army surgeon who, he wrote, had made him into a man. And this little notebook, said Julien to himself, has always been kept under lock and key! He went up to his room, burnt his manuscript and returned to the drawing-room. The brilliant rogues had left, only the men with medals remained.

Round the table, which the servants had just brought in ready set out, there were seven or eight women aged between thirty and thirty-five, exceedingly well born, exceedingly pious, and exceedingly affected. The dazzling Maréchale* de Fervaques came in making excuses for the lateness of the hour. It was past midnight; she went over and took a seat beside the marquise. Julien was deeply stirred: she had the eyes and the look of Mme de Rênal.

Mlle de La Mole still had a good gathering around her. She and her friends were busy making fun of the poor Comte de Thaler. He was the only son of the notorious Jew famous for the wealth he had amassed by lending money to kings* to make war on the common people. The Jew had just died, leaving his son an income of a hundred thousand crowns a month, and a name that was alas only too well known. This unusual position should have called for simplicity of character or a great deal of will-power.

Unfortunately the count was no more than a decent fellow adorned with all sorts of pretensions induced in him by his flatterers.

M de Caylus maintained that they had implanted in the count a resolve to ask for Mlle de La Mole's hand in marriage (she was being courted by the Marquis de Croisenois, who was to become a duke with an income of a hundred thousand pounds).

'Ah! don't accuse him of having any resolve,' said Norbert pityingly.

What this poor Comte de Thaler perhaps lacked the most was the faculty of will. This side of his character would have made him worthy of being a king. Constantly seeking counsel from everyone, he did not have the courage to follow any advice through to the end.

His face would have been enough on its own, Mlle de La Mole was saying, to fill her with eternal joy. It was a striking mixture of anxiety and disappointment; but from time to time you could very clearly discern in it surges of self-importance and of that decisive tone befitting the richest man in France, especially when he's rather good-looking and not yet thirty-six. 'He's timorously insolent,' said M. de Croisenois. The Comte de Caylus, Norbert and two or three young men with moustaches mocked him to their hearts' content without his noticing, and at length sent him packing as one o'clock was striking:

'Have you got your famous Arabs waiting at the door for you in this weather?' Norbert asked him.

'No; these horses are a new and much less costly pair,' replied M. de Thaler. 'I'm paying five thousand francs for the horse on the left, and the one on the right is only worth a hundred louis; but do me the honour of believing that it is only put into harness at night. The thing is, its trot is absolutely identical to the other one's.'

Norbert's comment made the count think that it was respectable for a man like himself to have a passion for horses, and that he shouldn't let his get wet. He set off, and the other gentlemen left a moment later, full of fun at his expense.

So, thought Julien as he heard them laughing on the stairs, I've been granted a glimpse of the opposite extreme from my situation! I haven't so much as an income of twenty louis, and I've been standing side by side with a man who has an income of twenty louis an hour, and they were poking fun at him... It's a sight to cure you of envy.

CHAPTER 5

Sensitivity and a great lady's piety

> An idea with any spark in it seems like a
> piece of rudeness there, so accustomed have
> people become to colourless words. Woe
> betide anyone who innovates in speech!
>
> FAUBLAS*

AFTER several months of ordeals, this was the point Julien
had reached on the day the steward of the household handed
him the third quarterly instalment of his salary. M. de La
Mole had put him in charge of supervising the administration
of his estates in Brittany and Normandy. Julien visited them
frequently. He was wholly in charge of the correspondence
relating to the notorious lawsuit with the Abbé de Frilair. M.
Pirard had briefed him.

On the basis of the short notes that the marquis scribbled in
the margins of all the various papers he received, Julien drafted
letters which were almost invariably signed.

His teachers at the theological college complained of his lack
of application, but none the less considered him to be one of
their most distinguished pupils. These different tasks, undertaken with all the keenness of frustrated ambition, had soon
robbed Julien of the fresh complexion he had brought from
the provinces. His pallor was an asset in the eyes of his young
contemporaries at the seminary; he found them much less
spiteful, much less inclined to worship Mammon than their
counterparts in Besançon; they thought he was suffering from
consumption. The marquis had given him a horse.

Fearful of being seen while out galloping, Julien had told
them that this was exercise ordered by the doctors. Father
Pirard had introduced him to several Jansenist societies. Julien
was astonished; the idea of religion was inextricably bound up
in his mind with that of hypocrisy and the hope of making
money. He admired these pious, stern men who don't think
about accounts. A number of Jansenists had befriended him
and were offering him advice. A new world was opening up

before him. In Jansenist circles he met Count Altamira, who was nearly six foot tall, a liberal sentenced to death in his own country, and a religious man. He was struck by this strange contrast between religious devotion and a love of liberty.

Relations were strained between Julien and the young count. Norbert had felt that Julien reacted too sharply to some of his friends' jokes. Having stepped beyond the bounds of propriety once or twice, Julien made a point of never addressing any remarks to Mlle Mathilde. Everyone was always perfectly polite to him at the Hôtel de La Mole, but he felt he was out of favour. His provincial common sense explained this outcome by appeal to the popular saying: *new's beautiful*.

He was perhaps a little more perspicacious than at first, or else the first magic of Parisian sophistication had worn off.

As soon as he stopped working he fell victim to deadly boredom; this is the withering effect of the politeness which distinguishes high society: it is admirable, but oh so measured, so perfectly calibrated in accordance with rank. Anyone with a sensitive nature sees straight through it.

No doubt you can reproach the provinces with their common or rather uncivil way of talking; but people do show a bit of feeling when they answer you. Julien never had his pride wounded at the Hôtel de La Mole, but he often felt close to tears at the end of the day. In the provinces, a waiter will take an interest in you if you have some kind of accident as you set foot in his café; but if there is something about this accident that is hurtful to your pride, the waiter, while expressing his sympathy for you, will find ten occasions to repeat the word causing you such agonies. In Paris, they are considerate enough not to laugh at you to your face, but you are always a stranger.

We shall pass over in silence a host of little adventures which would have made Julien look ridiculous if he had not been in some sense beneath ridicule. His exaggerated sensitivity made him commit thousands of blunders. All his pleasures were calculated ones: he practised pistol shooting every day, he was one of the good pupils of the most famous fencing masters. As soon as he had a moment to himself, instead of spending it reading as he used to do, he dashed to the riding school and asked for the most vicious horses. When he went out with the riding master he was almost invariably thrown off his horse.

The marquis found him easy to work with because of his dogged application, his silence and his intelligence; and little by little he entrusted him with the handling of any business that was the least bit tricky to sort out. At times when his soaring ambition left him some respite, the marquis was a shrewd businessman; with his ear close to the ground, he was in a position to speculate with success. He bought houses and forests; but he readily took offence. He gave away hundreds of louis and went to court over a few hundred francs. Rich men with noble hearts look to business for amusement, not results. The marquis needed a chief of general staff to introduce a system that was clear and easy to follow into all his financial affairs.

For all her restrained character, Mme de La Mole sometimes made fun of Julien. Great ladies are appalled by the *unpredictable* behaviour that heightened sensitivity produces; it is the very opposite of propriety. Once or twice the marquis spoke in Julien's defence: 'He may be ridiculous in your salon, but he scores in his office.' For his part Julien thought he had discovered the marquise's secret. She deigned to take an interest in everything as soon as the Baron de La Joumate was announced. He was a cold individual with an inscrutable countenance. He was short, thin, ugly, exceedingly well dressed, spent his life at Court and, as a rule, never said anything about anything. That was how his mind worked. Mme de La Mole would have been passionately happy, for the first time in her life, if she could have arranged for him to marry her daughter.

CHAPTER 6

A matter of accent

> Their lofty mission is to pass calm judgement on
> the minor events in the daily lives of nations. Their
> wisdom must forestall mighty anger over small
> causes, or over events that the voice of fame
> transfigures when it carries them afar.
>
> GRATIUS

FOR a newcomer who, out of pride, never asked any questions, Julien did not make himself look too foolish. One day, when he was driven into a café on the Rue Saint-Honoré by a sudden shower, a tall man in a beaver overcoat, surprised at his sullen stare, stared back at him exactly as Mlle Amanda's lover had done all that time ago in Besançon.

Julien had reproached himself too often with having let this first insult pass to put up with such a stare now. He demanded an explanation for it. The man in the overcoat immediately poured out a torrent of foul abuse at him: the whole café clustered round them; passers-by stopped by the door. Like a true provincial, Julien always carried a pair of small pistols on him as a precaution; he clenched them tightly inside his pocket. However he was sensible and did no more than repeat to his man at regular intervals: *Your address, sir! I despise you.*

The tenacity with which he stuck to these six words ended up by impressing the crowd.

'Damn it all! the fellow doing all the talking must give him his address!' Hearing this verdict repeated so often, the man in the overcoat flung five or six cards in Julien's face. Luckily none of them struck him; he had vowed he would only use his pistols if he was hit. The man went away, not without turning round from time to time to shake his fist and shout abuse at him.

Julien found himself bathed in sweat. So it's in the power of the meanest of mortals to get me as worked up as this! he said to himself in fury. How can I kill off my humiliating sensitivity?

What about finding a second? He didn't have any friends. He had had a number of acquaintances; but every time, after six weeks of seeing him, they had all become distant. I'm just not sociable, and now I'm cruelly punished for it, he reflected. At length he hit on the idea of seeking out a former lieutenant of the 96th called Liéven, a poor devil he often fenced with. Julien was quite open with him.

'I'm willing to be your second,' said Liéven, 'but on one condition: if you don't wound your man, you'll fight a duel with me, on the spot.'

'Agreed,' said Julien delightedly, and they went off in search of M. C. de Beauvoisis at the address indicated on his cards, in the depths of the Faubourg Saint-Germain.

It was seven o'clock in the morning. It was only when giving his name at the door that it occurred to Julien that this might be the young relative of Mme de Rênal's who had worked at the Embassy in Rome or Naples in the past, and had given a letter of introduction to the singer Geronimo.

Julien had handed a tall footman one of the cards flung at him on the previous day and one of his own.

He and his second were kept waiting a good three-quarters of an hour; at length they were introduced into a marvellously elegant suite, where they found a tall young man dressed like a doll; his features were handsome with all the perfection and the insignificance of a Greek statue. His strikingly narrow head was crowned with a pyramid of the loveliest fair hair. It had been curled with the greatest of care; not a hair was out of place. Having his hair curled like that, thought the lieutenant from the 96th, was what caused this cursed fop to keep us waiting. The colourful dressing gown, the morning trousers, everything down to the embroidered slippers was as it should be, and wonderfully soigné. His noble, empty face suggested that ideas would be conventional and rare: the cult of the agreeable gentleman, a horror of anything unexpected or humorous, a great deal of gravity.

Julien, who had had it explained to him by his lieutenant from the 96th that keeping someone waiting for so long after rudely throwing a visiting card in his face was yet another insult, strode briskly into M. de Beauvoisis's room. He intended to be insolent, but he would dearly have liked to be perfectly polite at the same time.

He was so struck by M. de Beauvoisis's gentle manners, by

his expression that was at once affected, self-important and smug, and by the marvellous elegance of his surroundings, that he abandoned in a flash any idea of being insolent. This wasn't his man from the day before. Such was his surprise at meeting so distinguished an individual in place of the vulgar character he had met in the café that he was at a loss for words. He handed him one of the cards that had been flung at him.

'That's my name,' said the fashionable young man, who was not induced to show much respect by the sight of Julien's black suit, worn at seven in the morning; 'but I don't understand, if I may make so bold...'

His way of uttering these last words brought back some of Julien's ill-temper.

'I've come to fight a duel with you, sir,' and he explained the whole affair straight out.

M. Charles de Beauvoisis, having given it due thought, was reasonably pleased with the cut of Julien's black suit. It comes from Staub's,* that's clear, he thought to himself as he listened to him speak; that waistcoat is in good taste, those boots are nice; but on the other hand, a black suit like that at this hour of the morning... ! All the better to escape bullets with, that must be it, said the Chevalier de Beauvoisis to himself.

Once he had produced this explanation for himself he resumed his exquisite politeness, addressing Julien almost as an equal. Their exchange was quite lengthy, the affair was a delicate one; but in the end Julien could not refuse to accept the obvious. The young man of such high birth standing before him did not have anything in common with the vulgar character who had insulted him the day before.

Julien felt an overwhelming reluctance to leave, and spun out his explanations. He observed the complacency of the Chevalier de Beauvoisis—that was the title he had used when referring to himself, being shocked that Julien should merely call him 'Mr'.

He admired his gravity, combined with a touch of discreet foppishness that never left him for a single moment. He was astonished at his curious way of moving his tongue as he pronounced his words... But all the same, none of this gave the slightest justification for picking a quarrel with him.

The young diplomat volunteered to fight with a very good grace, but the ex-lieutenant from the 96th who had been sitting there for an hour with his legs apart, his hands on his thighs and his elbows sticking out, decided that his friend M. Sorel was not the sort to pick a quarrel with a man for nothing, just because the man had had his visiting cards stolen.

Julien was in a very bad temper when they left. The Chevalier de Beauvoisis's carriage was waiting for him in the courtyard, in front of the porch; Julien chanced to look up and recognized in the coachman his man from the day before.

It was the matter of a moment for Julien to see him, grab him by his long coat, pull him off his seat and set about him with a horsewhip. Two footmen tried to defend their comrade; Julien was punched several times: at the very same moment he cocked one of his little pistols and fired at them; they took to their heels.

The Chevalier de Beauvoisis was coming downstairs with the most comic gravity, repeating in his upper-class accent: 'What's all this, what's all this?' He was clearly most curious, but diplomatic dignity did not allow him to show any more interest than that. When he learned what the matter was, haughtiness continued to do battle on his features with the slightly playful composure which must never leave a diplomat's face.

The lieutenant from the 96th realized that M. de Beauvoisis was game for a fight: he also wanted for reasons of diplomacy to make sure that his friend kept the advantage of taking the initiative. 'This time', he exclaimed, 'there's matter enough for a duel!' 'I should rather think so,' the diplomat replied.

'I'm dismissing that rogue,' he said to his footmen; 'someone else can take his seat.' The carriage door was opened: the chevalier insisted on doing Julien and his second the honours. They went and fetched one of M. de Beauvoisis's friends, who indicated a quiet spot to them. The conversation during the drive was really good. The only odd thing was the diplomat in his dressing gown.

These gentlemen, for all their wealth, thought Julien, aren't at all boring like the people who come to dinner with M. de La Mole; and I see why, he went on a moment later, they allow themselves to be improper. They were talking about the dancers that the public had acclaimed in a ballet performed the previous evening. These gentlemen alluded to some spicy anecdotes that Julien and his second the lieutenant from the 96th were totally ignorant of. Julien was not stupid enough to pretend he knew them; he admitted his ignorance with a good grace. His frankness appealed to the chevalier's friend; he related these anecdotes to him in the greatest of detail, and did it very well.

One thing astonished Julien beyond bounds. The carriage was held up for a moment by an altar of repose that was being put up in the middle of the road for the Corpus Christi day procession. These gentlemen took the liberty of cracking a number of jokes; the priest, according to them, was the son of an archbishop.* In the house of the Marquis de La Mole, who wanted to become a duke, no one would ever have dared utter such a thing.

The duel was over in an instant: Julien got a bullet in his arm; they bound it up for him with handkerchiefs; they moistened them with brandy and the Chevalier de Beauvoisis begged Julien very politely to allow him to accompany him home in the same carriage that had brought him. When Julien indicated the Hôtel de La Mole, the young diplomat and his friend exchanged glances. Julien's cab was there, but he found the conversation of these gentlemen infinitely more entertaining than that of the lieutenant from the 96th.

Goodness me! a duel—so that's all there is to it! Julien thought. How glad I am to have found that coachman again! What misery if I'd had to go on enduring that insult in a café! The entertaining conversation had hardly been interrupted. Julien realized then that diplomatic affectation does have its uses.

So boredom isn't inherent, he said to himself, in a conversation between people of high birth! These two make jokes about the Corpus Christi Day procession, they risk telling highly shocking anecdotes, and in picturesque detail too. The only thing totally lacking is any discussion of the political scene, and this lack is more than made up for by the elegance of their tone and the perfect appropriateness of their expressions.

Julien felt a strong liking for them. How glad I would be to see a good deal of these two!

No sooner had they taken leave of one another than the Chevalier de Beauvoisis sped off to find out all he could: it was not inspiring.

He was most curious to know his man; could he decently pay him a visit? What little information he could gather was not of an encouraging sort.

'This is all just frightful!' he said to his second. 'It's impossible for me to admit that I fought a duel with a mere secretary of M. de La Mole's, and what's more, because my coachman stole my visiting cards.'

'It's certain there'd be a risk of ridicule in all this.'

That very evening the Chevalier de Beauvoisis and his friend broadcast it everywhere that this M. Sorel, in any event an irreproachable young man, was the illegitimate son of a close friend of the Marquis de La Mole's. This fact gained acceptance without any difficulty. Once it was established, the young diplomat and his friend deigned to visit Julien once or twice during the fortnight he spent confined to his room. Julien confessed to them that he had only once in his life been to the Opera.

'That is dreadful,' they said to him, 'it's *the* place to go; the first time you go out, it simply must be to see *Count Ory*.'*

At the Opera the Chevalier de Beauvoisis introduced him to the famous singer Geronimo, who was enjoying great success at the time.

Julien was virtually wooing the chevalier's friendship; he was captivated by the young man's mixture of self-respect, mysterious complacency and foppishness. For instance, the chevalier stammered a little, because he had the honour of being on frequent visiting terms with a great lord who suffered from this impediment. Never had Julien seen amusing ridiculousness allied in a single individual with the perfection of manners that a poor provincial must strive to imitate.

He was seen at the Opera with the Chevalier de Beauvoisis; this acquaintance brought his name to people's lips.

'Well now!' M. de La Mole said to him one day, 'so I see

you're now the illegitimate son of a rich gentleman from the Franche-Comté, one of my intimate friends?'

The marquis cut Julien short as he tried to protest that he had not had any hand whatsoever in accrediting this rumour.

'M. de Beauvoisis didn't wish to have fought a duel with a carpenter's son.'

'I know, I know,' said M. de La Mole; 'it's up to me now to give substance to this tale, which suits my purposes. But I have a favour to ask of you, which will only take up half an hour of your time: on Opera days,* at eleven thirty, would you go and mingle with the people of fashion in the foyer as they come out? I observe that you sometimes still exhibit provincial mannerisms, and you need to get rid of them; besides, it's no bad thing to get to know—at least by sight—some of the important people I may one day send you to see on business. Call at the box-office and make yourself known; I've arranged for you to have the privilege of a free pass.'

CHAPTER 7

An attack of gout

And I was given promotion, not for deserving it,
but because my master had gout.

BERTOLOTTI*

THE reader may perhaps be surprised at this open and almost friendly tone; we had forgotten to say that for the past six weeks the marquis had been kept at home by an attack of gout.

Mlle de La Mole and her mother were at Hyères,* staying with the marquise's mother. Count Norbert only saw his father for brief moments; they were on excellent terms, but had nothing to say to each other. M. de La Mole, reduced to Julien, was astonished to find ideas in his head. He had him read the newspapers out loud to him. Soon the young secretary was in a position to select the interesting passages. There was a new paper* that the marquis could not abide; he had sworn never to read it, and every day he talked about it. Julien laughed. In his irritation at modern times, the marquis had Livy read aloud to him; he was entertained by Julien's improvised translation of the Latin text.

One day the marquis said in the tones of excessive politeness that often irked Julien:

'Allow me, my dear Sorel, to make you a gift of a blue suit: when you see fit to don it and to call upon me, I shall regard you as the younger brother of the Comte de Chaulnes, that is to say the son of my friend the old duke.'

Julien did not really understand what was going on; that same evening he tried out a visit wearing a blue suit. The marquis treated him as an equal. Julien had a heart worthy to appreciate true politeness, but he had no idea of nuances. He would have sworn, before the marquis had this whim, that it was impossible to be received by him with greater courtesy. What admirable talent! Julien said to himself; when he rose to go, the marquis made his apologies for being unable to see him out on account of his gout.

A strange idea preoccupied Julien: might he be making fun of me? he wondered. He went to seek advice from Father Pirard, who, being less polite than the marquis, merely whistled and changed the subject by way of reply. The following morning Julien presented himself to the marquis in a black suit, with his briefcase and his letters to be signed. He was received in the old manner. In the evening, with a blue suit, the tone was quite different, and every bit as polite as the day before.

'Since you aren't too bored during these visits you are kind enough to pay to a poor, sick old man,' the marquis said to him, 'what you should do is talk to him about all the little happenings in your life, but speak frankly, and without any other concern than to tell a clear and entertaining story. For it's vital to keep oneself entertained,' the marquis went on; 'that's the only real thing there is in life. It isn't every day that a man can save my life at the wars, or make me the gift of a million; but if I had Rivarol* here, next to my chaise-longue, every day he would spare me an hour of pain and boredom. I saw a lot of him in Hamburg during the Emigration.'*

And the marquis told Julien the anecdotes about Rivarol and the inhabitants of Hamburg; it took four of them together to understand one of his witticisms.

Reduced to the company of this little abbé, M. de La Mole tried to put some sparkle into him. He appealed to Julien's honour by tickling his pride. Since he was being asked for the truth, Julien resolved to tell all; but keeping two things back: his fanatical admiration for a name which put the marquis in an ill humour, and his total lack of faith, which hardly suited a future parish priest. His little affair with the Chevalier de Beauvoisis came at the right moment. The marquis laughed till he cried at the scene in the café in the Rue Saint-Honoré, with the coachman hurling foul abuse at him. It was a time of perfect openness in the relationship between master and protégé.

M. de La Mole became interested in Julien's strikingly unusual personality. To begin with, he flattered his ridiculous ways in order to enjoy them; he soon found it more interesting to correct, very gently, this young man's misguided ways of looking at things. Other provincials who come to Paris admire everything, thought the marquis; this fellow hates everything. They have too much affectation, he doesn't have enough, and fools take him for a fool.

The attack of gout was prolonged by the bitter cold of winter, and it lasted several months.

It's perfectly acceptable to become attached to a fine spaniel, the marquis reflected to himself; why am I so ashamed at becoming attached to this little abbé? He's original. I treat him like a son; all right! what's wrong with that? If it lasts, this caprice will cost me a diamond worth five hundred louis in my will.

Once the marquis had fathomed his protégé's resolute character, he entrusted him with some new piece of business daily.

Julien was alarmed to notice that this great lord was capable of giving him contradictory decisions on the same matter.

This might seriously compromise him. From then on Julien never worked with the marquis without bringing a register in which he wrote down decisions, and the marquis initialled them. Julien had taken on a clerk who transcribed the decisions relating to each affair into a special register. This register also received a copy of every letter.

At first this idea seemed the height of ridicule and tedium. But in less than two months, the marquis appreciated its advantages. Julien suggested employing a clerk who had recently worked for a banker, to keep a record in duplicate of all the income and expenditure from the estates that Julien was in charge of administering.

These measures shed so much light for the marquis on his own affairs that he was able to treat himself to the pleasure of engaging in two or three new pieces of speculation without the help of his broker, who robbed him.

'Take three thousand francs for yourself,' he said one day to his young minister.

'Sir, my conduct may be slandered.'

'What do you want, then?' retorted the marquis in annoyance.

'Be so good as to make out a warrant and write it in the

register in your own hand; this warrant will give me a sum of three thousand francs. Actually, it was the Reverend Father Pirard who thought up all this accounting.' The marquis, with the bored expression of the Marquis de Moncade listening to his steward M. Poisson's accounts,* wrote out the decision.

In the evening, when Julien appeared in his blue suit, there was never any talk of business. The marquis's displays of kindness were so flattering to our hero's pride, which was still rather touchy, that soon, in spite of himself, he felt a kind of attachment to this agreeable old gentleman. It was not that Julien was responsive, as this is understood in Paris; but nor was he a monster, and no one, since the death of the old army surgeon, had spoken to him with such kindness. He observed to his astonishment that out of politeness the marquis showed consideration for his pride in a way that the old army surgeon had never done. He realized in the end that the surgeon had more pride in his cross than the marquis did in his Blue Sash. The marquis's father was a great lord.

One day, at the end of one of his morning audiences, when he was dressed in his black suit and there for business, Julien happened to amuse the marquis, who kept him for a further two hours, and insisted on giving him some bank notes that his agent had just brought him from the Stock Exchange.

'I hope, your lordship, that I shall not fail to show the deep respect I owe you if I beseech you to let me say a word.'

'Speak, my dear fellow.'

'May his lordship deign to allow me to refuse this gift. The man in the black suit is not the one it is meant for, and it would utterly spoil the behaviour that his lordship is good enough to tolerate in the man in the blue suit.' He bowed with great respect and left the room without looking at the marquis.

This manifestation of Julien's character amused the marquis. He related it to Father Pirard that evening.

'I must finally confess something to you, my dear Father. I know whose son Julien is, and I authorize you not to keep secret what I confide in you.'

The behaviour he revealed this morning is noble, thought the marquis, and I am making him a nobleman.

Some time later, the marquis was at last able to go out.

'Go and spend two months in London,' he said to Julien. 'The special and other postal services will bring you the letters I receive, together with my notes. You will prepare the replies and send them back to me, putting each letter in with the reply to it. I've calculated that the delay will only be five days.'

As he sped along the road to Calais, Julien was amazed at the triviality of the so-called business he was being sent on.

We shall not describe the feeling of hatred and almost horror with which he set foot on English soil. The reader knows of his mad passion for Bonaparte. He took every officer for a Sir Hudson Lowe,* every great lord for a Lord Bathurst, ordering the infamies on St Helena and being rewarded for it with ten years in the Cabinet.

In London he at last experienced the heights of foppery. He had become acquainted with some young Russian nobles who initiated him.

'You are predestined for this, my dear Sorel,' they said to him; 'your natural look is the cold expression, *utterly remote from the sensation of the moment*, that we try so hard to adopt.'

'You haven't understood your century,' Prince Korasov said to him: '*always do the opposite of what is expected of you*. This, on my honour, is the only religion for our time. Don't be either mad or affected, for then acts of folly and affectation would be expected of you, and the precept would fail to be carried out.'

Julien was crowned with glory one day in the salon of the Duke of Fitz-Folke, who had invited him to dinner along with Prince Korasov. They had to wait for an hour. The way Julien behaved in the midst of the twenty people waiting there is still quoted by the young Embassy secretaries in London. His expression was priceless.

He determined, in spite of his dandy friends, to see the famous Philip Vane,* the only philosopher England has produced since Locke. He found him serving his seventh year in prison. The aristocracy doesn't fool around in this country, Julien thought; Vane is dishonoured, vilified etc.

Julien found him in fine spirits; the fury of the aristocracy kept him from being bored. There sits, said Julien to himself as he left the prison, the only cheerful man I've seen in England.

'*The idea that is of greatest use to tyrants is that of God*,' Vane had said to him...

We shall leave out the rest of his system as being too *cynical*.

On his return: 'What entertaining idea are you bringing back from England for me?' M. de La Mole asked him... He remained silent. 'What idea are you bringing back, entertaining or not?' insisted the marquis.

'*Primo*,' said Julien, 'the wisest Englishman has an hour of folly every day; he is visited by the demon of suicide, who is the god of the country.

'2° Wit and genius lose twenty-five per cent of their value on landing in England.

'3° Nothing in the world is as beautiful, as worthy of admiration, or as moving as English landscapes.'

'My turn,' said the marquis:

'*Primo*, why did you go and say at the Russian Ambassador's ball that there are three hundred thousand young men of twenty-five in France who passionately desire war? Do you think that's something our kings will like to hear?'

'One doesn't know what to do when talking to our great diplomats,' said Julien. 'They have a way of embarking on serious discussions. If you stick to the platitudes of the press, you are taken for a fool. If you allow yourself to say something true and novel, they are astonished, they don't know what to answer, and at seven o'clock the next day they have you informed through the First Secretary at the Embassy that you said the wrong thing.'

'Not bad,' said the marquis laughing. 'Anyway, I bet you, Mister profound thinker, that you haven't guessed what you went to England for.'

'Begging your pardon,' replied Julien; 'I went there to dine once a week with the King's Ambassador, who is the most civil of men.'

'You went to get the Legion of Honour cross that you see over there,' the marquis said to him. 'I don't wish to make you abandon your black suit, and I've grown accustomed to the more entertaining tone I've adopted with the man wearing the blue suit. Until further notice, take this as understood: when I see this cross, you will be the youngest son of my friend the Duc de Chaulnes, who, without realizing it, has been employed in the Diplomatic Service for the past six months. Take note', added the marquis with a very serious air, cutting short Julien's expressions of gratitude, 'that I do not wish to raise you from your position. It's always a mistake and a misfortune for the patron as well as for the protégé. When my lawsuits bore you, or you cease to suit my needs, I shall request a good living for you, like the one our good friend Father Pirard has, *and nothing more*,' the marquis added in a very curt tone of voice.

This cross set Julien's pride at rest; he spoke much more readily. He was less often inclined to believe himself singled out for insult by those remarks capable of some unflattering interpretation that anyone can let slip in an animated conversation.

This cross also earned him an unusual visit: that of the honourable Baron de Valenod, who had come to Paris to thank the Cabinet for his title, and to establish good relations. He was about to be appointed mayor of Verrières to replace M. de Rênal.

Julien had a good laugh, to himself, when M. de Valenod insinuated to him that M. de Rênal had just been discovered to be a Jacobin. The fact is that in a fresh round of elections that were in the offing, the new baron was the Government candidate, and in the electoral college of the département, which was in truth very reactionary, M. de Rênal was standing for the liberals.*

Julien tried in vain to discover anything about Mme de Rênal; the baron appeared to remember their former rivalry and was inscrutable. He ended up by asking Julien for his father's vote in the forthcoming elections. Julien promised to write.

'You should, noble sir, introduce me to his lordship the Marquis de La Mole.'

'Quite right, *I should*,' Julien thought; 'but a rogue like you...!'

'The truth is', he replied, 'that I'm too much of a new boy at the Hôtel de La Mole to take the initiative of introducing people.'

Julien used to tell the marquis everything: that evening he described Valenod's pretensions to him, and all his great deeds since 1814.

'Not only', replied M. de La Mole with a most serious air, 'will you introduce the new baron to me tomorrow, but I shall invite him to dinner the day after. He shall be one of our new prefects.'

'In that case', replied Julien coldly, 'I request the post of master of the workhouse for my father.'

'Well done!' said the marquis, resuming his gaiety; 'granted; I was expecting you to moralize. You're getting the hang of things.'

M. de Valenod informed Julien that the person who ran the lottery in Verrières had just died: Julien thought it amusing to give the office to M. de Cholin, the old fool whose petition he had picked up all that time ago in M. de La Mole's room. The marquis laughed wholeheartedly at the petition which Julien recited to him when getting him to sign the letter requesting this office from the Minister of Finance.

M. de Cholin had hardly been appointed when Julien learned that this office had been requested by a deputation from the département on behalf of M. Gros, the famous geometer: this generous man only had an income of fourteen hundred francs, and every year he had lent six hundred francs to the recently deceased holder of the office, to help him bring up his family.

Julien was amazed at what he had done. It doesn't matter, he said to himself, I shall have to resort to a good many other injustices if I want to make my way, and what's more, learn to hide them beneath fine sentimental phrases: poor M. Gros! *He* deserved the cross, I'm the one to get it, and I have to act in accordance with the desires of the Government who's giving it to me.

CHAPTER 8

What decoration distinguishes a man?

'Your water doesn't refresh me,' said the
thirsty genie. 'All the same, it's the coolest
well in the whole of Diarbekir.'

PELLICO*

ONE day Julien had just returned from the delightful estate at
Villequier on the banks of the Seine, which M. de La Mole
kept an interested eye on because it was the only one of all his
estates that had belonged to the famous Boniface de La Mole.
In the Paris house he found the marquise and her daughter,
who were just back from Hyères.

Julien was a dandy now, and understood the art of living in
Paris. He behaved with exemplary coldness towards Mlle de La
Mole. He appeared to have no recollection of the days when
she asked him so gaily for details of how he fell off his horse.

Mlle de La Mole found him taller and paler. His figure and
appearance no longer bore any trace of the provincial; this was
not the case with his conversation: it was noticeably still far
too serious and assertive. However, despite the measured tone,
his pride precluded any hint of subservience; it was just that
you felt he still regarded too many things as important. But
you could tell he was a man to defend his point of view.

'He lacks the flippant touch, but he does have a mind,' said
Mlle de La Mole to her father, as she joked with him about the
cross he had given Julien. 'My brother went on at you about
getting one for eighteen months, and he's a La Mole!'

'Yes, but Julien doesn't act as you'd expect him to, which
can't be said of the La Mole you're talking about.'

His grace the Duc de Retz was announced.

Mathilde felt herself overcome by an irresistible yawn; she
recognized the antique gilding and the familiar faces of her
father's salon. She conjured up an utterly tedious image of the
life she was about to resume in Paris. All the same, when in
Hyères she missed Paris.

Yet I'm nineteen! she thought: it's the age for happiness, so say all these idiots in gold leaf. She was looking at nine or ten volumes of new poetry which had mounted up on the drawing-room table during her visit to Provence. It was her misfortune to have a sharper intellect than M. de Croisenois, M. de Caylus, M. de Luz and her other friends. She could just imagine everything they would say to her about the wonderful sky in Provence, poetry, the South, etc., etc.

These lovely eyes in which dwelled the most profound boredom, and worse still, despair at ever finding any pleasure, alighted on Julien. He at least was not quite like anyone else.

'Monsieur Sorel,' she said in that bright, crisp and utterly unfeminine voice adopted by upper-class young women, 'Monsieur Sorel, are you coming to M. de Retz's ball this evening?'

'Mademoiselle, I haven't had the honour of being introduced to his grace.' (It was as if these words and this title stuck in the proud provincial's throat.)

'He has instructed my brother to take you along with him to his house; and if you were to come, you could give me some information about the Villequier estate; there's talk of going there in the spring. I'd like to know if the château is habitable, and if the surrounding countryside is as pretty as they claim. There are so many undeserved reputations!'

Julien made no reply.

'Come to the ball with my brother,' she added in very curt tones.

Julien bowed respectfully. So even in the middle of a ball, I'm accountable to all the members of the family. Aren't I being paid to engage in business? His bad temper added: What's more, God knows whether what I tell the daughter won't upset the plans made by the father, the brother or the mother! this is every bit the sovereign prince's Court. You'd have to be a real nonentity who at the same time would give nobody any cause for complaint.

How I dislike that tall girl! he thought as he watched Mlle de La Mole walk towards her mother, who had called her over to introduce her to a number of her women friends. She carries all fashions to extremes, her dress is falling off her shoulders... she's even paler than before she went away... What colourless hair, it's so fair! It's as if the light went straight through it.

How haughty she is the way she greets people, in the way she looks at them! What queenly gestures!

Mlle de La Mole had just called her brother over as he was leaving the drawing-room.

Count Norbert came up to Julien:

'My dear Sorel,' he said to him, 'where would you like me to pick you up at midnight for M. de Retz's ball? He's given me express instructions to bring you along.'

'I'm very aware to whom I owe such kindness,' Julien replied, bowing to the ground.

His bad temper, unable to find fault with the tone of civility and even interest which Norbert had adopted in speaking to him, began to get to work on the reply which he, Julien, had made to these obliging words. He detected in it a shade of servility.

That evening, when he arrived at the ball, he was struck by the magnificence of the Hôtel de Retz. The front courtyard was covered over with a great awning of crimson twill with gold stars on it: the height of elegance. Beneath this awning the courtyard was transformed into a grove of flowering orange trees and oleanders. As care had been taken to bury the pots sufficiently deep, the oleanders and oranges looked as if they were growing straight out of the ground. The pathway for carriages was strewn with sand.

The whole scene seemed amazing to our young provincial. He did not have the least inkling of such magnificence; in an instant his kindled imagination had left his bad temper thousands of miles behind. In the carriage on the way to the ball, Norbert had been cheerful while he, Julien, saw everything painted black; no sooner had they entered the courtyard than the roles were reversed.

All that Norbert noticed was the few details which, in the midst of such magnificence, it had not been possible to attend to. He totted up the expenditure on each item, and as the total mounted up, Julien observed that he became almost envious and quite put out.

Whereas Julien himself was won over, full of admiration and almost nervous with emotion when he reached the first of the rooms where the dancing was going on. People were crowding round the door into the second, and there was such a throng that he was unable to move forward. The décor in this second room represented the Alhambra palace in Grenada.

'She's the queen of the ball, you must agree,' a young man with a moustache was saying as his shoulder rammed into Julien's chest.

'Mlle Fourmont, who was the prettiest of them all throughout the winter,' replied the man next to him, 'can tell she's slipping into second place: look at her strange air.'

'She really does pull out all the stops to charm us. Just look at that gracious smile when she's dancing on her own in the quadrille. Word of honour, it's priceless.'

'Mlle de La Mole seems to be in full control of the pleasure she derives from her victory, which she's well aware of. It's as if she were afraid of charming the person talking to her.'

'Excellent! That's the art of seduction.'

Julien was making vain attempts to catch a glimpse of this seductive woman; seven or eight men taller than himself prevented him from seeing her.

'There's a good deal of coquettishness in her noble restraint,' said the young man with a moustache.

'And those big blue eyes which are lowered so slowly just when you'd think they were on the verge of giving away their secret,' his neighbour continued. 'My goodness, there's nothing so crafty.'

'Look how common the beautiful Mlle Fourmont seems beside her,' said a third man.

'This air of restraint signifies: what charm I should lay on for you, if you were the man to be worthy of me!'

'And who can be worthy of the sublime Mathilde?' asked the first speaker: 'some sovereign prince, handsome, witty, well-built, a hero in war and no older than twenty at the very most.'

'The illegitimate son of the Emperor of Russia... for whom, for the sake of this marriage, a kingdom would be found; or quite simply the Comte de Thaler, looking like a peasant dressed up...'

The doorway cleared and Julien was able to go through.

Since she has a reputation of being so remarkable in the eyes of these namby-pambys, it'd be worth my while to study her, he thought. I shall understand what makes perfection for that sort of person.

As he was looking round for her, Mathilde glanced at him. My duty calls me, Julien told himself; but there was no bad temper left except in his expression. Curiosity drove him forward with a pleasure soon increased by the low cut of Mathilde's dress round the shoulders—hardly very flattering to his pride, if the truth be told. There is something youthful about her beauty, he thought. Five or six young men, among whom Julien recognized the ones he had overheard by the door, stood between her and him.

'You, sir, who've been here all winter,' she said to him, 'isn't it true that this ball is the prettiest of the season?'

He made no reply.

'This quadrille of Coulon's* strikes me as admirable; and these ladies are dancing it perfectly.' The young men turned to see who the fortunate man was whose answer was so insistently sought. It was not an encouraging one.

'I should hardly qualify as a good judge, Mademoiselle; I spend my life writing: this is the first ball of such magnificence that I've ever seen.'

The young men with moustaches were scandalized.

'You are a wise man, Monsieur Sorel,' replied the lady with a greater show of interest; 'you observe all these balls, all these festivities, like a philosopher, like Jean-Jacques Rousseau. These follies amaze you without ensnaring you.'

A single name had just quenched the fire of Julien's imagination and driven all illusions from his heart. His mouth took on an expression of disdain that was maybe somewhat exaggerated.

'Jean-Jacques Rousseau', he replied, 'is no more than a fool in my eyes when he takes it upon himself to judge high society; he didn't understand it, and brought to it the heart of an upstart lackey.'

'He wrote *The Social Contract*,' said Mathilde in tones of veneration.

'An upstart who, while preaching the republic and the overthrow of the high offices of the monarchy, is over the moon if a duke alters the direction of his after-dinner stroll just to accompany one of the upstart's friends.'

'Oh yes! the Duc de Luxembourg at Montmorency accompanying a M. Coindet* on his way to Paris...', Mlle de La Mole elaborated, with the pleasure and abandon of the first sweet taste of pedantry. She was intoxicated with her learning, rather like the academician who discovered the existence of King Feretrius.* Julien's eye remained searching and severe. Mathilde had had a moment of enthusiasm; she was deeply put out by her partner's coldness. She was all the more astonished as it was she who customarily produced this effect on others.

At that moment the Marquis de Croisenois was making his way eagerly over towards Mlle de La Mole. For a moment he stood three paces away from her without being able to break through the throng. He looked at her with a smile at the obstacle in his path. The young Marquise de Rouvray was near him; she was a cousin of Mathilde's. She was leaning on the arm of her husband, who had only enjoyed matrimony for a fortnight. The Marquis de Rouvray, exceedingly young himself, showed all the foolish love that takes hold of a man who, on making a marriage of convenience entirely arranged by solicitors, discovers a perfectly lovely woman. M. de Rouvray was going to become a duke on the death a very old uncle.

While the Marquis de Croisenois, unable to break through the crowd, was gazing delightedly at Mathilde, she cast her large, heavenly blue eyes on him and his neighbours. What could be more insipid, she said to herself, than that whole group! There is Croisenois who has aspirations to marry me; he's gentle and polite, he has perfect manners like M. de Rouvray. Were it not for the boredom they inspire, these gentlemen would be most agreeable. He too will tag along behind me at the ball with that blinkered, contented expression. A year after our wedding, my carriage, my horses, my dresses, my château twenty leagues from Paris, all that sort of thing will be as perfect as it possibly can, just what's required to make a social climber die of envy—someone like the Comtesse de Roiville, for instance; and then what... ?

Mathilde was bored in anticipation. The Marquis de Croisenois managed to get near her, and he was talking away, but she let her mind wander without listening to him. The sound of his words merged in her ears with the hum of the ball. Her gaze went automatically after Julien, who had moved away with a respectful, though proud and discontented air. In a corner, far from the madding crowd, she spied Count Altamira, who had been condemned to death in his country, and is already familiar to the reader. Under Louis XIV a relative of his had married one of the princes de Conti; the memory of this gave him some protection from the Congregation police.

The only thing I can think of that distinguishes a man is a death sentence, Mathilde thought: it's all there is that can't be bought.

Ah! that's a witty saying I've just thought up! What a shame it didn't come out in such a way as to do me credit! Mathilde had too much taste to bring into the conversation a piece of wit prepared in advance; but she also had too much vanity not to be delighted with herself. A look of happiness replaced the appearance of boredom on her features. The Marquis de Croisenois, who was still talking to her, thought he glimpsed success and redoubled his eloquence.

What could an unkind person find objectionable in my witty remark? Mathilde asked herself. I'd reply to my critic: 'The title of baron or viscount is something money can buy; a cross is something you are given; my brother has just got one, and what did he do for it? Rank is something you can acquire. Ten years in the garrison, or a relative who is Minister of War, and you're a squadron commander like Norbert. A huge fortune...! now that's the most difficult of all, and consequently the most meritorious. Isn't it funny! It's the opposite of everything the books say... Well now! to get a fortune, you marry M. Rothschild's daughter.'

My witticism really is profound. A death sentence is the only thing that no one has yet thought of asking for.

'Do you know Count Altamira?' she asked M. de Croisenois.

She looked so much as if she were only just coming back to earth, and this question had so little bearing on anything the poor marquis had been saying to her for the past five minutes, that his politeness was quite thrown by it. Yet he was a man of wit and highly reputed as such.

Mathilde is very idiosyncratic, he thought; it's a disadvantage, but she has such a fine social position to offer her husband! I don't know how this Marquis de La Mole does it; he has connections with the top people in every party; he's a man who can't go into eclipse. Besides, this idiosyncrasy of Mathilde's can pass off as genius. Associated with high birth and a great deal of wealth, genius isn't a mark of ridicule, and in that case what a distinction! What's more, when she wants to she has just the right blend of wit, character and timing that perfect affability requires... As it is difficult to do two things well at the same time, the marquis answered Mathilde with a vacant expression as if he were repeating a lesson:

'Who doesn't know poor Altamira?' And he told her the story of his abortive, ridiculous and absurd conspiracy.

'Quite absurd!' said Mathilde as if talking to herself. 'But he did act. I want to see a real man; bring him over to me,' she said to the marquis, who was very shocked.

Count Altamira was one of the most open admirers of Mlle de La Mole's haughty and almost impertinent air; she was in his view one of the most beautiful young women in Paris.

'How beautiful she would be on a throne!' he said to M. de Croisenois; and made no difficulty about allowing himself to be led over to her.

There is no shortage of people in society who try to make out that nothing is in quite such poor taste as a conspiracy—it whiffs of Jacobins. And what could be more distasteful than an unsuccessful Jacobin?

The look in Mathilde's eyes mocked Altamira's liberalism just as M. de Croisenois did, but she listened to him with pleasure.

A conspirator at a ball—what a nice contrast, she thought. This one with his black moustache struck her as having the face of a lion at rest; but she soon noticed that his mind was fixed on one thing: *utility, admiration for utility*.

The young count did not consider anything worthy of his attention unless it was capable of giving his country a system of government by two Chambers. He was glad to leave Mathilde, the most attractive woman at the ball, because he saw a Peruvian general coming in.

Despairing of Europe, poor Altamira was reduced to thinking that when the States of South America are strong and powerful, they will be able to restore to Europe the liberty sent to them by Mirabeau.*[1]

A swirl of young men with moustaches had come up to Mathilde. She had indeed noticed that Altamira had not fallen under the spell, and felt miffed that he had moved away; she saw his black eyes flashing as he talked to the Peruvian general. Mlle de La Mole gazed at the young Frenchmen with that look of deep seriousness that none of her rivals could imitate. Which one of them, she thought, could get himself sentenced to death, even supposing all the odds were in his favour?

This strange look flattered those who did not have much intelligence, but made the others nervous. They feared the explosion of some caustic witticism that would not be easy to counter.

High birth bestows countless qualities whose absence would offend me: I can tell from the example of Julien, thought Mathilde; but it withers away those qualities of character that lead a man to be sentenced to death.

At that moment someone near her was saying: 'This Count Altamira is the second son of the Prince of San Nazaro-Pimentel; it was a Pimentel who tried to save Conradin,* who was beheaded in 1268. They're one of the noblest families in Naples.'

And that, said Mathilde to herself, proves my maxim very nicely: high birth takes away the strength of character without which a man doesn't get sentenced to death! So I'm predestined to think nonsense this evening. Since I'm just a woman like any other, all right then! I'll have to dance. She yielded to the entreaties of the marquis, who had been requesting a *galope** for the past hour. To take her mind off her failure in philosophy, Mathilde determined to be exemplarily charming. M. de Croisenois was thrilled.

But neither the dance, nor the desire to be attractive to one of the most comely men at Court, nor anything else could

---

[1] This page was composed on 25 July 1830* and printed on 4 August. [*Original*] *Publisher's note.*

distract Mathilde. She could not have been more successful. She was the queen of the ball, she saw this, but it left her cold.

What a colourless existence I shall lead with a person like Croisenois! she said to herself as he led her back to her seat an hour later... Where shall I find pleasure, she added sadly, if after six months' absence I get none in the midst of a ball that's the envy of all the women in Paris? And what's more, I'm surrounded here with the homage of a milieu that I couldn't conceivably imagine being better constituted. The only middle-class people here are a few peers and maybe one or two Juliens. And yet, she added with growing sadness, what advantages fate has given me: dazzling reputation, fortune, youth! alas, everything except happiness.

The most dubious of my assets are just the ones they've been telling me about all evening. My intellect I do believe in, for it's obvious that I scare them all. If they're brave enough to tackle a serious subject, five minutes of conversation leaves them quite gasping for breath, and seeming to make a great discovery out of something I've been telling them repeatedly for a whole hour. I'm beautiful, I do have the asset Mme de Staël* would have sacrificed everything for, and yet it's a fact that I'm dying of boredom. Is there any reason to think I'll be less bored when I've exchanged my name for that of the Marquis de Croisenois?

But goodness me! she added, feeling almost like tears, isn't he an ideal man? He's the masterpiece of this century's upbringing; you only have to look at him and he finds something pleasant and even witty to say to you; he's brave... But that Sorel is quite out of the ordinary, she said to herself, and the look of gloom in her eye became one of annoyance. I informed him I wanted to speak to him, and he doesn't deign to come back!

CHAPTER 9

The ball

The lavish clothes, the dazzling candles, the
perfumes: so many pretty arms and lovely
shoulders; bouquets of flowers, lilting tunes by
Rossini, paintings by Ciceri! I am beside myself!
Uzeri's Travels

'You're in a bad mood,' the Marquise de La Mole said to
her; 'I warn you, it's not becoming at a ball.'

'I've only got a headache,' replied Mathilde disdainfully,
'it's too hot in here.'

At that moment, as if to vindicate Mlle de La Mole, the old
Baron de Tolly was taken ill and collapsed; he had to be
carried away. Apoplexy was mentioned; it was an unpleasant
incident.

Mathilde took no notice. It was a matter of principle, with
her, never to pay any attention to the old, or indeed anyone
known to say dreary things.

She danced to escape the conversation about apoplexy,
which was not the trouble after all, since two days later the
baron turned up again.

But M. Sorel still hasn't come, she said to herself again after
she had finished dancing. She was almost looking round for
him when she caught sight of him in another room. Amazingly
enough, he seemed to have lost the air of imperturbable
coldness that came so naturally to him; he didn't look English
any more.

He's talking to Count Altamira, my man under sentence of
death! Mathilde said to herself. There's a look of smouldering
fire in his eye; he's like a prince in disguise; his expression is
prouder than ever.

Julien, still talking to Altamira, was coming over to where
she was; she gazed steadily at him, studying his features for a
sign of those high qualities that can earn a man the honour of
being sentenced to death.

As he was passing by her:

'Yes,' he said to Count Altamira, 'Danton* was a man!'

Oh heavens! Could he be a Danton? Mathilde wondered; but he has such a noble face, and Danton was such a horribly ugly individual, he was a butcher, I believe. Julien was still quite near her, and she did not hesitate to call him over; she was aware and proud of asking an extraordinary question for a young lady:

'Wasn't Danton a butcher?' she said to him.

'Yes, in some people's view,' Julien replied with an expression of the most undisguised disdain, his eyes still glinting from his conversation with Altamira; 'but unfortunately for people of high birth, he was a barrister at Méry-sur-Seine; in other words, Mademoiselle,' he added with a hostile expression, 'he began like a number of peers I see here. It's true that Danton had a tremendous disadvantage in the eyes of beauty: he was extremely ugly.'

These last words were spoken quickly, with an extraordinary and certainly most impolite expression.

Julien paused for a moment, bending forward a little from the waist, and with a proudly humble expression. He seemed to be saying: 'I'm paid to answer you, and I live off my pay.' He did not deign to look up at Mathilde. She, with her big eyes extraordinarily wide open and fixed upon him looked like his slave. At length, as the silence continued, he looked at her like a valet looking at his master—to take orders. Although his eyes stared straight into Mathilde's, which were still fixed on him with a strange look, he walked away with marked alacrity.

How could he, who is genuinely so handsome, Mathilde said to herself at length as she emerged from her musing, how could he praise ugliness like that! Never dwells on his own conduct! He's not like Caylus or Croisenois. This Sorel has something of the look my father adopts when he does such a good imitation of Napoleon at a ball. She had quite forgotten Danton. There's no getting away from it, this evening I'm bored. She seized her brother's arm and, to his great dismay, forced him to do a turn on the dance floor. It occurred to her she could follow the conversation between the condemned man and Julien.

There was a huge throng. She managed none the less to get

within two paces of them just as Altamira was making for a
tray in order to take an ice-cream. He was talking to Julien,
half turning towards him. He saw an arm in a brocade sleeve
taking one of the ices next to his. The braid seemed to catch
his attention: he turned round completely in order to see who
the arm belonged to. At that instant, those noble and innocent
eyes took on a mild expression of disdain.

'You see that man,' he said rather quietly to Julien; 'he's the
Prince of Araceli, the —— Ambassador. This morning he
requested my extradition* from M. de Nerval, your Foreign
Minister. Look, there he is over there playing whist. M. de
Nerval is rather inclined to hand me over, for we gave you two
or three conspirators in 1816. If I'm returned to my king, I'll
be hanged within twenty-four hours. And it'll be one or other
of those fine gentlemen with moustaches who'll *grab me*.'*

'Base wretches!' exclaimed Julien under his breath.

Mathilde did not miss a syllable of their conversation.
Boredom had vanished.

'Not as base as all that,' rejoined Count Altamira. 'I talked
to you about myself to fire your imagination. Look at the
Prince of Araceli; every five minutes he casts an eye on his
Golden Fleece; he can't get over the pleasure of seeing that
trinket on his chest. The poor man is basically an anachronism.
A hundred years ago the Fleece was a signal honour, but at
that time it would have been way out of his reach. Today,
among the men of high birth, it takes an Araceli to be delighted
with it. He would have had a whole town hanged to get it.'

'Was that the price he paid for it?' asked Julien anxiously.

'Not exactly,' replied Altamira coldly; 'he may have had
thirty or so rich landowners from his part of the world flung
into the river for their reputation as liberals.'

'What a monster!' said Julien again.

Mlle de La Mole, leaning forward with the keenest interest,
was so close to him that her lovely hair almost touched his
shoulder.

'How young you are!' replied Altamira. 'I was telling you
that I have a married sister in Provence; she's still pretty, she's
kind and gentle; and an excellent mother, faithful to all her
duties, pious but not a zealot.'

What's he driving at? wondered Mlle de La Mole.

'She's happy,' went on Count Altamira; 'she was happy in 1815. At that time I was hiding in her house, on her estate near Antibes. Well, when she heard of Marshal Ney's* execution, she started dancing!'

'Is that possible?' said Julien, dumbfounded.

'It's the partisan spirit,' replied Altamira. 'There are no genuine passions left in the nineteenth century: that's why people are so bored in France. They commit acts of the utmost cruelty, but without any cruelty at all.'

'Too bad!' said Julien; 'when you commit crimes, you should at least do it with enjoyment: that's the only good thing about them, and the only slight justification there is for them.'

Utterly forgetting everything she owed herself, Mlle de La Mole had stationed herself almost completely between Altamira and Julien. Her brother, who was giving her his arm in a habitual act of obedience, was gazing around the room, and to hide his awkwardness tried to look as if he was hemmed in by the crowd.

'You're right,' Altamira was saying; 'people do everything without enjoyment, and without remembering what they've done, even when it's a crime. I can point out to you as many as ten men at this ball who will be eternally damned as murderers. They've forgotten all about it, and so has society.[1]

'Several of them are moved to tears if their dog breaks a leg. At the Père-Lachaise Cemetery when flowers are flung on their graves, as you put it so nicely in Paris, we are told that they combined all the virtues of valiant knights, and we learn of the mighty deeds of their ancestors who lived under Henri IV.* If, in spite of the good offices of the Prince of Araceli, I am not hanged and I ever come to enjoy my fortune in Paris, I intend to invite you to dine with nine or ten revered and remorseless assassins.

'You and I shall be the only ones with untainted blood at this dinner, but I shall be despised and almost hated as a bloodthirsty monster and a Jacobin, and you will be despised

---

[1] Thus speaks the voice of discontent. Molière's note in *Tartuffe*. [Stendhal's note.]

quite simply as a man from the common people who has
intruded into good society.'

'Nothing could be more true,' said Mlle de La Mole.

Altamira looked at her in astonishment; Julien did not deign
to give her as much as a look.

'Mark you, the revolution I found myself leading', Altamira
went on, 'was a failure because I was unwilling to let three
heads roll, and to distribute among our followers seven or eight
millions which happened to be in a coffer I had the key to. My
king, who today is consumed with the desire to have me
hanged, and before the uprising was on intimate terms with
me, would have given me the Grand Sash of his Order if I had
let those three heads roll and distributed the money from the
coffers, for I should at least have had a half success, and my
country would have had a Charter as it stood... That's the way
of the world, it's a game of chess.'

'At that time', Julien volunteered, his eyes ablaze, 'you
didn't know the game; now...'

'I'd let heads roll, you mean, and I wouldn't be a Girondin*
as you insinuated to me the other day... ? I'll answer that one',
said Altamira with a look of sadness, 'when you've killed a
man in a duel, which I may say is far less nasty than having
him put to death by an executioner.'

'I'm telling you!' said Julien, 'the ends justify the means; if
instead of being an atom I had some sort of power, I'd have
three men hanged to save the lives of four.'

His eyes shone with the fire of conscience and scorn for the
idle judgements of men; they met Mlle de La Mole's right next
to him, and instead of changing into a gracious and civil look,
his scorn seemed to intensify.

She was deeply shocked at it; but it was no longer in her
power to forget Julien. She moved away in mortification,
dragging her brother with her.

I must drink some punch and dance a lot, she told herself;
I'll pick the best of the crowd, and make an impression at all
costs. Good, here comes that impertinent celebrity the Comte
de Fervaques. She accepted his invitation; they danced. It's a
matter of seeing, she thought, which of the two of us will be
the more impertinent; but so that I can make proper fun of

him, I must get him talking. Soon all the rest of the quadrille only danced for appearances' sake. No one wished to miss any of Mathilde's stinging repartee. M. de Fervaques was getting flustered, and as he could only produce elegant phrases instead of ideas, he was making faces; Mathilde, who was in a bad mood, was merciless to him and made an enemy out of him. She danced until daybreak and at length withdrew in a state of terrible fatigue. But in the carriage she went and used up the small amount of strength she had left on making herself sad and miserable. She'd been despised by Julien and couldn't despise him.

Julien was on top of the world. Swept off his feet unawares by the music, the flowers, the beautiful women, the elegance of it all, and more than anything, by his imagination, which dreamed of distinctions for himself and liberty for everyone.

'What a fine ball!' he remarked to the count; 'there's nothing missing.'

'Yes there is: thought,' replied Altamira.

And his face betrayed the kind of scorn that is all the more scathing because obvious efforts of politeness are being made to conceal it.

'You're right there, my lord. It's true, isn't it, that thought still turns to conspiracy?'

'I am here for the sake of my name. But everyone hates thought in your salons. It must never rise above the wit of a vaudeville couplet: then it is rewarded. But the man who thinks, and puts any energy and novelty into his sallies, gets termed a *cynic* by you people. Wasn't that what one of your judges called Courier?* You put him in prison, just like Béranger.* Anyone with any claim to distinction for his intellect, in your country, is booted into the police courts by the Congregation; and right-minded folk applaud.

'You see, your antiquated society puts appearances before everything else... You will never rise above military bravery; you will have men like Murat,* but never a single Washington. All I detect in France is vanity. A man who comes up with new ideas while speaking is bound to let slip the odd rash remark, and his host considers himself dishonoured.'

As he spoke, the count's carriage, which was taking Julien

home, drew up in front of the Hôtel de La Mole. Julien was starry-eyed about his conspirator. Altamira had paid him a fine compliment, obviously out of deep conviction: 'You haven't got the flippancy of the French, you understand the principle of *utility*.' It so happened that only two days before, Julien had seen *Marino Faliero*, a tragedy by Casimir Delavigne.*

Doesn't Israel Bertuccio have more character than all those noble Venetians? reflected our rebellious plebeian; and yet they are people whose lineage can be traced back unequivocally to the year 700, a century before Charlemagne, whereas the cream of the nobility at M. de Retz's ball this evening only goes back, and haltingly at that, as far as the thirteenth century. Well! in the midst of these nobles from Venice, with all the distinction of their birth, Israel Bertuccio is the man you remember!

A conspiracy wipes out all the titles conferred by the whims of society. A member of it immediately steps into the rank assigned him by his attitude towards death. Intelligence itself loses its power...

What would Danton be today, in this age of Valenods and Rênals? not even the crown prosecutor's deputy...

What am I saying! he'd have sold himself to the Congregation; he'd be a minister, for the great Danton did after all steal. Mirabeau was another one who sold himself. Napoleon had stolen millions in Italy, otherwise he'd have been stopped in his tracks by poverty, like Pichegru.* La Fayette was the only one who never stole. Do you have to steal, do you have to sell yourself? Julien wondered. This question stopped him in his tracks. He spent the rest of the night reading the history of the Revolution.

The next day as he wrote his letters in the library his thoughts were still on the conversation with Count Altamira.

In point of fact, he said to himself after daydreaming for a long while, if those liberal Spaniards* had compromised the people by committing crimes, they wouldn't have been so easy to sweep aside. They were proud and talkative children... just like me! exclaimed Julien suddenly as if waking up with a start.

What difficult thing have I ever done to give me the right to judge poor devils who, after all, for once in their lives, have shown nerve and begun to act? I'm like a man who, on rising from table, exclaims: 'Tomorrow I shall go without dinner; and it won't stop me being as strong and cheerful as I am today.' Who knows what it feels like to be right in the midst of a great action... ? These lofty thoughts were disturbed by the unexpected appearance of Mlle de La Mole coming into the library. He was so fired up by his admiration for the great qualities of Danton, Mirabeau and Carnot,* who managed not to be beaten, that his eyes alighted on Mlle de La Mole without thinking about her, without greeting her, almost without seeing her. When at length his big, wide-open eyes registered her presence, the look of fire in them died away. Mlle de La Mole was galled to observe it.

It was to no avail that she asked him for a volume of Vély's *History of France** that was sitting on the top shelf, thus obliging Julien to go and fetch the bigger of the two ladders. Julien had brought up the ladder; he had fetched the book and handed it to her, but he was still incapable of turning his thoughts to her. As he carried the ladder away, he was so preoccupied that he put his elbow through the front of a bookcase; the pieces of broken glass falling on to the floor brought him to himself at last. He hastened to make his excuses to Mlle de La Mole; he tried to be polite, but he was nothing more than polite. It was crystal clear to Mathilde that she had disturbed him, and that rather than talk to her, he would have preferred to go on thinking about what was on his mind before she appeared.

She looked intently at him and moved slowly away. Julien watched her go. He savoured the contrast between the simplicity of what she was wearing and the magnificent elegance of her attire the day before. The difference between the two facial expressions was almost as striking. The young lady who had been so haughty at the Duc de Retz's ball had now an almost pleading look. I really think, Julien said to himself, that this black dress enhances the beauty of her figure even more. She has the bearing of a queen; but why is she in mourning?

If I ask someone the reason for her mourning, I'll find myself committing yet one more piece of ineptitude. Julien had completely emerged from the depths of his enthusiasm. I must reread all the letters I did this morning; God knows what I'll find in the way of words left out and blunders. While he was reading the first of these letters with studied attention, he heard the rustle of a silk dress right next to him; he looked round sharply: Mlle de La Mole was standing two feet from his table, laughing. This second interruption annoyed Julien.

Mathilde herself had just become acutely aware that she meant nothing to this young man; her laughter was designed to hide her embarrassment, and she succeeded.

'It's obvious you're thinking about something really interesting, Monsieur Sorel. Could it be some curious anecdote about the conspiracy responsible for bringing Count Altamira here to Paris? Tell me what's going on: I'm dying to know. I'll be discreet, I swear I will!' She was astonished at this word as she heard herself uttering it. Good grief! was she pleading with an inferior? As her embarrassment grew, she added somewhat flippantly:

'What can possibly have turned you, who are usually so cold, into a being inspired—a sort of Michelangelo prophet?'

This sharp and indiscreet interrogation wounded Julien deeply and threw him back into his deranged state.

'Was Danton right to steal?' he asked her brusquely, with a look in his eyes that grew wilder every minute. 'Should the Piedmontese* or Spanish revolutionaries have compromised the common people by committing crimes? Have given away all the posts in the army, and all the military crosses, even to people who didn't deserve them? Wouldn't the people who had worn these crosses have feared the return of the king? Should they have plundered the Turin treasures? In short, mademoiselle,' he said, stepping up to her with a terrible expression, 'must a man who wants to wipe ignorance and crime from the face of the earth sweep over it like a tempest and wreak evil more or less at random?'

Mathilde was alarmed, and could not withstand his gaze; she stepped back two paces. She looked at him for an instant; then, ashamed of her alarm, she tripped lightly out of the library.

CHAPTER 10

Queen Marguerite

O love! what madness is so great that you
cannot persuade us to find pleasure in it.
Letters from a PORTUGUESE NUN.*

JULIEN reread his letters. When the dinner bell sounded:
How ridiculous I must have been in the eyes of that Parisian
doll! he said to himself; what madness to tell her straight what
I was thinking about! But perhaps not such madness after all.
On this occasion the truth was worthy of me.

Anyway, why did she come and question me about private
things! It was an indiscreet question coming from her. She
offended against etiquette. My thoughts about Danton aren't
part of the service her father pays me for.

When he reached the dining-room Julien was distracted
from his bad temper by the sight of M\ue de La Mole in her full
mourning, which he found all the more striking as no other
member of the family was in black.

When dinner was over he found himself completely
recovered from the fit of enthusiasm which had gripped him
all day. By a stroke of fortune, the academician who knew
Latin was one of the company. He's the man who'll be least
inclined to laugh at me, Julien told himself, if, as I assume,
my question about M\ue de La Mole's mourning is a sign of
ineptitude.

Mathilde was looking at him with a strange expression. Isn't
this just what Mme de Rênal told me about the flirtatiousness
of the women in this part of the world? thought Julien. I
wasn't nice to her this morning, I didn't give in to her whim
to engage in conversation. It puts me up in her esteem. I dare
say there'll be all hell to pay. Later on her disdainful haughtiness will find a way of taking revenge. I defy her to do her
worst. What a contrast with what I've lost! What delightful
spontaneity! What simplicity! I used to know her thoughts
before she did; I saw them taking shape; my only opponent in

her heart was her fear of her children dying; it was a reasonable
and natural feeling, one I cherished even, though I suffered on
account of it. I was a fool. The ideas I dreamed up about Paris
prevented me from appreciating this sublime woman.

What a difference, my God! What do I find here? Arid and
haughty vanity, all the shades of pride and nothing more.

They were leaving the table. I mustn't let my academician
get caught by someone else, Julien told himself. He went up
to him as they were moving into the garden, put on a gentle
and submissive air and joined in his fury at the success of
Hernani.*

'If only we were still in the days of *lettres de cachet*... !'* he
said.

'Then he wouldn't have dared,' exclaimed the academician
with a gesture like Talma.*

Remarking on a flower, Julien quoted a few words from
Virgil's *Georgics*, and declared that nothing could match the
poetry of the Abbé Delille. In short, he flattered the academician in all ways possible. After which, with an air of total
indifference:

'I suppose', he asked him, 'that Mlle de La Mole must have
received an inheritance from some uncle or other, and be in
mourning for him?'

'Goodness! you're a member of the household', said the
academician, stopping in his tracks, 'and you don't know about
her folly? As a matter of fact, it's strange that her mother
allows her to do things like this; but between ourselves,
strength of character isn't exactly what the members of this
family are renowned for. Mlle Mathilde has enough for all of
them put together, and she rules them all. Today is the 30th
of April!' And the academician stopped and gave Julien a
knowing look. Julien smiled with the most intelligent
expression he could muster.

What connection can there possibly be between ruling a
whole household, wearing a black dress and the 30th of April?
he wondered. I must be even more obtuse than I thought.

'I'll confess to you...' he said to the academician, keeping
the questioning look in his eye.

'Let's take a turn round the garden,' said the academician,

thrilled to glimpse an opportunity to indulge in lengthy and elegant narrative. 'Come now! Is it really possible that you don't know what happened on the 30th of April 1574?'

'Where do you mean?' asked Julien in astonishment.

'In the Place de Grève.'*

Julien was so astonished that this answer did not put him in the picture. Curiosity, and the expectation of some tragic interest, which were so in keeping with his character, gave him those shining eyes that a story-teller so likes to see in his listener. The academician, thrilled to find a virgin ear, related to Julien at length how on the 30th of April 1574 the handsomest man of his time, Boniface de La Mole,* and his friend Hannibal de Coconasso, a Piedmontese gentleman, had had their heads cut off in the Place de Grève. La Mole was the adored lover of Queen Marguerite of Navarre;* 'And note', added the academician, 'that Mlle de La Mole is called Mathilde-Marguerite. La Mole was also the Duc d'Alençon's* favourite and the intimate friend of his mistress's husband, the King of Navarre, later to become Henri IV. On Shrove Tuesday of that year 1574, the Court was at Saint-Germain with poor King Charles IX, who was in the throes of dying. La Mole determined to abduct his princely friends, who were being kept prisoners at Court by Queen Catherine de Medici.* He brought two hundred horses up beneath the walls of Saint-Germain; the Duc d'Alençon lost his nerve, and La Mole was thrown to the executioner.

'But what Mlle Mathilde finds so moving, something she revealed to me herself some seven or eight years ago when she was twelve, for she has a mind of her own, she does...!' And the academician raised his eyes to heaven. 'What struck her imagination in this political catastrophe was that Queen Marguerite of Navarre hid in a house on the Place de Grève and had the courage to send someone to the executioner to request the head of her lover. And at midnight on the following evening she took this head in her carriage, and went off to bury it herself in a chapel at the foot of Montmartre.'

'Really?' Julien exclaimed, genuinely moved.

'Mlle Mathilde despises her brother because, as you can see, he never spares a single thought for all this ancient history,

and never wears mourning on the 30th of April. Ever since
this famous execution, in memory of La Mole's close friendship with Coconasso who, like the good Italian he was, was
called Hannibal, all the men in this family are given this name.
And,' added the academician lowering his voice, 'this Coconasso, according to Charles IX himself, was one of the cruellest
assassins of the 24th of August 1572.* But how can it be, my
dear Sorel, that you are ignorant of these things, when you sit
at the family table?'

'So that's why twice at dinner Mlle de La Mole called her
brother Hannibal. I thought I must have misheard.'

'It was a reproach. It's strange that the Marquise puts up
with such follies... The man who marries that tall girl has got
some pretty rich things coming to him!'

This comment was followed by five or six satirical remarks.
The delight and the familiarity shining in the academician's
eyes shocked Julien. We're just like two servants busy running
down their masters, he thought. But nothing should surprise
me coming from this Academy man.

One day Julien had surprised him on his knees before the
Marquise de La Mole; he was asking her for a tobacconist's
licence for a nephew in the provinces. That evening, one of
Mlle de La Mole's little chambermaids, who was pursuing
Julien just as Elisa had once done, gave him the idea that her
mistress's mourning was not put on to attract attention. It was
a quirk which stemmed from the depths of her character. She
genuinely loved this La Mole, the beloved lover of the wittiest
queen of her century—a man who lost his life for attempting
to restore freedom to his friends. And what friends too! The
First Prince of the Blood* and Henri IV.

Accustomed as he was to the perfect spontaneity which was
the mark of all of Mme de Renâl's behaviour, Julien saw
nothing but affectation in all the women in Paris; and he only
had to feel the least bit melancholy to find nothing at all to say
to them. Mlle de La Mole was an exception.

He began to stop interpreting as emotional coldness the kind
of beauty that stems from a noble bearing. He had long
conversations with Mlle de La Mole, who sometimes went out
into the garden with him after dinner to stroll up and down

outside the open windows of the drawing-room. She told him one day that she was reading D'Aubigné's* *History*, and Brantôme. Strange reading matter, thought Julien; and the marquise doesn't allow her to read Walter Scott's novels!

One day, her eyes shining with the pleasure which denotes sincerity, she told him admiringly about something she had read in L'Etoile's* memoirs concerning a young woman who had lived in Henri III's reign:* finding her husband unfaithful, she had stabbed him to death.

Julien's self-esteem was flattered. A person who was surrounded by so much respect, and who, according to the academician, ruled the entire household, deigned to speak to him in a way which could almost be taken for friendship.

I was wrong, Julien soon thought; it isn't familiarity, I'm only the confidant in a tragedy, it's her need to talk. They take me for learned in this family. I'll go off and read Brantôme, D'Aubigné and L'Etoile. I'll be able to challenge some of the anecdotes Mlle de La Mole talks to me about. I want to get out of this role of passive confidant.

Little by little his conversations with this young lady of such imposing and yet such relaxed bearing became more interesting. He forgot his dreary role as a rebellious plebeian. He found her learned and even sound in her ideas. Her opinions in the garden were very different from the ones she professed in the drawing-room. With him she sometimes had moments of enthusiasm and frankness which were the absolute opposite of her usual manner, so haughty and so cold.

'The Wars of the League* were France's heroic age,' she said to him one day, her eyes glittering with inspiration and enthusiasm. 'At that time everyone fought to get the particular thing he wanted, to make his party triumph, and not just to win a boring cross like in the time of your emperor. You must agree that there was less egoism and petty-mindedness. I love that century.'

'And Boniface de La Mole was its hero,' he said.

'At any rate he was loved as it must perhaps be sweet to be loved. What woman alive nowadays would not be revolted to touch the head of her decapitated lover?'

Mme de La Mole summoned her daughter. If hypocrisy is to

be of service, it must remain hidden; and Julien, as you observe, had half-confessed to Mlle de La Mole his admiration for Napoleon.

This is the tremendous advantage they have over us, said Julien to himself when he was left alone in the garden. The history of their ancestors lifts them above vulgar sentiments, and they aren't always obliged to be thinking about their livelihood! How wretched! he added bitterly, I'm not worthy to reflect on these higher matters. My life is nothing but a series of hypocritical postures, because I haven't got an income of a thousand francs to buy my bread and butter.

'What are you dreaming of now, sir?' Mathilde asked him, running back outside.

Julien was tired of despising himself. His pride made him tell her openly what he was thinking. He flushed deeply when speaking of his poverty to a person with so much wealth. He tried to make it clear from his dignified tone that he wasn't asking for anything. He had never struck Mathilde as more attractive; she detected in him a sensitivity and openness which he often lacked.

Less than a month later, Julien was strolling pensively in the garden of the Hôtel de La Mole; but his face no longer showed the hardness and the philosophical arrogance stamped on it by the constant feeling of his own inferiority. He had just gone back to the door of the drawing-room with Mlle de La Mole, who maintained she had hurt her foot while dashing about with her brother.

She leaned on my arm in a rather special way! Julien said to himself. Am I a fop, or could it be true that she rather fancies me? She listens to me with such a sweet expression, even when I'm confessing all the sufferings of my pride to her! When you think how haughty she is with everyone! They'd be pretty astonished in the drawing-room to see her with a look like that on her face. It's quite certain she doesn't wear that sweet, kind expression for anyone else.

Julien tried not to let himself overestimate the significance of this strange friendship. He compared it himself to an armed encounter. Every day when they met up again, before resuming the almost intimate tones of the day before, it was as if they asked themselves: shall we be friends or enemies today? Julien had realized that to let this haughty girl insult him even once with impunity would be to lose everything. If I have to quarrel with her, isn't it better for it to happen straight away, in defending the legitimate rights of my pride, rather than in rebuffing the marks of scorn that would soon follow the slightest failure to uphold what I owe to my personal dignity?

Several times, on days when she was in a bad mood, Mathilde tried to adopt the manner of a great lady with him; she put a rare degree of subtlety into these attempts, but Julien rudely rebuffed them.

One day he interrupted her brusquely: 'Does Mlle de La Mole have some order to give her father's secretary?' he said to her. 'He is required to listen to her orders and to carry them out with respect; but beyond that, he is not obliged to say a single word to her. He is not paid to communicate his thoughts to her.'

This kind of behaviour, and the strange suspicions Julien was having, banished the boredom he regularly experienced in that magnificent drawing-room where people were yet afraid of everything, and it was not seemly to joke about anything.

It'd be funny if she were in love with me! Whether or not she loves me, Julien went on, I have an intimate confidante in a girl of intelligence who has the whole household in fear and trembling before her, so I see, and the Marquis de Croisenois more than anyone else. Such a polite, gentle and brave young man, who has all the advantages of birth and fortune put together, a single one of which would more than gladden my heart! He's madly in love with her, and is due to marry her. How many letters M. de La Mole has had me write to the two solicitors to arrange the contract! And yours truly, who feels just how subordinate he is with pen in hand, finds himself, two hours later in the garden, triumphing over this agreeable young man: for after all, her preference is striking, and very marked. Perhaps, too, she hates in him the future husband. She has pride enough for that. And the kindness she shows to me is earned in my capacity as a subordinate confidant.

Come off it! Either I'm mad, or she's making advances to me; the more coldly and respectfully I treat her, the more she seeks me out. It could be deliberate policy, a sort of affectation; but I see her eyes light up when I turn up unexpectedly. Do women in Paris have the art of feigning to such a degree? What does it matter to me! Appearances are on my side, so let's enjoy appearances. Goodness, she's beautiful! I do so like her big blue eyes, seen from close up, when they gaze at me as they so often do! What a difference between this spring and last, when I lived in misery, keeping myself going by sheer will-power in the midst of those hundreds of filthy, spiteful hypocrites! I was almost as spiteful as they are.

On days when he felt mistrustful: This girl is making fun of me, Julien thought. She's in league with her brother to mystify me. But she looks as if she so despises the lack of energy in that brother of hers! 'He's brave, but that's all there is to him,' she says to me. 'He doesn't have a single thought that dares to deviate from what's fashionable. I'm always the one who has to come to his defence.' A girl of nineteen! At that age is it possible to keep to a self-imposed hypocrisy every moment of the day?

On the other hand, when Mlle de La Mole fixes her big blue eyes on me with that strange look in them, Count Norbert invariably goes away. I find that suspect; shouldn't he be indignant at seeing his sister single out one of their household *domestics*? For that's how I've heard the Duc de Chaulnes speaking of me. This memory caused anger to wipe out all other feelings. Is it just a fondness this obsessive old duke has for old-fashioned ways of speaking?

So then, she's pretty! Julien went on with the look of a tiger. I shall have her and then make my exit, and woe betide anyone who disturbs me in my flight!

This idea became Julien's sole preoccupation; he was no longer able to think of anything else. His days passed by like hours.

Time and time again, when he was trying to deal with some matter of serious business, his mind would let everything drop, and he would wake up a quarter of an hour later with his heart pounding and his head in turmoil, fixated on this thought: Is she in love with me?

CHAPTER 11

The power of a young lady

*I admire her beauty, but I live in fear of
her mind*

MÉRIMÉE*

IF Julien had spent as much time studying what went on in
the drawing-room as he devoted to exaggerating Mathilde's
beauty, or to working himself into a passion against the innate
haughtiness of her family—which she laid aside on his
account—he would have understood what constituted her
power over her entourage. As soon as anyone displeased Mlle
de La Mole, she had a way of punishing the offender with a
joke that was so measured, so well chosen, so seemly on the
surface, and so appositely delivered, that the wound grew
greater every moment, the more you thought about it. It
gradually became unbearable to the afflicted self-esteem. As
she laid no store by many of the things that were genuinely
desired by the rest of the family, she always appeared imperturbable in their eyes. Aristocratic salons are a fine source of
quotations once you've stepped outside, but that's all; politeness in itself doesn't impress after the first few days. Julien
experienced this—after the first enchantment, the first astonishment. Politeness, he told himself, is only an absence of the
anger that would be occasioned by bad manners. Mathilde was
often bored, she would perhaps have been bored anywhere. So
sharpening an epigram was a distraction and a real pleasure for
her.

It was perhaps in a bid to find some slightly more amusing
victims than her immediate family, the academician and the
five or six other subordinates who curried favour with them,
that she had kindled hopes in the Marquis de Croisenois, the
Comte de Caylus and two or three other young men of the
greatest distinction. For her, they were nothing more than
fresh targets for her epigrams.

We shall admit with some distress, for we like Mathilde,

that she had received letters from several of them, and had on occasion replied. We hasten to add she is a character who constitutes an exception to the mores of this century. Lack of prudence is not generally a reproach to be levelled at pupils of the noble convent of the Sacred Heart.

One day the Marquis de Croisenois handed back to Mathilde a rather compromising letter she had written him the day before. He was hoping by this mark of the highest prudence to advance his affairs considerably. But imprudence was what Mathilde relished in her correspondence. She took pleasure in gambling with her fate. She did not speak to him for six weeks afterwards.

She was amused by these young men's letters; but in her opinion, they were all alike. It was always the deepest of passions, and the most melancholy.

'They're all the same perfect man, ready to set off for Palestine,' she said to her cousin. 'Can you think of anything more insipid? So these are the letters I shall be getting all my life! Letters like that can only change every twenty years, according to the kind of occupation in fashion. They must have been less colourless at the time of the Empire. Then, all those young men from high society had seen or engaged in actions that *really* were heroic. The Duc de N——, my uncle, was at Wagram.'*

'What wit do you need to strike someone with a sabre? And when this has happened to them, they talk about it so much!' said M‍lle de Sainte-Hérédité, Mathilde's cousin.

'Well! I enjoy these accounts. Being in a *real* battle, one of Napoleon's battles, where ten thousand soldiers got killed, that proves courage. Exposing yourself to danger elevates the soul and saves it from the boredom which seems to engulf my poor worshippers; and it's catching, this boredom is. Which one of them has it in mind to do something out of the ordinary? They're striving to win my hand, big deal! I'm rich, and my father will see to his son-in-law's advancement. Ah! would that he might find one who was the slightest bit amusing!'

Mathilde's lively, trenchant and picturesque way of looking at things ruined her style, as you can see. Often one of her expressions was felt to be a blot by her exquisitely polite friends. They would almost have admitted to themselves, if she had been less in fashion, that her speech was just a bit too colourful for feminine delicacy.

She, for her part, was most unjust towards the good-looking cavaliers who frequent the Bois de Boulogne. She viewed the future not with terror—that would have been a strong sentiment—but with a repugnance rare at her age.

What more could she wish for? Fortune, noble birth, intelligence, beauty—so they said and so she believed—had all been heaped upon her by the hand of Fate.

These were the thoughts of the most highly envied heiress of the Faubourg Saint-Germain when she began to take pleasure in going for walks with Julien. She was astonished at his pride; she admired the canniness of this ordinary commoner. He'll work his way up to becoming a bishop like the Abbé Maury,* she said to herself.

Soon the genuine, unfeigned resistance with which our hero greeted several of her ideas began to preoccupy her; she kept thinking about it; she related to her friend and confidante the finest details of their conversations, and felt that she never managed to convey their full flavour properly.

She had a sudden illumination: I'm fortunate enough to be in love, she said to herself one day, in a fit of unbelievable joy. I'm in love, I'm in love, it's obvious! At my age, where else should a young, beautiful and witty girl experience strong emotion, if not in love? It's no use, I'll never feel love for Croisenois, Caylus and *tutti quanti*. They're perfect, maybe too perfect; anyway, they bore me.

She ran through in her mind all the descriptions of passion she had read in *Manon Lescaut*,* *La Nouvelle Héloïse*, the *Letters from a Portuguese Nun*, etc. etc. There was no question, of course, of anything other than a grand passion: a passing fancy was unworthy of a girl of her age and her birth. She only bestowed the name of love on that heroic sentiment encountered in France in the days of Henri III and Bassompierre.* That kind of love did not yield basely before obstacles; quite the opposite, it caused great deeds to be done. What a misfortune for me that there isn't a real Court like Catherine de Medici's or Louis XIII's!* I feel ready for the boldest and the greatest ventures. What would I not do with a valiant king like Louis XIII sighing at my feet! I'd lead him into the Vendée,* as the Baron de Tolly is always saying, and from there he'd recapture his kingdom; and then no more Charter*... and Julien would help me. What's he lacking? A name and a fortune. He'd make a name for himself, and he'd acquire a fortune.

Croisenois lacks nothing; and he'll never be more than a half-Ultra, half-liberal duke all his life, an indecisive creature always keeping away from extremes, and *consequently in second place everywhere*.

What great action isn't *an extreme* at the moment when it is undertaken? Only when it is accomplished does it seems possible to ordinary mortals. Yes, it's love with all its miracles that's going to reign in my heart; I can feel it from the fire burning within me. Heaven owed me this favour. It won't have heaped all these advantages on a single individual in vain. My happiness will be worthy of me. Each one of my days will cease to be a cold replica of the one before. There's already proof of greatness and daring in being bold enough to love a man so far removed from me on the social scale. We shall see: will he continue to be worthy of me? At the first sign of weakness I see in him, I shall abandon him. A girl of my birth, with the chivalrous character too that people are good enough to credit me with (this was one of her father's expressions), must not behave like a silly fool.

Isn't that precisely the role I'd be playing if I loved the Marquis de Croisenois? I'd have a new edition of my cousins' happiness, which I despise so utterly. I know in advance everything the poor marquis would say to me, and everything I'd have to reply to him. What sort of a love is it that makes you yawn? Might as well go in for religion. I'd have a celebration to mark the signing of the contract, just like my youngest cousin had, with the grandparents getting all senti-mental—that is, if they weren't miffed because of a last-minute condition that had been slipped into the contract the day before by the other party's solicitor.

CHAPTER 12

Might he be a Danton?

The need to be on edge: such was the character of
the fair Marguerite de Valois, my aunt who soon
married the King of Navarre, whom we now soon
see reigning in France under the name of Henri IV. Her
need to gamble was the key to this amiable
princess's character; whence her quarrels and her
reconciliations, starting with her brothers from the
age of sixteen. Now what does a young lady have to
gamble with? Her most precious possession: her
reputation, the basis of esteem for the rest of her life.

Memoirs of the DUC D'ANGOULÈME*
natural son of Charles IX

JULIEN and I have no signed contract between us, no solicitor,
everything is heroic, everything will be born of chance. Apart
from noble birth, which he lacks, this is Marguerite de Valois's
love for young La Mole, the most distinguished man of his
time. Is it my fault if the young men at Court are such staunch
followers of *the conventional*, and turn pale at the mere idea of
any adventure in the least bit out of the ordinary? A little trip
to Greece or Africa* is the height of daring for them, and even
then they only know how to march with their troops. As soon
as they find themselves alone they're afraid, not of Bedouin
spears but of ridicule, and this fear drives them mad.

My little Julien, on the other hand, only likes acting on his
own. Never the slightest thought, in this privileged creature,
of turning to others for support and help! He despises others,
and that's why I don't despise him.

If, for all his poverty, Julien was noble, my love would
merely be vulgar folly, a boring misalliance; I'd want none of
it; it wouldn't have what characterizes grand passions: the
vastness of the difficulty to be overcome and the black uncertainty of the outcome.

Mlle de La Mole was so preoccupied with these fine arguments that the next day, without realizing it, she praised Julien

to the Marquis de Croisenois and her brother. Her eloquence went so far that it rankled with them.

'Watch out for that young man, who has so much energy,' exclaimed her brother. 'If the revolution starts up again, he'll have us all guillotined.'

She was careful not to reply, and hastened to tease her brother and the Marquis de Croisenois for their fear of energy—nothing more, basically, than fear of facing the unexpected, or terror of being caught short by the unexpected...

'Every time, gentlemen, every time it's fear of ridicule, the monster which unfortunately died in 1816.'*

'Ridicule no longer exists', M. de La Mole used to say, 'in a country with two political parties.'

His daughter had taken the point.

'So you see, gentlemen,' she said to Julien's enemies, 'you'll have been thoroughly frightened all your lives, and at the end you'll be told:

It was not a wolf, it was only its shadow.'*

Mathilde soon left them. Her brother's words appalled her; they worried her considerably; but by the next day she took them as the finest form of praise.

In this century, when all energy is dead, his energy frightens them. I'll repeat my brother's words to him; I want to see what his answer is. But I'll choose one of those moments when his eyes are shining. He can't lie to me then.

He'd be a Danton! she went on after her mind had rambled confusedly for a long time. *Well then! the Revolution would have started up again. What roles would Croisenois and my brother be playing in that case? It's laid down in advance: sublime resignation. They'd be heroic lambs, letting their throats be cut without a word. Their only fear as they died would be yet again of being in bad taste. My little Julien would blow out the brains of any Jacobin who came to arrest him, if he had the slightest hope of getting away. He's not afraid of being in bad taste, not he.*

This last thought made her pensive; it reawakened painful memories, and took away all her boldness. This thought reminded her of all the quips made by Messrs de Caylus, de Croisenois, de Luz and her brother. These gentlemen were unanimous in holding against Julien his ecclesiastical air: humble and hypocritical.

But, she resumed suddenly, with a gleam of joy in her eye, the bitterness and the frequency of their jokes prove, in spite of them, that he's the most distinguished man we've seen this winter. What do his faults, his ridiculous sides matter? He has greatness about him, and they are shocked by it, for all their kindness and indulgence. It's undoubtedly true that he's poor, and that he has studied to become a priest; while they are squadron commanders, and didn't need to pursue any studies; much easier for them.

In spite of all the disadvantages of his eternal black suit, and that ecclesiastical expression of his, which he actually has to have, poor boy, to avoid starving to death, his talent frightens them, nothing could be plainer. And the ecclesiastical expression vanishes as soon as we're alone together for a few moments. And when these gentlemen say something they think is subtle and unexpected, isn't their first glance directed at Julien? I've noticed that quite clearly. And yet they know full well that he never speaks to them unless questioned. I'm the only one he talks to unsolicited, he thinks I have a lofty mind. He only replies to their objections just enough to be polite. He lapses into deference right away. With me, he goes on discussing things for hours, he isn't sure of his ideas as long as I put forward the slightest objection to them. Anyway, all this winter no one has drawn pistols; all that's happened is a bit of verbal attention-seeking. Well, my father, who's a superior being, and will do great things for the fortunes of our house—my father respects Julien. The rest of them hate him, nobody despises him apart from my mother's pious women friends.

The Comte de Caylus had or pretended to have a great passion for horses; he spent his life in his stable, and often had lunch there. This great passion, coupled with his habit of never laughing, made him greatly respected among his friends: he was the eagle of their little circle.

As soon as they had gathered the next day behind Mme de La

Mole's sofa, without Julien there, M. de Caylus, backed by Croisenois and Norbert, roundly attacked Mathilde's good opinion of Julien, and this quite out of the blue, almost as soon as he saw Mlle de La Mole. She grasped this piece of subtlety from a mile off, and was charmed by it.

There they all are in league, she said to herself, against a man of genius who hasn't so much as ten louis in income, and can only answer them when he's questioned. They're afraid of him garbed in his black suit. What would it be like with epaulettes?

She had never been more brilliant. Right from the first skirmishes, she poured jocular sarcasm on Caylus and his allies. When the fire of these brilliant officers' jokes had died down:

'If tomorrow some country squire from the Franche-Comté mountains', she said to M. de Caylus, 'realizes that Julien is his natural son and gives him a name and a few thousand francs, in six weeks he'll have moustaches like you, gentlemen; in six months he'll be an officer in the Hussars like you, gentlemen. And then the greatness of his character won't be an object of ridicule any more. I see you reduced, your grace the future duke, to the old, bad argument that the Court nobility is superior to the nobility of the provinces. But what will you be left with, if I decide to push you to the limits, if I'm mischievous enough to give Julien a Spanish duke for a father, a prisoner of war in Besançon in Napoleon's day, who has prickings of conscience and recognizes him on his deathbed?'

All these suppositions about an illegitimate birth were felt to be in rather poor taste by Messrs de Caylus and de Croisenois. That was all they saw in Mathilde's line of reasoning.

However much Norbert was under her thumb, his sister's words were so clear that he put on a grave expression which, it must be admitted, ill suited his kind, smiling face. He plucked up the courage to say one or two words.

'Are you ill, my dear?' Mathilde answered with a serious little expression on her face. 'You must be feeling pretty bad to counter my joking with moralizing.

'Moralizing, you of all people! Are you canvassing for a job as prefect?'

Mathilde soon forgot the Comte de Caylus's look of annoyance, Norbert's bad temper and M. de Croisenois's silent despair. She had to make up her mind about a dreadful hypothesis which had just begun to obsess her.

Julien is pretty sincere with me, she said to herself; at his age, someone so low on fortune's ladder who suffers as he does through his astonishing ambition needs a woman for a friend. Maybe I am that friend; but I don't detect any love in him. With his boldness of character he would have spoken to me of his love.

This uncertainty, this debate with herself, which from then on filled Mathilde's every moment, and was fuelled with fresh arguments every time Julien spoke to her, completely banished those moments of boredom she was so prone to.

As the daughter of an intelligent man who might become a minister and restore their forests to the clergy,* Mlle de La Mole had been an object of the most excessive flattery while at the convent of the Sacred Heart. There is no remedy for this misfortune. She had been persuaded that because of all her advantages of birth, wealth, etc., she ought to be happier than other girls. This is the source of the boredom suffered by princes, and of all their follies.

Mathilde had not escaped the dire influence of this notion. However sharp you are, you can't be on your guard at ten years old against the flattery of a whole convent, especially when it has the appearance of being so well founded.

From that moment she had decided she was in love with Julien, she stopped feeling bored. Every day she congratulated herself on her decision to indulge in a grand passion. It's a pastime fraught with danger, she thought. So much the better! Thousands of times better!

Without a grand passion, I was languishing with boredom at the best time of my life, between sixteen and twenty. I've already wasted my best years; forced for my only pleasure to listen to my mother's friends rabbiting on—women who, I gather, were not so strict in Coblenz* in 1792 as their pronouncements are today.

It was while these great uncertainties were preying on Mathilde that Julien failed to understand the long gazes she fixed upon him. He certainly detected an increased coldness in Count Norbert's manners, and a fresh fit of haughtiness in Messrs de Caylus, de Luz and de Croisenois. He was accustomed to it. This misfortune sometimes befell him as a sequel to an evening when he had shone more brilliantly than befitted his station. Had it not been for the special reception which Mathilde gave him, and the curiosity aroused in him by this whole set-up, he would have avoided following these dazzling young men with moustaches into the garden when they accompanied Mlle de La Mole there after dinner.

Yes, there's no way I can hide it from myself, thought Julien, Mlle de La Mole has a strange way of looking at me. But even when her lovely blue eyes are staring at me wide open with the greatest of abandon, I always decipher in them traces of scrutiny, detachment and cruelty. Can it really be that *this* is love? What a contrast with the way Mme de Rênal would look at me!

One evening after dinner, Julien, who had followed M. de La Mole into his study, was making his way quickly back to the garden. As he drew up to Mathilde's group without signalling his presence, he overheard one or two words uttered very loud. She was tormenting her brother. Julien heard his name pronounced twice unmistakably. He appeared; a deep silence fell all of a sudden, and vain efforts were made to break it. Mlle de La Mole and her brother were too worked up to find any other subject of conversation. Messrs de Caylus, de Croisenois, de Luz and one of their friends struck Julien as being chilly as ice. He moved away.

CHAPTER 13

A plot

Unconnected remarks, chance encounters are
transformed into the most blatant proof in the eyes
of a man of imagination if he has any spark of fire
in his heart.

SCHILLER*

THE next day Julien again caught Norbert and his sister
talking about him. His arrival prompted a deathly silence,
as on the previous evening. His suspicions ran riot. Have
these agreeable young people by any chance undertaken to
make fun of me? That's much more likely, much more
natural, I must confess, than a putative passion of Mlle de
La Mole's for a poor devil of a secretary. In the first place,
do people of this sort have passions? Mystification is their
strong point. They're jealous of my wretched superiority in
using words. Being jealous is again one of their weaknesses.
Everything hangs together in this scheme of things. Mlle de
La Mole wants to persuade me that she's singling me out,
simply in order to produce a spectacle for the benefit of her
suitor.

This cruel suspicion altered the whole of Julien's psychological stance. His insight found a nascent feeling of love in his
heart, and had no difficulty in destroying it. This love was
based only on Mathilde's rare beauty, or rather on her queenly
ways and her wondrous style of dress. In this respect Julien
was still a social climber. A pretty woman from high society is,
so they maintain, what most astonishes a peasant with a sharp
mind when he reaches the upper classes of society. It was not
Mathilde's character that had set Julien dreaming these past
few days. He had enough sense to realize that he did not
understand her character at all. Everything he saw of it might
be no more than an outward appearance.

For instance, nothing in the whole world would have made
Mathilde miss Mass on a Sunday. She accompanied her
mother to church almost every day. If some rash guest in the

drawing-room of the Hôtel de La Mole forgot where he was
and allowed himself the remotest allusion to a joke against
the real or supposed interests of throne or altar, Mathilde
would instantly freeze into icy seriousness. Her look, always
so piercing, took on all the inscrutable hauteur of an old
family portrait.

But Julien had ascertained that she still had one or two of
the most philosophical of Voltaire's works in her room. He
himself often made off with a few volumes of the fine edition
in its magnificent binding. By separating each volume a little
from its neighbour, he concealed the absence of the one he was
taking, but he soon noticed that some other person was reading
Voltaire. He resorted to a ruse learned in the seminary, and
put a few strands of horsehair on the volumes he imagined
might be of interest to Mlle de La Mole. They disappeared for
weeks on end.

M. de La Mole, who had grown impatient with his bookseller for sending him all the *fake Memoirs** that came out,
instructed Julien to buy any new titles that were at all
titillating. But lest poison should spread through the household, the secretary had orders to deposit these books in a small
bookcase in the marquis's own room. He was soon quite
certain that these new books only had to be hostile to the
interests of throne and altar, and they would disappear in no
time. And it was scarcely Norbert who was the reader.

Exaggerating the significance of this discovery, Julien attributed a Machiavellian duplicity to Mlle de La Mole. This alleged
wickedness was one of her charms in his eyes, almost the only
psychological charm she had. Boredom with hypocrisy and the
language of virtue threw him into this excess.

What was happening was that he was whipping up his own
imagination rather than being carried away by love.

It was after losing himself in fantasies about the elegance
of Mlle de La Mole's figure, the excellent taste of her attire,
the whiteness of her hands, the beauty of her arms, the
*disinvoltura** of all her movements, that he found himself in
love. At that point, to complete the spell, he believed she was
a Catherine de Medici. Nothing was too profound or too
wicked for the character he imputed to her. She was the ideal

of the Maslons, the Frilairs and the Castanèdes he had admired in his youth. In short, for him she represented the ideal of Paris.

Was ever anything funnier than attributing profundity or wickedness to the Parisian character?

It's possible that this trio is making fun of me, thought Julien. You have very little understanding of his character if you can't already see the sullen and cold expression assumed by his gaze when it met Mathilde's. Bitter irony repelled the assurances of friendship that Mlle de La Mole was bold enough to venture on one or two occasions.

Stung by the sudden oddness of his response, this girl's heart, which was naturally cold, bored and receptive to things of the mind, became as passionate as it was in her nature to be. But there was also a great deal of pride in Mathilde's character, and the birth of a sentiment which made her whole happiness depend on someone else was accompanied by gloom and sadness.

Julien had already learned enough since his arrival in Paris to discern that this was not the arid sadness of boredom. Instead of being eager, as before, for parties, shows and all manners of entertainments, she shunned them.

Music sung by Frenchmen bored Mathilde to death, and yet Julien, who made it his duty to be present when people came out of the Opera, noticed that she arranged to be taken there as often as she could. He thought he detected that she had lost some of the perfect moderation that shone in all her actions. She sometimes answered her friends with jokes that were offensive, they were so caustically hard-hitting. It seemed to him that she had it in for the Marquis de Croisenois. This young man really must have an insane love of money—not to walk out on this girl, however rich she may be! Julien thought. And for his own part, incensed at the way male dignity was being insulted, he stepped up his coldness towards her. He often went so far as to produce replies that were scarcely civil.

However firm his resolve not to be taken in by Mathilde's signs of interest, they were so obvious on some days, and Julien, the scales falling from his eyes, was beginning to find her so pretty that he was sometimes quite embarrassed by it.

The skill and persistence shown by these young members of high society might end up getting the better of my inexperience, he said to himself; I must go away and put a stop to all this. The marquis had just entrusted him with the administration of a number of small estates and houses he owned in the lower Languedoc.* A journey was necessary: M. de La Mole gave his unwilling consent. Except in matters of high ambition, Julien had become his second self.

When you tot it all up, they haven't caught me out, Julien said to himself as he made ready to leave. Whether the jokes Mlle de La Mole makes at these gentlemen's expense are real or merely designed to boost my confidence, I've had my amusement from them.

If there isn't a conspiracy against the carpenter's son, Mlle de La Mole is unfathomable, but she is to the Marquis de Croisenois at least as much as to me. Yesterday, for instance, her ill-temper was real, and I had the pleasure of seeing her preference for me discountenance a young man who's as noble and rich as I'm a beggar and a plebeian. That's the finest of my triumphs; it'll keep me laughing in my post-chaise as I speed across the plains of the Languedoc.

He had kept his departure a secret, but Mathilde knew better than he did that he was going to leave Paris the next morning, and for a long while. She resorted to a dreadful headache, made worse by the stuffy air in the drawing-room. She walked about a good deal in the garden, and used her scathing jokes so effectively to harry Norbert, the Marquis de Croisenois, Caylus, de Luz and a few other young men who had dined at the Hôtel de La Mole, that she forced them to leave. She looked at Julien with a strange expression.

Looking at me like that may just be play-acting, thought Julien; but what about the fast breathing, what about all the emotion! Bah! he said to himself, who am I to pronounce on all these matters? I'm dealing with the most sublime and most subtle of all Parisian women. The fast breathing that was on the point of moving me will have been copied from Léontine Fay* whom she so admires.

They were left alone together; the conversation was visibly flagging. No! Julien has no feelings for me, said Mathilde to herself with real unhappiness.

As he was taking leave of her, she squeezed his arm tightly:

'You'll be getting a letter from me tonight,' she said to him in a tone of voice so altered that the sound was unrecognizable.

Julien was at once moved by this.

'My father', she went on, 'has a rightful esteem for the services you perform for him. *It's imperative* you don't leave tomorrow; find an excuse.' And off she ran.

Her figure was delightful. You couldn't imagine anyone with a daintier pair of feet, and she ran with a gracefulness that Julien found ravishing; but would you ever guess what his next thought was after she had completely disappeared from sight? He took offence at the peremptory tone in which she had uttered the phrase *it's imperative*. Louis XV on his deathbed was likewise stung to the quick by this phrase *it's imperative* tactlessly used by his physician in chief, and Louis XV was hardly a parvenu.

An hour later a footman handed Julien a letter; it was quite simply a declaration of love.

There isn't too much affectation in the style, Julien said to himself, attempting by his literary comments to contain the joy which made his cheeks go taut and forced him to laugh in spite of himself.

But me of all people, he suddenly exclaimed, passion being too strong to be contained, a poor peasant like me getting a declaration of love from a great lady!

On my side of the picture, things look pretty good, he added, suppressing his joy as much as he could. I've managed to preserve the dignity befitting my character. I haven't told her I love her. He began to study the shape of the letters; Mlle de La Mole had nice English handwriting.* He needed some sort of physical occupation to take his mind off a joy that was verging on delirium.

'Your departure forces me to speak... It would be more than my strength could bear not to see you any more.'

A sudden thought struck Julien like a discovery, interrupted his scrutiny of Mathilde's letter, and increased his joy twofold.

I've got the better of the Marquis de Croisenois, he exclaimed—me, with nothing but serious things to say! And he's so handsome! He's got a moustache and a fine uniform; he always comes up with some witty and subtle remark just at the right moment.

Julien spent a few exquisite moments; he wandered aimlessly through the garden, out of his mind with happiness.

Later he went up to his study and had himself announced to the Marquis de La Mole, who had fortunately not gone out. By showing him some papers marked as having just arrived from Normandy he had no difficulty in convincing him that in order to look after the Normandy lawsuits he needed to postpone his departure for the Languedoc.

'I'm so glad you're not leaving,' the marquis said to him when they had finished discussing business. '*I like having you around*.' Julien left the room; this remark made him feel uncomfortable.

And here am I about to seduce his daughter! to put a stop, maybe, to this marriage of hers with the Marquis de Croisenois, which is his great delight for the future: if he isn't a duke himself, at least his daughter will get a footstool.* It occurred to Julien that he should set off for the Languedoc in spite of Mathilde's letter, in spite of the explanation he had given the marquis. This flash of virtue soon vanished.

How kind I am, he said to himself, a plebeian like me taking pity on a family of this rank! when the Duc de Chaulnes calls me a domestic! How does the marquis increase his enormous fortune? By selling off some of his stocks when he finds out at Court that a *coup d'état* is going to be staged. And here am I, cast down on the bottom rung by a cruel Providence—giving me a noble heart and not so much as a thousand francs in income, in other words no bread to live on, *literally speaking no bread*; am I the one to refuse a pleasure on offer! A limpid spring welling up to quench my thirst in the burning desert of mediocrity I'm struggling to cross! Not on your life, I'm not that much of a fool; every man for himself in this desert of egoism they call life.

And he remembered a number of disdainful glances cast in his direction by Mme de La Mole, and especially by her *lady* friends.

The pleasure of triumphing over the Marquis de Croisenois finally succeeded in routing Julien's last recollection of virtue.

How I should like him to take offence! he said. How confidently I'd strike him now with my sword. And he made the gesture of someone thrusting in Seconde position. Before this I was a know-all, basely misusing a touch of pluck. After this letter, I'm his equal.

Yes, he said to himself, dwelling on the words with infinite voluptuousness, our respective worth—the marquis's and mine—has been weighed up, and the poor carpenter from the Jura has come out best.

Good! he exclaimed, there's the signature for my reply all waiting. Don't go imagining, Mlle de La Mole, that I'm forgetting my station. I'll make sure you understand and really feel that it's for the sake of a carpenter's son that you're betraying a descendant of the famous Guy de Croisenois who followed St Louis* to the Crusades.

Julien was unable to contain his joy. He was obliged to go down into the garden. His room where he had locked himself up seemed to him too cramped to breathe in.

Me, a poor peasant from the Jura, he repeated to himself over and over again, me, with this dismal black suit I'm condemned to wear for ever! Alas! twenty years ago I'd have worn a uniform like the rest of them! At that time a man like me had either been killed or was *a general by the age of thirty-six*. The letter which he was clutching in his hand gave him the stature and the stance of a hero. Nowadays, it's true, with a black suit like this, a man has a salary of a hundred thousand francs and the Blue Sash at forty, like Monsignor the Bishop of Beauvais.*

All right then! he said to himself, laughing like Mephistopheles, I've got more intelligence than they have; I can pick the right uniform for my century. And he felt a resurgence of ambition and attachment for the robes of the priesthood. How many cardinals were born beneath me and went on to reign! My fellow countryman Granvelle,* for instance.

Gradually Julien's agitation subsided; caution surfaced again. He said to himself, like his mentor Tartuffe, whose part he knew by heart:

I may believe such talk an honest ploy
....
I shall not trust the sound of words so sweet
Until she grants some token here and now
Of favours I so ardently desire
To vouch the truth of all her words imply.
                    Tartuffe, act IV, scene v

Tartuffe too was brought down by a woman, and he was no
worse than anyone else... My reply may be shown to someone... for which I can produce this remedy, he added, speaking
slowly in tones of controlled ferociousness—I'll start off with
the most vivid sentences from the sublime Mathilde's letter.

Yes, but four of M. de Croisenois's footmen pounce on me
and snatch the original from me.

No they don't, because I'm armed, and in the habit, as
people know, of firing at footmen.

All right then, one of them is plucky, he pounces on me.
He's been promised a hundred gold napoléons. I kill or wound
him, that's fine, just what they want. I'm thrown into prison
perfectly legally; I'm tried in the criminal court and sent off,
with all justice and fairness from the judges, to keep Messrs
Fontan and Magalon company in Poissy.* There I have to
sleep with four hundred beggars all lumped together... And
am I to feel any pity for these people! he exclaimed, jumping
impetuously to his feet. Do they have any for the lower orders
when they get their hands on them! This reflection was the
dying gasp of his gratitude towards M. de La Mole, which had
been tormenting him up till then, despite himself.

Steady on, good gentlemen, I understand this little piece of
Machiavellian cunning; Father Maslon or M. Castanède from
the seminary couldn't have done better. You'll get the *provocative* letter back from me, and I'll be the sequel to Colonel
Caron* at Colmar.

Wait a minute, gentlemen, I'm going to send the fateful
letter to the Reverend Father Pirard for safe-keeping in a well-
sealed envelope. He's an honourable man, and a Jansenist, and
as such immune from financial temptations. Yes, but he opens
letters... Fouqué's the person to send this one to.

Julien, it must be admitted, had a dreadful look in his eye

and a hideous countenance; it exuded unadulterated wickedness. He was the victim of misfortune at war with the whole of society.

To arms! Julien shouted out. And he leaped down the front steps of the Hôtel de La Mole in a single bound. He went into the writing clerk's booth on the street corner and gave him a good fright. 'Copy this!' he told him, handing him Mlle de La Mole's letter.

While the scribe was working, he himself wrote to Fouqué; he begged him to keep a precious object safe for him. But, he thought interrupting himself, the secret agency at the post office will open my letter and hand you back the one you're looking for... no, gentlemen. He went off and bought a fat Bible from a Protestant bookseller, hid Mathilde's letter very skilfully inside the cover, got the whole thing parcelled up, and his package left with the stage-coach, addressed to one of Fouqué's workmen, whose name was unknown to anyone in Paris.

This done, he went back to the Hôtel de La Mole joyful and lightfooted. Now for *the two of us!* he exclaimed, as he locked himself into his room and flung off his black suit:

'Indeed! mademoiselle,' he wrote to Mathilde, 'can this really be Mlle de La Mole who hands a letter via her father's manservant Arsène to a poor carpenter from the Jura—a most seductive letter no doubt meant to make fun of his gullibility...' And he copied out the most transparent sentences from the letter he had just received.

His reply would have been a credit to the Chevalier de Beauvoisis's diplomatic caution. It was still only ten o'clock; intoxicated with happiness and the feeling of his own power, so new to a poor devil like himself, Julien put in an appearance at the Italian Opera. He heard his friend Geronimo singing. Never had music brought him to such a pitch of exaltation. He was a god.[1]

---

[1] Esprit per. pré. gui. II. A. 30.* [Stendhal's footnote.]

CHAPTER 14

A young lady's thoughts

What bewilderment! What sleepless nights! Great
heavens! Am I going to make myself despicable?
He'll despise me himself. But he's leaving, he's going away.

                                    Alfred DE MUSSET*

IT was not without a struggle that Mathilde had written.
Whatever the origin of her interest in Julien, it soon got the
better of the pride which, ever since she had had any self-
awareness, had reigned supreme in her heart. This haughty,
cold individual was carried away for the first time in her life by
a passionate sentiment. But if it got the better of her pride, it
remained faithful to the habits of pride. Two months of
struggle and new sensations replenished, so to speak, the whole
of her psychological being.

Mathilde thought she glimpsed happiness. This vision,
which takes a total hold over courageous souls when they are
allied with superior minds, had to fight a long battle against a
sense of dignity and every feeling of common duty. One day
she went into her mother's room at seven in the morning and
begged her to let her take refuge in Villequier. The marquise
did not even deign to give her an answer, and suggested she
went back to bed. This was the last effort put up by ordinary
virtue and deference to generally accepted ideas.

The fear of doing wrong and upsetting notions held to be
sacred by people like Caylus, de Luz and Croisenois had
relatively little hold over her; such beings did not strike her as
capable of understanding her; she would have consulted them
if it had been a matter of buying a barouche or a piece of land.
Her real dread was lest Julien be displeased with her.

Perhaps, though, he only has the outward appearance of a
superior being?

She couldn't abide lack of character, it was her only
objection to the handsome young men who surrounded her.
The more they graciously mocked everything which deviates

from fashion, or which fails to follow it properly while thinking it does so, the more they damned themselves in her eyes.

They were brave, that was all. And anyway, brave in what sense? she asked herself: in duels, but a duel has become just a ceremony. Every bit of it is known in advance, even down to what you have to say as you succumb. Stretched out on the grass, hand on heart, you have to produce a generous pardon for your adversary and a word for an often imaginary fair lady, or one who'll go to the ball on the day of your death, for fear of arousing suspicions.

They'll brave danger at the head of a cavalry squadron all glinting with steel, but what about danger when it's solitary, out of the ordinary, unforeseen and really sordid?

Alas! Mathilde said to herself, Henri III's Court was where you found men who were noble in character as well as by birth! Ah! if Julien had fought at Jarnac* or Moncontour, I shouldn't have any more hesitation. In those days of vigour and strength, Frenchmen weren't namby-pambys. The day of battle was almost the one of least bewilderment.

Their life wasn't imprisoned like an Egyptian mummy inside an outer casing that was always common to everyone, always the same. Yes, she went on, it took more real courage to make one's way home alone at eleven at night after leaving the Hôtel de Soissons where Catherine de Medici lived, than it takes today to flit off to Algiers*. A man's life was a succession of hazards. Nowadays hazard has been driven out by civilization, the unexpected has gone. If it appears in ideas, there aren't enough epigrams to attack it; if it appears in events, there are no limits to the base acts we'd perpetrate out of fear. Whatever folly we are induced to commit by fear, excuses are found for it. What a degenerate and boring century! What would Boniface de La Mole have said in 1793 if, lifting his severed head out of his tomb, he had seen seventeen of his descendants letting themselves be rounded up like sheep and guillotined two days later? Death was certain, but it would have been in bad taste to defend oneself and kill even one or two Jacobins.* Ah! in France's heroic days, in Boniface de La Mole's century, Julien would have been the squadron commander and my brother the well-behaved young priest with moderation in his eyes and sweet reason on his lips.

A few months back, Mathilde had despaired of meeting anyone in the least different from the common pattern. She had derived some pleasure from allowing herself to write to a number of young men in society. This boldness, so unseemly, so imprudent in a girl, carried the risk of dishonouring her in the eyes of M. de Croisenois, the Duc de Chaulnes her grandfather and all the house of Chaulnes who, on seeing her intended marriage broken off, would have wanted to know the reason why. At that time Mathilde was unable to sleep on days when she had written one of her letters. But those letters had the excuse of being replies.

Now she was daring to say that she was in love. She was writing *on her own initiative* (what a terrible expression!) to a man from the lowest ranks of society.

This fact guaranteed that if discovered, she would be eternally dishonoured. Which of the women who called on her mother would have dared to take her side? What form of words could they have been given to repeat to take the sting from the dreadful derision of society salons?

And anyway, saying something was dreadful enough, but writing! *There are some things that cannot be put on paper*, Napoleon exclaimed on learning of the surrender of Baylen.* And it was Julien who had told her this saying! as if to teach her a lesson in advance.

But all this counted for nothing as yet: Mathilde's anguish had other causes. Heedless of the frightful effect on society, the inexpungible blot spreading derision, for it dishonoured her caste, Mathilde was about to write to a being of an utterly different nature from the Croisenois's, the de Luz's and the Caylus's.

The depth of Julien's character, the *unknown* in it, would have terrified her even if she had been starting up an ordinary social relationship with him. And she was actually about to make him her lover, perhaps even her lord and master!

Where will his claims end, if ever he can ask anything of me? Well! I shall say to myself like Medea: *In the midst of so many perils I still have MYSELF.**

Julien wasn't in the least in awe of noble blood, so she believed. More than this, perhaps he didn't feel any love at all for her!

In these last moments of terrible doubt, ideas of feminine pride came to her. Everything ought to be special in the fate of a girl like me, Mathilde exclaimed impatiently. The pride that had been instilled into her since the cradle was battling against virtue. It was at this moment that Julien's departure loomed up to bring everything to a head.

(Characters like this are fortunately very rare.)

Extremely late that evening Julien was mischievous enough to have a heavy trunk sent down to the porter's lodge; to carry it, he summoned the footman who was courting Mlle de La Mole's chambermaid. This move may have no effect, he said to himself, but if it succeeds, she'll think I'm gone. He fell asleep in high spirits over this joke. Mathilde did not sleep a wink.

Very early the next morning Julien left the house without being seen, but returned before eight o'clock.

He was scarcely in the library before Mlle de La Mole appeared at the door. He handed her his answer. He thought it his duty to speak to her; nothing was easier, at any rate, but Mlle de La Mole did not want to listen and dashed off. Julien was enchanted; he did not know what to say to her.

If all this isn't a game agreed on with Count Norbert, it's clear the cold look in my eyes is what has kindled the baroque love this girl of such high birth has taken it into her head to feel for me. I'd be rather more foolish than is appropriate if ever I allowed myself to be carried away to the point of feeling any liking for this tall, fair doll. This consideration left him more cold and calculating than ever before.

In the impending battle, he added, her pride in her birth will be like a high hill forming a military position between her and me. That's where I'll have to manœuvre. I did quite the wrong thing by staying in Paris; postponing my departure like this is degrading, and exposes me if all this is only a game. What was the risk in going? I'd have been mocking them, if they're mocking me. If her interest in me is at all genuine, I'd have increased it a hundredfold.

Mlle de La Mole's letter had given such a boost to Julien's vanity that, in the midst of all his laughter at what was happening to him, he had forgotten to think seriously about the expediency of his departure.

He was fated to have the kind of character that made him extremely sensitive about his mistakes. He was very put out by this one, and had almost given up thinking about the unbelievable victory that had preceded this little set-back, when, around nine o'clock, Mlle de La Mole appeared on the threshold of the library, threw him a letter and fled.

It looks as if it's going to be a romance by letter, he said as he picked up this one. The enemy is making a false move, so I shall order up coldness and virtue.

A definitive answer was being requested of him with a hauteur which increased his inner merriment. He gave himself the pleasure of mystifying, for two pages on end, any persons wishing to make fun of him, and he added a further joke, near the end of his reply, announcing that his departure was settled for the following morning.

When the letter was finished: the garden will provide a way for me to hand it over, he thought, and out he went. He looked at the window of Mlle de La Mole's room.

It was on the first floor, next to her mother's suite, but there was a large mezzanine floor separating it from the ground.

The first floor was so high that as he walked along the path under the limes with his letter in his hand, Julien could not be seen from Mlle de La Mole's window. The arched canopy formed by the beautifully trimmed lime trees cut off the view. Oh no! Julien said to himself in annoyance, yet another rash move! If they're bent on making fun of me, to be seen with a letter in my hand only furthers the cause of my enemies.

Norbert's room was exactly above his sister's, and if Julien stepped out from under the arch formed by the trimmed branches of the limes, the count and his friends could follow his every movement.

Mlle de La Mole appeared behind the window-pane; he showed a corner of his letter; she lowered her head. Julien immediately ran back up to his room, and happened to meet the fair Mathilde on the main staircase; she snatched his letter with perfect composure and laughter in her eyes.

What passion there was in poor Mme de Rênal's eyes, said Julien to himself, when she plucked up courage to take a letter from me, even after six months of intimacy. Not once, I think, did she she ever look at me with laughter in her eyes.

The rest of his response he did not formulate to himself with the same clarity; was he ashamed at the triviality of his motives? But then what a difference, his thoughts ran on, in the elegance of her day dress, in the elegance of her bearing! On seeing Mlle de La Mole from thirty yards away, a man of taste would guess what rank of society she belongs to. That's what you could call overt worth.

While he joked away, Julien was still not admitting to himself what was at the back of his mind: Mme de Rênal didn't have a Marquis de Croisenois to sacrifice for him. His only rival was that wretched sub-prefect M. Charcot, who had himself called de Maugiron, because there are no de Maugirons left.

At five o'clock Julien received a third letter; it was thrown to him from the door of the library. Mlle de La Mole again ran away. What an obsession with writing! he said to himself laughing, when it's so simple for us to talk! The enemy wants letters from me, it's obvious, and several of them! he was in no hurry to open this one. Yet more elegant phrases, he thought; but he grew pale when he read it. There were only eight lines.

I need to talk to you: I must talk to you, this evening; when the first hour after midnight strikes, be in the garden. Take the gardener's big ladder from beside the well; lean it up against my window and climb up to my room. There's a moon: never mind.

CHAPTER 15

Is it a plot?

Ah! how cruel is the interim between the
conceiving of a great plan and its execution! What
idle terrors! What waverings! Life is at stake!—
Much more is at stake: honour!

SCHILLER*

THIS is getting serious, thought Julien... and a little too
obvious, he added on reflection. So! This lovely young lady
can talk to me in the library with what amounts, thank
heavens, to total freedom; the marquis, afraid that I may show
him some of the accounts, never comes here. So! M. de La
Mole and Count Norbert, the only people ever to set foot here,
are out for most of the day; it's easy to observe the moment
when they return to the house, and the sublime Mathilde, for
whose hand a sovereign prince would not be too noble, is
wanting me to commit an abominable act of imprudence!

It's clear they want to bring about my downfall, or to make
fun of me at the very least. To begin with, they tried to use my
letters to destroy me; but these have proved circumspect. So
then! they need an action that's clearer than daylight. These
fine little gentlemen must just think me too stupid or too vain.
Hell! To climb up a ladder like that to a first floor twenty-five
foot from the ground on the brightest of moonlit nights!
There'll be time for everyone to see me, even from the
neighbouring houses. I'll be a fine sight on my ladder! Julien
went up to his room and began to pack his trunk, whistling
the while. He was resolved to leave without even answering.

But this wise resolve did not give him any inner peace. What
if by chance, he said to himself all of a sudden when his trunk
was shut, Mathilde was in good faith! then I'd be acting like
an utter coward in her eyes. I'm not a person of rank, am I? I
need sterling qualities, cash down, without the benefit of the
doubt, proved for sure by eloquent actions...

He spent a quarter of an hour in reflection. What's the point
in denying it? he said at last; I'll be a coward in her eyes. I'll

lose not only the most dazzling woman in high society, as they were all saying at the Duc de Retz's ball, but on top of that the divine pleasure of seeing the Marquis de Croisenois sacrificed for me—the son of a duke, and destined to become a duke himself. A charming young man with all the qualities I lack: a sense of appropriateness, birth, fortune...

This remorse will dog me all my life, not on her account— there are so many sweethearts!

...But there is only one honour!

as old Don Diego*says—and here I am clearly and distinctly retreating in the face of the first real danger that comes my way; for that duel with M. de Beauvoisis was something of a joke. This is quite different. I may be shot point-blank by a servant, but that's the lesser danger; I may be dishonoured.

This is getting serious, my lad, he added with a Gascon* accent and twinkle in his eye. *Knightly honour* is at stake. Never will a poor devil who's been cast as low down as I have by fortune ever get such an opportunity again; I shall have my successes, but they'll be of an inferior kind...

He reflected at length, walking up and down with brisk steps, stopping short from time to time. A magnificent marble bust of Cardinal Richelieu had been parked in his room, and his eye was drawn to it in spite of himself. This bust seemed to be looking at him sternly, as if reproaching him for lacking the daring that should come naturally to the French character. In your day, great man, would I have hesitated?

In the worst case, Julien said to himself at last, suppose all this is a trap, it's a pretty sinister one and pretty compromising for a young lady. They know I'm not the sort of man to keep quiet. So they'll have to kill me. That was all right in 1574, in Boniface de La Mole's day, but his present descendant would never dare. These people just aren't the same. Mlle de La Mole is so envied! Four hundred salons would reverberate with her shame tomorrow, and imagine the delight!

The servants are gossiping among themselves about the obvious favour shown to me; I know they are, I've heard them...

On the other hand, her letters...! They may believe I've got

them with me. They'll surprise me in her room and snatch
them from me. I'll have to face two, three or four men, who
knows? But where'll they get them from, these men? where in
Paris can you find underlings who'll keep quiet? They're afraid
of the law... Damn it all! It'll be Messrs Caylus, Croisenois
and de Luz themselves. The thought of this moment, and the
ridiculous figure I'll cut in their midst, must be what has
tempted them. Watch out for Abelard's fate,* Mister secretary!

Well, damn it all, gentlemen! You shall bear my marks, I'll
strike you in the face, like Caesar's soldiers did at Pharsala...
As for the letters, I can put them in a safe place.

Julien made copies of the latest two, hid them in a volume
of the fine edition of Voltaire in the library, and took the
originals off to the post himself.

When he got back: What a mad enterprise I'm about to fling
myself into! he said to himself in surprise and terror. He had
spent a quarter of an hour without facing up to the act awaiting
him that night.

But if I refuse, I'll despise myself afterwards! For the rest of
my life this act will be a major source of self-doubt, and for
me, doubt of this kind is the most searing of afflictions. Didn't
I suffer it on account of Amanda's lover! I think I'd find it
easier to forgive myself for an outright crime; once it was
confessed, I'd stop thinking about it.

Just think! I shall have been the rival of a man bearing one
of the finest names in France, and I shall myself, in all
cheerfulness, have declared myself to be his inferior! When it
comes down to it, it's cowardly not to go. That settles it,
exclaimed Julien, getting to his feet... besides, she's terribly
pretty.

If this isn't some treachery or other, what an act of folly
she's committing for me...! If it's just mystification, damn it
all, gentlemen! it's up to me to make the joke serious, and
that's what I'll do.

But what if they tie up my arms the moment I enter the
room; they may have set up some ingenious contraption!

It's like a duel, he said to himself laughing, you can parry
any blow, says my fencing master, but the good Lord, who
wants an end to it, makes one of the two forget to parry.

Anyway, here's something to answer them with: he drew his pocket pistols; and although the priming was fresh and still explosive, he replaced it.

There were still several hours to wait; to give himself something to do, Julien wrote to Fouqué:

My good friend, don't open the enclosed letter except in case of accident, if you hear word that something unusual has happened to me. In that case, delete the proper names from the manuscript I am sending you, and make eight copies of it which you are to send to the newspapers in Marseille, Bordeaux, Lyon, Brussels etc.; ten days later, get this manuscript printed and send the first copy to the Marquis de La Mole; and a fortnight later, scatter the other copies during the night in the streets of Verrières.

The little justificatory memorandum that Fouqué was only to open in case of accident was cast in the form of a story, and Julien drafted it so as to compromise Mlle de La Mole as little as possible, but ultimately he did give a very accurate picture of her involvement.

Julien was just finishing off sealing up his packet when the bell rang for dinner; it made his heart pound. His imagination, absorbed in the tale he had just composed, was entirely given over to tragic forebodings. He had visualized himself seized by servants, bound, and led off to a cellar with a gag in his mouth. There a servant kept him in custody, and if the family honour of these nobles required the adventure to have a tragic end, it was easy to put an end to everything with the sort of poison that leaves no trace; at which point they said he had died of an illness and carried him back dead to his room.

Moved like a playwright by his own story, Julien was genuinely afraid when he went into the dining-room. He looked at all the servants in full livery. He studied their countenances. Which are the ones that have been chosen for tonight's expedition? he wondered. In this family, memories of Henri III's Court are so pervasive, so often recalled, that if they believe they've been insulted, they'll act more decisively than other figures of their rank. He looked at Mlle de La Mole in order to read her family's plans in her eyes; she was pale, and her countenance came straight out of the Middle Ages. He had never seen her looking so grand; she was truly beautiful and imposing. It almost made him fall in love. *Pallida morte futura** he said to himself (her pallor portends her great designs).

It was to no avail that he made a point after dinner of taking a long stroll in the garden: there was no sign of Mlle de La Mole. Talking to her at that moment would have taken a great weight off his mind.

Why not admit it? he was afraid. As he was resolved to act, he unashamedly let this feeling take hold of him. Provided that when the time comes to act, I can summon up the necessary courage, he said to himself, does it matter what I may be feeling at this moment? He went off to reconnoitre the position, and test the weight of the ladder.

This is an instrument, he said to himself, laughing, which it's my destiny to use! here as in Verrières. What a difference! On that occasion, he added with a sigh, I wasn't obliged to be wary of the person for whose sake I was taking risks. What a difference too in the danger itself!

I could have been killed in M. de Rênal's garden without there being any dishonour in it for me. They could easily have made my death seem inexplicable. Here, just think of the abominable stories that'll be told in the salons of the Hôtel de Chaulnes, the Hôtel de Caylus, the Hôtel de Retz etc.— everywhere, in short. I shall be a monster for posterity.

For two or three years, he went on with a laugh, making fun of himself. But this idea was more than he could take. And what about me, where will I find justification? Even supposing Fouqué publishes my posthumous pamphlet, it'll be just one more piece of infamy. Imagine! I'm taken into a household, and in return for the hospitality I receive and the favours showered upon me, I publish a pamphlet on the goings-on there! I attack the women's honour! Ah! I'd rather a thousand times be a dupe!

That evening was excruciating.

CHAPTER 16

One o'clock in the morning

This garden was exceedingly large, and had been
laid out in perfect taste only a few years back. But the
trees were more than a century old. It had a rustic feel
about it.

MASSINGER*

HE was about to countermand his instructions to Fouqué
when eleven o'clock struck. He turned the key noisily in his
bedroom door, as if he were shutting himself in. He crept off
stealthily to observe what was happening in the rest of the
house, especially on the fourth floor, which was inhabited by
the servants. There was nothing out of the ordinary. One of
Mᵐᵉ de La Mole's chambermaids was holding a party, and the
servants were drinking punch in the best of spirits. The ones
who are laughing like that, thought Julien, can't be taking part
in the nocturnal expedition: they'd be more serious.

Finally he went and posted himself in a dark corner of the
garden. If their plan is to conceal their doings from the
household servants, they'll arrange for the men they've
instructed to take me by surprise to come in over the garden
wall.

If M. de Croisenois is keeping a cool head throughout this
business, he's bound to find it less compromising for the young
woman he wishes to marry to have me taken by surprise before
I've actually got into her room.

He made a reconnaissance in military fashion, with great
precision. My honour is at stake, he thought; if I commit any
kind of blunder, it'll be no excuse in my own eyes to tell
myself: I hadn't thought of that.

The weather was heartrendingly clear. The moon had risen
about eleven o'clock, and at half-past midnight it was shining
full on the side of the house overlooking the garden.

She's mad, Julien thought to himself; when one o'clock
struck, there was still light in Count Norbert's windows. Never

in all his life had Julien been so afraid; he could only see the dangers in the enterprise, and had no enthusiasm for it.

He fetched the enormous ladder, waited five minutes to allow time for a counter-order, and at five past one leaned the ladder against Mathilde's window. He climbed up quietly, pistol in hand, astonished not to be attacked. As he approached the window, it opened noiselessly:

'So you've come, sir,' Mathilde said to him with great emotion; 'I've been following your movements for the past hour.'

Julien was highly embarrassed; he did not know how to behave, he felt no love whatsoever. In his embarrassment, he thought he ought to be bold, and tried to kiss Mathilde.

'How dare you!' she said, pushing him away.

More than pleased to be given his cue to leave, he glanced hurriedly round about: the moon was so bright that it cast black shadows in Mlle de La Mole's room. There may very well be men hidden there that I can't see, he thought.

'What have you got in the side pocket of your suit?' Mathilde asked him, delighted to find a subject of conversation. She was suffering strangely; all the feelings of restraint and nervousness so natural to a girl of high birth had regained their hold, and were causing her torture.

'I've got all kinds of arms and pistols,' Julien replied, no less pleased to have something to say.

'You must draw up the ladder,' said Mathilde.

'It's huge; it may break the windows of the drawing-room below, or the mezzanine floor.'

'You mustn't break the windows,' Mathilde rejoined, trying in vain to adopt an everyday conversational tone; 'you could, it seems to me, lower the ladder by means of a rope that could be fixed to the top rung. I always keep a supply of ropes in my room.'

And this is a woman in love! thought Julien; she dares to declare her love! So much composure, so much wisdom in these precautions are a clear enough indication to me that I'm not scoring a victory over M. de Croisenois as I foolishly thought; I'm merely following in his footsteps. When it comes down to it, what do I care! Am I in love with her? I am scoring a victory over the marquis in this sense, that he'll be most annoyed to have a successor, and even more annoyed that this successor should be me. How disdainfully he stared at me yesterday evening at the Café Tortoni,* while pretending not to recognize me! What a hostile look he had as he went on to greet me, when he could no longer avoid doing so!

Julien had fixed the rope to the top rung of the ladder, and was letting it down gently, leaning a long way out from the balcony to ensure that it did not touch the windows. Just the moment to kill me, he thought, if someone is hiding in Mathilde's room; but a profound silence continued to reign everywhere.

The ladder touched the ground, and Julien managed to lay it down flat in the bed of exotic flowers running the length of the wall.

'What will my mother say', said Mathilde, 'when she sees her lovely plants all flattened...! You must throw down the rope,' she went on with great composure. 'If someone saw it going up to the balcony, it would be difficult to explain away.'

'And me? How me go 'way?' said Julien in a jocular tone, imitating Creole speech. (One of the household chambermaids was born in San Domingo.)

'You, you go through door,' said Mathilde, delighted at this idea.

Ah! how worthy this man is of all my love! she thought.

Julien had just let the rope drop into the garden when Mathilde squeezed his arm. He thought he was being grabbed by an enemy, and wheeled round sharply, drawing a dagger. She had thought she heard a window being opened. They stood motionless, holding their breath. The moon shone full upon them. The noise was not repeated, and they felt no further anxiety.

Then their embarrassment resumed; it was considerable on both sides. Julien made sure the door was shut with all its bolts; he did consider looking under the bed but didn't dare; one or two footmen could have been posted there. Eventually, fearing lest his caution reproach him at some future date, he did look.

Mathilde had succumbed to all the cruel anguish of acute nervousness. She loathed the situation she was in.

'What have you done with my letters?' she asked at last.

What a good opportunity to disconcert these gentlemen if they are eavesdropping, and to avoid the battle! thought Julien.

'The first one is hidden in a fat Protestant Bible being conveyed a good distance from here by yesterday evening's stage-coach.'

He spoke very clearly as he went into these details, in such a way as to be heard by the persons who might be hidden in the two large mahogany wardrobes that he hadn't dared to search.

'The other two are in the post, and bound for the same destination as the first.'

'Good God! why all these precautions?' asked Mathilde in astonishment.

Why on earth should I lie? thought Julien, and he confessed all his suspicions to her.

'So that explains why your letters were so cold, my love!' exclaimed Mathilde, sounding mad rather than tender.

Julien did not notice this nuance of tone. The familiarity of her words made him lose his head, or at any rate his suspicions vanished: he plucked up the courage to put his arms round this beautiful girl who inspired in him such respect. He was pushed away, but half-heartedly.

He appealed to his memory, just as he had done previously at Besançon with Amanda Binet, and recited several of the finest passages from *La Nouvelle Héloïse*.

'You have the heart of a man,' replied the lady, without paying much attention to his fine phrases; 'I wanted to put your bravery to the test, I must confess, my dearest. Your initial suspicions and your determination show you to be even more intrepid than I thought.'

It was costing Mathilde an effort to use terms of endearment, and she was clearly more preoccupied by this strange manner of speaking than with the meaning of what she was saying. The familiarity of her words, devoid of any tender tone, gave Julien no pleasure: he was astonished at the total absence of happiness; to induce it he eventually had recourse to his reason. He could see he was esteemed by this girl who had so much pride and never praised anyone unreservedly; this consideration enabled him to feel a form of happiness stemming from self-esteem.

It was not, admittedly, the sweet sensation enveloping his whole being that he had sometimes felt with Mme de Rênal. There was nothing tender about his feelings on this first occasion. It was the more intense happiness of ambition, and Julien was above all else ambitious. He talked again about the people he had suspected and the precautions he had devised. As he spoke, he was thinking about the means of taking advantage of his victory.

Mathilde, who was still highly embarrassed and seemed aghast at what she had done, appeared delighted to find a subject of conversation. They talked of ways of seeing each other again. Julien relished the resourcefulness and bravery he again demonstrated during the course of this discussion. They were dealing with people with great foresight; little Tanbeau was certainly a spy, but Mathilde and he weren't lacking in ingenuity either. What could be easier than meeting in the library to arrange everything?

'I can be seen in any part of the house without arousing suspicions,' Julien added, 'even to the point of going into Mme de La Mole's room.' This was the only way of reaching her daughter's room. If Mathilde thought it better for him to arrive by ladder every time, his heart would be wild with joy at exposing himself to this trivial danger.

Listening to him talk, Mathilde was shocked by his air of triumph. So he's my master! she said to herself. She was already racked by remorse. Her reason was appalled by the signal folly she had just committed. If she had been able to, she would have destroyed herself and Julien. When from time to time her will-power silenced her remorse, feelings of awkwardness and suffering modesty made her acutely unhappy. She had in no way foreseen the dreadful state she was in.

But I must say something to him, she told herself at length, it's part of the conventions; one speaks to one's lover. And then, to fulfil a duty, with a tenderness that was far more in the words she used than in the sound of her voice, she told him of the various resolutions she had taken concerning him over the past few days.

She had decided that if he was bold enough to reach her room with the help of the gardener's ladder, as instructed, she would be entirely his. But never had anyone adopted a colder or more polite tone of voice to say such tender things. Up until that point, the assignation had been chilly as ice. It was enough to put anyone right off love. What a moral lesson for a rash young girl! Is it worth sacrificing one's future for such a moment?

After much wavering, which might have struck a superficial observer as the effect of the most determined hatred, so difficult was it for a woman's feelings of self-respect to yield even to such strong determination on her part, in the end Mathilde gave herself to him as a compliant mistress.

To tell the truth, the excitement she showed was somewhat *contrived*. Passionate love was still rather more of a model to be imitated than a reality.

Mlle de La Mole thought she had a duty to fulfil towards herself and her lover. The poor fellow, she said to herself, has shown consummate bravery; he's got to be happy, or else I'm the one lacking character. But she would willingly have paid the price of an eternity of unhappiness to be spared the cruel obligation that was upon her.

Despite the terrible extent to which she was forcing herself, she kept perfect control over what she said.

Not a single regret or reproach emerged to spoil that night, which struck Julien as strange rather than happy. What a contrast, great heavens! with the last twenty-four hours he had spent in Verrières! These fine Parisian ways have found the secret of spoiling everything, even love, he said to himself with extreme injustice.

He was indulging in these reflections standing upright in one of the large mahogany wardrobes where she had put him at the first signs of noise from the adjoining suite, which was Mme de La Mole's. Mathilde followed her mother to Mass, the maids soon left the rooms, and Julien escaped easily before they returned to finish their work.

He got on his horse and sought out the most remote spots in

one of the forests near Paris. He was far more amazed than happy. The happiness which took hold of him from time to time was like that of a young sub-lieutenant who, at the outcome of some amazing action, has just been made a colonel on the spot by the commander in chief; he felt himself raised to a great height. Everything that had been above him the day before was at his side now, or else beneath him. The further away Julien rode, the more his happiness gradually increased.

If there was no tenderness in his heart, it was because, strange as this word may seem, in all her conduct towards him, Mathilde had been carrying out a duty. There had been nothing unexpected for her in any of the events of that night, apart from the unhappiness and the shame she had experienced, instead of the perfect bliss depicted in novels.

Could I have made a mistake? Could it be that I'm not in love with him after all? she wondered.

CHAPTER 17

An old sword

I now mean to be serious;—it is time
Since laughter now-a-days is deem'd too serious
A jest at vice by virtue's called a crime.
Don Juan, C. XIII

SHE did not appear at dinner. In the evening she came into
the drawing-room for a moment, but did not look at Julien.
This conduct struck him as strange; but, he thought, I don't
know their customs: she'll give me some good reason for all
this. Nevertheless, driven by the most extreme curiosity, he
studied the expression on Mathilde's face; he could not conceal
from himself that she had a hard, hostile look. She was
manifestly not the same woman who on the previous night had
felt or feigned moments of ecstasy that were too excessive to
be genuine.

The next day and the day after she showed the same
coldness; she did not look at him or notice his existence.
Julien, consumed by the most acute anxiety, could not have
been further from the feelings of triumph which were all he
had experienced on the first day. Could this by any chance, he
wondered, be a return to virtue? But this word was really
rather bourgeois for the haughty Mathilde.

In everyday situations she scarcely believes in religion,
thought Julien; she's attached to it as something beneficial to
the interests of her caste.

But may she not out of mere delicacy be reproaching herself
bitterly for the lapse she has committed? Julien believed
himself to be her first lover.

But, he said to himself at the other moments, it has to be
admitted that there's nothing innocent, uncomplicated or
tender in her behaviour; I've never seen her act more haugh-
tily. Could she despise me? It would be worthy of her to
reproach herself with what she has done for me, merely on
account of my lowly birth.

While Julien, filled with the prejudices he had drawn from

books and from his memories of Verrières, was pursuing the fantasy of a tender mistress who no longer thinks of her own existence once she has given happiness to her lover, Mathilde's vanity was furious with him.

As she had ceased to be bored over the past two months, she no longer dreaded boredom; so with no possible means of suspecting this, Julien had lost his chief advantage.

I've got myself a master! said Mlle de La Mole to herself, in the throes of the blackest spite. He's a man of honour, granted; but if I push his vanity to the limits, he'll take his revenge by making known the nature of our relationship. Mathilde had never before had a lover, and at this moment in life which gives some tender illusions even to the most arid of souls, she was at the mercy of the most bitter reflections.

He has a tremendous hold over me, since he reigns through terror and can inflict a dreadful punishment on me if I push him too far. The mere idea of this was enough to drive Mlle de La Mole to insult him. Courage was the foremost quality in her character. Nothing could be more certain to cause her some degree of agitation and cure her of a residual boredom that kept rearing its head than the idea that her whole existence was staked on the toss of a coin.

On the third day, since Mlle de La Mole persisted in not looking at him, Julien followed her after dinner into the billiard room, quite clearly against her will.

'Well, sir, so you think you've acquired some pretty strong rights over me,' she said to him with barely restrained anger, 'since in opposition to my quite plainly declared wishes, you presume to speak to me...? Do you know that no one in the world has ever dared as much?'

Nothing could have been more amusing than the dialogue between these two lovers; without realizing it they were impelled by feelings of the most dire hatred for each other. As neither of them was long-suffering by nature, and besides, they had the ways of polite society, they soon reached the point of declaring plainly to each other that they were breaking it off for good.

'I swear you eternal secrecy,' said Julien; 'I'd even add that I'll never address a word to you, if your reputation were not liable to suffer from so marked a change as that.' He bowed respectfully and left.

He did not find it too hard to carry out what he believed to be a duty; he was a long way from believing himself deeply in love with Mlle de La Mole. Doubtless he did not love her three days previously, when the lady had hidden him inside the large mahogany wardrobe. But everything soon changed inside him as soon as he saw himself estranged from her for ever.

His cruel memory began to go over the minutest details of that night which in real life had left him so cold.

During the very night after they had formally broken it off for ever Julien almost went mad on finding himself obliged to admit to himself that he loved Mlle de La Mole.

A terrible conflict followed this discovery: all his feelings were in turmoil.

Two days later, instead of lording it over M. de Croisenois, he was almost ready to fling his arms round him in tears.

Experience of misfortune gave him a glimmer of common sense; he decided to set off for the Languedoc, packed his trunk and went to the post-station.

He felt like collapsing when, on arrival at the mail-coach office, he was told that by some remarkable chance there was a seat the next day on the coach for Toulouse. He reserved it and went back to the Hôtel de La Mole to announce his departure to the marquis.

M. de La Mole had gone out. More dead than alive, Julien went into the library to wait for him. Imagine his reaction on finding Mlle de La Mole there!

On seeing him appear she assumed an unmistakable expression of cruelty.

Carried away by his unhappiness, thrown by surprise, Julien committed the weakness of saying to her, in the most tender and heartfelt of tones: 'So you don't love me any more?'

'I'm appalled at having given myself to the first man who came along,' said Mathilde, weeping with rage at herself.

'*The first man who came along*!' exclaimed Julien, and he rushed towards an old sword from the Middle Ages which was kept in the library as a curiosity.

His suffering, which he considered extreme at the instant he had addressed Mlle de La Mole, had just been increased a hundredfold by the tears of shame he saw her shed. He would have been the happiest of men to be able to kill her.

At the very instant when he had just drawn the sword with some difficulty from its ancient sheath, Mathilde, happy at such a novel sensation, advanced proudly towards him; her tears had dried up.

The image of the Marquis de La Mole his benefactor conjured itself up vividly before Julien's eyes. Me, kill his daughter! he said to himself, how appalling! He made as if to fling down the sword. It's quite certain, he thought, that she'll burst out laughing at the sight of this melodramatic gesture: the very idea served to restore all his composure to him. He gazed at the blade of the old sword curiously, as though looking for a rust mark, then he put it back in its sheath, and, with the utmost calm, replaced it on the gilded bronze nail which supported it.

This whole sequence, which was very slow towards the end, lasted a good minute; Mlle de La Mole watched him in amazement. So I've been on the verge of being killed by my lover! she was saying to herself.

This idea took her right back to the most heroic moments in the century of Charles IX* and Henri III.

She stood motionless in front of Julien, who had just put back the sword; she gazed at him with eyes which no longer held any hatred. It must be admitted that she was terribly attractive at that moment: certainly no woman had ever looked less like a Parisian doll (this expression summed up Julien's great objection to the women in this part of France).

I'm going to relapse into some form of weakness for him, thought Mathilde; this time round he would indeed believe himself my lord and master, after a relapse, and at the precise moment when I've just spoken so sternly to him. She fled.

Goodness, she's beautiful! said Julien as he saw her running away: this is the creature who was flinging herself into my arms with such frenzy less than a week ago... And those moments will never return! And it's all my fault! And, at the time of that encounter which was so out of the ordinary and so intriguing for me, my feelings were dead...! I must admit that I was born with a pretty insipid and wretched character.

The marquis appeared; Julien hastened to announce his departure.

'Where to?' asked M. de La Mole.

'The Languedoc.'

'Under no circumstances, if you please; you are destined for higher things; if you leave, it shall be for the North... indeed, in military terms, I confine you to your quarters. You will oblige me by never being absent for more than two or three hours at a time, I may need you at any moment.'

Julien bowed and withdrew without saying a word, leaving the marquis most astonished; he was in no state to talk, and locked himself into his room. There he was free to paint himself an exaggerated picture of his utterly atrocious fate.

So, he thought, I can't even go away! God knows how many days the marquis will keep me in Paris. God Almighty! What'll become of me? And not a single friend to turn to: Father Pirard wouldn't let me finish my first sentence, and Count Altamira would suggest I join some conspiracy or other.

And yet I'm out of my mind, I can feel it; I'm out of my mind!

Who can guide me, what'll become of me?

CHAPTER 18

Cruel moments

And she confesses it to me! She goes into the
minutest details! Her lovely eyes fixed on mine tell of
the love she felt for another!

SCHILLER

MADEMOISELLE de La Mole thought rapturously of nothing
but the thrill of having been on the point of being killed. She
went so far as to say to herself: he's worthy of being my
master, since he was on the point of killing me. How many
fine young men from high society would you have to fuse
together to get one passionate impulse like that?

It must be admitted that he looked very attractive when he
climbed on to the chair to put back the sword, in precisely the
same picturesque position that the interior designer had
arranged it! I wasn't that mad to love him after all.

At that moment, if some honourable means of renewing the
relationship had presented itself, she would have grasped it
with pleasure. Julien, locked in his room with two turns of the
key, was in the throes of the most violent despair. In his
wildest thoughts, he considered flinging himself at her feet. If
instead of hiding away in a remote place, he had wandered
about the garden or the house in such a way as to be available
for any opportunities that arose, he might perhaps have been
able in the matter of an instant to transform his appalling
misery into the most acute happiness.

But the worldly wisdom we reproach him with lacking
would have vetoed the sublime gesture of seizing the sword
which, at that moment, rendered him so fetching in Mlle de La
Mole's eyes. This caprice, which worked in Julien's favour,
lasted the whole day; Mathilde conjured up a delightful image
of the brief moments in which she had loved him, and she
regretted them.

In fact, she said to herself, my passion for this poor young
man only lasted from his point of view from an hour after
midnight, when I saw him coming up his ladder to my room

with all his pistols in the side pocket of his suit, until eight o'clock in the morning. It was a quarter of an hour later, when I was at Mass at St Valery's church,* that I began to think he would now believe himself my master, and might well try to make me obey by terrorizing me.

After dinner, far from shunning Julien, Mlle de La Mole spoke to him and more or less requested him to follow her into the garden; he obeyed. He could have done without this ordeal. Mathilde was unwittingly yielding to the love she was beginning to feel for him again. She derived intense pleasure from walking by his side, and she looked with curiosity at the hands which that very morning had seized the sword to kill her.

After such an action, after everything that had happened, it was out of the question to revert to their former mode of conversation.

Gradually Mathilde began to confide intimately in him about the state of her affections. She derived a strange enjoyment from this kind of conversation; in due course she told him about the passing fancies she had had for M. de Croisenois, for M. de Caylus...

'What! For M. de Caylus as well!' Julien exclaimed; and all the bitter jealousy of a jilted lover burst forth in this response. This was how Mathilde interpreted it, and she took no offence.

She continued to torture Julien by recounting her former feelings to him in the most picturesque detail, and in a voice that rang with the most intimate truth. He could tell that she was depicting something she saw before her very eyes. He observed to his chagrin that as she spoke she was making discoveries about her own heart.

The affliction of jealousy cannot go beyond this.

To suspect that a rival is loved is already cruel enough, but to have to hear a detailed confession of the love he inspires from the woman one adores is surely the ultimate in suffering.

O how Julien was punished, at that moment, for the surges of pride which had led him to put himself above the Caylus's and the Croisenois's! What intimate and heartfelt sorrow he experienced as he exaggerated to himself the least of their qualities! What ardent good faith he showed in despising his own self!

Mathilde seemed adorable to him; no form of words can adequately convey the excess of his admiration. As he walked by her side, he cast furtive glances at her hands, her arms, her queenly bearing. He was on the verge of falling at her feet, destroyed by love and misery, crying: Mercy!

And this beautiful young woman, so utterly superior, who once loved me, will no doubt soon be loving M. de Caylus!

Julien could not doubt Mlle de La Mole's sincerity; there was too obvious a ring of truth in everything she was saying. To make his misery absolutely complete, there were times when by concentrating on the feelings she had once entertained for M.de Caylus, Mathilde reached the point of speaking about him as if she loved him at the present moment. There certainly was love in her tone of voice; Julien discerned it clearly.

Had molten lead been poured down into his chest, he would have suffered less. How on earth, when he had reached these extremes of unhappiness, could the poor fellow have guessed that it was because she was talking to him that Mlle de La Mole derived such pleasure from thinking back to flutterings of love she had felt formerly for M. de Caylus or M. de Luz?

Nothing can possibly express Julien's feelings of anguish. He was listening to detailed confessions of love felt for others in the very lime walk where only a few days previously he had waited for one o'clock to strike in order to penetrate her room. No human being can endure a higher degree of misery.

This form of cruel intimacy lasted a good week. Mathilde would at times appear to seek out, at times merely not shun opportunities for talking to him; and the topic of conversation they both seemed to come back to with a sort of cruel relish was the account of the feelings she had entertained for others: she told him of the letters she had written, she even recalled for him her actual words, she recited whole sentences to him. Towards the end of the week she seemed to be gazing at Julien with a sort of mischievous glee. His sufferings were a source of intense enjoyment to her.

You can see that Julien had no experience of life, he hadn't even read any novels; if he had been a little less awkward and had said with some composure to this girl he so adored and who confided such strange things to him, 'Admit that although

I'm not the equal of all these gentlemen, nevertheless I'm the one you love...', perhaps she would have been glad to be seen through; at any rate, success would have depended entirely on the elegance with which Julien expressed this idea, and the moment he chose. Be that as it may, he was coming out rather well from a situation which was verging on the monotonous in Mathilde's eyes.

'You don't love me any more, and I adore you!' Julien said to her one day, distracted with love and unhappiness. This was more or less the greatest act of foolishness he could have committed.

His words destroyed in a flash all the pleasure Mlle de La Mole derived from talking to him about the state of her affections. She was beginning to be surprised that after all that had passed he did not take offence at what she was telling him; she was even reaching the stage of imagining, just when he said this foolish thing to her, that perhaps he didn't love her any more. Pride has no doubt extinguished his love, she said to herself. He's not the sort of man to let someone get away with preferring people like Caylus, de Luz, or Croisenois, whom he admits to be so superior to him. No, I shan't see him at my feet any more!

On the days leading up to this, in the naïvety of his misery, Julien had often voiced sincere praise for the brilliant qualitites of these gentlemen; he even went so far as to exaggerate them. This nuance had not escaped Mlle de La Mole, she was astonished by it, but did not guess the reason for it. In praising a rival he believed to be loved, Julien's frenetic nature was empathizing with the rival's happiness.

His frank, but oh so stupid words caused everything to change in a flash: Mathilde, sure of being loved, despised him utterly.

She was taking a stroll with him at the time of this inept remark; she walked away, and her last glance expressed the most terrible scorn. Back in the drawing-room she did not look at him again the whole evening. The next day this scorn took up all her emotional energy; gone was the impulse which for the past week had caused her to get such pleasure from treating Julien like the most intimate of friends; the sight of him was disagreeable to her. Mathilde's reaction reached the proportions of revulsion; nothing can possibly convey the extremes of scorn she felt when she set eyes on him.

Julien had understood nothing of what had been happening for the past week in Mathilde's heart, but he did discern this scorn. He had the good sense only to appear in her presence as rarely as possible, and he never looked at her.

But it was not without mortal suffering that he so to speak deprived himself of her presence. He thought he felt his misery increasing on account of it. The courage in a man's heart can't hold out beyond this, he said to himself. He spent his time by a little window in the rafters of the house; the shutters had been closed with care, and from there at least he could catch a glimpse of Mlle de La Mole when she appeared in the garden.

Just imagine how he felt when he saw her walking after dinner with M. de Caylus, M. de Luz or some other man for whom she had admitted feeling some flutterings of love in the past!

Julien had no conception of such an intensity of misery; he was on the verge of shouting out loud; this resilient character was finally shattered through and through.

Any thought unconnected with Mlle de La Mole had become hateful to him; he was incapable of writing the simplest of letters.

'You're not in your right mind,' the marquis told him.

Fearful of having his secret guessed, Julien spoke of illness and managed to be convincing. Fortunately for him, the marquis teased him at dinner about his forthcoming journey: Mathilde gathered that it might be very lengthy. Julien had been keeping out of her way for some days now, and her brilliant young men, who had everything lacking in the pale and sombre creature she had once loved, no longer had the power to rouse her from her dream-like state.

Any ordinary girl, she said to herself, would have sought out a partner among these young men who are the centre of attention in any salon; but one of the characteristics of genius is not to trail its inspiration in the rut traced by vulgar folk.

As the consort of a man like Julien, who only lacks some of the fortune I possess, I shall constantly be the focus of attention, I shan't go through life unnoticed. Far from constantly dreading a revolution like my cousins, who from fear of the common people don't dare scold a postillion who's driving them incompetently, I shall be sure of playing a part, and an important one too, for the man I've chosen has character and unbounded ambition. What does he lack? Friends, money? I'll provide them. But her mind treated Julien somewhat as an inferior being, who can be made to love one when it suits.

CHAPTER 19
The Opera Bouffe*

> O how this spring of love resembleth
> The uncertain glory of an April day;
> Which now shows all the beauty of the sun,
> And by and by a cloud takes all away!
>
> SHAKESPEARE

PREOCCUPIED by the future and the unusual role she was
hoping for, Mathilde soon reached the point of regretting the
dry, metaphysical discussions she often had with Julien. Weary
of such lofty thoughts, sometimes too she regretted the
moments of happiness she had experienced with him; these
last memories did not come without remorse, she was overwhelmed by it at times.

But if one is to lapse, she said to herself, it is worthy of a
girl like myself only to neglect my duty for a man of quality;
no one shall say it was his pretty moustache or his graceful
style on horseback that seduced me, but his profound discussions on the future awaiting France, his ideas on the parallel
that may be drawn between the events about to burst upon us
and the revolution of 1688 in England*. I've been seduced, she
replied to her remorse, I'm a weak woman, but at least I
haven't been led astray like some pretty little doll by external
attributes.

If there is a revolution, why shouldn't Julien Sorel play the
part of Roland,* and I that of Mme Roland? I prefer her role to
Mme de Staël's:* immoral conduct will hold you back in our
century. I'm adamant that no one shall reproach me with a
second lapse; I'd die of shame.

Mathilde's musings were not all as grave, admittedly, as the
thoughts we have just transcribed.

She would look at Julien and find delightful charm in his
most trivial actions.

Surely, she said to herself, I've succeeded in destroying the
remotest idea he might have had that he has any rights.

The look of unhappiness and deep passion on the poor boy's

face when he said those words of love to me a week ago more than prove it; I must concede that it was pretty extraordinary of me to take offence at a remark brimming with so much respect, so much passion. Am I not his wife? This word came very naturally, and, it must be admitted, was very pleasing. Julien still loved me after endless conversations in which I only talked to him—and with a great deal of cruelty, I agree—about the passing attraction which the boredom of my life had inspired in me for these young men from high society who give him such pangs of jealousy. Ah! if he knew what little danger they represent for me! How wan they strike me in comparison with him, and all exact copies one of another.

As she reflected thus, Mathilde was doodling with a pencil on a page in her album. One of the profiles she had just finished astonished and delighted her: it bore a striking resemblance to Julien. It's the voice of heaven! This is one of love's miracles, she exclaimed in rapture: without meaning to, I've done his portrait.

She ran off to her room, locked herself in, and applied herself assiduously, trying to do a portrait of Julien; but she did not succeed: the profile sketched by chance still remained the best likeness. Mathilde was delighted by this: she took it as clear proof of a grand passion.

She did not get up from her album until very late, when the marquise summoned her to go to the Italian Opera. She only had one thought in her head: to look everywhere for Julien so as to get her mother to entreat him to sit with them.

He did not turn up; the ladies only had vulgar mortals in their box. During the whole of the first act of the opera, Mathilde dreamed with the most intensely passionate rapture of the man she loved; but in the second act one of love's adages sung, admittedly, to a tune worthy of Cimarosa, pierced her heart. The heroine of the opera was saying: 'I must punish myself for the extremes of adoration I feel for him, I love him too much!'

From the moment she had heard this sublime aria* everything in the real world vanished for Mathilde. People spoke to her; she did not answer; her mother scolded her, she could scarcely bring herself to look at her. Her ecstasy reached a pitch of passionate exaltation, comparable in its power to the emotion that Julien had been feeling for her over the past few days. The divinely graceful aria filled every moment that she did not spend thinking directly about Julien; and how strikingly applicable she found the adage to her own situation. Thanks to her love of music, she felt that evening the way Mme de Rênal always did when thinking of Julien. Cerebral love doubtless has more wit than real love, but it only has brief moments of enthusiasm; it is too self-conscious, it is forever passing judgement on itself; far from leading thought astray, it is entirely constructed out of thoughts.

Once they were back home, despite everything Mme de La Mole could say, Mathilde claimed to be feverish, and spent part of the night practising this tune on her piano. She sang the words of the famous aria which had captivated her:

> Devo punirmi, devo punirmi,
> Se troppo amai, etc.*

The outcome of this night of folly was that she believed she had succeeded in triumphing over her love.

(This page will be detrimental to the unfortunate author in more ways than one. The unresponsive among you will accuse him of impropriety. But he isn't insulting the young women who dazzle the Paris salons by supposing that a single one of them is capable of the mad impulses which spoil Mathilde's character. She is a purely imaginary figure,* and besides, imagined quite without reference to the social customs which, in the succession of centuries, will guarantee nineteenth-century civilization a place of such distinction.

Caution is not what is lacking in the young women who adorned the balls this winter.

I do not think either that they can be accused of being too scornful of a brilliant fortune, horses, fine lands and everything else that secures an agreeable situation in society. Far from seeing all these advantages as merely boring, they generally covet them with the greatest of constancy, and if their hearts have any passion it is for them.

Nor is it love which directs the fortune of young men endowed with some talent like Julien; they latch on with an iron grip to a clique, and when the clique makes its fortune, all the good things in society rain down upon them. Woe betide the studious man who doesn't belong to any clique: even the most uncertain of minor successes will be held against him, and high virtue will triumph by robbing him. You see, sir, a novel is a mirror going along a main road. Sometimes it reflects into your eyes the azure of the sky, sometimes the mud of the quagmires on the road. And the man carrying the mirror in the basket on his back gets accused by you of being immoral! His mirror shows the mire, and you accuse the mirror! You'd do better to accuse the road where the quagmire is, and better still the inspector of roads who allows the water to stagnate and the quagmire to form.

Now that it is firmly agreed that Mathilde's character is impossible in our century, which is no less prudent than virtuous, I am less afraid of causing annoyance by continuing to recount the follies of this amiable girl.)

Throughout the whole of the following day she was on the look-out for opportunities to reassure herself of her triumph over her mad passion. Her great aim was to put Julien off in every way possible; but not a single one of his movements escaped her.

Julien was too miserable and above all too agitated to see through such a complicated manœuvre on the part of her passion; he was even less able to see all the ways in which it favoured him: he fell victim to it; his misery had never perhaps been so extreme. His actions were so little under the control of his mind that if some embittered philosopher had said to him: 'Make sure you take rapid advantage of it when things are going your way, with the kind of cerebral love you see in Paris, the same style of behaviour can't last more than two days', he would not have understood him. But whatever his state of exaltation, Julien had a sense of honour. His first duty was discretion; he realized this. To seek advice, to describe his torture to anybody at all would have been a blessed relief comparable to that felt by a poor wretch crossing a burning desert who receives a drop of ice-cold water from heaven. He recognized the danger, he felt afraid of responding with a flood

of tears to any indiscreet soul who might question him; he
locked himself away in his room.

He saw Mathilde taking a long stroll in the garden; when at
last she had left it, he went down there; he went over to a
rosebush where she had picked a flower.

The night was dark, he could give himself up fully to his
misery without fear of being seen. It was obvious to him that
Mlle de La Mole loved one of those young officers she had just
been talking to so gaily. She had loved *him* but she had
discovered how worthless he was.

And I am indeed worthless! Julien said to himself with total
conviction; all in all, I'm a pretty insipid creature—pretty
common, pretty boring to others, pretty unbearable to myself.
He was utterly disgusted with all his good qualitites, with all
the things he enjoyed with enthusiasm; and in this state of
topsy-turvy imagination, he was attempting to judge life with his
imagination. This error bears the mark of a superior man.

On several occasions the idea of suicide came to him; it was
a seductive image, like a delectable haven; it was the glass of
ice-cold water offered to the poor wretch dying of thirst and
heat in the desert.

My death will increase the scorn she feels for me! he
exclaimed. What a memory I'll leave behind!

Once he has sunk into this last abyss of misery, a human
being has no resources other than courage. Julien was not
inspired enough to say: I must be bold; but as he looked up at
Mathilde's bedroom window, he saw through the shutters that
she was putting out her light: he pictured this charming room
that he had only seen, alas! once in his life. His imagination
did not go any further.

One o'clock struck; to hear the sound of the bell and to say
to himself: I'm going to get the ladder and climb up, was the
matter of an instant.

It was a flash of genius; sound reasons came crowding in.
Can I possibly be more unhappy! he said to himself. He ran to
the ladder, the gardener had chained it up. Using the hammer
of one of his little pistols, which broke in the attempt, Julien,
endowed at that instant with superhuman strength, bent one
of the links in the chain securing the ladder; he had it at his

service in a matter of minutes, and positioned it against Mathilde's window.

She's going to get angry, to pour scorn on me, but what does it matter? I'll give her a kiss, then go up to my room and kill myself... my lips will touch her cheek before I die!

He flew up the ladder and knocked at the shutter; after a few seconds Mathilde heard him and tried to open the shutter; the ladder was in the way; Julien hung on to the iron hook used to fix the shutter open and, at the repeated risk of sending himself crashing to the ground, gave the ladder a violent jolt and shifted it slightly. Mathilde was able to open the shutter.

He threw himself into the room more dead than alive:

'So it's you, is it, my love!' she said, flinging herself into his arms...

... ...

Who can describe Julien's inordinate happiness? Mathilde's was almost as great.

She spoke up against herself, she denounced herself to him.

'Punish me for my appalling pride,' she said to him, hugging him in her arms till he could hardly breathe. 'You're my master, I'm your slave, I must ask your pardon on my knees for having tried to rebel.' She slipped out of his arms to fall at his feet. 'Yes, you're my master,' she said to him, still intoxicated with happiness and love. 'Reign over me for ever, punish your slave severely when she tries to rebel.'

At another moment she tore herself from his arms, lit the candle, and Julien had the greatest difficulty in the world in preventing her from cutting off all the hair on one side of her head.

'I want to remind myself', she told him, 'that I'm your servant: if ever any loathsome pride comes along to lead me astray, show me this hair and say:"it's no longer a matter of love, it's nothing to do with the emotion you happen to be feeling at this moment, you have sworn to obey, obey on your honour".'

But it is wiser to suppress the description of such excesses of folly and bliss.

Julien's virtue was a match for his happiness: 'I must go down by the ladder,' he said to Mathilde when he saw dawn breaking over the distant chimney-stacks in the east, beyond the gardens. 'The sacrifice I'm imposing on myself is worthy of you, I'm depriving myself of a few hours of the most amazing happiness a human soul can taste; I'm making this sacrifice for your reputation: if you know my heart, you'll understand how much I'm forcing myself. Will your attitude towards me always be the same as it is now? But honour calls, and that's enough. You should know that after our first assignation, not all suspicion fell on thieves. M. de La Mole has set up a watch in the garden. M. de Croisenois is surrounded with spies, it's known what he does every night...'

At the thought of this, Mathilde laughed riotously. Her mother and one of the women on duty were woken up; they suddenly spoke to her through the door. Julien looked at her; she turned pale as she scolded the chambermaid, and did not deign to answer her mother.

'But if they take it into their heads to open the window, they'll see the ladder!' Julien said to her.

He clasped her in his arms once more, flung himself onto the ladder and let himself slide rather than climbing down; in a flash he was on the ground.

Three seconds later the ladder was under the row of limes, and Mathilde's honour was saved. Coming to his senses, Julien found he was covered in blood and almost naked: he had wounded himself as he slid carelessly down.

The intensity of his happiness had restored all the energy of his character: had twenty men appeared before him, it would just have been one more pleasure to attack them single-handed at that moment. Fortunately his military prowess was not put to the test: he laid the ladder in its usual place; he put back the chain that secured it; he did not forget to remove the indentation left by the ladder in the bed of exotic flowers beneath Mathilde's window.

As he was running his hand in the dark over the soft earth to make sure that the indentation was completely removed, he felt something drop onto his hands: it was Mathilde's hair from one side that she had cut off and was throwing down to him.

She was at her window.

'This is what your servant sends you,' she said to him quite audibly, 'it's the sign of eternal obedience. I renounce the use of my reason, be my master.'

Julien in defeat was on the point of going to get the ladder again and climbing back up to her room. In the end reason got the upper hand.

Getting back into the house from the garden was no easy matter. He managed to force open a cellar door; once inside the house, he was obliged to break into his room as quietly as possible. In his turmoil he had left everything in the little room he had just abandoned so hastily, right down to his key which was in his suit pocket. 'So long', he thought, 'as she thinks to hide all those earthly remains!'

At length exhaustion got the better of happiness, and as the sun rose he fell into a deep sleep.

The bell for lunch woke him only with extreme difficulty; he made his appearance in the dining-room. Shortly afterwards Mathilde came in. It was a really happy moment for Julien's pride when he saw the love which shone from the eyes of this beautiful girl, the object of so much homage; but soon his prudence had occasion to be alarmed.

Using the short time she had had to attend to her hairstyle as an excuse, Mathilde had arranged her hair in such a way as to let Julien see at a glance the full extent of the sacrifice she had made him when she cut it off in the night. If so lovely a face could have been spoiled by anything, Mathilde would have achieved this: the whole of one side of her beautiful ash-blond hair was cut off half an inch from her scalp.

At lunch Mathilde's behaviour wholly matched this first act of imprudence. It was as if she had taken it upon herself to let everyone know of her mad passion for Julien. Fortunately that day M. de La Mole and the marquise were very preoccupied with the imminent award of some Blue Sashes, which did not include M. de Chaulnes. Towards the end of the meal, Mathilde, who was talking to Julien, let slip the term *master* when addressing him. He blushed to the roots of his hair.

Whether by chance or deliberately on Mme de La Mole's part, Mathilde was not alone for a single moment that day. In the evening, as they moved from the dining-room to the drawing-room, she nevertheless found a moment to say to Julien:

'Are you going to think it's an excuse on my part? Mama has just decided that one of her maids will spend the night in my room.'

That day went by in a flash. Julien was on top of the world. At seven o'clock the next morning he was already settled in the library; he hoped Mlle de La Mole would deign to put in an appearance; he had sent her an interminable letter.

He only saw her many hours later, at lunch. Her hair was arranged that day with the greatest of care; wondrous artistry had taken charge of concealing the place where the hair had been cut. She looked at Julien once or twice, but her gaze was calm and polite; there was no question of calling him *master* any more.

Julien's astonishment hampered his breathing... Mathilde seemed almost to be reproaching herself with everything she had done for him.

On careful consideration, she had decided that he was a being who, if not altogether common, none the less did not stand out sufficiently from the rest to deserve all the strange acts of folly she had ventured to commit for his sake. All in all, her thoughts were hardly on love: that day she was weary of loving.

As for Julien, his emotions swung wildly like those of a sixteen-year-old boy. Appalling doubt, astonishment and despair took hold of him in turn throughout that lunch which seemed to him to last an eternity.

As soon as he could decently get up from table, he rushed rather than ran to the stables, saddled his horse himself and set off at a gallop; he was afraid of disgracing himself by some act of weakness. I must kill my heart with physical exhaustion, he said to himself as he galloped through the woods at Meudon*. What have I done, what have I said to deserve such a fall from favour?

I mustn't do anything or say anything today, he thought on returning to the house, I must be as dead physically as I am mentally. Julien is no longer alive, it's his corpse that is still twitching.

CHAPTER 20

The Japanese vase

His heart does not understand to begin with how
acute is his unhappiness; he is more disturbed than
moved. But as his reason gradually returns, he feels
the depth of his misfortune. All the pleasures of life
are destroyed for him, he can only feel the sharp
prickings of despair tearing him apart. But what is
the use of talking of physical pain? What pain felt
by the body alone can be compared with this?

JEAN PAUL*

DINNER was being announced; Julien only just had time to
dress. In the drawing-room he found Mathilde, who was
earnestly entreating her brother and M. de Croisenois not to
go and spend the evening at Suresnes with the Maréchale de
Fervaques.

No one could have been more charming and more amiable
towards them. After dinner Messrs de Luz, de Caylus and
several of their friends turned up. It looked as if Mlle de La
Mole's resumption of the cult of sisterly affection went hand
in hand with that of the strictest propriety. Although the
weather was delightful that evening, she insisted on not going
out into the garden; she wanted everyone to stay by the couch
where Mme de La Mole was settled. The blue sofa was the
focus of the group, as in winter.

Mathilde had taken against the garden, or at any rate it
seemed utterly boring to her: it was linked with the memory
of Julien.

Unhappiness dulls the mind. Our hero was inept enough to
come over to the little wicker chair which had witnessed such
brilliant triumphs in the past. Today no one said a word to
him: his presence was as good as unnoticed, or worse. Those
of Mlle de La Mole's friends who were stationed near him at
the foot of the sofa made a point of turning their backs to him,
or at least that was how it struck him.

It's exactly like falling from favour at Court, he reflected.

He determined to spend a short while studying the people who presumed to crush him with their disdain.

M. de Luz had an uncle with an important post in the king's entourage, on the strength of which this handsome officer slipped the following amusing particular into the beginning of his conversation with every interlocutor who came up to him: his uncle had set off at seven o'clock for Saint-Cloud* and was banking on spending the night there. This detail was brought in with every sign of straightforwardness, but it never failed to appear.

As he observed M. de Croisenois with the severe eye of misfortune, Julien noticed the excessive influence which this amiable and kindly young man imputed to occult causes—to the point where he was saddened and annoyed if he found an event of any importance being ascribed to a simple, quite natural cause. There's a streak of madness in this, Julien said to himself. His character is strikingly like the Emperor Alexander's, as described to me by Prince Korasov. During his first year in Paris, when he was just out of the seminary, Julien was dazzled by the graceful accomplishments of all these amiable young men: they were so new to him, all he could do was admire them. Their true character was only just beginning to emerge to his gaze.

I'm playing an unworthy role here, he suddenly thought. It was a matter of getting up from his little wicker chair in a way that would not be too inept. He tried to improvise, but this meant asking something new of an imagination that was too preoccupied elsewhere. He had to resort to memory, and his was ill-endowed, it must be admitted, with resources of this kind: the poor fellow was still pretty lacking in social graces, and consequently displayed an exemplary ineptitude which everyone noticed when he rose to leave the drawing-room. Wretchedness was only too apparent in his whole manner. For the past three-quarters of an hour he had been playing the part of an unwelcome subordinate from whom no one takes the trouble of concealing what they think of him.

The critical observations he had just made on his rivals prevented him, however, from taking his misfortune too tragically; he did have, to bolster his pride, the memory of what had happened two days ago. Whatever their advantages over me, he thought as he went out alone into the garden, Mathilde has never been for any of them what she deigned to be for me twice in my life.

His wisdom stopped there. He had no understanding whatsoever of the character of the strange person whom chance had just made absolute mistress over his entire happiness.

He contented himself on the following day with killing himself and his horse with exhaustion. That evening he did not attempt to approach the blue sofa again; Mathilde was faithful to it. He noticed that Count Norbert didn't even deign to look at him when he ran across him in the house. He must be doing violence to his instincts, he thought, since he's naturally so polite.

Sleep for Julien would have been bliss. In spite of physical fatigue, his imagination was progressively invaded by all-too-bewitching memories. He did not have the wit to see that by indulging in these long rides on horseback through the woods on the outskirts of Paris, he was only acting upon himself and in no way upon Mathilde's heart or mind, so he was leaving it to chance to settle his fate.

It seemed to him that one thing would bring infinite relief to his suffering: to talk to Mathilde. Yet what would he dare say to her?

This was what he was musing deeply about at seven o'clock one morning when he suddenly saw her coming into the library.

'I know, sir, that you wish to speak to me.'

'Great heavens! Who told you so?'

'I just know, what does it matter to you? If you aren't a man of honour, you can ruin me, or at any rate try to; but this risk, which I don't believe to be real, certainly won't prevent me from being frank. I don't love you any more, sir, my mad imagination has been deceiving me...'

At this terrible blow, distracted with love and unhappiness, Julien tried to justify himself. Nothing could have been more absurd. Can one justify oneself for failing to be liked? But reason had no hold over his conduct any more. Some blind instinct drove him to delay the decision on his fate. It seemed to him that as long as he was talking, all was not over. Mathilde was not listening to his words, the sound of them irritated her, she couldn't see how he had the audacity to interrupt her.

Virtue and pride were both causing her remorse that made her equally wretched that morning. She was somehow devastated by the appalling idea of having given rights over herself to a little abbé, the son of a peasant. It's more or less, she said to herself at times when she was exaggerating her wretchedness, as if I had a lapse with one of the lackeys on my conscience.

With bold and proud characters, it is only a short step from anger at oneself to fury with others; fits of rage in such cases cause acute pleasure.

In a matter of moments, Mlle de La Mole reached the point of heaping upon Julien the most outrageous expressions of scorn. She was infinitely clever, and her cleverness excelled in the art of torturing the self-esteem of others, and inflicting cruel wounds upon it.

For the first time in his life Julien found himself subjected to the working of a superior mind fired by the most violent hatred of him. Far from having even the slightest thought of defending himself at that moment, he reached the stage of despising his own self. As he heard himself assailed with such cruel outbursts of scorn, so cleverly calculated to destroy any good opinion he might have of himself, it seemed to him that Mathilde was right and that her words did not go far enough.

As for her, she savoured to the full the pleasure her pride took in thus punishing herself and him for the adoration she had felt a few days before.

She had no need to improvise and think up from scratch the cruel things she said to him with such satisfaction. She was only repeating what the advocate for the party opposed to love had been saying in her heart for the past week.

Every word increased Julien's wretchedness a hundredfold. He tried to escape, but Mlle de La Mole held him back authoritatively by the arm.

'Be so good as to observe', he said to her, 'that you're talking very loud, you'll be overheard from the next room.'

'So what!' replied Mlle de La Mole arrogantly, 'who shall dare tell me I can be heard? I want to cure that petty pride of yours for ever of the ideas it may have got hold of concerning me.'

When Julien was able to leave the library, he was so astonished that it made him less aware of his misery. 'Oh well! she doesn't love me any more,' he repeated to himself out loud as if informing himself of his situation. She loved me for a week or ten days, so it seems, whereas I shall love her all my life.

Is this really possible, she meant nothing—nothing to me only a few days ago!

Mathilde's heart was awash with gloating pride; so she *had* been able to break it off irrevocably for ever! Triumphing so totally over such a powerful attraction would make her perfectly happy. As things are, this little gentleman will understand once and for all that he doesn't and never will have any hold over me. She was so happy that she genuinely felt no love any more at that moment.

After such an appalling and humiliating scene, love would have become impossible for anyone less passionate than Julien. Without deviating for a single instant from her duty to herself, Mlle de La Mole had made some nasty remarks to him, so well targeted as to appear true even when remembered in a calm frame of mind.

The conclusion Julien drew at first from such an astonishing scene was that Mathilde's pride knew no bounds. He firmly believed that everything was over between them for good and all, and yet at lunch the next day he was awkward and nervous in her presence. It was not a failing he could have been reproached with up until then. In small matters as in important ones, he knew precisely what it was his wish and desire to do, and he just carried it out.

That day, after lunch, when Mme de La Mole asked him for a seditious and at the same time rather rare pamphlet that her priest had brought her in secret that morning, Julien reached over to a side table for it and knocked over an old blue china vase, as hideous as they come.

Mme de La Mole sprang up with a cry of distress and came over to take a close look at the ruins of her beloved vase. 'It was antique Japanese porcelain,' she said, 'it came from my great-aunt the Abbess of Chelles;* it was a gift from the Dutch to the Duke of Orleans* while he was regent, and he gave it to his daughter...'

Mathilde had followed her mother over, delighted to find in smithereens this blue vase she thought horribly ugly. Julien was silent and not excessively disturbed; he found Mlle de La Mole right next to him.

'This vase', he said to her, 'is destroyed for ever, and the same goes for a sentiment which was once master of my heart; I beg you to accept my apologies for all the acts of folly it caused me to commit.' And he left the room.

'You'd really think', said Mme de La Mole as he walked off, 'that that M. Sorel is proud and pleased with what he's just done.'

These words went straight to Mathilde's heart. It's true, she said to herself, my mother has guessed right, that's just what he is feeling. Only then came an end to the joy caused by the scene she had had with him the day before. Oh well, it's all over, she told herself with apparent calm; it's taught me a great lesson; it was an appalling, humiliating mistake! It'll make me be good for the rest of my life.

Why wasn't I telling the truth? Julien thought; why does the love I felt for this mad creature go on tormenting me?

This love, far from dwindling to nothing as he hoped, grew in leaps and bounds. She's mad, it's true, he said to himself, but is she any the less adorable for it? Could anyone be prettier? Didn't everything the most elegant civilization can offer in the way of intense pleasures jostle, so to speak, to be represented in the person of Mlle de La Mole? These memories of past happiness swept Julian up and rapidly destroyed everything reason had accomplished.

Reason struggles in vain against memories of this kind; its stern attempts only increase their charm.

Twenty-four hours after shattering the old Japanese porcelain vase, Julien was decidedly one of the unhappiest of men.

CHAPTER 21

The secret memorandum*

For everything I describe I have seen; and if I may
have been deceived when I saw it, I am most
certainly not deceiving you when telling you of it.

Letter to the Author

THE marquis summoned him; M. de La Mole looked years
younger; there was a glint in his eye.

'Let's have a word about your memory,' he said to Julien,
'they say it's prodigious! Could you learn four pages off by
heart and go and recite them in London? But without altering
a single word...'

The marquis was crumpling up that day's copy of *La
Quotidienne** in annoyance, and trying in vain to conceal his
deeply serious expression—one that Julien had never seen on
his face before, even when the subject of his lawsuit with
Frilair came up. Julien had sufficient experience of life by then
to sense that he must appear to be completely taken in by the
careless tone he was being treated to.

'This issue of *La Quotidienne* is perhaps not very entertaining, but if his lordship is agreeable, tomorrow morning it will
be my privilege to recite it to him in its entirety.'

'What! Even the announcements?'

'Precisely so, and without a single word missing.'

'Do you give me your word on it?' asked the marquis with
sudden gravity.

'Yes, sir, fear of breaking it would be the only thing capable
of interfering with my memory.'

'You see, I forgot to put this question to you yesterday: I
shall not ask you to swear never to repeat what you are about
to hear; I know you too well to insult you like that. I have
already vouched for you; I'm going to take you along to a salon
in which twelve people will be gathered; you will make a note
of what each one says.

'Don't worry, it won't be a rambling conversation, each
person will speak in turn—I don't mean in ordered speeches,'

the marquis added, resuming the knowing and light-hearted look which came so naturally to him. 'While we are speaking, you will write twenty pages or so of notes; you will come back here with me and we'll reduce these twenty pages to four. These four pages will be what you'll recite to me tomorrow morning instead of that whole copy of *La Quotidienne*. You will leave immediately afterwards; you'll have to go post haste like a young man travelling for his own pleasure. Your aim will be to pass completely unnoticed. You will arrive in the entourage of an important personage. There you will need greater skill. It's a question of fooling his whole entourage; for among his secretaries and his servants there are people in the pay of our enemies, who are lying in wait for our agents to intercept them as they go about their business. You will have a letter of recommendation of no consequence.

'At the instant when his excellency looks at you, you will pull out my watch you see here, which I'll lend you for the journey. Take it on your person now, then that's dealt with, and give me yours.

'The duke himself will deign to write out at your dictation the four pages you'll have learned off by heart.

'Once that's done, but not before, please note, you will be at liberty, if his excellency questions you, to give him an account of the meeting you are about to take part in.

'What will keep you from getting bored during your journey is that between Paris and the minister's residence there are people who would like nothing better than to put a bullet into the Reverend Father Sorel. At which point his mission is over, and I foresee a long delay; for how, my dear fellow, are we to hear of your death? Your zeal cannot extend to sending us word of it.

'Run off at once and buy a complete set of clothes,' the marquis went on gravely. 'Adopt the fashion of two years ago. This evening you've got to look rather negligent in your dress. For the journey, on the other hand, you will be dressed as usual. Does this surprise you, are you canny enough to guess the reason? Yes, my good fellow, one of the venerable figures whose opinion you are going to hear is perfectly capable of passing on information, on the strength of which you may well find yourself one evening being given opium if not worse in some friendly inn where you have ordered supper.'

'It would be better', said Julien, 'to do an extra thirty leagues and not take the direct route. We're talking about Rome, I imagine...'

The marquis adopted an air of haughtiness and displeasure that Julien had not seen him wear in such an extreme form since that time at Bray-le-Haut.

'That, sir, you will find out when I see fit to tell you. I don't like questions.'

'It wasn't one,' Julien replied fervently; 'I swear it, sir, I was thinking out loud, I was running through my mind for the safest route.'

'Yes, it seems that your mind was quite elsewhere. Don't ever forget that an ambassador, even at your age, mustn't appear to be forcing confidences.'

Julien was very mortified: he was in the wrong. His self-esteem was looking for an excuse and failing to find one.

'You must realize', added M. de La Mole, 'that one invariably allows one's emotions to get involved when one has done something silly.'

An hour later Julien was in the marquis's antechamber, turned out in the manner of a subordinate, with out-of-date clothes, a cravat of dubious whiteness, and something ridiculously pompous about his whole appearance.

On seeing him the marquis burst out laughing, and only then was his faith in Julien completely vindicated. If this young man betrays me, M. de La Mole said to himself, who *can* I trust? And yet if you're involved in a lot of business, you have to trust someone. My son and his brilliant friends of the same ilk have enough courage and loyalty for a whole army; if it were a question of fighting, they would perish on the steps of the throne, they are competent in everything... except what's required at this juncture. Damned if I can imagine one of them being able to learn off four pages by heart and travel a hundred leagues without being discovered. Norbert would know how to get himself killed like his ancestors, but that's a conscript's privilege too...

The marquis fell to musing deeply: If it comes to getting killed, he sighed, this Sorel might be just as good as Norbert...

'Let's get into the carriage,' said the marquis as if to banish an unwelcome thought.

'Sir,' said Julien, 'while I was having this suit fitted, I learned the first page of today's *Quotidienne* off by heart.' The marquis took the newspaper. Julien recited his piece without getting a single word wrong. 'Good,' said the marquis, at his most diplomatic that evening; all this time the young man isn't noticing the streets we're passing through.

Eventually they found themselves in a large drawing-room of rather dismal appearance, partly panelled and partly hung with green velvet. In the middle of the room a sullen footman was just finishing setting up a large dinner-table, which he later converted into a conference table by means of a huge sheet of green baize all covered in ink stains, salvaged from some ministry or other.

The host was an enormous man whose name was never uttered; Julien thought he looked and talked like someone who had just had a heavy meal.

At a sign from the marquis, Julien had remained at the far end of the table. To cover up his embarrassment, he set about trimming some pens. Out of the corner of his eye he counted seven speakers, but he only got a back view of them. It struck him that two of them were addressing M. de La Mole as an equal, while the others seemed more or less respectful.

A new figure came in unannounced. This is odd, thought Julien, they don't announce people in this salon. Could it be that this precaution is being taken in my honour? Everyone got up to greet the newcomer. He was wearing the same extremely distinguished decoration as three of the other people already in the room. They spoke in rather low voices. To judge the newcomer, Julien was reduced to what he could glean from his features and his general bearing. He was short and stocky, with high colour, a glint in his eye, and no expression other than the viciousness of a wild boar.

Julien's attention was sharply distracted by the almost immediate arrival of a quite different individual. He was a tall, very thin man wearing three or four waistcoats. His gaze spelled reassurance and his gestures civility.

He's the very image of the old Bishop of Besançon, thought Julien. He was clearly a man of the Church, and he did not look more than fifty or fifty-five; no one could have had a more unctuous expression.

The young Bishop of Agde appeared, and looked most astonished when, on casting a glance over the people present, his eye alighted on Julien. He had not spoken to him since the ceremony at Bray-le-Haut. His look of surprise embarrassed and annoyed Julien. For goodness' sake! thought the latter, will it always work to my disadvantage to know someone? All these great lords I've never set eyes on before don't intimidate me in the least, and this young bishop's stare freezes me to the spot! There's no denying I'm a most peculiar and most unlucky individual.

Soon a small, very dark man came into the room with a great clatter, and began talking as soon as he had stepped inside the door; he had a swarthy complexion and a rather mad look about him. As soon as this relentless talker arrived the others gathered into small groups, seemingly to escape the boredom of listening to him.

As they moved away from the fireplace, people drew closer to the far end of the table where Julien was sitting. His expression became more and more embarrassed; for after all, try as he might, he could not fail to hear, and inexperienced as he was, he understood the full significance of the things that were being openly discussed; and how dearly the high-ranking figures he appeared to be observing must have wished them to remain secret!

Julien had already, working as slowly as possible, trimmed himself some twenty pens; this resource was going to run out on him. He looked in vain for an order in M. de La Mole's eyes; the marquis had forgotten him.

What I'm doing is ridiculous, Julien said to himself as he trimmed his pens; but people with such insignificant faces, who have such important concerns entrusted to them by others or by themselves, must be extremely touchy. I have an unfortunate way of looking at people that is somehow questioning and disrespectful, and it would surely annoy them. If I keep my eyes resolutely lowered, I'll look as if I'm taking in their every word.

His embarrassment was acute: he was hearing some very strange things.

CHAPTER 22

The discussion

The republic: for each individual today who would
sacrifice everything for the public good, there are
thousands and millions whose only experience is of
their own enjoyment and their vanity. A man is
respected in Paris for his carriage, not his virtue.

NAPOLEON, *Chronicle*

THE footman rushed in calling: 'His grace the Duke of ——'

'Be quiet, you *are* a fool,' said the duke as he came in. He
said it so well, and with so much majesty, that in spite of
himself Julien decided that knowing how to get angry with a
footman summed up all the wisdom of this important personage. Julien raised his eyes, then lowered them again at once.
He had surmised the newcomer's significance so well that he
trembled lest his glance be considered an indiscretion.

The duke was a man of fifty, dressed like a dandy, who
walked as if on springs. He had a narrow head, a big nose, and
a curved profile with all his features drawn forwards; no one
could have had more noble and more insignificant an air. His
arrival was the sign for the meeting to begin.

Julien was sharply interrupted in his observations of physiognomy by the voice of M. de La Mole. 'May I introduce
Father Julien Sorel,' the marquis was saying. 'He's gifted with
an astonishing memory; it's only an hour since I told him
about the mission he might be honoured with, and in order to
demonstrate his memory, he has learned the first page of *La
Quotidienne* off by heart.'

'Ah! the Foreign News section written by poor old N——,'
said the host. He seized the newspaper eagerly, and, giving
Julien a look that was comic, so hard was he trying to appear
important, 'Speak, sir,' he said.

There was a deathly hush, with all eyes riveted on Julien; he
recited so well that after twenty lines: 'That'll do,' said the
duke. The little man who looked like a wild boar sat down. He
was presiding, for he was no sooner seated than he pointed out

a card-table to Julien and signalled to him to bring it up close to him. Julien settled himself at it with the wherewithal to write. He counted twelve people seated round the green baize.

'M. Sorel,' said the duke, 'please withdraw into the next room; you'll be summoned back.'

The host took on a worried expression. 'The shutters aren't closed,' he said in a half-whisper to his neighbour. 'There's no need to look out of the window,' he called foolishly after Julien. Here I am in the thick of a conspiracy at the very least, thought the latter. Fortunately it isn't one of the kind that leads to the Place de Grève*. Even if there were danger in it, I owe this and more besides to the marquis. How glad I'd be if I were granted a chance to make up for all the sorrow my follies may one day cause him!

All the time he was thinking of his follies and his misfortune, he was looking at his surroundings in such as way as never to forget them. Only then did he remember that he hadn't heard the marquis tell the footman the name of the street, and the marquis had arranged for a cab to bring them here, which was unheard of for him.

For a long while Julien was left to his reflections. He was in a room hung with red velvet edged with wide gold braid. On the side table there was a large ivory crucifix, and on the mantlepiece a gilt-edged copy of M. de Maistre's book *On the Pope*,* magnificently bound. Julien opened it so as not to appear to be listening. At times voices were raised very loud in the next room. At last the door opened and he was called in.

'Consider, gentlemen,' said the chairman, 'that from now on we are speaking in front of the Duke of——. This gentleman', he said with a gesture in Julien's direction, 'is a young Levite devoted to our holy cause, who will easily be able, thanks to his astonishing memory, to transmit everything we say, down to the last word.

'It's this gentleman's turn to speak,' he said, indicating the individual with an unctuous expression who was wearing three or four waistcoats. Julien thought it would have been more natural to refer to the gentleman in the waistcoats by name. He took some paper and wrote down a great deal.

(At this point the author would have liked to put a page of

dots. 'That's not very accommodating,' said his publisher. 'And if you don't accommodate your readers' tastes it spells death for a frivolous work like this one.'

'Politics', replied the author, 'is a millstone round the neck of literature, which sinks it in less than six months. Politics in the midst of concerns of the imagination is like a pistol-shot in the middle of a concert. The noise is harsh without being dynamic. It doesn't blend in with the sound of any instrument. All this politics will mortally offend one half of my readers and bore the other, even though they found it quite special and dynamic in the morning paper...'

'If your characters don't talk politics', the publisher rejoined, 'they cease to be Frenchmen of 1830, and your book is no longer a mirror, as you would have it...')

The minutes taken by Julien were twenty-six pages long; here is a very colourless extract from them, for it was necessary, as always, to suppress the ridiculous excesses which would have struck readers as odious or scarcely credible (see *La Gazette des Tribunaux*).*

The man in the waistcoats with the unctuous look (he was perhaps a bishop) smiled frequently, and this gave his eyes with their flabby lids a strange gleam and a less indecisive expression than usual. This figure, whom they invited to speak first in front of the duke (but which duke? Julien wondered), apparently to expound the different viewpoints and carry out the function of assistant public prosecutor, struck Julien as lapsing into the hesitancy and inability to draw firm conclusions that such lawyers are often reproached with. During the course of the discussion, the duke himself went so far as to reproach him with this.

After several sentences of moralizing and indulgent philosophizing, the man in the waistcoats said:

'Noble England, guided by a great man, the immortal Pitt, spent forty billion francs to stem the revolution. If this gathering will allow me to allude quite frankly to a dismal subject, England did not realize clearly enough that with a man like Bonaparte, especially when all they had to put in his way was a handful of good intentions, the only decisive factor would have been individual initiative...'

'Ah! advocating assassination* again!' said the host uneasily.

'Spare us your sentimental homilies,' the chairman exclaimed in annoyance; his boar's eye glinted ferociously. 'Carry on,' he said to the man in the waistcoats. The chairman's cheeks and forehead turned crimson.

'Noble England', went on the spokesman, 'is crushed today, for before an Englishman can buy his bread, he is obliged to pay the interest on the forty billion francs used against the Jacobins. The country hasn't got a Pitt any more...'

'She does have the Duke of Wellington,' said a military gentleman who assumed an air of great importance.

'Silence, I beg you, gentlemen,' called out the chairman; 'if we argue any more, it'll have been pointless to call in M. Sorel.'

'We all know that you, sir, are not short of ideas,' said the duke, glaring at the interruption, from a man who had been one of Napoleon's generals. Julien realized that this comment alluded to something personal and highly offensive. Everyone smiled; the turncoat general looked beside himself with anger.

'There's no Pitt any more, gentlemen,' the spokesman went on, with the discouraged look of a man despairing of getting his listeners to see reason. And were there to be a new Pitt in England, you can't pull the wool over a nation's eyes twice in the same manner...'

'That's why a victorious general, a Bonaparte, is henceforth impossible in France,' interrupted the military man again.

This time round, neither the chairman nor the duke dared get angry, although Julien thought he read in their eyes that they would have dearly liked to. They lowered their gaze, and the duke was content with sighing in such a way as to be heard by all.

But the spokesman had taken umbrage.

'No one can wait for me to finish,' he said vehemently, completely dropping the smiling courtesy and measured language which Julien believed to be the expression of his character. 'No one can wait for me to finish; I'm not being given any credit for the effort I'm making not to offend anyone's ears, however long they may be. All right then, gentlemen, I shall be brief.'

'And I shall tell you in very blunt terms: England hasn't got a farthing left to further the good cause. Even if Pitt himself were to come back, all his genius would be of no avail to pull the wool over the English smallholders' eyes, for they know that the short Waterloo campaign on its own cost them a billion francs. Since you want plain speaking', the spokesman added, getting more and more animated, 'I say to you: '*Go out and seek your own help*,* for England hasn't got a guinea to give you, and when England doesn't pay, Austria, Russia and Prussia, who only have courage and not money, cannot wage more than a campaign or two against France.

'It is to be hoped that the young soldiers mustered by the forces of Jacobinism will be defeated in the first campaign, or maybe in the second; but in the third, at the cost of seeming a revolutionary in your biased eyes, in the third you'll get the soldiers of 1794,* who that time round weren't the press-ganged peasants of 1792.'

At this point interruptions fired off from three or four quarters at once.

'Sir,' said the chairman to Julien, 'go into the next room and copy out the beginning of the minutes you've taken.' Julien left the room, much to his regret. The spokesman had just touched on eventualities which formed the subject of his customary meditations.

They're afraid I'll laugh at them, he thought. When he was recalled, M. de La Mole was saying, with a seriousness which struck Julien, who knew him, as highly comic:

'...Yes, gentlemen, it's particularly appropriate to ask of this unfortunate nation:

Will it be a god, a table or a basin?

'*It will be a god*!* the fable-writer exclaims. You, gentlemen, seem to be the ones for whom these most noble and profound words are destined. Act on your own, and noble France will reappear much as our ancestors had created her and our eyes still saw her before the death of Louis XVI.*

'England—her noble lords, that is—loathes base Jacobinism as much as we do: without English gold, Austria, Russia and Prussia can only fight two or three battles. Will that be enough to bring about the desired occupation, like the one M. de Richelieu* so stupidly failed to exploit in 1817!* I don't think so.'

Here there was an interruption, but it was stifled by sounds of *sshh*! from everyone else. It again came from the former imperial general* who was after a Blue Sash, and wanted to cut a figure among the authors of the secret memorandum.

'I don't think so,' M. de La Mole resumed when the hubbub died down. He stressed the *I* in a tone of insolence that delighted Julien. That was well played, he said to himself, making his pen fly almost as fast as the marquis's speech. With a word said right, M. de La Mole destroys all twenty of this turncoat's campaigns.

'It isn't only to foreign hands', the marquis continued, 'that we can look for a fresh military occupation. All these young men writing inflammatory articles in *Le Globe** will provide you with three or four thousand young captains in whose midst there may be a Kléber,* a Hoche, a Jourdan, a Pichegru, but less well-intentioned.

'We failed to give him due honour,' said the chairman, 'His memory should have been made immortal.'

'We must ultimately have two parties in France,' M. de La Mole went on, 'but two parties not in name alone, two parties that are quite distinct, quite separate. Let's be clear who it is we must crush. On the one hand journalists, voters, public opinion, in short: youth and all its admirers. While its head is being turned by the sound of its idle words, we on our side have the sure advantage of feeding off the budget.'

Another interruption here.

'You, sir,' said M. de La Mole to the interrupter with admirable hauteur and polish, 'you don't "feed off it"—if the term shocks you—you devour forty thousand francs from the State budget and eighty thousand you receive from the civil list.

'Well, sir, since you drive me to it, let me boldly take you as an example. Like your noble ancestors who followed St Louis to the Crusades, you ought, in return for these hundred and twenty thousand francs, to have at least a regiment to show us—a company, or come now! a half-company, even if it had no more than fifty men in it ready to fight, and devoted to the good cause, in life and in death! You've only got lackeys who, if it came to an uprising, would frighten the daylights out of your good self.

'The throne, the altar, the nobility risk destruction tomorrow, until such time as you set up a force of five hundred *devoted* men in every département; and I mean devoted, not just with the true bravery of the French, but also the constancy of the Spaniards.

'Half of each band will have to consist of our children, our nephews, real gentlemen, that is. Each one of them will have at his side not some talkative petty bourgeois, ready to sport the red-white-and-blue emblem if 1815* repeats itself, but a good, straightforward, loyal peasant like Cathelineau;* our gentleman will have instructed him, they will have been suckled by the same nurse if possible. Let each one of us sacrifice a fifth of his income to set up this little band of five hundred devoted men in each département. Then you'll be able to count on a foreign occupation. Your foreign troops will never even get as far as Dijon if they aren't sure of finding five hundred friendly soldiers in every département.

'Foreign kings will only listen to you when you announce the presence of twenty thousand gentlemen ready to take up arms to open the gates of France to them. Guaranteeing this support is a burden, you'll tell me; gentlemen, our heads remain on our shoulders at this price. It's war to the death between freedom of the press and our existence as gentlemen. Become manufacturers or peasants, or take up your guns. Be cautious if you wish, but don't be stupid; open your eyes.

'*Form your battalions*, I'd say to you with a line from the Jacobins' song,* then some noble Gustave-Adolphe* will come along and, moved by the imminent threat to the cause of the monarchy, will speed three hundred leagues from his own country to do for you what Gustave did for the Protestant princes. Do you intend to go on producing talk and no action? In fifty years time there will only be presidents of republics in Europe, and not a single king. And with those four letters K–I–N–G, gone are priests and gentlemen. All I can see is *candidates* currying favour with grubby *majorities*.

'It's no use saying that at this moment France doesn't have an accredited general known and loved by all; that the army is only organized to serve the interests of throne and altar; that all the old troopers have been removed from it, whereas every single Prussian or Austrian regiment has fifty sub-officers who've been in the firing line.

'Two hundred thousand young men from the lower middle classes are infatuated with war...'

'A pax on unpalatable truths,' said a solemn individual complacently; he was apparently high up in the ecclesiastical ranks, for M. de La Mole smiled engagingly instead of getting angry, which was a very telling sign for Julien.

'A pax on unpalatable truths; let us sum up, gentlemen: a man with a gangrened leg that needs amputating is in no position to say to his surgeon: "this diseased leg is perfectly healthy." If you'll excuse the expression, gentlemen, the noble Duke of —— is our surgeon.'

At last the great name has been uttered, thought Julien; I shall be galloping off towards the —— tonight.*

CHAPTER 23

The clergy, forests and freedom

*The first law of every creature is self-preservation and
life. You sow hemlock and make out that you'll see corn
ripening!*

MACHIAVELLI

THE solemn individual went on: it was obvious he knew what
he was talking about; he expounded the following great truths
with a gentle, well-tempered eloquence which Julien appreciated enormously:

'1. England doesn't have a guinea to further our cause;
economics and Hume* are in fashion there. Even the *Saints**
won't give us any money, and Mr Brougham* will laugh at
us.

2. Impossible to get more than two campaigns out of the
kings of Europe without English gold; and two campaigns
won't suffice against the lower middle class.

3. Need to form an armed party in France, otherwise the
royalist cause in Europe won't risk even these two campaigns.

'The fourth point I venture to put to you as self-evident is
this:

*Quite impossible to form an armed party in France without the
clergy.* I say this boldly, because I'm going to prove it to you,
gentlemen. We must give everything to the clergy.

1. Because they are engaged in their business night and day,
and guided by men of great ability settled at a safe distance
from the storms three hundred leagues from your frontiers...'

'Ah! Rome, Rome!' exclaimed the host...

'Yes, sir, *Rome!*' the cardinal continued proudly. '*Pace* the
jokes of greater or lesser ingenuity that were in fashion when
you were young, let me declare openly, in 1830, that the
clergy, guided by Rome, is alone in being able to speak to the
lower orders.

'If fifty thousand priests repeat the same words on the day
appointed by the leaders, the common people, who, after all,
provide the soldiers, will be more moved by their priests'

words than by all the doggerel* in the world...' (This slighting allusion set off murmurs.)

'The clergy has greater understanding than you do,' the cardinal went on, raising his voice; 'all the steps you have taken to achieve this crucial aim, *having an armed party in France*, have been taken by us.' Here he threw in facts... 'Who sent eighty thousand rifles to the Vendée?*... etc., etc.

'As long as the clergy is deprived of its forests* it possesses nothing. When the first war comes along, the finance minister is going to send word to his agents that there's no more money available except for parish priests*. Basically, France is not a religious country, and she loves wars. Whoever it happens to be who gives her war will be doubly popular, because waging war means starving the Jesuits, as the common people would put it; and waging war means delivering those monsters of pride, the French, from the threat of foreign intervention.'

The cardinal's words were going down well... 'What is needed', he said, 'is for M. de Nerval* to leave the Cabinet: his name puts people's backs up unnecessarily.

At this, everyone stood up and spoke at once. They'll send me out again, Julien thought; but even the wise chairman had forgotten about Julien's presence and his very existence.

All eyes looked round for a man Julien recognized. It was M. de Nerval, the Prime Minister, whom he had glimpsed at the Duc de Retz's ball.

The commotion reached a peak, as the newspapers say when talking about the National Assembly. After a good quarter of an hour things quietened down somewhat.

Then M. de Nerval rose to his feet and, adopting the tones of an apostle:

'I shall not make out to you', he said in a strange voice, 'that I put no store by the premiership.

'It has been indicated to me, gentlemen, that my name doubles the Jacobins' numbers by turning a good many moderates against us. I should therefore readily step down; but the ways of the Lord are shown only to a few; and', he added, staring straight at the cardinal, 'I have a mission; heaven has said to me: "You shall lay your head on the block, or you shall restore the monarchy in France and reduce the

Chambers to what Parliament was under Louis XV",* and *that, gentlemen, is what I shall do.*'

He finished uttering and sat down; a deep silence fell.

There's a good actor, Julien thought. He again made the mistake, as he always did, of crediting people with too much intelligence. Roused by this stimulating evening's debates, and particularly by the sincerity of the discussion, at that moment M. de Nerval believed in his mission. For all his great courage, the man did not have any sense.

Midnight struck during the silence following the fine phrase: *that is what I shall do.* Julien found the striking of the clock somehow imposing and funereal. He was moved.

The discussion soon resumed with growing animation, and in particular with unbelievable openness. These people will have me poisoned, Julien thought at times. How can they say such things in front of a plebeian?

Two o'clock struck, and they were still talking. The host had been asleep for some time; M. de La Mole was obliged to ring for more candles. M. de Nerval, the minister, had left at a quarter to two, having taken frequent advantage of a mirror beside him to study Julien's face. His departure had seemed to put everyone at their ease.

While the candles were being renewed, 'God knows what that man is going to tell the king!' said the man in the waistcoats softly to his neighbour. 'He can make us look pretty ridiculous and ruin our future. You must admit he's got a rare degree of self-importance and even effrontery to turn up here. He used to come along before he rose to the Cabinet; but a portfolio changes everything: it swamps all a man's other interests, and he ought to have sensed this.'

No sooner was the minister gone than the general from Bonaparte's army had shut his eyes. Now he said something about his health and his wounds, looked at his watch and left.

'I'd lay a wager on it', said the man in the waistcoats, 'that the general is running after the minister; he's going to apologize for being here, and claim to be manipulating us.'

When the bleary-eyed servants had finished renewing the candles:

'Let us get down to our deliberations, gentlemen,' said the

chairman, 'we must stop trying to convince one another. We must think about the content of the memorandum which in forty-eight hours' time will be before the eyes of our friends across the border. We have talked about ministers. We can admit now that M. de Nerval has left us: what do we care about ministers? We shall dictate wishes to them.'

The cardinal showed his approval with a subtle smile.

'Nothing could be easier, it seems to me, than summing up our position,' said the young Bishop of Agde with the concentrated and forced vehemence of the most exalted fanaticism. He had kept silent up until then; his eyes, which Julien had been watching, had had a gentle and serene look in them to start with, but had begun to blaze after the first hour of discussion. Now his soul was overflowing like lava from Vesuvius.

'Between 1806 and 1814, the one thing England did wrong', he said 'was not to take direct, personal action against Napoleon. Once the man had created dukes and chamberlains, once he had restored the throne, the mission God had entrusted to him was over; he was ripe for sacrificial slaughter. The Holy Scriptures teach us in more places than one how to deal with tyrants.' (Here followed a number of quotations in Latin.)

'Today, gentleman, what has to be sacrificed is not a man, but Paris. The whole of France copies Paris. What's the use of arming your five hundred men per département? It's a risky and never-ending enterprise. What's the use of involving France in a business that is peculiar to Paris? Paris alone with its newspapers and its salons has committed the evil: let this new Babylon perish.

'There must be a decisive confrontation between the altar and Paris. Such a catastrophe would even be in the worldly interests of the throne. Why didn't Paris dare breathe a word under Bonaparte? The Saint-Roch cannon* has the answer to that one...'

....

It was not until three in the morning that Julien and M. de La Mole left.

The marquis felt embarrassed and tired. For the first time, when he addressed Julien, there was a note of entreaty in his voice. He wanted Julien's word for it that he would never disclose the excesses of zeal—that was the marquis's expression—which chance had just let him witness. 'Don't mention this to our friend abroad unless he really insists on knowing what our young hotheads are like. What does it matter to them if the State is overthrown? They will be cardinals, and take refuge in Rome. But nobles like us, in our châteaux, will be massacred by the peasants.'

The secret memorandum that the marquis drafted on the basis of Julien's twenty-six pages of minutes was not ready until a quarter to five.

'I'm absolutely dead beat,' said the marquis, 'and it shows clearly in this memorandum, which lacks clarity towards the end; I'm more dissatisfied with it than with anything I've ever done in my whole life. Let's think now, dear fellow,' he added, 'go and get a few hours' rest; and for fear of your being abducted, I'm going to lock you into your room myself.'

The next day the marquis took Julien to a remote château some distance from Paris. They were received by odd-looking hosts, whom Julien took to be priests. He was handed a passport which bore an assumed name, but did finally indicate the purpose of the journey which he had always pretended to be ignorant of. He took his seat in a barouche on his own.

The marquis had no worries about Julien's memory: he had recited the secret memorandum to him several times; but he was in great fear lest Julien be waylaid.

'Make sure you always keep up the appearance of a dandy travelling to while away the time,' he said to him warmly as he was leaving the drawing-room. 'There may have been several false brethren at our gathering yesterday.'

The journey was swift and very dreary. No sooner was Julien out of the marquis's sight than he forgot both the secret memorandum and his mission, and all his thoughts turned to Mathilde's disdain.

At a village several leagues beyond Metz, the postmaster came to him to say there were no horses. It was ten o'clock at night; most put out, Julien ordered some supper. He walked up and down in front of the door, and imperceptibly, without letting anyone see what he was doing, he slipped into the stable courtyard. He saw no horses there.

All the same, that man had a strange look, Julien said to himself; his vulgar eye was examining me.

He was beginning, as you see, not to believe every word of what was said to him. He was thinking of slipping away after supper; and with a view to learning at any rate something about the region, he left his room to go and warm himself in front of the kitchen fire. Just imagine his delight at finding Signor Geronimo, the famous singer, sitting there.

Ensconced in an armchair that he had had brought to the fireside for him, the Neapolitan was groaning out loud and talking more himself than the twenty German peasants put together who were crowding round him in open-mouthed astonishment.

'These people will be the ruin of me,' he called out to Julien, 'I've promised to sing in Mainz* tomorrow. Seven sovereign princes have flocked to listen to me. But let's go and take the air,' he added with a meaningful look.

When he was a hundred yards off down the road, and out of range of being overheard:

'Do you know what's going on?' he asked Julien; 'this postmaster is a rogue. While I was out walking, I gave twenty sous to a little urchin who told me everything. There are more than twelve horses in a stable at the far end of the village. They want to delay some courier or other.'

'Really?' said Julien innocently.

It wasn't everything to have discovered the fraud: they still had to leave; but this result Geronimo and his friend failed to achieve. 'Let's wait until tomorrow,' the singer said at last, 'they're suspicious of us. Perhaps one of us is the person they've got it in for. Tomorrow morning we order a good breakfast; while they prepare it we go for a walk, we slip away, we hire horses and get to the next post.'

'What about your luggage?' said Julien, who was thinking that perhaps Geronimo himself might have been sent to waylay him. There was nothing for it but to have supper and go to bed. Julien was still in his first deep sleep when he was woken with a start by the voices of two people talking quite uninhibitedly in his room.

He recognized the postmaster, wielding a dark lantern. The light was directed towards the trunk of the barouche, which Julien had had brought up to his room. Next to the postmaster was a man rummaging unperturbed in the open trunk. All Julien could make out were the sleeves of his coat, which were black and tight-fitting.

It's a cassock, he said to himself, and he quietly seized hold of two small pistols he had put under his pillow.

'Don't be afraid that he'll wake up, Father,' the postmaster was saying. 'The wine they were served was some of the one you yourself prepared.'

'I can't find any sign of papers,' replied the priest. 'Plenty of linen, essences, creams and other frivolities; he's a young man of the world, in pursuit of his pleasures. The envoy is more likely to be the other one, who puts on an Italian accent.'

The men moved closer to Julien to search the pockets of his travelling suit. He was very tempted to kill them as thieves. Nothing could have been less risky as far as the consequences went. He really wanted to. I *would* be a fool, he told himself, I'd compromise my mission. When his suit had been searched; 'He's no diplomat,' said the priest; he moved away, luckily for him.

If he touches me in my bed, he'd better watch out! Julien said to himself; he may very well come and stab me, and I won't put up with *that*.

The priest looked round. Julien had his eyes half open; imagine his astonishment: it was Father Castanède! Indeed, although the two people were trying to keep their voices down, he had fancied right from the start that he recognized one of the voices. Julien was seized with an overwhelming desire to purge the earth of one of its most dastardly scoundrels...

But what about my mission! he said to himself.

The priest and his acolyte went out. A quarter of an hour later, Julien pretended to wake up. He called for someone and woke the whole house.

'I've been poisoned!' he shouted, 'I'm in horrible agony!'

He wanted a pretext to go to Geronimo's assistance. He found him half-asphyxiated by the laudanum that was in the wine.

Fearing some funny business of this sort, at supper Julien had drunk some chocolate brought from Paris. He did not succeed in waking Geronimo sufficiently to persuade him to leave.

'If you gave me the whole kingdom of Naples', said the singer, 'I still wouldn't give up the bliss of sleeping right now.'

'But what about the seven sovereign princes!'

'Let them wait.'

Julien set off alone and arrived without further incident at the important dignitary's residence. He wasted a whole morning trying in vain to obtain an audience. By a stroke of good fortune, about four o'clock, the duke decided to take the air. Julien saw him going out on foot, and did not hesitate to go up to him to ask for alms. When he was a couple of paces from the important dignitary, he drew out the Marquis de La Mole's watch and displayed it ostentatiously. '*Follow me at a distance*', he was told, without so much as a glance.

A quarter of a league further on, the duke plunged into a little Café-hauss.*. It was in one of the rooms of this low-class inn that Julien had the honour of reciting his four pages to the duke. When he had finished: '*Begin again and go more slowly*,' he was told.

The prince took notes. '*Make your way on foot to the next post. Abandon your belongings and your barouche here. Get to Strasburg as best you can, and on the twenty-second of this month* (it was then the tenth) *be here at half past twelve noon in this same Café-hauss. Don't leave it now until half an hour is up. Silence!*'

These were the only words Julien heard. They were enough to imbue him with the utmost admiration. That's the way, he thought, to conduct business; what ever would this great statesman think if he heard the impassioned talkers of three days ago?

Julien spent two days getting to Strasburg: it did not seem to him that he had any business there. He made a great detour. If that devil of a Father Castanède recognized me, he's not a man to lose track of me that easily... And what a pleasure for him to make a fool of me and scupper my mission!

Father Castanède, chief of the Congregation's police* for the whole of the northern border, had fortunately not recognized him. And despite their zeal, the Jesuits in Strasburg did not think to put Julien under observation: with his cross fastened to his blue greatcoat, he had the air of a young soldier very taken with his personal appearance.

CHAPTER 24

Strasburg

Fascination! You have all the energy of love, all
its power to endure unhappiness. Only its
enchanting pleasures, its sweet delights are
outside your sphere. I could not say as I watched
her sleep: she is all mine, with her angelic beauty
and her sweet failings! Here she is delivered into
my power, just as heaven created her in its mercy
to delight a man's heart.

SCHILLER, *Ode*

FORCED to spend a week in Strasburg, Julien tried to keep
himself entertained by thoughts of military glory and devotion
to his country. Was he in love, then? he really didn't know,
but in his tortured mind he did find Mathilde absolute mistress
of his happiness and of his imagination. He needed all the
energy in his character to keep himself from sinking into
despair. Thinking about anything that didn't have some connection with Mlle de La Mole was beyond his powers. Ambition
or the simple triumphs of vanity used to take his mind off the
feelings inspired in him formerly by Mme de Rênal. Mathilde
had absorbed everything; he found her everywhere in the
future.

On all sides, in this future, Julien saw lack of success. This
individual we saw so full of presumption, so arrogant in
Verrières, had lapsed into ridiculous extremes of self-
disparagement.

Three days previously he would have taken pleasure in
killing Father Castanède, and here in Strasburg, if a child had
picked a quarrel with him, he would have decided the child
was in the right. Thinking back over the adversaries and
enemies he had encountered in his life, he felt every time that
he, Julien, had been in the wrong.

The reason was that now he had an implacable enemy in the
shape of that powerful imagination of his, which had previ-

ously been wholly engaged in depicting such brilliant success for him in the future.

The unmitigated solitude of a traveller's life increased the hold of his black imagination. What a treasure a friend would have been! But, Julien said to himself, is there any heart that beats for me? And even if I had a friend, doesn't honour bid me keep eternal silence?

He was out riding, miserably, in the countryside round Kehl; this little town on the banks of the Rhine has been immortalized by Desaix and Gouvion Saint-Cyr*. A German peasant was showing him the little streams, the paths and the islands in the Rhine made famous by the courage of those great generals. Using his left hand to guide the horse, Julien held open with his right hand the superb map which adorns the *Memoirs* of Marshal Saint-Cyr. A cheerful exclamation made him look up.

It was Prince Korasov, his friend from London who some months earlier had instructed him in the first principles of high foppery. Faithful to this great art, Korasov, who had arrived in Strasburg the day before, and in Kehl an hour ago, and who had never in his life read a word on the siege of 1796, began to explain everything to Julien. The German peasant stared at him astonished, for he knew enough French to make out the gross howlers perpetrated by the prince. Julien was a thousand miles away from what the peasant was thinking, he was looking in astonishment at this handsome young man, and admiring the graceful way he rode his horse.

Oh happy man! he said to himself. How well his breeches suit him; and what an elegant haircut! Alas! if I had been like that, perhaps when she'd loved me for three days she wouldn't have taken an aversion to me.

When the prince had finished his siege of Kehl: 'Your expression is like a Trappist's,' he said to Julien, 'you're exceeding the guidelines on gravity I explained to you in London. Looking miserable is never in good taste; looking bored is the done thing. If you're miserable, there must be something you're wanting, something that hasn't turned out right.

'*It's showing yourself to be inferior.* If you're bored, on the contrary, it's what tried in vain to please you that is inferior. So you must understand, old fellow, how serious it is to confuse the two.'

Julien flung a crown to the peasant who was listening to them open-mouthed.

'Good,' said the prince, 'there's graciousness, and a noble disdain! Very good!' And he set his horse at a gallop. Julien followed him, filled with dumb admiration.

Ah! if I'd been like that, she wouldn't have preferred Croisenois to me! The more his reason was shocked at the prince's ridiculous ways, the more he despised himself for not admiring them, and considered himself unfortunate in not having them. Self-loathing cannot be carried to greater extremes.

Finding him decidedly miserable, the prince said, when they got back to Strasburg: 'Come now! old fellow, have you lost all your money, or might you be in love with some little actress?'

Russians copy French customs, but always fifty years behind the times. They've now reached the century of Louis XV.

This joking about love brought tears to Julien's eyes: Why shouldn't I consult an amiable man like this? he asked himself all of a sudden.

'Well yes, actually, old fellow,' he said to the prince, 'here I am in Strasburg, as you see, very much in love, and even jilted. A delightful woman who lives in a nearby town called it off after three days of passion, and the reversal is killing me.'

He gave the prince a full account of Mathilde's behaviour and character, disguising the identities of the people involved.

'Don't go on to the end,' said Korasov: 'to give you confidence in your doctor, I shall finish off the confession. This young woman's husband is exceedingly wealthy, or rather *she* belongs to the highest-ranking nobility in the region. She must have something to be so proud about.'

Julien nodded, he was in no state to say any more.

'Very good,' said the prince, 'here are three rather bitter pills for you to swallow forthwith:

'1. Call daily on Madame..., what's her name?'

'Mme de Dubois.'

'What a name!' said the prince, bursting out laughing; 'I'm

so sorry, to you it's sublime. You must see Mme de Dubois every day; whatever you do, don't look cold and ill-humoured in her presence; remember the great principle of your century: be the opposite of what people expect. Behave exactly as you did a week before being honoured with her favours.'

'Ah! I didn't have anything to worry about then,' Julien exclaimed in despair, 'I thought I was taking pity on her...'

'Moths get burnt on candles,' the prince went on, 'it's a saying as old as the hills.

'1. You will see her every day;

'2. You will pay court to a woman of her acquaintance, but without putting on any outward signs of passion, d'you understand? I won't conceal from you that your role is a difficult one; you're acting a part, and if there's any suspicion of this, all is lost for you.'

'She's so intelligent, and I'm not! All is lost for me,' said Julien sadly.

'No, it's just that you're more in love than I thought. Mme de Dubois is deeply wrapped up in herself, like all women to whom heaven has given either too much nobility or too much money. She looks at herself instead of looking at you, and so she doesn't know you. During the two or three fits of passion for you that she induced in herself, by a great effort of the imagination, she was seeing in you the hero she had dreamed of, not what you really are...

'But the devil take it! this is elementary stuff, my dear Sorel, are you a total schoolboy...?

''Pon my word! let's go into this shop; look at that charming black collar: anyone would think it was designed by John Anderson of Burlington Street; do me the pleasure of taking it, and throwing out for good that sordid bit of black rope you have round your neck.

'Well now,' the prince went on as they stepped out of the finest haberdasher's shop in Strasburg, 'what sort of company does Mme de Dubois keep? For Christ's sake! What a name! Don't get angry, my dear Sorel, I can't help it... Who shall you make advances to?'

'A prude to end all prudes, the daughter of an immensely rich hosier. She has the loveliest eyes in the world, and I find them infinitely charming; she is surely one of the highest-ranking women in the region; but in the midst of all her grandeur, she blushes so much that she quite goes to pieces if anyone happens to mention business or shops. And unfortunately, her father was one of the best-known merchants in Strasburg.'

'And so if the subject of *trade* comes up,' the prince said, laughing, 'you can be sure that your fair lady is thinking of herself and not of you. This weak spot of hers is sheer heaven, and exceedingly useful; it will prevent you from having the slightest moment of folly in the presence of her lovely eyes. Success is assured.'

Julien was thinking of Mme de Fervaques, the marshal's widow, who was a frequent visitor at the Hôtel de La Mole. She was a beautiful foreigner who had married the marshal a year before he died. Her whole life seemed entirely geared towards getting people to forget that her father was in *trade*; and, to have something going for her in Paris, she had put herself at the head of the cohorts of virtue.

Julien had a sincere admiration for the prince; he would have given anything to have his foibles! The conversation between the two friends was endless; Korasov was delighted: never had a Frenchman listened to him for so long. So I've at last reached the point, said the prince to himself delightedly, where I'm listened to when I teach my masters a lesson!

'We're quite clear about this, aren't we?' he repeated to Julien for the tenth time, 'not the slightest hint of passion when you talk to the young beauty—the daughter of the Strasburg hosier—in Mme de Dubois's presence. On the other hand, there must be burning passion when you write. Reading a well-written love letter is the ultimate pleasure for a prude; it's a moment when she can be off her guard. She's not acting a part, she can dare to listen to her heart; so two letters a day.'

'Never, never!' said Julien despondently; 'I'd rather be pounded in a mortar than compose three fine phrases; I'm a corpse, dear fellow, don't hope for anything more from me. Let me die by the roadside.'

'Who's talking about composing fine phrases? In my writing-case I have six volumes of hand-written love letters. There are some for every possible kind of feminine character; I've got some for high virtue. Didn't Kalisky go wooing the prettiest Quaker lady in all England on Richmond Hill—you know, three leagues outside London?'

Julien was less miserable when he took leave of his friend at two o'clock in the morning.

The next day the prince sent for a clerk, and two days later Julien received fifty-three carefully numbered love letters, designed for the most sublime and dreary virtue.

'There aren't fifty-four of them', said the prince, 'because Kalisky got shown the door; but what does it matter to you to be harshly treated by the hosier's daughter, since all you want is to produce an effect on Mme de Dubois's heart?'

They went riding every day: the prince was mad about Julien. Not knowing what proof to give him of his sudden friendship, he eventually offered him the hand of one of his cousins, a rich heiress in Moscow; 'and once you're married,' he added, 'my influence and the cross you're wearing will make you a colonel in two years' time.'

'But this cross wasn't awarded by Napoleon, quite the opposite.'

'Who cares?' said the prince, 'He invented it, didn't he? It's still far and away the most distinguished in Europe.'

Julien was on the verge of accepting; but his duty summoned him back to the important dignitary; when he took leave of Korasov, he promised to write. He was given the answer to the secret memorandum he had brought, and he sped off in the direction of Paris; but no sooner had he been on his own for two days on end than the idea of leaving France and Mathilde struck him as torture worse than death. I won't marry the millions that Korasov is offering me, but I will take his advice.

After all, the art of seduction is his business; he's been thinking of nothing else for over fifteen years, for he's now thirty. No one could say he lacks wits; he's subtle and cunning; enthusiasm and poetry are out of the question in a character like his; he acts for other people; all the more reason for him to be right.

It's essential, I shall pay court to Mme de Fervaques.

She may well bore me a little, but I'll gaze at those lovely eyes of hers, which are so like the ones which loved me most in the whole world.

She's a foreigner; it'll be a new character to observe.

I'm mad, I'm going under, I must follow a friend's advice and not trust in myself.

CHAPTER 25

The Ministry of Virtue

But if I sample this pleasure with so much
prudence and circumspection, it won't be a
pleasure for me any more.

LOPE DE VEGA*

As soon as he was back in Paris, and had stepped out of M. de
La Mole's study, leaving him most put out by the despatches
in front of him, our hero hurried off to see Count Altamira.
To add to the distinction of being sentenced to death, this
handsome foreigner could also boast a high degree of gravity
and the good fortune of being religious; these two qualities,
and most importantly, the count's high birth, were entirely to
the liking of Mme de Fervaques, who saw a good deal of him.

Julien confessed gravely to him that he was deeply in love
with her.

'There you have the purest and the highest virtue,' Altamira
replied, 'just a trifle jesuitical and bombastic. There are days
when I understand each individual word she uses, but I don't
understand the whole sentence. She often makes me feel I
don't understand French as well as I'm said to. This is an
acquaintance which will put your name on people's lips; it will
make you count in society. But let's go and see Bustos,' said
Count Altamira, who was a systematic thinker, 'he has courted
the marshal's widow.'

Don Diego Bustos* wanted the matter explained to him at
length, and listened without a word, like a barrister in
chambers. He had the chubby face of a monk, with a
black moustache, and an air of incomparable gravity; apart
from that, he was every inch the good *carbonaro*.

'I understand,' he said to Julien at last. 'Has the Maréchale
de Fervaques had any lovers or hasn't she? Do you therefore
have any hope of success? That's the question. This is to admit
that for my part, I got nowhere. Now that it no longer rankles,
I reason things out like this: she's often ill-tempered, and as I
shall explain in a minute, she's really quite vindictive.

'I don't detect in her the bilious temperament of genius, which puts something like a veneer of passion over every action. On the contrary, it's the phlegmatic and calm manner characteristic of the Dutch which gives her such rare beauty and fresh colouring.'

Julien was growing impatient with the Spaniard's long-windedness and imperturbable phlegm; from time to time, in spite of himself, he let slip one or two monosyllables.

'Do you mind hearing me out?' Don Diego Bustos said to him gravely.

'Do forgive my *furia francese*,* I'm all ears,' said Julien.

'As I was saying, the maréchale is very prone to hatred; she is merciless in her pursuit of people she has never seen, lawyers, wretched men of letters who have composed songs like Collé,* you know?

> 'Tis my caprice
> To love Bernice, etc.*

And Julien had to listen to him reeling off the whole thing. The Spaniard was very glad of a chance to sing in French.

This divine song was never listened to with more impatience. When it was over: 'The marshal's widow', said Don Diego Bustos, 'had the author of this song sacked:

> 'One day the lover at the inn...'

Julien shuddered lest he should decide to sing it, but he was content with analysing it. It genuinely was sacrilegious and quite improper.

'When Mme de Fervaques took against this song,'* said Don Diego, 'I pointed out to her that a woman of her rank shouldn't read all the silly rubbish that gets published. Whatever the advances in piety and gravity, there will always be a good collection of drinking songs in France. When Mme de Fervaques had had the author, a poor devil on half pay, sacked from a position worth eighteen hundred francs, "Watch out," I said to her, "you've attacked this versemonger with your weapons; he may answer back with his verse: he'll write a song about virtue. The gilded salons will be on your side; people who enjoy a laugh will repeat his epigrams." Do you know, sir, what the maréchale replied to me? "In the cause of the Lord the whole of Paris would see me march to martyrdom; it would be a new spectacle in France. The common people would learn to respect quality. It would be the most glorious day in my life." Never had her eyes looked more glorious.'

'Aren't they magnificent!' Julien exclaimed.

'I see you're in love... So', Don Diego Bustos went on gravely, 'she doesn't have the bilious constitution which drives people to revenge. If she nevertheless enjoys causing harm, it's because she's unhappy; I suspect some *inner unhappiness* there. Might she not be a prude grown weary of her profession?

The Spaniard looked at him in silence for a full minute.

'That's the real question,' he added gravely, 'and that's where you can draw some hope. I thought a lot about it throughout the two years when I made myself her most humble servant. Your whole future—you, sir, who are in love—hangs on this great uncertainty: Is she a prude grown weary of her profession, and spiteful because she's unhappy?'

'Or alternatively,' said Altamira, emerging at last from his deep silence, 'is it something I've suggested to you over and over again? Quite simply French vanity; it's the memory of her father, the famous draper, which is causing such misery to this naturally morose and arid character. I suppose there's only one way for her to be happy; to live in Toledo, and be tormented by a confessor who conjures up daily visions of hell gaping open.'

As Julien was leaving: 'Altamira tells me you're one of us,' said Don Diego, more grave than ever. 'One day you'll help us win back our freedom, so I'm ready to help you with this little distraction. You need to know Mme de Fervaques's style; here are four letters in her hand.'

'I shall copy them out,' said Julien, 'and bring them back to you.'

'And no one shall ever learn through you a single word of what we have said?'

'Never, upon my honour!' Julien exclaimed.

'Then may God help you!' the Spaniard added; and he accompanied Altamira and Julien in silence right out on to the stairs.

This scene cheered our hero up a bit; he was on the verge of smiling. And here is the pious Altamira, he said to himself, helping me in an adulterous venture.

Throughout the whole of the grave conversation with Don Diego Bustos, Julien had been attentive to the hours struck by the clock on the Hôtel d'Aligre.*

The hour for dinner was drawing near, he was therefore going to see Mathilde again! He went home and dressed with great care.

First piece of stupidity, he said to himself as he went downstairs; I must follow the prince's prescription to the letter.

He went back up to his room and chose the plainest travelling outfit imaginable.

Now, he thought, there's the matter of how I look at her. It was only five thirty, and dinner was at six. He decided to go down to the drawing-room, which he found deserted. The sight of the blue sofa moved him to tears; soon his cheeks were burning hot. I must wear down this foolish hypersensitivity of mine, he told himself angrily; it might betray me. He picked up a newspaper to appear to be doing something, and went out three or four times from the drawing-room into the garden.

It was only in great fear and trembling, and when he was well hidden behind a large oak tree, that he dared to look up at Mlle de La Mole's window. It was hermetically shut; he almost collapsed, and stood leaning against the oak for some considerable time; then he walked over with tottering steps to look at the gardener's ladder again.

The link in the chain, which he had once forced open in circumstances, alas! so different from now, had not been repaired. Carried away by a mad impulse, Julien pressed it to his lips.

Having spent a long time wandering between the drawing-room and the garden, Julien found he was terribly tired; this was a first victory which he was keenly aware of. The look in my eyes will be listless and won't betray me! Gradually the dinner guests foregathered in the drawing-room; the door did not open once without causing dire turmoil in Julien's heart.

The company sat down to table. At last Mlle de La Mole

appeared, ever faithful to her habit of keeping people waiting. She blushed deeply on seeing Julien; no one had told her of his arrival. In accordance with Prince Korasov's advice, Julien looked at her hands: they were trembling. Agitated beyond measure as he was by this discovery, he was fortunate enough not to appear other than tired.

M. de La Mole praised him openly. The marquise spoke to him immediately afterwards, and complimented him on his look of fatigue. Julien kept saying to himself: I mustn't look at Mlle de La Mole too much, but then nor must I avoid looking at her either. I must appear to be the way I really was a week before my misfortune... He had occasion to be satisfied with his success, and he stayed on in the drawing-room. For the first time he was attentive towards his hostess, and made every effort to draw out the men in her company, and to keep up a lively conversation.

His civility was rewarded: at about eight o'clock the Maréchale de Fervaques was announced. Julien slipped away and soon reappeared, dressed with the greatest care. Mme de La Mole was infinitely appreciative of this mark of respect, and made a point of showing him her satisfaction by telling Mme de Fervaques about his journey. Julien seated himself next to the maréchale in such a way as to keep his eyes hidden from Mathilde. From this position, following all the rules of the art, he made Mme de Fervaques the target of his most dumbfounded admiration. A tirade on this sentiment formed the opening of the first of the fifty-three letters presented to him by Prince Korasov.

The maréchale announced that she was going to the Opera-Buffa.* Julien made his way there in haste; he ran into the Chevalier de Beauvoisis, who took him off to a box reserved for gentlemen of the royal household, which just happened to be next to Mme de Fervaques's box. Julien kept on gazing at her. It's vital, he said to himself on returning home, that I keep a siege diary; otherwise I might forget my attacking moves. He forced himself to write two or three pages on this boring subject, and in so doing succeeded—most miraculously!—in almost not thinking about Mlle de La Mole.

Mathilde had almost forgotten him while he was off on his

journey. After all, he's only a common sort of person, she thought; his name will always remind me of the greatest lapse in my life. I must revert in good faith to vulgar notions of chaste behaviour and honour; a woman has everything to lose by forgetting them. She appeared willing to agree at last to the conclusion of the settlement with the Marquis de Croisenois, which had been drawn up ready for so long. He was beside himself with joy; he would have been most astonished to be told that resignation lay at the bottom of Mathilde's disposition towards him, which made him so proud.

All Mlle de La Mole's ideas changed on seeing Julien. In reality, *he's* my husband, she told herself; if I revert in good faith to notions of chaste behaviour, then *he's* the one I must marry.

She was expecting unwelcome entreaties and wretched looks from Julien; she prepared her responses: for surely when they got up from dinner, he would try to have a few words with her. Quite the contrary, he stayed put in the drawing-room, his eyes didn't even turn towards the garden, God alone knows at what cost! It's better to have it out with him right away, thought Mlle de La Mole; she went into the garden alone, Julien did not appear. Mathilde came over and strolled by the French windows of the drawing-room; she saw him utterly taken up with describing to Mme de Fervaques the old ruined castles that crown the hillsides along the Rhine and give them such character. He was beginning to make quite a good showing at the sentimental and picturesque turn of phrase that is called *wit* in certain salons.

Prince Korasov would have been thoroughly proud if he had happened to be in Paris: that evening went exactly as he had predicted.

He would have approved of Julien's conduct on the following days.

An intrigue among the members of the clandestine government* was about to make a number of Blue Sashes available; Mme de Fervaques insisted on her great-uncle's becoming a knight of the order. M. de La Mole laid the same claim on behalf of his father-in-law; they united their efforts, and the maréchale came to the Hôtel de La Mole almost every day. It was from her that Julien learned that the marquis was about to become a minister: he was offering the *Camarilla** a most ingenious plan for abolishing the Charter, without any upheaval, in the space of three years.

Julien could expect to be made a bishop if M. de La Mole got into the Cabinet; but to his eyes all these great concerns had been somehow shrouded in a veil. His imagination only glimpsed them dimly now, in the far distance so to speak. The dreadful misfortune which was making him obsessional caused him to see all life's concerns wrapped up in his relationship with Mlle de La Mole. He reckoned that after five or six years of careful effort, he would manage to make her love him again.

His calm and rational mind had sunk, as you observe, into a state of total derangement. Of the many qualities that had distinguished him formerly, all that remained was a degree of persistence. Outwardly faithful to the plan of conduct laid down by Prince Korasov, he would seat himself every evening quite close to Mme de Fervaques's chair, but it was quite beyond him to find anything to say to her.

The effort he was putting in to appear cured in Mathilde's eyes swallowed up all his emotional energy, and he sat beside the marshal's widow like a creature barely alive; even his eyes, as happens in extreme physical suffering, had lost all their fire.

As Mme de La Mole's attitude was always a mere replica of the opinions of a husband who might make her a duchess, for some days now she had been praising Julien's qualities to the skies.

CHAPTER 26

Propriety in love

> There also was of course in Adeline
> That calm patrician polish in the address,
> Which ne'er can pass the equinoctial line
> Of any thing which Nature would express:
> Just as a Mandarin finds nothing fine,
> At least his manner suffers not to guess
> That any thing he views can greatly please.
> *Don Juan*, C. XIII, st. 84

THERE'S a streak of madness in the attitude of this entire family, thought the maréchale; they're infatuated with this young priest of theirs, whose only qualification is listening— with rather lovely eyes, it's true.

Julien for his part took Mme de Fervaques's ways as an almost perfect example of that *patrician calm* which radiates punctilious civility and, even more so, declares the impossibility of any powerful emotion. Any unpredictable reactions, any failure of self control, would have scandalized Mme de Fervaques almost as much as a lack of majesty towards her inferiors. The slightest outward sign of emotion would have struck her as some kind of *moral inebriation* to be ashamed of, and most prejudicial to the duties that a person of high rank owes to herself. Her great pleasure was talking about the king's latest hunt, her favourite book the *Memoirs* of the Duc de Saint-Simon,* especially the part concerned with genealogy.

Julien knew which part of the room, given the arrangement of the lights, was flattering to Mme de Fervaques's type of beauty. He made sure he was there before her, but took great care to turn his chair in such a way as not to see Mathilde. Astonished at the constancy with which he was hiding from her, one day she left the blue sofa and brought her needlework over to a little table next to the maréchale's chair. Julien got a fairly close view of her from underneath Mme de Fervaques's hat. Those eyes, which controlled his destiny, alarmed him at first, then jolted him out of his habitual apathy; he talked, and very well too.

He addressed his words to the maréchale, but his sole aim was to produce an effect on Mathilde. He grew so animated that Mme de Fervaques found she no longer understood what he was saying.

That was a preliminary point in his favour. If it had occurred to Julien to back it up with a few sentences of German mysticism, high religiosity and Jesuitry, the maréchale would have classed him on the spot as one of the superior men whose calling it is to regenerate our century.

Since he's sufficiently ill-mannered, Mlle de La Mole said to herself, to talk for as long as this, and with so much ardour, to Mme de Fervaques, I shan't listen to him any more. For the whole of the rest of that evening she kept her word, although with difficulty.

At midnight when Mathilde took her mother's candlestick to accompany her up to her room, Mme de La Mole paused on the stairs to produce a full-blown eulogy of Julien. This put the finishing touches to Mathilde's ill-temper; she was unable to fall asleep. One thought calmed her down: Someone I despise can still be a man of great worth in the maréchale's eyes.

As for Julien, he had done something, he was less miserable; his eyes alighted by chance on the Russian-leather case in which Prince Korasov had enclosed his present of fifty-three love letters. Julien saw in a note at the bottom of the first letter: *Number One is to be sent a week after the first meeting*.

I've fallen behind! Julien exclaimed, for I've been seeing Mme de Fervaques for some time now. He settled down at once to copying out this first love letter; it was a homily full of pronouncements on virtue, and deadly dull; Julien was fortunate enough to fall asleep at the second page.

Some hours later, bright sunlight surprised him slumped over the table. One of the hardest moments in his life was when, each morning on waking up, he *learned of* his wretchedness. That day, he was almost laughing as he finished copying out his letter. Is it possible, he said to himself, that there ever existed a young man who writes like this! He counted several sentences nine lines long. At the end of the original, he saw a note in pencil:

These letters are to be delivered personally: on horseback, with black tie and blue greatcoat. Letter to be handed to the porter with a contrite air and look of deep melancholy. If any chambermaid is sighted, eyes to be furtively wiped. Speak to the chambermaid.

All this was faithfully executed.

What I'm doing takes some nerve, Julien thought as he left the Hôtel de Fervaques, but so much the worse for Korasov. Daring to write to such a notorious pillar of virtue! I shall be treated by her with the utmost disdain, and nothing will amuse me more. It's ultimately the only comedy I can appreciate. Yes, heaping ridicule on that most odious creature I call *myself* will amuse me. If I followed my own lights, I'd commit some crime or other to distract myself.

For the past month, the most wonderful moment in Julien's life had been when he put his horse back in the stable. Korasov had expressly forbidden him to glance, on any pretext whatsoever, at the mistress who had abandoned him. But the sound she knew so well of that horse's hoofs, Julien's way of cracking his whip at the stable door to summon a groom, sometimes drew Mathilde over to her window, behind the curtain. The lace was so fine that Julien could see through. By looking up in a certain way from under the brim of his hat, he could see Mathilde's figure without seeing her eyes. Consequently, he said to himself, she can't see mine, and that doesn't count as looking at her.

That evening, Mme de Fervaques behaved towards him exactly as if she had not received the philosophical, mystical and religious disquisition which he had handed to her porter that morning with such melancholy. On the previous day, chance had shown Julien how to be eloquent; he positioned himself in such a way as to see Mathilde's eyes. She, for her part, left the blue sofa the moment Mme de Fervaques arrived: she was deserting her habitual company. M. de Croisenois showed consternation at this latest whim; his obvious suffering took the keen edge off Julien's misery.

This unexpected turn in his life made him talk like an angel;

and as self-regard worms its way even into hearts that are temples of the most august virtue: Mme de La Mole is right, the maréchale said to herself as she climbed into her carriage again, there is something distinguished about this young priest. It must be that, to start with, my presence intimidated him. In point of fact, everything one comes across in this house is rather frivolous; such virtue as I see here has had the helping hand of old age, and badly needed the frosts of passing years. This young man must have the discernment to have seen the difference; he writes well; but I very much fear that the entreaty he makes in his letter for me to enlighten him with my advice will turn out to be none other than a sentiment that is unaware of its own nature.

Nevertheless, how many conversations have begun like this! What makes me augur well of this one is the difference between his style and that of the young men whose letters I have had the opportunity of reading. One can't help seeing spirituality, deep seriousness and real conviction in the prose of this young Levite; he must have the sweet virtue of Massillon.*

CHAPTER 27

The best positions in the Church

Services! talents! qualities! bah! Join a coterie.

TELEMACHUS*

THUS the thought of a bishopric was associated for the first time with Julien in the mind of a woman who was sooner or later to be handing out the best positions in the Church of France. This trump card she held would scarcely have swayed Julien; at that moment his thoughts did not rise to anything beyond his present plight. Everything made it worse; the sight of his room, for instance, had become unbearable to him. In the evening, when he returned to it with his candle, every piece of furniture, every little embellishment seemed to acquire a voice to acquaint him sourly with some fresh detail of his misery.

That day as he came in: I've got forced labour to do, he said to himself with an eagerness he had not detected in himself for a long while; let's hope the second letter will be as tedious as the first.

It was more so. What he was copying seemed to him so absurd that he found himself transcribing it line by line without thinking of the meaning.

It's even more bombastic, he said to himself, than the official documents relating to the treaty of Munster, which my instructor in diplomacy made me copy out in London.

Only then did he remember Mme de Fervaques's letters: he had forgotten to hand back the originals to the grave Spaniard Don Diego Bustos. He looked them out; they were genuinely almost as amphigoric as the ones written by the young Russian nobleman. Vagueness was total. They said everything, yet said nothing. This is the aeolian harp of style, Julien thought. In the midst of the most lofty thoughts on nothingness, death, infinity etc., the only thing real I discern is an appalling fear of ridicule.

The solitary scene we have just summed up was repeated for

a fortnight on end. Falling asleep as he copied out a sort of commentary on the Apocalypse, going off the next day with a melancholy air to deliver a letter, putting his horse back in the stable with the hope of catching sight of Mathilde's dress, working, putting in an appearance at the Opera in the evening when Mme de Fervaques did not come to the Hôtel de La Mole, such were the monotonous events in Julien's life. It was more interesting when Mme de Fervaques called on the marquise; then he could snatch a glimpse of Mathilde's eyes under one of the wings of the widow's hat, and he waxed eloquent. His picturesque and sentimental phrases were beginning to take a turn that was at once more striking and more elegant.

He was well aware that what he was saying was absurd in Mathilde's eyes, but he wanted her to be struck by the elegance of his diction. The more what I say is false, the more I must make her admire me, Julien thought; and then, with appalling nerve, he exaggerated certain aspects of nature. He soon observed that in order not to appear vulgar in the maréchale's eyes, he had above all to avoid straightforward and rational ideas. He went on in this vein, or else cut short his amplifications, according as he read success or indifference in the eyes of the two great ladies he had to please.

All in all, his life was less dreadful than when his days were spent in idleness.

But, he said to himself one evening, here I am copying out the fifteenth of these appalling disquisitions; the first fourteen have been faithfully remitted to Mme de Fervaques's porter. I shall have the honour of filling up all the pigeon-holes in her desk. And yet she treats me exactly as if I wasn't writing to her! How will all this end? Could my constancy bore her as much as it does me? You just have to admit that this Russian friend of Korasov's who was in love with the fair Quaker lady from Richmond was a terror in his time; it simply isn't possible to be more deadly.

Like all the mediocre beings who chance to witness the manœuvres of a great general, Julien did not understand the first thing about the attack mounted by the young Russian on the heart of the fair Englishwoman. The first forty letters were designed merely to obtain forgiveness for having made so bold as to write at all. The point was to get this gentle creature, who might perhaps be bored beyond measure, into the habit of receiving letters that were perhaps a trifle less insipid than her everyday life.

One morning, Julien was handed a letter; he recognized Mme de Fervaques's crest, and broke the seal with a haste that would have seemed quite impossible to him a few days previously: it was only an invitation to dinner.

He hastened to consult Prince Korasov's instructions. Unfortunately, the young Russian had tried to be as frivolous as Dorat,* when what was required was to be straightforward and intelligible; Julien was unable to surmise what stance he should adopt at Mme de Fervaques's dinner party.

The drawing-room was of the utmost magnificence, gilded like the Gallery of Diana at the Tuileries, with oil paintings on the panelling. There were lighter patches on these pictures. Julien learned later that the subjects had struck the mistress of the house as lacking in propriety, and she had had the pictures corrected.* *What a moral century*! he thought.

In the drawing-room he noticed three of the important figures who had taken part in composing the secret memorandum. One of them, Monsignor the Bishop of ——,* Mme de Fervaques's uncle, held the list of ecclesiastical benefices, and rumour had it that he never refused his niece anything. What an enormous step forward I've taken, Julien said to himself with a melancholy smile, and how indifferent I am to it! Here I am having dinner with the famous Bishop of ——.

The dinner was mediocre and the conversation exasperating. This table is like the contents of a bad book, Julien thought. All the most important subjects of human thought are confidently tackled. But you have only to listen for three minutes to wonder which carries the day: the speaker's bombast or his appalling ignorance.

The reader has doubtless forgotten that little man of letters called Tanbeau, the academician's nephew and a future professor, whose job it seemed to be to poison the salon at the Hôtel de La Mole with his base slander.

It was through this little man that Julien had the first inkling that Mme de Fervaques, while not replying to his letters, might

well take an indulgent view of the sentiment that dictated
them. M. Tanbeau's black soul was ravaged at the thought of
Julien's successes; but since from another point of view a man
of quality cannot be in two places at once, any more than a
fool can, if Sorel becomes the mistress of the sublime maréchale, said the future professor to himself, she will find him an
advantageous situation in the Church, and I shall be rid of him
at the Hôtel de La Mole.

Father Pirard also gave Julien lengthy sermons on his
successes at the Hôtel de Fervaques. There was *sectarian
jealousy* between the austere Jansenist and the Jesuit, revivalist
and monarchist salon of the virtuous maréchale.

CHAPTER 28

Manon Lescaut

Now once he was thoroughly convinced of the
foolishness and asinine stupidity of the prior, he
usually managed fairly well by calling white black
and black white.

LICHTEMBERG*

THE Russian instructions laid down categorically that one was
never to contradict out loud the person one was writing to.
One was not, on any pretext whatsoever, to forsake a stance of
the most ecstatic admiration; the letters always worked from
this assumption.

One evening at the Opera, in Mme de Fervaques's box, Julien
was praising to the skies the ballet based on Manon Lescaut.*
His only reason for talking in this way was that he found the
work of no interest.

The maréchale said that this ballet was much inferior to the
Abbé Prévost's novel.

Goodness! thought Julien both astonished and amused, a
lady of such high virtue praising a novel! Mme de Fervaques
openly professed, two or three times a week, the most utter
scorn for writers who by means of these insipid works try to
corrupt a young generation that is, alas! only too prone to be
led astray by the senses.

'In this immoral and dangerous genre', the maréchale went
on, '*Manon Lescaut*, so I'm told, ranks high on the list. The
weaknesses and the well-deserved anguish of a most criminal
character are depicted there, so I'm told, with a truthfulness
which has some depth in it; which didn't stop your Bonaparte
from declaring on St Helena that it's a novel written for
lackeys.'

These words restored all Julien's mental energy. Someone
has tried to discredit me in the maréchale's eyes; they've told
her about my enthusiasm for Napoleon. She's sufficiently put
out at this fact to yield to the temptation of letting me know
how she feels. This discovery kept him amused all evening and

made him amusing. As he took leave of the maréchale in the foyer of the Opera: 'Remember, sir,' she said to him, 'that devotion to Bonaparte is incompatible with devotion to me; the most that is allowed is to accept him as a necessity imposed by Providence. Anyway, the man's soul was too rigid to appreciate artistic masterpieces.'

Devotion to me! Julien repeated to himself; that means nothing, or means everything. Here you have mysteries of language that are quite beyond our poor provincials. And he thought a lot about Mme de Rênal as he copied out an inordinately long letter intended for the maréchale.

'Why is it', she asked him the next day with a look of indifference that he found contrived and unconvincing, 'that you talked to me about 'London' and 'Richmond' in a letter you wrote yesterday, so it seems, on returning from the Opera?'

Julien was very embarrassed; he had done his copying line by line, without thinking about what he was writing, and had apparently forgotten to replace the words 'London' and 'Richmond' from the original with 'Paris' and 'Saint-Cloud'. He made two or three attempts at a sentence in reply, but was unable to finish any of them; he felt on the verge of breaking into helpless laughter. At length, as he fumbled for words, he hit upon this idea: 'Exalted by discussion of the most sublime, the most weighty concerns of the human soul, my own may have had a moment's distraction while writing to you.'

The impression I'm creating is such, he said to himself, that I'd do well to spare myself its irksome repercussions for the remainder of the evening. He left the Hôtel de Fervaques at the double. Later on that evening, when he looked over the original of the letter he had copied out the previous day, he soon came to the ill-fated place where the young Russian spoke of London and Richmond. Julien was most astonished to find this letter almost tender.

It was the contrast between the apparent frivolity of his conversation and the sublime, almost apocalyptic profundity of his letters that had caused him to be singled out. The length of his sentences was especially pleasing to the maréchale; *this* isn't the jerky style made fashionable by Voltaire, that immoral man! Although our hero did everything in the world to banish any kind of common sense from his conversation, it still had an antimonarchist and ungodly flavour which did not escape Mme de Fervaques. Surrounded by eminently moral figures, who frequently, however, did not have so much as a single idea per evening, this lady was deeply struck by anything resembling novelty; but at the same time she thought it incumbent upon her to take offence. She called this failing *bearing the mark of worldly frivolity*...

But salons like this are only worth a visit when one has something to solicit. The full boredom of the uneventful life that Julien was leading is no doubt shared by the reader. These are the lowlands of our journey.

During all the time taken up in Julien's life by the Fervaques episode, Mlle de la Mole found it necessary to take herself firmly in hand in order not to think about him. She was in the throes of violent inner conflicts; sometimes she flattered herself that she despised this most dreary young man; but in spite of herself his conversation enthralled her. What astonished her above all was his perfect falseness; he didn't utter a single word to the maréchale that wasn't a lie, or at least an appalling travesty of his way of thinking, which Mathilde was so perfectly familiar with on virtually every topic. This Machiavellian streak impressed her. What profundity! she said to herself; what a contrast with the bombastic idiots or the common rogues like M. Tanbeau who talk in this style!

Nevertheless, some days were quite dreadful for Julien. It was in fulfilment of the most painful of duties that he made his daily appearance in the maréchale's salon. His efforts to play a part succeeded in draining him of all emotional strength. Often, at night, as he crossed the vast courtyard of the Hôtel de Fervaques, it was only through sheer character and reasoning power that he just managed to keep himself from sinking into despair.

I overcame despair in the seminary, he told himself: and yet what a dreadful prospect I had in front of me at the time! I either succeeded or failed in making my fortune, but in either case I saw myself condemned to spend the whole of my life in the intimate company of the most despicable and revolting creatures on earth. The following spring, a mere eleven months later, I was perhaps the happiest young man in my age-group.

But as often as not all this fine reasoning was ineffectual against the horrors of reality. Every day he saw Mathilde at lunch and dinner. From the numerous letters dictated to him by M. de La Mole, he knew she was on the point of marrying M. de Croisenois. This amiable young man was already making an appearance twice a day at the Hôtel de La Mole: the jealous eye of a jilted lover did not miss a single one of his movements.

When he thought he had noticed Mlle de La Mole treating her suitor well, Julien could not help looking lovingly at his pistols when he returned to his room.

Ah! how much wiser I would be, he said to himself, to remove my name from my linen and go off to some solitary forest twenty leagues from Paris and end this execrable life! As a stranger in the region, my death would stay hidden for a fortnight, and who would spare a thought for me after a fortnight!

This line of reasoning was very sensible. But the next day, a glimpse of Mathilde's arm visible between the sleeve of her dress and her glove was enough to plunge our young philosopher into memories of a cruel sort, which none the less maintained his attachment to life. All right! he said to himself at that point, I'll follow this Russian policy to the bitter end. How will it all finish?

As regards the maréchale, once I've copied out these fifty-three letters, I shall certainly not write any others.

As regards Mathilde, six weeks of painful play-acting like this will either make no difference to her anger, or will win me a moment's reconciliation. God Almighty! I'd die of happiness! And he was unable to finish his train of thought.

When, after a long spell of dreaming, he managed to pick up the thread of his argument, he said to himself: So then, I'd win a day's happiness, after which she would revert to her cruel ways, founded, alas! on my meagre capacity to please her, and I'd have no resources left, I'd be ruined, destroyed for ever…

What guarantee can she offer me with a character like hers? Alas! my unworthiness is the key to everything. My manners will be wanting in elegance, my way of talking will be heavy and monotonous. God Almighty! Why am I me?

CHAPTER 29

Boredom

To sacrifice oneself to one's passion, fair enough;
but to passions one does not feel! O wretched nineteenth
century!

HAVING at first read Julien's long letters without any pleasure,
Mme de Fervaques was beginning to be preoccupied by them,
but one thing distressed her: What a shame M. Sorel isn't a
proper priest! One could admit him to some sort of intimacy;
but with that cross, and the almost bourgeois suit he wears,
one lays oneself open to cruel questions, and what is one to
reply? She did not finish her train of thought: *some malicious
woman from my circle of friends may assume and even spread
the rumour that he's a little cousin of subordinate rank, a
relative of my father's, some merchant decorated by the
National Guard.*

Up until the time she had set eyes on Julien, Mme de
Fervaques's greatest pleasure had been to write the word
maréchale beside her name. Thereafter, the unhealthy, hyper-
sensitive vanity of a social climber fought against a nascent
attraction.

It would be so easy for me, said the maréchale to herself, *to
make him a vicar-general in some diocese near Paris! But plain
M. Sorel, and what's more, petty secretary to M. de La Mole!
it's most distressing.*

For the first time, this creature *who was fearful of everything*
was moved by an interest alien to her pretensions to rank and
social superiority. Her old porter noticed that when he brought
her a letter from the handsome young man who looked so sad,
he was sure to see the maréchale lose the abstracted and
displeased look she was always careful to adopt at the appearance of any of her servants.

Being bored with a way of life that was always seeking to
make an impression on an audience, without any genuine
heartfelt enjoyment of this kind of success, had become so

intolerable to the lady since having Julien in her thoughts, that for the chambermaids not to be ill-treated for a whole day on end, it was sufficient if, in the course of the previous evening, she had spent an hour with this unusual young man. His growing influence survived some anonymous letters, very well written ones too. It was to no avail that little Tanbeau furnished Messrs de Luz, de Croisenois, and de Caylus with two or three cunning items of slander which these gentlemen took pleasure in spreading, without really taking a view on the truth of the accusations. The maréchale, whose mind was not constituted to resist these vulgar practices, confided her doubts in Mathilde, and was always consoled.

One day, having asked three times whether there were any letters, Mme de Fervaques made up her mind abruptly to reply to Julien. It was a victory for boredom. At the second letter, the maréchale was almost stopped in her tracks by the impropriety of writing such a vulgar address in her own hand: *To Monsieur Sorel, c/o Monsieur le Marquis de la Mole.*

'Will you please', she said curtly to Julien that evening, 'bring me some envelopes with your address written on them.'

Here I am set up as a manservant-cum-lover, Julien thought, and as he bowed he took pleasure in putting on a face like Arsène, the marquis's old valet de chambre.

That same evening he brought some envelopes, and the next day, very early in the morning, he received a third letter: he read five or six lines at the beginning, and two or three towards the end. It was four pages of tiny, close-written script.

Gradually, the lady adopted the sweet habit of writing almost every day. Julien answered with faithful copies of the Russian letters, and such is the advantage of a bombastic style that Mme de Fervaques was not in the least astonished at the lack of connection between the answers and her letters.

Just imagine how it would have irked her pride if little Tanbeau, who had taken it upon himself to spy on Julien's movements, had been able to inform her that all these unopened letters were flung at random into Julien's drawer.

One morning, the porter was on his way to the library with a letter to him from the maréchale; Mathilde ran into the man, saw the letter and the address on it in Julien's hand. She went into the library as the porter was coming out: the letter was still on the edge of the table; Julien, who was very busy writing, had not put it in his drawer.

'This is something I will not put up with,' Mathilde exclaimed, seizing the letter; 'you're forgetting all about me, and I'm your bride. Your conduct is appalling, sir.'

At these words, her pride, astonished at the dreadful impropriety of what she had done, choked her; she burst into tears, and soon seemed to Julien to be quite unable to breathe.

Surprised and disconcerted, Julien did not perceive clearly what this scene betokened in the way of wondrous good fortune for him. He helped Mathilde to sit down; she almost let herself go in his arms.

The first instant when he noticed this movement was one of intense joy. The second was a thought for Korasov: I may lose everything by a single word.

His arms stiffened, so painful was the effort imposed by strategy. I mustn't even allow myself to clasp to my heart this lovely, yielding body, or she'll despise and ill-treat me. What an appalling character!

And as he cursed Mathilde's character, he loved her infinitely more for it; he seemed to be holding a queen in his arms.

Julien's impassive coldness increased the pangs of pride which wounded Mlle de La Mole to the quick. She did not have anything like the necessary composure to try to guess from his eyes what his feelings were for her at that moment. She could not bring herself to look at him; she was in fear and trembling of being greeted with an expression of scorn.

Sitting motionless on the sofa in the library, with her head turned away from Julien, she was racked with the most acute anguish that pride and love can inflict on a human soul. What an atrocious step she had just taken!

It was my peculiar fate, wretched woman that I am! to see my most improper advances rebuffed! And rebuffed by whom? added her grief-crazed pride. Rebuffed by a servant of my father's.

'I won't put up with this,' she said out loud.

And, rising to her feet in fury, she opened the drawer of

Julien's table which stood a couple of feet from her. She remained frozen to the spot in horror when she saw nine or ten unopened letters identical in every respect to the one which the porter had just brought up. In all the addresses she recognized Julien's handwriting, more or less disguised.

'So,' she exclaimed, quite beside herself, 'not only are you on close terms with her, but you despise her, what's more. You, a nobody, despising Mme la Maréchale de Fervaques!

'Ah! forgive me, darling,' she added, flinging herself down and clasping his knees, 'despise me if you want, but please love me, I can't go on living deprived of your love.' And she fell down in a dead faint.

Here she is then, this proud creature, lying at my feet! said Julien to himself.

CHAPTER 30

A box at the Opera Bouffe

As the blackest sky
Foretells the heaviest tempest
Don Juan, C. I, st. 73

IN the midst of all these great upheavals, Julien was more astonished than happy. Mathilde's insults showed him how wise the Russian strategy was. *Speak little, act little*, this is my only means of salvation.

He lifted Mathilde up, and without saying a word laid her on the sofa again. Gradually she was overcome with tears.

To hide her embarrassment, she picked up Mme de Fervaques's letters; slowly she unsealed them. She started visibly when she recognized the maréchale's writing. She turned over the pages of the letters without reading them: most of them covered six sheets.

'Answer me this, at least,' Mathilde said at length in the most pleading of tones, but without daring to look at Julien. 'You're well aware that I have my pride; it's the misfortune of my position and even of my character, I'll admit; so Mme de Fervaques has stolen your heart from me... Has she made all the sacrifices for you that this ill-fated love misled me into making?'

A dismal silence was Julien's only answer. What right has she, he was thinking, to ask me to commit an indiscretion unworthy of a gentleman?

Mathilde tried to read the letters; her tear-filled eyes made it impossible.

For a month now she had been unhappy, but so proud a character was nowhere near admitting her feelings to herself. Chance alone had brought on this outburst. For a moment jealousy and love had triumphed over pride. She was seated on the sofa, very close to him too. He saw her hair and her alabaster neck; for a second he forgot what he owed to himself;

he slipped his arm round her waist and almost clasped her to his chest.

She turned her head slowly towards him: he was astonished at the intense anguish in her eyes, to the point where their usual look was unrecognizable.

Julien felt his strength abandoning him, so mortally painful was the act of courage he demanded of himself.

Those eyes will soon express nothing but the coldest disdain, Julien said to himself, if I allow myself to give in to the happiness of loving her. And yet, in a faint voice, with phrases she scarcely had the strength to finish, she was at that very moment expressing yet again to him her heartfelt regret at actions dictated, she supposed, by too much pride.

'I have my pride too,' Julien said to her in a barely audible voice, and his features betrayed that he was on the verge of physical collapse.

Mathilde turned eagerly towards him. To hear his voice caused her happiness such as she had almost ceased to hope for. At that moment, she only remembered her haughtiness to curse it, she would have liked to find unusual, scarcely credible forms of behaviour to prove to him the extent of her adoration for him and her hatred of herself.

'It's probably on account of my pride', Julien went on, 'that you favoured me for a brief while; it's certainly on account of my courageous firmness befitting a man that you respect me at this moment. I may feel love for the maréchale...'

Mathilde shuddered; her eyes took on a strange expression. She was about to hear her sentence pronounced. This reflex did not escape Julien; he felt his courage weaken.

Ah! he said to himself as he listened to the sound of the idle words his mouth was uttering just as he would have done an extraneous noise; if only I could smother those pale cheeks with kisses, and you not feel it!

'I may feel love for the maréchale,' he went on... and his voice faltered even more; 'but I certainly don't have any decisive proof of her interest in me...'

Mathilde looked at him: he withstood this look, or at any rate he hoped his face hadn't given him away. He felt himself imbued with love right into the innermost recesses of his heart.

Never had he adored her to this extent; he was almost as crazy as Mathilde. If she had been able to muster enough composure and courage to engineer it, he would have fallen at her feet, renouncing all idle role-playing. He had enough strength to enable him to carry on talking. Ah! Korasov, he exclaimed inwardly, why aren't you here! How much I'm in need of some word to guide my conduct! Meanwhile his voice was saying:

'In the absence of any other sentiment, gratitude would be enough to make me feel affection for the maréchale; she was indulgent towards me, she consoled me when I was being scorned elsewhere... I may indeed not have unlimited faith in certain appearances which are no doubt extremely flattering, but perhaps also very short-lived.'

'Oh! Good God!' exclaimed Mathilde.

'Well, what guarantee can you give me?' Julien went on in an urgent, firm voice that seemed to dispense for a moment with the cautious cloak of diplomacy. 'What guarantee, what god can vouch for it that the position you seem inclined to reinstate me in at this moment will last more than a couple of days?'

'The extremity of my love, and of my unhappiness if you don't love me any more,' she said to him, grasping his hands and turning towards him.

The brusque movement she had just made had caused her cape to slip a little: Julien could see her lovely shoulders. Her slightly dishevelled hair conjured up a blissful memory for him...

He was about to yield. One rash word, he said to himself, and I start up another long sequence of days spent in despair. Mᵐᵉ de Rênal used to find reasons for doing what her heart dictated: this girl from high society only lets her heart be moved when she has proved to herself with sound reasons that it ought to be moved.

He saw this truth in a flash, and in a flash too he found courage once more.

He withdrew his hands that Mathilde was squeezing in hers, and with marked respect he moved a little away from her. A man's courage cannot do more than this. He busied himself next with gathering up all the letters from Mme de Fervaques that were lying scattered on the sofa, and it was with a show of extreme politeness—so cruel at that moment—that he added:

'Mademoiselle de La Mole will deign to allow me to think all this over.' He walked quickly away and left the library; she heard him shut all the doors in turn.

The monster is totally unmoved, she said to herself...

But what am I saying, monster! He's wise, prudent and good; *I'm* the one with more wrong on my side than can possibly be imagined.

This frame of mind persisted. Mathilde was almost happy that day, for she was entirely given over to love; it was as if her inner self had never been in turmoil from pride, and what pride it was!

She shuddered with horror when, that evening in the drawing-room, a footman announced Mme de Fervaques; the man's voice struck her as sinister. She could not bear the sight of the maréchale, and rapidly moved away. Julien, feeling little pride in his painfully won victory, had not trusted the look in his own eyes, and had not dined at the Hôtel de La Mole.

His love and happiness increased swiftly as the moment of battle receded; he had already reached the point of blaming himself. How could I have resisted her, he said to himself; what if she were to stop loving me! An instant can change that proud spirit, and it has to be admitted that I've treated her abominably.

That evening, he felt he simply had to put in an appearance in Mme de Fervaques's box at the Opera Bouffe. She had expressly invited him: Mathilde would not fail to learn of his presence or his rude absence. In spite of the cogency of this argument, he did not have the strength, at the beginning of the evening, to immerse himself in the social scene. Talking would deprive him of half his happiness.

Ten o'clock struck: he absolutely had to show his face.

By a piece of good fortune he found the maréchale's box full of women, and he was relegated to a position near the door, completely hidden by all the hats. This saved him from making a fool of himself; the divine strains of Caroline's despair in the *Matrimonio Segreto** reduced him to tears. Mme de Fervaques saw these tears; they formed such a contrast with the masculine firmness of his usual countenance that this great lady's soul, long since saturated with all that is most corrosive in a social climber's pride, was actually touched by them. What little was left in her of a woman's heart drove her to speak. She wanted at that moment to enjoy the sound of his voice.

'Have you seen the La Mole ladies?' she asked him, 'they're in a box on the third row.' Julien at once leant out over the stalls, supporting himself rather impolitely on the front of the box: he saw Mathilde; her eyes were glistening with tears.

And yet it isn't their day for the opera, Julien thought; what keenness!

Mathilde had persuaded her mother to come to the Opera Bouffe, although the box which one of the lady devotees of the family had hastened to offer them was in a most unsuitable row. She wanted to see if Julien would spend that evening with the maréchale.

CHAPTER 31

Frightening her

So this is the fine miracle of your
civilization! You have turned love into an
ordinary matter.

BARNAVE

JULIEN ran to Mme de La Mole's box. The first sight to meet
his gaze was Mathilde's tear-filled eyes; she was crying quite
openly. There were only people of subordinate rank there: the
friend who had lent her box and some men of her acquaintance.
Mathilde put her hand on Julien's; she seemed to have
forgotten all fear of her mother. Almost choking with tears,
the only word she said to him was: 'Guarantees!'

Whatever happens I mustn't speak to her, Julien told
himself, deeply moved for his own part, and trying as best he
could to conceal his eyes behind his hand, using the chandelier
which dazzles the third row of boxes as his excuse. If I speak,
she won't be able to doubt the intensity of my emotion any
more: the sound of my voice will betray me, everything may
yet be lost.

His struggles were far more painful than in the morning; he
had had time to become stirred to the depths of his being. He
was afraid of seeing Mathilde get piqued through vanity.
Intoxicated with love and desire, he took it upon himself not
to speak to her.

This, in my opinion, is one of the finest traits of his
character; an individual capable of taking such a hold over
himself can go far, *si fata sinant.**

Mlle de La Mole insisted on driving Julien home. Fortunately
it was raining heavily. But the marquise had seated him
opposite her and talked to him continuously, preventing him
from saying a word to her daughter. It was as if the marquise
was taking care of Julien's happiness; no longer fearful of
losing everything through the intensity of his emotion, he gave
himself over to it in frenzy.

Shall I dare to relate that on returning to his room Julien

flung himself on to his knees and planted kisses all over the love letters donated by Prince Korasov?

O great man! how much I owe you! he exclaimed in his frenzy.

Gradually he regained a degree of composure. He compared himself to a general who has half won a great battle. The advantage is certain, and very considerable, he said to himself; but what will happen tomorrow? everything can be lost in an instant.

With a passionate gesture he opened the *Memoirs dictated on St Helena* by Napoleon,* and for two long hours he forced himself to read them; only his eyes were reading, but no matter, he forced himself to do it. During this strange reading process, his head and his heart had ascended to the sphere of all that is loftiest, and were working away unknown to him. This heart is quite unlike Mme de Rênal's, he said to himself, but he did not go any further.

FRIGHTEN HER, he exclaimed suddenly, flinging the book away. The enemy will only obey me in so far as I frighten her, and then she won't dare despise me.

He walked up and down his little room, wild with joy. In all truth, this happiness stemmed more from self-satisfaction than from love.

Frighten her! he repeated to himself proudly, and he was right to feel proud. Even in her happiest moments, Mme de Rênal always doubted that my love was equal to hers. Here, I've got a demon to subjugate, so I must *subjugate*.

He knew perfectly well that the next day Mathilde would be in the library from eight in the morning; he did not put in an appearance until nine, burning with love, but keeping his heart firmly under the control of his head. Not a single minute passed maybe without his repeating to himself: Keep this great doubt always nagging at her: Does he love me? Her brilliant position, the flatteries of everyone who speaks to her, incline her *a little too readily* to reassure herself.

He found her sitting on the sofa, pale and calm, but apparently in no state to make a single movement. She held out her hand to him:

'Julien, I've offended you, it's true; you may be angry with me...?'

Julien was not expecting so straightforward a tone as this. He was on the verge of betraying himself.

'You want guarantees, my dear,' she added after a silence she had hoped would be broken; 'that is fair. Abduct me, let's leave for London... I shall be ruined for ever, dishonoured'... She had the strength of will to withdraw the hand she had held out to Julien, and to cover her eyes with it. All her inner feelings of restraint and feminine virtue had returned to her 'Go on! dishonour me,' she said at length with a sigh, 'it's *a guarantee.*'

Yesterday I was happy because I had the guts to be strict with myself, Julien thought. After a brief moment's silence, he had enough hold over his emotions to say in icy tones:

'Once we're on the road for London, once you're dishonoured, to use your expression, who can vouch that you will love me? That my presence in the post-chaise won't seem unwelcome to you? I'm not a monster; to have ruined you in the eyes of public opinion will be just one more misfortune for me. It's not your position in society that's the obstacle, it's unfortunately your character. Can you vouch to yourself that you will love me in a week's time?'

(Ah! let her love me for a week, just a week, Julien murmured to himself, and I'll die of happiness. What do I care about the future, what do I care about life? and this divine happiness can start this instant if I want, it's entirely up to me!)

Mathilde saw he was plunged in thought.

'So I'm utterly unworthy of you,' she said taking his hand.

Julien kissed her, but instantly the iron hand of duty gripped his heart. If she sees how much I adore her, I'll lose her. And, before withdrawing from her embrace, he had resumed all the dignity befitting a man.

That day and the following days he managed to hide the intensity of his bliss; there were moments when he refused himself even the pleasure of clasping her in his arms.

At other moments, delirious happiness got the better of any advice prudence could give.

There was a honeysuckle bower, designed to hide the ladder, where he had been accustomed to station himself in the garden to keep a distant watch on Mathilde's shutters and to weep at her inconstancy. A very big oak stood close by, and the trunk of this tree prevented indiscreet eyes from seeing him.

As he walked with Mathilde by this very spot which reminded him so vividly of the intensity of his misery, the contrast between past despair and present bliss was too much for his temperament; tears flooded his eyes and, raising his loved one's hand to his lips: 'This is where I lived with my thoughts on you; from here I would look at those shutters, I would wait for hours on end for the lucky moment when I would see this hand of yours opening them...'

His weakness was total. He depicted to her in true colours that cannot be invented the intensity of the despair he had felt then. Brief interjections bore witness to his present happiness which had put an end to this terrible suffering...

What am I doing, my God! Julien said to himself, suddenly coming to his senses. I'm ruining everything.

In the excess of his alarm, he thought he could already detect less love in Mlle de La Mole's eyes. It was an illusion; but Julien's face changed swiftly and became deathly pale. His eyes grew dull for an instant and an expression of arrogance not untainted with cruelty soon replaced the look of most genuine and most unrestrained love.

'What's the matter with you, my dearest?' Mathilde asked him with tenderness and anxiety.

'I'm lying,' said Julien in annoyance, 'and I'm lying to you. I blame myself for it, and yet heaven knows I have enough esteem for you not to lie. You love me, you are devoted to me, and I don't need to talk in flowery phrases to please you.'

'My God! Are all the ravishing things you've been saying to me for the last two minutes just flowery phrases?'

'And I blame myself acutely for them, my dearest. I composed them once for a woman who loved me and bored me... It's the flaw in my character, I'm denouncing myself to you of my own accord, please forgive me.'

Bitter tears poured down Mathilde's cheeks.

'As soon as some slight thing that has shocked me forces me

into a moment's daydreaming', Julien went on, 'my loathsome memory, which I curse at this very moment, offers me its resources, and I misuse them.'

'So I've unwittingly just done something that must have displeased you?' Mathilde said with charming simplicity.

'One day, I remember, as you passed by these honeysuckle bushes, you picked a flower: M. de Luz took it from you, and you let him have it. I was right there.'

'M. de Luz? That's impossible,' Mathilde replied, with the peremptoriness that came so naturally to her: 'I don't behave like that.'

'I'm sure you did,' Julien retorted sharply.

'Oh well! it's true, my dearest,' said Mathilde, sadly lowering her eyes. She knew for certain that for some months now she hadn't allowed M. de Luz to do any such thing.

Julien looked at her with indescribable tenderness: No, he said to himself, she doesn't love me *any the less*.

That evening, she reproached him jokingly with his fondness for Mme de Fervaques: 'a bourgeois loving a social climber! Hearts of that sort are maybe the only ones that my Julien can't drive mad. She had turned you into a real dandy,' she said, fondling his hair.

During the time he thought Mathilde despised him, Julien had become one of the most elegantly dressed men in Paris. But he had an additional advantage over people of that sort: once he was ready attired, he did not give his appearance another thought.

One thing vexed Mathilde: Julien continued to copy out the Russian letters and send them to the maréchale.

CHAPTER 32

The tiger

Alas! why these things and not others?

BEAUMARCHAIS*

AN English traveller tells of living at close quarters with a
tiger; he had reared it and used to stroke it, but he always kept
a loaded pistol on his table.

Julien only abandoned himself to the intensity of his happiness at moments when Mathilde could not see it reflected in
his eyes. He was punctilious in his duty of addressing a harsh
word to her from time to time.

When Mathilde's gentleness, which he observed with astonishment, and her excessive devotion were on the point of
robbing him of all control over himself, he had the strength of
purpose to leave her company forthwith.

For the first time ever, Mathilde felt what it was to love.

Life, which for her had always plodded along like a tortoise,
was now on the wing.

Since, however, it was necessary for pride to surface in some
way or another, she was anxious to expose herself with temerity
to all the dangers her love might put in her way. Julien was the
one to show caution; and it was only when there was some
question of danger that she did not yield to his will; but while
submissive and almost humble with him, she behaved that
much more arrogantly towards all those members of the
household who had dealings with her, whether family or
servants.

In the evening in the drawing-room, in a gathering of sixty
people, she would call Julien over in order to talk to him
personally and at length.

When little Tanbeau settled down beside them one day, she
begged him to go to the library to fetch her the volume of
Smollett containing the revolution of 1688; and as he hesitated:
'And don't be in any hurry over it,' she added with an

expression of insulting arrogance which was balm to Julien's soul.

'Did you notice the little monster's look?' he asked her.

'His uncle has put in ten or twelve years' service in this salon, otherwise I'd have him booted out on the spot.'

Her behaviour towards Messrs de Croisenois, de Luz, etc., while perfectly polite in a formal sense, was hardly less provocative in substance. Mathilde bitterly regretted confiding so much in Julien early on, all the more so since she did not dare confess to him that she had exaggerated the almost totally innocent displays of interest with which these gentlemen had been favoured.

Despite all her fine resolve, her woman's pride would daily prevent her from saying to Julien: 'It was because I was talking to you that I took pleasure in describing my weakness in not withdrawing my hand when M. de Croisenois, as he rested his on a marble table, happened to brush gently against mine.'

Today, one of these gentlemen had hardly to speak to her for a few moments before she found she had a question to ask Julien, and this was a pretext for keeping him by her side.

She discovered she was pregnant and announced it delightedly to Julien.

'Will you still have doubts about me now? Isn't this a guarantee? I'm your wife for ever.'

This announcement filled Julien with deep astonishment. He was on the verge of forgetting the principle governing his behaviour. How can I be deliberately cold and offensive towards this poor girl who's ruining herself for me? If she looked at all unwell, even on days when the terrible voice of wisdom made itself heard, he found he did not have the heart any more to utter one of those cruel remarks to her that were so essential, in his experience, to make their love last.

'I want to write to my father,' Mathilde said to him one day; 'he's more than a father to me; he's a friend, and as such, I should find it unworthy of you and me to try to deceive him, even for a moment.'

'My God! What are you about to do? said Julien in alarm.

'My duty,' she replied, her eyes shining with joy.

She was more magnanimous, it appeared, than her lover.

'But he'll turn me out of the house in ignominy!'

'He has every right to, and we must accept this. I shall give you my arm and we'll leave by the carriage door, in broad daylight.'

The astonished Julien begged her to postpone this step for a week.

'That I cannot do,' she replied, 'honour calls; I've seen where my duty lies, and I must follow it, right away, too.'

'All right then! I order to you to postpone it,' Julien said at length. 'Your honour is safe, I'm your husband. Both of our situations are going to be changed by this crucial step. I too am acting within my rights. Today is Tuesday; next Tuesday is the Duc de Retz's day; in the evening, when M. de La Mole comes home, the porter will hand him the fateful letter... All he thinks about is making you a duchess, I'm sure of it; just imagine his grief!'

'Do you mean: "just imagine his thirst for revenge"?'

'I am entitled to pity my benefactor, to be upset about hurting him; but I do not and never will fear anyone.'

Mathilde gave in. This was the first time since she had announced her new situation to Julien that he had spoken authoritatively to her; never had he loved her so much. It was a source of happiness for the tender side of his nature to seize upon Mathilde's state to excuse him from the need to say cruel things to her. The thought of confessing to M. de La Mole disturbed him deeply. Was he going to be separated from Mathilde? And however painful it might be for her to see him go, when a month had passed by would she still be thinking about him?

He was in almost equal dread of the just reproaches he was liable to incur from the marquis.

That evening, he imparted this second source of grief to Mathilde, and then led astray by his love, he also confessed the first.

She changed colour.

'Do you really mean', she said 'that spending six months apart from me would cause you misery?'

'Tremendous misery, it's the only misfortune in the world I contemplate with terror.'

Mathilde was happy indeed. Julien had played his part so assiduously that he had succeeded in making her think that of the two of them, she was the one who loved the most.

The fateful Tuesday came round. At midnight, on returning home, the marquis found a letter addressed in such a way as to make him open it himself, and only when no witnesses were present.

Dear Papa,

All social ties are broken off between us, all that remains are ties of nature. After my husband, you are and always will be the person who is dearest to me. Tears are welling up in my eyes as I think of the suffering I am causing you, but to avoid my shame becoming public, to give you time to take thought and to act, I could not any longer postpone the confession I owe you. If your friendship towards me, which I know to be deep, is willing to grant me a small allowance, I shall go and settle wherever you wish, in Switzerland, for instance, with my husband. His name is so obscure that no one will recognize your daughter in Mme Sorel, the daughter-in-law of a carpenter from Verrières. This is the name it has cost me so much to put in writing. I fear for Julien the consequences of your anger, which is justified at first sight. I shall not be a duchess, papa; but I knew this when I fell in love with him; for I was the first to love—I did the seducing. I have inherited from you too lofty a character to waste my attention on anything that is or strikes me as vulgar. To please you, I tried to entertain thoughts of M. de Croisenois, but it was no use. Why had you put true worth before my eyes? You said as much to me yourself on my return from Hyères: 'young Sorel is the only person I find amusing.' The poor fellow is as wretched as I am, if that is possible, at the suffering this letter is causing you. I cannot prevent you from feeling angered as a father; but please continue to love me as a friend.

Julien respected me. If he spoke to me from time to time, it was exclusively on account of his deep gratitude towards you: for the dignity inherent in his character inclines him only ever to respond officially to anything that is so far above him. He has an acute, innate sense of differences in social status. I was the one—I confess it with a blush to my closest friend, and never will such a confession be made to anyone else—I was the one who squeezed his arm one day in the garden.

In twenty-four hours' time, why should you be angry with him? My lapse is irreparable. If you insist on it, I shall be the intermediary for his assurances of profound respect and despair at incurring your displeasure. You will see no more of him; but I shall go and join him wherever he wishes. That is his right, and my duty; he is the father of my child. If your kindness is willing to grant us six thousand francs to live on, I shall accept them gratefully: if not, Julien intends to settle in Besançon, where he will embark on a career as teacher of Latin and literature. However low his starting-point, I am convinced that he will rise high. With him, I have no fear of remaining in obscurity. If there is a revolution, I am sure that his will be a leading role. Could you say as much for any of the men who have asked for my hand? They have fine estates! I cannot see this circumstance alone as a reason for admiration. My Julien would rise to a high position even under the present regime, if he had a million and my father's protection…

Mathilde, knowing the marquis to be a man who acted on first impulse, had written eight pages.

What's to be done? Julien wondered while the Marquis de La Mole was reading this letter; where lies 1) my duty, 2) my interest? My debt to him is enormous: but for him, I'd have been a subordinate rogue, and not enough of a rogue to escape being hated and persecuted by others. He's given me a place in high society. My *necessary* acts of roguery will be 1) more infrequent, 2) less infamous. That counts for more than if he'd given me a million. I owe him this cross and the reputation for diplomatic services that put me above other people.

If he had his pen in his hand to lay down my conduct, what would he write…?

Julien was brusquely interrupted by M. de La Mole's old manservant.

'The marquis wants to see you at once, dressed or undressed.'

The manservant added in a low voice as he walked along beside Julien:

'He's beside himself with rage, watch out.'

CHAPTER 33

The infernal torment of weakness

In cutting this diamond, a careless jeweller removed
some of its brightest glints. In the Middle Ages—what
am I saying?—even under Richelieu, a Frenchman had
strength of will.

MIRABEAU

JULIEN found the marquis in a fury: for the first time in his
life, perhaps, this nobleman was vulgar; he assailed Julien with
all the insults that came to his lips. Our hero was astonished
and irritated, but his gratitude was not shaken. Just think how
many wonderful plans which the poor man has been cherishing
in his inmost thoughts are falling in ruins at a stroke before his
very eyes! But I owe it to him to reply; my silence would
increase his anger. Tartuffe's part supplied the reply.

'*I am no angel**... I have served you well, you have rewarded
me generously... I was grateful, but I'm twenty-two... In this
household, my thoughts were only understood by you and this
delightful person...'

'You monster!!' exclaimed the marquis. 'Delightful!
Delightful! The day you first found her delightful you ought
to have fled.'

'I tried to; that was the time I asked you to let me leave for
the Languedoc.'

Weary of striding up and down in fury, the marquis flung
himself into an armchair, overcome with sorrow; Julien heard
him mutter to himself: 'Really he isn't a wicked man.'

'No, I'm not, where you are concerned,' Julien exclaimed,
falling down at the marquis's knees. But he was excessively
ashamed of this gesture and very soon got up again.

The marquis was genuinely out of his mind. At the sight of
this gesture, he again began to assail Julien with dreadful
insults worthy of a cab-driver. The novelty of these swear-
words was perhaps a distraction.

'What! my daughter's to be called Mme Sorel! What! my
daughter's not going to be a duchess!' Every time these ideas

came to him as clearly as this, M. de La Mole went through torture, and his instinctive reactions were no longer under the control of his will. Julien was afraid of being thrashed.

In his lucid phases, and as he began to get used to the idea of his misfortune, the marquis's reproaches to Julien were quite reasonable:

'You should have fled, sir,' he said to him... 'It was your duty to flee... You're the lowest of the low.'

Julien went over to the table and wrote:

My life has long been unbearable to me; I am ending it. I beg my lord Marquis to accept both my protestations of boundless gratitude and my apologies for the embarrassment that my death in his house may cause.

'I humbly beg your lordship to deign to cast an eye over this paper... Kill me,' said Julien, 'or have your manservant do it. It's one o'clock in the morning, I'll go and walk up and down in the garden near the far wall.'

'Oh go to hell!' the marquis shouted after him as he left.

I understand, thought Julien; he wouldn't be displeased if I spared his manservant the business of seeing to my death... Let him kill me, fair enough, I'll offer him this by way of satisfaction... But, damn it all, I love life... my duty is to my son.

This idea, which struck his imagination with such clarity for the first time, absorbed him totally after the first few minutes of walking up and down, during which he had been aware of nothing but danger.

This interest, which was so new to him, turned him into a creature of caution. I need advice on how to behave towards this impetuous man... His reason is gone, he's capable of anything. Fouqué is too far away, and besides, he wouldn't understand what moves the heart of someone like the marquis.

Count Altamira... Can I be sure of silence for ever? Seeking advice mustn't constitute an action that complicates my position. Alas! the only person left is the dour Abbé Pirard... His mind has been narrowed by Jansenism... A Jesuit rogue would have some worldly wisdom, and would fit the bill better...

M. Pirard is capable of thrashing me at the mere mention of the misdeed.

The genius of Tartuffe came to Julien's rescue: Right, then, I'll go and make confession to him. This was the final decision he took in the garden after walking about for a good two hours. He no longer believed he might be surprised by a gunshot; he was succumbing to sleep.

Very early the next morning, Julien was several leagues away from Paris, knocking at the stern Jansenist's door. He found, much to his astonishment, that the latter was not unduly surprised by his revelation.

I ought perhaps to blame myself, the priest thought, more concerned than angry. 'I had suspected this love. My friendship for you, you wretched boy, prevented me from warning the father...'

'What's he going to do?' Julien asked eagerly.

(He felt great warmth towards the priest at that moment, and would have found a scene very painful.)

'I can see three courses of action,' Julien went on: '1) M. de La Mole can have me killed;' and he told of the suicide note he had left with the marquis; '2) he can have me shot point-blank by Count Norbert, who would challenge me to a duel.'

'Would you accept?' said the priest, getting up in fury.

'You're not letting me finish. I should most certainly never shoot at my benefactor's son.

'3) He can send me away. If he says to me: "Go to Edinburgh or New York", I shall obey. Then Mlle de La Mole's situation can be concealed; but I shall not allow my son to be done away with.'

'And that, make no doubt about it, will be the first thing that corrupt man thinks of...'

Back in Paris Mathilde was in despair. She had seen her father at about seven o'clock. He had shown her Julien's letter, and she was in in fear and trembling lest he had decided that the noble way was to put an end to his life: And without my permission? she said to herself with anguish that was in fact a form of anger.

'If he is dead, I shall die,' she told her father. '*You* will be the cause of my death... You will perhaps be glad of it... But this I swear to his spirit: I shall first of all go into mourning, and be *M. Sorel's widow* in public; I shall send out announcements, you can count on that... You won't find me faint-hearted or cowardly.'

Her love reached the proportions of folly. It was M. de La Mole's turn to be astounded.

He began to view events with some sort of reason. Mathilde did not appear at lunch. The marquis was relieved of a tremendous weight on his mind, and was in particular most flattered when he observed that she had said nothing to her mother.

Julien was just dismounting from his horse. Mathilde summoned him and flung herself into his arms almost in front of her chambermaid. Julien was not very grateful for this passionate demonstration; he had emerged in a highly diplomatic and calculating frame of mind from his long conference with Father Pirard. His imagination was dulled from calculating possible moves. With tears in her eyes, Mathilde informed him that she had seen his suicide note.

'My father may change his mind; be so good as to set off this very instant for Villequier. Get back on your horse and leave the house before they get up from lunch.'

As Julien's look of cold astonishment remained unaltered, she had a fit of tears.

'Leave me to run our affairs, darling,' she exclaimed passionately, clasping him in her arms. 'You know perfectly well that I'm not undertaking this separation from you voluntarily. Write to me via my chambermaid, make sure the address is in an unknown hand; and I shall write reams back. Farewell! You must flee.'

Her last words wounded Julien; he obeyed all the same. There's something inevitable about it, he thought: even in their best moments, these people have the knack of rubbing me up the wrong way.

Mathilde strongly resisted all the *prudent* courses of action suggested by her father. She was never willing to engage in negotiations on any basis other than this: she would be Mme Sorel, and would live in poverty with her husband in Switzerland, or in her father's house in Paris. She utterly rejected the suggestion of a clandestine confinement.

'That would lay me open to slander and dishonour. Two months after our wedding, I shall go on a journey with my husband, and it'll be easy for us to assume that my son was born after a respectable interval.'

Greeted at first by outbursts of anger, this firmness eventually succeeded in instilling doubts into the marquis.

In a moment of tenderness:

'Well now!' he said to his daughter, 'here is a certificate for an annuity of ten thousand pounds; send it to your Julien, and let him hurry up and make it impossible for me to take it back.

To *obey* Mathilde, whose love of being in command was familiar to him, Julien had made an unnecessary journey of forty leagues: he was at Villequier, settling the farmers' accounts: this benefaction from the marquis was a pretext for him to return. He went to seek asylum with Father Pirard, who, in his absence, had become Mathilde's most useful ally. Every time Father Pirard was questioned by the marquis, he demonstrated to him that any course of action other than a public marriage would be a crime in the sight of God.

'And fortunately,' the priest added, 'wordly wisdom is in agreement on this occasion with religion. Could one count for a moment, with Mlle de La Mole's impetuous character, on her maintaining secrecy if she hadn't imposed it on herself? If you don't accept the open step of a public marriage, society will talk for far longer about this strange misalliance. You must tell all in one go, without there being the slightest mystery—in appearance or in reality.'

'That's right,' said the marquis thoughtfully. 'In this scenario, talk of their marriage three days after the event will be nothing but the burbling of people without an idea in their heads. The thing to do is take advantage of some great anti-Jacobin measure by the Government so that the whole thing can slip by unnoticed in the aftermath.'

Two or three of M. de La Mole's friends shared Father Pirard's way of thinking. The great obstacle, to their minds, was Mathilde's resolute character. But after all these fine arguments, the marquis in his heart of hearts could not get used to the idea of renouncing the hope of a *footstool** for his daughter.

His memory and his imagination were full of the rakish and treacherous deeds of all kinds that had still been possible in his youth. To give in to necessity, to fear the law struck him as an absurd and demeaning thing for a man of his rank. He was paying dearly now for the bewitching dreams he had indulged in for the past ten years about the future of this beloved daughter.

Who could have foreseen it? he said to himself. A daughter with such an arrogant character, with such a superior cast of mind, more proud than I am of the name she bears! Whose hand had been requested of me in advance by all the most illustrious nobles in France!

You have to throw caution to the winds. This century is destined to cast everything into confusion! We're heading for chaos.

CHAPTER 34

A man of intelligence

The prefect riding along on his horse said to
himself: Why shouldn't I be a minister, or head of
the Cabinet, or a duke? This is how I shall wage war
...In this way I'd have innovators put in chains...

LE GLOBE

No argument is strong enough to break the hold of ten years
of enjoyable dreaming. The marquis did not think it reasonable
to be angry, but could not bring himself to forgive. If only this
Julien could die by accident, he said to himself at times... His
grieving imagination thus found some solace in pursuing the
most absurd fantasies. They counteracted the effect of Father
Pirard's sensible reasoning. A month went by in this fashion
without any step forward in the settlement.

In this family matter, as in politics, the marquis had brilliant
insights which filled him with enthusiasm for three days on
end. At such times some course of action would fail to appeal
to him because it was backed by sound arguments; but then
arguments only found favour with him in so far as they
supported his preferred plan. For three days running he
worked with all the ardour and enthusiasm of a poet to bring
things to a certain point; the next day he had forgotten all
about it.

At first Julien was disconcerted by the marquis's delays; but
after a few weeks he began to surmise that in this matter M.
de La Mole did not have any firm plans.

Mme de La Mole and the rest of the household believed that
Julien was off travelling in the provinces, seeing to the
administration of the estates; he was hiding in Father Pirard's
presbytery, and seeing Mathilde almost every day. She went to
see her father for an hour every morning, but sometimes they
let whole weeks go by without discussing the matter that was
constantly on their minds.

'I don't want to know that man's whereabouts,' the marquis
said to her one day. 'Send him this letter.' Mathilde read:

The Languedoc estates bring in 20,600 francs. I make over 10,600 francs to my daughter and 10,000 francs to M. Julien Sorel. I am of course donating the estates themselves. Instruct the solicitor to draw up two separate deeds of gift, and to bring them to me tomorrow; after which, no further dealings between us. Ah! sir, was I to expect all this?

La Mole.

'Thank you very much indeed,' said Mathilde brightly. 'We shall settle in the Château d'Aiguillon,* between Agen and Marmande. They say the region is as beautiful as Italy.'

This gift came as a great surprise to Julien. He was no longer the stern and cold man we knew earlier. The fate of his son took up all his thoughts in anticipation. This fortune, unexpected and pretty substantial for someone so poor, gave him ambitions. He saw himself and his wife enjoying an income of 36,000 pounds between them. As for Mathilde, all her emotion was absorbed in adoration of her husband, for that was how her pride always referred to Julien. Her great, her sole ambition was to have her marriage recognized. She spent her days exaggerating to herself the great prudence she had shown in throwing in her lot with that of a superior man. In her mind, personal distinction was all the fashion.

The effect of almost continuous absence, multifarious business, and scant time available for talking of love, was to complete the good work of the wise strategy Julien had devised earlier.

Mathilde finally grew impatient at seeing so little of the man she had reached the point of genuinely loving.

In a moment of bad temper she wrote to her father, and began her letter like Othello.*

That I have preferred Julien to the delights society offered the daughter of Monsieur le Marquis de La Mole is amply proved by my choice. These pleasures of esteem and petty vanity mean nothing to me. I have been living apart from my husband for almost six weeks now. That is a sufficient demonstration of my respect for you. I shall leave my family home by next Thursday. Your generous gifts have made us rich. No one knows my secret apart from the respectable Abbé Pirard. I shall go to his house, he will marry us, and an hour after the ceremony we shall be on our way to the Languedoc, and we shall never set foot in Paris again except on your orders. But what pierces me to the heart is the thought that all this will make a stinging anecdote to tell against me, and against you. May not the epigrams of a foolish public force our splendid Norbert to pick a quarrel with Julien? If that happened, I know him, I should have no influence over him. We should find in him shades of the rebellious plebeian. Dear father, I beseech you on my knees: come and witness the celebration of our marriage in Father Pirard's church next Thursday. The sting will be taken out of this malicious anecdote, and the threat to the lives of your only son and my husband will be removed, etc., etc.

The marquis was thrown by this letter into a state of curious embarrassment. So the time had come at last for him *to make up his mind*. All his little habits, all his ordinary friends had lost their influence.

In this strange situation, the broad traits of his character, imprinted by the events of his youth, resumed all their hold over him. The misfortunes of the Emigration had turned him into a man of imagination. Having spent two years enjoying an immense fortune and all the honours of the Court, he had been cast by the events of 1790 into the appalling hardships of the Emigration. Learning the hard way had radically altered the character of the twenty-two-year-old marquis. Basically, he stood assertively in the midst of his present wealth, rather than being dominated by it. But this very imagination which had saved his soul from being consumed by the gangrene of gold, had made him fall prey to a mad desire to see his daughter adorned with a fine title.

During the six weeks which had just elapsed, there had been moments when the marquis, on an impulse, had decided to make Julien rich; Julien's poverty struck him as unworthy, as dishonourable for him, M. de La Mole, and out of the question for the husband of his daughter; he flung his money away. The following day, his imagination took another turn, and it seemed to him that Julien would heed the silent message of this financial generosity, would change his name, exile himself to America, and write to tell Mathilde that as far as she was concerned he was dead. M. de La Mole imagined this letter already written, and pictured its effect on his daughter's character...

On the day he was awakened from these youthful fantasies by the *real* letter from Mathilde, he had considered at length killing Julien or having him removed, and then began dreaming of setting up a brilliant fortune for him. He would bestow on him the name of one of his estates; and why shouldn't he pass on his peerage to him? The Duc de Chaulnes, his father-in-law, had spoken to him several times, ever since his only son had been killed in Spain, of his desire to hand on his title to Norbert...

One can't deny that Julien has an unusual gift for business, he's adventurous, perhaps even *brilliant*, the marquis said to himself... But in the depths of his character I detect something that alarms me. This is the impression he gives everyone, so there must genuinely be something there (the more difficult it was to pin down what was genuinely there, the more it alarmed the imaginative faculties of the old marquis).

As my daughter put it to me so shrewdly the other day (in a letter we have suppressed): 'Julien has not given his allegiance to any salon or any coterie.' He's got no one lined up to side with him against me, or any resource whatsoever if I abandon him... But is this a sign of ignorance of the present state of society...? On two or three occasions I have said to him: 'No one has any realistic expectations of making his way without the backing of the salons...'

No, he doesn't have the shrewd and cunning genius of an attorney who never loses a minute or an opportunity... He doesn't have anything of Louis XI's* character. On the other hand, I hear him him uttering maxims that are the opposite of generous... I'm at sea... Might he be repeating these maxims for his own benefit to serve as a *dike* against his passions?

At any rate, one thing stands out: he can't abide scorn, that's my hold over him.

He doesn't worship high birth, it's true, he doesn't respect us out of instinct... He's at fault there; but anyway, the only thing that the soul of a seminarist should find it hard to abide is the lack of creature comforts and money. He's quite different, he can't bear scorn at any price.

Put on the spot by his daughter's letter, M. de La Mole recognized the need to come to a decision: Well, this is the big question: did Julien's audacity go so far as embarking on courtship of my daughter because he knows I love her more than anything, and I have an income of a hundred thousand crowns?

Mathilde protests to the contrary... No, Mister Julien, this is a point on which I don't wish to be deluded.

Was it a case of genuine, unexpected love? Or was it a vulgar desire to rise to a high position in society? Mathilde is perspicacious, she sensed right away that this suspicion could damn him in my eyes, hence her avowal: she was the one who took it into her head to fall in love first...

Could a girl with such a proud spirit forget herself to the point of making physical advances...! Squeezing his arm in the garden one evening—how dreadful! As if she hadn't had hundreds of less improper ways of letting him know that he was someone special.

Making excuses is an admission of guilt; I mistrust Mathilde... That day, the marquis's reasoning was more conclusive than usual. However, habit got the better of him and he resolved to gain time by writing to his daughter. For communication took place by letter from one side of the house to the other. M. de La Mole did not dare discuss matters with Mathilde face to face and stand up to her. He was afraid of ending everything by a sudden concession.

LETTER

Make sure you do not commit any fresh acts of folly; here is a lieutenant's commission in the Hussars for M. le Chevalier Julien Sorel de La Vernaye. You see what I am doing for him. Do not stand in my way, do not ask me any questions. He must leave in the next twenty-four hours, to present himself in Strasburg where his regiment is stationed. Here is a warrant from my banker; I wish to be obeyed.

Mathilde's love and joy knew no bounds; she determined to take advantage of victory, and replied forthwith:

M. de La Vernaye would be at your feet, overcome with gratitude, if he knew all the things you are deigning to do for him. But in the midst of all this generosity, my father has forgotten me; your daughter's honour is in danger. An indiscreet word can cause an eternal blot—one that an income of twenty thousand crowns would not expunge. I shall not send the commission to M. de La Vernaye unless you give me your word that some time in the next month my marriage will be celebrated in public, at Villequier. I beg you not to delay any longer, because shortly thereafter your daughter will only be able to appear in public under the name of Mme de La Vernaye. How much I thank you, dear Papa, for sparing me the name of Sorel, etc., etc.

The reply was unexpected.

Obey, or I retract everything. Tremble, rash girl. I do not yet know what sort of person your Julien is, and you yourself know even less than I do. He must leave for Strasburg, and take care not to put a foot wrong. I shall make known my wishes in the next fortnight.

So stern a reply astonished Mathilde. *I do not know Julien*; this phrase plunged her into a reverie which soon offered her the most bewitching of hypotheses; but she took them for the truth. My Julien hasn't cloaked his mind in the mean, petty *uniform* of the salons, and my father doesn't believe in his superiority, precisely because of what proves it...

All the same, if I don't give in to this passing display of toughness, I foresee the possibility of a public scene; a scandal will lower my standing in society, and may make me less attractive in Julien's eyes. After the scandal... poverty for ten years; and the folly of choosing a husband for his personal qualities can only escape ridicule by the most dazzling opulence. If I live a long way away from my father, at his age he may forget me... Norbert will marry a charming and clever woman: Louis XIV was captivated in his old age by the Duchess of Burgundy...*

She had made up her mind to obey, but was careful not to impart her father's letter to Julien; his unruly character might have driven him to some act of folly.

That evening, when she informed Julien that he was a lieutenant in the Hussars, his joy knew no bounds. To picture it, just consider his lifelong ambition and the passion he now felt for his son. The change of name filled him with astonishment.

When you come to think about it, he reflected, my story's

ended, and all the credit goes to me alone. I've succeeded in
making this monster of pride fall in love with me, he added,
glancing at Mathilde; her father can't live without her, nor she
without me.

CHAPTER 35

A storm

O God, give me mediocrity!
MIRABEAU

HIS mind was elsewhere; he responded only half-heartedly to her displays of great tenderness. He remained silent and morose. Mathilde had never looked up to him so much, never found him so lovable. She feared some subtle quirk of his pride that would go and upset the whole situation.

Almost every morning she saw Father Pirard coming to the house. Mightn't Julien through him have gained some insight into her father's intentions! Mightn't the marquis himself have written to him on the whim of a moment? After a stroke of good fortune like this, how was Julien's stern expression to be explained? She did not dare question him.

She *did not dare*! she, Mathilde! From that moment on there entered into her feelings for Julien something ill-defined, something unexpected, almost like terror. This arid soul experienced passion as fully as is possible in someone brought up in the midst of the surfeit of civilization that Paris worships.

Early the next morning Julien was at Father Pirard's presbytery. Post horses were making their way into the courtyard with a dilapidated chaise hired from the nearest station.

'An equipage like this is no longer appropriate,' said the stern priest with a scowl. 'Here are twenty thousand francs as a gift from M. de La Mole; he invites you to spend them within a year, endeavouring, however, to avoid making a fool of yourself in so far as possible.' (Such a considerable sum of money lavished on a young man was viewed by the priest as nothing less than an invitation to sin.)

'The marquis adds: "M. Julien de La Vernaye will be assumed to have received this money from his father, to whom there is no need to refer otherwise. M. de La Vernaye will perhaps see fit to give a present to M. Sorel, a carpenter in Verrières, who cared for him as a child..." I can see to this part of the instructions,' the priest added. 'I have at last persuaded M. de La Mole to reach a settlement with the Abbé de Frilair, who is such a Jesuit. His influence is decidely too much of a match for us. Implicit recognition of your noble birth by this man who rules Besançon will be one of the tacit conditions of the settlement.'

Julien could no longer control his feelings, and embraced the priest: he saw himself recognized.

'Come, come!' said M. Pirard, rebuffing him; 'what is the meaning of this worldly vanity ?... As for Sorel and his sons, I shall offer them, in my own name, an annuity of five hundred francs, to be paid to each one of them for as long as I am satisfied with them.'

Julien had already become cold and aloof. He expressed his thanks, but in very vague terms that made no commitment. Could it really be possible, he wondered, that I might be the natural son of some great lord driven into exile in our mountains by the terrible Napoleon? This idea seemed less improbable to him with every passing moment... My hatred for my father would be proof of it... I shouldn't be a monster any more!

Only a few days after this monologue, the fifteenth regiment of Hussars,* one of the most brilliant in the army, was lined up in battle formation on the parade ground in Strasburg. M. le Chevalier de La Vernaye was mounted on the finest horse in Alsace, which had cost him six thousand francs. He was being presented as a lieutenant without ever having been a sub-lieutenant except on the books of a regiment he had never heard of.

His impassive expression, the stern, almost fierce look in his eyes, his pallor and his imperturbable composure launched his reputation right from the very first day. A little while later, his perfect, restrained civility, his skill with pistols and swords, which he displayed without too much affectation, banished any thought of joking out loud at his expense. After five or six days of wavering, public opinion in the regiment declared itself in his favour. 'This young man has everything,' said the old officers mockingly, 'except youth'.

From Strasburg Julien wrote to M. Chélan, the former priest of Verrières, who was now verging on extreme old age:

You will have learned with joy, I do not doubt, of the events which moved my family to make me rich. Here is a sum of five hundred francs which I beg you to distribute without fuss, or any mention whatsoever of my name, to the unfortunate souls who are poor now as I once was, and whom you no doubt help just as you once helped me.

Julien was intoxicated with ambition, not with vanity; he nevertheless devoted a good deal of his attention to external appearances. His horses, his uniforms, his servants' livery were punctiliously maintained in a way which would have been a credit to the fastidiousness of a great English lord. He was hardly a lieutenant, promoted through favouritism a mere two days ago, and he was already calculating that to be a commander-in-chief at thirty at the very latest, like all great generals, it was essential at twenty-three to be more than a lieutenant. He thought of nothing but glory, and his son.

He was in the throes of the most unbridled ambition when he was surprised by a young footman from the Hôtel de La Mole, who arrived with a despatch.

'All is lost,' wrote Mathilde:

Come as quickly as possible, sacrifice everything, desert if need be. Immediately on arrival, wait for me in a cab near the little gate into the garden, outside n° —— in —— street. I shall come out and speak to you; maybe I shall be able to slip you into the garden. All is lost, and, I fear, irredeemably so; count on me, you will find me devoted and steadfast. I love you.

In a matter of moments Julien obtained leave from the colonel and left Strasburg at full gallop; but the terrible anxiety devouring him did not allow him to continue this form of travel beyond Metz. He flung himself into a post-chaise; and it was with almost unbelievable speed that he arrived at the spot indicated to him, near the little gate into the garden of the Hôtel de La Mole. The gate opened, and at the same instant Mathilde, forgetting all self-respect, flung herself into his arms. Fortunately it was only five o'clock in the morning and the street was still deserted.

'All is lost; my father, fearing my tears, went off during the night on Thursday. Where to? No one knows. Here's his letter; read it.' And she stepped up into the cab with Julien.

I could have forgiven everything, except the scheme to seduce you because you are rich. There, wretched daughter, you have the terrible truth. I give you my word of honour that I shall never consent to any marriage with this man. I shall guarantee him an income of ten thousand pounds if he is willing to live a long way off, outside the frontiers of France, or better still in America. Read the letter I have just received in response to the enquiries I had made. The impudent wretch had urged me himself to write to Mme de Rênal. I shall never read a word from you on the subject of this man. I am filled with loathing for Paris and yourself. I urge you to shroud the impending event in the deepest secrecy. Renounce in all sincerity a worthless man, and you will find a father once more.

'Where is the letter from Mme de Rênal?' Julien asked coldly.

'Here it is. I didn't want to show it to you, darling, until you'd been prepared for it.'

LETTER

What I owe to the sacred cause of religion and morality forces me, sir, into the painful course of action that I am carrying out in writing to you now; a precept which cannot err orders me to do injury to my neighbour at this moment, but in order to avoid a greater scandal. The suffering which this causes me must be overcome by my sense of duty. I'm afraid, sir, the conduct of the person about whom you ask me to tell you the whole truth may well have struck an outsider as puzzling or perhaps even perfectly decent. This individual may have thought fit to conceal or disguise part of the real situation—prudence dictated this as well as religion. But his conduct, which you desire to be acquainted with, has in fact been extremely blameworthy, much more so than I can ever express. Being poor and grasping, this man used the most consummate hypocrisy, and resorted to the seduction of a weak and unhappy woman in his attempt to acquire status and to turn himself into a somebody. It is part of my painful duty to add that I have no choice but to believe that M. J— has no religious principles. In all conscience, I am obliged to think that one of his means of getting on in a household is to try to seduce the woman who wields most influence. Concealed beneath an appearance of disinterestedness and shrouded in phrases taken from novels, his one and only great aim is to succeed in gaining control over the master of the house and his fortune. He leaves behind him a trail of suffering and eternal regrets, etc., etc., etc.

This letter was extremely long and half-obliterated by tears, and it was indeed in Mme de Rênal's hand; it was even written with more care than usual.

'I cannot blame M. de La Mole,' Julien said when he had finished it; he is fair-minded and prudent. What father would want to give his beloved daughter to such a man! Farewell!'

Julien leaped down out of the cab and ran to his post-chaise, which was stopped at the end of the street. Mathilde, whom he seemed to have forgotten, went after him for a few steps; but the stares of the shopkeepers who came out into their doorways, and who all knew her, forced her to go back in haste into the garden.

Julien had set off for Verrières. On this swift journey he was unable to write to Mathilde as he was planning; his hand only made an illegible scrawl on the paper.

He arrived in Verrières on a Sunday morning. He sought out the local gunsmith, who complimented him profusely on his recent fortune. It was the latest local news.

Julien had great difficulty in getting him to understand that he wanted a pair of pistols. At his request the gunsmith loaded the pistols.

The *three chimes* were being sounded on the church bells; in villages throughout France this is the well-known signal which, after the various peals of the morning, announces the immediate start of Mass.

Julien made his way into the new church in Verrières. All the high windows in the building were draped with crimson hangings. Julien found himself a few paces behind Mme de Rênal's pew. It seemed to him that she was praying fervently. The sight of this woman who had loved him so much made Julien's arm tremble to such an extent that he was unable at first to carry out his design. I can't do it, he told himself; physically, I just can't do it.

At that moment the young priest who was officiating at the Mass rang the bell for the *Elevation*. Mme de Rênal lowered her head, which became almost completely hidden for an instant behind the folds of her shawl. Julien no longer recognized her so clearly; he fired a shot at her and missed; he fired a second shot: she fell.

CHAPTER 36
Sorry details

Do not expect any weakness on my part. I have
taken my revenge. I have deserved death and
here I am. Pray for my soul.

SCHILLER

JULIEN stood motionless with unseeing eyes. When he came
to himself a little, he observed all the faithful fleeing out of the
church; the priest had left the altar. Julien began to walk away
quite slowly behind a small cluster of women who were making
their way out, screaming and shouting. A woman trying to get
away faster than the others pushed him roughly, and he fell
down. His feet had got caught in a chair knocked over by the
crowd; as he was getting up, he felt himself grasped round the
neck; it was a police officer in full uniform arresting him.
Julien made an automatic gesture to reach for his little pistols,
but a second officer was grabbing hold of him by the arms.

He was led away to the prison. They went into a room, he
was handcuffed and left alone; the door was shut on him with
two turns of the key; all this was carried out very fast, and he
responded with indifference.

'Fancy that, it's all over,' he said out loud when he came
back to this senses... 'Yes, in a fortnight's time the guillotine...
or killing myself between now and then.'

His reasoning did not go beyond this; his head felt as if it
were being gripped with great force. He looked to see if anyone
was holding him. After a few moments he fell into a deep
sleep.

Mme de Rênal was not mortally wounded. The first bullet
had pierced her hat; as she was turning round, the second shot
had been fired. The bullet had struck her on the shoulder,
and, amazingly enough, had rebounded off the shoulder-blade,
fracturing it nevertheless, and had hit a gothic pillar, chipping
a huge piece of stone off it.

When, after a long and painful session dressing the wound,
the surgeon, a grave man, told Mme de Rênal: 'I can vouch for

your life as surely as I can for my own', she was deeply distressed.

For a long while now she had sincerely wished for death. Her letter to M. de La Mole, which she had been forced to write by her present confessor, had been the final blow for a creature weakened by such relentless misery. The source of her misery was Julien's absence; her name for it was *remorse*. Her confessor, a fervent and virtuous young priest newly arrived from Dijon, was not taken in.

To die like this, but not by my own hand, is *not* a sin, Mme de Rênal reflected. God will perhaps forgive me for rejoicing at my death. She did not dare add: and dying at Julien's hand is the summit of bliss.

As soon as she was rid of the presence of the surgeon and all her friends who had flocked to see her, she summoned Elisa her maid.

'The gaoler', she told her, blushing deeply, 'is a cruel man. He will no doubt ill-treat him, thinking he is doing me a favour... I can't bear the thought of it. Couldn't you go to the gaoler, as if on your own initiative, and give him this little parcel containing a few louis? You can tell him that it's against the principles of religion for him to ill-treat him... The main thing is that he mustn't go round talking about this money he's been sent.'

The incident we have just related was responsible for the humane treatment Julien received at the hands of the town gaoler in Verrières; it was still the same M. Noiroud, that perfect ministry official, whom we observed in such a fine state of fright at the appearance of M. Appert.

A judge presented himself at the prison.

'I caused death with premeditation,' Julien told him; 'I bought the pistols from —— the gunsmith, and had him load them. Article 1342 of the Penal Code* is explicit; I deserve death, and I am ready for it.'

Astonished at the tenor of this reply, the judge made a point of questioning the accused repeatedly, to get him to *trip himself up* in his answers.

'But don't you see', Julien said to him with a smile, 'that I am declaring myself to be as guilty as you could wish? Come now, sir, you shall not miss the prey you are stalking. You shall have the pleasure of sentencing me. Please spare me your presence.'

There is one tedious duty left for me to carry out, Julien thought: I must write to Mlle de La Mole.

'I have taken my revenge,' he wrote to her:

Unfortunately, my name will appear in the press, and I shall not be able to escape from this world incognito. I shall die in two months' time. Vengeance was appalling, as is the pain of being separated from you. From this moment on, I forbid myself to write or utter your name. You must never speak of me, even to my son: silence is the only way to honour me. For the ordinary run of mortals, I shall be a common murderer... Allow me to speak the truth at this solemn, final moment: you will forget me. This great catastrophe, which I advise you never to speak of to any living soul, will have exhausted for several years to come all the romantic and over-adventurous yearnings I observed in your character. You were made to live with the heroes of the Middle Ages; you must show their strength of character. Let the impending event take place in secret without compromising you. You will assume a false name and confide in no one. If you are in dire need of a friend's help, I bequeath you Father Pirard.

Do not speak to anyone else, especially not people of your class: the de Luz's, the Caylus's of this world.

A year after my death, please marry M. de Croisenois; I entreat you, I order you to as your husband. Do not write to me, I should not answer you. Far less evil than Iago, so it seems to me, I shall none the less echo his words: *From this time forth I never will speak word.**

I shall not be observed to speak or write further; you will have had my last words together with my last acts of adoration.

J. S.

It was after sending off this letter that Julien, somewhat restored to his senses, was for the first time extremely unhappy. Each one of the hopes nurtured by his ambition had to be successively plucked from his heart by the solemn words: I am going to die. Death in itself was not *horrendous* in his eyes. His whole life had been nothing but a lengthy preparation for misfortune, and he had not omitted to consider the one which passes for the greatest of them all.

Just imagine! he said to himself: if in sixty days' time I had to fight a duel with a man of great skill at arms, would I be so feeble as to think about it constantly, and with terror in my soul?

He spent more than an hour trying to study himself thoroughly in his new light.

When he had seen clearly into the depths of his soul, and the truth appeared before his eyes as distinctly as one of the pillars of his prison, he turned his thoughts to remorse.

Why should I feel any? I was atrociously wronged; I committed murder, I deserve death, but that's all there is to it. I'm going to die after settling my account with the human race. I'm not leaving any unfulfilled obligations behind me, I don't owe anything to anyone; the only shameful feature of my death is the instrument of it: that alone; it's true, is amply sufficient to shame me in the eyes of the bourgeois citizens of Verrières; but from an intellectual point of view, what could be more despicable! One means remains open to me to win esteem in their eyes: flinging gold coins to the people as I walk to the scaffold. Associated with the idea of *gold*, I shall remain a resplendent memory for them.

After following this line of reasoning, which a minute later struck him as self-evident, Julien said to himself: I have nothing left to do on earth, and he fell into a deep sleep.

At about nine o'clock in the evening the gaoler woke him up by bringing him supper.

'What are they saying in Verrières?'

'Monsieur Julien, the oath I swore before the crucifix at the crown courthouse, the day I was invested with my office, obliges me to keep silence.'

He said nothing, but went on standing there. The sight of this vulgar hypocrisy amused Julien. I must make him wait a good long time, he thought, for the five francs he wants for selling me his conscience.

When the gaoler saw the meal coming to an end with no attempt being made to win him over:

'The friendship I feel for you, Monsieur Julien,' he said with a gentle, contrived expression, 'obliges me to speak; though they say it's against the interests of justice, because it may help you prepare your defence... Monsieur Julien, who is good at heart, will be very glad to learn from me that Mme de Rênal is getting better.'

'What! isn't she dead!' Julien exclaimed, quite beside himself.

'What! you knew nothing about it!' said the gaoler with a dumbfounded expression which soon became one of happy greed. 'It'll be only right and proper for Sir to give something to the surgeon who, according to the law and to justice, shouldn't have spoken. But to please Sir, I went to his house, and he told me everything...'

'Yes, yes, so the wound isn't mortal,' Julien said impatiently, 'd'you vouch for it with your life, you wretch?'

The gaoler, a giant six foot high, took fright and retreated towards the door. Julien saw that he was going about it the wrong way to get at the truth, he sat down again and tossed M. Noiroud a gold napoléon.

As Julien gradually became convinced by the man's story that Mme de Rênal's wound was not mortal, he felt himself giving way to tears.

'Leave the room!' he said brusquely.

The gaoler obeyed. As soon as the door was shut: 'Oh God! she isn't dead!' Julien exclaimed; and he fell on his knees in floods of tears.

In that solemn moment, he was a believer. What do priests and their hypocrisies matter? Can they in any way detract from the truth and the sublimeness of the idea of God?

Only then did Julien begin to repent the crime he had committed. By a coincidence which saved him from despair, that moment had also brought an end at last to the state of physical tension and near madness in which he had been engulfed since leaving Paris for Verrières.

His tears flowed from a generous source; he was in no doubt about the conviction awaiting him.

So she will live! he said to himself... She will live to forgive and to love me...

Very late the next morning when the gaoler woke him up:

'That must be a really stout heart you've got there, Monsieur Julien,' the man said to him. 'I came in twice and didn't want to wake you. Here are two bottles of excellent wine sent you by M. Maslon our priest.'

'Maslon? is that rogue still here?' Julien asked.

'Yes, sir,' the gaoler replied lowering his voice, 'but don't talk so loud, it could turn out badly for you.'

Julien laughed heartily.

'At the stage I've reached, good fellow, you're the only one who could harm me if you stopped being kind and humane... You will be well paid,' Julien said, interrupting himself and resuming his imperious manner. This manner was instantly justified by the gift of a coin.

M. Noiroud again recounted—in the greatest detail, what's more—everything he had found out about Mme de Rênal; but he did not mention Mlle Elisa's visit.

The man was base and servile in the extreme. An idea flashed across Julien's mind: This hideous giant of a fellow can only earn three or four hundred francs, for his prison doesn't get much custom; I can guarantee him ten thousand francs if he's willing to escape to Switzerland with me... The difficulty will be to persuade him of my good faith. The idea of the lengthy discussion he would have to have with such a vile creature filled Julien with disgust, and he turned his thoughts elsewhere.

By evening the moment had passed. A post-chaise came to fetch him at midnight. He was thoroughly satisfied with the police officers who accompanied him on his journey. The next morning, when he arrived at the prison in Besançon, the authorities were good enough to house him in the upper storey of a gothic keep. He judged the architecture to date from the beginning of the fourteenth century; he admired its gracefulness and striking elegance. Through a narrow gap between two walls on the far side of a long courtyard, a magnificent view could be glimpsed.

On the following day he was formally interrogated, after which he was left in peace for several days. His mind was at rest. Everything seemed quite straightforward to him in his case: I intended to kill, so I must be killed.

His thoughts did not pursue this line of reasoning any further. The trial, the irksome necessity of appearing in public, his defence—he considered all these as minor inconveniences, tedious ceremonies that it would be time enough to think about on the day itself. Nor did the moment of death give him greater pause: I'll think about it after the trial. Life was not in the least boring for him, he considered everything in a new light. He had no ambition left. He only thought occasionally about Mlle de La Mole. His remorse preoccupied him a good deal, and often confronted him with the image of Mme de Rênal, especially in the night-time stillness that was only broken, in this high keep, by the cry of the white-tailed eagle!

He gave thanks to heaven that he hadn't wounded her to death. It's an astonishing thing! he said to himself, I thought that by writing that letter to M. de La Mole she had destroyed my future happiness for ever, and less than a fortnight from the date of that letter I'm no longer concerned about all the things that preoccupied me then... An income of two or three thousand pounds to live quietly in a mountainous spot like Vergy... I was happy then... I didn't know how happy I was!

At other moments he leaped up from his chair. If I'd wounded Mme de Rênal to death, I would have killed myself... I need this certainty in order not to find myself repugnant.

To kill myself... that is the great question, he reflected. These judges, who are so formalistic, so dogged in their pursuit of the poor accused, who would have the best of citizens hanged in order to fasten a medal to their coats... I should escape from their power, from their insults in bad French,* which the local newspaper will call eloquence.

I may live for another five or six weeks, give or take a bit... Kill myself! most certainly not, he said to himself a few days later, Napoleon went on living...

Besides, I'm finding life enjoyable; this place is quiet; I don't have any tedious visitors, he added laughing, and he began to make a note of the books he wanted to have sent from Paris.

CHAPTER 37

A keep

The tomb of a friend
STERNE*

HE heard a loud noise in the corridor; it was not a time when people came up to his prison; the white-tailed eagle flew off with a cry, the door opened and the venerable Father Chélan, trembling all over and leaning on a stick, flung himself into his arms.

'Ah! God Almighty! is this possible, my child... Monster! I should say.'

And the kind old man was unable to utter another word. Julien was afraid he would collapse. He was obliged to walk him over to a chair. The hand of time had fallen heavily on this once energetic man. He struck Julien as no more than a shadow of his former self.

When he had got his breath back: 'It was only the day before yesterday that I got your letter from Strasburg with your five hundred francs for the poor of Verrières; it was delivered to me in the mountains at Liveru where I'm living in retirement with my nephew Jean. Yesterday I learned of the catastrophe... Oh heavens! is it possible!' and the old man no longer wept, his face looked utterly vacant, and he added mechanically: 'You'll need your five hundred francs, I've brought them back for you.'

'I need to see you, Father!' Julien exclaimed, very touched. 'I've got money to spare.'

But he was unable to elicit any coherent response from him after that. Now and again M. Chélan shed a few tears which trickled silently down his cheeks; then he looked at Julien, and seemed somehow dazed to see him take hold of his hands and raise them to his lips. This countenance that had been so full of life before, and had so energetically portrayed the noblest of feelings could not now shake off a look of total apathy. A peasant of some description soon came to fetch the old man.

'He mustn't be over-tired,' he said to Julien, who gathered that this was the nephew. This apparition left Julien plunged in cruel suffering which kept tears at bay. Everything seemed irreparably gloomy to him; his heart felt like ice in his chest.

This was the cruellest moment he had experienced since the crime. He had just seen death in all its hideousness. All illusions of spiritual grandeur and generosity had melted away like clouds before a storm.

This terrible state lasted several hours. Someone who has been psychologically poisoned needs physical remedies and champagne. Julien would have considered himself a coward for resorting to them. Towards the end of a horrendous day when he did nothing but pace up and down his narrow tower: I'm utterly mad! he exclaimed. Only if I had to die like everyone else should the sight of this poor old man have plunged me into such terrible gloom; but a quick death in the prime of life is precisely a guarantee against this sorry decrepitude.

Whatever arguments he put to himself, Julien found himself feeling emotional, as if he were a coward, and he was consequently upset by this visit.

There was nothing rugged and grandiose left in him, no more Roman virtue; death appeared as way above him now, and as something less easy.

This shall be my thermometer, he told himself. Tonight I'm ten degrees below the courage that will take me on a level path to the guillotine. I had it this morning, that sort of courage. Anyway, what does it matter! As long as it returns to me at the crucial moment. This thermometer idea amused him, and ended up by taking his mind off his plight.

On waking the next morning he was ashamed of the previous day. My happiness, my peace of mind are at stake. He almost resolved to write to the public prosecutor to request that no one be admitted to see him. What about Fouqué? he thought. If he takes it upon himself to come to Besançon, just think how distressed he'd be!

It was some two months now since he had last thought about Fouqué. I was a real fool at Strasburg, my thoughts didn't go beyond the collar of my suit. He was greatly preoccupied by the memory of Fouqué, and it left him feeling more tender. He paced up and down in agitation. Here I am now well and truly twenty degrees below the death level... If this feebleness increases, I'll be better off killing myself. What a delight for the Father Maslons and the Valenods if I die like a menial wretch!

Fouqué came; this unpretentious, kind man was beside himself with grief. His only idea when he had one was to sell all his possessions to bribe the gaoler and engineer Julien's escape. He talked to him at length of M. de Lavalette's escape.*

'You're distressing me,' Julien said to him; 'M. de Lavalette was innocent, whereas I'm guilty. Without meaning to, you're rubbing in the difference...

'But is it true! Honestly? You'd sell all your possessions?' Julien asked, suddenly becoming observant and suspicious again.

Fouqué was delighted to see his friend responding at last to his great idea, and he gave him a lengthy account, down to the last hundred francs, of what he would make from each one of his holdings.

What a sublime effort from a country landowner. Think what he's sacrificing for me now—all those economies, all those stingy little half-measures that made me squirm so much when I observed him engaged in them! One of those fine young men I saw at the Hôtel de La Mole, who all read *René*,* wouldn't have any of these absurd characteristics; but apart from the ones who are very young, and whose wealth is inherited, what's more, so they don't know the value of money, which of these fine Parisians would be capable of a sacrifice like this?

All Fouqué's bad grammar,* all his unrefined gestures vanished: Julien flung himself into his arms. Never had the provinces, when compared with Paris, received a finer accolade. Fouqué, delighted by the momentary enthusiasm he saw in his friend's eyes, took it for consent to make a getaway.

This vision of the *sublime* restored to Julien all the strength Father Chélan's sudden appearance had robbed him of. He was still very young; but in my opinion he was a fine specimen. Instead of going from tenderness to cunning, like most men, age would have given him a kindly disposition that is easily moved; he would have grown out of his exaggerated mistrustfulness... But what's the use of these idle predictions?

The interrogations became more frequent despite Julien's efforts: all his answers tended in the direction of curtailing the case: 'I have committed murder, or at any rate I intended to inflict death, and it was premeditated, too,' he repeated every day. But the judge was a stickler for form above all else. Julien's declarations did nothing to curtail the interrogations; the judge felt wounded in his self-esteem. Julien did not discover that there had been a move to transfer him to a dreadful cell, and that it was thanks to Fouqué's intervention that he was allowed to remain in his nice room a hundred and eighty steps up the tower.

The Abbé de Frilair was one of the important people who ordered their stocks of firewood from Fouqué. The good merchant managed to gain an entry to the all-powerful vicar-general. To his unutterable delight, M. de Frilair announced to him that he had been touched by Julien's good qualities and the services he had performed at the seminary in the past, and that he was planning to speak favourably to the judges on his behalf. Fouqué glimpsed a hope of saving his friend, and on his departure, prostrating himself before the vicar-general, he begged him to use a sum of ten louis for saying Masses to implore the acquittal of the accused.

Fouqué was making a singular error of judgement. M. de Frilair was in no way a Valenod. He refused, and even tried to insinuate to the good peasant that he would do better to keep his money. Seeing that it was impossible to make himself clear without being imprudent, he advised him to give away this sum in alms, for the poor prisoners who did literally lack everything.

This Julien is a strange creature, his action is inexplicable, thought M. de Frilair, and nothing should be so where I am concerned... Perhaps it will be possible to make a martyr of him... In any event, I'll get to the bottom of this affair, and I may even find an opportunity of giving a good fright to that Mme de Rênal who has no respect for us, and in fact loathes me... Perhaps I'll discover some way in all this of bringing about a sensational reconciliation with M. de La Mole, who has a soft spot for this little seminarist.

The settlement of the lawsuit had been signed a few weeks earlier, and the Abbé Pirard had left Besançon again, after making a point of mentioning Julien's mysterious birth, on the very day when the wretch was murdering Mme de Rênal in the church at Verrières.

Julien saw only one unpleasant event now between him and death: a visit from his father. He consulted Fouqué about writing to the public prosecutor to get a dispensation from all visits. Such repugnance at the thought of seeing your own father, and at a time like this too, profoundly shocked the timber merchant's honest, bourgeois heart.

It gave him a sudden insight into why so many people felt passionate hatred for his friend. Out of respect for misfortune he concealed his feelings on the matter.

'In any event', he answered coldly, 'this privacy order wouldn't apply in the case of your father.'

CHAPTER 38

A powerful man

> But there is so much mystery in her ways and so
> much elegance in her figure! Who can she be?
> SCHILLER

THE doors of the keep opened very early the next morning. Julien was woken with a start.

Oh Lord! he thought, here comes my father. What an unpleasant scene!

At that same moment a woman in peasant's clothes flung herself into his arms. He recognized her with difficulty: it was Mlle de La Mole.

'You beast, I only found out from your letter where you were. Until I actually got to Verrières I was completely in the dark about what *you* call your crime, but is really a noble act of revenge which shows what a lofty heart you have beating here inside your chest...'

In spite of his prejudices against Mlle de La Mole, which in point of fact he did not admit openly to himself, Julien found her very attractive. How could he fail to see in her whole way of behaving and talking a nobility and disinterestedness beyond anything a petty and vulgar spirit could have risen to? Once more it was a queen he loved, and after a brief pause, he said to her with a rare nobility of diction and thought:

'The future was very vividly mapped out before my eyes. After my death I had you getting married again to M. de Croisenois, who would have accepted a widow. The noble but rather romantic nature of this charming widow would have been taken by surprise and won over to the cult of humdrum prudence by a striking and tragic event of deep significance for her, and she would have deigned to appreciate the very real qualities of the young marquis. You would have resigned yourself to being happy the way other people are: esteem, wealth, high rank... But, dear Mathilde, if anyone gets wind of your arrival in Besançon, it will be a mortal blow for M. de

La Mole, and that's something I shall never forgive myself. I've caused him so much grief already! The academician will say that he nurtured a serpent in his bosom.'

'I must admit I was hardly expecting so much cold reasoning, so much concern for the future,' said Mlle de La Mole, somewhat annoyed. 'My maid, who's almost as cautious as you are, took out a passport for herself, and I came post-haste under the name of Mme Michelet.'

'And was it as easy as that for Mme Michelet to reach me?'

'Ah! you're still the same superior man I singled out! First of all I offered a hundred francs to a judge's secretary who claimed it was impossible for me to gain entry into this keep. But once he had the money, this honest fellow kept me waiting, raised objections—I thought he had it in mind to rob me...' She paused.

'Well?' said Julien.

'Don't get angry, Julien dearest,' she said kissing him, 'I was obliged to reveal my name to the secretary who took me for a working girl from Paris who was in love with the handsome Julien... Honestly, those were his very words. I swore to him that I was your wife, and I shall get a permit to see you every day.'

This is total madness, Julien thought, I couldn't prevent it. After all, M. de La Mole is such a great nobleman that public opinion will find a way of excusing the young colonel who marries this charming widow. My imminent death will cover it all up. And he yielded rapturously to Mathilde's love; it was madness, it was uplifting, it was something quite unique. She offered in all seriousness to kill herself with him.

After this first flood of passion, when she had feasted her eyes on Julien to her heart's content, she was suddenly seized with burning curiosity. She scrutinized her lover and found him far more impressive than she had imagined. Boniface de La Mole seemed to her to have been resurrected, only more heroic.

Mathilde went to see the foremost barristers in the region, and insulted them by offering them gold too crudely; but they accepted in the end.

She soon came to the view that where shady matters of great

import were concerned, everything in Besançon depended on
the Abbé de Frilair.

Under the obscure name of Mme Michelet, she found unsur-
mountable difficulties at first in getting through to the all-
powerful Congregationist.* But rumour spread through the
town of the beauty of a young milliner who was madly in love,
and had come down from Paris to Besançon to console the
young priest Julien Sorel.

Mathilde hurried about alone on foot in the streets of
Besançon; she hoped not to be recognized. In any event, she
thought it would do no harm to her cause to make a great
impression on the local populace. In her madness she imagined
starting up a popular uprising to rescue Julien on the way to
the scaffold. Mlle de La Mole fancied she was wearing simple
attire appropriate for a grieving woman; in fact it was such as
to catch everyone's eye.

She had become the object of everyone's attention in Besançon when, after a week of petitioning, she obtained an audience
with M. de Frilair.

For all her courage, she associated influential Congregationists so strongly with the idea of inveterate and circumspect
wickedness that she trembled as she rang the door of the
bishop's palace. She was scarcely capable of walking when she
had to go up the staircase leading to the first vicar-general's
apartment. The solitude of the episcopal palace sent a chill
through her spine. What if I sit down on a chair, and the chair
grabs me by the arms: I'll be gone for good. Who will my maid
be able to turn to for news of me? The captain of the
gendarmerie won't lift a finger... I'm all alone in this big town!

As soon as she glanced into the apartment, Mlle de La Mole
felt reassured. First of all, the door had been opened for her
by a footman in a most elegant livery. The room where she
was asked to wait boasted a refined and delicate luxury having
nothing in common with vulgar magnificence, and in Paris at
any rate only to be found in the best houses. No sooner did
she catch sight of M. de Frilair coming over to her with a look
of smooth affability on his face then all her fantasies about a
horrendous crime vanished. She did not even detect on his
handsome face any trace of that energetic and somewhat

uncouth virtue that Parisian society finds so antipathetic. The half-smile flickering over the features of the priest whose power in Besançon was absolute heralded a man of refinement, a learned prelate, a skilled administrator. Mathilde felt she might have been in Paris.

It took M. de Frilair but few moments to get Mathilde to confess that she was the daughter of his powerful adversary the Marquis de la Mole.

'I am indeed not Mme Michelet,' she said, reverting fully to her superior manner, 'and this revelation costs me very little, since I have come to consult you, sir, about the possibility of procuring the escape of M. de La Vernaye. In the first place he's only guilty of an act of momentary folly; the woman he shot is making a good recovery. Secondly, to bribe the lower orders, I can hand over fifty thousand francs right away, and pledge myself to produce double that amount. Finally, my gratitude and that of my family will leave nothing undone to repay someone who has saved M. de la Vernaye.'

M. de Frilair seemed astonished at this name. Mathilde showed him several letters from the Ministry of War addressed to M. Julien Sorel de la Vernaye.

'As you see, sir, my father had assumed responsibility for his fortune. I married him in secret, and my father wished him to be a high-ranking officer before announcing a marriage that is somewhat unusual for a La Mole.'

Mathilde noticed that M. de Frilair's expression of kindness and gentle gaiety faded rapidly as he made important discoveries. A look of cunning mingled with profound insincerity came over his face.

The priest was having doubts; he slowly reread the official documents.

What advantage can I derive from these strange confessions? he wondered. Here I am all of a sudden on intimate terms with a friend of the famous Maréchale de Fervaques, the all-powerful niece of Monsignor the Bishop of ——,* through whose offices one becomes a bishop in France. What I saw as belonging to the remote future is unexpectedly in the offing. This opportunity may bring me to the culmination of all my desires.

At first Mathilde was alarmed by the sudden change that had come over the features of this all-powerful man with whom she found herself alone in a remote apartment. But what of it! she said to herself in a little while, wouldn't the worst outcome have been to make no impression at all on the cold egoism of a priest sated with power and pleasure?

Dazzled by the rapid route to a bishopric that unexpectedly opened up before his eyes, and astonished at Mathilde's talents, M. de Frilair dropped his guard for a moment. Mlle de La Mole almost had him at her feet, ambitious and keen to the point of trembling with nerves.

Everything is becoming clear, she thought, nothing will be impossible here for a friend of Mme de Fervaques. In spite of a feeling of jealousy that was still very painful, she summoned up the courage to explain that Julien was a close friend of the maréchale's, and encountered Monsignor the Bishop of —— almost daily at her house.

'If a list of thirty-six jurors were to be drawn by lot four or five times in succession from among the worthy inhabitants of this département,' said the vicar-general with a steely glint of ambition in his eyes and deliberate emphasis on each word, 'I should consider myself most unlucky if in each list I didn't get nine or ten friends, and the most intelligent of the bunch too. I should almost always have a majority, indeed more than that, even for a verdict of guilty; so you see, mademoiselle, it will be an easy matter for me to obtain an acquittal...'

The priest broke off suddenly, as if amazed at the sound of his own voice; he was confiding things that are never said to the profane.

But it was his turn to strike Mathilde speechless when he informed her that what most astonished and intrigued Besançon society about Julien's strange adventure was that he had once inspired a great passion in Mme de Rênal, and had shared it for a considerable while. M. de Frilair easily perceived the deep turmoil produced by his story.

I've got my revenge! he thought. Here at last is a way of manipulating this most determined little lady; I was in fear and trembling of failure. Her aristocratic and headstrong manner made him doubly sensitive to the rare beauty he saw almost pleading before him. He resumed all his self-control and did not hesitate to turn the knife in her wounded heart.

'I shouldn't be surprised in the end', he told her casually, 'if we were to learn that jealousy caused M. Sorel to fire two shots at this woman he once loved so much. She is far from lacking in charms, and she had recently been seeing a great deal of a certain Abbé Marquinot from Dijon, a sort of Jansenist—devoid of morals, as they all are.'

M. de Frilair took voluptuous pleasure in inflicting slow torture on the heart of this pretty girl whose weak point he had unexpectedly discovered.

'Why', he said, fixing his burning eyes on Mathilde, 'should M. Sorel have chosen the church, if not because precisely at that moment his rival was celebrating Mass there? Everyone credits your fortunate protégé with limitless intelligence, exceeded only by his caution. What could have been simpler than to have hidden in M. de Rênal's gardens which he knows so well? There, with virtual certainty of not being seen, caught or suspected, he could have killed the woman he was jealous of.'

This seemingly sound argument finally succeeded in causing Mathilde to lose all control of herself. Her haughty spirit, imbued through and through, nevertheless, with all the arid caution which is taken in high society as a faithful reflection of the human heart, was constitutionally incapable of understanding in a flash the pleasure that comes from scorning all caution—an experience that can be so intense for a passionate spirit. Among the upper classes of Parisian society where Mathilde had grown up, passion only very rarely manages to divest itself of caution, and people choose the fifth floor when they decide to fling themselves out of the window.

The Abbé de Frilair was at last sure of his hold over Mathilde. He intimated to her (lying no doubt) that he could answer fully for the public ministry in charge of bringing the prosecution against Julien.

After the thirty-six jurors had been drawn by lot for the assizes, he would make a direct, personal approach to at least thirty of their number.

If Mathilde had not seemed so attractive to M. de Frilair, he would not have spoken so openly to her until the fifth or sixth interview.

CHAPTER 39

Politicking

March 31, 1676. He that endeavoured to kil his
sister in our house, had before kild a man, & it had
cost his father 500 escus to get him off, by their
secret distribution gaining the favour of the
Counsellors.

LOCKE, *Travels in France**

ON leaving the bishop's palace, Mathilde did not hesitate to
send a missive to Mme de Fervaques; fear of compromising
herself did not hold her back for a single second. She entreated
her rival to procure a letter for M. de Frilair, written from
start to finish in the hand of Monsignor the Bishop of ——.
She went so far as to beseech her to come with all speed in
person to Besançon. This was a heroic action on the part of a
jealous and proud spirit.

Acting on Fouqué's advice, she had been prudent enough
not to tell Julien about the steps she was taking. Her presence
was disturbing enough for him as it was. More of a gentleman
now that death was near than he had been in his lifetime, he
felt remorse not only about M. de La Mole, but also for
Mathilde.

How dreadful! he said to himself, when I'm with her I find
my mind wandering at times, and even getting bored. She's
sacrificing her reputation for me, and this is how I reward
her! So does this mean I'm a swine? The question would
scarcely have bothered him when he was ambitious; at that
time the only thing he regarded as shameful was not achieving
success.

His moral unease in Mathilde's company was all the more
pronounced as he inspired in her at that moment the most
outlandish and demented passion. She talked of nothing else
but the strange sacrifices she wanted to make to save him.

Uplifted by a sentiment she was proud of, and one which
quite got the better of her arrogance, she would have liked to
let no moment of her life go by without filling it with some

remarkable act. The strangest projects entailing great risk to herself filled her long conversations with Julien. The gaolers, well paid, let her reign supreme in the prison. Mathilde's ideas did not stop at the sacrifice of her own reputation; she didn't care if she proclaimed her condition to the whole of society. Flinging herself on her knees in front of the king's galloping horses to beg for Julien's reprieve, attracting the monarch's attention at the repeated risk of being trampled to death, was one of the lesser flights of fancy of this exalted and fearless imagination. With the aid of her friends in the king's service, she was certain to be allowed into the reserved areas in the park at Saint-Cloud.

Julien felt himself most unworthy of such devotion; he was in all honesty tired of heroism. It would have taken tenderness of a straightforward, innocent, almost timid variety to have touched him, whereas on the contrary the notion of an audience—of *other people*—was indispensable to Mathilde's haughty spirit.

In the midst of all her anguish, of all her fears for the life of this lover whom she had no desire to survive, she felt a secret need to amaze the public by the excess of her love and the sublime character of her exploits.

Julien was getting irritated at not finding himself moved by all this heroism. Just think what would have happened if he had found out about all the crazy ideas with which Mathilde assailed the mind of the devoted but eminently reasonable and essentially limited Fouqué!

Fouqué did not quite know what to criticize in Mathilde's devotion; for he would himself have sacrificed the whole of his fortune and exposed his life to the greatest of risks to save Julien. He was flabbergasted at the amount of gold that Mathilde flung away. For the first few days, the sums she spent like this made a deep impression on Fouqué, who regarded money with all the veneration of a provincial.

In the end he found out that Mlle de La Mole's plans frequently altered, and to his great relief he hit upon an epithet to denigrate this character he found so tiring: she was *changeable*. From this qualification to the term *unsound*—the greatest anathema in the provinces—there is but one small step.

It's most odd, Julien said to himself one day as Mathilde was leaving his prison, that such an ardent passion, and one directed at me, should leave me so cold! And I adored her two months ago! I had indeed read that the approach of death detaches you from everything; but it's awful to feel ungrateful and not to be able to do anything about it. Does it mean I'm an egoist?' He subjected himself to the most humiliating reproaches on this score.

Ambition had died in his heart, and another passion had risen from its ashes there; he called it remorse at having murdered Mme de Rênal.

In actual fact, he was desperately in love with her. He felt an extraordinary happiness when, left entirely alone with no fear of interruption, he could give himself over completely to the memory of the happy days he had spent long ago in Verrières or at Vergy. The most minor incidents from those times that had flown by too fast had an irresistible freshness and charm for him. He never thought of his successes in Paris; they made him feel uncomfortable.

The drift of Julien's emotions, which grew rapidly more marked, was half-perceived by Mathilde in her jealousy. She could see very clearly that she had to fight his love of solitude. Sometimes in a voice of terror she uttered the name of Mme de Rênal. She saw Julien tremble. Her passion from then on knew no limits or measure.

If he dies, I die after him, she said to herself with all possible sincerity. What would the Paris salons say on seeing a girl of my rank carry to such a point her adoration of a lover destined to die? To find sentiments like this, you have to go back to the heroic age; it was passions of this sort that made hearts throb in the century of Charles IX and Henri III.

In the midst of the most intense moments of rapture, when she was clasping Julien's head to her heart: Oh how dreadful! she said to herself in horror, can this lovely head be destined to roll! Well, she added, burning with a heroism not devoid of happiness, these lips of mine, now pressed to these pretty locks, will be stone cold less than twenty-four hours afterwards.

The memories of these moments of heroism and appalling

ecstasy held her in an invincible grip. The idea of suicide, so absorbing in itself, and hitherto so remote from this haughty spirit, infiltrated it and soon reigned with absolute power. No, the blood of my ancestors hasn't come down to me lukewarm, Mathilde said to herself with pride.

'I have a favour to ask you,' her lover said to her one day: 'put your child out to nurse in Verrières, and Mme de Rênal will keep an eye on the nurse.'

'What you are saying there is very hard...' And Mathilde turned pale.

'So it is, and I apologize a thousand times, my love,' exclaimed Julien coming out of his daydream and clasping her in his arms.

After drying her tears, he returned to his idea, but more skilfully. He had steered the conversation into melancholy philosophizing. He was talking of a future that was shortly to be cut off for him.

'One has to admit, my dearest, that passions are an accident of life, but this accident only occurs with superior spirits... The death of my son would really be a blessing for your family's pride, this is what subordinates will sense. Negligence will be the lot of this child of misfortune and shame... I hope that at a time I don't wish to specify, but have the courage to perceive, you will obey my last requests: you will marry the Marquis de Croisenois.'

'What! Dishonoured!'

'Dishonour won't get a hold on a name like yours. You'll be a widow, a madman's widow, that's all. I'll go further: not having money as its motive, my crime will not entail any dishonour. Perhaps by that time some enlightened legislator will have wrested from the prejudices of his contemporaries the suppression of the death penalty.* Some friendly voice will then say, to quote an example: "Look, Mlle de La Mole's first husband was a madman, but not a wicked man or a criminal. It was absurd to cut off his head..." And then my memory won't be infamous; at least not after a while. Your position in society, your fortune and, allow me to say so, your genius, will enable M. de Croisenois, once he's your husband, to play a role he couldn't aspire to on his own. He only possesses birth and bravery, and these qualities by themselves, which produced a man of accomplishment in 1729, are an anachronism a century later, and only give rise to pretensions. You need other things besides to become a leader of the youth of France.

'You will put your resolute and enterprising character to the service of the political party in which you choose to launch your husband. You will be able to succeed the Chevreuses and the Longuevilles of the Fronde*... But by then, my dear, the celestial fire which blazes within you at this moment will have died down a bit.

'Allow me to say this to you,' he added after a good many other preparatory remarks, 'in fifteen years' time you will regard the love you once felt for me as an excusable moment of folly, but as folly nevertheless...'

All of a sudden he broke off and became wistful. He found himself once again contemplating a thought that was utterly shocking in regard to Mathilde: in fifteen years' time Mme de Rênal will adore my son, and you will have forgotten him.

CHAPTER 40

Tranquillity

It is because I was mad then that today I am wise. O
philosopher, you who take an instantaneous view
of things, how short are your perspectives! Your
eye is not designed to follow the underground
workings of passions.

W. GOETHE

THIS conversation was interrupted by a formal interrogation
followed by a meeting with the counsel for the defence.

These moments were the only wholly disagreeable ones in a
life free of care and filled with tender dreaming.

'It's a case of murder, and murder with premeditation,'
Julien said to both the magistrate and the barrister. 'I'm
extremely sorry about it, gentlemen,' he added with a smile,
'but this reduces your task to a very small matter.'

When it comes down to it, Julien reflected when he had
managed to get rid of these two individuals, I must be brave,
and braver it seems than these two men. They regard this duel,
with its fatal outcome, as the ultimate in misfortune, as the
king of terrors,* and I shall only think seriously about it on the
day itself.

It's because I've experienced a greater misfortune, Julien
continued his inner philosophizing. I suffered in an altogether
different way during my first journey to Strasburg, when I
thought Mathilde had abandoned me... And to think that I so
passionately desired the perfect intimacy that leaves me so cold
today!... In fact I'm happier alone than when this beautiful
girl shares my solitude...

The barrister, a man guided by rules and formalities,
thought he was mad, and believed along with the public that
jealousy was what had made him take up a pistol. One day he
risked hinting to Julien that this allegation, true or false, would
be an excellent basis for the defence. But the accused instantly
became passionate and incisive again.

'If you value your life, sir,' exclaimed Julien, beside himself, 'remember never to utter this abominable lie again.' The cautious barrister feared for a moment that he was going to be murdered.

He was preparing his speech, because the day of decision was rapidly approaching. Besançon and the whole département talked of nothing but this *cause célèbre*. Julien was unaware of this detail; he had requested that no one should ever mention this sort of thing to him.

That day, when Fouqué and Mathilde had wanted to inform him of certain public rumours of a kind, so they thought, to give rise to hope, Julien had cut them short at the very first mention.

'Leave me with my life of the imagination. Your petty pestering, your details of real life, which all upset me to some degree, would drag me down from heaven. Each person dies as best he may; my wish is not to think of death except in my own way. What do I care about *other people*? My ties with *other people* are going to be abruptly severed. For pity's sake, don't talk to me about any of them any more: it's quite enough to see the judge and the barrister.'

In fact, he said to himself, it seems that my destiny is to die dreaming. A nonentity like myself, who is sure to be forgotten in a fortnight's time, would be a real sucker, you have to admit, to get all theatrical...

It's strange all the same that I've only understood the art of enjoying life since seeing the end so close at hand.

He spent these final days walking about on the narrow terrace at the top of the tower, smoking some excellent cigars that Mathilde had had brought over from Holland by courier, and quite unaware that his appearance was awaited every day by all the telescopes in town. His thoughts were in Vergy. He never spoke of Mme de Rênal to Fouqué, but on two or three occasions his friend told him that she was making a rapid recovery, and this comment reverberated in his heart.

While Julien's spirit was almost always wholly in the realm of ideas, Mathilde, concerned with reality as befits an aristocratic temperament, had succeeded in bringing about such a degree of intimacy in the direct correspondence between Mme

de Fervaques and M. de Frilair that by this time the great word *bishopric* had already been uttered.

The venerable prelate in charge of the list of benefices added as a postscript to one of his niece's letters: *This poor fellow Sorel is just a scatterbrain, I hope he will be restored to us.*

At the sight of these lines M. de Frilair went almost wild with delight. He did not doubt he could save Julien.

'Were it not for this Jacobin law* which stipulates that an interminable list of jurors be drawn up, and has no other real purpose than to remove all influence from people of good birth,' he said to Mathilde the day before the thirty-six jurors were to be drawn by lot for the assizes, 'I should have answered for the *verdict*. Didn't I get Father N acquitted...'

It was a pleasure the next day for M. de Frilair to discover among the names that had come out of the urn five Congregationists from Besançon, and among the strangers to the town the names of M. Valenod, M. de Moirod and M. de Cholin. 'I can answer first of all for these eight jurors here,' he told Mathilde. The first five are *machines*. Valenod is my agent, Moirod owes everything to me, and de Cholin is an idiot who's afraid of everything.'

The newspaper broadcast the names of the jurors throughout the département, and Mme de Rênal, to the unutterable horror of her husband, determined to go to Besançon. The most that M. de Rênal could obtain was that she would not leave her bed, so as to avoid the unpleasantness of being called as a witness.

'You do not understand my position,' said the former mayor of Verrières, 'I am now a liberal by *defection*,* as they say; there's no doubting that that rascal Valenod and M. de Frilair will easily obtain from the public prosecutor and the judges everything that can possibly be disagreeable for me.'

Mme de Rênal gave in readily to her husband's orders. If I made an appearance at the assize court, she said to herself, I'd look as if I were seeking vengeance.

Despite all the promises of caution which she had given her confessor and her husband, no sooner had she set foot in Besançon than she wrote in her own hand to each one of the thirty-six jurors:

I shall not appear on the day of the trial, sir, because my presence might be prejudicial to M. Sorel's case. My one desire in the world, and it is passionately held, is that he should be saved. Be in no doubt about it, the appalling idea that on my account an innocent man had been put to death would poison the rest of my life and probably shorten it. How could you condemn him to death while *I* am alive? No, society probably does not have the right to take life, especially not the life of a person like Julien Sorel. Everyone in Verrières has witnessed his moments of derangement. This poor young man has powerful enemies; but, even among his enemies (and how numerous they are!), who would cast any doubt on his admirable talents and his profound learning? This is no ordinary citizen that you are about to judge, sir. For almost eighteen months we all knew him as pious, dutiful and conscientious; but two or three times a year he was seized by fits of melancholy which bordered on derangement. The entire town of Verrières, all our neighbours at Vergy where we spend the summer season, my whole family, and the esteemed sub-prefect himself will bear witness to his exemplary piety; he knows the entire Holy Bible by heart. Would an ungodly person have applied himself for years to learning the holy book? My sons will have the honour of handing you this letter: they are children. Deign to question them, sir; they will supply you in regard to this poor young man with all the details that might still be necessary to convince you of how barbarous it would be to condemn him. Far indeed from avenging me, you would deal me a death blow.

What will his enemies be able to say to counter this fact? The wound that resulted from one of those moments of folly that even my children observed in their tutor is so minor that after less than two months it has allowed me to travel by post horses from Verrières to Besançon. If I learn, sir, that you have even the slightest hesitation about rescuing from the barbarity of the law a person who is so little guilty, I shall rise from my bed, where I am confined solely by my husband's orders, and I shall go and fling myself at your feet.

Declare, sir, that the premeditation is not established, and you will not have to reproach yourself with the blood of an innocent man, etc., etc.

CHAPTER 41
The trial

The country will remember this famous case for a
long time to come. Concern for the accused
reached an extraordinary level: the reason being
that his crime was astonishing and yet not
appalling. Even had it been, this young man was
so handsome! His great destiny, so soon ended,
heightened the sympathy. Will they condemn
him? The women asked the men of their
acquaintance, and they were seen to turn pale as
they waited for the reply.

SAINTE-BEUVE

AT last came the day so dreaded by Mme de Rênal and
Mathilde.

The unaccustomed appearance of the town increased their
terror, and did not fail to shake even Fouqué's stalwart nerves.
The whole province had flocked to Besançon to see this
romantic case tried.

For several days there had been no more room in the inns.
The presiding judge was overwhelmed with requests for tickets
for the assizes; all the ladies of the town wanted to watch the
trial; Julien's portrait was hawked in the streets, etc. etc.

Mathilde was holding in reserve for this supreme moment a
letter written from start to finish in the hand of Monsignor the
Bishop of ——. This prelate, who was the head of the Church
in France and appointed bishops, deigned to ask for Julien's
acquittal. On the eve of the trial, Mathilde took this letter to
the all-powerful vicar-general.

At the end of the meeting, as she broke into tears on taking
her leave: 'I shall answer for the jury's verdict,' M. de Frilair
told her, finally abandoning his diplomatic reserve, and close
to being moved himself. 'Among the twelve individuals
instructed to examine whether your protégé's crime is established, and above all whether there was any premeditation, I
can count on six friends who have my personal interests at

heart, and I have given them to understand that my promotion to a bishopric depends on them. Baron Valenod, whom I have made mayor of Verrières, can answer fully for two of his subordinates, M. de Moirod and M. Cholin. In all truth Fate has given us two most unsound jurors to try this case; but although ultra-liberals, they are faithful to my orders on important occasions, and they have been asked on my behalf to vote with M. Valenod. I have discovered that a sixth juror, an immensely rich manufacturer and a liberal prattler, is secretly after a contract from the Ministry of War, and no doubt he would not wish to displease me. I have had him informed that M. de Valenod has my final word.'

'And what sort of man is this M. Valenod?' asked Mathilde uneasily.

'If you knew him you could have no doubts about a successful outcome. He's a bold, impudent and vulgar talker, made to be a leader of fools. The events of 1814* wrested him from destitution, and I shall make a prefect of him. He's capable of thrashing the other jurors if they won't vote his way.'

Mathilde was somewhat reassured.

Another discussion awaited her in the course of the evening. To avoid prolonging a disagreeable scene which in his view could only have one outcome, Julien was determined not to make a speech.

'My counsel will speak, that's quite sufficient,' he said to Mathilde. 'I'll be held up as a spectacle to all my enemies for long enough as it is. These provincials have been scandalized by the rapid rise to fortune I owe to you, and believe you me, there isn't a single one of them who doesn't wish to see me sentenced, but will feel free to blub like a baby when I'm led off to execution.'

'They wish to see you humiliated, that's only too true,' replied Mathilde, 'but I don't believe them to be cruel. My presence in Besançon and the sight of my grief has aroused the interest of all the women; your handsome face will do the rest. If you say a word in the presence of your judges, the whole of the public gallery will be on your side,' etc. etc.

At nine o'clock the next day, when Julien came down from

his prison to go to the great hall in the law courts, the police had considerable difficulty in pushing aside the enormous crowd thronging the courtyard. Julien had slept well, he was extremely calm, and his only feeling was one of philosophical pity for this crowd of envious souls who, without any cruelty, were going to applaud his death sentence. He was very surprised when, after spending over a quarter of an hour trapped in the midst of the throng, he was obliged to recognize that his presence inspired a feeling of tender pity in the crowd. He did not hear a single unpleasant remark. These provincials are less nasty than I thought, he said to himself.

On entering the courtroom he was struck by the elegance of the architecture. It was in pure gothic style, with a host of pretty little columns carved into the stone with the utmost skill. He imagined himself in England.

But soon his whole attention was taken up by a dozen or even fifteen pretty women filling the three galleries above the judges and the jury, right opposite the dock. On turning round to face the public, he saw that the circular gallery overlooking the amphitheatre was filled with women: most of them were young, and struck him as very pretty; their glistening eyes were full of concern. The crowd in the rest of the courtroom was immense; people were fighting at the doors, and the sentries were unable to impose silence.

When all the eyes that were looking for Julien noticed his presence as he took up his place on the slightly raised bench reserved for the accused, he was greeted by a murmur of astonishment and tender concern.

You wouldn't have thought him more than twenty that day; he was dressed very simply but with perfect elegance; the arrangement of his hair round his forehead was most fetching; Mathilde had insisted on seeing to his appearance herself. Julien's pallor was extreme. He had hardly sat down in the dock before he heard people saying all around him: 'Goodness! how young he is!... But he's only a boy... He looks far nicer than his portrait.'

'Accused,' said the officer sitting on his right, 'can you see those six ladies sitting up in that gallery?' He pointed to a little gallery projecting over the part of the amphitheatre where the jury sit. 'That's the prefect's wife,' the officer went on, 'next to her is the Marquise de M——, she's a good friend to you, I heard her talking to the examining magistrate. Next along is Mme Derville...'

'Mme Derville!' exclaimed Julien, and his brow flushed deeply. On leaving here, he thought, she'll write to Mme de Rênal. He was unaware of Mme de Rênal's arrival in Besançon.

The witnesses were very soon heard. At the first word of the charge read out by the assistant public prosecutor, two of the ladies sitting in the small gallery right opposite Julien burst into tears. You don't find Mme Derville getting emotional like that, Julien thought. He noticed however that her face was very red.

The assistant public prosecutor was indulging in pathos in bad French* on the barbarity of the crime that had been committed; Julien observed that Mme Derville's neighbours looked strongly disapproving. Several members of the jury, apparently known to these ladies, were speaking to them and seemed to be reassuring them. This must be a good sign, Julien thought.

Up until then he had felt himself imbued with unmitigated scorn for all the men present at the trial. The assistant public prosecutor's insipid rhetoric heightened this feeling of disgust. But gradually Julien's emotional coldness vanished in the face of the obvious signs of interest which he aroused.

He was pleased with his counsel's resolute expression. 'No fine words,' he said to him under his breath as he was about to begin speaking.

'All the bombast stolen from Bossuet that was wheeled out to attack you has worked in your favour,' said the barrister. Indeed, he had hardly been speaking for five minutes before almost all the women had their handkerchiefs in their hands. Encouraged by this, the counsel directed some extremely powerful words to the jury. Julien trembled; he felt himself on the verge of tears. Good God! what will my enemies say?

He was about to give in to the emotion overwhelming him, when fortunately for him he caught an insolent glance from Baron de Valenod.

That pompous underling has a glint in his eye, he said to

himself; what a triumph for a base mind like his! If my crime had only had this one result, I ought to curse it. God knows what he'll say about me to Mme de Rênal!

This idea dispelled all others. Shortly afterwards Julien was called back to reality by signs of assent from the public. His counsel had just finished his speech. Julien remembered that it was the done thing to shake him by the hand. Time had flown by.

Refreshments were brought to the barrister and the accused. Only then was Julien struck by something: no woman had left the courtroom to go to dinner.

'I must say, I'm absolutely starving,' said the barrister, 'what about you?'

'I am too,' Julien replied.

'Do you see, there's the prefect's wife getting her dinner too,' the barrister said to him, pointing out the little gallery. 'Keep up your spirits, everything's going well.' The hearing resumed.

As the judge was summing up, midnight struck. He was obliged to break off his speech; in the midst of the silence fraught with tension everywhere, the resounding chime of the clock filled the courtroom.

This is my last day starting now, Julien thought. Soon he felt himself fired by the idea of duty. He had controlled his emotion up until then, and kept his resolve not to speak; but when the presiding judge asked him if he had anything to add, he rose to his feet. He could see straight across into Mme Derville's eyes, and under the lights they seemed to him to be glistening. Could she be crying, by any chance? he wondered.

'Gentlemen of the jury,

My horror of scorn, which I thought I could face at the moment of death, compels me to speak. Gentlemen, I do not have the honour of belonging to your class, you see in me a peasant who has rebelled against his lowly lot.

'I am not asking you for any mercy,' Julien went on in a firmer voice. 'I have no illusions, death awaits me: it will be a just death. I was capable of attempting to kill the woman most worthy of everyone's respect and everyone's esteem. Mme de Rênal had been like a mother to me. My crime is appalling, and it was *premeditated*. I therefore deserve to die, gentlemen of the jury. But if I were less guilty, I see around me men who have no time for any pity that my youth might deserve, and who will wish to punish in me and for ever discourage this generation of young men who, being born into an inferior class and in some sense ground down by poverty, have the good fortune to get themselves a decent education, and the audacity to mingle in what the rich in their arrogance call society.

'That is my crime, gentlemen, and it will be punished all the more severely as I am not being tried by my peers. I do not see on the jury's benches any peasant who has grown rich, but only outraged members of the bourgeoisie...'

For twenty minutes Julien spoke in this vein, he unburdened himself of everything he had bottled up; the assistant public prosecutor, who was aspiring to favours from the aristocracy, was fuming on his bench; but in spite of the rather abstract terms in which Julien had couched his arguments, all the women were giving way to tears. Mme Derville herself had her handkerchief over her eyes. Before winding up, Julien turned once more to premeditation, to his repentance, and to the respect and boundless filial devotion that in happier times he had felt for Mme de Rênal... Mme Derville uttered a cry and fainted.

One o'clock was striking as the jury withdrew into their room. No woman had forsaken her seat; a number of men had tears in their eyes. Talk was very animated to start with, but gradually, as the jury's decision was long in coming, universal fatigue began to bring calm to the assembly. It was a solemn moment; the lamps cast a dimmer light. Julien, who was very tired, heard people near him discussing whether this delay was a good or a bad sign. He saw with pleasure that everyone was on his side; there was no sign of the jury returning, and still no woman left the courtroom.

As two o'clock finished striking, a great stir was heard. The little door of the jury's room opened. Baron de Valenod came forward with a grave, theatrical step followed by all the members of the jury. He coughed, then declared that upon his soul and conscience the unanimous verdict of the jury was that Julien Sorel was guilty of murder, and of murder with premeditation: this verdict carried the death penalty; the sentence was read out a moment later. Julien looked at his watch and remembered M. de Lavalette:* it was a quarter past two. Today is Friday, he thought.

Yes, but it's a happy day for our Valenod, who has sentenced me... I'm too closely guarded for Mathilde to be able to rescue me as Mme de Lavalette did... So, three days from now, at this same time, I shall know what there is to know about the *great question-mark*.

At that moment he heard a cry and was brought back to the affairs of this world. The women around him were sobbing; he saw that all faces were turned towards a little balcony carved into the top of a gothic pilaster. He learned later that Mathilde had concealed herself there. As the cry was not repeated, everyone turned back to look at Julien again, whom the officers were trying to get out through the crowd.

Let's try not to give this scoundrel Valenod any grounds for laughter, thought Julien. What a contrite and hypocritical expression he had when he pronounced the verdict that carries the death penalty! Whereas that poor president of the assizes, for all his years of being a judge, had tears in his eyes as he sentenced me. What a thrill for our Valenod to get his revenge for our old rivalry over Mme de Rênal!... So I'll never see her again! It's all over... A last farewell is impossible between us, I feel it in my bones... How happy I'd have been to tell her what repugnance I feel for my crime!

Just these words: 'I consider myself justly condemned.'

CHAPTER 42*

WHEN Julien had been taken back to prison, he had been put in a room reserved for those under sentence of death.

Although he was someone who usually noticed the minutest detail, he had failed to observe that they were not taking him back up to his tower. He was imagining what he would say to Mme de Rênal if he had the good fortune to see her before the last moment. He thought she would interrupt him, and he wanted to be able in his opening words to convey to her just how much he repented. After such an action, how can I persuade her that I love no one but her? For after all, I tried to kill her out of ambition, or love for Mathilde.

As he got into bed he discovered that the sheets were made of a coarse material. The scales fell from his eyes. Ah! I'm in a cell, he said to himself, because I've been condemned to death. That's only right.

Count Altamira told me that Danton, on the eve of his death, declared in his loud voice: 'It's odd, the verb *to guillotine* can't be conjugated in all its tenses; you can certainly say: I shall be guillotined, you shall be guillotined, but no one says: I have been guillotined.'

Why not, Julien continued, if there is an afterlife?... Count upon it, if I find the Christians' God, I'm done for: he's a despot, and as such, he's full of thoughts of vengeance; his Bible talks of nothing but dreadful punishments. I've never loved him; I've never even wanted to believe that anyone could love him sincerely. He's merciless (and Julien recalled several passages from the Bible). He'll punish me quite abominably...

But what if I find Fénelon's* God! Maybe he'll say to me: 'Much shall be forgiven thee, for thou hast loved much...'*

Have I loved much? Ah! I loved Mme de Rênal, but I behaved appallingly. There, as elsewhere, simple and unassuming worth was abandoned for glittering show...

But then again, what a prospect!... Colonel in the Hussars, if we were at war; secretary of a legation in peacetime; then ambassador... for I'd soon have become familiar with international affairs..., and even if I'd been a mere fool, does the

Marquis de la Mole's son-in-law have any rivalry to fear? All my follies would have been forgiven, or rather considered to be qualities. A man of quality, enjoying the grandest of lifestyles in Vienna or London...

'Not exactly, sir, guillotined in three days' time.'

Julien laughed heartily at this quip from his intellect. In all truth, man has two selves in him, he thought. Who the devil was it thinking up that sly comment?

'Yes, I grant you! good fellow, guillotined in three days' time,' he replied to the interrupter. 'M. de Cholin will hire a window, going halves with Father Maslon. Well now, which of these two worthies will be robbing the other over the cost of hiring this window?

This passage from Rotrou's *Venceslas* suddenly came back to him.

LADISLAS. ... My soul is all prepared.
THE KING, *Ladislas's father*. The scaffold likewise; thither bear your head.

A fine answer! he thought, and fell asleep. He was woken in the morning by someone embracing him tightly.

What, already! said Julien, opening a wild eye. He thought he was in the executioner's hands.

It was Mathilde. Luckily she didn't understand me. This reflection restored all his composure. He found Mathilde changed as if by six months of illness: she was genuinely unrecognizable.

'That unspeakable Frilair has betrayed me,' she said to him, wringing her hands; fury prevented her from crying.

'Wasn't I fine yesterday when I made my speech?' replied Julien. 'I was improvising, and for the first time in my life too! It's true there's every fear that it may also be the last!'

At that moment Julien was playing upon Mathilde's character with all the composure of a skilled pianist running his fingers over a piano... 'I lack the advantage of an illustrious birth, it's true,' he went on, 'but Mathilde's great spirit has raised her lover to her height. Do you believe that Boniface de la Mole cut a better figure in front of his judges?'

Mathilde was tender, that day, without affectation, like a poor girl living somewhere up on the fifth floor; but she was unable to get any simpler words out of him. Without knowing it, he was paying her back the torment that she had often inflicted on him.

No one knows the source of the Nile, Julien said to himself. It hasn't been granted to mortal eyes to see the king of rivers in the state of a simple stream: thus no human eye shall see Julien weak, first and foremost because he isn't. But my heart is easily touched; the most ordinary of words, said in tones of sincerity, can fill my voice with emotion and even make my tears flow. How often have I been despised by the stony-hearted for this failing! They thought I was imploring them: *that* is what's intolerable.

They say that at the foot of the scaffold Danton was moved by the memory of his wife; but Danton had given strength to a nation of frivolous young upstarts, and prevented the enemy from reaching Paris...* I'm the only one who knows what I might have done... For everyone else, I'm nothing more than a QUESTION-MARK.

If Mme de Rênal were here, in my cell, instead of Mathilde, would I have been able to answer for myself? The excess of my despair and my repentance would have been interpreted by the likes of Valenod and all the patricians in the neighbourhood as a base fear of death; they're so proud, these weak characters who are kept above temptations by their financial situation! 'You see what it means', M. de Moirod and M. de Cholin would have said, having just sentenced me to death, 'to be born a carpenter's son! A man may become learned and skilful—but his feelings!... Decent feelings can't be acquired.' Even with poor Mathilde here, who's crying now, or rather who can't cry any more, he said looking at her red eyes... and he clasped her in his arms: the sight of genuine sorrow made him forget his syllogism... She's been crying all night, maybe, he thought; but one day how ashamed she'll be of this memory! She'll regard herself as having been led astray, in her early youth, by the base attitudes of a plebeian... Friend Croisenois is feeble enough to marry her, and damn it all, he'll do the right thing. She'll cast him in a role,

> By virtue of that right
> Which a strong mind, ambitious beyond bound
> Wields o'er the grosser minds of common men.*

Come on! this is comic: ever since I've been facing death, all the lines of verse I've ever known in my life have been coming back to me. It must be a sign of decadence...

Mathilde was repeating to him in a listless voice: 'He's there in the next room.' At last he paid attention to these words. Her voice is feeble, he thought, but her imperious character is still all there in her tone. She's talking quietly so as not to get angry.

'Who's there, then?' he asked her gently.

'Your counsel, to get you to sign your appeal.'

'I shan't appeal.'

'What do you mean, you won't appeal?' she said getting up, her eyes blazing with anger, 'And why not, may I ask?'

'Because at this moment I feel the strength in me to die without letting people laugh too much at my expense. Who can guarantee that in two months' time, after a long stay in this dank cell, I shall be in an equally good frame of mind? I foresee meetings with priests, with my father... Nothing in the world can possibly be as unpleasant for me. Why not die!'

This unexpected vexation revived all the haughty side of Mathilde's character. She had been unable to see the Abbé de Frilair before the cells in the Besançon prison were opened to visitors; her fury fell on Julien. She adored him, and for a good quarter of an hour he was again confronted, in her imprecations against his character, in her regrets at having loved him, with the full force of that arrogant spirit which had heaped such poignant insults on him on that earlier occasion in the library of the Hôtel de la Mole.

'Heaven owed it to the glory of your race to have you born a man,' he said to her.

But as far as I'm concerned, he thought, I'd be a real fool to spend two months more in this revolting place, a target for all the most vile and humiliating fabrications of the patrician faction,[1]—and my only solace being the imprecations of this

---

[1] This is a Jacobin speaking. [Stendhal's footnote.]

mad woman... Well, two mornings from now, I'm fighting a duel with a man known for his imperturbability and his remarkable skill... 'Quite remarkable,' said the Mephistophelian voice; 'he never misses.'

Oh well, so be it! Fair enough. (Mathilde was continuing to be eloquent.) No, by God, he said to himself, I shan't appeal.

Once this resolve was made, he fell to musing... The postman on his round will bring the newspaper at six o'clock as usual; at eight, after M. de Rênal has read it, Elisa will come tiptoeing in to put it on her bed. Later she'll wake up: suddenly, as she reads, she'll be overcome with emotion; her pretty hand will tremble; she'll read as far as these words... *At five past ten he had ceased to exist.*

She'll weep bitterly, I know her; it won't make any difference that I tried to murder her, everything will be forgotten. And the person whose life I tried to take will be the only one to weep sincerely at my death.

Ah! how's that for an antithesis! he thought, and for a good quarter of an hour while Mathilde continued to make a scene at him, his thoughts dwelled entirely on Mme de Rênal. In spite of himself, and though he often replied to what Mathilde was saying to him, he could not get his mind away from the memory of the bedroom in Verrières. He could see the *Besançon Gazette* on the orange taffeta quilt. He could see that white hand clutching it convulsively; he could see Mme de Rênal weeping... He followed the trace of each tear down that charming face.

As Mlle de La Mole was unable to get Julien to agree to anything, she called in his counsel. Fortunately he had been an army captain during the Italian campaign of 1796, when he had fought alongside Manuel.*

For form's sake he argued against the condemned man's resolve. Julien, wanting to treat him with respect, spelled out all his reasons to him.

'Upon my word, a man is entitled to think as you do,' said M. Félix Vaneau to him in the end (that was the barrister's name). 'But you have three full days to appeal, and it is my duty to come back every day. If a volcano opened up under the prison in the next two months, you would be saved. You may die of illness,' he said, looking at Julien.

Julien shook him by the hand. 'Thank you kindly, you're a good fellow. I shall think about all this.'

And when Mathilde at last left with the barrister, he felt much more warmly disposed towards the barrister than to her.

CHAPTER 43

An hour later, he was woken from a deep sleep by the sensation of tears running over his hand.

Ah! it's Mathilde again, he thought, only half-awake. She's come, as theory prescribes, to attack my resolve with tender sentiments. Weary at the prospect of this new scene in the pathetic mode, he did not open his eyes. Belphégor's lines* as he flees his wife flashed into his mind.

He heard a strange sigh; he opened his eyes: it was Mᵐᵉ de Rênal.

'Darling! I'm seeing you again before I die, is it an illusion?' he exclaimed, throwing himself at her feet.

'But forgive me, madam, I'm nothing but a murderer in your eyes,' he said the very next moment, coming to his senses.

'Sir... I have come to beseech you to appeal, I know that you are unwilling to...' Her sobs were choking her; she was unable to speak.

'Deign to forgive me.'

'If you want me to forgive you, my love,' she said, rising and flinging herself into his arms, 'appeal at once against your sentence.'

Julien was smothering her in kisses.

'Will you come and see me every day during those two months?'

'I swear to you I will. Every day, unless my husband forbids it.'

'I'll sign!' Julien exclaimed. 'Oh heavens! you forgive me! Is it possible!'

He clasped her in his arms; he was out of his mind. She gave a little cry.

'It's nothing,' she said, 'you hurt me.'

'Your shoulder!' Julien exclaimed, bursting into tears. He moved back a little, and covered her hand with burning kisses. 'Who could have foretold this the last time I saw you, in your room in Verrières?'

'Who could have foretold then that I would send M. de la Mole that vile letter?'

'I want you to know that I've always loved you, that you are the only one I've loved.'

'Can that really be!' exclaimed Mme de Rênal, delighted in her turn. She leaned against Julien who was at her knees, and for a long time they wept in silence.

At no time in his life had Julien experienced a moment like this.

Much later, when they were able to speak:

'What about that young woman Mme Michelet,' said Mme de Rênal, 'or rather that Mlle de La Mole, for in all honesty I'm beginning to believe this strange romance!'

'It's only true on the face of it,' Julien replied. 'She's my wife, but she isn't my beloved.'

By means of countless interruptions on both sides, they managed with great difficulty to tell each other what they did not know. The letter sent to M. de la Mole had been written by the young priest who was Mme de Rênal's confessor, and then copied out by her.

'What a dreadful thing I was forced to do by religion!' she said. 'And what's more, I toned down the most appalling passages in the letter...'

Julien's demonstrations of ecstasy and his evident happiness proved to her how completely he forgave her. Never before had he been so wild with love.

'And yet I think of myself as pious,' she said to him as the conversation continued. 'I believe sincerely in God; I believe equally, and I even have proof of it, that the sin I'm committing is appalling, and as soon as I see you, even after you've fired two shots at me...' At this point, despite her resistance, Julien smothered her with kisses.

'Don't do that,' she went on, 'I want to discuss everything with you for fear of forgetting it... As soon as I see you, all my obligations disappear, and I become nothing but love for you, or rather the word love is too weak. I feel for you what I should feel exclusively for God: a mixture of respect, love and obedience. In all honesty I don't know what you inspire in me. If you told me to stab the gaoler, the crime would be committed before I had time to think. Explain that to me lucidly before I leave you: I want to see clearly into my heart;

for in two months' time we must part... Talking of which, are we to part?' she asked him, smiling.

'I shall retract my word,' Julien exclaimed rising to his feet; 'I shall not appeal against the death sentence, if by poison, knife, pistol, charcoal* or any other means whatsoever you try to end or interfere with your life.'

A sudden change came over Mme de Rênal's face; the most intense tenderness faded into deep musing.

'What if we were to die right away?' she said to him at length.

'Who knows what awaits us in the next world?' Julien replied. 'Perhaps torments, perhaps nothing at all. Can't we spend two months together in a delightful way? Two months is a good many days. I shall never have been so happy!'

'You'll never have been so happy!'

'Never,' Julien repeated in delight, 'and I'm speaking to you just as I speak to myself. God keep me from exaggerating.'

'Speaking to me like that is as good as an order,' she said with a timid and melancholy smile.

'Well then! you are to swear, by the love you feel for me, not to make any attempt on your life by direct or indirect means... Consider', he went on, 'that you have to live for my son, whom Mathilde will abandon to servants as soon as she becomes Marquise de Croisenois.'

'I swear,' she replied coldly, 'but I want to take your appeal away with me, written and signed by your own hand. I shall go in person to the public prosecutor.'

'Be careful, you'll compromise yourself.'

'Now that I've taken the step of coming to see you in your prison, I shall for ever after be the heroine of idle tales in Besançon, and the whole of the Franche-Comté,' she said with a deeply sorrowful look. 'The bounds of strict propriety have been overstepped... I'm a woman who's lost her honour; it's true that I did it for you...'

Her voice was so sad that Julien kissed her with a happiness that was quite new to him. This was no longer the intoxication of love, it was extreme gratitude. He had just perceived, for the very first time, the full extent of the sacrifice she had made for him.

Some charitable soul informed M. de Rênal, no doubt, of the lengthy visits his wife was making to Julien's prison; for when three days were up he sent his carriage for her, with the express order to return forthwith to Verrières.

This cruel separation had been a bad start to Julien's day. He was informed two or three hours later that a certain priest given to intrigue, who had none the less failed to make any headway among the Jesuits in Besançon, had posted himself that morning outside the prison gate, in the street. It was raining hard, and out there this man had set himself up to play the martyr. Julien was out of sorts; this bit of stupidity touched him deeply.

He had already refused a visit from his priest in the morning, but the man had taken it into his head to receive Julien's confession and then win notoriety among the young women in Besançon with all the secrets he would claim to have been told.

He was proclaiming in a loud voice that he was going to spend all day and night outside the prison gate: 'God has sent me to touch the heart of this latterday apostate...'* And the common people, always curious about any spectacle, were beginning to gather round.

'Yes, my brothers,' he said to them, 'I shall spend the day here, and the night, and every following day and night likewise. The Holy Spirit has spoken to me; I have a mission from on high, I am the one who must save young Sorel's soul. Join me in prayer,' etc. etc.

Julien lived in dread of scandal and anything that might draw attention to him. He considered there and then seizing the opportunity to escape from the world unnoticed; but he had some hope of seeing Mme de Rênal again, and he was madly in love.

The prison gate was in one of the busiest streets. The idea of this mud-spattered priest drumming up a crowd and a scandal tortured his innermost being—And without a doubt he's repeating my name time and time again! This moment was more painful to him than death.

Once or twice at hourly intervals he summoned a warder who was devoted to him and sent him off to see if the priest was still at the prison gate.

'Sir, he's down on both knees in the mud,' the warder told him every time. 'He's praying out loud and saying litanies for your soul...' Impertinent fellow! thought Julien. At that moment he did indeed hear a dull murmur; it was the crowd joining in the litanies. As a final onslaught on his patience, he saw the warder himself move his lips as he repeated the Latin words. 'They're beginning to say', added the warder, 'that you must have a heart of stone to refuse the help of this holy man.'

'Oh my country! How barbarous you still are!' Julien exclaimed beside himself with anger. And he continued his reflections out loud, paying no attention to the warder's presence.

'That fellow wants an article in the newspaper, and he's sure to get it.

'Ah! cursed provincials! In Paris I wouldn't be subjected to all these vexations. People there are more adept at charlatanism.

'Show in this holy priest,' he said at last to the warder, and the sweat was streaming down his forehead. The warder crossed himself and went out in great delight.

The holy priest turned out to be horribly ugly, and even more horribly spattered in mud. The cold rain falling outside heightened the gloom and dankness of the cell. The priest tried to embrace Julien, and began to get sentimental as he talked to him. The most vile hypocrisy was only too apparent; Julien had never been so angry in all his life.

A quarter of an hour after the priest had come in, Julien found himself a complete coward. For the first time death struck him as horrendous. He thought of the state of putrefaction his body would be in two days after the execution, etc. etc.

He was about to betray himself by some sign of weakness, or fling himself at the priest and strangle him with his chain, when he had the idea of begging the holy man to go and say a Mass for him—a proper Mass worth forty francs—that very same day.

Now as it was almost noon,* the priest made off in haste.

CHAPTER 44

As soon as he had left, Julien wept bitterly, and wept at having to die. Gradually he admitted to himself that if Mme de Rênal had been in Besançon, he would have confessed his weakness to her...

At the point where he was most regretting the absence of the woman he adored, he heard Mathilde's footsteps.

The worst thing about prison, he thought, is not being able to shut your door. Everything Mathilde told him only served to exasperate him.

She informed him that on the day of the trial, M. de Valenod, with his appointment as prefect in his pocket, had dared to flout M. de Frilair and indulge in the pleasure of condemning Julien to death.

'"Whatever came over your friend," M. de Frilair has just said to me, "to go and rouse and attack the petty vanity of this *bourgeois aristocracy*! Why speak of *caste*? He showed them what they had to do in their own political interest: these ninnies hadn't thought of it, and were ready to weep. This 'caste solidarity' served to obscure from their gaze the horror of condemning to death. It must be admitted that M. Sorel is very new to politics. If we don't succeed in saving him by an appeal for pardon, his death will be a kind of suicide..."'

Mathilde was scarcely in a position to tell Julien something she did not as yet suspect: that the Abbé de Frilair, seeing there was no hope for Julien, thought it would serve his own ambition if he aspired to become his successor.

Almost beside himself with impotent rage and annoyance, Julien said to Mathilde: 'Go and hear a Mass for me, and leave me in peace for a while.' Mathilde, who was already highly jealous of Mme de Rênal's visits, and had just learned of her departure, understood the reason for Julien's bad temper and burst into tears.

Her distress was genuine; Julien could see this, and it only made him more exasperated. He had an overriding need for solitude, and how was he to procure it?

At length, having tried all forms of reasoning to touch his

emotions, Mathilde left him alone, but at almost the same moment Fouqué appeared.

'I need to be alone,' he said to this faithful friend... And on seeing him hesitate: 'I'm drafting a statement for my appeal for pardon... as far as other things go... do me a favour, don't ever speak to me about death. If I need you to do anything particular for me on the day, leave it up to me to raise the matter.'

When Julien had at last procured solitude, he found he was more burdened and more cowardly than before. The little strength remaining in this weakened spirit had been exhaused in concealing his state from Mlle de La Mole and Fouqué.

Towards evening he took comfort in this thought:

If this morning, at the moment when death seemed so hideous to me, they had come to announce that it was time for the execution, *the eye of the public would have been a spur to glory*, maybe my walk would have had something stiff about it, like that of a nervous fop stepping into a salon. One or two perceptive people, if such exist among these provincials, might have been able to guess my weakness... but no one would have *seen it*.

And he felt relieved of part of his misery. I'm a coward at this moment, he chanted over and over again to himself, but no one shall know it.

An event that was almost more disagreeable still was awaiting him on the following day. For some time now his father had been saying he would visit him, and on that day, before Julien woke, the white-haired old carpenter appeared in his cell.

A feeling of weakness came over Julien; he was expecting the most disagreeable of reproaches. To put the finishing touches to his wretchedness, he was experiencing an acute sense of guilt that morning at not loving his father.

Chance has put us side by side on this earth, he said to himself while the warder was tidying up the cell, and we have caused each other just about all the hurt we could. Here he comes when I'm facing death to deliver the final blow.

The old man's stern reproaches began as soon as they were on their own.

Julien was unable to restrain his tears. What unworthy weakness! he said to himself in fury. He'll go around everywhere exaggerating my lack of courage; what a triumph for the likes of Valenod and all the ingratiating hypocrites who rule Verrières! They're really powerful in France, they have all the social advantages on their side. Up till now I was at least able to say to myself: 'They get money, admittedly, and every form of honour is heaped upon them, but *I* am noble in spirit.'

And now here's a witness who'll be believed by everyone, and will certify to all Verrières, with much exaggeration too, that I showed weakness in the face of death! I shall have been a coward in this ordeal that they all understand!

Julien was on the verge of despair. He did not know how to get rid of his father. And shamming in such a way as to deceive this most perspicacious old man was at that moment quite beyond his strength.

His mind ran rapidly over all the possibilities.

'*I've got some savings put by!*' he exclaimed suddenly.

This piece of inspiration completely altered the old man's countenance and Julien's position.

'How should I dispose of them?' Julien went on more calmly: the effect produced had dispelled all his feelings of inferiority.

The old carpenter was burning with a desire not to let slip this money, a share of which Julien seemed to wish to leave to his brothers. He spoke at length and with passion. Julien was able to indulge in mockery.

'Well now! the Almighty has inspired me in the matter of my will. I shall give a thousand francs to each of my brothers and the rest to you.'

'Very well,' said the old man, 'the rest is my due; but since God has granted you the grace of touching your heart, if you wish to die a good Christian, it's fitting that you pay your debts. There's still the cost of your food and education that I advanced you and you are forgetting...'

'That's fatherly love for you!' Julien repeated to himself in great dismay when he was at last alone. Soon the gaoler appeared.

'Sir, after parents have visited, I always bring my guests a bottle of good champagne. It's a bit dear, six francs a bottle, but it warms the spirit.'

'Bring in three glasses,' Julien replied with childlike eagerness, 'and show in two of the prisoners I hear walking up and down the corridor.'

The gaoler brought him two relapsed convicts who were preparing to return to hard labour. They were cheery scoundrels who were really most remarkable for their shrewdness, their courage and their phlegm.

'If you give me twenty francs,' said one of them to Julien, 'I'll tell you my life story in detail. It's *brilliant*.'

'But won't you lie to me?'

'That I won't,' he answered. 'My friend here, who'll be envious of my twenty francs, will denounce me if I invent anything.'

His story was appalling. It showed a heart full of courage, but with only one passion left: money.

After they had gone Julien was no longer the same man. All his anger at himself had disappeared. The dreadful suffering, poisoned by cowardice, which had taken hold of him since Mme de Rênal's departure, had turned to melancholy.

As I came to be less taken in by appearances, he said to himself, I'd have seen that the Paris salons are inhabited by honest folk like my father, or cunning rascals like these convicts. They're right, men from the salons never get up in the morning with this agonizing thought: 'How am I going to get my dinner?' And they boast of their honesty! And from the ranks of the jury they proudly condemn the man who's stolen a silver spoon and fork because he felt faint with hunger.

But if it's at Court, if it's a matter of losing or winning a ministerial portfolio, my honest salon gentlemen are reduced to exactly the same crimes as the ones those two convicts were driven to by the need to get their dinner...

There's no such thing as *natural rights*:* this term is nothing but a bit of antiquated rubbish worthy of the assistant public prosecutor who was hounding me the other day, and whose ancestor was made rich by land which Louis XIV confiscated from the Protestants.* There is only a *right* when there is a law to forbid you doing something on pain of punishment. Before the advent of laws, the only thing *natural* is the might of the lion or the need of the creature suffering hunger or cold, *need* in short... No, the people who are honoured are no more than rogues who've had the good fortune not to be caught red-handed. The accuser unleashed on me by society was made rich by an act of infamy... I attempted murder, and I'm justly condemned; but leaving aside this one action, that fellow Valenod who condemned me is a hundred times more harmful to society.

So then! Julien went on sadly but without anger, my father, for all his avarice, is a better man than all of these. He's never loved me. And now it's the last straw when I go and dishonour him through my ignominious death. What is known as *avarice*—this fear of going short of money, this exaggerated view of the malevolence of mankind—makes him see a prodigious source of comfort and security in a sum of three or four hundred louis that I may be leaving him. One Sunday after dinner he'll show his gold to all the people in Verrières who envy him. 'At this price', his expression will say to them, 'which one of you would not be delighted to have a son guillotined?'

This philosophy might well be sound, but it was of a kind to make him wish for death. Five long days went by like this. He was polite and gentle with Mathilde, who, he could see, was driven to distraction by the most acute jealousy. One evening Julien thought seriously about taking his own life. His spirit was sapped by the deep misery he had been plunged into by Mme de Rênal's departure. Nothing appealed to him any more, either in real life or in the realms of imagination. Lack of exercise was beginning to impair his health and make his character weak and over-intense like some young German student's. He was losing that manly detachment which rebuffs with a forceful oath certain ill-becoming thoughts that besiege the minds of the unfortunate.

I love truth... Where is it?... Hypocrisy everywhere, or at any rate charlatanism, even among those of greatest virtue, even among the really great. And his lips pursed in disgust... No! man can't trust man.

Mme de ——, who was collecting for her poor orphans, told me that Prince So-and-So had just given ten louis—a lie. But what am I saying? Napoleon on St Helena!... Pure charlatanism, a proclamation in favour of the King of Rome.*

For Christ's sake! if a man like that, and what's more at a time when misfortune should recall him sternly to his duty, descends into charlatanism, what can you expect from the rest of the species?...

Where is truth? In religion... Yes, he added with the bitter smile of utmost scorn, in the mouths of the Maslons, the Frilairs and the Castanèdes of this world... Maybe in true Christianity, where priests would be given no more pay than the apostles got?... But St Paul's pay was the pleasure of giving commands, of speaking and being spoken of...

Ah! if there were a true religion... Poor fool that I am! I see a gothic cathedral, and ancient stained-glass windows; my feeble heart conjures up a picture of the priest who is the keeper of these windows... My soul would understand him, my soul needs him... All I find is a fop with dirty hair... minus the charm, a Chevalier de Beauvoisis.

But a real priest, a Massillon, a Fénelon... Massillon consecrated Dubois.* Saint-Simon's *Memoirs* have spoilt Fénelon for me... But I mean a real priest... Then tender souls would have a meeting-point in this world... We wouldn't be isolated... This good priest would talk to us about God. But which God? Not the one in the Bible, a cruel little despot thirsting after vengeance... no, Voltaire's God, righteous, good, infinite...

He was disturbed by all the memories of this Bible that he knew by heart... But how, when *two or three are gathered together*, can you believe in the great name of GOD, after the terrible abuse made of it by our priests?

To live in isolation!... What torment!...

I'm going mad, and starting to be unfair, Julien said to himself, striking his forehead. I'm isolated here in this cell, but I didn't *live in isolation* on earth, I had a strong sense of *duty*. The duty I had prescribed for myself, for right or for wrong... was like a solid tree-trunk I leaned against during the storm; I swayed, I was buffeted. After all, I was only a man... But I wasn't swept away.

It's the dank air in this cell which makes me think of isolation...

And why go on being a hypocrite while cursing hypocrisy? It isn't death, or the cell, or the dank air that are getting me down, it's the absence of Mme de Rênal! If in Verrières I were obliged, in order to see her, to live for weeks on end hidden in the cellars of the house, would I complain?

'The influence of my contemporaries is getting the better of me,' he said out loud, with a bitter smile. 'Talking to myself only days away from death, I'm still a hypocrite... O nineteenth century!'

...A huntsman fires a shot in the forest, his prey falls to the ground, he rushes forward to seize it. His shoe strikes an anthill two foot high and destroys the ants' home, scattering ants and their eggs far and wide... The most philosophically inclined among the ants will never be able to understand this huge and terrible black object—the huntsman's boot—which has suddenly broken into their dwelling with incredible speed, in the wake of a dreadful noise accompanied by a shower of red sparks...

...That's what death, life and eternity are like—very simple things for anyone with sensory organs on a scale to apprehend them...

A mayfly hatches at nine o'clock in the morning in high summer, and dies at five in the evening; how should it understand the word *night*?

Give it five more hours of existence, and it will see and understand what night is.

That's what I am like, I shall die at twenty-three. Give me five more years, to live with Mme de Rênal.

And he began to laugh like Mephistopheles. What madness to debate these great questions!

1. I'm being hypocritical as though there were someone there to listen to me.

2. I'm forgetting to live and to love, when there are so few days left for me to live... Alas! Mme de Rênal isn't here; maybe her husband won't let her come back to Besançon, any more and continue to dishonour herself.

This is what's causing my isolation, not the absence of a

righteous good, all-powerful God who isn't cruel and thirsting for vengeance.

Ah! if he existed... Alas! I'd fall at his feet. 'I have deserved death,' I'd say to him; 'but Almighty God, bountiful God, merciful God, give me back the woman I love!'

Night was well advanced by then. After Julien had slept peacefully for an hour or two, Fouqué arrived.

Julien felt strong and resolute like a man who can see clearly into the depths of his soul.

CHAPTER 45

'I don't want to play a nasty trick on poor Father Chas-Bernard by summoning him here,' he said to Fouqué. 'It'd put him off his dinner for three days. But try to find me a Jansenist who's a friend of M. Pirard and impervious to intrigue.'

Fouqué was waiting impatiently for this opening. Julien acquitted himself with propriety of everything that is owed to public opinion—in the provinces. Thanks to the Abbé de Frilair, and despite his bad choice of confessor, Julien in his cell was the protégé of the Congregation; if he had handled things better, he might have engineered his escape. But the bad air in the cell was having its effect, and his mental powers were dwindling. This increased his happiness at Mme de Rênal's return.

'My first duty is to you,' she said, kissing him. 'I ran away from Verrières...'

Julien had no petty pride where she was concerned, and he recounted all his moments of weakness to her. She showed him all her kindness and charm.

That evening, as soon as she had left his prison, she summoned to her aunt's house the priest who had latched on to Julien like a predator; as he wished for nothing better than to gain credit with young women belonging to high society in Besançon, Mme de Rênal easily persuaded him to go and make a novena* at Bray-le-Haut Abbey.

No words could express the wild excesses of Julien's love.

By paying in gold, and using and abusing the credit of her aunt, who was a devout woman with wealth and a good name, Mme de Rênal obtained leave to see him twice a day.

News of this fanned Mathilde's jealousy to a pitch of mad frenzy. M. de Frilair had admitted to her that his considerable credit simply did not extend to flouting propriety to the point of getting permission for her to see her friend more than once a day. Mathilde had Mme de Rênal followed to discover her every movement. M. de Frilair was exhausting all the resources of a very crafty mind in order to prove to Mathilde that Julien was unworthy of her.

In the midst of all these torments, she only loved him the more, and almost every day she made a hideous scene.

Julien wanted at all costs to behave like a gentleman right to the last with this poor girl he had so strangely compromised; but at every moment his frenzied love for Mme de Rênal got the better of him. When bad arguments failed to persuade Mathilde of the innocence of her rival's visits, he said to himself: the end of the drama must be very near now; I can be excused for not being better at dissembling.

Mlle de La Mole learned of the death of the Marquis de Croisenois. M. de Thaler with all his wealth had taken the liberty of making some disagreeable remarks about Mathilde's disappearance. M. de Croisenois went and begged him to retract them; M. de Thaler showed him some anonymous letters addressed to himself, which were full of details put together with such skill that it was impossible for the poor marquis not to glimpse the truth.

M. de Thaler took the liberty of making some jokes quite lacking in subtlety. Mad with anger and misery, M. de Croisenois demanded so much by way of reparations that the millionaire preferred a duel. Stupidity triumphed, and one of Paris's most likeable young men met his death before reaching twenty-four.

This death had a strange and unhealthy effect on Julien's weakened spirit.

'Poor Croisenois', he said to Mathilde, 'was really most reasonable, and behaved like a gentleman towards us; when you were acting so rashly in your mother's salon, he ought to have hated me and picked a quarrel; for hatred bred of scorn is usually ferocious.'

M. de Croisenois's death altered all Julien's ideas about Mathilde's future; he spent several days trying to prove to her that she ought to accept the hand of M. de Luz. 'He's a shy man, and not too jesuitical,' he said, 'and he'll no doubt throw in his chance with the rest. His is a darker and more persistent ambition than poor Croisenois's, and with no duchy in the family, he won't make any difficulties about marrying Julien Sorel's widow.'

'A widow who despises grand passions at that,' Mathilde

retorted coldly, 'for she's lived long enough to see her lover prefer another woman to her after six months, and a woman who's the origin of all their suffering.'

'You're being unfair: Mme de Rênal's visits will supply the barrister from Paris with some striking lines for my appeal; he'll depict the murderer honoured by the attentions of his victim. This may have some effect, and perhaps one day you'll see me as the subject of some melodrama, etc. etc.'

Furious jealousy that was impossible to avenge, persistent and hopeless misery (for even supposing Julien were saved, how was she to win back his heart?), shame and pain at loving this faithless lover more than ever before, had cast Mlle de La Mole into a gloomy silence from which neither the zealous attentions of M. de Frilair nor the blunt frankness of Fouqué were able to shake her.

Julien on the other hand, apart from the moments usurped by Mathilde's presence, lived for love and had scarcely a thought for the future. Through the strange workings of this passion in its most extreme form, when totally devoid of sham, Mme de Rênal almost shared his carefree outlook and his gentle cheerfulness.

'In those early days', Julien would say to her, 'when I could have been so happy on our walks in the woods round Vergy, an unbridled ambition carried me off to imaginary realms. Instead of pressing to my heart this lovely arm of yours which lay so close to my lips, I let the future snatch me away from you. I was deep in the countless battles I would have to fight to build a colossal fortune... No, I should have died without knowing happiness if you hadn't come to see me here in prison.'

Two incidents occurred which disturbed this peaceful life of theirs. Julien's confessor, for all his Jansenism, was not immune to an intrigue hatched by the Jesuits, and unknowingly became their instrument.

He came to tell Julien one day that unless he wished to fall into the dire sin of suicide, he had to take all possible steps to obtain a pardon. Now as the clergy had a great deal of influence with the Ministry of Justice in Paris, this offered an easy solution: Julien must be converted with great show.

'With great show!' Julien repeated. 'Ah! I've caught you at it, you too, Father—play-acting like a missionary...'

'Your age,' the Jansenist went on gravely, 'the attractive looks bestowed on you by Providence, the very motive for your crime, which remains inexplicable, the heroic actions that Mlle de La Mole is generously performing in your interest, everything, in short, down to the astonishing friendship shown you by your victim—everything has contributed to making you the hero of the young women in Besançon. They've forgotten everything for your sake, even politics...

'Your conversion would strike a chord in their hearts and make a deep impression here. You can be of major use to religion, and am I to be the one to hesitate for the frivolous reason that the Jesuits would take the same line in a similar instance! Thus, even in this particular case which eludes their rapacious grasp, they could still cause harm! Let it not be so... The tears shed as a result of your conversion will wipe out the corrosive effect of ten editions of the impious works of Voltaire.'

'And what shall I be left with', Julien answered coldly, 'if I despise myself? I was ambitious, I don't want to blame myself; at that time I acted in accordance with the conventions of the day. But now I'm living from one moment to the next. And from the way things look, I'd make myself most unhappy if I went in for an act of cowardice...'

The other incident, which affected Julien in a quite different way, was of Mme de Rênal's doing. One or other of the scheming ladies among her friends had managed to persuade this innocent and timid soul that it was her duty to set off for Saint-Cloud, and go and prostrate herself before King Charles X.*

She had determined on the sacrifice of parting from Julien, and after so great an effort, the unpleasantness of making a spectacle of herself, which at other times would have struck her as worse than death, no longer meant anything to her.

'I shall go to the king, I shall admit for all to hear that you are my lover: the life of a man, and a man like Julien, should outweigh all other considerations. I shall say that jealousy was what made you try to take my life. There are plenty of examples of poor young men in this predicament saved by the humanity of the jury, or of the king...'

'I won't ever see you again, I'll have you locked out of my prison, and sure as anything I'll kill myself out of despair the very next day, unless you swear to me that you won't take any action that makes a public spectacle of us both. This idea of going to Paris doesn't come from you. Tell me the name of the little schemer who suggested it to you...

'Let's be happy for the small number of days left in this short life. Let's hide ourselves away; my crime is only too patent. Mlle de La Mole has unlimited credit in Paris; believe me, she's doing what is humanly possible. Here in the provinces I have everyone rich and respected lined up against me. Your action would antagonize even further these rich and essentially conventional people, who have life so easy... Don't let us become a laughing-stock for the Maslons, the Valenods and countless other worthier folk.'

The bad air in the cell was becoming unbearable to Julien. By good fortune, on the day he was told that he had to die, the countryside was rejoicing in bright sunshine, and Julien was in courageous vein. Stepping out in the fresh air was a delicious sensation for him, like a walk on land for the sailor who has spent long at sea. Here we go, everything's all right, he told himself, I'm not lacking in courage.

Never had his head looked so poetic as at the moment it was due to fall. The sweetest moments he had experienced in those early days in the woods in Vergy crowded back into his mind with great vigour.

Everything happened simply, appropriately, and with no affectation on his part.

Two days earlier he had said to Fouqué:

'As far as emotion goes, I can't answer for it; this cell is so ugly, so dank, it brings on attacks of fever in which I no longer recognize myself. But fear—never! I shan't be seen to turn pale.'

He had seen to it in advance that on the morning of the last day, Fouqué would take Mathilde and Mme de Rênal away.

'Take them off in the same carriage,' he had instructed him. 'See to it that the post horses keep up a steady gallop. They'll fall into each other's arms, or else will show each other mortal hatred. In either case, the poor women will have their minds taken off their appalling grief for a while.'

Julien had extracted a solemn promise from Mme de Rênal that she would live in order to look after Mathilde's son.

'Who knows? Perhaps we go on having sensations after our death,' were his words to Fouqué one day. 'I'd rather like to rest, and rest is the word for it, in that little grotto in the high mountain overlooking Verrières. On several occasions, as I've told you, when I had withdrawn for the night into that grotto, and was gazing down into the distance over the richest provinces in France, my heart was fired with ambition; at that time it was my passion... Anyway, this grotto means a great deal to me, and no one would deny that its situation is most attractive to a philosopher's soul... Now then! these good Congregationists in Besançon make money out of everything; if you go about it right, they'll sell you my remains...'

Fouqué succeeded in this sad bargain. He was spending the night alone in his room beside the body of his friend, when to his great surprise he saw Mathilde at the door. Only a few hours before he had left her ten leagues away from Besançon. She had a wild look in her eyes.

'I want to see him,' she said.

Fouqué did not have the strength to speak or get up. He pointed at a large blue coat there on the floor; it enveloped what remained of Julien.

She flung herself on her knees. The memory of Boniface de La Mole and Marguerite de Navarre must have given her superhuman courage. Her trembling hands opened the coat. Fouqué looked away.

He heard Mathilde walking hurriedly about the room. She was lighting a number of candles. When Fouqué had the strength to look at her, she had placed Julien's head on a little marble table in front of her, and she was kissing his forehead...

Mathilde followed her lover all the way to the tomb he had chosen for himself. A large number of priests escorted the bier, and, unknown to anyone, alone in her black-draped carriage, she carried on her lap the head of the man she had loved so much.

Having made their way like this almost to the summit of one of the highest mountains in the Jura, in the middle of the night, twenty priests celebrated a Mass for the dead in the little grotto magnificently lit by an infinite array of candles. All the inhabitants of the little mountain villages along the path of the procession had followed on behind, drawn to it by the striking character of this strange ceremony.

Mathilde made her appearance in the midst of them, wearing long mourning attire, and at the end of the service she had several thousand five-franc coins flung to the crowd.

Left alone with Fouqué, she insisted on burying the head of her lover with her own hands. It almost drove Fouqué out of his mind with grief.

Through Mathilde's good offices the wild grotto was adorned with marbles sculpted at great expense in Italy.

Mme de Rênal was faithful to her promise. She did not seek in any way at all to take her own life; but three days after Julien, she died with her children in her arms.

THE END[1]

[1] The disadvantage with the reign of public opinion—which, incidentally, procures *Liberty*—is that it meddles in things that are not its concern, for instance: private life. This explains the gloom in America and England. To avoid interfering with private life, the author has invented a little town, Verrières; and whenever he needed a bishop, a jury or an assize court, he situated them all in Besançon, where he has never set foot. [Stendhal's footnote.]

EXPLANATORY NOTES

CURRENCY

franc: basic unit of the French monetary system since 1803.

pound (Fr. *livre*): older unit still used in Stendhal's time as the equivalent of a franc.

crown (Fr. *écu*): silver coin of variable worth, commonly either 3 or 6 francs.

louis or *napoléon*: gold coin worth 20 francs.

centime: coin worth one hundredth of a franc.

sou: coin worth 5 centimes.

DISTANCES

league (Fr. *lieue*): a variable measure, usually about 4 kilometres.

1 *to the Happy Few*: this dedication is in English in the original. It appears on the last page of the novel, at the end of the table of contents (printed according to French custom at the back of the book). It occurs similarly elsewhere in Stendhal's writings. He is believed to have borrowed it not so much from Shakespeare ('we few, we happy few, we band of brothers', *Henry V*, IV. iii) as from Goldsmith's *Vicar of Wakefield*: 'tracts . . . read only by the happy *few*' (ch.ii).

2 *Publisher's Note*: fictitious.

2 *events of July*: the 1830 revolution which put Louis-Philippe on the French throne in place of Charles X.

2 *1827*: the novel was in fact written in 1829–30.

3 *Danton*: 1759–94, leading statesman and orator of the French Revolution (1789). Like the majority of Stendhal's epigraphs, this one appears to have been invented by him to suit his own text: only 15 of the 73 epigraphs in the novel have been traced to the works of the authors credited with them.

3 *Franche-Comté*: one of the former provinces in eastern France, extending from Burgundy to the Swiss border (capital: Besançon). Although there are two places called Verrières in this region, Stendhal's little town bears no resemblance to either of them. Some critics have identified Dole (on the road from Besançon to Dijon) as the model for Verrières. Others point out

that many of the features of the locality described by Stendhal are more reminiscent of the French Alps near Grenoble than of the Jura.

3 *Mulhouse tradition*: production of painted fabrics had started in Mulhouse in the mid-18th c. and spread throughout the Rhine valley and surrounding mountain regions.

4 *orders of knighthood*: visible as insignia worn on the coat.

5 *conquered by Louis XIV*: in 1678.

5 *events of 1815*: final defeat of Napoleon at Waterloo, and Second Restoration of Louis XVIII. Under the Restoration, the new industrial ethos was championed by the liberal party, from which M. de Rênal strongly dissociates himself.

5 *182– elections*: the general election of 1824, which consolidated the power of the Ultra-royalists.

6 *mindless*: Stendhal's italicization is sometimes idiosyncratic, and is not always followed in this translation.

7 *Barnave*: 1761–93, born in Grenoble; friend of Stendhal's family. Revolutionary orator in favour of constitutional monarchy. See also epigraphs to chapters I. 19, 24, II. 31.

8 *Ultra*: the Ultras, or pure royalists, stood for the ideals of counter-revolution and the Catholic establishment. Their leader, Villèle, was head of the Cabinet from 1822 to 1827.

8 *Saint-Germain-en-Laye*: the château of Saint-Germain-en-Laye, département of Seine-et-Oise, was built in 1539 and served as a royal residence. It has a famous terrace by Le Nôtre (1613–1700).

8 *Jacobin*: member of a revolutionary political society founded in Paris in 1790. The name derives from their meeting-place: a former 'Jacobin' (Dominican) convent. The Jacobins advocated absolute power for the people.

8 *Legion of Honour*: founded by Napoleon in 1802 to reward civil and military exploits. The Legion of Honour cross is attached to a red ribbon.

9 *M. Appert*: a well-known figure of the period. His campaigns for prison reform took him round prisons throughout France.

11 *Fleury*: the Abbé Fleury (1640–1723) was Louis XV's confessor and author of an *Ecclesiastical History*.

12 *eight hundred pounds*: for a note on currency, see p. 530.

12 *at the age of eighty*: at the end of the 1820s, old priests educated

in the Gallican, or French, tradition found themselves the victims of a wave of hostility from the younger Ultramontane clergy whose absolute allegiance was to the pope. These intrigues were particularly prevalent in the Franche-Comté.

14 *voted 'no' to the Empire*: in the plebiscite held before Napoleon was crowned emperor in Dec. 1804, there were 3,572,329 votes in favour of the Empire, 2,569 against.

14 *carpenter's son*: the French term *charpentier* denotes someone who typically prepares and assembles timber frames for use in building construction. I have translated it here by the English 'carpenter' (now archaic in this sense), in order to preserve the biblical resonance of the expression 'carpenter's son', recurrently applied to Julien.

15 *impressionable*: this translates the French *inégal* which appears in the original edition. Castex corrects it to *égal* (even-tempered) on the grounds that *inégal* does not fit Mme de Rênal's character. I think that this correction is not justified by close reading of the text.

15 *Duke of Orleans*: Philippe-Egalité (1747–93) was a supporter of the Revolution, voted for the death of his cousin Louis XVI, and was himself executed. His son Louis-Philippe (1773–1850) became King of France in 1830.

15 *Mme de Montesson*: married Philippe-Egalité in secret. *Mme de Genlis*: 1746–1830, niece of Mme de Montesson and governess to the children of her marriage to Philippe-Egalité. She wrote a number of books on education. *M. Ducrest*: nephew of Mme de Montesson and brother of Mme de Genlis. He was responsible for renovating the Palais-Royal (Paris residence of the House of Orleans) and adding its distinctive galleries.

17 *Machiavelli*: 1469–1527. 'And will I be at fault if it is so?'

17 *good lady*: the French expression used (*ma femme*) is not refined usage. Stendhal comments in the margin of his personal copy of the novel that M. de R. does not refer to his wife as 'Mme de Rênal' (in upper-class tradition).

17 *abbé*: a term originally denoting an abbot in the Catholic Church, but later extended to anyone wearing ecclesiastical dress, whether or not he had been ordained as a priest. Abbés without ecclesiastical duties were frequently employed as private tutors. They wore either a black suit with frock-coat, or a cassock (hence M. de Rênal's uncertainty about Julien's dress).

19 *St Helena Chronicle*: the *Mémorial de Sainte-Hélène* (1823) was compiled by the Comte de Las Cases, Napoleon's secretary, who accompanied him to St Helena and kept a record of their conversations.

21 *Ennius*: 239–169 BC. [*Unus homo nobis*] *cunctando restituit rem*: 'By delaying he [one man] saved the republic [for us].' Reference to Quintus Fabius Maximus Cunctator, who ultimately defeated Hannibal by never offering him pitched battle.

22 *Rousseau*: 1712–78, French Enlightenment philosopher and writer. His major works include *La Nouvelle Héloïse* (1761), an epistolary novel; the *Contrat Social* (1762), a treatise on political philosophy; and his *Confessions* (posthumous), a sentimental, self-justificatory autobiography.

22 *On the Pope*: Joseph de Maistre (1753–1821) was an opponent of the Revolution and a staunch defender of the monarchy and the pope. His book was widely read by the young guard of Ultramontane priests.

24 *thirty-six francs*: so that the monthly wage could be paid in everyday *écu* coins, each worth 3 or 6 francs.

25 *make a Station*: perform the requisite devotions in front of one of the fourteen images representing successive incidents in Christ's Passion.

25 *Lodi bridge, Arcola and Rivoli*: victories by Napoleon over the Austrians; the first two in 1796, the latter in 1797.

25 *Congregation*: name given by Stendhal's contemporaries to the *Association des Chevaliers de la Foi* ('Association of Knights of the Faith'), a Jesuit-inspired secret society whose true identity or even existence was unknown to the general public. It had a network across France, and was deeply involved in reactionary politics. The term *congrégation* was also used to refer to the pious associations officially established by the Concordat of 1801 and dedicated to charitable works, particularly the *Congrégation de la Vierge* and its various affiliates. Since the secret Congregation found it expedient to shelter behind the activities of the latter, and membership was in many instances overlapping, it is not surprising that the general public often grouped all these bodies together indiscriminately under the one term *congrégation*.

25 *Le Constitutionnel*: founded in 1815, it favoured constitutional monarchy and became the mouthpiece of the liberal opposition.

26 *Mme de Beauharnais*: 1763–1814, the future Empress Josephine.

She was first married to the Vicomte de Beauharnais, who was executed in 1794. She then married General Bonaparte in 1796. They were divorced in 1809.

29 *Mozart (Figaro)*: 'I no longer know what I am, or what I'm doing.'

36 *sub-prefect*: official representing central government at the level of the district (*arrondissement*). The prefect heads a département (see n. to p. 106 below).

37 *Elective Affinities*: the title of a novel by Goethe (1808), dealing with the attractions of a married couple for two other people.

37 *feast of St Louis*: 25 Aug.

41 *Théâtre de Madame*: vaudeville theatre in Paris built in 1820.

41 *Aveyron*: département in S.W. France at the southern end of the Massif Central.

42 *the late Prince de Condé*: Louis-Joseph, Prince de Condé (1736–1818), organized a counter-revolutionary army in 1792.

43 *Besenval's Memoirs*: published in 1805–6, they give a detailed picture of pre-revolutionary France.

44 *de visu*: 'by sight' (Latin).

44 *La Quotidienne*: Ultra-royalist newspaper founded in 1792.

44 *Jacobin*: see n. to p. 8.

45 *mezzo-termine*: 'compromise' (Italian).

48 *Don Juan*: *Don Juan*, the poem by Byron (1788–1824), appeared in 1819.

50 *leagues*: for distances, see p. 530.

52 *Gabrielle*: the legend of the *Châtelaine de Vergy* exists in numerous versions. In the original 13th-c. French verse romance, as also in the tale in the *Heptameron* by Marguerite de Navarre (1492–1549), the lady dies of grief, believing in error that her lover has disclosed their love to another woman; whereupon the lover kills himself. Later versions are more gruesome: the lover perishes first, and the jealous husband serves up his heart to the lady at dinner. Realizing what she has eaten, she starves herself to death. In 1804 Stendhal had seen a stage adaptation of the story, *Gabrielle de Vergy* by Dormont de Belloy (first performed in 1777). A modern French version of the 13th-c. legend was published in 1829. The real village of Vergy is not in the Franche-Comté but in Burgundy, near Dijon.

52 *Tuileries*: the Palais des Tuileries, begun in 1564, was the Paris residence of the French monarchy. It was partially burned down by the Commune in 1871, and finally destroyed in 1882. Only parts of the gardens remain.

53 *M. Godart's excellent study*: Jean-Baptiste Godart, *Histoire Naturelle des lépidoptères en France*. The work was unfinished when the author died in 1823.

56 *Strombeck*: the Baron de Strombeck was a personal friend of Stendhal's. Guérin (1774–1833) exhibited his painting of Dido and Aeneas at the Salon of 1817. It depicts Dido listening to Aeneas in the presence of her sister.

58 *Charles the Bold*: 1433–77, Duke of Burgundy from 1467.

60 *the Robespierres of this world*: Robespierre (1758–94) was a key figure in the French Revolution. He instigated the Terror in 1793, and met his own death on the scaffold.

66 *More than fifty crowns*: 56 écus worth 3 francs each would represent the extra sum of 168 francs offered by M. de Rênal.

73 *Sieyès*: 1748–1836, churchman and politician; author of a famous pamphlet on the *Tiers Etat* (1789), and one of the organizers of Napoleon's *coup d'état* of Nov. 1799.

77 *Pontarlier*: town close to the Swiss border on the road from Neuchâtel to Dijon.

80 *Saint-Réal*: Abbé de Saint-Réal (1639–92), French historian. The ascription to him of this key aesthetic formulation is false, and critics have seen in it a pun on the name Saint-Réal: a founding father of the doctrine of realism, or the 'Holy Real'.

85 *Polidori*: Byron's doctor and secretary. Stendhal met them both in Milan in 1816.

87 *Corneille*: 'L'amour / Fait les égalités et ne les cherche pas.' These lines are attributed by Stendhal to Corneille (1606–84), but they in fact come from *Venceslas*, a play by Rotrou (1609–50).

89 *Love's Blazon*: in literal translation this medieval verse reads:
Love in Latin gives *amor*;
So then from love ensueth death [*la mort*],
And, as its heralds, care which gnaws [*qui mord*],
Grief, sorrow, trickery, sin, remorse [*remords*].

94 *provincial saying*: fictitious?

99 *Robespierre*: see n. to p. 60.

100 *Voltaire*: 1694–1788, philosopher and writer of the French
    Enlightenment; mordant critic of all forms of religious and
    political humbug.

100 *Louis XV*: 1710–74, came to the throne in 1715.

100 *Chamber of Deputies*: lower house of the French Parliament.
    Deputies were chosen by electoral colleges, themselves elected by
    citizens paying sufficient taxes to qualify as primary electors.

101 *Fontenoy*: victory of the French over the English and the Dutch
    in 1745.

101 *peculiar institution*: reference to one of the local pious associations
    sponsored by the official Congregation to enlist the lower orders
    (see n. to p. 25 above). They were believed by liberals to turn
    servants into spies.

101 *as equals*: shown in French by the use of the 'familiar' pronoun
    tu.

102 *Richelieu*: 1585–1642, cardinal and statesman. He entered Louis
    XIII's council in 1624 and played a major role in shaping the
    absolute monarchy and centralizing French administration. (The
    Duc de Richelieu (see n. to p. 394) had been prime minister in
    Mme de Rênal's own time, but the cardinal is a more plausible
    model for her to choose.)

105 *Bray-le-Haut*: fictitious.

105 *Jansenist*: follower of the doctrine of Cornelius Jansenius
    (1585–1638) on divine grace, predestination, and the perverseness
    of the human will. The history of the French Catholic Church
    was marked by hostility between Jesuits and Jansenists.

106 *département*: the French Constitution of 1789 abolished the old
    French provinces and divided the territory of France into 83
    départements.

107 *Leipzig*: site of the battle of the Nations in 1813 between
    Napoleon and the Allies. *Montmirail*: Napoleonic victory of 1814.

108 *Revolution*: that of 1789.

108 *Restoration*: see n. to p. 5 above.

108 *Agde*: French port on the Mediterranean coast.

113 *a sky-blue sash*: see n. to p. 212 below.

113 *ardent chapel*: the French expression *chapelle ardente* is the stan-
    dard term for a mortuary chapel lit by candles.

114 *St Clement*: the real St Clement was pope from 88 to 97, and was not a military figure. There are no surviving effigies of him.

115 *Philip the Good*: 1396–1497, Duke of Burgundy from 1419.

116 *'93 of cursed memory*: during the Terror of 1793, the National Guard in Lyon revolted, imprisoned the mayor and massacred 200 local Jacobins.

116 *lottery office*: the royal lottery, founded in 1776, abolished in 1836.

116 *yesserdy*: the French word *hier* is misspelt *yert* and italicized by Stendhal.

125 *Guardate alla pagine 130*: 'look at page 130'.

125 *spelling mistakes*: not reproduced by Stendhal in the text of the letter.

129 *red morocco case*: Stendhal specifies a case used to hold a single glass. It was customary for a suitor to have a crystal glass engraved with appropriate verses, and to present this to his beloved in a case as a love-token. Mme de Rênal might well have received such a case from her husband.

133 *Casino*: Stendhal's uncle had frequented an Ultra-royalist circle in Grenoble called the *Casino*.

134 *making her eat his heart*: see n. to p. 52.

140 *That man taking refuge on his roof*: allusion to a notorious incident in the Isère in 1816, when a liberal innkeeper who had fallen foul of the Ultras tried to escape arrest by climbing on to a neighbour's roof, and was shot dead.

143 *Malagrida*: 1689–1761, Italian Jesuit burned in Lisbon by the Inquisition on account of his seditious writings. This quotation is generally (and elsewhere by Stendhal) attributed to the diplomat Talleyrand (1754–1838).

144 *edicate*: the French verb *éduquer* (italicized by Stendhal) had been stigmatized by Voltaire, and was still considered vulgar in the 1860s by the lexicographer Littré.

144 *King Philip*: Philip II of Macedon (382–336 BC) employed Aristotle as tutor to his son Alexander. M. de Maugiron's compliment to Julien is modelled directly on the text of an apocryphal letter from King Philip to Aristotle, quoted in 19th-c. biographies of Aristotle.

148 *the last mission*: the Catholic Church organized a number of propaganda missions in the provinces during the Restoration.

148 *Ligorio's new theology*: St Alphonsus Liguori (1696–1787) was a Neapolitan bishop and missionary who founded the Congregation of the Most Holy Redeemer (1732). He was an outspoken critic of Jansenism.

149 *La Fontaine*: 1621–95. French poet whose *Fables* have long been an obligatory ingredient in French children's education.

149 *Messire Jean Chouart*: the priest in the fable 'The Priest and the Dead Man' (VII, 11): accompanying a coffin to the cemetery, he is thinking covetously of the luxuries he will be able to buy with the money he earns from this funeral, when a sudden jolt smashes his head against the coffin, and he accompanies the dead man to the grave. The annotated edition of the *Fables* published in 1818 by the writer Charles Nodier (1780–1844) gives a reactionary, monarchist commentary on the fables.

150 *Gros*: the geometer Louis-Gabriel Gros (1765–1812) had given tuition in mathematics to the young Stendhal, unbeknown to his parents, since Gros held Jansenist views. He was deeply admired by Stendhal.

152 *cabaret*: modest establishment serving wine and food, where it would be fashionable and deliberately daring for people of the Rênals' class to dine.

153 *medical practitioners*: the French term *officier de santé* was applied from 1803 to 1892 to doctors who did not have the title of *docteur en médecine*.

155 *Brotherhood of St Joseph . . . etc.*: officially registered pious associations (see n. to p. 25).

156 *The Woes of a Civil Servant*: this chapter has a slightly different title in the table of contents.

156 *Casti*: 1724–1803, Italian writer. 'The pleasure of holding one's head high all year round is well worth buying at the price of one or two quarters of an hour that have to be endured.'

156 *Charter*: France was granted a Charter by Louis XVIII in 1814.

157 *commune*: smallest administrative subdivision of a département.

157 *Mad the man who trusts her*: the couplet attributed to François I (1494–1547): *Souvent femme varie / Bien fol qui s'y fie* is recorded by Brantôme (see n. to p. 316). It was given notoriety in 1832 by Victor Hugo in his portrayal of François I in *Le Roi s'amuse*, and features in *Rigoletto* (based on Hugo's play).

159 *Congregation*: see n. to p. 25.

159 *Mr Five-and-Ninety*: reference to a magistrate from Marseille, M. Mérindol, who, in a court case against the pamphleteer Barthélemy in January 1830, let slip the regional form *nonante-cinq* (instead of the standard *quatre-vingt-quinze*). He was mercilessly ridiculed by Barthélemy in a poem, and by the whole of the liberal press.

160 *Signor Geronimo*: probably modelled on the Italian singer Lablache (1794–1858), who arrived in France around May 1830 to sing the role of Don Geronimo in Cimarosa's *Matrimonio Segreto* (first performed in Paris in Nov. 1830).

160 *Zingarelli*: Italian composer and director of the Conservatory in Naples where Lablache had studied music.

160 *Giovannone*: Giovanni Stile was appointed director of San-Carlino in 1810.

161 *credete a me*: 'do believe me'.

162 *carta canta!*: 'This paper proclaims them!'

170 *siege of 1674*: Besançon, which belonged to Spain, was besieged by Louis XIV's troops for 27 days in 1674. It finally became French under the terms of the treaty of Nijmegen in 1678.

173 *La Nouvelle Héloïse*: see n. to p. 22 above.

174 *Dôle*: Genlis is well beyond Dole (*sic*) on the road from Besançon to Dijon.

177 *Besançon Valenod*: Stendhal is here putting words into the mouth of the 'purveyor of dinners' at the Besançon seminary (see p. 188)—the counterpart of M. Valenod in the workhouse in Verrières. The French has a pun on the term *soumission* ('submission'), which means both 'submissiveness' and (as a commercial term) 'tender'.

180 *Intelligenti pauca*: (Latin) 'Few words [are needed] for one who understands'.

180 *Bossuet*: 1627–1704, Bishop of Meaux, theologian, and orator famous for the eloquence of his sermons. He supported Louis XIV against Protestantism, and championed the Gallican cause. *Arnault*: Antoine Arnauld, 1612–94, theologian; key figure in the Jansenist movement associated with the convent of Port-Royal *Fleury*: see n. to p. 11. Stendhal's grandfather was shocked to note that contemporary priests were ignorant of the writings of this famous Church historian.

180 *Vale et me ama*: (Latin) 'Farewell, and grant me your affection.'

181 (*Do you speak Latin?*): the translations given in the text are
Stendhal's.

183 *Unam Ecclesiam*: 'One Church': this bull is an invention of
Stendhal's.

185 *Young*: Edward Young, 1681–1765, author of *Night Thoughts*,
and *Love of Fame, the Universal Passion*. This epigraph and the
one to ch. 28 (both quoted in French) appear to be fictitious; I
have translated them 'back' into English.

186 *Mount Verna*: Mount Alverino.

187 *government by two Chambers*: established by the Charter of 1814.

187 *books are her real enemies*: in 1827 a law was passed at the
instigation of the clerical faction to curb freedom of the press.

187 *Sieyès*: see n. to p. 73.

187 *Grégoire*: the Abbé Grégoire, 1750–1831, was Bishop of Blois and
a member of the Convention during the Revolution. He was
elected deputy for Grenoble in 1819.

190 *Sixtus V*: Felice Peretti, 1520–90, religious reformer, elected
pope in 1585. He had spent the previous 15 years in semi-
disgrace, pretending to be dumb and lame, and was chosen as a
compromise candidate who appeared to offer little threat. On
election, however, he immediately resumed full possession of his
faculties.

191 *Abbé Delille*: 1738–1813, French poet and translator of Virgil.
Stendhal met him in his youth, and may have heard this anecdote
at first hand.

191 *Guercino*: 1591–1666, Italian fresco painter.

195 *Diderot*: 1713–84, French Enlightenment philosopher.

200 *the use of arms*: Stendhal commented in a letter to Strich in 1825
on the fact that since 1817 young peasants in seminaries throughout France had been instructed in the use of arms to prepare
them for the eventuality of a civil war if the Jesuits were driven
from France.

200 *Incedo per ignes*: 'I go forward through the flames' (Horace).

203 *Barême's genius*: the reference is to B. F. Barrême (1640–1702),
French mathematician.

203 *altars of repose*: small altar on which the priest puts the consecrated sacrament, particularly during a procession.

206 *The Precursor*: newspaper published in Lyon, and widely read in Paris, particularly in liberal circles.

209 *The only king remembered by the crowd*: ('Le seul roi dont le peuple ait gardé la mémoire') this line of verse from the *Eulogie of Voltaire* by Gudin de la Brenellerie (1738–1812) had been inscribed on the base of the statue of Henri IV (1553–1610) by the Pont-Neuf in Paris.

212 *Blue Sash*: the *cordon bleu* of the *Ordre du Saint-Esprit* (Order of the Holy Spirit), an order of knighthood founded by Henri III in 1578, abolished in 1791, and re-established between 1815 and 1830. The cross was fastened to a wide, azure-blue ribbon worn as a sash across the right shoulder.

215 *Emigration*: adversaries of the Revolution took refuge abroad after 1789.

216 *Mary Magdalene*: reference to the poet Delphine Gay, 1804–55, who recited her poetry in the salons of the period.

219 *Sacred Heart of Jesus*: devotion founded by a visitation nun, St Marguerite-Marie Alacoque (1647–90). It was much favoured by the Congregation in the 1820s. Stendhal commented in 1825 on the unscrupulous way in which the Jesuits used the gory image of the Sacred Heart to manipulate the emotions of women in the provinces.

220 *Marie Alacoque*: see preceding n.

221 *particular Cabinet*: at the beginning of 1828 an Ultra right-wing faction had tried to take over the Cabinet, against the wishes of the country as expressed in recent elections.

222 *in pace*: (Latin: 'in peace') reference to underground cells used to lock up dissident monks.

239 *Sainte-Beuve*: 1804–69, French writer and critic.

239 *Virgil*: 'O countryside, when shall I gaze on you?' The quotation is in fact from Horace (*Satires*, II. vi. 60).

240 *Mirabeau*: the Comte de Mirabeau, 1749–91 (son of the economist and physiocrat Marquis de Mirabeau), was a leading figure of the Third Estate. An advocate of constitutional monarchy, he used his oratorical powers to steer a dangerous course between the revolutionaries and the Court. One of his triumphs was to get the Constituent Assembly to vote for a patriotic levy.

240 *last election*: the liberal opposition gained ground at the expense of the Ultras in the general election of 1827.

240 pious associations: see n. to p. 25.

242 *Saint-Philippe du Roule*: fashionable church situated (in present-day Paris) between the Boulevard Haussmann and the Avenue des Champs-Elysées.

243 *Concordat*: agreement between Napoleon and Pope Pius VII (1801) setting out the terms under which the Catholic Church would be given recognition by the French State. The alienation of Church lands was made permanent, but the State assumed responsibility for the payment of clerical salaries.

244 *Malmaison*: château situated to the west of Paris; residence of Napoleon, and then of the Empress Josephine after their divorce (1809).

244 *walls . . . which break up the park*: the Swedish banker Haguermann, who had purchased Malmaison, undertook building work in 1830 to separate the original layout of the château from the extensions built in the grounds by the Empress Josephine.

245 *Spanish War*: France invaded Spain in 1823 to restore the Bourbon king.

246 *Place de Grève*: square in Paris where public executions took place. Renamed Place de l'Hôtel de Ville in 1806.

246 *Moreri*: 1643–80, author of a *Grand Dictionnaire historique* (1674).

246 *Adsum qui feci*: Virgil, *Aeneid*, IX. 427: 'I am here who was the cause of it.'

247 *Philip II*: King of Spain, 1556–98. *Henry VIII*: King of England, 1509–47.

248 *Cardinal Dubois*: 1656–1723, cardinal and politician. Tutor to the Duke of Orleans; prime minister in 1722.

249 *Robespierre and his cart*: see n. to p. 60. The cart was that used to convey victims to the guillotine.

249 *Faubourg Saint-Germain*: neighbourhood of Paris surrounding the church of Saint-Germain-des-Prés on the south bank of the Seine.

249 *Voltaire's death*: 1778.

250 *Kant*: German philosopher, 1724–1804.

250 *nil mirari*: *nil admirari* ('do not marvel at anything'), Horace, *Epistles*, 1.6.

251 *Henry III's friend*: Boniface de la Mole, 1530–74.

252 *Père-Lachaise*: cemetery where many of the famous are buried:

opened in 1804 at Ménilmontant (on the eastern outskirts of Paris) on land that had formerly belonged to Louis XIV's confessor, the Père de La Chaise.

252 *Marshal Ney*: 1769–1815, renowned for his exploits in the revolutionary wars and those of the Empire. Created a peer of France by Louis XVIII, he deserted to Napoleon during the Hundred Days and was court-martialled for treason at the Second Restoration.

253 *possible*: in the original French, Julien writes *cela* ('that') with a double ll: *cella*—a common mistake among French native speakers unsure of their spelling. Stendhal remembered committing it himself when first employed at the ministry of war on his arrival in Paris at the age of 16.

254 *St Charles's day*: 4 Nov.

256 *Académie des Inscriptions*: founded by Colbert in 1663 for the pursuit of historical and archeological learning.

257 *Chapelle*: 1626–86, French poet. *Molière*: 1622–73, French dramatist.

258 *Reina*: Francesco Reina, 1772–1826: Italian lawyer, scholar and patriot much admired by Stendhal.

258 *Voltaire's Princess of Babylon*: 1768; an oriental extravaganza depicting the tumultuous adventures of a dazzlingly beautiful princess and her bold suitor.

259 *Bois de Boulogne*: wood on the western edge of Paris where it was fashionable to go riding.

259 *Rue du Bac*: long narrow street running from the Seine through the Faubourg Saint-Germain to the Rue de Sèvres.

260 *Place Louis XVI*: now Place de la Concorde. In 1828 a monument was erected on the spot where Louis XVI had been guillotined.

262 *Ronsard*: 1524–85, French poet.

262 *You can only lean . . .* : maxim attributed to Talleyrand (see n. to p. 267).

263 *new colleagues*: 77 new peers were created in Nov. 1827—a move which displeased the extreme Ultras.

263 *Béranger*: 1780–1857, writer of patriotic political songs. He had been condemned in 1828 to 9 months' imprisonment and a fine of 10,000 francs for three seditious songs. The liberal paper *Le Constitutionnel* tried to raise a public subscription to pay the fine.

263 . . . *freely on any subject*: this long sentence is an echo of Figaro's monologue in Beaumarchais's *Marriage of Figaro* (V.3).

264 *La Quotidienne . . . La Gazette de France*: the latter was an Ultra-royalist newspaper, engaged in 1830 in a major campaign against *La Quotidienne*, the other extreme right-wing paper, which supported Charles X's current minister Polignac. *La Gazette de France* advocated the inclusion of the ex-minister Villèle in the Cabinet.

264 *rode in the king's carriages*: this was a highly exclusive privilege granted to certain members of the nobility under the Ancien Régime, but it had lost some of its distinction by 1830.

267 *Abbé de Pradt*: 1759–1837, churchman, diplomat and political writer. He opposed the Revolution and emigrated, but later rallied to Napoleon, becoming his chaplain and his ambassador to Warsaw. He returned to the royalist fold with the Restoration of Louis XVIII. *Talleyrand*: 1754–1838, prelate and diplomat; minister of foreign affairs under Napoleon. He was responsible for forming a provisional government in 1814 and summoning Louis XVIII to the throne; he played a major part in negotiating the treaty of Vienna in 1815. *Pozzo di Borgo*: 1764–1842, Corsican diplomat who became privy councillor to Alexander I of Russia, and worked for the defeat of Napoleon.

267 *great poet*: the name *Sainclair* echoes the Saint-Clair who is the hero of a tale published by Mérimée (1803–70) in January 1830. Commentators have noted characteristics of both Mérimée and Lamartine (1790–1869) in Stendhal's 'great poet'. Lamartine had abandoned his earlier Ultra stance in favour of more liberal views by 1829; he was officially admitted to the Académie Française in April 1830.

268 *Baron Bâton*: *bâton* is the French word for 'stick, rod'.

268 *Duc de Bouillon*: 1555–1623, Protestant supporter of Henri IV. *Bouillon* is the French word for 'broth'.

268 *most subtle man of this century*: Talleyrand (see n. to p. 267) has been suggested as the model for this portrait.

269 *Tartuffe*: the main character of Molière's play *Tartuffe* (1669) is a consummate hypocrite who attempts to marry his protector's daughter and seduce his wife by pretending to be deeply devout. The play was immensely popular between 1815 and 1830, and was used by liberals as an anticlerical weapon.

269 *like Bazilio*: it is in fact Bartholo (in Beaumarchais's *Marriage of*

Figaro, 1784) who comments that a certain lodging place must be a thieves' den if Basilio lives there.

270 *electoral colleges*: see n. to p. 100 above.

270 *decisive manœuvre*: reference to the 1827 elections, in which a number of instances of high-level fraud had come to light.

270 *Comte*: famous conjurer of the period.

271 *greatest poet of the age*: reference to Béranger (see n. to p. 263 above).

271 *M. de Nerval*: see n. to p. 398.

271 *Lord Holland*: 1773–1840. Whig peer associated with a number of political reforms. He sympathized with the French Revolution and protested at the Allies' imprisonment of Napoleon.

272 *new king of England*: William IV acceded to the throne in June 1830.

272 *Duc de Castries*: 1727–1800, minister for the navy from 1780 to 1787. *d'Alembert*: 1717–83, French Enlightenment philosopher, mathematician and writer.

272 *Maréchale*: the title designates the wife of a marshal.

272 *lending money to kings*: Baron James de Rothschild, nicknamed 'kings' moneylender', raised large sums in 1823 to support the Spanish War, in which the rebel general Riego was hanged by Ferdinand VII.

275 *Faublas*: *The Amorous Adventures of the Chevalier de Faublas* is a novel by the politician and writer Louvet de Coudray, 1760–97.

280 *Staub's*: the most fashionable Parisian tailor of the time.

282 *son of an archbishop*: Catholic clergy are celibate.

283 *Count Ory*: opera by Rossini, first performed in 1828 and put on again with great splendour at the Tuileries in the spring of 1830.

284 *Opera days*: Mondays, Wednesdays and Fridays.

285 *Bertolotti*: editor of the Piedmontese literary journal *Lo Spettatore* to which Stendhal had contributed in 1816.

285 *Hyères*: port on the Mediterranean coast.

285 *new paper*: plausibly *Le National*, founded in 1829, and hostile to the Ultra-right.

286 *Rivarol*: 1753–1801, literary figure with a reputation for wit. He is remembered chiefly for his *Discourse on the Universality of the*

French Language, awarded a prize by the Berlin Academy in 1786.

286 *Emigration*: see n. to p. 215.

288 *M. Poisson's accounts*: reference to a scene in *L'Ecole des bourgeois* by d'Allainval (1700–53). First performed in 1728, this comedy of manners, depicting nobles and parvenus at loggerheads, was given 162 performances between 1801 and 1837.

289 *Lowe . . . Bathurst*: Bathurst was minister for the colonies from 1815 to 1825, and was responsible for appointing Lowe to the governorship of St Helena in April 1816.

289 *Vane*: fictitious. Critics have suggested that Stendhal modelled this character on Richard Carlile, a follower of Jeremy Bentham. Carlile was in prison in 1817 when Stendhal first visited London.

291 *standing for the liberals*: in the 1827 elections a royalist faction joined forces with the liberal opposition, and became known as the right-wing defection.

293 *Pellico*: Silvio Pellico, 1788–1854, Italian writer imprisoned in the Spielberg in Brünn for Carbonarism. Stendhal had made his acquaintance in Milan in 1816.

297 *Coulon's*: the Coulons were a family of ballroom dancers famous at the time.

298 *accompanying a M. Coindet*: reference to a passage in Rousseau's *Confessions* (Book X).

298 *King Feretrius*: the liberal press in the 1820s was merciless in its mockery of M. Laurentie, editor of the Ultra newspaper *La Quotidienne*, for a howler he had committed in a scholarly treatise on the Roman historians: ignorant of the expression *Jupiter Feretrius* (*Feretrius* is a conventional epithet of disputed meaning), he had conjured a King Feretrius out of the Latin sentence he was attempting to translate.

301 *Mirabeau*: see n. to p. 240.

301 *Conradin*: Conrad V (1252–68), last of the Hohenstaufen dynasty, was King of Sicily from 1254, and was beheaded on the orders of the King of Naples.

301 *galope*: this dance was all the rage in the late 1820s.

301 *25 July 1830*: it was on this day that Charles X and his minister Polignac published a set of repressive measures which triggered off the July Revolution, bringing France a greater measure of liberty under Louis-Philippe.

302 *Mme de Staël*: 1766–1817, French writer. She had an influential salon in Paris at the beginning of the Revolution, but was later forced into exile by Napoleon. She held progressive views on politics and on the position of women in society.

304 *Danton*: see n. to p. 3.

305 *extradition*: plausibly an allusion to the Galotti affair, which received widespread coverage in the press in 1830. The Prince of Castelcicala, Neapolitan chargé d'affaires in Paris, had requested the extradition of a conspirator named Galotti who had sought political asylum in Corsica.

305 *grab me*: the slang term *empoigner* was the cause of a topical scandal in 1823: it was used in public by the chief gendarme when he expelled a deputy from the Chamber.

306 *Ney*: see n. to p. 252.

306 *Henri IV*: 1553–1610, King of Navarre (Henri III) from 1562, and of France (Henri IV) from 1589. Married Marguerite de Valois, daughter of Henri II.

307 *Girondin*: member of a political group formed in 1791 around the deputies from the Gironde. The Girondins represented moderation in the Convention, and opposed the massacres of the Terror.

308 *Courier*: Paul-Louis Courier, 1772–1825, author of pamphlets against the Restoration. He was sentenced to two months' imprisonment in 1821, and accused of 'cynicism' by the crown prosecutor at his trial.

308 *Béranger*: see n. to p. 263.

308 *Murat*: 1767–1815, marshal in Napoleon's armies; married Napoleon's sister Caroline; King of Naples from 1808.

309 *Delavigne*: 1793–1843, French poet and dramatist. *Marino Faliero* was first performed in May 1829 and widely discussed in the press for its political overtones. The plot centres on the character of Israel Bertuccio, a 'man of the people' who hatches a plot against the Venetian nobility in 1335.

309 *Pichegru*: 1761–1804, commander of the Rhine army under Napoleon. He later betrayed the Revolution by establishing contact with the émigré forces. *La Fayette*: 1757–1834, French general and politician. He took part in the American War of Independence, and supported the French revolutions of 1789 and 1830 as a liberal royalist.

309 *liberal Spaniards*: reference to an uprising in 1829 by a group of

liberals in Catalonia against Ferdinand VII. It was severely repressed.

310 *Carnot*: 1753–1823, mathematician and leading figure of the Revolution. He organized the Republican armies and planned military strategy. He was exiled by the Restoration.

310 *Vély's History of France*: publication of this history began in 1755 and was completed after Vély's death in 1759.

311 *Piedmontese . . . revolutionaries*: reference to the 1821 uprising.

312 *Letters from a Portuguese nun*: a collection of passionate love letters which appeared in 1669 purporting to be a translation of the correspondence of Mariana Alcoforado, a Portuguese nun.

313 *Hernani*: drama by Victor Hugo (1802–85) which caused a well-prepared uproar at its first performance in 1830 because it deliberately violated the conventions of French classical theatre. It became a focal point for the hostility between traditionalists and the emerging Romantic movement.

313 *lettres de cachet*: letters bearing the king's seal and containing a peremptory order of imprisonment or exile.

313 *Talma*: 1763–1826, French tragic actor much admired by Napoleon.

314 *Place de Grève*: see n. to p. 246.

314 *Boniface de la Mole*: see n. to p. 251.

314 *Marguerite of Navarre*: Marguerite de Valois, 1553–1615 (known as *la Reine Margot*), daughter of Henri II of France and Catherine de Medici, and sister of Charles IX, Henri III and the Duc d'Alençon. She married Henri III of Navarre (later Henri IV of France, grandson of the earlier Marguerite de Navarre who was sister to François I). Renowned for her wit, beauty and amorous adventures, she wrote poetry and a volume of memoirs.

314 *Duc d'Alençon*: 1554–84, son of Henri II and Catherine de Medici, and brother of Marguerite de Navarre.

314 *Catherine de Medici*: 1519–89, wife of Henri II and mother of François II, Charles IX, Henri III (Duc d'Anjou), Marguerite de Valois and the Duc d'Alençon. She acted as regent during Charles IX's minority, and was a ruthless politician. Her motive for imprisoning her son the Duc d'Alençon and her son-in-law Henri de Navarre was to thwart a plot to substitute the Duc d'Alençon for the Duc d'Anjou (who had become King of Poland) as heir to the ailing Charles IX.

315 *24th of August 1572*: St Bartholomew's day. Date of the massacre of Protestants ordered by Charles IX at the instigation of Catherine de Medici.

315 *First Prince of the Blood*: the Duc d'Alençon.

316 *d'Aubigné*: 1552–1630, French writer and historian; companion-at-arms of Henri IV. His account of La Mole's plot was published in 1660. *Brantôme*: 1560–1614, French historian; chamberlain of the Duc d'Alençon. His minutely detailed chronicle of Court life contains an account of La Mole's adventures.

316 *L'Etoile*: 1546–1611, French chronicler. His *Journal d'un bourgeois de Paris sous Henri III* is a daily record of the period 1574–1610.

316 *Henri III's reign*: 1574–89.

316 *the League*: the *Sainte Ligue* was a Catholic confederation founded by the Duc de Guise to defend Catholicism against the Calvinist movement when Henri III made peace with the Protestants in 1576. There ensued a religious war in which the Guises tried to seize the throne. It ended when Henri IV finally renounced Calvinism in 1593.

320 *Mérimée*: 1803–70, French writer best known for his short stories.

321 *Wagram*: defeat of the Archduke Charles of Austria by Napoleon on 6 July 1809.

322 *Abbé Maury*: 1746–1817; a cobbler's son who rose to become bishop, then cardinal.

322 *Manon Lescaut*: novel by the Abbé Prévost (1697–1763), published in 1731.

322 *Bassompierre*: 1579–1646, marshal of France and diplomat.

322 *Louis XIII*: 1601–43; reigned from 1610.

323 *Vendée*: département on the west coast of France. Royalist stronghold during the Revolution, and site of a counter-revolutionary uprising in 1793–5.

323 *Charter*: see n. to p. 156.

324 *Duc d'Angoulême*: Charles de Valois, 1573–1650, illegitimate son of Charles IX and Marie Touchet. His *Memoirs* document the reigns of Henri III and Henri IV.

324 *A little trip to Greece or Africa*: like Lord Byron, many young men from different parts of Europe went to Greece from 1821 onwards to fight in the War of Independence against Turkey. French

troops set off for North Africa in May 1830 and seized Algiers on 4 July.

325 *died in 1816*: reference to the dissolution of the newly elected Chamber by Louis XVIII, because it had an ungovernable reactionary majority. Stendhal explains in his correspondence that the broad left/right split in party politics after 1816 killed off ridicule by replacing a single aristocratic stereotype (from which one was ridiculed for deviating) with alternative models which guaranteed that one man's fool would be another's hero.

325 *. . . only its shadow*: La Fontaine, *The Shepherd and his Flock* (*Fables*, IX, 19).

328 *restore their forests to the clergy*: a continuing grievance of the Ultras: the Revolution had dispossessed the Church of its forests, and the liberals succeeded in thwarting proposals to hand them back in the early days of the Restoration.

328 *Coblenz*: reputed to be a place of loose morals.

330 *Schiller*: 1759–1805. Critics have seen in this epigraph (not identified in Schiller's works) a free interpretation by Stendhal of the following lines from Shakespeare's *Othello* (III.3): 'Trifles light as air / Seem to the jealous confirmations strong / As proofs from holy writ.'

331 *fake Memoirs*: There was such a vogue for memoirs in 1829–30 that numerous fake ones of famous people were published and avidly read.

331 *disinvoltura*: 'carefree abandon' (Italian).

333 *Languedoc*: former province in south-western and central-southern France.

333 *Léontine Fay*: famous actress of the time.

334 *English handwriting*: French term for a cursive, right-leaning script widely taught in France.

335 *footstool*: reference to the ancient privilege of being seated at Court in the presence of the king and queen, which had recently been reinstated.

336 *St Louis*: Louis IX, 1214–70, King of France from 1226.

336 *Bishop of Beauvais*: consecrated in 1825 at the age of 40.

336 *Granvelle*: Antoine Perrenot de Granvelle (1517–86), born in Besançon, became Bishop of Arras, and went on to be a minister of the Emperor Charles V. His father had in fact also served in the same capacity.

337 *in Poissy*: Fontan and Magalon, editors of a satirical publication, were imprisoned in 1824 and later condemned to hard labour in the prison at Poissy for criticizing the Government.

337 *Colonel Caron*: French officer executed in 1822, after being framed by the police and accused of insurrection.

338 *Esprit per. pré. gui. II.A. 30*: Stendhal's cryptic note has been deciphered as: Esprit per[d] pré[fecture]. Gui[zot]. 11 août 1830. ('Wit loses Prefecture. Guizot. 11 August 1830'). Stendhal had applied to Guizot (an official at the ministry of the interior) for a post as prefect, and been turned down. He took pleasure in alluding cryptically to this rejection in a footnote to his novel, and also in the header at the top of the page in question (not included in this translation because of pagination constraints), which reads: L'ESPRIT PERD. He was appointed consul at Trieste a few weeks later.

339 *Alfred de Musset*: 1810–57, French writer.

340 *Jarnac . . . Moncontour*: victories won in 1569 by the Catholics, led by the Duc d'Anjou (the future Henri III), over the Protestant forces of the Prince de Condé and Admiral Coligny respectively.

340 *Algiers*: see n. to p. 325.

340 *Jacobins*: see n. to p. 8.

341 *surrender of Baylen*: General Dupont signed a disastrous capitulation at Bailén in Andalucia in 1808.

341 *. . . MYSELF*: echo of a line from Corneille's tragedy *Médée*, 1635 (I. 5).

345 *Schiller*: Critics have noted similarities between this epigraph (not identified in Schiller's works) and the following lines from Shakespeare's *Julius Caesar*: 'Between the acting of a dreadful thing / And the first motion, all the interim / Is like a phantasm, or a hideous dream' (II.1).

346 *Don Diego*: the father of the hero Rodrigue in Corneille's play *Le Cid* (1636) says to his son: 'We only have one honour. There are so many sweethearts!' (III.6).

346 *Gascon*: people from Gascony (former duchy in S.W. France) have a reputation for humour and bragging.

347 *Abelard's fate*: Pierre Abélard (1079–1142) was a scholastic philosopher best remembered for his ill-fated passion for his pupil Héloïse. Her uncle took revenge by breaking into Abélard's room at dead of night and castrating him.

349 *Pallida morte futura*: 'Pale with her approaching death' (Virgil, *Aeneid*, IV. 643).

350 *Massinger*: 1584–1640, English dramatist.

352 *Café Tortoni*: fashionable café on the Boulevard des Italiens.

360 *Charles IX*: 1550–74; reigned from 1560 under the regency of his mother Catherine de Medici. *Henri III*: see n. to p. 340.

363 *St Valery's church*: in the Rue de Bourgogne (now no longer standing).

368 *The Opera Bouffe*: also known as the Italian Opera, and situated on the Boulevard des Italiens. Like the Grand Opera, it was a meeting-place for the aristocracy.

368 *the revolution of 1688 in England*: comparisons between Restoration France and England under James II were a recurrent theme in the French press at the end of the 1820s. Whether Charles X might suffer a fate similar to that of James II in 1688 was a live topic.

368 *Roland*: Roland de la Platière (1734–93), politician. He was minister of the interior in 1792 and supported the Girondins (see n. to. p. 307). He committed suicide on learning of his wife's execution. *M*ᵐᵉ *Roland*: 1754–93. She had an influential political salon frequented by Girondins, and perished on the scaffold.

368 *M*ᵐᵉ *de Staël*: see n. to p. 302.

369 *this sublime aria*: the opera appears to be fictitious.

370 *Devo punirmi* . . . : 'I must punish myself, I must punish myself, if I've loved too much.'

370 *a purely imaginary figure*: despite these protestations, a recent society scandal had provided Stendhal with a model for Mathilde's behaviour. In Jan. 1830, Marie de Neuville, the 17-year-old niece of a former Government minister, had eloped to London with Edouard Grasset, a commoner who had made a name for himself by fighting in the War of Greek Independence. After a brief escapade, she returned to her family and refused to marry Grasset.

376 *Meudon*: on the S.W. outskirts of Paris.

377 *Jean Paul*: Johann Paul Richter, 1763–1825.

378 *Saint-Cloud*: château on a hillside overlooking the Seine on the western outskirts of Paris, built by Louis XIV's brother, with gardens by Le Nôtre. Napoleon used it as a summer palace, and it

was adopted as a Parisian residence by Louis XVIII and Charles X.

382 *Chelles*: town near Meaux on the Marne, to the east of Paris. The abbey is now in ruins.

382 *Duke of Orleans*: Philippe III (1674–1723) was Louis XV's regent from 1715 to 1723.

383 *secret memorandum*: in 1829–30 the liberal press warned of an ultra-reactionary plot to call upon foreign powers to intervene against the threat of renewed revolution in France. The campaign alluded specifically to a 'Secret Memorandum'. The king's aide-de-camp, the Duc de Fitz-James (from whom Stendhal borrowed many attributes for his portrayal of the Marquis de la Mole), left in haste on a mission to Germany in July 1830 after the French Government suffered a severe electoral defeat. Scholars have recognized a number of contemporary political figures in the characters in this scene.

383 *La Quotidienne*: see n. to p. 264.

390 *Place de Grève*: see n. to p. 246.

390 *On the Pope*: see n. to p. 22.

391 *La Gazette des Tribunaux*: a publication which appeared every weekday, containing full reports on court proceedings.

392 *advocating assassination*: the idea of resorting to drastic measures to rid Europe of Bonaparte was openly voiced abroad in 1814–15.

393 *Go out and seek your own help*: the French sentence echoes a proverb *Aide-toi, le ciel t'aidera* which had been adopted as the name of a liberal society formed in 1827.

393 *1794*: year of sweeping victories for the revolutionary armies.

393 *It will be a god!*: La Fontaine, *Fables*, IX, 6: 'The Sculptor and the Statue of Jupiter'. The sculptor contemplates his block of marble and wonders what his chisel will make of it.

393 *Louis XVI*: reigned 1774–91; guillotined 1793.

394 *M. de Richelieu*: the Duc de Richelieu (1766–1822) was prime minister twice under Louis XVIII, and represented France at the Congress of Aix-la-Chapelle.

394 *1817*: Allied forces occupied France from 1815 (Congress of Vienna) until 1818.

394 *former imperial general*: modelled on General Bourmont, minister of war in 1829, who had deserted Napoleon at Waterloo.

394 *Le Globe*: review which voiced the anti-establishment opinions of a group of gifted young writers in the late 1820s.

394 *Kléber*: 1753–1800, French general who commanded the revolutionary armies in the Vendée, the Rhine and in Egypt. *Hoche*: 1768–97, French general who commanded the revolutionary armies in the Moselle and the Vendée. *Jourdan*: 1762–1833, marshal of France who defeated the Austrians at Fleurus in 1794, and headed the revolutionary armies in Spain. *Pichegru*: see n. to p. 309.

395 *1815*: Napoleon's former soldiers rallied round him when he landed from Elba and marched on Paris in March 1815 at the beginning of the Hundred Days.

395 *Cathelineau*: 1759–93, leader of the counter-revolutionary uprising in 1793.

395 *Jacobins' song*: the *Marseillaise*.

395 *Gustave-Adolphe*: King of Sweden, 1594–1632. Intervened in the Thirty Years War on the side of the German Protestant princes against the Holy Roman Emperor.

396 *towards the . . . tonight*: see n. to p. 402 on *Mainz*.

397 *Hume*: 1711–76, Scottish philosopher and historian.

397 *Saints*: strict dissenters.

397 *Mr Brougham*: Lord Brougham, 1778–1868; lord chancellor from 1830 to 1834. He was admired by Stendhal for his liberalism.

398 *doggerel*: reference to the *Marseillaise* quoted in the previous chapter.

398 *Vendée*: see n. to p. 328.

398 *clergy . . . forests*: see n. to p. 328.

398 *parish priests*: one of the terms of the Concordat of 1801 was the payment of clerical salaries by the State.

398 *Nerval*: modelled on the Prince de Polignac, 1780–1847. He served as foreign minister, and prime minister from Aug. 1829 until his reactionary measures brought about the downfall of Charles X. He had a reputation for mysticism.

399 *under Louis XV*: the regional Parliaments were suppressed from 1770 to 1774.

400 *Saint-Roch cannon*: in 1795 a detachment of the National Guard

trying to storm the Convention was dispersed from the steps of Saint-Roch, a church off the Rue Saint-Honoré, by a single small cannon manned by the revolutionary forces.

402 *Mainz*: this reference to Mainz is the key to the unknown destination of Julien's mission. The last sentence of II. 22 can be read as 'I shall be galloping off to the [Grand Duchy of Hesse] tonight'. The Duke of —— then plausibly becomes the Austrian statesman Prince Metternich (1773–1859), who resided in Hesse and was backed by the forces of the Holy Alliance. He opposed the development of liberal movements in Europe in the 1820s.

404 *Café-hauss*: Stendhal's version of the German *Kaffeehaus*.

405 *the Congregation's police*: see n. to p. 25.

407 *Gouvion Saint-Cyr*: 1764–1830, marshal of France. With General Desaix (1768–1800) he defended Kehl against the Austrians in 1796. He served as minister of war under Louis XVIII. His *Mémoires sur les campagnes des armées du Rhin et Moselle* appeared in 1829.

413 *Lope de Vega*: 1562–1635, Spanish writer.

413 *Don Diego Bustos*: Stendhal may have modelled this character on the Spanish republican Don Bastos, who appears in Lebrun's play the *Cid d'Andalousie*. This was first performed in 1825, after being banned for over 4 years by the censorship on account of a scene where Don Bastos strikes the King of Spain in the dark.

413 *carbonaro*: member of an Italian secret political society formed in the early years of the 19th c. to promote republican ideals.

414 *furia francese*: 'French ardour' (Italian).

414 *Collé*: 1709–83, song-writer and dramatist.

414 *'Tis my caprice . . . etc.*: *J'ai la marotte / D'aimer Marote, etc.*

414 *took against this song*: critics have detected here an allusion to the treatment of the song-writer Béranger (see n. to p. 263) by Mme du Cayla, 1785–1852, Louis XVIII's mistress. Before his conviction in 1828, he had been remanded in 1821 for offences against public morality and against the person of the king, and had been sacked from a position worth 1,800 francs a year, to which he had been appointed under Napoleon. The song in question depicts the king's virility in scurrilous terms which neither the monarch nor his mistress could have been expected to appreciate. In 1822 Béranger attacked Mme du Cayla herself in another song. She was noted for her striking beauty, her religious devotion, and her

prudishness, which she displayed with great *éclat* in her salon. In these respects she may provide a model for Mme de Fervaques.

416 *Hôtel d'Aligre*: situated on the Rue de Richelieu near the Palais-Royal.

417 *Opera-Buffa*: the Opera Bouffe, or comic opera.

418 *clandestine government*: name given under Louis XVIII to the Ultra faction which backed the Comte d'Artois (the future Charles X).

419 *Camarilla*: Spanish term designating the extremist supporters of Ferdinand VII. The expression was applied to the Ultra faction in France in 1830.

420 *Saint-Simon*: 1675–1755. His *Memoirs* span the period 1694–1723, and contain a detailed account, from a traditional monarchist perspective, of Court life and the chief characters involved.

423 *Massillon*: 1663–1742, French preacher.

424 *Telemachus: Les Aventures de Télémaque*, 1699; written by Fénelon (see n. to p. 504) for the edification of the young Duke of Burgundy.

426 *Dorat*: 1734–80, French poet; prolific writer of elegant froth.

426 *had the pictures corrected*: Mme du Cayla (see n. to p. 414) was on close terms with the minister for the arts, who made a point of rectifying the indecency of statues and paintings in public places.

426 *Bishop of* ——: one of Mme du Cayla's protégés (though not her uncle) was the Bishop of Hermopolis, Monsignor Frayssinous (1765–1841). At her instigation, Louis XVIII made him minister for ecclesiastical affairs in 1824. He held this office until 1828, and was again given responsibility for Church positions in 1829.

428 *Lichtemberg*: 1744–99, German physicist and satirical writer.

428 *the ballet based on Manon Lescaut*: a grand spectacle first performed in May 1830. The libretto (based on the novel by the Abbé Prévost, see n. to p. 322) is by Scribe (1791–1861), and the score by Halévy (1799–1862).

432 *Girodet*: 1767–1824, French painter. His literary writings and part of his correspondence were published in 1829.

439 *Matrimonio Segreto*: *The Secret Marriage*, opera by Cimarosa (1749–1801). The heroine Caroline becomes secretly engaged to one of her father's subordinates.

441 *si fata sinant*: 'if the Fates allow' (Virgil, *Aeneid*, 1.19)

442 *Memoirs dictated . . . by Napoleon*: the 8-vol. *Mémoires de Napoléon à Sainte-Hélène* were compiled by Gourgaud and Montholon (two officers who had accompanied Napoleon to St Helena), and published 1822–7.

446 *Beaumarchais*: 1732–99, French dramatist; author of the *Mariage de Figaro* (1784), from which this epigraph is taken (V.3).

451 *I am no angel*: Molière, *Tartuffe* (III.3).

456 *a footstool*: see n. to p. 335.

458 *Château d'Aiguillon*: built in the 17th c.

458 *like Othello*: echo of Desdemona's speech to the Venetian Senate (I.3).

460 *Louis XI*: 1423–83; reigned from 1461. In his strife with his great lords and his feud with Charles the Bold he displayed cold, calculating cunning.

462 *Duchess of Burgundy*: Adelaide of Savoy had married Louis XIV's grandson Louis of Burgundy in 1697, and the old king delighted in her company.

465 *fifteenth regiment of Hussars*: there were only 14.

470 *Article 1342 of the Penal Code*: the Penal Code of 1810 contained only 484 articles. Article 295 deals with 'murder', defined as 'voluntary homicide'. Article 296 deals with 'assassinat', defined as 'murder committed with premeditation'.

471 *From this time forth I never will speak word*: Othello, V. 2 (quoted in English by Stendhal).

475 *bad French*: a survey conducted in 1794 revealed that 6 million Frenchmen spoke no French at all, and another 6 million spoke it very imperfectly; only 3 million were judged to speak it correctly. Despite the attempts of the Revolution to eradicate the various regional dialects in favour of a national language, French in 1830 was still a second language for large sections of the population.

476 *Sterne*: 1713–68.

478 *Lavalette's escape*: Lavalette (1769–1830) was an important figure in Napoleon's army and civil administration. He was condemned to death in 1815 for his part in engineering Napoleon's comeback, but managed to escape from prison by changing clothes with his wife. He was smuggled into Bavaria, where he remained until

granted a pardon in 1822. Sadly, his wife had by this time lost her reason, and never recognized him when he returned to Paris.

478 *René*: novel by Chateaubriand (1768–1848), published in 1802. Its hero suffers from world-weariness.

478 *Fouqué's bad grammar*: see n. to p. 475 on *bad French*.

483 *Congregationist*: member of the Congregation (see n. to p. 25).

484 *Bishop of* ——: see n. to p. 426.

488 *Locke*: quoted in French by Stendhal. *The Life of John Locke with Extracts from his Correspondence, Journals and Commonplace Books* was published by Lord King in 1829.

491 *suppression of the death penalty*: this was a subject of contemporary debate. Victor Hugo had published a poem entitled 'The Last Days of a Condemned Man' in 1829.

492 *the Fronde*: name of an uprising of nobles against Cardinal Mazarin during Louis XIV's minority (1648–52). The Duchesse de Chevreuse (1600–79) and the Duchesse de Longueville (1619–79) were leading figures in the movement.

493 *king of terrors*: Job 18: 14.

495 *Jacobin law*: the law of 2 May 1827 had extended the list of those eligible for jury service.

495 *liberal by defection*: see n. to p. 291 on the 1827 elections.

498 *events of 1814*: fall of Napoleon and Restoration of Louis XVIII.

500 *bad French*: see n. to p. 475.

503 *Lavalette*: see n. to p. 478. Lavalette glanced at his watch as his death sentence was read out.

504 *Chapter 42*: the last 4 chapters have neither title nor epigraph.

504 *Fénelon's God*: Fénelon (1651–1715), prelate and writer. His *Maxims of the Saints* (1697) were condemned by the Church for Quietism.

504 *thou hast loved much*: echo of Christ's words to Mary Magdalene (Luke 7: 47)

506 *Danton . . . prevented the enemy from reaching Paris*: the Jacobins, led by Danton, set up the Insurrectionary Commune on 10 Aug. 1792. Prussian forces marched on France in July 1792, but were defeated by the revolutionary armies at Valmy on 20 Sept.

507 *. . . of common men*: lines quoted (with a minor inaccuracy) from Voltaire's play *Mahomet*, 1741 (II. 5): 'Du droit qu'un esprit

ferme et vaste en ses desseins / A sur l'esprit grossier des vulgaires humains.'

508 *Manuel*: 1775–1827; barrister and liberal deputy under the Restoration. He fought in the revolutionary armies from 1792 to 1797.

510 *Belphégor's lines*: '. . . le nœud du mariage / Damne aussi dru qu'aucuns autres estats' ('The marriage bond / Damns as surely as any other state'), from La Fontaine's tale *Belphégor* (v,7), in which a demon sent to Earth to investigate the marriage state discovers that conjugal life is not a bed of roses.

512 *charcoal*: presumably from the fumes. Carbon monoxide poisoning was a recognized hazard of cooking on charcoal stoves and chafing dishes.

513 *latterday apostate*: comparison of Julien with Julian the Apostate (331–63): Roman emperor from 361), who forsook Christianity for paganism.

514 *almost noon*: Mass could not be celebrated after noon.

518 *natural rights*: reference to Rousseau's *Social Contract* (see n. to p. 22).

518 *confiscated from the Protestants*: to hand out to nobles in favour at Court.

520 *King of Rome*: Napoleon II (1811–32), son of Napoleon by his second wife Marie-Louise, was proclaimed King of Rome at his birth. Napoleon abdicated in his favour in both 1814 and 1815.

520 *Dubois*: in 1720 Massillon (see n. to p. 423) officiated under Cardinal de Rohan at the consecration of Cardinal Dubois (see n. to p. 248).

523 *novena*: 9 days of ritual prayer.

526 *Charles X*: 1757–1836; reigned 1824–30.

American Literature

British and Irish Literature

Children's Literature

Classics and Ancient Literature

Colonial Literature

Eastern Literature

European Literature

Gothic Literature

History

Medieval Literature

Oxford English Drama

Poetry

Philosophy

Politics

Religion

The Oxford Shakespeare

A complete list of Oxford World's Classics, including Authors in Context, Oxford English Drama, and the Oxford Shakespeare, is available in the UK from the Marketing Services Department, Oxford University Press, Great Clarendon Street, Oxford OX2 6DP, or visit the website at www.oup.com/uk/worldsclassics.

In the USA, visit www.oup.com/us/owc for a complete title list.

Oxford World's Classics are available from all good bookshops. In case of difficulty, customers in the UK should contact Oxford University Press Bookshop, 116 High Street, Oxford OX1 4BR.